MEN OF inked

THROTTLE ME • HOOK ME • THROTTLED • RESIST ME

www.chellebliss.com

CHELLE BLISS

USA TODAY BESTSELLING AUTHOR

Dear Reader,

Thank you for downloading the Men of Inked Volume One.

Just a word warning…this is **<u>NOT</u>** a clean romance. If you're offended by profanity and sex, this may not be the read for you.

The Men of Inked is a saga revolving around a fun, loving, and devoted Italian family.

Happy reading!

ABOUT THE AUTHOR

Chelle's a full-time writer, time-waster extraordinaire, social media addict, coffee fiend, and ex-history teacher.

To learn more about Chelle's books, please visit menofinked.com.

Where to Follow Me:

facebook.com/authorchellebliss1

bookbub.com/authors/chelle-bliss

instagram.com/authorchellebliss

x.com/ChelleBliss1

goodreads.com/chellebliss

amazon.com/author/chellebliss

pinterest.com/chellebliss10

Do you LOVE audiobooks?

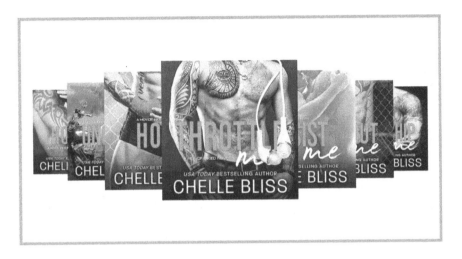

To check out my entire audio library, please visit *menofinked.com/audio* for more information.

THROTTLE me

A MEN OF INKED NOVEL

WALL STREET JOURNAL & USA TODAY BESTSELLING AUTHOR

CHELLE BLISS

1

THE DARKNESS

SUZY

THE MOONLIGHT FILTERED THROUGH THE PINE TREES LINING THE FIELDS, leaving shadows on the pavement. The crisp air that had been missing for months caressed my skin. Cranking up the radio, I sang along to Justin Timberlake's "Rock Your Body." It was just the cool breeze, JT, and me. I couldn't wait to crawl in my bed and close my eyes, getting lost in a dream world that had nothing to do with my current reality.

The night had been perfect. I'd had dinner and drinks with my best friend, Sophia, and although I was exhausted from a long workday, I felt a sense of serenity. Spending time with Sophia always made me happy. She was like a sister to me, especially when she had lived with me for over a year. I felt like part of me had been missing since the day she moved out, leaving me behind.

Dancing in the seat, screaming out the lyrics, I thought about how I wanted someone that would do everything the song described. No one had ever made me feel the way that JT sang about women. The steering wheel shook in my hands and a screeching sound pulled me out of my JT trance.

"Damn it," I said, hitting the steering wheel with my palm.

The orange flash from my hazards blinked against the dark pavement as I pulled off the road and my car sputtered to a stop. Bad luck seemed to follow me. I squeezed the steering wheel, trying to calm my frazzled nerves. I knew the day would come, the day my car would die, but I prayed it would happen after my next paycheck…no such luck.

Resting my head on the wheel, I closed my eyes, taking a deep breath. "Great, just fucking great." I rocked back and forth, feeling sorry for myself, hitting my head on the cool plastic. I thought about whom to call or where to walk. I hadn't passed a gas station or even a damn streetlight in miles. Without picking up my head, I reached for my phone, bringing it to my eyes.

"Shit." The screen wouldn't power on after I hit every button I could think to press. It was useless. It was dead and now I was totally stranded. What else could possibly go wrong? Sighing, I sat up and glanced in the rearview mirror, but only the shadows from the trees filled my view. No cars, neon signs, or streetlights. Fuck.

I placed my hand on my chest to feel the beat of my heart, which was so hard I swear it was audible. Visions from slasher movies flooded my mind. Girl deserted on the side of the road until she's found by a handsome stranger that ends up being a serial killer.

Should I start walking to God knows where? Do I just sit there and wait for a stranger to offer me help? I never liked feeling helpless—I was too smart to be helpless, but it was the only thing I felt in this moment. It could be hours before someone found me in my car.

I grabbed my purse, dead phone, and keys, and climbed out of the car. My feet ached in the extra-high heels I wore. Leaning against the car, I gave my feet a moment to adjust, as I looked in both directions. Neither of my options were good and I was exhausted. My feet fucking screamed from standing still. Thank God I could sleep in tomorrow after the way this evening was ending. There was a gas station a couple miles back—better to go with what I knew than to walk into an uncertain future. I tapped the lock button on my key chain one more time, helping relieve my OCD need to double-check everything, before I started walking away.

Barely clearing the trunk, a single light came over a small hill in the distance, hurting my eyes with the brightness. The roar of the engine grew louder as the distance closed. I waved my arms as a figure came into view, but the asshole biker drove right passed me as I screamed,

"Hey! Hey!" The wind from his bike caused the dust on the road to kick up and fill my mouth.

I turned around, coughing, and screamed toward the bike. I knew it was pointless. There was no way in hell he'd heard me yelling above the roar of his bike, but he had to see me. The red taillight lit up the road as he turned the bike in my direction. I swallowed hard, unsure if this was my best idea of the night—but I'd already made too many mistakes to dwell on that. He was my only hope of getting home.

I stood there like a deer in headlights, unable to move, as I gaped at him. My hands trembled as the figure on the bike came to a stop. The engine was almost deafening, as I took in the sight of him on the machine. The bike was a Harley, a Fat Boy, with no windshield, chrome handlebars, and a dark body. He wore black boots, dark jeans, and a dark t-shirt. He was large and muscular, and I sucked in a breath as my eyes reached his handsome and rugged face. A playful grin danced on his lips as he watched me ogle him. Fucking hell.

"Need some help, lady?" he asked, removing his helmet, running his fingers through his disheveled hair. The dark peaks stood up on the top, the sides were short and clipped, and the color matched the sky—dark. I couldn't see his eyes; a pair of tinted glasses hid them. Could serial killers be so sexy?

"Um, do you have a cell phone I could use to call for a ride?" I asked without taking a step in his direction. *Don't get too close—leave room to run.* Who the fuck was I kidding? I couldn't make it five feet in these damn shoes.

"Sure." As he leaned back on his bike, I studied his body as he dug in his pocket. The skintight jeans showed his muscles through the denim fabric. Everything clung to him. I wanted to poke him to see if he felt as hard as he looked. What the fuck was wrong with me?

I was too busy staring to notice what he was holding out for me. "Lady, you wanted my phone?"

Snapping back to reality with the sound of his deep voice, I took a step toward him, reaching for the phone. "Oh, sorry."

My fingertips grazed his palm, and a tiny shock passed between us. His fingers closed on my hand as I pulled away. My heartbeat, which had calmed, now began to pound feverishly in my chest. It had to be my hormones. I hadn't had sex in God knows how long—I stopped counting after three months. The man in front of me wasn't my type, but his sex appeal wasn't lost on me. He looked like a whole lot of trouble, and I didn't need that in my life.

I stepped back, keeping my eyes trained on him, as I dialed the only person close enough to help—Sophia. The phone rang and his eyes traveled up and down the length of my body—with each ring, my stomach began to turn. I didn't have anyone else to call.

Tapping the end button, I sighed. "There's no answer. Thanks." I gave him a sheepish smile as I handed him the phone.

"Let me take a look and see if there's anything I can do. Okay?" he asked, as he began angling the bike to shine the headlights on the hood.

"Sure." I hit the unlock button on my car key before climbing in. I put the key in the ignition, but stayed aware of his proximity. No one would hear me scream if he tried to kill me. I couldn't let my guard down.

He put the kickstand down, climbed off the bike, and placed the helmet on the seat. Pulling the hood latch next to my seat, I watched him from the relative darkness of my car, my face hidden by shadows. He was large, larger than he looked sitting on the Harley. He had to be more than a foot taller than me, and looked more solid with the bike illuminating his body. I stared at him, mouth open slightly, my breathing shallow as I looked at him like a piece of meat through the gap between the hood. He oozed masculinity and ruggedness, and I tried to picture him without all the skintight clothes. The muscles in his arm rippled as he touched the parts under the hood.

What would it be like to be with a man like him? Every man I'd dated just didn't work out. They were nice guys, but the spark I wanted was always missing. People think I'm a good girl, and I am, but my mind is filled with dirty thoughts that I could never share with a mate. I'd shared them with Sophia, but she doesn't count. No one had ever done anything fantasy-worthy with me. I can barely speak the words that are needed to describe the things I want done to me, or that I'd want to do to another person in this world.

"Ma'am," he said, snapping me out of the evaluation of my sex life, or lack thereof.

"Sorry, yes?"

"Can you try and start it for me, please?" he said, leaning over the hood, his hands placed on either side of the opening. "Now," he said. The car churned and churned. "Stop," I heard him yell over the screeching noise. He moved methodically around the engine. "Try it again." I turned the key, causing the engine to rattle, but not start.

He stood, rubbing the back of his neck as curses spilled from his lips. The only thing I could see was his crotch. I stared, motionless. His t-shirt covered the belt loops and stopped just above his groin. Damn. He filled out those jeans. He had to be big. Everything about him was big—he couldn't, just couldn't, have a small cock, could he?

The last guy that I'd slept with was more the size of a party pickle. It was the most unsatisfying sexual experience of my life. He was a teacher, and I wanted someone who was educated and self-sufficient, but he was boring in and out of the bedroom. I thought I'd found that with Derek, Mr. Pickle, but I was wrong. He was a wreck, and filled with more mental issues than anyone I'd ever know. He was germophobic, which was problematic when having sex. He'd jump right out of bed immediately after sex to shower and wash the dirty off. I sighed to myself, remembering his need to be clean—never mind that he was an asshole, too.

The hood of my car made a loud thump as the man slammed it. "Your car is a little tricky. Foreign cars can be complicated. I can't seem to get it to start," he said, walking toward the driver-side door.

"It's okay. Thanks for trying." I climbed out, not wanting to be trapped inside. What the hell was I going to do now?

"I was heading to the bar up the road. Want to join me?" He smiled and tilted his head as he studied me. "You can call a tow truck from there. It may take a while for them to get out here."

I couldn't think of any other option. He was my only hope, my saving grace from the dark roadside, and a means to an end. There were worse things than climbing on the back of his motorcycle and wrapping my arms around him. "Okay, but I've never been on a bike."

"Never? How is that even possible?" he asked, shaking his head, a small laugh escaping his lips. His teeth sparkled in the light, straight and white. His jaw was strong, his cheekbones jutted out more when he smiled, and a small dimple formed on the left side of his face.

I looked down at the ground, my cheeks heated. "I don't know. I just never knew anyone that had one and I find them totally scary."

"It's not far from here and there isn't much traffic. I'll keep you safe," he said, holding out his helmet.

My stomach fluttered as I closed the car door and thought about my first motorcycle ride. The black, round helmet felt cool against my fingers as I took it from him. I scrunched my eyebrows together as I studied it. I didn't know if there was a front or a back, or how to put it on.

"Here, let me help you," he said as he reached for the helmet, removing it from my grip. His hand touched mine and I felt the spark again. Not a real spark, but electricity that I felt with every fiber of my being from the slightest touch. My body wanted his touch, but my mind was throwing up the caution flag.

Placing it gently on my head, he ran his rough fingers down the straps, almost caressing my skin, to adjust it to fit my face. I inhaled deeply, trying to fill all my senses with him. He smelled different than any other man I'd smelled. He didn't smell of cheap cologne, but there was a spicy, woodsy scent that reminded me of home. I closed my eyes and relished the feel of his warm skin against mine.

"All done. Are you ready?" he asked.

I opened my eyes, heat creeping up my neck, as I had been lost in his touch. "Yes." I prayed my voice didn't betray me.

He climbed on the bike, sliding forward, making room for me. "Lift your leg and climb on."

Placing my hand on his shoulder to help balance myself, I followed his instructions; my body slid forward, smashing against him. Rock solid. He turned his head, looking me in the eyes. "Put your feet on the pegs and wrap your arms around me. I don't bite—well, unless you want me to." He smirked, and my heart felt like it was doing the tango in my chest as I pressed against his back. He didn't just say that to me, did he? I lifted my feet off the ground, turning over complete control to the stranger I was entrusting with my life. I locked my hands together, completely wrapped around him.

"Ready?"

"Wait! I don't even know your name. I mean, I'm putting my life in your hands and I don't even know who you are." I gripped his body tighter, clinging to him.

I couldn't hear his laughter, but I felt the rumble of it from deep in his chest. "My friends call me City, sugar." He throttled the engine and my heart skipped a beat. Fear gripped me—there was no turning back now.

My grip became viselike, fear overcoming any need to be cool or seem calm in front of him. He patted my hands before the bike began to move, and I couldn't bear to look. I buried my face in his back, avoiding any chance of seeing the road. The wind caressed my skin, causing it to feel like ice compared to the warmth my palms experienced. Did this man have any soft spots? I flexed my fingers against his chest, wanting to feel his hardness, praying like hell I made it seem natural and not like I was molesting him.

The bike picked up speed, and my heart thundered against his back. I gripped him harder, holding on for dear life, the sound of the engine drowning out everything else around me, except the two of us. He leaned into the bike, his ass moving snugly between my legs. I didn't dare move. He was warm, comfortable, and I enjoyed every minute my body touched his. I closed my eyes, trying to not think about the movement of the bike underneath us—the slight shift and unevenness of the road made me feel off balance.

The noise of the engine changed, and I finally peeked over his shoulder. The parking lot of the Neon Cowboy was packed with bikes and was the brightest thing for miles. I'd driven by it dozens of times, but never thought about stopping. This wasn't the type of bar for kids on speedy, foreign-made bikes, but a place for tough bikers to hang out, drink beer, and pick up chicks.

City backed the bike into an empty spot, and I could feel my body begin to tremble from the fear that finally began to seep through my veins. I did it. I rode on a motorcycle, and with a stranger, no less. My breath was harsh as I blinked slowly and tried to calm myself down.

"You can climb off now, sugar." His legs were straddling the bike and he held the handlebars, securing the bike for me. "Enjoy your first ride?"

I released my hands from the security of his body and hoisted myself off on trembling legs. "It was the single most terrifying thing I've ever experienced," I said, thankful when my feet were firmly on the ground. I stood, trying to get my body to stop shaking and my heart to slow down before walking inside the bar with him at my side.

"If that's the scariest thing you've ever experienced, you need to get out more, sugar. I took it slow with you." He grinned, and my stomach plummeted from his sinful smile. I wanted to see him above me naked and moving in and out of my body slowly, almost at a torturous pace. Everything about him made my body convulse and scream for attention. He wasn't my type. I preferred a bookworm and a man that liked to spend an evening inside watching a movie or playing Scrabble, not riding like a bat out of hell on a Fat Boy to hang out at a bar. I wasn't a barfly and never would be.

The outdoor lights gave me a full view of the man that called himself City. His hair was darker than I originally thought, almost jet black, and an inch long on the top, brushing against his forehead as he shook it out. It was a mess from the wind, with the front hanging over his forehead. I couldn't tell the color of his eyes; they were still hidden behind the tinted lenses of his glasses.

"Yeah, lucky me." I chuckled and tried to play it cool, even though my body shook. If that was slow, I didn't think I wanted to know what his idea of fast and hard were—or did I? Fuck me. He had my brain all jumbled.

After removing the helmet, I ran my fingers through my hair, trying to straighten it after the wild ride. He laughed as he crawled off the bike, taking the helmet from my hands, and placed it on the seat. I watched, mesmerized, as he removed his glasses and put them inside a small bag hanging from the side of the bike. I wanted to see his eyes, and the entire man without a mask or veil.

"Ready, babe?" He motioned toward the door.

I wanted to scream no, but I didn't have a choice. I could never walk into this sort of place on my own.

"Yeah, ready as I'll ever be." I started walking toward the door and felt a hand on my arm, stopping me in my tracks. I looked at his fingers wrapped around my arm and turned toward him. "What are you doing?"

"You can't just walk into a place like this. You're an outsider. They'll eat you alive in there. I don't want anyone giving you shit. We have to make them believe you're with me so they leave you the fuck alone. Unless you want the attention?" he asked with a crooked eyebrow.

"I don't." I didn't mind the idea of making everyone in the bar think we were together. City was hot and seemed like a nice guy; he did stop to help me when he could've driven right by me.

"Just stay by my side and follow my lead. I know these people and I don't want them sniffing around you. They look for easy prey," he said, giving me a smile that made my body tingle and my sex convulse.

"Okay, I'll stick to you like glue and follow your lead." Jesus, I sounded like a dork. I've always been a bookworm. I was national honor society member, and when all my friends were partying, I stayed in my dorm to study.

City nestled me against his side, tucking me between his body and arm. I moved with him, trying to keep up with his fluid movements, but my legs were so short I felt like I almost had to jog to keep time with him. He opened the door and I was immediately hit with a smoky smell, loud, twangy music, and a dozen set of eyes looking directly at us.

Randomly people yelled out "City" throughout the bar, giving me a clue that he was a regular. I felt like I'd entered a seedy version of *Cheers* and City was Norm, only sexy and muscular. He leaned down, placing his mouth next to my ear. I felt his hot breath before I could hear his words.

"Stick close and show no fear," he whispered, causing goose bumps to break out across my skin. "Let's say hello then we'll call a tow for you."

City looked big enough to handle any man in this place, but I didn't want to take that chance. I concentrated on breathing, keeping my chin up, and watching where I walked. The floor was filled with peanut shells and dust, and it made the walk in the stilettos even more treacherous than normal. I could barely walk when I bought them, but they looked too sexy to pass up.

We walked to a table filled with men all wearing their leather vests, covered in patches. They were unshaven, as dangerously sexy as City, with mischievous smiles on their faces. "Who's this lovely lady, City?" one man asked. His eyes raked up my body, stopping at my breasts before he looked at my face.

"This is Sunshine. Don't even fucking think about it, Tank, she's with me," City said with a smile on his face as he pulled me closer.

Sunshine? I'd never told him my name and he never asked. I didn't like the way Tank looked at me. Thank God he wasn't the one driving by while I was stranded. He looked at me like I was a piece of meat, a meal for his enjoyment.

Tank put his hands up in surrender. "Dude, I'd never. Chill the fuck out. I'm just enjoying the view," he said, his eyes moving from City to me, and not being coy about his visual molestation.

City squeezed my waist. "Sunshine, this is Tank, the asshole. This is Hog, Frisco, and Bear," he said, pointing to each of the men.

The nicknames didn't seem to fit any of the men, except Bear. His arms were hairy and he was big, huge, in fact, with dark hair and a fuzzy face. He looked huggable and kind, with soft hazel eyes.

"Hi," I said, looking at each of them quickly, but I didn't try to memorize their names.

"I didn't know you were bringing a woman tonight, City," Bear said.

"Wilder shit *has* happened, Bear," City said, pulling me closer, leaving no space between us.

"She doesn't look like your usual taste, my friend." Bear smirked. "I don't mean that shitty, girl, I just mean you're one fine piece of ass and too good for that low-life motherfucker. You should be sitting on my lap." He patted his leg, and I wanted to find an exit. I looked down and studied my clothes. I didn't wear the trashy clothes some of the women in here wore, but I looked classy, sexy even, with not a hint of nerd to be found.

City moved toward Bear, and my heart sank as he began to speak. "Show some respect, you asshole. That's not how you talk to a lady." City stood inches from Bear's face. "Apologize to the lady. *Now*." City towered over him as Bear stayed rooted in his chair.

Bear looked at me, and I could see him swallow hard before he spoke. "I'm sorry, Sunshine. I was just kidding around. I really am an asshole. Forgive me, please."

"No harm done, Bear," I said with a fake smile, hoping to calm the situation.

"We're going to sit at the bar." City looked at Bear, not moving his eyes.

"Come on, dude, sit with us. Don't mind Bear. He's a total dick. Make his ass go sit at the bar," Frisco said.

"Sunshine and I want to be alone. I'll catch you guys another night," City said, pressing his hand against my back, guiding me away from the table and the large bar area.

"I'm sorry. They can be childish dicks. Bear doesn't have a filter," he said as he pulled out a chair for me. City had manners. Not many of the men I dated did something as simple as pull out a chair for a lady—it was a lost art. "He's a good guy, but sometimes his mouth runs and he doesn't think before he speaks."

"It's okay, really…it is. Thanks for sticking up for me," I said to him as I sat down, pulling my stool closer to the bar. "Why did you call me Sunshine?"

"Well, I don't know your name and you remind me of sunshine—your hair is golden and your smile glows. Just sounded right. I had to come up with something on the fly," he said. "I hope you didn't mind." He shrugged and grabbed the menu lying nearby.

"I didn't mind, but my name is Suzy."

"What would you like, Suzy?"

I wanted to say "you," because somehow this man made me lose my grip on reality. "Virgin daiquiri, please."

"Virgin? Really?" His brows shot up and the corner of his mouth twitched.

"I already had a drink tonight. I just want something sweet, no liquor."

"Do you want something to eat?" he asked. "You a vegetarian too?" He laughed.

"Shut up." I smacked him on the arm. "I'm good. I just want to call a tow truck."

"Gotcha." He pulled out his phone and placed it on the bar. "Hey, darlin', can you put in an order for a cheeseburger, a beer, and a virgin daiquiri?" he asked the bartender.

"Sure thing, handsome," she said, walking away, slowly swaying her hips to grab attention. I turned to City to see if he was watching her, but he was staring at me instead, and my mouth felt dry and scratchy.

"You want to call Triple A or someone else?" he asked without taking his eyes off me. They were an amazing shade of blue, and I couldn't look away. I'd always loved my blue eyes, but his were almost turquoise. I felt like he was staring through me, into me, seeing everything I hid under the surface. I wanted him, but I didn't want to admit my attraction. I *couldn't* admit it.

"Triple A is good," I said, reaching for my purse to find my membership card. I fumbled with my wallet, finding the card behind everything else inside. I could feel his eyes on me; he studied me and it made me nervous. What was he thinking? I dialed the number as I swiveled away from him, needing to avert his stare.

"Hello, Triple A, how can I help you?"

I could barely hear the tiny female voice above the loud classic rock that pulsed throughout the smoky bar. City chatted with the bartender as I tried to drown them out and give my location and details about my car. They wouldn't be able to make it out to my car until morning. Fuck. I thanked her for helping me before hitting the end button.

"What'd they say?" City asked with a sincere look as the bartender sashayed away from us.

"They won't make it out here until morning because they're busy and we're in the middle of nowhere. I'm to leave it unlocked so they can get in and put it in neutral or something. I don't know how it works. I've never had my car towed before." Now what the hell was I going to do? I was stranded at the Neon Cowboy with Mr. Sexalicious and my dirty thoughts.

"I'll bring you back to your car when I'm done eating. I guess you'll need a lift home too?" he asked, sipping his drink as he eyed me.

I smiled at him. Though I hated the thought of him going out of his way, and I wasn't that comfortable with a stranger knowing where I lived, I couldn't say no. "I'd appreciate it, if you don't mind."

"Not at all, Suzy. I can't just leave you here and walk out the door. I got ya, babe." He turned his stool toward me and leaned into my space. "Where do you want me to take you after we leave? Home?" He quirked an eyebrow, waiting for my response, and held me in place with his hard stare.

Home? Whose home was he referring to? City looked to be the type that had different women falling out of his bed every morning…or maybe he kicked them out before he fell asleep. His fingers brushed against the top of my hand and my internal dialogue evaporated.

"Where. Do. You. Live?" The laughter he tried to hide behind his hand made it clear that I'd sat there longer in thought than I had realized.

I cleared my throat. "I need to unlock my car then I need a lift home. I live about fifteen minutes north. Is that okay? I mean, I don't want to—" He put his finger over my lips and stopped me mid-sentence.

"Doesn't matter, I'll take you anywhere," he said with a sly grin that made my pulse race and my body heat. He licked his lips, and I stared like an idiot. My sex convulsed at the thought of his lips on my skin. What the fuck was wrong with me? Every movement he made and word he spoke turned sexual, as if permeating my brain. I needed to get laid; this man was not hitting on me, was he?

"You want some? I can't eat it all," he said as the plate was placed in front of him.

I shook my head and picked up my drink, trying to cool my body off from the internal fire caused by City. The cool, sweet strawberry slush danced across my tongue and slid down my throat.

I swirled the red straw in my mouth, trying to occupy my mind. His arms flexed as he lifted the burger to his mouth, forearms covered with tattoos. The left arm had various designs woven together—a koi fish, a tiger, and a couple of other nature-themed pieces that seemed to move across his skin, and his right arm had a city skyline. I wanted to touch his arms and run my fingers across his ink. He looked big everywhere, and my gaze drifted down his body and lingered at his crotch. I wondered if his motorcycle and tattoos made up for shortcomings elsewhere, but I couldn't believe a man like him was tiny. There was no way in hell he had a party...

"Pickle?"

I blinked and moved my eyes away from his crotch to his eyes. *Pickle?* He held it and motioned for me to take it.

"No. Thanks, though. You eat it," I said, feeling like he was reading my mind. God, I hoped he didn't see me staring at his crotch. I sucked down the rest of my drink, wishing now that it did have alcohol in it. Maybe then I wouldn't feel so embarrassed. "I noticed your tattoos. What's the one on your right arm?"

15

"That's the Chicago skyline," he said, as he took another bite.

"You from there?"

"Born and bred, baby." He grunted and continued to chew. I couldn't take my eyes off his mouth. Watching him eat was erotic to me; his lips moved as he chewed, and he sucked each finger in his mouth to clean off the juices that flowed from the sandwich. Damn. It *had* been too long since I'd had sex—when eating becomes sexual. Houston, we have a problem.

2

RAY OF SUNSHINE

CITY

I COULD'VE EASILY STARTED HER CAR, BUT I DIDN'T WANT TO. HER beauty caught my eye and I wanted to know more about her. Shit, I wanted to fuck her. I couldn't just drive away and leave her out there to fend for herself. I'm a dick usually, but I couldn't just leave her there.

She looked helpless as I almost drove by her. When the lights of my bike shone on her, dirty thoughts flooded my mind. She had on "fuck me" heels with a short-as-hell skirt and a lacy white tank top that instantly made my dick hard. Her hair fell across the top of her breasts and sparkled in the light. It was golden, and I wanted to pull it while my cock was buried deep inside of her.

I pretended to come to her rescue and try to help, but I wanted to keep her as long as I could. I'd have one of the guys at the bar tow her car back to her place.

I could see fear in her eyes when we walked in tonight. They were large like saucers, her mouth hung open, and she looked around the room like she'd never been in a bar before. The guys here could be assholes, especially when a beautiful woman enters the room. Bear was always a total prick, but he did have a point. I wanted to fuck her and I wanted it dirty.

17

"How about I buy you a real drink? Just one. You aren't driving tonight, so what's the harm?"

I watched as she chewed her lip. "I guess you're right. My week's been crappy. I could use something…stronger," she said, blowing out a puff of air, causing her hair to move.

"Well, let's change that. Bad date?" I asked. I looked at her shoes before moving up her entire body and stopping at her face. "How can I make it better?"

Her lips parted and her chest heaved as she sucked air in quickly. "It's not so bad anymore. Tonight started out great, I went out with a girlfriend of mine, but it's just my friggin' car that put the icing on the cake."

Friggin'? Did grown women really use that word?

"I'm sure the car is no big deal," I said as I motioned for the bartender. "Know what you want?"

"Martini. A sweet one, please." She polished off her *virgin* daiquiri. She didn't swear and barely drank liquor; she wasn't like most girls I knew—even her clothes weren't as sexy as I'd expect for a girl her age.

"What can I get you, honey?" Sandy asked.

"Sunshine here will take a sweet martini, Sandy. Anything you can make flavored, preferably." I looked over at Suzy. "Right?"

"Yes, thank you." She looked out of place in a bar like this, but I wanted her at my side. She appeared to be a good girl with a clean mouth, but I could tell her mind was littered with filthy thoughts. She looked at me—no, stared at me—watching every movement and studying my entire body. She wanted me as much as I wanted her, even though she didn't want to admit it or couldn't. "You come here a lot, huh? Everyone seems to know you."

"The guys and I hang out here a couple nights a week after work, and it's close to my house. It's just a place I like to come to relax and unwind a bit after a long day."

She licked her lips, and I swear to fuckin' Christ my cock twitched. I adjusted myself, trying to stop a full-on hard-on from catching her eye. I watched her legs as she shifted in her seat, rubbing them together before crossing them. I had her and I knew it, but the trick was to not scare her off.

"What do you do, City?" She glanced at her hands, trying not to look at me.

"I'm an artist. You?" I left it at that—sounded classier than "I'm a tattoo artist." I was an artist at heart, but my canvas was human skin.

"Teacher. What kind of artist?"

She didn't look like any schoolteacher I'd ever had. I wouldn't have been able to pay attention in class with her walking around in heels and stretching to write on the chalkboard. "Tattoo," I said as I pointed at the artwork on my arm. "You have any?"

"Tattoos?" she asked as her eyebrows rose and her eyes grew wide.

"Yeah, by the look on your face I'd say the answer is 'no.'"

"Oh no." She laughed. "Needles scare the heck out of me." Grabbing her drink, she gulped down half the martini without even blinking.

"Do you swear?" I asked as she set the glass back on the bar.

"What?" She gaped at me.

"Do you swear? Simple question. You've said 'heck' and 'friggin'' so far, but nothing dirty."

"Oh, um, yeah, I swear." Her cheeks turned pink and a small smile spread across her face. "I'm just used to watching my words with the kids around all day."

"Prove it," I said, staring in her sapphire eyes.

"What? Why?"

"'Cause I need to know if it's in you. Are you all good girl? Or is there something more underneath dying to come out?" I hid the smile and laughter that were so close to breaking free from my lips. The pink of her cheeks spread across her face. I knew I'd embarrassed her, but fuck, I needed to know if I stood a chance.

"Yes, I swear. What do you think I am? I'm not a child, City." She glared at me as she raised the drink to her lips and wrapped them around the rim. Fuck. I wanted those lips wrapped around my dick, taking me deep and sucking me off.

"Never said you were, babe. Do you drink besides tonight?" I asked, now smiling because I knew she was upset. I liked the fire I saw in her eyes when I pointed out her good-girl qualities—she obviously didn't like being labeled.

"Sometimes. I'm just responsible. I don't drink and drive. My dad used to be a cop, and it was drilled into my head at an early age." The words she spoke hit me like a ton of bricks. Drunk driving was the one thing in the world that caused my blood to boil.

Good-girl teacher with a cop father? Just my luck. "Nothin' wrong with that. Virgin daiquiris aren't always your thing, then?"

"Why? Do I have to be a drinker? I mean, does it make me less of an adult?"

"No, Suzy. Just trying to get a feel for who you are—*what* you are."

Her shoulders slumped and she seemed to relax a bit with my words.

"Want another drink? You downed that one quick." She'd surprised me with how fast she polished it off, so my question about her drinking had been answered, but I wanted to watch her get a little pissed.

"One more and then I'm done," she said.

"You order your drink and I'm going to go talk to my friend over there real quick. He's a mechanic. I'll see what he can do with your car tonight." Standing, I motioned to Sandy and pointed to Suzy.

"Okay, don't leave me alone here too long."

"Promise, two minutes, tops." I walked away from Suzy as Sandy approached. The vultures would swoop in soon enough in my absence.

"Bored with Sunshine over there, buddy?" Tank asked as he kicked back in his chair as the others laughed. Tank's smile was wide, and the laughter only encouraged him further. "I can step in if you'd like. I wouldn't mind spending the night with that sweet flower."

I sat down in my usual seat next to Bear. "You can fuck off tonight." I pointed at Tank. "I don't need your shit." Tank just grinned. I knew he was fucking around, but it pissed me the fuck off. I'd known Tank for years, and although he could be a pain in the ass, he had a heart of gold.

"Easy there, City. What the fuck crawled up your ass and died?" Bear said.

"Nothing, man, long day. Sorry, brother."

"Sweet on that girl, huh? Never knew you were such an uptight dick, let alone overprotective of a woman," Bear said.

"I'm not, but fuck, the shit that comes out of your mouth just pisses me off at times."

"Sorry. Just fuckin' with you."

"We're cool." I slapped Bear on the shoulder, hoping to change the mood. No matter what assholes the guys could be, they were still my friends. They always had my back. "I need a favor, Tank."

"Name it."

"Her car's down the road and isn't starting. It's an easy fix to get it moving again, but there's some other issue with it. Think you could take care of it for me and drop it by her place tomorrow?"

"Sure. Whatever you need. You want me to just get it running or fix it for her?"

"Fix it and I'll pay for the repair. Don't let her pay for anything. Just drop it in her driveway."

"Gotcha, kid. I'll need her keys," he said as he popped open a peanut and threw the shell on the floor.

"I'll get them to you before we head out. Thanks, man." I stood quickly, needing to get back to Suzy. I'd already been gone too long.

"Night. Enjoy the Sunshine. Don't get burned," Bear said. *Motherfucker.*

A man stood over Suzy, invading her personal space, as she backed away as far as possible without falling off the stool. He looked greasy, with long, straggly hair, a dirty top, and stained pants, and he was covered in old, faded tattoos. I'd seen the motherfucker here before, and it never ended well. He always creeped women out, and someone always tossed him on his ass after he had one too many.

"Excuse me," I said as I stood behind him and waited for him to turn his attention toward me.

"What?" he asked without turning around.

"The lady doesn't want to talk to you." I squeezed my hands into fists and tried to keep my temper down for Suzy's sake.

"I didn't ask your opinion."

Her eyes were wide, and she slowly shook her head at me. The anger was clearly evident on my face. I felt like I was breathing fire at this point.

"Get the fuck away from my girl or it won't end well for you." I crossed my arms over my chest and stood there, unmoving. If it weren't for Suzy I would've laid the motherfucker out by now, but she didn't seem like the bar-fight type of girl.

He squinted at her and looked pissed off, but what the fuck did I care? "I don't see your name on her, dick."

"What's going on over here?" Bear said behind me as I grabbed the bastard by the collar, getting ready to pound his fucking face into a bloody mess.

"This asshole is bothering my girl. I think he needs to be taught a lesson." I tightened my grip on the material that hung from his body.

I could see his Adam's apple bob as he swallowed. I knew Bear would seal the deal, and the fucker would move on without me having to punch his fucking lights out. "Sorry, guys. You should be more careful about leaving your property unattended. Next time it may not be here when you get back. Would be a shame for something to happen to this beautiful creature." The fucking bastard smirked.

My fist landed against his face before I realized what I'd done. The fucker deserved far worse than a punch to his jaw. He was a sleazy-ass motherfucker bothering someone that obviously didn't want to be touched. "Get the fuck out of here! Now!" I yelled as he lay on the floor holding his jaw.

"Let's go, asshat. Time for you to leave." Bear picked him up and pulled him toward the door with his feet dragging across the wood planks. "Don't fucking show your face in here again if you know what's good for you."

I shook my hand as pain shot through my fingers. I knew I'd feel that punch for a couple of days, but it was worth it to lay that scumbag out and get him away from Suzy. "Are you okay?" I asked her as I flexed my fingers and studied her face.

"Yeah, I'm fine. Thank you for saving me, again." She smiled at me and looked at my hand. Her smile faded as she saw the way I moved my fingers. "Are you okay?"

"Yeah, bastard had a bony-ass jaw, is all," I said, shaking out the last pain in my knuckles.

She reached out and held my hand. "Sandy, can we get some ice over here?" she asked over her shoulder as she stroked my fingers and rubbed my knuckles with her soft, warm hands. I wanted to close my eyes and relish the feel of her skin against mine. I wanted to touch her. I ached to kiss her, but this wasn't the place.

"Really, that's not necessary. I just want to make sure you're okay, Suzy." I didn't stop her from touching me. I could feel the heat from her skin even after her fingers had moved on to another part of my hand. My hands always hurt from working for hours on designs, so the fist to the jaw didn't help them feel any better. I touched her cheek with my free hand, and she moved into my touch and searched for the contact. "You are okay, right?"

"Yeah, that guy was creepy, but he didn't hurt me. Thank you for coming back when you did."

"Sorry, I should've paid attention and shouldn't have left you. I didn't offend you with being possessive and calling you my girl? "

"Oh, no. I've never had anyone say that about me, ever." Her lips turned down as she concentrated on my hands. How could no one ever call her "my girl"?

"Hey." I held her chin and forced her to look at me. "Every girl should hear those words in her lifetime." I didn't smile. I wanted her to know I was dead serious.

"Yeah, well, I haven't." She let go of my hand and turned away from me, pulling out of my grip.

I didn't think I'd ever used those words when speaking of a woman, except Joni. A sharp pain hit me square in the chest as I thought of my ex, the only woman I'd ever loved. I had a reaction to Suzy like I did when I met Joni, and seeing another man bothering her made me see red. I wanted to protect her, unlike I had with Joni. I cleared my throat and shook my head, trying to rid myself of my lost love. "Well, it's not too late for it to happen. I didn't think I'd be sitting in a bar tonight talking to such a beautiful woman, but here I am. Your story has yet to be written."

"I'll never give up on my fairytale," she said as she let go of my hand and picked up her martini, swallowing the last drops. "Is it hot in here?" She pulled on her tank top, moving it back and forth to cool her skin. Every time the material moved away from her flesh, I'd get a peek of breast, and I had to force myself not to stare.

"Want to take a ride on the bike to cool off?" I asked. I wanted to feel her body against mine again, hugging my hips with her thighs, her arms wrapped around me.

She rubbed her forehead. "I'm feeling a bit lightheaded. I shouldn't have had two drinks."

"I'll make sure you don't fall off the bike. Just hold on tight and I'll get you home safely." I touched her knee, wanting to see if she'd pull away from me, but she didn't. The skin was soft and smooth, and I wanted to run my hands up her thighs and watch her head fall back in ecstasy. I wanted to take her home and have my way with her, but I couldn't just ask her.

"What about my car?" she asked breathily as I pulled my hand away. My touch had an effect on her, based on the tone of her voice. She wasn't good at hiding her feelings.

"I talked to Tank about it. He's going to take care of it tonight and drop it off in the morning. He just needs your keys."

"Really? He'd do that for me?" Her eyebrows shot up and her lips parted.

"Yes, and for me. Keys?" I held out my hand to her, ready to ditch this fucking place.

She dug through her purse, pulled out her keys, and placed them in my hand. She brushed her hair over her shoulder. I wanted to sink my teeth into her. I wanted to hear her moan, breathless underneath me. She truly was beautiful. She had an understated sex appeal to her. She didn't flaunt the beauty of her body, and I didn't think she even had a clue how fuckin' hot I found her. She was the girl next door, the untouched bookworm that every guy wanted to conquer. I wanted to make her dirty. I wanted to make her scream filthy words while I fucked her. I wanted to corrupt this girl in the worst possible way. She would be a challenge, and maybe I'd found someone worthy of my time.

"How will he know where I live?" she asked.

"Registration in the glove box." I twirled the keys in my finger and held my hand out for her to take. "Ready?"

"Duh," she said as she shook her head and grabbed my hand. All I could do was laugh. She wobbled on the high heels as she reached out and grabbed my shirt to steady herself. Sex didn't ooze off of her. There was a quirkiness that I couldn't put my finger on, but the sex kitten was there somewhere underneath the surface.

"Home?" I wanted to ask her "your place or mine," but I didn't think she was that type of girl. My life had become an endless parade of those girls, and there wasn't one thing that said "take me home and fuck me" about Suzy.

"Yes," she said.

I motioned to Tank, and he walked toward us before we made it to the door. "Her car is two miles south, man. Can you have it done by tomorrow?" I asked as I placed the keys in his hand.

"Sure, buddy. I'll have it at her place as early as possible."

"Thanks," I said as I shook his hand.

"Crap," she said.

"What?" I asked as we both looked at her.

"I have to cancel my tow," she said.

"Here." I handed her my phone. "Call them back before we hit the road."

"Thanks." She walked away on shaky legs; the drinks must have had a greater effect on her than I had thought. She leaned on a table with the phone in her ear and her ass sticking out. Her skirt rode up, giving me a view of the back of her legs. The muscles flexed and moved as she swayed back and forth. I couldn't imagine being tipsy and walking in those pointy fucking shoes. Women were insane.

"Make sure her car is running good before you bring it back, got it? No shit-ass job, Tank. I don't want her breaking down on the side of the road again."

"Got it. I don't do half-ass work, City. Got a thing for this girl?"

"I don't have a thing for her—my dick does, but she's just another woman. Stop busting my balls and do me this favor."

Tank laughed. "Sure. I gotcha. I'll take care of the car and you take care of her—get her home safely." He winked at me.

I rolled my eyes and spoke through clenched teeth. "I'm always a gentleman, Tank."

"Like fuck you are, man. Kind, at times, a gentleman, never," I heard him say as he walked away, twirling her keys in his fingers.

"Okay, all done. Let's bounce," she said as she touched my shoulder.

Did she just say *bounce*? Fuck me runnin'. I was in trouble with this girl. I knew it from the moment I saw her, but my cock didn't want to be the voice of reason. It never did—traitorous fucker. "Let's get you out of here and out of those shoes, Suzy." I wrapped my arms around her waist and helped her to the door.

3

DOWN & DIRTY

SUZY

Did I just say *bounce*? Hello, the nineties want their phrase back. I'd never been the cool girl, the one that attracted the sexy guy, but hell, tonight I was in rare form. My legs felt like jelly as we walked out of the Neon Cowboy into the parking lot. I was thankful for the coolness of night and the fresh air. City made me nervous, and made every part of my body scream for his touch.

I couldn't take my eyes off his fine ass as he grabbed the helmet and turned toward me. "Can you do the helmet yourself or do you want me to do it for you?" he asked with his head cocked and a smile on his lips.

I just wanted him to touch me. "Can you do it, please? I'm worried I won't do it right."

"No problem, beautiful."

I closed my eyes. I could feel my body sway no matter how hard I tried to stand still. I felt amazing, like I was flying on a cloud. I opened my eyes to peek at him as he adjusted the straps. The world seemed to spin faster every time I closed my eyes. His fingers touched my skin and I swear electricity flowed through his hand. I wanted more—needed more.

"All right, sexy. All ready." Sexy? Oh God, I wanted this man. I watched as he climbed on the bike and held out his hand to me.

"Here goes nothing," I whispered before grabbing him and climbing on the bike.

"Hold on tight." He scooted back into my legs; my entire body felt like it was on fire as I wrapped my arms around his torso and locked my fingers together. His muscles moved underneath my fingertips and I wanted to rub them—no, I wanted to lick them. I squeezed my legs together, leaving no space between us as I leaned forward, resting my breasts against his back.

"Where am I going?" he asked as he started the bike and cranked the engine.

Please don't let me be wrong. "Your place." I held my breath as soon as I said the words and waited for him to laugh.

"You sure?" he asked in an even tone, but didn't turn around.

I'd never been so reckless about anything in my life. "Yes, unless you don't want to…" Did I read the signs wrong? *God, what an idiot I am.*

"Are you fucking crazy? I've been dying to crawl inside of you since I saw you on the road. Hold on, sugar, you're in for one hell of a ride."

I tried to control my breathing, thinking about his words, but it was useless. Excitement filled me, and thankfully the couple of drinks helped give me courage to go home with this sexy-ass man…or stupidity, but in this moment all I could think of is what the night held.

I held on for dear life as we cruised down the country roads toward his place. I didn't even know where he lived, and I wasn't paying attention to anything but his body and how it felt against me and under my hands. Images of him naked flooded my brain as my heart raced in my chest almost as fast as the bike moved. I got lost in time and didn't seem to worry as much as I concentrated only on his hardness.

I peeled my face from his back as the bike slowed, and I looked around as he backed up. A small white single-story house with green shutters lay before us. His home was on a large plot of land from what I could see. The street was far away from the structure, with a long driveway connecting the two.

"Change your mind, princess?" he asked.

"No, I meant every word." My voice shook and my entire body seemed to quake.

"Climb off first, use my shoulders."

I grabbed his shoulders and could feel the hardness. He was covered in muscle. I hadn't felt one squishy part the entire time I had my hands on him. I'd always describe myself as a tad fluffy. I wasn't lean and muscular, I did have curves and some softness to my body, but not City—he was ripped. I pushed myself off, using his shoulders as leverage, and the gravel driveway made my ability to stand still and straight almost impossible. The drinks didn't help either, and the killer shoes I had on didn't allow me to grip the ground any easier.

I watched as he climbed off the bike, his muscles rippling and shifting with each movement. My mouth watered at the thoughts of touching him and being his for a night. He moved toward me, and I swallowed hard. The closer he moved, the quicker my heart pounded in my chest, and I closed my eyes out of fear and anticipation. I puckered my lips and waited for him to kiss me, but nothing.

"I need to take your helmet off." *For the love of God, please help me disappear.* I'd forgotten about the helmet, and had to look like a complete idiot standing there with my eyes closed, waiting for a kiss, swaying in the wind, and wearing the damn thing. I'd been so wrapped up in the moment that all I could think about was him—kissing him, seeing him naked, touching him…just him. I smiled and could feel the heat creep into my cheeks. Butterflies filled my stomach, and I closed my eyes, hoping the embarrassing scene that just occurred would be quickly forgotten. I could hear him softly chuckling as he undid the straps and pulled it off my head. "Cute."

I opened my eyes and squinted at him. "Cute? What the heck is cute?"

"You." He tapped my nose, and I rolled my eyes.

"Freaking great."

"Yep, you're cute. Innocent, but fucking dying to be bad." He placed the helmet on the bike, turning his attention back at me. He touched my chin, pulling my face up to look him in the eyes. The rough skin of his thumb glided across my cheek, and I inhaled quickly. "I'm going to make you swear if it's the last thing I do. You're going to be screaming curse words tonight."

Everything in my body ignited at once—my heart pounded, my hands shook, and I stood there on trembling legs, feeling his nearness. The man stole my breath and made me lose all ability to communicate. He wrapped his solid arms around me, pulling my chest against his rock-hard torso, his lips hovering over mine. His hot breath brushed against my mouth as his fingers rested against my throat. My pulse raced under his fingertips, his touch making the rapid beating of my heart increase. Everything ceased to exist as he nipped my bottom lip, sending a jolt of pleasure throughout my body.

An overwhelming craving for more took hold, and I melted into him. A small moan escaped as his lips crushed against mine. Gripping his shoulders, I tipped my head back, giving him deeper access to my mouth. I wanted everything he had to give—all doubts vanished and were replaced by sheer need.

Lust consumed me as he ravaged my mouth and commanded the kiss, deep, warm, and hard. The warmth of his fingers on the back of my neck sent goose bumps across my flesh. Wanting his heat, needing more contact, I lifted the back of his shirt and swept my fingers across his silky skin. There was a cavern near his spine, the outer edges rimmed in hard muscle that flexed underneath my touch. I brushed the edge of his pants with my fingers, sweeping them inside, grazing his skin with my fingernails. His hold on my neck tightened, and he groaned in my mouth. We fed each other air, leaving no room or moment to absorb anything else but each other.

I wanted all this man had to give. I wanted his promise of making me scream words that I didn't use. Bending down and grabbing my ass, he scooped me into his arms, never breaking the contact with my mouth. My stomach flipped like on a rollercoaster, the movement and excitement taking over my senses. The anticipation bubbled inside me as he carried me toward his house, and eventually his bedroom.

I wrapped my legs around his waist, hooking my ankles together, and felt his hardness against my core. With each step it rubbed against my clit, the friction driving me close to the brink of orgasm, until he raised my body to his abdomen. The key scraping against the lock sent a thrill through me—*I'm doing this... really doing this.* Running my fingers through his hair, I bit his lip before opening my eyes.

"Suzy has claws?" he asked against my lips, his breath warm as it caressed my face. I squeezed my eyes shut, hoping that we wouldn't hold a conversation at this moment. I didn't want to talk or chicken out. City was the most gorgeous man I had ever kissed, let alone slept with. "Want it rough, beautiful, or soft and slow?" he asked with a hard squeeze of my ass, kicking the door closed.

I sucked in a breath, not sure how to respond. No one had ever asked me what I wanted before this moment. "Um," I mumbled into his neck.

Peeling me off his chest, he looked me in the eyes. "No one ever ask you what you wanted before?"

What the fuck? Could he read my mind? "No." I looked down, trying to avoid his gaze. I felt too transparent, and I couldn't stand the thought of being figured out.

He whispered in my ear as he ground his hardness against me: "Tell me what you want and it's yours."

I bit my lip and stared at him. There was no smile or smirk on his face. City looked like a man possessed, and I had no doubts he'd deliver on his offer. I didn't know what I wanted, but I knew I wanted him any way he'd give it to me. What was his idea of rough? Fuck. "Can I have both?"

His eyes sparkled as his smile reached his baby blues. Anxiety filled my body at the thought of him naked and inside me. My breathing became labored with the knowledge that we were inching closer to our final destination. The lights were off as he carried me through the house. He nipped at my neck as I tried to take in my surroundings. His footsteps and our breathing were the only sound as he carried me.

Light filled the room and momentarily blinded me. As my eyes adjusted, I looked around the bedroom before he placed me gently on the bed. The large room had white walls; a large, framed Harley poster hung above the dresser and was the only visible decoration in the room. Dangling my feet over the bed, I noticed that the only color in the room was from the black comforter and the rich auburn wood flooring. City lifted his shirt as he watched me look around, but didn't say a word as he approached. I swallowed hard as I took in his magnificent, tanned torso.

I was speechless, and for me that's a rarity. The six-pack he sported made my mouth water, and my fingers itched to touch it. As he approached, I could clearly see the intricate art on his chest and arms. A black dragon filled his right ribcage, and black tribal designs decorated his right shoulder, looking richer against his dark skin. I never cared much for tattoos, but on him they fit and were freaking amazing.

A twinkle caught my eye, and I leaned forward to get a better view of his chest. There were barbells running through each of his nipples, and I was shell-shocked. Tattoos had become part of the social norm, but piercings still were a bit of a taboo in my mind. Not taboo in that I found them revolting, just the opposite. I wanted to play with them like a new toy at Christmas.

"Still a yes, princess?" he asked as he stood between my legs.

"Yes." My voice was a little stronger now, my resolve more certain than it had been when I'd squeaked out the words before we pulled out of the Neon Cowboy.

He leaned over me, pushing me into the mattress. My face was buried in his chest as he reached toward the nightstand, and I couldn't help myself—I licked the metal around his nipple. As he leaned into my tongue, the sound of his groan filled the room, and the sound of plastic alerted me he'd grabbed a condom. There was no turning back now; I'd be his for the night—at least he was prepared.

"Like what you see?" he asked, his lips twitching at the corners.

He knew he looked good. I was sure he'd never had a moment where he doubted his hotness or sexual prowess.

"Your artwork is amazing and the piercings are just—wow." I didn't know what else to say. I loved everything that I saw and couldn't wait to see the rest.

Hovering over my body, he stared into my eyes and lingered just out of reach of my lips. Placing my hands on his chest, I felt the solidness of his body before digging my fingernails into his flesh. His fingers touched my stomach, and I knew what I wanted. I didn't want slow, but fast and hard...all night long.

The initial softness of his kiss caught me off guard. I expected it to be demanding from the start, but his lips explored mine, testing my resolve to stay the course. He kissed perfectly. A hint of tongue swiped against my bottom lip, looking for entrance, and I willingly granted him access. Our tongues tangled together as his hand explored my body. I wanted him —I craved his touch. I moaned as his hand rubbed against the lacy fabric of my bra. I writhed under his fingers as they skillfully worked my nipple, pulling and twisting.

He broke the kiss, and I felt like I could breathe again. "Sit up," he commanded.

I didn't hesitate. I pushed myself up as he backed away and studied me. His expression made me nervous—but it wasn't critical—as he soaked me in. His lips turned up as his eyes roamed my body, and I could tell that he only had one thing on his mind. He leaned forward, grabbed the bottom of my shirt, and started to lift. "Arms, babe," he said as I sat up in front of him.

I moved quickly as his fingers inched closer to my bra. I couldn't do anything but stare at the cocky grin on his face while he undressed me. He didn't look like any other man I'd ever been with. Having him undress me was the single most erotic moment of my life. His smell surrounded me, a mixture of earth, sweat, and musk. When I thought my heart couldn't beat any faster, his fingertips caressed my collarbone, and it skipped a beat before thundering in an erratic rhythm. I wanted to get down on my knees and pray that I lived through this experience.

"Breathe," he said.

I inhaled quickly, not realizing I'd been holding my breath. I wanted to cover my body, but his lopsided grin made me do the opposite.

He wrapped his hand around my neck and kissed me. My toes curled from the passion in his kiss. I felt a hunger, like I was about to be devoured by him. Pressing my body into his, I became his meal, willingly offering myself.

Our hands and mouths became entwined, and the sound of our hard breath and lips tugging and pulling filled the air. I opened my eyes to look at him, and became entranced by his mouth. I watched as he kissed me, and took in all of his features. His long brown lashes lay against his protruding cheekbones, and were brought out by full, dark eyebrows. A shadow had developed on his jaw line and joined with his sideburns, and I couldn't keep my finger away any longer.

The facial hair tickled my skin as I ran my finger down the roughness to the edge of his mouth. I could feel our lips move under the pads of my fingers. Our hands explored each other feverishly, learning the curves and spots that made one another twitch and shake. There was a delicious torture to the touching and kissing.

My clit ached as his hand inched up my thigh and brushed against my underwear. I gasped in his mouth as his fingers dug into the material and ripped it from my skin. I didn't care that they were my best underwear that I saved for special occasions; I wanted him inside me. He cupped my sex, applying pressure as I moaned and my head fell back. I didn't have the ability to hold it up as he began running his fingers through my wetness.

"Oh God," I said, as my eyes rolled back and my lids fluttered closed.

Warmth surrounded my nipple as his mouth closed around it, and he sucked in a pulsating rhythm. I dug my nails into his skin, needing something to hold. I cried out as his teeth captured the throbbing tip and bit down. Slowly his finger prodded my entrance before slipping inside at an agonizing pace. I needed to be filled and wanted the friction of his palm to relieve the ache between my legs.

I ground my hips into his palm, begging for more, as he pulled his fingers out and thrust them back in. I wanted to palm his cock through his jeans, but his body was too long and his crotch too far away. I grabbed his hair, fisting it in my hand, and he moaned, causing the vibration against my nipple to push me to the edge. His warm, rough palm stroked my clit as he worked his fingers in and out, massaging my G-spot. Pants and moans fell from my lips as he worked my body like a well-choreographed dance number.

I couldn't stop my body from twitching as my release crashed over me unexpectedly. I screamed his name as the ripples of pleasure cascaded throughout me. I gulped for air, trying to catch my breath as my aftershocks squeezed his finger and tried to suck him deeper.

"Jesus," I muttered, wiping a bit of drool from the corner of my lips. I'd never had an orgasm so intense. No one had ever found my G-spot, let alone touched it with such skill. I lay panting with my skirt on as he climbed off the bed and began unbuckling his belt.

"You ain't seen nothing yet, sugar." His deep laugh filled the room.

"Oh, um." My stomach flipped. I needed to move. "No, let me," I said. He moved his hands away from the metal and closer to the bed. Crawling catlike, I positioned myself right in front of him and tucked my feet underneath my ass. I unbuckled his belt slowly, pulling it out of the loops in a teasing motion. Movement caused my eyes to look downward; straining against the restrictive denim I could see a long, thick bulge.

"Like what ya see?"

Fuck. "Uh huh," I said, swallowing roughly. I touched his stomach and slowly slid my fingers down his skin before grabbing for the button. "You sure about this?" I thought I'd turn the tables a bit. He kept asking me if I was sure, but hell, I knew what I wanted, and it was him.

"Mm hmm," he said with a smile on his face and a twinkle in his eye as he rested his hands on his sides.

He grinned like he knew something I didn't. A small patch of hair lined the top of his jeans—happy trail indeed. I unbuttoned his jeans and slowly unzipped them with fingers more steady than I thought possible. The clicking of the zipper passing by each tooth as I took my time and made my heart race. I savored the moment, freeing his hard-on. I leaned forward and pressed my lips to the soft, dark hair that had been trapped underneath the fabric. His body shook at the contact and his fingers tangled in my hair. The denim of his jeans was rough against my palm as I slid up his massive thigh to palm him. A small bump at the tip gave me pause before I looped my fingertips in the sides, licking a path from his belly button to the zipper.

I tugged the material down his skin as I kept my mouth attached to his abdomen. I backed away as the material slid down and his shaft sprang free. My heart stopped and I sucked in a breath, my eyes growing wide.

Jesus. "What the…" What the fuck? I stared in wonderment. Not only was the man blessed with a large member, but also he added to it, decorated it. A large metal loop with a ball hung from the tip. I was eye to eye with it, and couldn't imagine why any man would do that to his body.

"You can touch it." He laughed. "It won't hurt you," he said, moving his abdomen in my direction.

"I've never seen anything like it." I reached out and ran my finger across the shiny metal jutting out. "Will I feel it?" I felt like a complete idiot, but I'd never seen one in person, let alone had sex with someone that had extra parts.

"It will give you a different sensation at first, closest to your opening…some pressure, maybe."

I didn't want to touch it with my finger, so I stuck out my tongue and licked around the cool, sleek hardware. His hips jerked and his shaft lurched from the contact. I reached out and fisted his shaft in my hands, being mindful of the metal protruding from it as I worked it with my hands and mouth in unison. He was rock hard.

"Fuck," he moaned as I slid it out of my mouth and flicked the piercing with my tongue.

I stopped and looked at him, but didn't let go. "Did I hurt you?" His head was tipped back, with his arm outstretched, still with a handful of hair in his grasp.

"Sugar, you can't hurt me. Take all of me."

I smiled at him, and the name "sugar" made me feel all gooey inside. No one had been so forward with me, and it made wetness pool against the fabric of my skirt. I inched closer, stroking him, and held him firm in my grasp. His musky scent was intoxicating.

I knew I couldn't fit the entire thing, but I'd try like hell. I moved forward, allowing more to slide across my tongue, causing his body to tremble and his breathing to turn hard and fast.

"Fuck, baby. That's the spot. Just like that." He fisted my hair roughly, causing my eyes to water.

I moaned against his cock, and he released a shaky breath. I tried to draw him in a little deeper with each stroke of my lips against his warm, smooth skin. I stopped when the metal hit my teeth, flicking it, as his hips shook in my grasp. His hand moved in my hair, pulling and pushing me, controlling the speed as I gagged each time the head hit the back of my throat. I opened my eyes and looked up at him. His mouth was opened slightly, his chest heaved from heavy breath, and goose bumps covered his flesh. Saltiness caressed my tongue as I worked the tip with precision.

"I want to taste you." His words caused warmth to pool between my legs and my core to spasm.

"But I'm not done," I said, looking at him, confused, my hands stroking his shaft. "Don't you want me to finish?" My brows knitted together as I looked at him. He grinned and unclenched his fist from my hair.

"We aren't done. I want to bury my face between your legs and make you scream again."

Well shit, who could say no to that?

"Did I do something wrong?" I shook my head as I looked down at my knees.

His hand gripped my chin, tipping it back, and stared into my eyes. "Suzy, you didn't do anything wrong. Fuck, it was perfect. I want to lick, suck, and then fuck ya, sugar." The words left me breathy and wanton. I felt beautiful and wanted.

He guided my face to his and crushed his lips against mine, sucking my tongue in his mouth as he pulled the skirt down my hips. "Tell me you want me to taste you," he said against my lips.

I swallowed hard; words, again, escaped me.

"Say it, Suzy." With one hand filled with my hair and the other wrapped around my back, he held me in place and left me with nowhere to go. Talking wasn't something that I was used to during sex, and he definitely brought me beyond my comfort zone. "I'm waiting." He bit my lip and brought me back to the moment.

"Taste me," I said, unable to look anywhere but into his dark eyes.

His grip tightened, pulling my head back as he released his hold on my back and began to lay my body back. I felt like a Raggedy Ann doll; I was putty in his hands. My heart hammered in my chest with anticipation as I waited for his mouth to kiss my flesh. He grabbed my legs underneath my knees and pulled my body to the end of the bed as he knelt on the floor. Gripping the sheets, needing something to hold, I tipped my head back and closed my eyes. Heat flooded my cheeks with the thought of him staring at my pussy. I lifted my head and looked at him as he smiled and ran his hands along my thighs, licking his lips, and absorbed the view in front of him. Not in one spot, but all of me; his eyes roamed over my body before his head leaned forward, and I closed my eyes, unable to look. My body convulsed as his lips touched the delicate skin just to the right of my sex, enough to cause my body to crave more. Suckling the spot where my legs met my core, my body began to tremble. His hands slid down my legs, my entire body was on fire, and I ached for more. I needed more, but this felt more like a tease. He gripped my ankles and lifted my legs, placing each one on his shoulders.

His finger ran through my wetness as his tongue flicked my throbbing clit. My body shot up; I was unable to control the movement caused by the pleasure that shot through my body. His mouth clamped down as his finger slid inside me. His hands were large, but I wanted more of him as my core sucked his fingers inside. He drew me into his mouth and laid his tongue against my flesh, moving it around in circles. My breathing sounded shaky and I tried not to cry out in ecstasy, as I was so close to the tipping point.

Adding a second finger made me feel stretched to the limit, almost to the point of pain. How in the hell would I handle all he had to offer? Swirling his tongue around my clit, his fingers caressing my aching flesh, he slid his hand under my ass, his fingers digging into my skin, as he tilted my hips. My eyes rolled back as his fingers and tongue made all coherent thought disappear. I was so lost in the moment that I didn't notice his mouth leave my body as his fingers stopped.

"Do you want me?" he growled against my clit, and my eyes opened and became drawn to his stare.

I trembled and tried to steady my breath. "Yes."

"Yes, what? What do you want?" he asked, his eyes not moving from mine, his entire body still.

"Have sex with me." I knew what he wanted me to say—he wanted me to use the F word, and I hadn't, couldn't.

"Suzy." He drew out my name and flicked his tongue against me. "You know what I want to hear. Tell me exactly what you want." He withdrew his fingers and tongue, leaving me panting for more.

I closed my eyes and exhaled, needing a moment to gather my thoughts. They were just words, and ones I said every day but never during sex. Drawing in a shaky breath, I said, "I want you. Fuck me, City."

4

WICKED WAYS

CITY

THERE'S SOMETHING ABOUT CORRUPTING SOMEONE IN THE PUREST FORM. She didn't swear, or didn't like to, but the sound of it made my cock grow hard. She looked fucking beautiful laid out across my bed with her flowing blonde hair and her blue eyes sparkling in the vibrant lighting of the room. She wasn't muscular from working out, or too thin, like a crack addict, from being strung out. Her body could best be described as a classic hourglass—large breasts and curvy hips joined by a tiny waist. She looked almost angelic, her white skin against the black comforter.

I reached under her torso, cupping the crook of her arms, and tossed her up the bed. "Wow." She laughed as she bounced against the mattress. "You just moved me like I weighed nothing."

"You're like a feather," I said, crawling up her body and reaching for the condom on my nightstand.

She giggled, her eyes growing wide as I tore the condom wrapper open between my teeth. There was something so fucking innocent about her, and I wanted to crawl inside of her goodness and never leave.

I nested between her legs, resting one arm under her body, trying not to crush her under my weight. "Laugh while you can, sweet girl," I murmured against her lips. "I'm going to make you scream all those dirty words you're too scared to say."

Her eyes were like saucers as I slid the condom over my piercing and down my shaft. Her pussy glistened as I nudged her legs farther apart with my knees. I wanted to tear her up, own her body, and make her mine for the night. I didn't wait for a reply before placing my lips over hers, consuming her, and coaxing her tongue into my mouth. I could spend hours kissing her, exploring every crevice, and be happy, but my balls were heavy and throbbed, needing the release. Capturing her nipple with my fingers, I pinched it lightly and rolled it between the tips. She moaned in my mouth, and my dick jumped to attention, aching to be inside her.

My mouth never left hers as I captured all of the sounds that escaped; those were mine and only mine to devour. Her body writhed under my relentless pursuit of her nipple and the overwhelming onslaught of my fingers against her delicate flesh. I wanted to make her come like this, but I knew there would be time for that later.

Her throat was soft underneath my tongue, and I inhaled the sweet smell of her perfume, stopping near her collarbone before sinking my teeth into her flesh. Her body moved, her hips rose off the bed, and her pussy nudged my cock—an open invitation.

"What do you want?" I said, as I bit down on the flesh of her shoulder.

"You."

"What part of me?" I didn't want to make this easy on her. I got a secret thrill out of watching her squirm with each question or prompt.

"Your penis."

Jesus...seriously? Normally I'd think it was all an act, but this girl was as good as they came, and I'd have my work cut out for me. I liked the idea of a conquest, someone that I could corrupt and make my own.

"The other word. I won't fuck you until you do." I could have blue balls by then, but eventually she'd say it. I wouldn't give in until she did.

I captured her nipple between my teeth, clamping down on the tip as I flicked it with my tongue.

"City, please," she said as she grabbed my shoulder almost breaking the skin with her nails.

I held her nipple with my teeth. "Say it."

"I can't." She pushed her pussy against me. "Just do it." I gave it right back as I ground my cock against her wetness. "Oh, God," she moaned.

"He ain't gonna help you now. Say the word, and it's yours." I sucked the tip harder.

"I want your c..."

"Say it and I'll slide it in that hot, wet pussy and make you scream. That shit I can guarantee." I slid my stiff shaft against her, touching her clit with each stroke. "Say it."

"Cock," she exhaled. "I want your cock."

"That wasn't so bad, was it?" I asked as I smiled against her skin. I knew she was uncomfortable, but I didn't give a fuck. She seemed like the type of girl that lived in a very controlled world; set limits for herself and never crossed them. I'd help her go beyond her imaginary lines.

I kissed her deeply and nudged her opening with the tip of my cock as she wrapped her legs around my back, almost pushing me inside of her. She knew what she wanted. She forced me inside of her with a moan and a whimper.

Her body felt warm and slick, and a shiver ran down my spine as I entered her. I wanted to thrust inside, wanted to be balls deep, but also wanted to be in control of the pace. I licked her lips and stared into her eyes as I pushed in slowly, until I couldn't go any further. I was still for a moment and just relished the feeling of being in her—exactly where I'd wanted to be since the moment I saw her.

She looked beautiful lying on my pillow with her blonde hair framing her face like a golden crown. Her blue eyes shimmered in the light and her cheeks were tinged pink from the excitement, could have been lust. I needed to move. I wanted to make her scream. I pulled out of her slowly as her nails dug into my shoulder, and thrust my dick inside of her, unable to stop myself.

She mewled and moaned with each stroke, as I picked up the pace, unable to take it slow. I wanted to watch her, see her face, as I fucked her. I leaned back and pulled her legs from my back and placed her feet against my shoulders. I smiled at her and licked my thumb.

"Want more?" I said as I pulled out of her.

"Yes." Her voice was breathy and whisper quiet.

I placed my thumb against her swollen clit and began to move it in small circles. "Oh, God," she moaned as her pussy convulsed around my shaft.

"Do you wanna come?" I asked, pulling out again, just leaving the tip inside.

Licking her lips, she looked at me with glassy eyes as she panted, "Yes."

"Do you want me to fuck you?" I asked as I denied her the very thing she wanted most—my cock and her orgasm.

"Please," she whispered.

"Say it." My lips twitched as I tried to stop the smile and laughter that wanted to escape as her face turned pink. "It's a simple phrase. You want my cock? Tell me what you want me to do with it."

She opened her eyes and exhaled before quickly saying, "Fuck me."

"Gladly." I thrust inside of her and moved my thumb rhythmically against her swollen clit as her body twitched and her head pushed deeper into the pillow. I wrapped my free hand around her thigh, gripping it as I assaulted her.

"Your pussy feels so fucking good," I moaned. I didn't go easy on her —she wasn't breakable. I increased the pace as her breathing became more jagged and her body began to glisten in the light. I could feel her body milking me, wanting more, and in that moment I stopped.

"Hey," she yelled, and her eyes opened, showing more passion and hatred than I thought possible. "I was so close."

I didn't speak, but pulled her legs tighter against my torso. Her feet were near my face and her legs were flush against me. I gripped her legs, allowing me to hold her and stop her from moving. I pounded into her, battering her body. I watched in awe as her tits bounced from the force of my body slamming into her.

She began to yell, "Oh, God."

"That's right, sugar. Let go. Feel all of me. I want you so fucking bad."

I used every muscle in my body to fuck her. I wanted her to know I possessed her and owned her orgasm in this moment. Her body began to tremble as her leg muscles tightened and flexed against me. I gripped her legs tighter, not wanting her to move.

"Fuck," spilled from her lips, and I couldn't control myself any longer. I didn't have to coax her into saying the word, but my cock had pushed her over the edge.

"You're so fucking tight," I said as I watched her body on the edge of orgasm—covered in sweat, skin flushed, and mouth open, lost in sensation.

She reached up and touched her breast, pushing herself over the edge as I thrust into her harder than I had before. "Oh God. Oh God, don't fucking stop," she wailed.

Her naked body before me, her dirty mouth, and watching her touch herself caused my balls to tighten, and the orgasm ripped through me. I shook and moaned as I pounded into her, her insides gripping me. Every part of my body tingled, and small aftershocks shook me to my very core.

I needed to catch my breath. The only sounds that filled the room were our gasps for air and the snap of the condom. "Fucking hell. That was amazing," I said as I kissed her ankle, running my hands up her legs.

"I've never..." she said.

"Never what?"

5

ONLY IN MY FANTASIES

SUZY

"NEVER EXPERIENCED ANYTHING LIKE THAT," I SAID. HOW TO EXPLAIN IT without sounding pathetic? Damn, nothing in my life had compared to having sex with him. I'd had a few one-night stands in college, but those boys didn't exactly know what they were doing.

City was rough and controlling, and I loved it. I stared at his beautiful body as he knelt before me, his skin glistening with sweat, his muscles moving in unison as he tried to catch his breath. I wanted to take a picture and always remember how he looked—sweaty and sexy as hell.

"That's nothing compared to what I could do to you," he said in a husky tone as he wiped the sweat from his brow. I wanted to lick the sweat off his body. I wanted to do things with him that I normally didn't even think about doing to anyone in my life. He was different.

"Hell," I said, unable to think of anything else. He could do better? Was that even possible?

"Maybe you'll let me show you sometime." A smile crept across his face, but it wasn't a sweet smile. This guy definitely had tricks up his sleeves. My heart raced at the thought of feeling him inside me again.

"You want to see me again?" I asked, unable to believe his words. We were polar opposites, and I didn't know why he'd want to see me again.

"Why wouldn't I?" His eyebrows turned down as his nose wrinkled.

I covered my eyes, feeling like an asshole. "I dunno. I thought this was just a one-night thing."

"I won't lie, I thought it would be just a one-night 'thing.' I wanted you from the moment I blew by you on the road." He moved next to me, wrapping his arm around my body. "You're not like any of my friends or the women I know."

"Well, I've met some of the people you hang out with." I frowned, thinking about some of the guys he'd surrounded himself with. Most of them seemed shady as heck. "They look more like my class full of under-achievers or someone I'd see on *America's Most Wanted*. Not my type."

"They look that bad?" he said in my ear. His low tone made my exhausted body buzz again.

"They're kinda scary, City. They remind me of criminals," I whispered.

He laughed. "Funny shit, sugar. They look scarier than they are." He nuzzled into my shoulder, burying his face in my hair. "I don't hang out with all those guys. Many of them are customers—some of them are my best clients. I stop there on the way home sometimes for a drink. Some of them are friendly and, well, some you've seen are assholes."

"You can say that again."

His body shook and I felt the vibration from his silent laughter. "I spend more time with my family than with those douchebags at the bar." He brushed the hair off my cheek and ran his fingers down my throat before he rested his palm on my chest. I felt exposed. "Are you cold?" he asked as I shivered.

"A bit," I lied. I wanted to cover my body.

"Did you want to leave?" He yawned.

"Um, I'm sure you're tired. I can stay if you want. It's up to you." I didn't want to leave this hot, hunky man and go home to my empty bed. *Don't kick me out like a piece of trash.*

He grabbed the blankets and covered our bodies. Yes! Inside I was doing cartwheels and screaming with excitement. He pulled me against his side and wrapped me in his arms. His body felt hard and comfortable. I rested my forehead against his jaw and could hear his heart beating in

CHELLE BLISS

his chest. The sheets were the softest cotton I had ever felt—not really what I had expected. I thought he'd be more of a flannel guy, or those scratchy sheets you find in hotels.

"Comfortable?" he asked with a long, content exhale.

"Very." I hadn't slept in the arms of a man in years. Usually I didn't fit just right, or they were so bony that my head hurt resting against their body, but City was built to sleep on. He was built for anything that involved two bodies.

I didn't quite know where to rest my hand. Did I put it on his chest or leave it at my side? Sophia wasn't going to believe this story when I tell her. She knew me as the good girl that lived in my controlled environment, unable or unwilling to move, but City was like a tsunami that started slowly and built into a giant wrecking ball of sin.

"Hand, babe."

"What?" I mumbled against his chest.

"Gimme your hand."

I moved my hand from my thigh and held it out to him, trying not to touch his skin. Grasping it, he placed my palm on his rock-hard chest, and put his hand on top. "Perfect," he said.

I didn't have any grand illusions, and I wasn't delusional. I knew I'd only have this night with City. We weren't meant to be—he wasn't what I was looking for. He wasn't the type of guy that was part of my master plan. I'd just lie here and enjoy the night in his arms.

I listened as his breathing slowed and changed. His hand twitched against mine as he squeezed my fingers and drifted into a deeper sleep. I felt exhausted, but I almost didn't want to sleep. I didn't want to miss a minute of staring at his body.

Thoughts flooded my mind while I listened to his deep breaths. I wanted to see him again, but would it be a waste of time? Did I want to go down a dead-end street and become attached to him? I knew I could fall for him. Even though I wanted to find someone to spend my life with and have that great happily ever after, I didn't open my heart to just anyone. Heartache was something I avoided at all costs. There wasn't a need to risk my heart if the certain outcome would be disastrous. The war of words continued in my head for a few minutes, until I finally decided to enjoy the moment and worry about the rest tomorrow.

***

The sound of metal clinking woke me, and I sat up in a panic. I thought someone had broken in while I slept. Looking around the room, I realized I wasn't in my bedroom. Last night hadn't been a dream. Reaching over, I felt the sheet where he had lain, and it was cold to the touch. Sunlight streamed through the sheer white drapes and bounced off the walls, amplifying the light. The room was tidy, except for our clothing from last night strewn about the floor.

My body ached as I stretched, trying to relieve the pain from my muscles being over used the night before. I needed something to wear and had to find a bathroom. I tiptoed out of bed and wrapped the sheet around my body to keep the cold at bay. A flannel shirt hung on the back of his door, and I grabbed it and held it up to my face, burying it in the soft material. The hint of cologne and the muskiness of his skin made my pussy clench. I dropped the sheet, wrapped the flannel around my body, and rubbed my cheek against the wrist cuff. I felt surrounded by City.

Walking to the door that I thought was the bathroom, I opened it and found his closet. Fuck. It was filled with t-shirts, jeans, and hoodies. I studied the contents, running my hand over the soft materials as they hung, before I closed the door. There were only two doors in his room, and neither of them led to a bathroom.

My reflection in the mirror hanging on the back of the door made me cringe. My blonde hair was in tangles and looked a mess, and my eyes looked tired from the night in his bed. A messy ponytail helped to tame my mane, making me feel presentable. Good enough. Opening the door, I peered into the hallway before tiptoeing into the hall. A loud, long creak filled the air as I took my first step.

"You up?" he yelled from the kitchen.

"Yes," I said, trying not to sound annoyed. "Be right there."

"I'm fixing breakfast. Take your time." I could hear dishes, cups, and all kinds of movement in the kitchen. I didn't think I'd ever had anyone besides my mom, Sophia, and Kayden make me breakfast. The smell of bacon and something sweet drifted down the hall and made my stomach grumble.

An old claw-foot bathtub and white pedestal sink filled the white and black room. He didn't seem too fond of color, which I found odd, since he described himself as an artist. Everything was clean and sparkling. I could tell that he took pride in his home. I searched his bathroom, looking for an extra toothbrush, but tried not to make noise. A knock sounded at the door and I jumped, knocking over some bottles under the sink and smacking my head against something hard. "Shit," I said as I rubbed my head.

"You okay? Did you need something?"

"I'm fine." So not fine. He caught me snooping and probably heard the bang from my head. "I wanted a toothbrush, do you have a spare?" I put my head in my hand, feeling like a fool but thankful that he didn't witness the event.

"There's an extra one in the medicine cabinet. Help yourself." I could hear his footsteps quiet as he walked away.

My face was still red as I left the bathroom and walked into the kitchen, trying to avoid City's eyes.

"Eggs, pancakes, and bacon okay?"

He looked amazing. He wore a pair of black track pants and a smile.

My stomach rumbled over seeing all the food he had prepared. "Did you cook for an army?" I asked.

"Didn't know what you liked, so I made a little bit of everything." He put the spatula on the counter and walked toward me. He was so damn hot. I licked my lips and closed my eyes.

I could feel his hot breath on my lips, and I smelled his scent. "I'm gonna fuck you, right here, right now. Yes or no?"

OMG, OMG, OMG, yes, yes, yes!

I swallowed hard and nodded before I leaned forward.

"Words, Suzy. Now the answer needs to be 'yes, fuck me, City' or 'no, I don't want to.'"

How would I ever say no to this man? I thought about the possibility of never seeing him again, and I wanted one last shot at him.

"Yes, fuck me, City," I whispered against his lips.

His mouth crushed mine and I could taste the coffee and sugar on his tongue. I could only hear our breath as the world around us fell away. His hands trailed up my thighs and cupped my ass. Fuck, this man was pure sin, and I wanted to be his minion.

He broke the kiss and looked in my eyes. I could hear his breathing, fast and hard. "Hands on the counter," he said with a commanding tone. *Yes, sir. Gladly.*

I turned my back to him and placed my palms on the edge. He pushed down on my back and lifted my hips. I rested my head on the cold tile and waited. Looking behind me, I watched as he pulled down his pants before palming his shaft. I heard a crinkling noise coming from his pocket. He'd planned this—he had a condom ready to go. *Lord, help me with this man.* Could I resist him?

I started to stand up when I heard, "Back down, sugar." I closed my eyes and followed his command. I felt him stroke my opening, and I sighed. When did I turn into a big ole pile of mush with a guy? He slid inside of me easily; I was slick and ready for him.

He grabbed my hips, holding me tightly as his hardness worked like a machine inside of me. I gripped the counter and my fingers began to tingle from my death grip. He felt amazing, caressing my insides with the metal piercing. My muscles ached as I stood on my tiptoes. He pounded into me, the sound of our skin slapping filling the air, his grunts ringing in my ears. His grip intensified and became almost painful.

"Fuck, your pussy is so damn tight," he growled.

"I love your cock," I moaned. That just slipped out—like it was something I said every day.

"I love being buried in your sweet pussy, sugar."

All the dirty words and the feeling of him stroking my depths pushed me over the edge. My body began to shake, and I moaned, "City."

I heard a loud crack and my ass began to sting. Did he just slap my ass? The pain began to radiate throughout my body and made my orgasm grow and build. My grip began to slip as my insides clenched against his length. *Crack.* Fucking hell.

"Fuck," he yelled as his stroke became more intense and erratic. I could feel him grow harder inside me as he slammed me against the counter. He rested his head against my back as we both stood there immobile for a moment.

"You got me all kinds of crazy, Suzy," he said, breathing heavy.

"Makes two of us." I was thankful the tile was cold. My body was covered in moisture and my skin was hot from the pounding I had just taken. He pulled out, and I instantly felt the loss of him. I waited for my feet to uncramp before trying to stagger to a chair. He removed the condom with a quick snap and tossed it in the trash. I swayed to my seat, thankful that it was only a few steps away. He adjusted himself inside his pants and walked to the stove with a devilish grin on his face.

"Pancake?" His blue eyes stared into mine as he held the pan up, asking permission to slip it on my plate.

I forgot how hungry I'd felt when I walked in. How did the man just fuck me like a maniac and now he was cooking like Guy Fieri?

"Yes. I never met a meal I didn't like." I silently prayed to God the jitters that filled my stomach would subside long enough to eat the giant meal he'd prepared.

"I love hearing shit like that. My sister is so fucking picky it makes me batshit crazy."

I buttered my pancake and watched him out of the corner of my eye as he grabbed the pan of eggs off the stove. An awkward silence filled the room as I looked at my plate. He'd just had his cock in me as the food sat on the stove, and now what? I wanted to keep the conversation flowing, and figured I'd follow his lead.

"Just one sister?" I asked.

"Just the one, but I have three brothers too. Eggs?"

"Everything," I said, moving my pancake to make room for the eggs and bacon. "Five kids, wow, your mother must be an amazing woman."

"Yeah, I think we caused most of the gray hair on her head, which she now dyes to keep her youthful appearance. We aren't the traditional Italian family. You have any brothers or sisters?" he asked, plopping the eggs on his plate and then putting the pan back on the stove.

"A sister, she doesn't live here. She's still up north, where we grew up." I poured the syrup on my single golden pancake before cutting a chunk.

I envied City. He had a big family and they had a bond that I'd never had with mine. He had something I always wanted.

"Ah, I can't imagine only having one. We're kinda a gang. We do everything together." He stuffed the eggs in his mouth and grabbed a piece of bacon. "You've missed out."

I loved that it seemed easy between us; we were comfortable, and he made me feel that way. "I guess so, but I have some friends that I'm closer to than any of my family." I placed the forkful of buttery goodness in my mouth and let it sit on my tongue a minute before I chewed it. "My mom's kinda a flake, and my dad works all the time, so I just have my friends."

"Damn, that fucking sucks. My family gets together every Sunday for dinner, and it's usually a bit loud."

"Every Sunday?" I saw my parents every week, but sometimes it was only for an hour, and dinners only happened on holidays.

I tried to go slow, not wanting to eat everything on my plate. I didn't want to look like a pig, but I was starving.

"Every Sunday. It's required, or my parents think something is wrong. Sometimes my grandparents come over and it turns into an all-day affair. Mom usually wakes up early to make the sauce and meatballs. We're required to be there at one for an early dinner."

It sounded nice. I'd never had anything like that in my life—never knew families did that kind of thing, besides in the movies.

"Hmm, that sounds like fun." I ate my breakfast and thought about all the family things I'd missed out in my life. My parents seemed too busy to deal with us at times, let alone have me over for dinner every Sunday. I knew they loved my sister and me, but we didn't have the close-knit family that City had described.

"It is, but I work with my brothers and sister and sometimes it gets to be too much. So, babe, do I get to take you on a proper date?"

"Oh, sorry," I said. "I'd love to go on a date with you. I mean, we already..." I moved my hand around, lost for the right word to describe what we did the night before.

"Fucked." He laughed. "I don't know if I will ever get over your good-girl thing you have going on."

"I'm not a good girl, City." I wasn't, and I knew it. Good girls didn't think about the things I did. They didn't want the things I wanted, and they sure as hell didn't go home with strangers. "What we did last night wouldn't have happened if I was a good girl." I smiled at him.

"You're a woman, Suzy. Sex doesn't make you a bad girl; it makes you human. That shit was explosive last night, and this morning I needed

51

to be in you again. I wouldn't change a goddamn thing." He must have sensed I was uncomfortable with the entire conversation. "I don't think you're bad. If someone does, then fuck them. I don't give a shit what anyone thinks about me."

"I know. It's not always so easy." I wanted to change the subject. "Do you want me to call my friend to pick me up?" I didn't want to dissect my qualities at the moment.

"I'll take you home after you're done, okay?"

"Thank you. I have a ton of things to do today." I had to grade papers —it was the end of the grading period, and grades were due on Monday morning. I had to make lesson plans and pay the bills before the weekend ended. My work never ended, not even on the weekends. Teachers don't walk out the door on Friday and leave it all behind—we work on the weekends and walk through the door on Monday prepared to teach the budding students not always so interested in learning. I sighed, thinking about all the work I had to do, but I was the only one that could get it done.

"No problem. I have to get to work by noon, so no rush."

I wiped my mouth unable to consume another morsel. "Where do you tattoo?"

"Inked. Ever hear of it?"

"I drive by it every day on the way to work, I think." I remembered seeing the sign, but had never set foot inside. "Looks like a nice place."

"Ever been?"

"Oh, no. I meant from the street. Doesn't look like the other shops in the area. Yours is pretty. How long have you worked there?"

"I don't think I've ever heard it described that way. My sister does all the decorating. We own the shop and opened it about five years ago."

Well, maybe he wasn't the starving artist I thought he was.

"Why don't you stop by sometime? I'd love to pop your cherry." I started choking. "Ink, babe, I'd love to give you your first tattoo." He laughed.

I patted my chest and coughed. "Maybe someday I'll let you. My parents are just anti-tattoo, and I never found anything I'd want to look at for a lifetime. How'd you pick yours?"

"Each one signifies something in my life." He pointed to the city skyline on his arm. "This is a reminder of where my family comes from, Chicago. It's where I grew up, and I go back every summer to visit my friends. It's part of me in more ways than one." He laughed and rubbed the tattoo on his arm.

"And the fish?"

"Ah, the koi. Well, that one I had my brother, Anthony, do when we opened the shop. It's a symbol of determination and power to achieve goals. We always talked about opening our own shop, and we'd finally achieved it. Plus, I fucking love the color orange."

"Looking at your house, I'd think you loved white."

He picked up my plate and laughed. "This place is only temporary. I don't see a point in splashing color on the walls. I'm surrounded by color all day at work. It's calming to come home to an empty canvas." Artists —complex creatures.

"I understand. My walls are actually white except for one blue wall in my bedroom. I'm not the typical bubblegum-pink girl."

He began to clean the kitchen and put the dishes in the dishwasher. His muscles rippled and flexed with each movement. My mouth watered as I remembered what it felt like for him to be above me and in me—I wanted more of him.

"I'll finish cleaning up. You go get ready to hit the road, okay?"

I could get used to being waited on. Mind-blowing sex? Check. Good cook? Check. Sexy as hell? Check. Manly, yet nice? Check. He had all the right qualities and kind of reminded me of Kayden. I didn't want Kayden, but I wanted someone that cared enough to take care of me.

"I'll just be a minute," I said as I stood from the table. "I don't want to take up any more of your time."

"Take all the time you want. I can't get fired if I'm late." He laughed as he kicked the dishwasher closed. "By the way, is Suzy your full name?"

I hated my full name. It sounded stuffy and old. "No."

"Spill."

"It's Suzette."

"Now that's sexy as fuck. *Suzette*." It rolled off his tongue, and I felt the moisture from my core begin to pool. Fuck, he'd made me a total cock-loving whore, and I wanted to hear him scream my name.

"Right." Looking over at his beautiful skin and taut muscles, I drank him in—memorized the picture before I walked out the door, leaving him to finish and to get the hell out of here. He could definitely become a weak spot if I didn't put distance between us. That yin and yang bullshit didn't really work in real life.

6

TOO GOOD TO BE TRUE

CITY

I SHUT THE BIKE OFF AND WAITED FOR HER TO CLIMB DOWN. SHE TRIED TO remove the helmet on her own and stood there looking as drop-dead fucking gorgeous as she did last night. She fumbled with the straps, trying to pull it off, but she frowned and her fingers began to move frantically. "Lemme get that for you," I said as I motioned for her to move closer.

"Sorry," she said, blowing a puff of air out.

"It's my pleasure, trust me." I winked and watched her cheeks pinken. I worked the straps apart slowly, trying to prolong the ending to our time together. I felt like she was going to give me the brush off. Her body language didn't match the last twelve hours. I needed to set another date with her and dig deeper into the woman she was instead of who she pretended to be.

"Thanks," she said, trying to look me in the eyes.

"There. So, about the real date. How about tonight?" I asked. I didn't see a point in wasting time. I wanted her in my bed again—or against the counter.

"Um, I guess tonight is good." She looked at me and then to her feet.

"Sugar, it's just a date. A real date—no strings attached." I grabbed her chin to look into her sky-blue eyes. "We kinda missed that part of

55

getting to know each other before I took you. I'll pick you up at nine. Wear something warm."

"Okay, I'll be ready. Want me to drive?" She looked at my bike, wrinkling her nose, and then noticed her car. "Wait, how did my car get here already? I totally forgot about it breaking down. What the heck?"

"Tank fixed it for you and delivered it about an hour ago. It's all ready, but to answer your question, no. We're taking the bike."

"Oh. Do you have his number so I can pay him?" she asked, her eyes wide as she chewed her lip.

"I got it. He did it as a favor to me."

"Oh, I couldn't. Let me pay you for it, then."

"Suzy, let me do something nice for you. Really, it wasn't a problem. Tank and I worked it out. I don't want you broken down again on a dark country road."

"I know. I just try and watch my money. I was going to get it fixed."

"Well, now it is. Nine tonight, and warm clothes." I leaned forward and kissed her lips. I grabbed the back of her neck and drew her closer. The light, sweet scent of her perfume filled my nostrils, as I tasted her lips. Everything about her was fucking sweet, and I wanted more. I consumed her mouth and commanded her body with my kiss. I wanted to leave her weak in the knees and wanting more when I drove away. I broke the kiss, but kept my hand in place and watched her as she stood there with puckered lips and her eyes closed. Exactly the response I wanted.

"Sugar," I said, smiling at her as her eyes fluttered open.

"Oh, sorry. I say that a lot around you." Her cheeks turned pink as she bit her lip.

"We'll finish that kiss later. I can't wait to crawl back inside that delicious pussy of yours tonight. Digits," I said before she had a chance to walk away. I programmed her number in my phone and sent her a text as she walked in her house. She'd be back for more.

I started the engine, revving it a couple times before pushing backwards and down the drive. She waved with a sweet smile on her face. My cock ached as I thought about all the dirty shit I wanted to do to her. I watched her in my side mirror as she watched me drive away. I had her.

***

"Where the fuck you been, Joey?" Mikey said as I walked through the door of Inked.

We opened Inked about five years ago. Everyone in my family has an artistic streak, and we didn't trust outsiders with our money. Growing up, my father had drilled that mantra in our heads. Don't trust others when you can do it yourself. We agreed that there would be no outsiders unless absolutely necessary. Problem with it, though, was that you could never fire family, especially when they're part-owners. Mike had the spaz gene. He was known for overreacting.

"I had to drop someone off, shithead. Who made you boss?" I asked as I set my stuff down at my workstation.

"You're typically here early. I started to get worried. You could've called or something, asshole."

"Don't get your panties in a bunch, Mom. I'm here now, so shut the fuck up."

Mikey threw his hands in the air—showing his surrender or disgust, I couldn't tell. He was the shop manager since he had absolutely no artistic talent, but he was one hell of a piercer. His real passion was fighting. He had joined the circuit years ago and often traveled out of town for a fight. Fighting with your hands and tattooing do not mix. My hands were precious to me. I needed them to work my magic and see the smiles on the faces of my customers.

"Mom called to remind us about tomorrow," Anthony said as he walked out of the employee-only area. Anthony is my oldest brother and probably the most unsettled. He's an amazing tattooist, but he's a musician. He dreamed of hitting it big, but for now he was ours.

"What the fuck?" Mikey said.

"How could we forget? It's only been the same day for thirty years," Izzy said as she unpacked her machine.

Izzy's the youngest and the only girl beside my mom. My parents kept trying until finally they had the little princess they always dreamed about, after having four boys climbing the walls and roughhousing. She was girly and kind, but if you crossed Izzy, she'd kick your ass. We were all overprotective of her, but we were scared of her too. In my family, the ladies ruled the roost and weren't to be crossed. She got that commanding personality from my mom, and led with an iron fist.

"Let's run down the schedule before I open the doors," Mikey said, leaning over the counter, looking toward the work area.

I listened to Mikey babble on about the clients of the day. I already knew my lineup. I had to finish a back tat I'd been working on for months, and a girl wanted me to fix her bad choice in a tramp stamp.

My mind kept wandering to Suzette. My mom would be happy if I brought a good girl home for once—someone that could give her grand-children someday. I was not ready for that. My dick was doing the thinking instead of my head. *Get your head on straight, man—too much pussy out there to settle.* I was getting a little ahead of myself, but Suzy may have been the first respectable girl I'd met in a long time. I never brought women I'd dated or slept with around my family. None of them had a future with me, and I didn't feel the need to subject my family to an intruder or an outsider.

"Joey." My sister stood, her face invading my personal space.

"What, Iz?" I looked up and noticed her squinty eyes as she studied me.

"What are you grinning about?"

"Nothing."

"Oh, bullshit." She pointed at me and tapped me on the forehead. "You've met someone. Spill it, brother."

"There's nothing to tell. You think you're a mind reader, but you aren't, sis."

"I've known you my entire life. You walk around here all moody and serious, but today I'd say you're almost glowing, ya big pansy ass."

"Fuck off, love."

"Ooooh, jackpot. Who is she?" A giant smile crept across her face as she leaned forward and stared in my eyes. She wasn't going to let it go. Everyone stopped what they were doing to listen to what I had to say, and Isabella's impending inquisition.

"Fine, Iz. I met her last night and I'm taking her out tonight. Happy?"

Iz twirled around and giggled like a schoolgirl. "Extremely, big brother." She kissed me on the cheek. I leaned back in my chair and watched as my sister celebrated like I was about to walk down the aisle.

"Don't get ahead of yourself, Iz. It's just a date."

"Oh, now come on. I can tell by the look on your face that she's a little bit more than just a simple date. I want the deets."

Grunting, I crossed my arms over my chest. "She was stranded and I stopped to help her. I brought her home and I'm taking her out tonight, simple as that."

"Hmmm."

She came closer, not believing a word that I spoke.

"Izzy, leave it at that."

"Who is she?"

"She's a school teacher, but I don't know much about her."

"You've had sex with this girl. I can tell." Izzy poked me in the chest. "You can't hide anything from me."

"Well, shit, Iz. That's none of your business, really." The door chimed as my client walked through the door. I was thankful that I had a reason to end the conversation and save the grilling for another day. But I wouldn't get too comfortable. I knew my sister's interrogation would happen sooner rather than later.

***

The shop had a buzz today. Everyone had smiles on their faces. The fall weather always made people happy. I had been coloring in a beautiful flower that I had inked on a client, Michelle, a week ago, but she couldn't take any more pain to finish it that day.

"It's healing nice, darlin'." I wiped the blood and ink off her skin.

"Yeah, I can't wait to see it finished. Sorry I pussied out the other day, City." She closed her eyes as the needle poked the still-healing skin.

"Hey, it's cool. I've seen huge men in tears getting a tattoo. I rather you walk away than pass the fuck out."

Her eyes opened and she started to laugh. "Really? Guys have actually cried?"

"Yes, like little babies. So no worries. Now hold still so I don't fuck this up." I patted her leg with my rubber gloves and set out to finish the beautiful tattoo.

I loved working with color. Flowers weren't normally my thing; I loved animals and intricate designs, but flowers were a challenge and were laced with bold colors.

My phone vibrated on the table and I glanced at it as I dabbed the needle in the pink liquid.

Suzy: *I can't make it tonight. Sorry, City.*

Fuck, she was brushing me off. I couldn't stop and text her back. Little Ms. Suzy would have to wait. I'd have to remind her of how good it felt inside her and how fucking hard she milked me.

"Something wrong, City?" Michelle asked.

"Nah, darlin'. Just thinking about something."

"Didn't mess up my tattoo, did you?"

"Hell no. I don't fuck up."

"Thinking about a girl?" Her eyebrows wiggled up and down.

"A woman." I didn't look up as I spoke to her, and I kept my eyes glued to her tattoo so I didn't have to eat my fucking words.

"Lucky cunt," she muttered.

"What?" I'd heard her loud and clear, but just wanted to see if she'd 'fess up.

"Oh, nothing. Wanna talk about her?"

"Nope. I'm good. Shit's between her and I, Michelle."

I had to get in that pretty little head of Suzy's. I knew I scared the fuck out of her and I should. I wasn't her type or some clean-cut cock-sucker. I knew how to please a woman, take care of myself, and have a good time. I just couldn't give her a chance to run away like a scared little princess.

Time felt like it stood still as I colored in the same area over and over again to get the shade just right. A small hint of gray near the pistil and I had finished this flower of torture. I wiped off the ink and patted her calf. "All done. Take a look."

She glided her hands down her legs in a seductive manner, but I didn't take the bait. "It's beautiful. You're fucking amazing." Not going there—not with this one.

I grabbed my phone, needing to change Suzy's mind about tonight.

Me: *Come on, it's Saturday night. Live a little, sugar.*

I washed my hands as Michelle sat back down and stared at the finished masterpiece.

"You remember what I said last time about taking care of the tattoo? Stay out of the sun, don't go in the pool or ocean until it heals, and keep it clean. Let me cover it for your trip home first. You can pay up front. Iz can check you out." After grabbing a new pair of gloves, I covered the area with a dressing.

"Don't you want to check me out?"

I could hear the hurt in her voice, but fuck no, I didn't want to check her out. I only had one person on my mind, and it was Suzy Goodie Two-shoes.

"Pfft, fine." Michelle stomped off as I grabbed my phone and typed another message.

Suzy: I don't think it's a good idea. I had a great time with you. Thanks for your help.

Like hell I'd let her off that easy. She was going to be mine again.

Me: I'll be there at nine—be ready. No ifs, ands, or buts.

Suzy: City—No.

Me: Boyfriend?

Suzy: No. I'm not a cheater. I don't think we'd work out—we're just not right.

Me: Sugar, it felt right this morning when my cock was buried inside of you and you screamed my name. Nine. No strings—just FUN. You know the word, right?

I cleaned my workstation and prepped for my next willing victim. I wouldn't let her weasel out of a night of fun. She didn't respond right away, but I knew that she would. She had to be thinking about the way she looked at me when I was buried inside her. I knew I had her. I just had to get beyond all her brains and rules. I had to reel her in. I knew my last sentence would agitate the hell out of her. I didn't think people besides the fuckheads in her class challenged her very often. I wasn't a boy and didn't know how to take no for an answer.

Suzy: Nine.

Gotcha.

***

Suzy opened the door with a smile on her face and a killer outfit.

"Hey. You look amazing." She had on furry boots, skintight jeans, and a fluffy, oversized sweater.

She eyed me up and down, studying my outfit. "I guess I'm dressed okay."

"I'm not a fancy guy. I wear my jeans, t-shirt, and boots or sandals."

She made a face at me—what the fuck was that about?

"You never dress up?" she asked, as she locked the front door and turned to face me.

"Only when necessary. Tonight it isn't." I sat on the bike and held out the helmet. "Want to do it yourself?"

She plopped it on her head. I laughed as she fiddled with the straps. "Want help?"

"No...I'm perfectly capable of doing it myself." She fastened the buckle under her chin. "See?" The helmet slid forward, covering her eyes. "Damn it."

I couldn't help myself; I burst into laughter. "Come here, lemme help."

Her lips pursed with annoyance.

"Don't worry, sugar, you'll get the hang of it."

"I'm not used to all this..." She motioned to the bike, her eyes still hidden as I pulled her toward me.

"Live a little. Learn to let go."

Her lips turned up in a smile. "Not that you know, but I'm a total control freak."

"We'll work on that." I pushed the helmet on top of her head and grabbed the straps.

"I'm perfect just the way I am." She squinted at me, which made it harder for me to stop laughing. The pissed-off-teacher look made my dick rock hard and my balls ache.

"I didn't mean it that way. I mean you need to learn to have some fun," I said, grabbing her chin after fixing the fasteners.

"I have plenty of fun, for your information."

"Climb on, sugar." I patted the seat. "What do you like to do for fun?"

Her hand touched my shoulder as she hoisted her leg over the bike. "Well, I like to read. I go out with my friends sometimes. Um, I like to hang out at the pool. I like to play games. I do plenty of fun things." Her body rested against mine and I closed my eyes. *Down, boy—not tonight.* She didn't mention one thing that resembled fun in my book.

"What about a club? Concerts? Parties?" A girl her age should've experienced a couple things in her life. She went to college and had to live a little...I mean, fuck. "I know you've never ridden a bike before."

"I don't dance. Concerts, a couple of times in college, and parties? Do work parties count?" She clasped her hands around my chest and sealed the gap between our bodies.

"Everyone can dance. I saw how your body moved last night, babe. You can dance." I turned the key and throttled the engine.

She swatted my chest. "Hush."

I'd embarrassed her. Good—I needed to push her. I wanted to learn what she was really all about. The good-girl bullshit worked for me, but I needed to know there was a sinner underneath that polished veneer.

"Well, tonight we're going to add a few check marks to your life." I moved my body, leaving no space between us.

"What are we doing?" she asked against my back, already hiding her face.

"Heading to the beach."

"It's dark, though."

"Exactly."

I drove slowly through her neighborhood, waiting for the right moment to pay her back for the smack on my chest. I hit the open country road at the end of her development and gunned the bike. Glancing in the side mirror, I could only see her blonde hair blowing in the wind.

I sped up, and she pinched my pec and yelled, "Stop!"

I didn't listen, pretending the wind made it impossible to hear. I pointed at my ear and shook my head. "I can't hear you."

"Slow down," she yelped.

Stopping at the red light, I turned to look at her. "There's no one around. We're safe—I promise."

"I don't know if I can ever get used to riding on this dang thing."

"Do you trust me?"

"What?"

"Trust, sugar. Simple question."

She sighed. "I do."

"Then enjoy the ride. It's freeing and there's nothing like it in the world. Ready? Hold on." I gunned the bike, but not enough to lose control, as she screamed in my ear. I couldn't stop myself from laughing.

She still had a stranglehold on my chest as we rolled into the beach-front bar. I squeezed the bike into the only single space available. Charlie's was the place to be seen on a Saturday night, and by the looks of it, half of the town was there.

"Can I open my eyes now?" she asked, her voice muffled from my jacket.

"We're here. Off you go." I pried her fingers apart and patted them.

"Charlie's?" She climbed off the bike and unlatched the helmet quicker than I thought possible.

"Yes. Have you been?"

"No." She looked around the parking lot.

"Hey," I said as I grabbed her chin. "It's okay. I'll give you plenty of firsts." I smiled at her. "I like the idea of showing you new things." There were so many things I wanted to do to her. I wanted to ruin her in every possible way. Fuck the lawyers and the boring motherfuckers.

"I rarely come down to the beach, let alone at night."

"Well, tonight there's a DJ, and I want to dance with you."

"Oh," she said, her eyes wide in shock. "I told you, I can't dance."

"You can and you will. Might take a couple of those sweet drinks you like, but you'll do it."

"Oh, suck it."

"I plan on it." I smirked at her and grabbed her hand.

7

I'M NOT TOO UPTIGHT, AM I?

SUZY

DID I KNOW WHAT A GOOD TIME WAS ANYMORE? I WENT TO COLLEGE AND knew how to live it up and let go. My life had become so wrapped up in work and finishing my master's degree that I kind of forgot what it meant to let go and unwind. I'd always put more pressure on myself, wanting to get ahead in life, not wanting to worry about paying the next bill. I lived comfortably and I was happy with that. I enjoyed staying home and reading a good book. Hell, it was cheaper than going out to a bar and drinking. I needed to watch my pennies, and drinking them just felt silly.

"I'll take a margarita," I said to the bartender, reaching in my purse, but City put his hand over mine.

"I'll take a Yuengling, please," he said to the bartender, and then he looked at me and said, "I got this, Suzy."

"I can pay for myself."

"We're on a date, sugar. I pay when we're on a date. Put your money away—I'll find another way for you to pay me back." Butterflies filled my stomach as he said the last word in my ear close enough that I felt the vibration.

I grabbed my drink, letting the cool liquid slide down my throat. I needed liquid courage if he thought I would dance with him tonight. Dancing and me didn't mix, never had. I never knew what to do with my hands, and I always felt like everyone watched me—it freaked me the hell out. If he wanted to dance, I'd give him exactly what he asked, and make an ass of myself to prove him wrong.

City picked up his beer and studied me. Why did he have to be so damn sexy? I didn't want to like him, but I did. His cockiness wasn't like the other men I'd dated; it had nothing to do with his career or his material possessions. No, his was natural and sexual.

"I'd like to say you should slow down, but fuck it, I like when you're tipsy." He sipped his beer and leaned against the bar.

"I don't see you tearing it up."

"I can't, I'm driving and I don't drive drunk. Have to keep a clear head when you're on a bike." He ran his finger over the rim of the bottle, and all I could do was stare at him.

The band took the stage, and everyone clapped as the lead singer began to speak. "Thank you. Thank you," he said as he motioned for the crowd to quiet down. The guitarist began to play, and the crowd grew quiet. A soulful melody filled the air as the lead singer began to sway. The rhythm was intoxicating, and if I were home, I'd be dancing around my living room making a total ass of myself without any witnesses.

"Finish your drink." City's lips were set in a hard line, and I knew what he wanted.

"Think you can handle all this?" I motioned up and down my body. Fuck, how else could I stall?

"I know I can." He licked his lips, and I didn't want it to affect me, but he got to me. "I remember the way you moved against my cock, sugar." He brushed the hair off my shoulder, and my spine tingled.

My face grew flush as images of last night flashed in my mind. I didn't respond to him as I polished off the last sip of my margarita. "I warned you." I shrugged and smiled. *Here goes nothin'—let's show this big boy whatcha got.*

Holding hands, we walked to the middle of the dance floor. The music wasn't the right tempo for a slow dance or to shake my booty, as Sophia used to call it. I didn't really know what to do as I stood there and looked around. He wrapped his arm around my back and pulled me close. "Feel the music. Follow my body."

Every inch of his front touched mine as he began to move with the music. Wrapping my arms around his neck, letting his body guide mine to the beat, it struck me how well the man could move. His body rubbing against mine caused my nipples to harden, and a familiar ache between my legs returned. The memory of how he felt inside me, moving in the same rhythm, made my knees feel weak as he held me against his torso. I let him move my body—I became pliable in his hands.

"See? You got moves," he said in my ear as I buried my face in his chest.

I didn't know if the liquor had given me the ability to move with the music or if it was the man holding me, but I'd never moved this gracefully in my life. I looked up into his eyes, and he stared at me with the side of his mouth turned up in a grin. Why did this sexy-ass man, who lived life totally opposite of me, want me? We didn't fit—we didn't make sense on paper, but that didn't stop my body from reacting to him, no matter how hard my mind said to ignore his charms.

"You think too much. Stop making a list of why you shouldn't be here. Feel the reasons you should," he said, and kissed my lips, distracting me as he pressed his erection into my stomach. My doubts vanished. I leaned into his body and grabbed his pecs, toying with the piercings underneath his shirt. "Don't start something you don't want to finish, Suzette," he whispered against my lips.

"I always follow through, City." I smirked and winked before pressing my lips against his. I couldn't resist him, at least not in person. I'd live for tonight and deal with the fallout tomorrow. Our bodies slowed as we kissed. He ran his fingers through my hair and then fisted it, tipping my head back to give him deeper access.

I breathed his air, no room left between us, as he held my body to his. He pulled back and left only a small gap between us, not releasing his hold on me entirely. "I want to taste you."

Fuck me. Every bit of my body felt hot and damp. I wanted City more than I had last night. "You do?" No one had ever talked to me like he did.

"I will." I could see his eyes change with his words, his pupils fully dilated. "I don't make false promises."

I swallowed hard, unable to stop the barrage of sexy images from invading my thoughts. Why can't he be a lawyer or something other than a biker tattoo guy? He probably wouldn't have this effect on me if he was anything other than who he was —City.

"Stop thinking and dance." He released his hold on my hair and swung me out, pulling me back against his body with a thump. *Christ have mercy on my soul.*

For once in my life, I felt like I could actually dance. The music was slow and sensual, and let me move without feeling like an idiot. We touched each other constantly and didn't lose eye contact.

The music slowed and everyone began to clap. "For our next song…" the lead singer said.

"Want another drink, sugar?"

"Yes, I'm parched." City had me all kinds of crazy. I felt like I was drooling, but my mouth screamed for something cool, and my body needed a break from the foreplay on the dance floor.

City motioned to the bartender, snapped his fingers, and pointed at me. "Aren't you getting one?" I asked.

"Just a water. I'm driving, remember." I respected him for sticking to his original plan. "Plus, I'd rather get you a little liquored up. We have an appointment down on that swing." He pointed in the distance to a dark object.

"What's out there?" I asked, squinting and trying to get a better look, but the beach was shrouded in darkness except for the glimmer of the moon on the ocean.

"Darkness."

"And?"

"You. Me. Darkness." The corner of his mouth tipped up, and I swear to God his eyes almost twinkled.

The bartender placed the margarita in front of me and I picked it up, needing a diversion. I ran my tongue along the salt before taking a mouthful of the cool, sweet liquid in my mouth. I swallowed fast, and the alcohol burned my throat on the way down. I looked at City, and he was watching me intently, curiously. I licked the rim again, letting the salt dance on my tongue, and saw his chest expand as he breathed in quickly.

"Keep doing that, sugar, and I won't let you take another sip."

"What? This?" I licked the rim again, keeping my eyes trained on him, and let my tongue drift as far as I could.

"Fuck," he muttered, running his hand across his face.

Two can play a naughty game, City. I may not be the hussy he was used to being with, but I knew how to get a man's attention.

Smiling against the glass as I took another sip and looked away, I pretended to be uninterested. The salt tasted good, mixed with the sweet, tangy drink as I let the liquid linger on my tongue before swallowing it. My legs felt tingly as the liquor spread throughout my system.

"Damn," I said, my face becoming flushed.

"What's wrong?" He raised an eyebrow, cocking his head.

"Strong drink. Guess the first one never left my system," I said, tipping it back again and sucking down the last bit of liquid.

"That's it. Come on, Suzy. I got something for you to lick." He grabbed my hand and started to tug me away from the bar.

"I can't," I protested as I set the glass on the bar.

"Oh, yes you can. You said you always follow through, and I'm cashing in on that promise, sugar." Butterflies filled my stomach with the knowledge that we were not going to be watching the waves. City had plans for me, and I couldn't back out now.

We reached the last step on the deck, and I stopped before my feet hit the sand. "Wait." My hand fell from his. "My boots. I don't want them to get ruined." I tried to give an innocent smile. I really didn't want to ruin them. They cost me more money than I wanted to admit.

He grunted and moved closer to me. We were eye to eye, with him flat on the beach and me perched on the step. He didn't say a word as he reached down and picked me up. I laughed as he pulled me against his chest. "Wrap your arms around me."

My laughter stopped as I wrapped my arms around his neck and stared at his face. City was beautiful; his dark features and ice-blue eyes that looked clear in the moonlight stole my breath. His jaw had a shadow from the stubble, and I ran my fingertips across it, remembering the night before. His lips were full and beautiful and screamed to be kissed. His eyebrows were manly, yet neat—no waxing, but he groomed them. His dark hair flopped with each step, and I couldn't help but smile. He was everything I wanted and exactly the type I ran away from.

City sat down on the swing, still holding me in his arms. "Straddle me," he growled in my ear as the swing moved back and forth.

"But people can see us." I looked around as my heart thumped in my chest.

"Could you see the swing from up there?" He smirked.

"No, I couldn't, but if someone catches us we could get in trouble."

"Sugar, we won't get in trouble and no one's going to find us. Trust me. Now straddle me."

I scanned the deck area, and he was right—no one was looking for us, or even seemed to notice that there was anyone on the beach.

"You a regular here, big boy?" I said as I adjusted my body.

"I only come out here to be alone. You're the first girl I've ever brought here."

"Hard to believe that I could be your first in anything."

"Sugar, no bullshit. You gonna kiss me or what?" he asked, grabbing my chin.

"Depends on the what," I said giggling, as he squeezed my waist, pulling me close, our noses touching.

"You talk big, little girl. I'm going to get that taste I've been looking forward to."

8

ANGLES

CITY

I COULDN'T STOP THE THOUGHT OF SUZY MOANING ON MY LAP, FACING away from me last night as I finger-fucked her. She was hesitant at first, nervous someone would see us, as I unzipped her pants enough to slide my fingertips inside. I wiped any thoughts out of her mind with a few strokes of my fingers. I watched her face as she rested her head against my shoulder—I watched her eyes roll back, and a small sound escaped her lips. "Quiet, sugar," I whispered in her ear, and she obeyed. Stroking her insides, circling her clit until her body shook and her pussy clamped down on my fingers.

She didn't move at first as I withdrew my fingers from her lace panties and brought them to my lips, wrapping my lips around them as I sucked her juices, and she stared at me with an open mouth and wide eyes.

"Mm. Taste yourself on me." I bent down and pressed my lips to hers, dragging my tongue across her bottom lip.

"City." She moaned in my mouth.

Reaching up and pulling her face to mine, I crushed my lips to hers.

"Joey. What the fuck?" Something hit my shoulder, and I blinked.

"What the fuck, Iz."

"Your dopey ass has been sitting there in fucking La-La Land for ten minutes grinning like a fucking mental patient. Snap. The. Fuck. Out."

"Couldn't just leave me there?" I asked. "And Iz, stop fucking hitting me. You're the only person that I let get away with that shit. You're always poking me with those bony-ass fingers."

"It's time to eat. Mama's been calling for everyone to come to the table." She rolled her eyes at me before walking away.

"I'm coming, Ma." I adjusted my dick in my jeans. My mind had become a little too engrossed in my fantasy, and the relief I needed would have to wait. I climbed off the couch and slid my hand in my pocket, looking for the phone that vibrated against my dick.

Suzy: I love your idea of or what.

Based on her message, I could tell I wasn't the only one thinking about our time on the beach.

"Iz, what the hell do you call the what, where, when, why, and how in English?"

She looked at me confused as I sat down at the table. "Trying to impress the teacher?" She giggled.

"Just answer the question, please." I sighed and stared at her, placing the phone on the table.

"What teacher?" Ma asked.

"Iz, what's it called? Throw me a bone."

"Interrogatives." My sister rolled her eyes before turning to face our mother. "He's schtuppin' a teacher, Ma."

"Isabella! That's not appropriate at the dinner table." My mom set the lasagna on the table. "I want details, Joseph." Ma winked at me.

Me: Wait until you feel the rest of my interrogatives.

I placed the phone on the table and looked around the room. Everyone had their eyes glued on me instead of the meal, as they usually were. "What?"

"You're smiling as you type—who is she, Joseph?" Ma said as she dished out the first steaming slice of heaven to my father.

"Just a woman, Ma." I held up my plate as I waited to be served. My mother was traditional in many ways, refusing to let us serve ourselves. She was the one to dish out the food and to sit last.

She held the lasagna over my plate. "I've never seen you like this. You want your piece, baby? You hungry?"

"Hell yes." I licked my lips and moved my plate closer to the piece hovering just out of reach.

"Then you're going to tell me about her, yes? No information means no food." She held the slice of lasagna to her nose and inhaled it. "Mm, it would be a shame for you to miss out on this meal."

I sighed. Women—the root of the evil in this world. If pussy wasn't so fucking perfect I'd swear off them for eternity.

"Fine, Ma. I'll tell you about her after we eat. Can I please have a piece now?"

"Sure, baby. You can help me wash the dishes and tell me all about *her*."

Fuck. "You're an asshole, Iz." Throwing me under the bus with Dean? Still seeing him?

"Bella, you better not still be seeing that man. He's nothing but trouble," my mother said.

Iz glared at me across the table. Served her little gossipy ass right for airing my shit at the dinner table.

The conversation turned to sports and football, as it always did on Sunday. My grilling was soon forgotten as my brothers and Dad stuffed their faces and rubbed their stomachs. I finished my lasagna, wiping my plate clean with a piece of garlic bread, before picking up my phone again.

Suzy: WTF. I teach math—no clue what an interrogative is. Hello— I don't get your angle.

Me: At the end of my linear path I have a point for you.

Did that make sense or did I just make a complete ass of myself? Fuck. This girl had me all fucked up. My parents always wanted their children to "settle down" and make babies, but I'd always been more interested in perfecting my skills and not wanting to get tied down, at least not after Joni. We didn't marry young and follow their path in life, and I thought my parents were secretly proud of us for waiting. They were happily married and have been for over forty years—they tied the knot right out of high school. Times were different.

Suzy: Oooh, you know just the right things to say to a girl.

73

Me: Tuesday night = (dinner) + my linear path + your diameter

"Joey, grab your plate. We have a date with a sink and some dishes," Ma said from behind me. I looked up at her and saw her smiling and reading over my shoulder. Fuck.

Suzy: No can do—grad classes. I'll take a rain check.

I turned off my screen and placed it in my pocket. Nothing was secret or sacred in this fucking house.

"Everybody bring your plates in the kitchen. Come on. Clear off the table," Ma said. The room filled with grumbles, but we all knew the drill. Thirty years later we didn't need to be told what our roles were in this family. My father was the figurehead, my mother told everyone what to do, and we did as told without giving lip.

Ma waited for me by the sink as I set my plate on the counter. "Did you find someone?" She was beaming.

"I just met her, Ma," I shooed her to the side so I could start tackling the dishes.

She threw the dishrag over her shoulder and eyed me. "Baby, the heart knows what the heart wants. Your sister told me you've been acting differently. It's written all over your face. Sometimes fate steps in and throws you off the course we've set in life."

"Don't go crocheting baby blankets yet, Ma."

She placed her hand on my shoulder as I scrubbed and avoided eye contact. "Joseph, I know the man you are. I know you're guarded with your heart after Joni, but you have to open again sometime. You need to find someone to trust in life. Is this girl worthy of that trust? Is she worth the risk?"

"Ma, I barely know the chick."

"Tsk, tsk. Someone doth protest too much." She kissed my cheek, ruffling my hair. That shit made me crazy, but with my hands full of soap I had no other option but to let her do as she wished.

"I can see you're not going to stop. She seems like a good person. She's different, Ma. She seems genuine, but I'm not rushing into anything."

"What about her? Is she madly in love with my baby boy?"

"Ma." I should hate her calling me her baby boy, but my mother could call me anything in the world. I adored the woman. "She isn't jumping on the Joey train. I don't think she really wants to see me."

"What? Why not?" She leaned against the counter, crossing her arms. "You're perfect."

"That's 'cause I'm your kid. I'm hardly perfect, Ma." I cleaned the last dish and placed it in the rack to dry. "You don't really know everything about me, no matter what you think."

"I know more than you think, sweetheart. Iz has loose lips, you know." I could beat my little sister's ass. I'm sure she doesn't tell my ma about all her love affairs. "I know you're quite the ladies' man. I'm not judging you, Joey. You never bring any girls around, but I know you."

Fucking Iz. "When and if I find the one, Ma, you'll be the first to know." I kissed her cheek, and her radiant smile lit up the room. "Suzy sees me as a tattoo artist that rides a motorcycle and hangs out in shithole bars. I don't exactly rank up there on her boyfriend material checklist."

"I kinda like this girl already." She giggled. I loved hearing the sound of her laughter. "She doesn't know everything about you and our family?" She raised her eyebrow.

"No, I don't tell anyone about us, Ma."

"Checklists are made to be changed. She needs to know the Joey I do. Are you going to ask her out? Make her yours?"

"That's what I was trying to do at the table, but she has class."

"Ah, a smart girl too. Joey, don't ask a girl out through text message. That's what's wrong with you kids today. She needs to hear your voice when you ask. Texting is too impersonal, and I'll never understand it. Call the girl."

"I will. I'll call her later. Happy?"

My ma wrapped her arms around me and said, "Very."

9

BROKEN RULES

SUZY

I COULDN'T GET HIM OUT OF MY MIND, AND IT HAD BEEN LESS THAN twenty-four hours since he dropped me off with a soul-stealing kiss. His cocky smile, his muscles, the way he touched me stayed with me long after he left. No one had made me want to break a rule more than he did. No matter how hard I tried to concentrate on my lesson plans for the upcoming quarter, my mind drifted to him.

Trying to quiet my brain, I flipped on *Catfish* as I crawled in bed. It had been my guilty pleasure since this show began. I loved watching the train wrecks and the broken hearts of those that thought they fell in love with someone, only to find out that they weren't who they pretended to be.

I used to tease Sophia and Kayden, my old roommates, mercilessly about how different their little tryst in New Orleans could've turned out. Their situation was different; they had mutual friends and had checked each other out, so they felt it was a sure thing.

On paper, Kayden and Sophia didn't work—it wasn't a match made in heaven—but their love was undeniable. It was electric. Sophia followed her heart, and his pull was inescapable for her. She fell for him hook, line, and sinker. I never understood it until I got to know Kayden. He wasn't anything like I thought—his heart was pure, but his path in life

76

had been different than mine. I'd never believe Sophia would find a guy without a college education and a criminal record to fall in love with, but they were the happiest couple I knew, and I wanted that kind of love.

My checklist had been realistic in theory, but City had me questioning my method and requirements. I'd dated men that fit on paper, but the chemistry lacked. City was just so City. I was approaching the end of my twenties, sitting in bed, eating bonbons, and watching *Catfish* alone.

I am happy, aren't I?

My phone began to move across my nightstand. I popped the last morsel of chocolaty goodness in my mouth. "Herlo?"

"Hey, Suzette." The vibration of his voice through the phone made my heart skip a beat as I swallowed the chocolate slowly. Damn, why did I have to eat that last piece before I answered? *Herlo?* I sounded like I had a speech problem.

"Oh, hey. How are you?" I grabbed the water on my nightstand and washed down the last bit of candy.

"I'm well, sugar. Whatcha doin'?" I heard rustling in the background. Were those his sheets? Was he naked?

"Just watching television, and I'm about to go to sleep, you?" I wiped the chocolate from my lips and licked my finger. These little bitches were so damn tasty.

"I just crawled in bed. What are you wearing?" he asked in a smooth timbre.

OMG, he didn't just ask me that. I looked down. I had my ratty go-to clothes for when I lounged around the house. "Um, a tank top and flannel pajama pants."

I could hear him laughing. "Really?"

"Yeah, why? What are you *wearing*?" *Please don't say you're naked.*

"Nothing, sugar." *Damn it all to hell.* "You still there?"

"Yeah." I knew he could hear the change in my tone, as it came out all breathy and quiet.

"When can I see you again?" he asked.

"I don't know, City." I wanted, *God* how I wanted to scream now, but I needed to think about him—us.

"Don't deny you want me, Suzy. I can hear it in your voice. You're thinking of my cock inside you and your lips on mine."

My breath hitched as the images played like a movie in my mind. "I won't deny it, but that doesn't make it right," I said, moving down in the sheets and turning off the television.

"I'm not asking you to be my girlfriend, Suzette. I remember you having an earth-shattering time yesterday. I can still hear the sound you made when I made you come against my fingers." A small moan escaped his lips.

My heart ached when he said he didn't want me to be his girlfriend. What the hell? *Stay on course—do not waiver from the list.*

"It was the sexiest fucking sound I've ever heard, sugar. The way your eyes rolled back and your body rocked into my hand. Fuck."

I squeaked. *OMG, lemme die.* "City."

"The taste of you on my tongue after. Fucking perfect. I'm rock hard thinking about you."

"You are?" I whispered.

"Rock fucking hard." His breathing changed like it had when he fucked me. I could never forget the sounds the man made when he came. "Friday night, Suzy. No excuses this time."

"Okay. Friday."

"Good. I'll be thinking about that sweet pussy all week, sugar. Sweet dreams." His words were drawn out and his tone was sexy as hell.

"Night," I whispered back before the phone went quiet and his harsh breath disappeared. Listening to the man turned me on, and I wanted to run to his house and have sex with him, but I didn't. Reaching into my nightstand, I grabbed my trusty battery-operated boyfriend of the last five years and thought of City as I climaxed. The orgasm didn't compare to the one I'd had under his deft fingers. He fucking ruined one of my simple pleasures.

***

Fuck Monday mornings. I never wanted to get out of bed. I pulled in the school parking lot five minutes late before throwing my bags down in my classroom, and I headed to the copier to be prepped for class that started in ten minutes. Damn. I hated being rushed.

I tapped my finger against the copy machine as it slowly churned out each piece of paper. People walked in and out of the teacher work area with quick hellos and "happy Mondays."

"What are you grinning about? It's Monday and you never smile, bitch," Sophia said behind me.

"I wasn't smiling." I turned around to see her grinning like a loon that had just escaped the funny farm.

"Oh, you were, sister. What happened?" Sophia always looked so put together and breathtaking.

"I have so much to tell you. I'll come see you during my planning period."

"By the look on your face I'd think you got laid this weekend. I'm not talking about a boring bullshit fucking either. You got *fucked*," she whispered in my face. I felt my face flush. "You did, don't lie, and I want every last detail."

The homeroom warning bell blared, and I started to panic, grabbing my papers in a crazy heap. "I'll be up third period. I'm going to be late, Sophia. I gotta run, babe."

"I'll hunt your ass down if you don't show up," Sophia said as I reached the door.

"I'll be there, whore. Shut it."

***

Sophia shut the door to her office. "Tell me, and I mean all of it."

Sitting on the comfy old couch in her office, I rested my head against the wall. "What do you want to know?"

"Don't play coy with me. You know more about my sex life than anyone else in the world. I want all the information, starting with who and when."

Sophia sat at her desk and rested her head on her hand. "I met him Friday night."

"Friday night? I don't remember you meeting someone," she said, her eyes looking upward as she replayed our time at the martini bar.

"After I left you. My car crapped out and this drop-dead gorgeous man stopped to help me."

"Helped you out of your panties too, I presume?" She giggled and slapped the desk.

"Eventually." I laughed. "I called you, but you didn't answer. I went with him on his bike to call a tow, and ended up having a drink or two."

"Bike? Like the ones the drunks ride around here with the electric motors, or are we talking smokin' hot Harley action?"

"Smokin' hot."

"His name?"

"City, but it's a nickname. When we left he asked where I wanted to go, and I told him I wanted him to take me to his house. I'd had too much to drink, because you know that just isn't me."

"Whatever. You're dying to be naughty but those uptight pricks you date are missionary men. Bleh. Keep talking," she commanded.

"Pushy wench, aren't you? When he undresses, girl..." I sighed. "Oh. My. God. His body is covered in tattoos, his nipples are pierced, and he, and he..." I covered my mouth and tried to hide my grin.

"Breathe, Suzy. He what?"

"His penis was pierced too." I swallowed, remembering how it looked.

"Oh, now I'm enthralled. So your ass breaks down, is rescued by a sexy-ass biker with tats and piercings, and..."

"I slept with him. More than once. I stayed the night, and he had me before breakfast too."

"Have you talked to him since?"

"Yes, we went on a date Saturday night, and he wants to take me out again on Friday."

"I know that look. What's the problem?"

"He's just not...isn't what I'm looking for." I frowned.

"Suzy, baby, listen to me. Do you like this man?"

"Yes."

"As you would say, did he make your body tingle and make you scream?"

"Yes, more times than I can count."

"Do you want to see him again?"

"I do, but—"

"Fuck buts, girl."

"He's a tattoo artist and lives in an old house. He just doesn't fit my checklist. He's a biker, Sophia. What could we possibly have in common?"

"You and your damn lists. If I had a list I wouldn't have Kayden and Jett. I can't imagine my life without them. We can't always control everything in life; sometimes life jumps up and smacks us in the face."

"I know, Soph. He scares me," I whispered.

"Has he hurt you?" She stood and walked toward me with her eyebrows drawn together and her mouth set in a hard line.

"No. I mean, I'm scared I could fall for him. I've never been with anyone like him, and I want to see him again. I've never had *that* spark, and with him it's like lightning."

Sophia sat down next to me and grabbed my face. "You listen to me, Suzy. You're young and have your whole life ahead of you. If you want to be with him, then do it. Stop trying to fit everyone in your mold. Rules are made to be broken. Give the guy a chance, babe. He's not asking you to marry him, is he?"

"No, he said he's not asking me to be his girlfriend either."

"Kayden wasn't looking for a girlfriend, but here we are, engaged with a baby. Sometimes life doesn't give us what we're looking for, but it gives us what is supposed to be. We just have to be willing to take the plunge. Live a little. Take a risk for once."

I smiled and hugged her. "You're right, Sophia, but I need some time and distance. So, Kayden still makes you happy even after everything?"

"I wouldn't trade a moment I've had with him. He's everything to me. My life's complete, Suzy. You need to find that guy that makes you feel whole. The one that gives you a reason to wake up each morning."

"So I should just enjoy the ride?" I wiggled my eyebrows at Sophia and laughed.

"In a matter of speaking, yes. Was it beautiful?"

"What?"

"His dick, Suzy. I've never seen a pierced one in person."

"Oh my God, it was the most beautiful thing I'd ever seen."

"I'm so excited for you, Suz." She bounced on the cushion, causing both of our bodies to shake. "When are you seeing him again?"

"Friday night. He didn't give me an option to say no."

"Smart man. You're such a pussy at times—listen to your heart and not your mind for once, got me?"

"Yes, Mom. I understand."

"Oh, and Suzy?"

"Yes?" I turned and looked at the grinning Sophia.

"I want pictures."

"You're such a whore." I laughed as I walked out the door.

ANTICIPATION

CITY

ME: ARE YOU IN BED?

   Suzy: Yes, you?

   Me: Yep, just lying here thinking about you. 24 hours until I hear you scream my name again.

We'd been texting all day. I never looked forward to a simple phone call or text from any chick. I ached for her. I lived with a perpetual boner now. We didn't have an exclusive deal, but the other girls didn't seem to do it for me anymore. My dick didn't ache for them. It wanted Suzy and her tight, sweet pussy.

   Suzy: What's your real name?

I thought I told her my name, but maybe I hadn't.

   Me: Joseph.

   Suzy: Can I call you Joe or Joey?

   Me: You can call me anything you want, sugar.

   Suzy: Joey. It suits you.

I never felt like a Joey—it seemed childish, and the nickname City seemed to fit me better.

   Me: Tank top and PJ pants?

   Suzy: Yes. Y?

   Me: Just want to know how to picture you as I stroke myself.

Craving the release, I stroked quicker, gripping it in my hand. I didn't want to come too quickly tomorrow night—I wanted to savor her and feast on her body.

Me: I'm going to picture you with your legs on my shoulders and your beautiful tits bouncing from my dick, slamming into you.

I stroked myself as I waited for her reply, caressing the tip, toying with the ring, giving it a tug.

Suzy: That's sexy. I can't wait to suck on you. Feel your velvety hardness in my mouth.

Oh, the little girl could be dirty. Time to push the envelope.

Me: Tell me one of your fantasies.

I wanted there to be a bad girl underneath—someone that wanted to get dirty with me. I stroked my shaft slowly and pictured her tight cunt milking me.

Suzy: Really?

Nothing was easy with this one.

Me: Yes, pick one.

Suzy: I always wanted someone to take me from behind and for him to hold my wrists at my side so I can't move.

Fuck me, it was a start at least. I wanted to pound her into next week. I wanted her so bad I thought my dick would break in my hand.

Me: What else? More.

Suzy: I always heard choking was amazing.

I stroked my cock faster and harder than I had before. I pictured my hands wrapped around her throat, watching her face turn pink, and feeling her clawing my chest as I rammed my cock into her. The warm liquid spurted, landing on my abdomen before I could stop.

Me: Fuck, sugar. You just made me come so fuckin' hard.

Suzy: OMG.

Me: Are you touching yourself?

I grabbed my shirt off the floor and wiped up the mess that I created lost in my mental fuckfest.

Suzy: Yes! You do things to me, Joey, things I've never felt before.

Me: Wait till tomorrow, sugar. Put a finger inside yourself.

No reply. She must be following my command. *Fucking perfect.*

Me: Don't type; just watch the screen, Suzette.

Me: I'm going to fuck you from behind and hold your wrists so tight in my grip that your fingers will go numb. My cock's going to throb inside of you—hit every spot that makes you scream, sugar.

How in the fuck was I getting a boner already?

Me: When I see your body grow flush and dew on your skin, I'm going to wrap my hands around your throat from behind and apply pressure until you're gasping for air and milking my cock for more.

Me: Come for me, sugar.

I lay in bed and pictured her touching herself. *Down, boy—fuck.*

Suzy: You're bad for me, Joey.

Me: Who the fuck wants to be good? Sweet dreams, beautiful.

Suzy: Night, Joey. I'm looking forward to the ride tomorrow night bahaha

I turned off my ringer and stared at the ceiling. I planned to give her more than she could handle and make all of her fantasies come true. Suzy was getting to me and cracking the well-built wall around my heart I'd created after Joni's death. *Air—I need air.* I jumped out of bed and put on a t-shirt and jeans. I needed to think, and I did that best on the open road.

I revved the engine a couple of times, put on my riding glasses, and cracked my neck. The roads were clear. The cold weather kept most of the snowbirds that traveled south off the roads, especially at night. I kicked the bike in top speed and felt the wind lash my exposed skin and blow through my hair.

I rode for over an hour, winding through the country roads before pulling in my driveway after midnight. My muscles vibrated and I felt exhausted. My mind was too tired to think of anything but my bed.

***

After grabbing my keys and jacket off the couch, I headed outside. Even though the calendar read October, the air was sticky and the sun made my skin burn—but I knew there would be a chill in the air tonight. Florida's winters were bipolar. Sometimes hot, sometimes cold—a totally fucking guessing game to keep you on your toes.

I tried to use Suzy's crazy-ass fucking method—I made a mental checklist while I drove. She had pros—fucking beauty, smart as hell, kick-ass career, independent, kind, innocent—but she also had cons. She was too fucking innocent and she could crush my heart into a million fucking pieces. *Think, man. She has to have other fucking flaws.* I liked the geeky girl underneath the hot, beautiful body. She wasn't used up and bitter from her experiences.

I walked in the shop early to find Mikey sitting at the front desk, rifling through the papers. "Morning, Mikey."

"Hey, bro, how's it hanging?"

"Little to the left," I said, adjusting myself.

"Never pegged you for a lefty. Thought maybe down the middle."

"Fucker, how could it hang down the middle? You need your head checked or some shit?"

"You know, maybe you weren't blessed with the Gallo family genes. Just sayin.'"

"Dumb fuck. You've seen my dick—you pierced the motherfucker for me."

Mikey chuckled. "I know, fucker. Just yanking your fucking chain. Touchy this morning, aren't we?"

I threw my bag next to my chair and walked up to the desk.

"Not touchy, Mike. This fuckin' girl is stuck in my head."

Mikey shook his head and started to laugh. "Ah, she's cracking that cold, dead heart of yours?"

"Fuck, I don't know. I'm seeing her again tonight. What the fuck am I doing, man?"

"Pussy. She got good shit, huh?" He grinned.

"Platinum pussy. Has my brain all fuckin' jumbled up, man."

"Never thought I'd see the day."

"Makes two of us," I mumbled.

"Listen, you want anyone else fucking her?" he asked as he placed his hand on my shoulder. He was always into love and touching, and it made me batshit crazy.

The thought of anyone else touching Suzy made me want to fucking vomit, or beat the shit out of the bastard. "Fuck no, I want to be the only one inside her. I don't like sloppy seconds."

"Well, there's your answer."

"Fucking hell." I shook my head and stared at the floor.

"Doesn't mean you have to marry her, Joey. Just make sure she doesn't want to fuck anyone else. Make her yours—take the leap."

"For once, Mikey, you're right. Fucking miracle." I couldn't deny it anymore. I wanted her and couldn't stand the thought of anyone else touching her or kissing her beautiful lips.

"You know I always got your back. It's been years, man. Joni would want you to be happy." He grabbed the schedule off the counter as the door chimed and the rest of the Gallo pack walked through the doors. "Would they have been friends—Joni and this girl?"

They had some similarities. Joni would think Suzy was funny as hell and sweet. "Yeah, they probably would have liked each other."

"She doesn't want you alone, wherever she is."

"Thanks, Mikey." Waiting for everyone to get settled, I grabbed my phone and sent Suzy a message about tonight.

Me: *You're mine tonight, Suzette.*

11

FRIDAY ~ WORLDS COLLIDE

SUZY

THE DAY DRAGGED ON, AND THE STUDENTS WERE IN A FOUL MOOD. I needed the weekend to start. When the lunchtime bell rang, I walked in my office, plopping in my chair as I let my head fall back. "Jesus," I muttered. I closed my eyes for a moment and listened to the stillness in the air, since the kids had cleared the building. Two more class periods—I could do it.

I opened my drawer, grabbed my container of leftover pasta, and searched for my phone. I hoped City messaged me—I needed something to brighten up this shit day. I looked at the screen and my stomach fluttered. I was "his" tonight. What did he mean? Sexually?

I never liked to be called Suzette, but the way it sounded coming out of his mouth made my breath hitch. He always seemed to whisper it in my ear or say it against my lips, and it drove me crazy. I wanted to hear him say my name tonight.

Me: Only tonight?

Hell, did I just sound needy?

City: All things are possible.

What the hell did that mean?

"Hello. Suzy, you in here?" I heard Sophia calling from the door.

"In my office," I yelled, grabbing a forkful of noodles.

88

Sophia stood in the doorway and made a sound of disgust. "I don't know how you eat that Ragu shit cold. Bleh." She scrunched her nose, opened her mouth, and stuck her finger inside, pretending to gag.

"Hey, Mama Guido, what are you doing slumming it down here?" I stuck the noodle in my mouth and made a face at her.

"Kayden and I were talking, and we wanted to know if you and the cock piercing wanted to come over for a barbecue tonight?"

"You just want to molest him with your eyes."

"No, I don't. I have my hunk. Kayden still makes me tingle thinking about him." She made a silly face and shook her body like just the thought of him brought her pleasure. "I want to meet this guy and see if he's worthy of my little Suzy. Plus, Kayden could use a little pick-me-up. Maybe they can be friends and we can double date." She rested her body against the door with her leg crossed in front of the other and her arms folded. I always had a hard time saying no to Sophia.

"Well, I'd have to ask him. I don't know what he had planned."

"Send me an email after you ask him. It'll be fun. Don't take no for an answer. You've piqued my curiosity about this man that has you all types of insane. I mean, sweetie, I've always known you were crazy, but he has you questioning everything in your perfect little mapped out life. I must meet him."

"Fine, Soph. Let me ask him."

Me: BBQ at my friends' place tonight. You game?

"There, I asked. It's up to him now. Happy?" I grabbed a huge forkful and slowly placed it in my mouth—anything to gross Sophia out. She was the queen of sauce and meatballs. I missed when the house used to fill with the smell of her cooking. I'd come home after a long day and Kayden would have something divine on the stove. Now it was Ragu and me against the world.

"Ugh, I can't stand here and watch you eat that shit."

My phone chirped. "Wait," I said as she walked away from my office. "Incoming."

"So?"

City: Sounds fanfuckingtastic. What time shall I give you a "ride"?

"Um," I said as I felt the heat creep into my cheeks. "He wants to know what time we should arrive."

CHELLE BLISS

"He talks all proper like that?"

"Nope, but that's all you're getting. Time, please?"

She sighed. "Eight, okay? If you're gonna be late just let me know, whoreface. Bye," she said as the door closed behind her.

Me: Sophia said to be there at eight. Pick me up around ten till to be there on time—Sophia doesn't do late.

I knew that Sophia would take one look at City and practically be doing cartwheels. She'd never liked any man I had seen since we became friends. I flipped through the paperwork from my mailbox this morning as I waited for City to respond.

City: I'll be there at six thirty. Be ready for me, because I'm hard as a fuckin' rock. I have plans for that pussy before we go to the BBQ.

OMG, OMG, OMG.

Me: I'll be waiting with bells on.

Five minutes left before the next barrage of hooligans walked through the door. My afternoon classes were murder. They weren't bad kids, but they were challenging and mentally draining.

City: Naked—no fucking bells.

A fire ignited in my body as I read the screen. *It's on like Donkey Kong.*

12

PASSING THE TEST

CITY

"Coming," a female voice from inside yelled.

"I remember you saying those very words twenty minutes ago," I growled in Suzy's ear.

Her cheeks turned a rosy shade of pink as she bit her lip, trying to hide her smile. Suzy pushed her hair off her shoulders and fixed her shirt, as though she wanted everything perfect and in place.

"Stop fidgeting, sugar."

"Oh my God, I can't. Sophia is going to take one look at me and know what we did," she said, dabbing her fingers at the corner of her lips.

"If she doesn't, then I didn't do it right."

A beautiful brunette opened the door with a smile. She looked me over, starting at my face, and then her eyes raked over my body. I felt almost violated by the way she appraised me. She looked at Suzy with a devilish grin and opened her arms. The girls exchanged hugs and whispered words that I couldn't hear, but Sophia's eyes didn't leave mine.

"Sophia, this is City."

"Nice to meet you, Sophia." I extended my hand to her. Sophia's hair was pulled back in a sloppy bun that sat on top of her head. She had a bright white smile and kind eyes.

She placed her hand in mine. "Nice to finally meet you, City. I've heard *all* about you." She winked.

A grin crept across my face—I guessed I got the thumbs-up from her friend. "Nice things, I hope."

"She spoke very *big* of you." She giggled, and I felt my cheeks heat. I could tell these girls together were going to be a handful. "Come on in. Kayden and Jett are out on the patio starting the grill."

I extended my arm for Suzy to walk in front of me, and I watched both girls walk inside as I stayed close behind. They lived in a small apartment that was decorated with mismatched pieces that all worked. *SportsCenter* was on the television, and baby things were scattered everywhere.

"Don't mind the mess. Children have a way of overtaking everything, no matter how small." Sophia waved her hands around and picked up small toys off the floor before tossing them in a basket near the television stand.

The door to the patio opened and a tall, muscular man holding a baby walked into the living room. His head was clean-shaven, and he looked like someone that I'd find down at the Neon Cowboy—or a guy who would walk in my shop for some work.

"Kayden, baby, Suzy brought her new beau, City."

Kayden eyed me warily. I held out my hand to him. "Nice to meet you, Kayden. Suzy talks very highly of you and Sophia."

Kayden placed the baby in the crook of his left arm before extending his right hand to me. "Glad to meet you, City." He squeezed my hand tightly, almost to the point of pain, but I didn't dare pull away. I knew the fuckin' macho bullshit. He was staking his claim on Sophia and giving me a silent warning with Suzy.

"Oh, Jett, come here, baby." Reaching for Jett, Suzy plucked him from Kayden's arms.

"No hello, Suzy? How are you, Kayden? I've missed you, Kayden. Just oooh, Jett." Kayden laughed.

"Oh now, Kayden, you know I love you. Gimme a kiss," she said, puckering her lips and closing her eyes.

My heart raced with the thought of Kayden placing his lips on hers. I squeezed my hands into fists. They were just friends. Kayden planted a kiss on her cheek as he rubbed the head of his child before walking into the kitchen and wrapping his arms around his wife.

"He's gotten so big," Suzy said as she bounced the baby in her arms, patting his butt. She looked natural with a child in her arms, like it was something she did every day. Her eyes lit up as Jett gripped her thumb.

"He's growing like a weed," Sophia said from the kitchen. "What do you guys want to drink? City, what can I get you?"

"I'll take a beer if you got one."

Suzy's eyes grew wide and her nostrils flared, and I didn't know what I said, but obviously I'd fucked up somehow. "But it's okay if you don't. I'll really drink anything."

"Coming right up. Suzy? Virgin daiquiri, babe?" Sophia snickered as she opened the fridge and began to dig around.

"What did I say wrong?" I whispered in her ear.

"Kayden doesn't drink. He's an alcoholic and has been clean for about a year now." She looked at Kayden and Sophia before returning her attention on the cooing baby in her arms.

"I didn't know. Shit, you should've given me a heads-up, sugar."

"I'm sorry. It just slipped my mind."

"It's okay, City. It's not something the ladies like to talk about. It's always the giant elephant in the room," Kayden said as he handed me the beer. "I can be around alcohol and not drink." He sat down on the couch and put his feet up on the coffee table. "Sit down; let the ladies work their magic in the kitchen. We'll take care of the meat, like God intended."

"I don't want to hear about your meat, Kayden." Suzy snickered.

"Kitchen, Suzy, but let Sophia cook." He pointed at her then toward the kitchen, and snapped his fingers.

"I can cook, Kayden," she said as she rubbed her nose against the baby's face before handing the baby to Kayden and walking away.

"City, Suzy can't cook a lick. She's the queen of pre-made. Just an FYI," he said as he cradled the baby and ran his finger along the chubby cheek.

Sitting on the couch, I set my beer on my knee and relaxed. "Eh, I can cook, so it's not a deal-breaker for me. Bucs fan?"

"Fuck no, Browns fan born and bred." He stretched out, placing his free hand behind his head.

"No shit? You like an underdog or abuse?" I smiled before lifting the beer to my lips.

"I stay true to my roots, you?"

"Bears fan. No other way to be."

"They've had some fuckin' horrible seasons, but the Browns have the market cornered on losing."

"Give ya that," I said as I tipped my beer toward him. "Suzy said you three lived together."

"Yep, for a while. She was a lifesaver, and I owe her. Don't fucking break her heart—I'll beat the fuck out of you." He laughed. "Seriously, you'll have a few more holes to match the ones you currently have."

What? I could see the girls had talked about me in detail. "Not my plan," I said. "Suzy isn't like other girls."

Suzy leaned against the counter and watched Sophia as they chatted. They looked over at us and started laughing.

"No, she's not. She's kind, pure, and too trusting. I feel like she's my little sister, and I'll protect her like she's my family."

"Gotcha. Loud and clear."

"You boys done with your pissing match?" Sophia said as she walked in the room with a plate of burgers. "These won't cook themselves."

"Let me handle the meat," Kayden said, handing Jett back to Suzy.

"That's what she said." Sophia chuckled. Kayden grabbed the plate from her and kissed her on the lips. She looked at him with a dopy grin as he backed away.

"If you're a good girl, I'll let you handle my meat later."

"Not in front of our guests," Sophia said as she smacked him on the shoulder.

"They're kind of nauseating aren't they?" Suzy stood next to me and rocked Jett in her arms. His eyes were almost closed as he sucked his fingers.

"A bit." I felt content with the three of them. I could almost feel the bond that they had, the love for each other.

"They've endured more than most people have in a lifetime, and they came out on the other side with an unbreakable bond. Someday I'll tell you their story. If fate is real, they're the perfect example. They were made for each other." She smiled as she watched them on the patio.

They touched each other and kissed, never moving apart. His actions portrayed adoration for his woman. "Are they married?"

"Not yet. Someday, I hope. They've both been married before, and they use that as an excuse not to *rush into things*." She curled her lips up and rolled her eyes. "I remind them that they have a baby. I guess I'm old-fashioned." She shrugged.

I made sure not to fuck that up. I never fucked without a condom or took that kind of risk. "I was brought up that way too, but you can't deny what they have. I'm sure they'll do it in time."

***

The evening was relaxing, and I liked talking with Kayden. He didn't bullshit, and Sophia was something else. She was a spitfire, and loved to tease Suzy mercilessly. "Did I pass the test with your friends?" I asked as we climbed on my bike.

"You did well. You got the thumbs-up from Sophia."

"She's not the one I'm worried about."

"Kayden? Oh, please. He likes to talk all his macho crap, but he's the sappy one. He just wants me happy, City."

"He said he'd kick my ass if I broke your heart, sugar."

She wrapped her arms around me as I walked the bike away from the building, trying not to be too noisy. "Kayden's been known to take matters into his own hands, but I'll set him straight about us," she said in my ear, chuckling.

"Whatcha mean?" I said as I started the engine.

"Oh, nothing." She rested her head against my shoulder and toyed with my nipple piercing. It was the first time I didn't feel her tense against my body when riding on the back of the bike. Maybe she was finally letting go and enjoying herself without overanalyzing the situation.

13

FORK IN THE ROAD

SUZY

I HAD BECOME USED TO BEING THE THIRD WHEEL AROUND SOPHIA AND Kayden, but tonight everything just felt right. Kayden and City had laughed and talked about sports for hours as Sophia and I talked about work and Jett.

I didn't want to be alone anymore, and I couldn't waste time with City. My heart ached around Kayden and Sophia, and I envied them, wanted what they had—that great love, the one that you can feel and almost touch, and I wouldn't settle for anything less. I had to walk away from City and move forward in my life.

Tears formed in my eyes while I thought about having to give him up as we pulled in and I climbed off the bike. I put my helmet on the bike and started to walk away from City. I didn't want him to see the glistening in my eyes.

"Where you hurrying off to?" Reaching out, he grabbed my wrist, pulling me into his arms.

"Nowhere, I was just going to unlock the door." I shrugged, keeping my arms down and not melting into his touch.

"You okay, sugar?" he asked, looking at my eyes with a question on his face.

"Yeah. The wind made my eyes water." I smiled at him.

"Glasses will block the wind. We'll have to get you a pair."

Thank God he bought that crock of shit. He wrapped his arms around me, smashing my face in his t-shirt. I inhaled, enjoying the musky scent in the material. I closed my eyes and luxuriated in the smell of him.

"Maybe." I felt shitty and my heart ached. Why bother buying me glasses? I didn't plan to spend the rest of my life riding on the back of his bike. Although Sophia and Kayden were opposites, they worked, but City and I didn't have a future.

"What's wrong?" he asked, squeezing me tighter.

"Nothing. I'm just tired." I squeezed him back and relished in the feel of his tight muscles. *Don't say it; don't look like a girl whose head is filled with fairytales.*

"Sugar, that's bullshit. You've never walked away from me or been snippy. Your sparkle's gone. Spill."

Don't do it. He isn't your knight in shining armor riding in on a white horse.

Shifting my weight, I stared at the ground, trying to avoid his gaze. "Nothing, City. I just need sleep. I swear." That lie felt easier than I'd thought.

"Look me in the eyes and say that." He pulled my chin up, forcing me to look into the clear azure eyes that showed sadness. I swallowed hard and steadied my breathing. I knew he could read me like an open book, everyone could, and I had to pull this off. *Don't cry or blink, girl —breathe.*

"I'm just tired, really." I stood on my tiptoes and placed my lips against his. This would be the last time I'd kiss him. I couldn't spend more time with him without risking my heart. I could fall in love with him easily, but I wouldn't risk the heartbreak that would follow. "Call me tomorrow?" I said as I backed away.

"You don't want me to come in, beautiful?" he asked, drawing his brows together and studying my face.

"Not tonight, City. I want to crawl in bed and drift off. If you come in, I know what will happen." I grinned at him as a sly smile spread across his face. He ran his finger down my cheek, and I wanted to lean in to it— I wanted more. "No, no. Don't even think about it." I giggled as he tried pulling me into a kiss. "Down, tiger."

"Tomorrow then," he said as he kissed me on the lips.

I instantly felt the loss of his heat as he let go of my body, and I looked at him. He really was beautiful. He looked like every girl's fantasy with his bike behind him, hard muscles, dreamy eyes, and kindness. I couldn't let myself fall any deeper for him. Every time my phone rang, my text alert chirped, or I stood in his presence, my heart raced. My heart and body responded to him, but my mind kept saying *run*. He wasn't the type that settled down and had a family, and I couldn't blame him. He was a playboy that led a different life than I did. He was on a different path.

I stood at a fork in the road—travel down the path of heartbreak and further immerse myself in his world, or make a clean break and continue on my journey to my ultimate destination of happiness and the love I couldn't live without.

"Tomorrow, big boy," I said with a meek smile, and waved to him before disappearing inside the house without watching him drive away. I threw my keys on the table, walking through the darkened house to my bedroom. My eyes felt heavy, and they burned from the tears that wanted to break free.

The roar of his engine made the walls in my bedroom rattle. I'd never hear that sound again without thinking of him and feeling butterflies in my stomach. He'd altered my thoughts and invaded my mind.

I undressed and put on my favorite comfy pajamas, catching a glimpse of my reflection in the mirror. I wanted to turn back the clock to a time when life felt simpler. When I didn't know the pure animal magnetism and sexual chemistry like I felt with him, but I couldn't. He ruined me and stole that from me.

My phone vibrated as I turned it in my hand and caught a glimpse of his message.

City: It's tomorrow—one minute after midnight.

Setting the phone on my nightstand, I stared at the empty bed and thought of how different the night could've been.

Me: Night, City. Drive safely.

I crawled under the sheets, loving the crisp material against my skin. I stared at the ceiling and watched the fan whirl, causing a shadow to form against the white background. I couldn't fall asleep, and turned on the television, praying that the mindless entertainment would help calm my thoughts and help me forget him.

My phone danced across the wooden surface. *Don't pick it up.* I couldn't do it. I wanted to see if I could break free of him—quit cold turkey like a junkie. I had to try to put distance between us. I'd only known him a week, but he invaded my life.

Flipping through the channels, I stopped on a show about a group of bikers. I'd heard about the show but never found interest in it until now. I couldn't bring myself to turn it off. Every man on the screen reminded me of him. The roar of the engines made my heart flutter and my stomach hurt. Curling on my side, I hugged the pillow as tears poured out, plopping on the material. I wanted to feel the wind in my hair and my arms wrapped around his body, but it could never happen again. My eyes burned as I gave in and drifted off to the sound of roaring engines.

***

I woke to a couple of messages from City wishing me good morning and asking when I could see him again. Leaving my phone on my nightstand, I made a glass of tea and sat on my front step sipping the warm cinnamon liquid. The neighborhood was quiet as a few couples walked down the sidewalks and children played in the front yard down the street. I stared at the sun shimmering off the wet grass and thought about him. I couldn't sit here all day and think about him. I had to find something to do today to keep my mind off him and move toward my future.

I needed a shower, had to wash his scent off me and start my day. No more wallowing in self-pity and the whirlwind that I'd lived for the last week. I grabbed my phone off the nightstand, but there were no new messages from City. Maybe he got the hint after I didn't send him a good morning text.

The ringing of my phone made me jump as I waited for the water to warm. I walked to the phone slowly and peeked at the screen—relief flooded me as I saw that it was Derek and not City.

"Hey," I said, as I stood there naked, staring in the mirror, the fog blurring my reflection.

"Hi, Suzy. What are you doing later?" Derek had a deep voice, but it didn't have half the effect on me that City's voice did.

"Not much, just about to jump in the shower. What's up?"

His sharp intake of air made it evident that he had just pictured me naked. "I wanted to know if you wanted to go to dinner tonight and maybe play some mini-golf. Do you want to go with me?"

"Oh, well..." I gnawed on my thumbnail and debated a date with Derek. He worked on paper, and we ran in the same circles. Our worlds were similar and we could relate to each other. Maybe he was the path that I needed to follow—or at least he'd help keep my mind off City.

"Come on, Suzy. We'll have fun. What do you say?" His voice was hopeful. Couldn't blame a guy for being persistent—he'd never taken no for an answer.

"Okay, Derek." I ran my hands down the bare skin between my breasts, loving the feel of the softness. I instantly felt like crap for saying yes when all I wanted to do was run to City.

"It's a date. I'll pick you up at six."

"See you at six."

"Great. I can't wait to see you tonight. Bye for now, Suzy."

"Bye, Derek." I heard him celebrating his victory before the line went dead.

I stood in the shower and daydreamed about City before touching myself, relieving the ache between my legs. The orgasm wasn't as satisfying as I had hoped. It dulled the need I felt for City. I craved the earth-shattering orgasms I felt under his deft fingertips, but I couldn't let my sexual desire cloud my judgment.

City sent me two more text messages before Derek picked me up for dinner. I ignored the urge to reply and finished my makeup, smacking my red lipstick together before running the brush through my hair one last time. The tight black miniskirt and yellow tank top helped show off my fading tan. Soon the winter cold and weakened sun would cause my skin to return to its almost ghostly shade of white. Grabbing my strappy black stilettos out of the closet, I thought of that last time I'd worn them—the night City rode into my life. I put my favorite Reef sandals in my purse for later, when my feet ached and we played mini-golf.

The chime of the doorbell snapped me out of my memories of the first night in City's bed. Opening the door, I took in the sight of Derek in a pair of khaki dress pants and crisp white linen shirt, with his toes peeking out from the fabric around his feet. His smile beamed as his eyes roamed my body, taking in my outfit before stopping on my breasts. He licked his lips before he settled on my face with a goofy smile.

"Wow, you look sexy, Suzy." His nostrils flared as his gaze drifted down my body again.

The way he looked at me made my skin crawl. "Thanks, you look great too." He did look nice, but not heart-stopping or panty-dropping.

He held out his hand to me. "Ready?"

I placed my fingers against his smooth palm, "Yeah," I said, although I was anything but.

Derek opened the door to his beat-up Nissan Altima, waiting for me to climb in before he kissed my hand and slammed the door.

I sighed as I watched him walk around the car, a brilliant and victorious smile on his face. "God, this is a horrible idea," I mumbled to myself as he opened the door and climbed in.

"What did you say?" he asked as he climbed in, closed the door, and looked at me.

"Just saying how hungry I am. Where are we eating?"

He brushed the hair off my shoulder, gliding his fingertips across my skin, lingering longer than felt comfortable. My body involuntarily moved away from his touch. "Sorry," he said as he turned away and gripped the steering wheel, his knuckles whitening from his firm grasp. "We're going to Paesano's for some Italian, if that's okay with you?"

"Sounds great."

I stared out the window, watching the trees pass by as Derek chattered about work. I looked forward to my weekends and escaping the stress and my job, but that was all Derek wanted to talk about. I listened to his words and answered when asked a question, but he already bored me. Thankful that the drive to the restaurant wasn't long, I climbed out of the car as Derek jogged to me and grabbed my arm, hooking them together.

The conversation during dinner was stagnant. We didn't have much in common besides work. It became evident as he talked about video games. My idea of a great night did not involve playing a mindless game on the television. When the food finally arrived, I found myself thankful for the silence as he shoveled the food in his mouth without care. He ate like a pig, with sauce from his pasta dribbling on his chin and resting at the corners of his mouth. I moved the food around on my plate, trying not to stare.

"You want to go for some drinks after here or you want to go to mini-golf?" he asked with a full mouth, a small piece of pasta falling in his lap.

Why the hell did I think this was a good idea? "Drinks sound great." I prayed that a few drinks would make him interesting and have the evening end on a high note.

We skipped dessert and headed to Club Karma for drinks. The club had opened a couple months ago, but I hadn't set foot inside. It had a big-city feel, not like the typical small-town hangouts. The walls were blood red, decorated with black-and-white photos of couples in various sexual positions and states of undress. Colorful lights bounced off the shiny black tile floor as dancers moved their bodies against each other. There were small seating areas with couches filled with couples laughing and touching, and a large bar on the opposite side of the entrance.

"Drink first?" Derek asked. I nodded and looked around as he guided me through the overcrowded space. Derek rested his body against the bar, his arm touching my skin. "You want to dance?" he shouted in my ear above the music.

I shook my head and waited for the bartender to come in our direction. A large mirror hung above the liquor bottles on the wall behind the serving area. Watching people dance with such erotic and methodical moves made me think of City and our dance last weekend. I never felt sexy on the dance floor, but with him I had been able to feel the music instead of thinking of my next move.

I ordered a martini, wanting the alcohol over a virgin daiquiri, needing to forget City and find a way to make Derek more palatable. His arm brushed against my back as he rested his hand on the bar, effectively trapping me. I ignored him, staring into the mirror as the bartender placed my drink on the bar.

I took a sip, testing the sweetness of the raspberry martini. This whole night had been a bad idea. I knew it from the moment I accepted his invitation to dinner. I wouldn't have said yes to him if I weren't trying to forget the tall, muscular Italian man.

"Suzy," Derek whispered in my ear, further invading my personal space.

"What?" I said into the glass still pressed against my lips.

"Drink up, babe, because I can't wait to get you out there." Derek bobbed his head like a character in a skit from *Saturday Night Live*. I could see his reflection in the mirror, and my cheeks felt heated at the thought of someone seeing me with him.

"Uh huh." I didn't turn to look at him but kept my eyes on the scene in the mirror, like I was watching a television show. I'd find a way to stall. I couldn't go on to the dance floor with him. No way in hell would that happen. He didn't have the ability to make me dance like City had, and his awkward movements would only draw more awareness to us, when all I wanted to do was blend in.

His fingers touched the skin of my arms and hand as I fought every urge to kick him in the balls. He rambled on about his clubbing days in college and how he mastered the dance floor and people would stop to watch him "bust a move." Almost spitting my drink out, I broke out into laughter, tears forming in my eyes. I could imagine the scene. Derek thought people stopped to admire his ability, when in actuality they were stunned or entertained beyond belief.

"What's so funny?" His lips were turned into a frown as he moved his head away from mine and stared at me.

"Oh, nothing, Derek. Just something I remembered from college." God, I had always been a shitty liar, but I didn't want to hurt his feelings. The man had confidence, and who was I to kill it?

"Ah, okay. I thought you were laughing at me." He shrugged before sipping his beer and wiping his lips on his shoulder. "Come on, just one dance," he begged, and released me from my human cage.

I sloshed the pink liquid in my glass, now half drained, and lifted it to my lips. I owed him at least one dance for his efforts. I swallowed the last mouthful and placed it on the bar. "Just one."

His eyes lit up as he grabbed my hand and pulled me toward the writhing bodies in the middle of the room. The beat of the music made me unable to feel my pulse, even though I knew it had to be hammering. I wanted to throw up at the thought of anyone watching me make an ass out of myself. Just as we reached the spot that Derek wanted, dead center, the DJ switched songs. Fuck, why me? A sad, slow melody filled the air as Derek pulled me into an embrace. I'd rather make a complete asshole out of myself with a wicked beat that didn't require touching.

"Perfect," he said, wrapping his arms around me, his hands resting a little too close to my ass.

Placing my hands on his shoulders, I tried to keep some distance between us, but Derek didn't get the hint. His body felt nothing like City's; there was no hardness to it. Derek's hands roamed my back as he swayed our bodies side to side to the music, and I gave in, letting him control our movement. He didn't speak as he moved us back and forth to the beat. Time passed slowly, and I felt like I had been wrapped in his arms for hours with no escape.

When the song ended, Derek broke the embrace and backed up to look at me. He gave me a silly grin, "Thank you."

"For what?" I yelled as the music began to thump through the speakers.

"The dance, Suzy. I loved having you in my arms," he said, as he reached for my hand and kissed the top.

"You're a sweet guy, Derek." I blushed. He wasn't a bad guy—he just wasn't City.

"Another drink?"

"If I didn't know any better, Derek, I'd think you're trying to get me drunk."

He smiled, his face turning pink as he pushed on my back and led me off the dance floor. "Can't blame a guy for trying."

We passed a set of couches, and something drew my attention. There before me was a woman in a skintight, barely there dress with red stiletto heels and long brown hair. The woman didn't draw my attention, but the man whose lap she sat on was City. He didn't notice me as he talked to her, giving her his total attention. His hand rested on her ass as she nibbled on his lips. I wanted to throw up. He didn't seem to have a problem forgetting me.

Bile rose in my throat at the sight of the two of them together. I'd spent the entire day trying to forget him without success, but he had moved on to someone else. "I'll take you up on that offer, Derek." No longer able to watch City with another woman, I walked to the bar with

Derek right behind me. Derek only had eyes for me tonight, and the smile on his face made it clear that I had made him happy with my response.

Even though I had been the one that ignored him, it still stung to see him enjoying the company of another woman. "What'll it be, sweetheart?" the bartender asked me as she leaned against the bar with a smile.

"Shot of anything sweet and another raspberry martini, please."

"I'll have another Miller," Derek said before she walked away. "A shot, huh?"

"It's Saturday night and I could use a little something stronger."

"I didn't know you were a drinker, Suzy." He grabbed our drinks, pushing mine in front of me before throwing down a twenty for the bartender.

"I'm not, but what the hell. Why not?" I shrugged before picking up the shot and smelling it. Raspberry something or other, but I wasn't quite sure. It would do the job and help dull the pang of jealousy I felt from seeing City with the girl in red. "To life and love," I said, raising my glass before swallowing the sweet concoction.

Derek tipped his beer in my direction and watched me as he raised it to his lips. "Why aren't you taken?" he asked from behind the brown bottle.

I shrugged. "Looking for the right one." The martini sloshed the glass as I brought it to my lips too quickly. One drink and a shot and I didn't give a fuck that some of it splashed on my breasts. Tears stung my eyes as I gulped the martini and hoped that it would put my brain in a temporary haze. The feel of a hand touching my breast caused me to jerk, sending the last bit of raspberry heaven to the floor. "What the fuck?" I said, looking down to see Derek's hand move away from my breast.

"Sorry." He grinned. "Just thought I'd help you with that little spill." He sucked on his fingers as he stared at my chest.

I snarled as I put my face close to his. "No matter how drunk I am, you don't touch me without asking. Am I clear?"

"Yes, ma'am," he said, raising his hand to salute me.

What a cocksucker. Poking him in the chest, I spoke very slowly. "I mean it, smartass. Do. Not. Touch. Me." Turning away, I looked in the mirror and saw the red dress still sitting on City's lap, and my fingernails dug into the wooden bar.

"Okay, Suzy. Let me make it up to you, since I made you spill your drink. Let me buy you another?"

I closed my eyes, rubbing the bridge of my nose, before turning my attention back to Derek. "I don't think so, Derek. Will you just take me home?"

"One more, Suzy. I swear I'll keep my hands to myself. I don't want the night to end like this. Please."

I studied his face, and he looked genuine, with a sad smile and pleading eyes. I held up my index finger to him. "One more and then I want to go."

"Excellent." He raised his hand in the air and snapped his fingers, grabbing the attention of the bartender.

As I leaned against the bar, my eyes kept wandering back to the mirror. The third martini was easier to drink; my legs felt weak and the bar became necessary to keep me from tipping over. Derek chattered in my ear and kept his distance as we polished off our third drinks.

"Ready?" he asked as he set the empty bottle on the counter.

"Are you okay to drive?" I asked. I may be drunk, but I knew enough to ask.

"Yeah, I can handle more than three beers, babe."

Hearing the word "babe" come out his mouth when he spoke made me want to throw up on his shoes. Everything about him made me crazy, and I knew that I'd never go on another date with Derek. On paper he seemed right, but in person he was a creepy mess that revolted me and did nothing for my libido.

"Okay, let's go." I grabbed my purse and walked on unsteady legs toward the door, leaving Derek to walk behind me.

"You want to hold my hand?"

"Why?" I stopped and turned to face him, almost falling over. I'd had too much to drink and didn't realize it until now.

"Because you're walking funny. Just hold on to my arm until we get to the car." He held out his hand and waited for me to take it.

He didn't grin or smile, and I believed he was sincere in his offer. Clearly the alcohol had made my brain fuzzy. I didn't hold his hand, but snaked my arm through his and leaned on his body as I swayed through the parking lot, thankful when we made it to his car.

Leaning against the car, I waited for him to open the door. I closed my eyes and soaked in the feel of the cool air against my warm, clammy skin. The air inside the club had felt stagnant. My anger and hurt over City made my body feel flushed and caused me to sweat. I had done this. I pushed City away. I had been an idiot, and I knew it when I saw him with her in his arms.

Derek's lips were on mine before I could react. I pushed at him, hitting his chest as he trapped me between him and the car. My arms felt like jelly, and I couldn't gauge how hard I was hitting him as the beat of my heart filled my ears. "Stop," I mumbled between breaks in the kiss, but he didn't stop crushing his body against mine harder. His lips moved over my cheek to my neck as he grabbed my breast and squeezed. "Derek, stop, damn it!" I yelled, hitting him in the ribs.

"You know you want it, Suzy," he said against my neck.

"I don't! Stop!" I pushed against him again, but his weight was too much. I swung and connected with his face with a loud smack. My hand stung from the contact.

His face moved away from my neck, and he looked me in the eyes. He glared at me with his mouth set in a firm line. "You hit me. What the fuck? I'm just giving you what you want, baby."

Clearly I had sent the wrong signals, or he was just a dumbass. "Get the fuck off me."

"You're such a prick tease in this outfit tonight. You can deny it all you want, but I know you want me."

"I do—"

His lips were on me again before I could stop him. I struggled against him, bending my knee up to make contact with his balls, but hit nothing as his body flew backward.

City held Derek by the throat, bringing him to eye level. "Why don't you pick on someone your own size, motherfucker?" City said with a look of pure hatred.

"This has nothing to do with you, man," Derek spat. "This is between the lady and me." Derek clawed at City's hands, trying to escape his grip.

City turned toward me. "He your boyfriend?" His eyes moved over my body, taking in my outfit. I shook my head, my hands gripping the car, not moving. "You want him to touch you?" He looked at Derek and back to me.

Derek's face had turned a deep shade of red, on the verge of purple, as City's grip increased. "No! I told him to stop!" I said. "But I work with the scumbag. Don't hurt him."

City growled; his chest heaved with rough breaths while deciding his next action. "Fuck," he muttered before dropping Derek to the ground.

Derek gasped for air as he tried to stand, but collapsed on his hands and knees. Air filled my lungs, and I realized I had held my breath, waiting for City to beat the hell out of Derek before my eyes. Did he deserve it? Hell yes, but I didn't want to witness it or deal with the aftermath.

City stood in front of me, his hands clenched at his side as he stared at me. The hard features of his face looked more pronounced by his anger. His cheeks flexed, his nostrils flaring as he studied me. "What the fuck, Suzy? I called you and you don't fucking answer and then you're here with this fucking prick and almost let him maul you in a parking lot." Running his fingers through his hair, he turned and looked at Derek before returning his attention back to me.

"I'm sorr-ry." I didn't know what else to say. I didn't have an excuse. "I didn't know I had to answer to you. You seemed to have your hands full inside, anyway." I snarled as I spoke.

"What the fuck are you talking about?"

"Brunette, red dress, almost dry-humping you on the couch. Ring any bells?" Who the fuck was he to question my actions?

"Fuck." His arms flexed as he clenched his hands into a hard fist at his sides. "Kaylee means nothing to me."

"Neither do I, I suppose."

"Woman, you have no idea what the fuck you're talking about." He stepped closer, and my body instantly registered his nearness, moisture pooling between my legs.

I swallowed, the dryness in my mouth making it hard to move anything down my throat. "I saw your hands on her ass as she kissed you. How the hell do you explain that? It seems women have no value to you."

"Shut your mouth, Suzy. I followed you out here because I saw you stumbling out of here with someone I didn't know. I came here to check on you. Kaylee is no one, hear me now, *no one*. I didn't come here with her or ask her to sit on my lap. I was trying to be nice to her."

"Well, if nice means you feel her up, I'd say you were very kind to her."

"Suzy, listen to me. I called you and asked you back out. You blew me off. What was I supposed to do? Sit home and wait for you to call?"

Breath escaped me as he closed the small space between us.

Tears began to stream down my cheeks as I took in the enormity of the situation. If City hadn't stopped Derek, would I have been able to get away from him? He just saved me, and I was being a total bitch. The sob tore through my chest as I broke down. City wrapped his arms around me and kissed my forehead. He felt so right against my body. I felt safe and comfortable with him, no matter how much we didn't seem to fit on paper. He said nothing, but made sounds to calm me as I buried my face into the soft material of his t-shirt. My fingers found the piercing on his nipple as I toyed with it and tried to catch my breath.

"Can I take you home, sugar?" he asked with his face buried in my hair.

"Yes," I whimpered, clinging to him like a lifeline.

Without speaking, he drew me into his arms, carrying me across the parking lot. I melted into him, resting my head against his shoulder. The thought of Kaylee still stung, but I couldn't be mad at him anymore. He saved me from a totally fucked-up night, and for that he'd earned my forgiveness. The jostling movement as he placed my bottom on the cool seat of his bike made my stomach churn. I said nothing as he put the helmet on my head and fastened the harness against my chin. He had the right mix of pissed-off male and swoon-worthy alpha to make any girl's heart go pitter-patter.

"Can you hold on?" he asked as he held my chin between his fingertips.

"Yes." My tone was breathy and betrayed me with the sound of need.

He climbed on the bike, scooting his ass between my legs and gripping the handlebars. I molded my torso against his and interlaced my fingers. The usual jitters I felt anticipating the ride ahead didn't register.

"Hold on, sugar." He throttled the engine and took off for the short drive to my house. The cool air whipped my hair around as I nuzzled against his warm back. My mind grew blank with the movement of the bike and the roar of the engine. I allowed myself to get lost in the moment and the sensation of the vibrations from the bike—and the feel of City between my legs.

Lost in the City coma, I didn't notice as we pulled into my development and weaved through the winding streets to my house. Maybe I'd drifted off, but I wanted to stay like this forever—wrapped around his body, in a stress-free haze of contentment. I mumbled against his shirt as he turned off the bike, placing his feet on the ground, securing it and tapping my hands. "Sugar, we're here."

"Mm hmm," I said into his back before raising my head and looking through blurry eyes at my house. I sat up, letting go of his chest before wiping the drool off my lips. "Thanks, City. I don't know what would've happened tonight if it weren't for you." I started to climb off the bike but didn't have the energy, and plopped back against the seat with an "oomph."

City laughed as he climbed off, pulling me off the bike, cradling me in his arms. "Can I come in?" he asked, brushing his nose against my cheek.

"Depends. You mad at me?" I asked, praying he said no.

"I'm not mad. We gotta talk, Suzy." His eyes begged me to let him in as his brow furrowed.

"Okay." I rested my head against his hard chest and rubbed my palm against his pec.

I handed him the keys as we approached the door. Anger was no longer visible, but the tilted grin I'd grown accustomed to had vanished. He kicked off his boots before he walked across my white carpet, placing me on the couch. The couch dipped from his weight, but I couldn't look him in the eye. I fiddled with my fingers as the silence became deafening. The alcohol-induced haze had started to wear off, and I felt a small buzz.

"Why the hell didn't you call me today? I thought we made plans. What the fuck did I do wrong?" His words made me cringe; sadness was evident in his voice.

"I wanted to put distance between us. You didn't do anything wrong." I shook my head, meeting his eyes.

"Distance? What for?" His eyebrows drew together as the skin wrinkled in between.

"I just don't think we'll work out." I shrugged.

"Woman, you think too damn much, and it's fucked up. Blew my ass off for that douchebag tonight, and how'd that shit turn out for you?" He paused before continuing. "What makes you think we don't have a shot?"

I looked away from him, unable to look him in the eyes. "We're just so different, City. I don't see a future between us, and at my age, I'm looking forward. I don't live life by the seat of my pants like you. We have nothing in common and we run in different worlds." Water clouded my vision as I stared at the wall across the room. I blinked, trying to clear the tears from my eyes.

Sighing, he reached for my face, touching my cheek and pulling my face in his direction. "Look at me, sugar." His eyes moved around my face. "I don't know how you think I live, and you sure as hell don't know who I am. We're getting to know each other, but you shut me out without a reason. You said it yourself, Sophia and Kayden are opposites but they work. Why couldn't we?"

I drew in a shaky breath, his words making my heart ache. "I know I said that, but I don't know, City."

"What don't you know? Talk to me." His hand closed over my fist in my lap as he stroked his thumb across my sensitive skin.

"I like you a lot. So much that it scares me, and I don't know if I could deal with the heartbreak when you walk out of my life." A tear slid down my cheek as I spoke.

"You never gave us a chance to see if we could work." His finger slid across my skin, wiping the tear away.

"You're not a one-woman man. I could tell that about you, and I don't work that way. I don't want to share you."

"Suzy, I'm not a whore. Since I met you last week I haven't been with anyone else. I don't want anyone else, just you."

"I'd like to believe that, but you looked a little too cozy with Karen tonight."

"Kaylee, not Karen. I'll be totally honest with you about her. I had sex with her twice in my life. Not my proudest moment, but she offered and I accepted. She wants to be my girlfriend, and I've told her no. I'm very clear with her that she and I are nothing and never will be. Should I have pushed her ass on the floor when she sat on my lap?"

"No, I guess not." I didn't want to think about the visual I had of another woman sitting on him and fawning.

"I wanted to be with you tonight. You blew me off. We had such a nice time last night, and as soon as I brought you home, you shut down."

"I don't know, City," I said.

"Joey."

"Joey, I watched Kayden and Sophia all night. They reminded me of what I want someday. I want someone that's going to love me and be mine alone. I want to be important to someone," I said, staring into his eyes without blinking, worried another tear would slip down my cheek.

"It's what everyone wants—"

"Let me finish." I shook my head. "I like you, Joey. No one has ever made me feel the way you do, but I can't risk falling for you. I can't have my heart broken." I bit my lip, trying to focus on pain instead of sadness. I didn't want tears to flow freely. "I think it's best if we stop now. The time we've spent together has been amazing, but I can't do it anymore. I can't lie to myself."

"May I speak now?" He smiled at me, but it was a sad smile.

"Yes."

"Do you think I'm incapable of love?" He stared at me, waiting for an answer, his mouth set in a firm line.

"No, I just don't think it's who you are *now*, and I can't wait around for that part of you. It wouldn't be fair to either of us."

"Suzette." Formal names always meant something serious. "I never allowed myself to think of a future with anyone, but last night I saw a world of possibilities. I realized what I was missing out on—I want what Kayden and Sophia have." He squeezed my fingers, and I watched his thumb rub the back of my hand. "Look at me. I've never allowed myself to get close to anyone in years, but your innocence and sweetness have pierced my heart."

"Oh," I said, my eyes growing wide with surprise.

"I didn't want to rush into anything with you. I don't want to ruin anything, but you need to understand where I'm coming from. You need to know my past." His Adam's apple bobbed in his throat as he swallowed before continuing. "I have been in love before. I had a fiancée and I thought my entire life was made. Plans don't always work out exactly as we think."

"I'm sorry," I said, breaking a hand free from his grip, touching his cheek, running my thumb across the rough stubble.

"It was a long time ago. We were in college and her name was Joni. We were high school sweethearts." He closed his eyes, and I could see the pain on his beautiful features. "I loved her more than anything in the world, and she was ripped from my life."

My heart skipped with the thought that anyone could break his heart.

"A fucking drunk driver hit her on her way home from work and she was killed instantly." He hung his head, hiding his face from my view. I could only imagine the pain that he'd felt losing his love that day in such a brutal manner. "I've never allowed myself to get that close to anyone after she died. It fuckin' wrecked me, and I didn't know if I'd ever fully heal."

"I'm sorry, Joey." I kissed his cheek, allowing him the time to gather his thoughts and hide a small part of himself.

His eyes rose to meet mine. "You remind me a lot of Joni…your kindness and playful nature. It's infectious. You two would've been good friends. She was my light, and I couldn't remember life without her until the day she died. I thought the heartbreak would kill me, Suzy. I've been so scared to open myself to anyone again, but you made me want to try. Don't shut me out. I can't promise forever, yet, but I want you to be mine, Suzy."

My breath caught. "What do you mean?"

"Woman, I swear sometimes I have to spell shit out to you. For a smart girl, sometimes you amaze me." He chuckled. "I want you to be my girlfriend. Mine and only mine. I'd planned to ask you tonight before you blew me off."

Yes, yes, yes! "What about you?" I asked. Would he see other girls? My heart couldn't take that.

"Just you, Suzy. I want a full commitment, and it's a two-way street. Your body is mine…no one else's. I haven't wanted to be with only one person in a long time."

"Okay," I whispered, a smile creeping across my lips. My body vibrated with excitement as his words sank in. City wanted me to be his girlfriend. Wow.

"So, you'll be my girlfriend?" he asked.

"Yes," I said as I crawled into his lap. "I've never wanted anything more," I said against his lips.

"Mine," he growled as he crushed his mouth to my lips. The kiss felt different than the others. There was a hunger behind it—a claiming.

City lifted my body as he stood. Wrapping my arms around his neck, I kissed him back with more passion than I had before. I wanted him more than I ever did. I wanted to make love to him and convey all the passion I felt for him—I wanted to heal him. He may have been broken, but I'd help his heart heal and show him all the love I had to offer.

14

STITCHES

CITY

SHARING THE LOSS OF JONI WAS EASIER THAN I'D THOUGHT. I RARELY spoke about her, and only my family knew about my past. I felt Suzy needed to know to understand. I owed it to her. I'd let it go beyond a casual relationship by meeting her friends and seeing her more than once. Fuck, I'd seen her more than any woman that I'd allowed in my bed since Joni.

Placing her feet on the bedroom floor, she slid down my body before standing, leaning against me. Her soft eyes stared into mine as the corners of her mouth turned up into a smile. Cradling my face in her hands, she rose on her tiptoes and touched her lips to mine. She tasted sweet, and my body craved more. We kissed with our eyes open, and I watched as her pupils dilated and her blinking slowed. Her hands began to move, and I heard the fabric of her shirt rustle as her knuckles brushed against my abdomen. I grabbed her hands, stilling them. "I undress you," I said, and her hands went slack at her side.

She swallowed, smiling at me before lifting her arms. Pulling up her shirt, I exposed her soft belly before the white lace of her bra became visible, her hard nipples calling for my mouth. I dropped her shirt to the floor behind her and ran my hands down her still-raised arms, over her collarbone, over her breasts, stopping at her nipples. I palmed her breasts in my hands and felt the heaviness in them. Her breathing changed as I ran my thumbs over her hardened nipples and stared in her eyes. Her mouth opened, and she sucked in a quick breath as her head fell back.

I wanted to take her hard and fast, but after the talk we'd just had, I knew I had to show her the gentler side of sex. I couldn't be rough with her, not this time at least. I had to show her that I cared for her and didn't think of her as a fuck toy.

I forced my hands to leave her breasts and moved them over her soft stomach, hooking my fingers inside the cloth hugging her hips, as I pulled her skirt down her legs, to reveal matching white lace panties. I kissed the delicate material and placed my knees on the floor. She stood there and swayed, but didn't move.

"Feet, sugar." I tapped the tops of her feet as I waited for her to react. I could hear her giggle above me as she crawled out of her skirt, and the sound of it made my heart skip a beat. Innocence and bliss. I grabbed her hips and moved her body until the back of her knees hit the soft mattress. She sat down and looked at me with wide eyes.

"Lie back," I growled as I held her knees, spreading them wide. "I want to taste that sweet pussy of yours. I'm going to devour you until you're begging for my dick, sugar." I grinned at her. I could hold out an eternity feasting on her body—worshipping her center with my tongue.

She rested on her elbows and smirked at me as I sat between her knees. "All the way down, sugar." I squeezed her knees in warning.

"Damn, you're pretty between my legs. I just wanted to watch you," she said with a playful grin on her face.

"Keep your eyes on me." I reached for her lace panties and wrapped my fingertips inside the material.

"Wait," she said as I began to move the material away from her body.

I pulled quickly, and the material disintegrated in my hands.

"Well, crap, those were expensive." She blew out a breath.

"I'll buy you new ones, sugar. No more talking; my mouth has other things to do that are more important." My hands glided down her legs, pulling them apart as they reached her knees. I moved my mouth to the soft, sensitive skin of her thigh and licked, causing her body to shudder.

I could smell her arousal, and the sweet scent of her pussy made my dick ache. I kissed and licked to the V where her leg connected to her body, only inches from her pussy. Sucking her flesh in my mouth, I lapped at her juices as I twirled my tongue over the smooth skin and listened to her tiny moans. Continuing the slow, sensual assault on her body, I gripped her knees as I ran my tongue across her pussy, but didn't stop to pay her engorged clit any attention. I stopped at the same exact spot on her right leg, pulling the skin into my mouth to leave a mark. I hadn't given a hickey since high school, but I wanted to leave something to remind her of who owned her body.

"You're killing me," she said, all breathy. I smiled against her skin as I bit down on the flesh and she flinched. "Jesus," she yelped, and the bed dipped as her back dropped against the mattress.

My tongue soothed the red skin where my teeth had left a mark, leaving no doubt where I'd been and to whom she belonged. I couldn't wait any longer to taste her and feel her on my tongue as I moved toward her heat, inhaling her scent before my mouth descended on her body. I buried my nose in her blonde hair and smelled her sweetness. My flat tongue rested against her clit as I began to circle it with my tongue, but I denied her the contact she wanted. I sucked her lips into my mouth, like a starved man, tasting her wetness on my tongue. Her fingers laced in my hair and pushed my face into her core.

I dipped my tongue into her wetness and swallowed her arousal. I didn't think I could ever get enough of her taste. I wanted to hear her scream and couldn't wait any longer. I licked upward, capturing the last drops from her pussy as I sucked her clit hard.

She moaned, pulling my face harder against her body, writhing under my touch. I pushed two fingers inside her and her body stilled. Her pussy clenched against my fingers as I thrust them inside her. Her body arched and she gripped the sheets as she moaned. Moving my palm against her skin, I placed my fingertips on her nipple. Pinching it, my grip pulsated against her stiff peak, and it tipped her over the edge. She lifted her head, and her body grew rigid as her breathing became erratic and shaky.

I stared at her face, watching her fall into oblivion, overcome by the orgasm gripping her body. She dropped her head on the pillow as her eyes opened, sucking in a shuddering breath. Listening to her ragged breaths, I grabbed the condom from my back pocket before standing and removing my clothing.

The look on her face was one of a predator staring at their prey. I stroked my cock and stared at her body, waiting to be filled. Her mouth opened as she stared at my hand, and I stroked it with a firm grip, catching the piercing as I touched the tip.

"You want me inside you, sugar?" I asked in a slow, deep tone as I stood at the foot of the bed stroking myself.

"Well," she said, caressing her skin and licking her lips. "I mean, your fingers are magic and your mouth is divine…"

I held up my free hand. "Shhh, sugar. No more talking. The only sound I want to hear is you screaming my name as you come on my dick."

"Oh," she said, her eyes still glued to my shaft like she'd never seen it before. She was so easy to fluster. I tore the condom wrapper open with my teeth and rolled it over my aching member. I couldn't wait any longer to be inside her luscious cunt and seek my release.

I moved up her body and nestled between her legs. "For the first time, I'm taking you as mine." I laid my palm against her pussy, cupping it as I gripped it in its entirety. "No one else gets to touch you understand, Suzette?" I asked with my lips against hers.

"Yes, Joseph. It's yours and only yours," she said, staring in my eyes.

I kissed her and claimed her body as mine, fucking her with passion. I took her slow and gentle, showing her body the attention it deserved, and worshipped her in a way she'd never experienced before collapsing on the mattress.

I stretched out in bed and stared at the ceiling as she went to get ready for bed. She walked out of the bathroom in a t-shirt, but I wanted to feel her skin against mine as we slept. "No clothes."

"What do you mean?" she asked as she touched the edge of the mattress.

"When you sleep in bed with me, I don't want you wearing clothes. They're a barrier I don't want to deal with—I want all of you whenever I want you, even in the middle of the night." I patted the mattress.

"Underwear?" She smiled and lifted the shirt.

"No underwear either. Strip and get your fine ass in this bed." She didn't move, looking at me with a silly smile. "Do it," I said, eyeing her.

"But—"

"No, buts, sugar. I've seen every inch of your body, even that beautiful little asshole of yours. That'll be mine someday too."

Her smile faded, but her eyes twinkled as she stepped out of her panties and threw her nightshirt on the floor. She curled against my body and rested her head on my shoulder.

"Hand, sugar."

She placed her hand on my chest, not forgetting where I'd put it the first night we spent together. My heartbeat thudded below her palm as I rested my hand on top of hers. I placed my lips against her forehead. "Sweet dreams, beautiful."

"Night, Joey," she said as she yawned. Her breathing changed quickly as she drifted to sleep.

I listened to her tiny breaths as she slept beside me, wrapped in my arms, and curled into my body. I held her hand against my chest and felt her fingertips rub my skin. I felt my eyes grow heavy as I rubbed her hand and tangled my fingers in her hair.

***

I felt someone staring at me as I opened my eyes in the darkness. "You awake?" she whispered.

"I am now," I said, moving my fingers in her hair. "What's wrong, sugar?"

"I couldn't sleep. I didn't want to wake you, but I…"

"What's bothering that pretty little head of yours?" I moved my fingers out of her hair and rubbed the soft skin of her arms, thrumming my fingers back and forth rhythmically.

"I'm just scared," she whispered.

"Of me?" I moved my head away to see her face barely lit by moonlight cascading through the blinds.

"Not really." She rubbed my chest. "I've had boyfriends, but only a couple. I've never felt about them the way I feel about you, Joey. It scares the piss out of me."

"How did you feel about them?" I asked, more curious about how she felt about me than the previous men in my shoes.

"They were nice, but I didn't get butterflies every time I saw them.

We'd go days without talking, and I was fine with that, but with you I'm always checking my phone for a message. I'm feeling needy with you, Joey, and I don't like it."

"Sugar." I reached for her chin, drawing her shadowed eyes toward my face. "That's not needy. Needy and clingy is if you're up my ass all day and want to know my every move. Needy is when you show up at my house all hours of the night and at the shop during the day." I shook my head and smirked at her. "You're not needy. Wipe that shit from your mind."

"If you say so. It's just a new feeling for me. If I overstep or act like a crazy person, please tell me." The worry in her eyes began to ease.

"Deal." I kissed her forehead, lingering over the soft flesh with my lips.

"What was your longest relationship?" I asked. I hadn't been the pillar of normal relationship behavior since I lost Joni, but I had an inkling that she had been just as unlucky in love as I had been.

"Four months," she whispered.

"Did you love him?"

"I think I loved him, but a week after I said those words to him, he left me. He's the only man I've ever said that to—he broke my heart."

I rubbed my hand up her arms to soothe her while she spoke.

"I've never really allowed myself to get that close to anyone after that. It was during my freshman year in college, and after that breakup, I just spent my time studying and avoiding anything that felt like it could lead to a relationship." She yawned and burrowed her body a little closer to mine.

"I understand heartbreak and wanting to guard your heart from the pain. I've lived it for more years than I'd like to admit." I pulled her closer, leaving no space between us. "Let's just take this slow. It's best for both of us."

"Slow," she said, as she reached up and rubbed my face. I pulled her hand back to my chest and held it against my heart.

I could hear her breathing change as sleep took her. I closed my eyes, content and happy for the first time since Joni had last slept in my arms. I looked forward to what tomorrow held.

15

TATTOOS AND TORMENT

SUZY

"How'd it go with Mr. Piercings?" Sophia chuckled in the phone as I chewed my bagel.

"He gave me a little going-away present this morning before he headed home to change." I chomped down, letting the cream cheese slide across my tongue.

"Oooh, someone had a sleepover. I like him, Suz. He looks badass, but I can see a kind heart underneath. Reminds me a bit of Kayden, but I hope without the other bullshit."

I swallowed down the dry leftover bagel. "I almost messed everything up with him, Sophia." I grabbed the glass of milk off the counter, taking a sip, while I waited for her to scream at me.

"Are you fucking crazy? Why in the hell would you do that? What happened?" she yelled, her shrill voice causing my ear to throb.

"I just didn't see us going anywhere, and I didn't want to get too attached to him. I ignored him yesterday and ended up going on a date with Derek instead."

"Derek? What the fuck, Suzy? You know that guy gives me the creeps."

I sighed as I leaned against the counter, wanting to smash my head into the gray Formica for being so stupid. "I know. I just wanted to forget City—epic disaster that I'll tell you about someday. Anyway, City came to my rescue and took me home."

"Well, thank Christ for small miracles."

"He asked me to be his girlfriend, Sophia. Can you believe that?"

"I do. You're an amazing girl, little mama. Any man would be lucky to have you as his woman. City was smart enough to realize it. Kayden was the same way with me, but his hard exterior melted. Sometimes you just have to roll with it to get to the good stuff. Nothing in life is risk free, Suzy."

"I know, Sophia. My entire body vibrates when I'm around him, and my stomach fills with butterflies. I've never felt that way with anyone, and it scares the crap out of me. I tried to push him away, but he didn't let me."

"You must have some fine shit."

I choked on my milk, and it started to come out my nose as I wiped my face. "What in the heck are you talking about, woman?"

"Well, you tried to get rid of him, and I know you usually hold true to your plan, so I know you didn't relent first and he came to you. Most guys would just say fuck that and walk away without looking back, but you must have something special that made him come back for more. Huh, who knew?" She giggled.

"Shut it, whore. We had a long talk about relationships and love when he brought me home. He's been hurt before and hasn't had a real girlfriend in years."

"We've all been hurt before. It's part of love. If you never hurt, then you've never truly been in love before, Suzy. What happened to him?"

"His fiancée died," I said, putting my cup in the dishwasher. I leaned against the counter and rested the phone against my shoulder.

"Wow, that's horrible. I couldn't image losing Kayden. I'd be a complete and total mess. I don't know if I'd love anyone the way I love him. I couldn't allow myself to love anyone that way again if he was ripped from my life."

"Yeah, I just wonder if he'll be able to make room in his heart for me. I'll always be competing with her for his love, I'm afraid."

"It's not a competition, sweetheart. There's room for both of you. He's taking a risk with you—just give him time to deal with his feelings. Don't rush into the L-word."

"You did with Kayden," I said, smiling even though she couldn't see me.

"I know." She sighed. "I couldn't imagine anyone else in my life. Kayden was it for me, babe. He ruined me and I could never be without him—I knew that after our first weekend together. It felt like all the planets aligned. I was finally with the man I was meant to be with my entire life."

"I'm just going to enjoy his glorious body filled with extra holes and pretty pictures. Jesus, girl, you should see his fine ass naked."

"Did you say ass?" she asked, sounding shocked.

"I am an adult, Sophia. I do swear."

"I think City's dick stirred your brain and altered your thought pattern. My Suzy sunshine never uses profanity," she bellowed.

"Suck it."

"What am I sucking?" she asked.

"Kayden's dong." I started laughing at how immature that sounded.

"Listen, whore, no matter what you do—do not fucking say 'I want to suck your dong' to City. His hard-on would vanish, as he would fall on the floor in a fit of laughter. It's not sexy, not at all. Funny as fuck? Yes, but not come here and fuck me talk. Got it?"

"I know. Just wanted to see what you'd say."

"Silly, girl. Oh, and don't call it a penis. Use the dirtiest, crudest words you can think of when you speak to him. Men love it dirty and raw. If you can find it in the health teacher's textbook, avoid it like the plague."

"Got it. All right, I'm going to go get ready."

"Where you going so early? Your ass usually isn't out of bed before noon, and it's only eleven."

"I have grocery shopping to do today, and I feel like browsing at a couple of stores. I plan to look at all the things I'll never be able to buy. A girl can dream, right?"

"Grocery shop today and window browse tomorrow. I'm so glad we have a long weekend, and I want to go shopping and have a girl's day out. We need to practice your dirty talk."

"Don't you want to stay home with him and Jett?" I asked, walking in my bedroom, searching my closet for something to wear.

"Nah, let them have some male bonding time. What time you want to pick me up tomorrow?" she asked.

"Noon, okay?"

"I'll be waiting for you, my pretty." She cackled as she hung up the phone, and I shook my head. Sophia was going to make it a very long day.

***

"Come on, you big pussy, let's go inside," Sophia said, yanking my arm as we sat in the parking lot of Inked. Once Sophia had something in her mind, she was like an Italian woman I knew—totally unbendable.

"Sophia, please. It's not nice to surprise him at work. What happen with the 'no cling' stuff?" I shook my head and put all my weight on the seat.

"It's not clingy. I want a damn tattoo. I want to surprise Kayden, and I never get a chance. I either have the baby or him with me. I'd rather him do it than some stranger. Please get out of the car before I pull you out by your hair."

Her hands were on her hips and she was giving me the pushy teacher look that always cracked me up. Sophia was just as much of a softy as I was, but her look was nastier and usually made people do as they were told.

"Fine, but when it all implodes I'm blaming your bossy butt." I closed the doors and hit my remote twice, making sure that no one could steal my collection of vintage hip-hop cassettes.

Sophia whistled as we approached the door. "This is a nice shop, not like most of the shit-ass tattoo places around here." She grabbed the door handle, and my palms began to sweat as my heart pounded in my chest, causing my breathing to grow ragged.

"Can I help you ladies?" a man asked. He looked like a younger version of City. His muscles bulged from under his shirt; his arms, covered in tattoos, flexed as he rose from his chair.

"I'd like to get a tattoo today. Any possibility of that?" Sophia asked.

Looking around the shop as Sophia spoke with the one of the Gallo boys, I took in all the vibrant colors on the walls—reds and oranges with yellow on the ceilings. No white space invaded this realm of his life.

I walked over to the beautiful artwork on the walls to get a closer look. The pieces on the wall were body parts that had been decorated with some of the most stunning work I'd ever seen. I turned my head and my stomach dropped. City was sitting next to a beautiful brunette with his hand on her breast and his face only inches away. They were laughing and talking, but he didn't see me. They looked comfortable together, like there was something between them, or maybe there had been at some point. My heart thumped against my chest and I felt flushed looking at them.

I walked back by the desk quickly and grabbed Sophia's arm. "Can we go, please?" I asked quietly.

She turned around and gave me a confused look. "What's wrong?"

"He's touching some girl's boob and I just can't look at it. It hurts to see it."

She touched my shoulder. "Babe, it's a boob. He's an artist and some girls like tattoos on their breasts. It's like a gynie looking at a snatch; it's just another body part. Don't get caught up in what you think you see." She smiled.

"You're crude. It was more how they were looking at each other." I shrugged.

"Was he looking at her or what he was doing?" She eyed me.

"He was looking at her breast, for Christ's sake."

"He was looking at his lines. Calm the fuck down before you have a coronary. Lemme see." She pushed me back and peered through the doorway to the tattoo area. "Look," she said, yanking my arm and pulling my body to see what she saw. "He's concentrating on his artwork." She held my body so I couldn't move, and forced me to view City touching someone else.

"Call me a prude, but I don't want to see it." I pulled away from her grip. "I'll go wait in the car—you get your tattoo or whatever. I can't be in here, Sophia."

"God, you're so dramatic. Get over your shit. He's not fucking the bitch in the chair, he's creating a masterpiece." She looked pissed at me. "Suit yourself, go wait in the car and I'll be out in a bit."

I pushed the door open as I heard Sophia say, "Hey, City."

Damn it. I wanted her to leave with me. I knew she was going to spill her guts, or should I say mine, and tell him everything that happened. I sat in my car and waited for over an hour. I tilted the seat back and closed my eyes, enjoying the warmth of the sun. I cracked the window an inch so I could feel the cold rush of wind on my face every so often.

"What are you doing, sugar?"

I jumped, his voice waking me from a nightmare. His face was buried in someone else's legs, kissing them with his mouth like he had done to me the night before.

"You scared the crap out of me. Jesus." I placed my hand over my eyes to block out the sun as I looked out the window to see his beautiful body.

"Why aren't you inside with Sophia? What the fuck are you doing out here alone? You didn't want to see me?" He looked hurt, but I couldn't get the visual of him with the woman's boob out of my mind.

"I thought it was best if I waited out here."

"Are you going to open your door so we can talk face to face? Or am I going to talk to you through glass like it's a prison visit?"

"You looked like you had your hands full," I said, and looked out the front windshield, avoiding his glare. "I'm sure you have more boobs to fondle." What the hell was wrong with me? The pang of jealousy hit me hard, and it felt foreign. I had never been a jealous person. No one had evoked this kind of emotion before him.

"Open the damn door, Suzy." He pulled on the handle, bending down to peer through the window. "So that's what it is. You're jealous?" He laughed.

I wanted to smack that shit-eating grin off his face. He looked so smug. "I'm not jealous." When had I reverted to acting like a childish crazy person? *Get a grip.* I knew it was only part of his job, but it was foreign to me, and I couldn't wrap my mind around the image and reality.

"Sugar, come on. I wasn't looking at her breast. I was working, for shit's sake. It's a piece of canvas to me. Don't be jealous—although I kinda like that emotion in you. Shows me that you care."

"I need time to process it all. Did you start Sophia's tattoo?" I asked, wondering how long I'd have to sit here.

"She needed a break. I won't go back in and finish until you get that fine ass out of that car and we talk about this."

The man knew how to hold me hostage. I closed my eyes and took a deep breath before unlocking the door.

City pulled on the handle, opening the door before crouching down next to me. "Sugar, look at me." The grin on his face made me want to smack him. "Only you. She's a married woman with children, and I've known her for years. I wasn't staring at her nipples—I watch my lines. If I make a mistake, it can't be fixed. Outta the car, Suzy." He backed away and waited for me to climb out.

Closing the door behind me, I leaned against it before he placed his arms on either side of my body, pinning me against the car. Rubbing his crotch against my stomach, he said, "You're the only one that does this to me."

I wanted to stake my claim and ward off any woman that thought he could be theirs. His hand snaked around my neck, gripping me roughly as he crushed his lips against mine. My lips parted, granting him access as he pushed his stiff shaft against me.

He broke the kiss and searched my eyes. "Are we good?"

"I just didn't like seeing it, City, especially so soon after seeing you with Kaylee. It's going to take some getting used to for me." I could get lost in his crystal blue eyes. "I'm sorry I was so childish," I said as I leaned my forehead against his cheek.

"Childish and jealous," he stated. "I'll be patient with you, but I'm going to make you pay later for your little temper tantrum." He laughed.

"What do you have in mind?" I asked with a cocked eyebrow and a grin.

"It's on a need-to-know basis, sugar, and you don't need to know… yet." He licked my bottom lip and grabbed my hand, pulling me to the shop door.

"That's not fair, City."

"Sometimes life isn't fair, sugar. I can guarantee that you'll be screaming through it, and it won't be out of pain, unless you're into that sort of thing." He waggled his eyebrows and chuckled.

Oh, hell. I knew trouble when I saw it, and it was standing right in front of me. City would be the death of me, but hell, at least I could say it was fun while it lasted. I did the thing I never, ever did—I took the plunge and jumped in feet first without holding my nose.

16

FANTASIES

CITY

I HAD PLANS FOR MY LITTLE DARLING. SHE NEEDED TO PAY FOR HER temper tantrum, but I wanted to give her plenty of time to think about her actions and worry about what was ahead of her.

Suzy stared at the ground as we walked through the door of Inked. Mikey sat at the desk and was engrossed in his work until I cleared my throat. He looked up, a smile breaking out across his face.

"Suzy, this is my brother Mikey."

"Michael," he said, holding out his hand.

Suzy smiled at him and placed her hand in his. "Nice to meet you, Michael."

"Pleasure is all mine." He brought her hand up to his mouth and kissed it.

"Hey, dickhead, break this shit up. Suzy's mine." I smacked his shoulder and gave him a glare.

"I'm just giving her a proper welcome, bro. Chill the fuck out," Mikey said, looking at me with a smarmy grin. *Asshole.*

"Do you want to come in the back or stay out here with *Mikey*?" I emphasized "Mikey" just to get under his skin. He'd always been Mikey, but he didn't like the nickname when women were nearby.

"I'll keep you company," he piped in, and I turned to give him the look of death.

"Um, I don't know. I don't really like blood. Is it bloody?" she asked.

"Not too bad, sugar. Tattoos are done with needles, so there's some." I pulled her close and buried my face in her hair, inhaling her sweet, flowery scent.

"I think I better wait out here," she said into my chest.

"I'll keep her company—no worries, Joey." The fucker winked at me, and I wanted to punch him in the face. I knew he was just fucking with me, because one thing my brother sure as fuck wasn't was a woman stealer. He wouldn't try and fuck Suzy or take her from me, but it still grated on my fucking nerves.

I'd never felt so territorial over someone, and especially not as quickly as I had with Suzy. Maybe it was her similarities to Joni or her kind heart, but I didn't want anything bad to happen to her, and I sure as hell didn't want to lose the opportunity to get to know everything about her.

"I'll be done soon with Sophia. I just have to finish the color." I kissed her, making sure to leave her breathless and her mind only filled with thoughts of me before I left her in the capable hands of my wanker little brother. "Don't let Mikey fool you. He's not as innocent as he looks."

"I figured that. I'm not completely naïve." I chuckled, because she was that naïve. Mikey had the look of a kindhearted person, with his charming, boyish good looks, but I'd seen him beat the piss out of men almost twice his size.

"Okay, sugar. Just don't believe a goddamn thing that comes out of that mouth of his, got me?" I smiled at her, and all I wanted to do is take her home and fuck her brains out, but I had to finish Sophia's tattoo and leave these two to talk.

"Gotcha, big guy. Go finish that tattoo so I can get her home to Kayden before he starts blowing up her phone. I'll be okay."

"I still have plans for you, sugar. I haven't forgotten. Catch ya in a few." I slapped her ass hard enough for it to sting. She yelped and jumped from the quick swat.

"Dang, City," she said as she rubbed her ass, and I laughed as I walked to the back of the shop.

Sophia was typing on her phone, and looked up as I approached.

"Get the pussy out of the car?" she asked as I pulled on my gloves.

"Yeah, we had a little talk." I laughed. I sat down and grabbed my machine and dipped the needle in the yellow ink.

"You have to understand her, City. She's not like most girls. She's in a class all her own," Sophia said as she looked up from her phone.

"Whatcha mean, darlin'?" I asked, rubbing the salve over the design before placing the needle against her skin.

"She hasn't really had a boyfriend or been in love. Shit, I'd never been truly in love with someone until I met Kayden. She's not used to any of this. God, I'm so fucking this up, but you're fucking killing me with that needle, City." She giggled.

"Just a little bit longer. Tell me more about her, Sophia. You guys were with each other, like, twenty-four-seven there for a while. What don't I know about her? What won't she tell me about herself?" I looked down and shaded in the beautiful hibiscus on her hip with shades of pinks and yellows.

"Well, where should I start? I'm sure you've figured out she doesn't swear, but trust me, that girl has one dirty-ass mind." She laid her head back in the chair and her body grew less tense. Talking seemed to help people get their mind off the needle scraping against their skin.

"Really? This I gotta hear."

"I don't want to give away all her secrets, but she needs a guy like you."

"What's that mean?" I had an idea, but I wanted to hear her best friend say it.

"Suzy is a control freak. She needs someone that won't give in to her, but—and this is a big but—she also needs someone that's going to care about what she wants. She's been with men that don't really live up to the promises in the sack, or make her feel like a freak."

Now she fucking intrigued me. "What would make her feel like a freak?"

"She has this fantasy about being kidnapped and sold into slavery."

She whispered the last words, and I looked up at her. I almost fucking choked. "Suzy?"

"Don't be so shocked, Joey. She just wants to be owned, if you know what I mean. She may be a control freak, but in the sack she wants to be used and controlled. Think you're up to the challenge?" She moved her eyebrows up and down, with the biggest smile plastered on her face.

"I think I'm just what the doctor ordered. Tell me more—this shit is good."

"She has fantasies, but will probably never share them with you."

"Why not?"

"No one has ever asked her, so don't expect her to just cough up that shit. You have to pull it out of her."

"Got it."

"Just don't break her heart, City, or I'll crush your balls. Got me?"

"Loud and clear, and I think you'd do it too, Sophia." Sophia didn't seem like the type to not follow through on her words. She reminded me of those strict teachers that you didn't want to fuck around in class and get that pissed-off-teacher look from, but I knew she was sweet too, 'cause Suzy wouldn't be friends with someone who wasn't.

"Oh, I have no issues inflicting bodily harm when necessary."

"Kayden must be one hell of a guy to handle you, Sophia."

"He's complicated."

"Suzy mentioned something along those lines about Kayden." I dipped the gun into the black to finish the shading as I hit the home stretch on the design on her leg.

"I normally wouldn't take as much shit as I did from him, but when you love someone and you know you're meant to be with them, you stick it through. I couldn't abandon him in his time of need. Someday I'll tell you the whole story, 'cause it's a long fucking tale."

"Almost done, just a few more lines. Was it worth it?" I knew the answer, but I wanted to hear her say it was worth the struggle that I feel she had to endure to find the love of her life.

"I wouldn't trade a moment of our fucked-up journey. We were meant to be together. I don't regret a second of my time with him."

I liked hearing about Kayden and Sophia. All my friends and siblings were single and had been put through the wringer. I wanted to hear that it was possible to find love in today's jaded world.

I put the machine on the table and began to wipe the tattoo to clean her skin so she could get a good look at it. "There ya go, darling. Hop up and look in the mirror." I leaned back in my chair and stretched my back.

Sophia jumped up and walked up to the mirror, holding the side of her pants down. It was beautiful and permanent.

"Whatcha think?"

"Oh my God, City. It's amazing. I fucking love it." She turned to the side and stood closer to the mirror. "The color's amazing."

"Will Kayden like it?" I asked. I was sure he'd love it; what man wouldn't love their woman to have their name on their skin? She was marked and his forever.

"He's going to freak out. The guy has a thing for tats, and he has my name on him. I can't wait to show him." She just stood there and stared in the mirror with a giant smile across her face.

"He does?"

"Yep, huge down his leg. There's no way to cover that shit up, either. He's mine forever and I'm his," she said as she walked back over to the chair.

"I never advise anyone to tattoo a boyfriend or girlfriend's name on their body. It's asking for disaster. You're brave."

"Brave? I'm never leaving that man, City. No one will ever love me like he does."

"I've seen the chemistry you two have. I did my part in warning you, but I can't deny you the design you want." I rubbed the salve on her skin and covered it to keep it clean. "You know how this works and about after-care?"

"Yep, it's my fifth tattoo. I got this shit."

"Well then, darling, you're all done."

"I have to use the ladies' room. Where is it?" she asked.

"Down the hall to the right. I'm going to go check on Suzy." I wanted to see her and make sure Mikey kept his paws off her.

I pulled my gloves off with a snap and threw them on the table. I cracked my neck and rounded the corner to see Mikey and Suzy sitting in the chairs talking and a little closer than I'd normally feel comfortable with—but this was Mikey.

They began to laugh. "Oh stop, Michael, you're killing me." She covered her mouth and slapped her knee.

"I shit you not," Mikey said, then looked up at me and cleared his throat. "Oh, big brother. How'd things go?"

"What the fuck are you two talking about?" I knew Mikey wanted to find any way to embarrass me; my family was fantastic for that shit.

"Nothing at all."

Suzy's face turned red, and she could barely look me in the eyes without breaking out into a fit of laughter. "Don't you worry, we're just sharing family memories."

Cocksucker. Someday I'd make him pay for this shit. I wouldn't normally give a fuck, but I didn't want Suzy to think of me in the way Mikey had probably described me. Thank the motherfucking gods that the rest of the group wasn't here today. Izzy would be all over Suzy, grilling her and filling her head with stories that should stay in the past. "That's what I'm afraid of."

"No worries. Michael was just reminiscing," she said between her fingers, trying to hide her laughter.

I wanted to choke the motherfucker. I knew he had a knack for making shit up just for his amusement and my embarrassment. I rubbed the back of my neck, trying to stop myself from punching him in the face.

"Where's Sophia?" Suzy asked, getting up from her seat.

"She's using the ladies' room. Go back and see the work I did on her." I kissed her, patting her ass as she walked away. "What the fuck did you tell her?" I said to Mikey.

He started to laugh as he stood. "Oh, nothing."

"Bullshit. What lies did you fill her head with, asswad?"

"I told her you slept with a teddy bear and sucked your thumb until you were ten." He doubled over in laughter, and I saw red.

"You're a dickhead, Mikey. Why do you always do this shit to me?" I closed my eyes and calmed my breathing.

"You never got all worked up before. You must really like this one." He plopped his ass in the chair and pulled himself up to the desk.

"Fuck you."

"Oh, testy. Definitely a boner for that blonde bombshell. Hey, you told my last girlfriend that I pissed my bed until high school. All's fair in love and war, rat bastard."

I burst into laughter. That was the last time that woman came around the family. She broke up with Mikey shortly after our Sunday dinner. "You didn't even like her. You were just fucking her." I heard the door creak, and Suzy and Sophia emerged with smiles on their faces. "Guess you're right, I deserved it, but for fuck's sake—I really like this girl. Don't fuck it up for me. Got me?" I said, leaning over the desk so only he could hear.

"Righto. Don't get your panties in a wad, man." Mikey stood quickly, and smiled as the ladies walked up to the desk. "Everything okay, ladies?"

Sophia's smile couldn't be any bigger. "Fabulous. You did such an amazing job, City. I fuckin' love it, and Kayden's going to be shocked as hell."

"Kayden?" Mikey said, his voice filled with curiosity.

"Yes, Kayden, my boyfriend and father of my baby."

"Fuck, all the good ones are taken," Mikey muttered as he walked away.

"I'm glad you're happy. Let me know what Kayden thinks about it."

Sophia wrapped her arms around me and said, "Thank you."

"Anytime, babe. I'm your man if you ever need any more work. Give that some time to heal. You're going to be sore for a couple of weeks. The hip is tender. Watch what type of clothing you wear, too."

Suzy stood off to the side and smiled at us both. I couldn't wait to get her alone later, but I still had work to do. "Come here, sugar." I held my hand out to her, and she placed her tiny fingers in my palm.

I wrapped her in my arms and pulled her body against mine. "I haven't forgotten that I owe you for your little display earlier." Her eyes went wide as she stared at me. "I never break a promise, either, sugar." I kissed her and rubbed my dick against her stomach. I couldn't wait to bury myself in her pretty little cunt. "I'll be over around eight. Be ready." I smiled and said goodbye as the two girls walked out of the shop in a fit of giggles.

17

WANTS AND DESIRES

SUZY

I COLLAPSED ON THE BED, EXHAUSTED, SWEATY, AND OUT OF BREATH. City stretched out next to me, hands behind his head, a smug-ass grin stretching his lips. "What's that look?" I asked.

"I fuckin' rocked your world."

"Cocky much?" He fucking did, too. I'd never come so hard or as much as I had with him. He knew all the right things to do and all the perfect places to touch. "If that was your punishment, it didn't work."

"Oh, I don't know about that. I heard you yelp a few times when I smacked your ass." He laughed.

I stared at the ceiling and thought about his words, remembering the stinging feeling of his hand landing on my ass. It set my skin on fire and made everything more intense.

"More out of shock than hurt. You surprised the heck out of me."

City turned on his side, rested his head on his hand, and gazed at me. He ran his fingertips across my stomach, and my flesh broke out in goose bumps. "I hope it's not the last surprise I ever give you."

I closed my eyes and wanted to stay in this moment forever.

"Whatcha thinking about, sugar?"

I opened my eyes and looked into his beautiful blue eyes. "You, Joe. You're just so, so...I don't know how to describe you." I sighed.

"Unlike anyone you've ever been with?" He arched his eyebrow.

"Yeah, and I don't know if that's a good thing, either." I didn't want to say that he also made me half neurotic. The jealously I'd felt in the tattoo shop was something foreign to me, and I didn't like it—not one bit. I barely knew him, and it gutted me to think of him with someone else. I was starting to question my sanity.

"Oh...it's good. The way you screamed my name couldn't be anything but good, sugar."

My face flushed, and warmth crawled down my skin. I had never been a yeller or made much noise at all, but then again, I'd never had a reason to before.

"Don't be embarrassed." He pulled me against his body and kissed my temple as he fisted my hair.

I couldn't escape him—his smell, skin, and warmth. Everything about him made me want more, and I couldn't block it from my mind or wish it away.

"Want me to go?" he whispered in my ear.

"No!" I opened my eyes quickly, turning toward him. My lips brushed against his. I didn't close my eyes and neither did he—we stared in each other's eyes for a moment as I melted into his body.

"Stop overthinking shit, Suzette. You want to be with me?"

"You scare the hell out of me, honestly."

"Why?" He brushed the hair from my face, and my skin tingled from the innocent touch.

"Like you said—you're unlike anyone I've ever known. You're like one giant damn mystery to me."

"I'm an open book. I don't hide my feelings and I don't pussyfoot around shit. I do what I have to and I say what's on my mind."

"I guess I'm just not used to someone being so...so..."

"Cocky, sexy, manly?" He chuckled and started to grab my side, causing me to break out into laughter.

"Stop!" I couldn't catch my breath.

"You think too damn much instead of saying what's on your mind."

"Okay, okay," I puffed out through my giggle, with tears running down my face. His hands stilled at my side and his tongue darted out and licked the tear from my cheek.

"Like that. No one has ever done that."

"Sugar, maybe I need to ask what they have done to you. I feel that list is shorter than what they did do. Have you come during sex before?"

I didn't want to answer that question. "Um."

"Yes or no?" I felt like his azure eyes were staring into my soul and trying to unwrap all of my secrets.

"Not really." I gave him a shy smile, not wanting to divulge that no one had ever gotten me off like he did. City was cocky enough without thinking he was my own personal sex god.

"Hmm. Did you come with me or were you faking that shit?"

Oh, here we go. "I did and I sure as hell wasn't faking—I never fake it."

"Besides me, ever? Without having to do it yourself?"

"No, no one has ever really cared if I did."

"Fucking assholes." He shook his head. "Why do women date assholes like that? I know no one's ever smacked your ass. What do you want that no one has ever done to you?"

Oh my God. I couldn't be any more embarrassed than I felt in this moment. "I don't know."

"That's bullshit, sugar. Everyone has fantasies." He nuzzled my hair, and I didn't feel so under the microscope, but I didn't want him to laugh at me.

"Tell me one of yours." I stroked his arms and traced the tattoos on his skin. The artwork really was beautiful. My parents always told me that tattoos were trashy, but on City they were works of art. They were a timeline of his life, and I wanted to peel back the layers and hear the story.

"I want to fuck you on my bike."

My breath caught in my throat. The thought of him taking me on his bike hadn't even crossed my mind, but now the image was burned into my brain.

"I want you spread eagle, my face planted between your legs, licking every ounce of wetness from your body before sinking my dick in you." The vibration of his words in my ear caused wetness to pool between my legs. Damn him. "Your turn." I knew he had a smile on his face without even seeing it. *Bastard.*

I sighed. "Where do I begin? God, this is so embarrassing."

"Sugar, if you can't share your fantasies with your boyfriend, who can you?"

One point, City—Suzy, Zero. "I swear I need to have my head examined." I covered my eyes with my hands. City would think I was nuts.

"Out with it. Sophia told me you two read a lot of those smut books. Fantasies can become reality, sugar."

"It's just so weird. You're going to think I'm completely insane."

He stroked my arm as I tried to cover my face. His body shifted as he moved my hand away from my eyes.

"I gotta know now. I can call Sophia and ask, or you can tell me. Give me the naughtiest thing you've always wanted."

I swallowed and shut my eyes. I didn't want to see his reaction when he heard this one. "Fine. I have this fantasy of being taken against my will."

He didn't gasp or scream, but very calmly said, "Rape or kidnapping?"

I opened my eyes and turned to look at him. He had a grin on his face, and the butterflies dancing in my stomach calmed. "Kidnap. I know it's weird," I mumbled.

"No, Suzette. It's not weird at all. We all have our kinks and fantasies. Okay, so kidnap and then what?" He looked so damn eager to hear the rest, like he was hanging on my every word. How could I not share the rest?

"Do you honestly want to know?"

"Yes."

"I've read so many amazing books that deal with kidnapping and being owned by someone. I don't really want some crazy person to kidnap me, but the books make it seem appealing and sexy as heck."

"I'll see what I can do to make that happen."

"Oh, God."

"I won't surprise you, you'll know when it's coming—when I'm coming for you."

He pulled my body against his, our skin touching, his hands pressed into my back; he made me feel normal about wanting something so taboo.

He smelled so good. His masculine and musky scent mixed with the smell of sex. I didn't think I could ever get enough of him.

His hand glided up my back, on to the nape of my neck as he grabbed a fistful of hair. The feel of his calloused hands against my skin and the prick of pain on my scalp felt like electricity throughout my body. Holding my head still with his firm grip on my hair, he looked into my eyes. The brilliant blue of his almost glowed in the light and burned with passion. "As for being owned, I plan to own every inch of your body. You *are* mine, sugar, don't forget that shit. I'm going to fucking ruin you."

Why the hell did that sound so amazing? Damn trashy books altered my sense of right and wrong. I wanted him to own me—ruin me.

I was lost in thought until his lips crashed against mine. His kiss wasn't gentle or kind, but demanding and all-consuming. My body molded around him as I wrapped my leg around his waist.

"I'm going to be rough, Suzette," he said against my lips.

I searched his eyes and could see the lust and need within. "I'm yours," I whispered.

He grabbed my torso and flipped me on my stomach. He moved faster than I thought possible, and he was behind me in a moment. He grabbed my hips and pulled my ass in the air. "Stomach down, sugar." He pushed on the small of my back. "Head too, only your ass in the air." I buried my face in the sheets and could smell him on the fabric.

I started to hyperventilate. I'd had sex doggie style, but this was something different—new. His fingers raked through my wetness, stroking my clit and squeezing it lightly. A jolt coursed through my body, and I cried out.

Smack. "Don't move," he said, rubbing my ass with one hand and pinching my clit with the other. "Unless you want another swat on the ass."

I wanted to squirm or rub against him like a cat in heat, but the sting of his last swat kept me rooted in place. His hand left my ass, and I turned to look at him. His tall, muscular body stood on the bed, and he stroked his cock. The metal piercing at the tip would disappear in his hand. His beautiful black hair was a mess and lay across his forehead, and the light reflected off his eyes. I could stare at him for hours—he was everything my mother told me to steer clear of in life. Just looking at the man made my panties wet. *I'm so screwed.*

I was so exposed in this position. My ass and pussy were on display for him. He pumped his hardness in his fist as he positioned himself behind me. I could feel the head rub through my wetness. His cock was hard as it poked at my entrance. I closed my eyes and held my breath as I waited for him to fill me. I instantly felt the loss of his body, and opened one eye to see what he was doing.

"What's wrong?" I asked, staring at him just standing there, stroking the shaft as he looked at me.

"Relax, sugar. I'll make it fanfuckingtastic." He rubbed my ass, and I knew his words were true.

I relaxed my muscles and closed my eyes as I felt his hand on me again. The head of his dick touched my opening, and I wanted him inside me. I gripped the sheets and braced myself for the impaling I was about to endure. He rested his hand on the top of my ass as he pushed himself inside. I felt stuffed, and I knew he wasn't fully seated inside. I squeezed the sheets tighter as the sensation of him became overwhelming, and more intense than I'd felt before.

His body slammed into mine as he pumped in and out. His body worked like a well-oiled machine, and his shaft was the piston battering my insides. The tip hit parts of my body that had never been touched before, and I wanted to crawl away—the fight-or-flight instinct started to kick in. My ass stung as the sound of his hand striking my ass filled my ears.

"Ass up, Suzette," he growled, grabbing my hips and molding my body exactly how he wanted it without going out of rhythm.

I bit my lip. I wanted to cry out. I wanted to crawl away. I didn't know if I could take one more minute as I reached back and grabbed his ankles. I dug my nails into his skin and grounded myself. I had to fight every urge in my body to flee.

I could feel every inch of him as it moved inside my body. His breathing was harsh and quick, and I buried my face in the sheets to stop from crying out. My muscles tightened as I felt an orgasm building inside me, but how? He hadn't even touched my clit in this position, and I hadn't touched myself.

CHELLE BLISS

His speed increased and his hips slammed against the sore spot left by his hand. He grabbed my hips and pulled me closer, allowing himself to be buried to the hilt.

"Fuck, your cunt is so tight." His fingers dug in my hip as I was held captive by his hands. "I can feel it squeezing my cock. Fuck, sugar," he said as he pulled my body against him to meet his thrust.

I squeezed my eyes shut as a moan escaped my mouth that I could no longer hold. I needed to yell as the orgasm crashed over me, my body becoming rigid. My core gripped his shaft as the aftershocks tore through me, and his rhythm became more intense, and eventually more erratic. He moaned and my body became limp, but I kept my ass in the air because of his rock-hard grip.

His body twitched against me before he pulled out and collapsed on the bed. "Fuck," he muttered.

My body ached. Rolling over, I stretched out across the mattress and rested my arm across his body. Our labored breathing filled the air. My hand rose and fell with his chest as I gulped for air and tried to swallow the cotton taste from my mouth.

Neither of us spoke as we lay there. City had been more than I could ever imagine. I liked being with him. He was easy to be around. He made me feel beautiful and wanted. I needed to turn my brain off and stop thinking of the reasons I should run away from him and enjoy our time together.

I felt like I was in a dream world, half awake as City rolled over and placed his arms around me. He kissed my face and whispered, "Night, beautiful," in my ear.

18

FAMILY HEADACHES

CITY

WE SPENT A FEW NIGHTS TOGETHER DURING THE WEEK—WORK TOOK UP our days and kept us apart, but the evenings were filled with fucking her raw and leaving no doubt in her mind of my feelings toward her. Saturday she had a wedding to attend that she'd already RSVPed to and couldn't change.

As I locked up the shop, my phone chimed.

Bear: Get your pussy ass over to the Cowboy. Where the fuck you been, man?

Suzy would be gone until around midnight, and a drink with the guys was in order.

Me: Headed that way, asshole. Save me a seat and you better have a fucking cold beer waiting for me.

Shoving the phone in my pocket, I climbed on the bike and headed toward the Neon Cowboy. Steam rose from the dampened streets as the tires parted the mist. The moonlight flashed through the trees lighting my path. The cool breeze felt good against my flesh as I barreled down the road to hang with my guys.

Walking in the bar, I took in the familiar smell of smoke, the sound of the country guitar, and the murmur of the crowd, and I realized how much I'd missed this place.

"Yo," Bear yelled, grabbing my attention. "I almost sent a search party looking for your ass," he said as I approached the table. Tank and the others laughed.

"I've been busy, fucker." A frosty glass sat waiting for me, as I'd hoped it would be.

"Busy nestled between that sweet blonde ass, I assume," Tank said as he twirled the beer bottle between his fingers.

"You're just jealous because you gotta pay for your pussy, shithead."

He shrugged, bringing the bottle to his lips. "Less complicated that way. I just wanna bust a nut without the cuddling and whining."

"You're an asshole." Frisco laughed, slapping Tank on the shoulder, causing the bottle to move from his lips.

"Fucker, you made me spill my beer."

Frisco covered his mouth with his hand as his eyes turned into small slits. We called him Frisco because he hailed from sunny California and grew up in the San Francisco area. His features were unique—his Chinese mother and American father were both evident in his features. His eyes were almond-shaped and dark, his hair pin straight, cropped at the top, and coal black. He was taller than me, and thin with a slight, muscular build.

"So, City, tell us about the li'l woman? How are things going?" Bear asked.

I leaned back in my chair and rested the beer against my knee. "Fucking perfect."

"You're serious about this one?" He raised an eyebrow and studied me.

Everyone at the table stopped, turning their attention to me. "Serious as a motherfuckin' heart attack." I sipped my beer, looking at their faces. Frisco smiled, Bear's mouth hung open, and Tank scowled. "What?" I said, moving the bottle from my lips.

"Didn't think I'd see the fucking day, dude," Bear said with a sappy grin.

"She's too pretty to be with your loser ass," Tank piped in before I could speak.

"Fuck off, Tank."

"I'm happy for you, man. This calls for another round." Tank raised his fingers to his lips and whistled. He was so crass, but the girl always ran when she heard him call. "Another round, sweet cheeks," he said as he patted her on the bottom.

"Hey, City. Nice to finally have a gentleman back in here." She winked at me before turning her attention back to Tank. "Anything for you, handsome?" she said, running her fingers down the side of Tank's face. He blushed as he placed his order.

"You know your ass would give up this shithole for a piece of that every night," I said to Tank as he watched her ass swaying in her Daisy Dukes as she walked toward the bar.

"Won't deny that shit." He laughed before slapping the table roughly, causing all the bottles to jump.

We talked for hours about motorcycles, tattoos, women, and, of course, the bar. The guys filled me in on the events of the last week. It was always the same old bullshit—bar fights, hook-ups, and booze. The town was so small that everyone knew each other's business, and word spread like wildfire.

"Fuck," Bear hissed. "Speaking of bitches, Kaylee was in here looking for your ass."

"What the fuck? When?" I gripped the bottle in my hand, trying to control my anger.

"Last night. Mumbling some bullshit about how she was yours. Spreading that shit around here like it was the gospel. I told her to fuck off," Bear said, leaning back like he was about to beat on his chest.

"She's a fucking train wreck. Stuck my dick in her twice and she won't let me fucking forget it. I'll set her ass straight, unless one of you boys wants to take her off my hands?" I looked around the table and waited for someone to accept.

"Fuck no, that bitch makes my skin crawl. Hate clingy women," Frisco said, shaking his head.

"My dick, my problem," I said, feeling the phone vibrate in my pocket. Pulling it out, I glanced at the screen under the table.

Suzy: Drunk and tired. Sophia's taking me home, but you're welcome to join me.

"Ball and chain wrangling your ass in?" Tank asked.

"Such a ball buster. It's late and I worked all day. I'm heading home.

145

Thanks for the drink, Bear." I shook his hand and turned to Frisco. "Good to see you again, buddy. Tank, it's been real."

"Whipped," Tank mumbled as I stood to leave.

I left the guys to end the evening how they always did. Bitching about life and women. Thankful that my night wouldn't end like it had for countless years, I sent Suzy a text.

Me: Leave the door unlocked. I'll meet you in bed.

When I arrived, Suzy was half dressed and passed out across the bed. Her mouth hung open, hair was half covering her face, and her dress was halfway off, exposing her breasts. It took everything in me not to snap a picture of her and remind her of it later, but I didn't want to be a dick.

"Wake up, sugar." I grabbed her leg, pulling her body down the bed. She mumbled but didn't wake. I pulled the hem of her dress, removing the clingy material. I rarely had the ability to just stare at her body without her trying to cover her skin. I stood and looked at her—white skin, perky breasts, and long, muscular legs. She was a vision.

Gathering her in my arms, I placed her head on the pillow before I removed my clothes and climbed in next to her.

"City," she muttered as she shimmied her ass into my dick.

"Fuck." I sighed. My cock throbbed from the warmth of her soft cheeks rubbing against it. "Go back to sleep, sugar." I pulled her tighter, burying my face in her hair before drifting off to sleep to her soft snores.

***

"How's the shop doing?" my father asked as we sat around the dining room table. Today was gnocchi, and it always sat in my gut like a ton of fucking bricks.

"We're doing good, Pop. We're turning a profit and we're constantly booked when I can get everyone to show up for work," Mike said before shoveling in a heaping forkful of gnocchi.

"Mike, you aren't always there either, so don't be a martyr and skip the bullshit." Anthony pointed his fork at Mikey before stabbing the gnocchi on his plate.

"We all have other shit to do. The shop is for fun and to have something of our own, so get off our damn backs, Mike. You aren't the *boss*,'" Izzy said emphasizing the word to sound like a great big "fuck you." "You just aren't an artist like the rest of us." She picked up the wine glass and brought it to her lips to hide her smile. Izzy always had been a spitfire.

My mother and father sat at the opposite ends of the table and exchanged looks as my siblings had a war of words. As children, we battled with our fists and usually one of us ended up bloodied, but now we used our mouths. Sometimes words leave a greater mark than any punch ever could.

"I'm every bit an artist as you are, baby sister. I just prefer to use my hands for other things. I may not draw pretty pictures, but I can pierce anything and knock a bastard on their ass in a single punch."

My father cleared his throat. "Is the shop too much?" he asked.

I needed to speak up. The shop was doing great and we all got along. Sundays often made us crabby because we wanted to do anything but be trapped in this house. A one-weekend reprieve would be fucking mind-blowing—and a totally bullshit improbability. "Pop, the shop's great. We're packed. Everyone shows up on the days they have appointments. I'm there more than anyone and I know the business the best. Mike may organize shit, but I know what happens inside the walls of Inked." I soaked my garlic bread in my mother's homemade sauce, which had spread out around my plate. "We need to keep ourselves busy during the day, and the shop has more than done that."

"Good, son. I'm proud of all of you. You could be sitting on your asses at home, but you're business owners and successful—not to mention your other hobbies." *Oh fuck.* Everyone hated to have their true passions and dream careers referred to as a "hobby."

I heard forks drop to the table and clatter off the dishes. Such drama queens in this goddamn room.

"Sorry about that. It's not what I meant." My father looked down at his plate, concentrating on his food, but I could see the smile on his face. He loved a good punch to the gut and ego whenever possible.

"I have a big fight coming up after the first of the year," Mikey piped in, to show my dad how far he'd risen.

"Around here?"

147

"New York. I got the call yesterday. I've been training for months for this opportunity."

"That's fantastic, son. Wish your mother and I could see it."

My mother looked green at the thought of her son being in a closed ring beating the piss out of someone—or getting the shit beat out of him. I'd put my money on Mikey in any fight, but I know my mother still thought of him as her baby. Fuck, we were all her babies.

"Michael, why can't you be like your brother? Go into music or something without violence and bloodshed?" She dabbed her lips with her napkin and then placed it on the table.

"Ma, I'm great at it and I love it. It's my dream to be a well-known ass kicker."

Pop reached over and slapped him on the back. I was surprised he didn't start beating on his chest at how proud he was of his ass-kicking son.

"I just don't like the whole idea. Become a musician or something else."

"Tone deaf," Mikey mumbled as he placed more food in his mouth.

My mother sighed and fidgeted with her fork on the table. "I was fine with it when I thought it was just a hobby or a passing phase, but now, I'm scared for you, Michael."

"No worries, Ma. I got this shit. You'll see." He grinned at her and flexed his muscles. "It's going to be on pay-per-view, so you'll be able to watch, Pop. I'm not the headliner, but they show all the opening fights before the main event."

"I'll have to have the guys over to watch my son kick some ass."

I rolled my eyes and hoped someone would change the conversation.

"Anyone talk to Thomas this week?" Mom asked.

Not the topic I would've liked, but anything to not hear about Mr. Badass and his upcoming match.

"I did, Ma, he texted me. It's hard for him to call with work," Anthony said.

She sighed and closed her eyes, pinching the bridge of her nose. "I worry most about him. He's in such danger every day, and I don't like him being so far away. I need all my children around this table every week."

I could see the pain on her face. She worried about my brother. He'd been an undercover cop for the last year. He was trying to infiltrate a motorcycle group notorious in Florida for drug trafficking and gun smuggling. He rarely called or texted in order to keep his cover, otherwise his life would end.

Why the fuck my brother risked his life was beyond me. It's one thing to work the streets every day walking a beat, but to go undercover and be discovered was something cops rarely fucking came back from. If something happened to him, my mother would never recover. Tommy had always been an adrenaline junkie, but this was extreme. Jump off a fucking bridge or skydive like normal people; don't risk being shot in the fucking head when they realize you're there to help bring them down.

"He said he's fine, Ma. He said not to worry and he's well and living the life. You know, Tommy would have made a great actor. He can bullshit the best of them." Izzy always tried to console my mother about Tommy's work, but it was always there—the worry. We all felt it like a ton of bricks, waiting for the phone call that he was missing, but thankfully it hadn't happened.

"I know, baby girl." My mom smiled at Izzy. "He could always charm the ladies."

"Speaking of charmer, Ma, Joey's girl was at the shop yesterday and I missed it." Izzy pouted and winked at me. She knew she'd just thrown me under the goddamn bus, and my mom would have a shitload of questions...again.

"Still seeing her, Joseph?" Her face lit up. I knew she was already picking out the baby names, but fucking hell, I wasn't ready for that shit.

"Yes, Ma." I hated talking about this shit with anyone, especially my mother.

"Is she your girlfriend?"

I sighed, wanting to reach over and choke that shit-eatin' grin off Izzy's face. "Yes."

"Don't chase her away because she isn't Joni. You hear me?"

"Yes, Ma."

"I met her, Ma." *Fucking Mikey.*

"What's she like, Michael?" My mom knew she wasn't going to get much more out of me than she had last week in the kitchen. She knew to ask the blabbermouth of the group.

"She's beautiful and deserves so much better than that punk." His head moved in my direction, and I wanted to bitch-slap him.

"Better as in you, Mikey?" I eyed him.

"Calm down, bro. She's a nice girl, Ma. Reminds me a bit of Joni. Innocent, and her laughter is infectious. You'll like her." He grinned at me.

What a fucking asshole.

"You'll have to bring her for Sunday dinner soon, Joseph." Exactly what I didn't want to do. I didn't want her to be around my crazy-ass siblings, especially Izzy. Iz was dying for another girl, since the testosterone to estrogen level was off balance.

"Maybe soon. I don't want to get ahead of myself."

"The holidays are coming up. Christmas, maybe. Is she a Catholic girl?"

Already planning the wedding ceremony. Religion weighed heavily in an Italian family—christenings, baptisms, weddings…everything seemed to revolve around the church.

"Ma, you haven't been to church in years," I said flatly.

"I know, but it's still important. It makes life easier. Is she Italian?"

"I never asked." I grabbed my plate and headed for the kitchen. I could hear the giggles from the table as my mother and sister always liked to rag on me most of all. No one was in a relationship in the group, but for some reason I was always the target.

I didn't know where Suzy and I stood and what the future held for us. She was always so wrapped up in her fucking thoughts and second-guessing our relationship. She couldn't get beyond the tattooed façade and the beat-up shack I called home. I needed to know that I was enough for her. I wanted to be liked for me—the good, bad, and the ugly.

19

FRIDAY COUNTDOWN

SUZY

I COULD HARDLY CONTAIN MY EXCITEMENT ALL WEEK. CITY AND I talked every night on the phone and texted during the day. I couldn't stay away from him and couldn't get him out of my mind. I tried to keep myself busy and find reasons not to be with him, but it didn't work. I was falling for the man, and falling hard.

Growing up, my mother had drilled in my head that I needed to find a man with a stable job. I needed to settle down, have a family, and live the American dream. I tried for years to find that man, the perfect mold, but all of them were just...boring as hell.

I'd never been willing to settle for anything less than perfect. A picket fence and a beautiful home are worthless if you dread going home to the one you're supposed to spend your life with. I prefer being single to the doldrums in which some of my friends currently dwelled. Sophia and Kayden were the happiest couple I knew, and they were complete opposites—they were the yin to the other's yang.

The students cleared the building as soon as the last bell blared at two in the afternoon on Friday. I had another thirty minutes left and couldn't seem to function. All I could think of was tonight and what could be— what would be. I couldn't stare at the clock and watch another minute tick away. I knew Sophia would be tidying up the library, and I needed to talk to her. She'd questioned me all week about City and when I'd see him again, but I hadn't told her the plan we had. I needed her opinion.

The lights in the library were dimmed, but I could see her wandering around, returning books to their rightful spots. I took a deep breath and walked through the door to the torrent of questions I knew I'd face.

"Sophia," I called out. I didn't want to scare the hell out of her. I knew most of the staff had snuck out early, but the two of us never took the chance at losing our jobs for a few minutes of our time.

She turned the corner with a stack of books in her hand and a smile on her face. "Hey, Suzy Q, what are you doing up here? Don't you have any big plans for tonight?" She winked at me. I couldn't hide the smile on my face. I felt like the electricity and joy radiated off my body. "How many hours until you see him?"

"Maybe I'm not going to see him tonight." I was so full of shit, and I knew I couldn't fool Sophia, but sometimes I hated that she could read me like an open book.

"Whatever, whore. It's written all over your face. You're going to get some cock tonight, and by the red creeping across your cheeks, I'd say it's fucking amazing."

"Do you hear how you talk in a school?"

"Prude ass. Every child has run away from this place screaming at two. There isn't a soul within earshot except for us. What time are you meeting him tonight?"

"We're meeting at seven." I plopped down on one of the comfy couches as Sophia placed the books on the table and sat down next to me.

"My feet are freaking killing me in these damn heels." She kicked off her shoes and rubbed her feet. "What's the plan tonight?"

"I don't even know if I can repeat it." I shrugged. My stomach was a jumbled mess from just thinking about the possibilities.

"You can and you will. This is me, girl. I know all your darkest secrets. Shit, you used to lie in bed with Kayden and me and grill us on our sex life. We have no secrets. I know you're a kinky bitch underneath that polished veneer."

"It's your fault. I was happy with my bland sex life and you had to go and ruin me with all those trashy novels."

"Stop changing the subject. What's the plan with the sexy-as-sin City?" She grinned and waggled her eyebrows up and down.

I'd always wanted sex that was worthy of girl talk, and for years, I'd lived off the stories that Sophia and my other friends had shared with me. City had made sex worth talking about; I'd finally have some wild stories to share.

"I kind of shared one of my fantasies with him and he's going to make it happen tonight." I covered my eyes with my hand, avoiding her stare. I was scared to tell her any more, but she knew every fantasy I had and always reassured me that I was normal, that my sanity hadn't been replaced by impure thoughts.

"Oh my God. Tell me, tell me." She practically bounced on the couch cushion. "Don't hold back now, bitch." She slapped my arm.

"I told him the darkest one."

"You didn't?"

I grinned, and my cheeks almost hurt from the smile that had been plastered on my face all day. "I did, and he said I'd have it."

"Kidnapping?" She looked shocked, but I saw the twinkle in her eye.

"I can't believe I told him, but yes. Oh my God, it's happening tonight, Sophia."

"I'm so proud of you." She wrapped her arms around me. "My baby's all grown up." She squeezed me and ran her palm down the back of my head. "Tell me more. I want to hear about him. Now."

"We're going to meet at the Neon Cowboy, that biker bar out in the country. We're going to have some dinner and drinks before I leave alone and he makes it become a reality."

"You're going to chicken out. Oh God, he's giving you time to change your mind." She stood up and started pacing the room.

"Calm down, Sophia. I'm not going to chicken out. I've wanted someone like him, and tonight I'm getting more than I could ever dream of—my fantasy becoming a reality."

"You've never done this shit. You're like I used to be—Ms. Missionary Style. I expect details tomorrow, and I mean a full report."

"Yes, ma'am. I'll give you a full briefing."

"I want every last fucking detail too, got me?"

"I got ya, Sophia. I better go get my stuff and head home. I want to rest a bit before I see him."

"Good luck with resting." She snickered.

"I know. I could barely sleep last night." I sighed.

"I used to get that way when I would see Kayden after time apart. There's no feeling like it." She smiled and hugged me. "Now go. I have to finish up and get home to my fantasy man."

"You still feel that way about Kayden after all this time?"

"I still get butterflies when I see him, Suzy. That's the difference, you know—that feeling has never gone away. I'm still get excited like the first time we met."

"I envy you, Sophia."

"You'll find your Kayden, babe. I think you may already have, if you don't let your stupid OCD checklist get in the way." She tapped me on the forehead.

"I got to go. We'll debate my sanity and compulsions another day." I waved to her as I walked out the door. "Later, Soph."

"Don't forget to call me, Suzy, or I'll hunt your ass down," she yelled to me as the door closed behind me.

***

"Hey, sugar." His voice filled my car via speakerphone, but he didn't sound as excited as I felt.

"Hey, City. I'm almost to the bar."

"I'm going to be fifteen minutes late. Fuck, I'm sorry. The tattoo I was working on took longer than I thought. Can you wait for me in the parking lot?"

Damn. That bar gave me the heebie-jeebies, and I didn't fit in, not even in the parking lot. "Yeah, City. I wouldn't dream of walking in there alone." I felt sick. "This isn't part of your plan, is it?"

"Hell no! We're still having some drinks first. I need you to not over-think everything tonight. I want you a little tipsy for what I have planned." He laughed.

The excitement took over, and all second thoughts vanished. "Okay, City. I'll be waiting for you."

"Do not go inside alone. Understand me?"

"I won't. I promise."

"See you soon, sugar."

After tossing my phone on the passenger seat, I rolled down the window, welcoming the cool air against my clammy skin. The events of the night played through my mind. City would be my kidnapper. My lungs burned as I screamed along with the song on the radio, "Dark Horse" by Katy Perry, the bass causing my windows to rattle with each beat.

Pulling into a spot hidden in the shadows, I turned off the lights and waited for City to arrive. In the rearview mirror I saw my face glistening from the humidity in the air, and I wanted to look flawless. City had seen me at my worst, but I wanted to look beautiful for him in front of his friends.

The lighted mirror behind my visor was more forgiving as I blotted my face with an old napkin I found in the glove box. My lips lacked color as I smacked them together, making kissy lips. After slathering on some Buxom lip gloss from my purse, I rubbed my lips together with a pop. They tingled as the peppermint oil started to plump my lips, soaking into my skin.

A loud knock on the window made me jump, and I hit my head on the visor. "Shit," I said. I turned to get a glimpse at my knight in shining armor, but it wasn't City outside my car. It was a guy that looked vaguely familiar. He stood there staring at me, and alarm bells went off in my head.

I cracked my window an inch, thankful I had rolled them up when I arrived. "Can I help you?"

"Why's such a pretty lady sitting out here alone? Come inside, beautiful."

Hell, he creeped me out. "I'm waiting for someone." I didn't want to hold a conversation with him. His hair was a mess, gray hair lined his face, and dirt was smeared across his tattered t-shirt. A sour smell caused me to wrinkle my nose—he was the asshole that wouldn't leave me alone the first time I came here, until City and Bear stepped in. Shit, where was City?

"You can wait inside, let me buy you a drink." His face came closer to

155

the window, and I could smell the alcohol on his breath, mixing with the body odor that I couldn't escape. My heart raced and my palms started to sweat. *Just stay in the car.*

"Thanks, but I'm going to wait here." I couldn't stand looking at him anymore. Why won't he just go away? I heard a motorcycle pull in the parking lot and come to a screeching halt next to my car. Peering through the passenger window, I saw City climbing off his bike quickly and coming at the scumbag outside my window.

"Get the fuck away from her," City roared as he stood toe to toe with the asshole.

"I just asked her to come inside for a drink." He looked City in the eye and didn't move. He must have had a death wish.

"She doesn't want to be bothered. Go the fuck home, you drunk bastard. Stop bothering all the ladies here, or at least *mine*. Do I need to beat that message in your stupid-ass head?" City grabbed his shirt, crumpling it in his fist.

The man threw his hands up in surrender and tried to back away, but City had a firm grip on his shirt.

"Come on, man. I didn't know she's yours. You need to keep better track of her. Pretty things disappear all the time around here." He grinned, and my skin began to crawl.

"Beat it, jackass. Next time I won't speak. I'll just bash your fucking head in so the only thing you can do with that mouth is drink through a goddamn straw." City released him and shoved him backward. The man stumbled before falling on his ass.

City opened my car door and held out his hand, but I couldn't take my eyes off the guy on the ground. The look he gave me was pure hatred.

"Come on, sugar. I'm here, he won't bother you."

Placing my hand in his, I didn't say a word as I closed my door. I stayed close as we approached the bar. My nerves were shot, and I needed that drink more than ever.

He stopped, grabbing my arm and turning me to face him. "Are you okay, Suzy?"

"Yeah, Joey. He didn't hurt me, but he's creepy as hell."

He wrapped his arms around me, cocooning me. Melting into him, I buried my face in his shirt. Unlike the man from the parking lot, City smelled amazing—the mix of musky cologne with his natural scent. My hand drifted across his chest until I found the piercing I'd become fond of touching.

"Sugar, keep doing that and we won't make it through the first drink before I take you in the bathroom and fuck you raw."

I leaned back with a smirk on my face. "I can't help myself. It's nice to finally touch you after such a long week." I buried my face in his shirt again, not letting go of the little metal object attached to his body.

"I have another piercing that could use some attention," he said through clenched teeth as he ground his cock against me.

"Nah, I'm good. Drink first, then you can do anything you want to me."

Did I just say that? I needed to learn to filter my promises—he was not a bland and boring lover, he liked his sex hard and fast, and he had mentioned my ass. *Don't even think about it.*

"Anything?" he whispered.

"Within reason." I smiled against his chest—thank God my face was hidden.

"That's my girl. Always thinking." He laughed and wrapped me under his arm before walking through the doors of the Neon Cowboy and into the firing squad of males that had egos to protect and manhood to show off. *Lord, help me.*

***

The guys I'd met the first night insisted that we sit with them. I reassured City that it was fine as long as he never left my side. The asshole in the parking lot had already put me on edge, and a tableful of strangers didn't help put my mind at ease.

Bear and Tank talked me into lemon drop shots and beer. I couldn't exactly order my virgin daiquiri sitting at table full of bikers. I tried to fit in, calm my nerves, and get in the right frame of mind for my "kidnapping." I listened to them talk about bikes and tats—a world foreign to me, but still entertaining. They looked scary, but they were good guys that just wanted to hang out, drink beer, and bullshit.

Bear looked just like his nickname—wild, curly, overgrown hair; a

CHELLE BLISS

beard; big and burly. When he stood, I could picture him like a grizzly bear on its hind legs ready to attack. When he spoke about his kids and old lady, he reminded me more of a teddy bear. I quickly learned my first impression of him had been wrong, and I needed to be more open-minded. Wilder shit had happened.

"What are you two kids doing tonight?" Bear asked as he washed down the last sip of beer.

I felt the heat crawling up my face, and I couldn't answer his question. I sat there and stared at City. I'd let him field that question.

"Nothing much, Bear. Just going to kidnap this beautiful creature and use her how I see fit." He winked at me and looked at Bear with a cocky smile.

I glanced around the table, and everyone was staring at me. I was sure the picture in their mind was accurate, minus the actual kidnapping part.

Bear slapped City on the back. "That's my boy," he said with a laugh.

City leaned over and nuzzled his face in my hair. "Why don't you head out and I'll find you, sugar," he whispered in my ear. I shivered at his words. I wanted him to play this game.

I turned my face and kissed him on the lips. "Yes, sir. Catch me if you can." The guys at the table started to hoot and holler as I stood from the table, almost knocking over my chair as City caught it. "Sorry about that," I said as I stood on shaky legs.

"Get going, sugar." City swatted me on the ass, and I yelped. I shouldn't have done that last shot.

I kept my eyes on the floor, making sure not to trip on my way out the door. My eyesight felt fuzzy, and my head was cloudy from the vodka. I turned to look back at City before walking out the door. Every man at that table stared at me. City looked excited as he winked at me with a tilted grin that made my panties wet, but the rest of them looked in shock. Maybe City had clued them in on our little role-playing adventure that lay ahead.

I smiled and waved; the cool air touched my skin as I walked outside to wait for my captor to find me. My heart thundered and my stomach gurgled as I made my way toward my car. I was ready for him.

158

20

WHAT DREAMS ARE MADE OF...

CITY

"Were you being fucking serious?" Tank leaned forward.

"About what? Using her?"

"Fuck, all of it," he said with an eyebrow raised and one side of his mouth curved in a smile.

"All of it. I got to go, boys. Time to go find my victim for the night." I stood from the table and threw a fifty down. "You gentleman have a good night with that image rolling around in your head right now."

They couldn't even begin to process what we were really going to do. They thought "kidnap" was just a nice way of saying I was going to take her away from the bar and have sex with her, but I was going to literally kidnap her.

"Can one of you take my bike home tonight and I'll grab it in the morning?" I asked before walking away.

"I'll take it," Bear said. "I'll tow it to Tank's shop."

"Thanks, man—my dick thanks you too." I laughed as I tossed him the keys.

"At least someone's prick will be happy tonight," Bear mumbled as he placed the keys in his jacket pocket.

I didn't say anything, but couldn't stop laughing. Poor bastards.

CHELLE BLISS

I rolled my neck as I headed for the door, cracking it almost like I was prepping for a game. I'd give Suzy everything she wanted and more.

"City!" a voice rang through the crowd. *Fuck.* "City!" A hand waved above the crowd, and I knew the voice but pretended not to hear her.

I didn't turn around, but walked faster until a hand wrapped around my arm.

"Oh, Kaylee, I didn't see you."

"I was screaming your name," she huffed, trying to catch her breath.

"Didn't hear you, either. I'm in a hurry and got to go."

"I've missed you, City." She tried to wrap her arms around me, but I grabbed them and forced them away.

"Stop, Kaylee. I really don't have time for this shit."

"You've always had time for me before." She pouted and tried to play the guilt card.

"I don't now. I have to go meet my girlfriend," I said, hoping she'd get the fucking hint.

"Girlfriend? Since when?" She looked in shock as she held my arm, digging her nails into my flesh.

"Bye, Kaylee. I don't have time for a goddamn chitchat. My girl's waiting for me, and I don't mean you."

I left her there with her mouth open and gulping for air like a fish. I needed to get to Suzy. I'd already left her entirely too long outside by herself. Damn it. She had to be in knots by now, but then again, it probably helped build her excitement.

Rubbing my face as I walked outside, I couldn't believe fucking Kaylee. I was supposed to be only moments behind Suzy; she'd fumbled with her keys trying to unlock her car when I grabbed her from behind. She could've changed her mind and gone home with the amount of time that had elapsed.

Her car was parked in the same spot, but her door was open and she wasn't inside. I looked around—where the fuck was she? I studied every inch of the parking lot, but couldn't see her. My heart thundered in my chest. I felt sick. I heard a muffled cry, but couldn't tell where it came from over the street noise. "Suzy," I screamed, panic taking hold.

Her purse lay on the ground near her car; I just had to find her. I couldn't stand there and wait any longer. I had to move. I ran into the

160

woods behind her car and surveyed the area. I listened for any sound; a man's voice caught my attention—faint but enough to pull my gaze to behind the bar.

I ran in the direction of the noise and saw a man on top of a woman, Suzy, raising his fist before striking her. "You bitch," he seethed. It was the motherfucker that had bothered her earlier when I arrived.

I grabbed him by the throat before he could land another blow and slammed his body to the ground. The force of his head connecting with the concrete made a horrific sound from his skull cracking. Straddling him, I pummeled him with my fists, feeding off the sound of his jawbone crunching underneath my knuckles. He moaned, but I didn't give a fuck. He hit a woman, *my* woman. I punched him again then grabbed his head, and I wanted to bash it into the cement to watch all of his blood ooze out, but a pair of hands began to pull me off him, stopping me.

"City, you're going to fuckin' kill him," Bear said as he tried to pull me back.

"Fuckin' bastard deserves to die." I moved my hand to punch him again, but Bear grabbed my wrist.

"Goddamn, man. He's out cold. Get the fuck away from him and take care of your girl."

Suzy. I had been so busy beating the fuck out of him, lost in my anger, I forgot to check on her. She lay on the cement with her eyes closed, not moving. She was limp in my arms as I cradled her against my chest. Blood dripped from her lip and nose, and I brushed the hair from her eyes to look for more damage. She had a red mark that would turn into a bruise near her temple.

"Suzy," I whispered, brushing my fingers across her face. "Suzy, wake up, sugar." I gathered her legs off the cold ground and placed her in my lap.

I looked at Bear as he stood over me with wide eyes. "Call an ambulance, Bear."

"On it, buddy." He stood over the asshole lying on the ground unconscious, and I saw Bear kick him. "The attacker is knocked out on the ground. I'll keep him restrained," Bear said to the person on the phone.

"Suzy, come on, sweetie. Wake up, beautiful." I kissed her warm lips. This was my fucking fault. "I'm so sorry, Suzy." *Fuck.* Her clothes were in place, nothing was torn, but they had dirt on them from being on the ground.

Her eyes started to open, and I felt like I could breathe again. I smiled at her, touching her cheek. "City," she said with a shaky voice. Her arms started to move, reaching for me.

"Don't move, sugar. Wait for the ambulance." I didn't want her to injure herself worse than that fucker may have already done.

"What happened?" She stared at me with her big, beautiful blue eyes. I could see the confusion and hurt in them.

"I'm sorry, Suzy. I got held up inside and I showed up too late. This wouldn't have happened if I didn't force you to live out one of your fantasies."

She smiled sweetly at me. "Ouch." Her tongue slid across her lip and stopped on the blood.

"You're bleeding, sugar. Just lie still until the paramedics can check you out."

"What about?" She didn't have to finish the sentence—I knew what she wanted to know.

"He won't hurt you anymore."

She closed her eyes and a tear slid down her cheek. "What did you do, City?"

"I gave the fucker a taste of his own medicine. He's out cold." I wiped the tear away from her cheek with my thumb.

"Is he"—her lip began to tremble—"dead?"

"He's alive. I wanted to kill the prick, but Bear pulled me off him." Sobs tore through her as her body began to shake. "Shh, I got you. No one's going to hurt you ever again, Suzy."

I held her until the paramedics arrived, and a second ambulance pulled in a moment later. Two men pulled her from my grasp, assessing her injuries before placing her on a stretcher and completing their evaluation. I watched as they checked the fucker's body on the ground. Fuck him. I hoped the bastard fucking died.

"We need to take her to the hospital. She's sustained some head injuries and we want to make sure it's not serious," the EMT said. "Would you like to meet us there?"

"I'll follow you." I looked over his shoulder and saw them loading Suzy into the ambulance. "Can I speak to her first?"

"Yes, quickly, so we can leave."

I climbed in the ambulance and crouched down next to the stretcher. Her body was strapped in and machines were attached to her arms. Suzy looked worse with the lights shining on her face. "Sugar, you want me to go with you or follow them?"

"Take my car, City. I don't want it here, please."

I leaned over and kissed her. My heart felt like it was going to explode in my chest. "I got it. I'll be right behind you. Don't worry," I said, not wanting to leave her, but wanting to obey her wishes.

She gave me a weak smile before I climbed out and headed for her car, moving as fast I could to be by her side. I had to beg for her forgiveness, and I prayed her injuries weren't serious. I could never live with myself. I found Suzy's phone lying by her purse, and I knew what I had to do. I dialed Kayden and Sophia and knew there would be hell to pay.

21

SOMETIMES SHIT NEEDS TO STAY FICTION

SUZY

Time seemed to pass in slow motion as a flurry of doctors and nurses poked and prodded me. I repeated the story of what happened so many times I could've recited it in my sleep.

"One more time, ma'am. What happened to you tonight?" the doctor asked as he placed a small light in my eyes.

I sighed and wanted to tell him to fuck off as he moved the light back and forth, momentarily blinding me. "Do I have to say it again? I've told you the story already." My patience was wearing thin.

"I need to make sure you have no memory issues from the blow to your head. Last time, I swear."

"You said that last time we did this." I rolled my eyes.

The doctor snickered. "I guess there's no short-term memory problems."

"My boyfriend and I were at a bar tonight, and I walked out before he did. I thought he was right behind me, and when I unlocked my car someone grabbed me from behind. By the time I realized what was happening, I was already on the ground and tried to fight back, but it was no use. I don't remember much else."

A police officer stood in the corner and scribbled on a little notepad as I spoke.

"I remember waking up in Joey's arms and then the ambulance arriving."

I couldn't give the truth. My boyfriend was supposed to kidnap me as we played out my fantasy for him to abduct me and make me his sex slave. Who did shit like that?

"We're just going to keep you here overnight for observation. You have a couple of bruised ribs, the laceration on your lip, and a concussion, but nothing that will cause long-term damage," the doctor said, staring at his clipboard. "We'll get you into a regular room as soon as possible so you can rest. We will release you in the morning."

"Is anyone here to see me?" I couldn't believe that City hadn't shown up, or anyone for that matter.

"Yes, but he's been instructed to wait outside until we complete your assessment."

"Can he come in now, please?"

My body ached, my face throbbed, and my head pounded from the aftereffects of the attack. I wanted to rest my eyes and turn off the light, but I needed to talk to City. I had to find out what happened, and why he wasn't the one to find me alone in the parking lot.

"Yes, I'll have the nurses talk with him and send him in. I'll see you tomorrow, Ms. McCarthy."

"Thanks," I said with a fake smile. I had nothing to be thankful for. All I wanted to do was crawl in my own bed and sleep against City's body. Crunchy hospital sheets, plastic mattresses, and thin blankets were not my idea of comfortable.

I threw my head back onto the thin pillow, squeezing my eyes shut. I wanted to cry, but I didn't have any tears left.

"Ma'am," the officer said, and cleared his throat. "I've taken down your statement, but I may need more details. We have your attacker in custody and the statement of Joseph Gallo and another gentleman, but we may still need your side to fill in the gaps. Here's my card. Call me when you can talk. It can wait until you're home and more comfortable." He smiled at me, and I could see he was genuine.

"I'll call you, sir. I just don't feel like talking about it anymore tonight." I rubbed my eyes. The lights were making my headache worse, and I wanted to sleep.

"No problem, ma'am."

Drawing back the curtain to leave, I caught a glimpse of City. A frown was visible as he looked at me. I could see the pain on his face. His hands appeared swollen, and red dotted his knuckles—blood from the pounding he must have given to the asshole.

"Hey," he said as he approached my bed.

"Hey yourself."

"Are you okay, sugar?" He sat down on the bed and held my hand.

"I'm okay, City. They're just keeping me for observation." I shrugged.

Touching my cheek with the rough pads of his fingers, he studied my face. His eyes roamed over every inch, stopping on my lips and cheekbone. "God, I'm so sorry, Suzy. It's all my fault." Deep lines appeared on his forehead.

"It wasn't your fault. You meant well. I give you an A for effort, but a D in completion, big boy." I smirked. I couldn't really be mad at him.

"Don't make jokes, sugar." He tried to keep a straight face, but I saw a small smile tug at the corner of his lips. "I could've lost you tonight." He squeezed my hand.

"What happened to you? You were supposed to be only a minute behind me, Joey." Closing my eyes, I remembered the fear I felt when I realized it wasn't City grabbing me from behind.

"I was on my way out of the bar after joking with the guys, but I got held up. I tried to get away as quickly as possible. I didn't want you to be outside alone. I should've never taken you to that bar. Fuck." He rubbed his face, "What happened before I got there, sugar?"

Tears began to fill my eyes as I spoke. I couldn't hold them back. "I pretended to drop my keys when I heard someone behind me. I thought it was you. As I bent down to pick them up, he grabbed me by the hair and knocked me off balance." I paused, trying to steady my voice. "He pulled me by my hair behind the building, and I tried to get free of him. I kicked and screamed, but no one heard me. He hit me in the face and called me names. I could taste the blood in my mouth. I don't remember anything else until I woke up in your arms." I cuddled into City, needing the feeling of safety.

"Shh, sugar. I'll never let anything bad happen to you again." He crawled in the bed and wrapped his arms around me. I cried in his chest until there were no more tears left. He stroked my hair, kissing my head, rocking me until I calmed.

"Where is she?" Sophia's voice woke me from my peaceful slumber. "I don't give a shit, I want to see her now."

Jesus.

"Ma'am, you can't go in there."

The curtain opened in one quick motion, and a scared Sophia appeared. "Oh my God, Suzy. I've been worried sick about you." She rushed to my bedside.

I saw movement out of the corner of my eye—Kayden. He looked pissed. More pissed than I'd ever seen him, and I'd seen him pretty crazy at times over the years.

"I'm okay, Sophia. Just some scrapes and bruises. I'll heal."

"You could've been killed, for shit's sake. And you." She glared at City, pointing at him. "You were supposed to protect her from shit like this. How could you let her go outside alone?"

"It's not his fault," I said, but she held up her hand.

"Well?" she asked.

"City, may I speak to you for a moment?" Kayden asked in a calm voice.

I didn't like pissed-off-looking and calm-sounding Kayden. "You both need to back off," I said.

"Suzy, this is between City and me. I won't keep him long," Kayden said.

I looked at City, silently pleading with him not to go. He squeezed my hand as he slid off the bed. "I'll be right back, don't worry." He gave me a wink and a smile before leaving with Kayden.

"Let the boys talk. What the fuck happened, Suzy?" Sophia sat down next to me, tilting her head before she grabbed my hand. "God, I was out of my mind when City called. This is all my fault."

"It's no one's fault, Sophia. I walked out and everything was going perfectly. I guess City got held up for a second, and that's all it took." I wiped the remaining tears off my cheek. "The same creep had bothered

167

me before and must've been waiting for me. It was stupid to think we could live out that fantasy. It's not as sexy as it sounds anymore."

"Fuck, it's my fault." She hung her head.

"Sophia, why would it be your fault?"

"I kinda told him about your fantasy." She didn't look me in the eyes.

"You did what?"

She stood up and moved out of reach. "When he was doing my tattoo, I told him that you don't like to share your fantasies, and told him about your kidnapping thing you've been dying to live out."

Jesus Christ. "Sophia, I know we're best friends and all, but that was between you, me, and Kayden." I took a deep breath and tried not to be angry. Sophia loved me, and so did Kayden. We always talked about sex, and they were the two people in the world that never judged me. Kayden was the only male that let me pick his brain on the subject, and he answered honestly without making me feel like an idiot. "I'm a little embarrassed here. I thank you for trying to give me what I want, but that was my secret to tell."

"If it would've worked out, he would've knocked your socks off, babe. City is exactly the type of guy you need to be with. Don't let this experience put doubt in that pretty little head of yours. He was a wreck, Suzy. I feel a little shitty now that I got bitchy with him. He really cares for you, my little OCD friend."

I laughed. I always made Sophia insane with all my little quirks and lists. The woman lived life by the seat of her pants, and I wanted everything planned. I had lists for my lists, and I would even include her on my lists when we lived together. "I know he cares, Sophia. I saw the pain in his eyes tonight. I don't think I've ever seen anyone so afraid for me before."

I could hear the murmured voices of Kayden and City but couldn't make out the words. "What is he saying to City?"

"You know Kayden is very protective of you. He's just having a man-to-man."

"I'm not a child, Sophia. Kayden better be nice." I crossed my arms over my chest.

"Kayden's always nice. They're just chatting." She smiled, but I could see the worry on her face.

Life had become so complicated, and my plans seemed to unravel before my eyes. I felt like Sophia on the rollercoaster she experienced when falling in love with Kayden. She put her hands up and screamed through the ride, while I wanted to jump off and keep my feet on the ground.

22

WHO'S THE BOSS?

CITY

"HOW IN THE FUCK COULD YOU LET HER WALK OUTSIDE ALONE?" KAYDEN stood toe to toe with me. I didn't blame him—he cared for Suzy.

"Kayden, I know, man. I was supposed to be right behind her. Everything got fucked up." I kept eye contact with him. I wouldn't show weakness, even though I knew the entire thing happened because of Kaylee and my past. My fucking cock always caused trouble.

"Yeah, I'd say. If anything happens to her, City, I'll kick your ass. I may look small compared to you, but I'll crush you. Hear that shit."

I clenched my hands, stopping myself from beating his ass right here in the hospital. I knew he wouldn't hit me. Throwing down with Kayden would only drive a wedge between Suzy and me. I'd let him say his piece. "Got it loud and clear, Kayden. I'll protect her with my life."

"I know you didn't mean for any of it to happen, City, but I expect more." He stepped back. "She's like a sister to me. Just protect her and we won't have an issue. I don't want to be a dick, but I had to tell you that you fucked up."

"I know, and I will, Kayden. I'm happy that you love her and you'll look out for her if I'm not around. I know I fucked up and I'll do everything in my power to make it up to her."

"Are you planning on breaking her heart, man?" He crossed his arms over his chest and stared. "If this shit is just a game to you, then you need to end it now."

"Fuck no, but I don't know where her head is right now." I rubbed my eyes, exhausted from the events of tonight.

"Don't give her a choice, City. She's quick to overthink everything. She needs a little push sometimes."

"I'm happy to show her the way. Are we good, man?" I asked. "I need to get back to her."

"Yeah, we're good." He held out his hand to me.

"Thanks, man." I shook his hand.

I walked through the curtain to the girls whispering on the bed. "Hey, ladies," Kayden said behind me. "Suzy, how are you, love?" He walked in front of me and stood next to her bed.

I stood at the foot of the bed and watched them as they interacted. They were a family, anyone could see that. There was a love and a shared past that brought them together. They chatted as I stood there, transfixed. Suzy looked battered, with bruises and a split lip. It would take forever for the effects to fade from her beautiful face.

"We have a room ready for you," a nurse said as she entered the small space.

"Oh, great," Sophia said. "We better head home, Suzy. Sleep well, and we'll stop by tomorrow to see you." She kissed Suzy on the cheek, and Kayden did the same.

"Night, Suzy." Kayden turned to me. "City, make sure she's okay tonight. Don't leave her alone." He wrapped his arm around Sophia.

"I wouldn't be anywhere else, Kayden."

"I love you guys. City will take good care of me. Go home—Jett will be up soon."

"Bye, love," Sophia said before they walked out.

I sat down next to her as the nurse started to unhook the machines. "Hey, sugar. How are you really feeling?"

"Sore." She winced as she moved her limbs. "Can you find a mirror? I want to see my face."

Oh God. Her face was swollen, with a small amount of dried blood in the corner of her mouth. I didn't want her to see herself all bruised. "I'll find one soon. Wait until you're moved."

"You can follow, sir. We're taking her to the second floor for the night." The nurse removed the brake on the bed as I stood and moved out of the way.

"I'm not leaving her side, ma'am," I said as Suzy laid her head on the pillow and smiled at me. I wouldn't leave her tonight.

The trip to her room was quick, and the nurse left us alone and didn't ask any questions. I sat down in the chair next to her as she yawned. My eyes felt heavy and my mind cloudy.

"Will you sleep up here with me? I mean, there isn't much room, but I want you to hold me tonight. I need you."

How could I say no to anything she asked? I'd stand on my head all night if it made her fucking happy. "Anything you want, sugar." I kicked off my shoes, climbing in the small twin bed before lying on my side, pulling her face to my chest. "Try to sleep. I'm not going anywhere."

The tiny bed was perfect as I cradled her in my arms. She gripped my shirt, resting her face against my shoulder. I enveloped her in my arms, I wanted her to feel safe, and I needed to know that she was okay.

Listening to her breath as she slept, I smelled her hair, but it had the scent of the cigarette smoke from the bar, and dirt. Her body twitched as she whimpered in her sleep. I wanted to crawl inside her dream and rescue her.

I flexed my hands; the stiffness from the bruises and small cuts made me wince. It wasn't anything I hadn't felt before, but I couldn't work for a couple of days until they healed. After pulling my phone from my pocket, I adjusted her body without waking her then sent Anthony a message. My other siblings would be in a panic and the entire crew would be here, but Anthony I could count on to keep the information low key—at least for tonight.

Me: Won't be in tomorrow. Tell Mikey to reschedule my appointments. Thanks, bro.

Anthony had a gig in Clearwater, and he was a sure bet to get the information.

Anthony: I told him, he's with me.

Fuck. Might as well have put it on the evening news or taken out a fucking billboard. Mikey would have a million questions and would want details.

Anthony: What the fuck happened? Not like you to not work.

I didn't want to give them the details, but I had to give enough to get them off my back. I didn't have a fucking choice in the matter. I'd have to cancel dinner with the family. My mother would want to know why—no one got out of dinner without a legitimate excuse. I wanted to stay with Suzy for the weekend and make sure she was okay before I let her be alone.

Me: Situation at the bar tonight. I need to stay with Suzy. Tell Mom I can't make it and clear my schedule for a couple days at least.

Anthony: WTF happened? You okay?

Suzy didn't move as I typed with one hand, trying not to break the embrace.

Me: Beat the shit out of some fucker that attacked her. She's in the hospital for the night and I want to stay with her after she's released. Don't tell anyone. I don't want them to flip out.

Anthony: Gotcha, but Mom is going to want details. Which hospital?

Me: County Hospital, but we're okay. My hands are just swollen. I'll be fine.

Anthony: Gotcha. Mum's the word.

Nothing stayed a secret in my family. It was like the mafia party line. I knew Mikey had probably read over Anthony's shoulder, and soon the entire brigade would be on high alert. I set the phone above my pillow and closed my eyes, wrapping Suzy in my arms.

I tried to think about happy things, Suzy's laugh or how she kissed me, but all I could think of was her limp body and bloodied face in my arms. I kept opening my eyes to remind myself that she was okay. I waited for exhaustion to take me and wipe that vision from my mind.

The sound of plastic squeaking against the tile floor woke me early in the morning. "Sorry, I didn't mean to wake you," a nurse said as she moved to the IV stand.

I grunted and waited for her to leave before closing my eyes again. Hospitals aren't the place for rest. The movement outside the room is constant, alarms and announcements echo through the halls, and people talk loud enough to wake the dead. I felt like a Mack truck had hit me.

My back was stiff, my eyes burned, and my hands throbbed. I wanted to get the fuck out of here and crawl in a real bed with her.

A quiet knock caused Suzy to stir, and my mother stood in the doorway. Fucking brothers—always mama's boys.

"Hey," she said, smiling.

I held put my finger to my lips, hoping not to wake Suzy as my ma entered the room. "It's early, Ma. What are you doing here?" I whispered.

"Your brother told me something happened and that you were here with Suzy. You know I can't sleep good when I worry about my children." She stood next to the bed, looking at Suzy's face against my chest.

"I'm fine, Ma. I couldn't leave her and I want to stay with her when she gets out for a couple days. I didn't think Mikey would put out an all-points bulletin."

"Always so quick to blame Michael, aren't you, Joseph? It was Anthony that texted me. I just wanted to stop and see if you two were okay." She shook her head at me.

When did my mother learn how to text?

"We will be as soon as we get out of this shithole."

"What happened, son?" My mom pulled up a chair and waited for my answer.

"Someone assaulted her. When I found her, I kicked his ass." I didn't want to meet my mother's eyes. She was the only person in the world I never wanted to disappoint. I wasn't a mama's boy, but in an Italian family a mother is the queen bee, top dog, and wore the pants. Even my father bowed down to her and cherished the ground she walked on. He wasn't a pussy, and could kick ass in his youth, but Mrs. Gallo wasn't a person any of us wanted to piss off. "Trust me, Ma, he looks worse than me."

She wrinkled her nose; she never liked to think of any of her children fighting, even Mikey. "Where were you?"

"Neon Cowboy, and we were on our way out after having a couple drinks." I definitely didn't want to share that I'd planned to kidnap my girlfriend. Sex wasn't something I talked to my mother about, and usually not even my father.

"I told you I hate that damn bar. There's nothing but trouble in *those* types of places. Haven't you learned anything from Thomas?" She wasn't mad, but I could see the fear in her eyes.

"Yes, Ma. I have friends there, clients even, and I like it there. I'm not going to stop hanging out there because of the what-ifs."

"Is she okay, son?" She peeked over my shoulder, her eyes growing wide as she took in the sight of Suzy's face.

"Yeah, she'll heal. Just waiting for the doctor to come and release her. I won't be there Sunday, but I promise to be there next week."

"Sure, baby. Can I drop off food, at least? That way you can spend time taking care of her without having to cook."

How could I say no to my mother? When she offered food it was the highest honor. She lived to cook and take care of her family. If I said no, it would be an enormous insult and there would be hell to pay.

"Sure, Ma. I'd love if you'd stop by with some food." I didn't entirely mean that statement, but I knew it would make her happy.

"I'm going to go and let you two rest. I don't want to wake her. I'll call you later, Joseph." She stood up and kissed my forehead. She was the only person in the world that I'd let treat me like a child. No matter how many times I told her I wasn't, she just made it all the more unbearable, smothering me with her love.

"Okay, Ma. Thanks."

"I love you, Joseph. Take care of that one."

"Love you too, Ma."

She walked out of the room and I ran my fingers over the bruises on Suzy's face. They were brighter in color and more visible than they had been the night before. She began to stir at my touch, and her eyes opened. The side crinkled from the smile on her face.

"You stayed?"

"Where else would I go, sugar?"

She closed her eyes and made a sound like "I don't know" as she smashed her face in my chest and inhaled. "Can we get out of here?"

"I'll go see if I can get the doctor to discharge you. Let me get up."

She winced as I helped her move out of my arms and climbed off the bed. "You're going to spend all day in bed when I get you out of here."

"Oooh, that sounds so sexy." She laughed and held her side.

"Bad girl, you're injured—rest only." I was happy to see that her spirit hadn't vanished with the attack. "Be right back or I'll break you out of this joint."

I found a nurse sitting at a desk and pleaded with her to process the paperwork quicker than normal. "You can help her get dressed to speed up the process if you'd like, sir," the nurse said as she typed.

"Sure, we'll be waiting, ma'am." I returned to the room to find Suzy trying to climb out of bed. "What the hell are you doing?" I said, rushing to her side.

"I needed to pee." She looked up at me with a shy, embarrassed smile.

"I'll help you, sugar. Then we got to get you dressed."

"Fine. I hate having to need help to walk, City. This is a little ridiculous."

"It's what I'm here for. You're *mine* and I'm going to take care of you this weekend. No arguments. Got it?" I waited for her reply before taking her hand.

"Yes, sir. I'm yours for the weekend. I thought it would be a bit different, but…" She shrugged.

"Makes two of us. Come on, sweetheart." I helped her to the bathroom and then grabbed her clothes. I hit them a couple times to get the dirt off before she dressed.

"I need a shower," she said as she hobbled out of the bathroom.

"I'll help you as soon as we get you home."

"You're the boss."

I liked the sound of those words coming out of her mouth. I wouldn't take any lip from her this weekend. She was *mine*.

23

MOUTH-WATERING GOODNESS

SUZY

I SETTLED IN MY BED, THANKFUL TO BE HOME, AND WATCHED CITY AS HE undressed. I'd never been with a man that I couldn't stop staring at. I wanted the image etched in my brain. His muscular build flexed as he took off his pants. The tattoos on his torso and arms moved, and I was mesmerized as if watching a movie. I ached to tug on the bar that hung from his nipple, salivated to taste his flesh, and shivered at the thought of him inside me.

He kicked his pants in the air and caught them. "Don't look at me like that, sugar." His shaft bobbed, catching my attention; my mouth suddenly felt dry.

I blinked and looked at his face. "Like what? I was just thinking about how skilled you are at catching your pants." I giggled.

"You just looked at my dick in a way that makes me want to jam it down your throat." He grinned at me, and even though my face hurt, I wanted nothing more than for him to do that to me. "Not today, sugar."

"Tomorrow?" I raised my eyebrows, hoping that I could entice him, or at least get a promise of something before the weekend ended.

"We'll see. I decide when and how. What can I get you?"

"Your cock." I knew when I said dirty words that he couldn't resist me. If he continued to deny me, I sure as hell wouldn't make it easy on him.

He rubbed his face and muttered something I couldn't quite make out. "Want something to drink or eat?"

He stood there, buck-naked and mouth-wateringly delicious, and waited for my answer. How could I think of water when his beautiful body was on full display? I shook my head and patted the mattress with a crooked smile.

"Tomorrow, sugar."

A pout hung on my lips, but inside I was happy to at least get a concession. "Good enough. I don't have anything in the fridge, City. I didn't think I'd be here much this weekend." Admitting to an Italian man that you lacked even the staples in your pantry wasn't easy.

"My mother wants to drop off food later. Are you okay with that?"

"Really?" My mother had never brought me food, even when I had the flu. I always fended for myself, even if it meant crawling to the kitchen to grab a glass of water. His mother, a woman I'd never met, would bring me food, and I had a twinge of jealousy. What would it have been like to grow up in a house like his?

"I can call her anytime and she'll drop something off. You just say the word."

"Word, word, word! Does your mom use Ragu like mine?" My mother never cooked from scratch. As a child I thought Chef Boyardee was the bee's knees, until I grew up and realized it was closer to vomit in a can.

City laughed, and his smile made my chest ache. "Don't even mention the word Ragu to her. She'll have a mental breakdown."

"Good to know," I said. "Remind me to never cook for her, okay?"

City grabbed his phone as he crawled in bed. "Hey, Ma. Suzy's going to rest for a bit, but we'd love for you to drop by with some food." I could hear her talking on the phone, and it reminded me of Charlie Brown's teacher. I couldn't make out the words, but I heard a garbled voice as I put my head on his chest. I played with the piercing, which earned me a stern look. "I'll text you her address. Thanks, Ma."

He put the phone down and stared at me, but I just smiled. "What?" I asked innocently.

"You must've hit your head harder than I thought."

"Maybe." I kissed his nipple, tugging on the hoop with my lips. He inhaled sharply as I bit down.

"Sugar, not now. I'm trying to be real good here, and you're not in any shape right now to do the things to you I want. Later, when you've rested and had something to eat, I'll give you more than you can handle...*if* I feel you're up to it."

"Party killer," I said, as I laid my head back down in the crook of his arm.

"Be a good girl and sleep." His fingertips trailed down my back, leaving a wake of warmth against my skin. I closed my eyes and enjoyed the feel of his hands on me, even if it wasn't the way I wanted.

***

I didn't know how long I slept, but when I woke up, I was alone in the bed. His side was still warm. My muscles rebelled and ached as I stretched. "Damn," I whispered, wanting to move without pain.

The doorbell rang and my heart started to pound—*his mother.* I didn't look presentable, and my face had to be a mess. I'd stared at it in horror this morning at the hospital. This wasn't the way I wanted to meet his mom.

I could hear them talking in the kitchen. The door cracked open and I turned my head, praying it was City. "Hey, sugar, ma's here. Do you want to meet her?"

"I look like crap, City. I can't have her see me like this."

He sat down next to me. "Sugar, she was at the hospital this morning. She's seen your face. She's not going to stare at you."

I sighed. "You didn't tell me."

"Sorry. Come on, just a quick hello. She made you lasagna." He brushed the hair away from my face, following the curve of my cheek.

I'd do anything this man asked me to. A smile, touch, or kiss and I was totally and utterly his. "Let me get dressed and I'll come out."

Meeting parents always scared me to death, and it meant a step deeper into a relationship. His mother obviously loved her son enough to bring us food, and I wanted to at least thank her for her kindness.

I looked into the mirror, touched the stitching on my lip with my tongue, noticing the coppery taste of blood. There was no need to bother with makeup. I couldn't look any worse than I did, and if she liked me now then I'd knock her socks off when she saw me at my best. Dressed in my favorite hoodie and sweats, I walked out to meet Mrs. Gallo.

"There she is," City said, standing from the couch with a smile plastered on his face.

Mrs. Gallo stood up and turned around. Her face was lit up and she looked like the mom I always wanted. She had long, wavy brown hair, big brown eyes, and a kind smile. "Suzy, it's so nice to finally meet you," she said as she wrapped her arms around me. "I'm sorry for how we're meeting, sweetheart. How are you feeling?"

"Thank you, Mrs. Gallo, I'm feeling much better." I moved to sit next to City, and grabbed his hand. "Thank you for making me lasagna. It's one of my favorites."

"My pleasure. Food always helps make everything better," she said.

"Italian motto," City muttered, and I laughed.

"I'm going to get going now and leave you two kids to enjoy your food. I just wanted to say hello. Is there anything else I can do before I leave?"

"No, ma'am, you've done more than I can ask for."

"Mrs. G or Maria, please. You need anything, just have Joseph call me."

"Joseph." I laughed. It sounded so serious, and fit him well.

"Watch it," he said in a playful tone, and squeezed my hand.

We all stood and hugged his mother goodbye. We walked to the door and watched her leave. I pictured her climbing into a minivan, even though she didn't have small children. I never pegged her for a woman that drove a Mercedes. I dreamed of a new Honda and knew it would be a budget killer...maybe someday.

"Your mom is great," I said as I wrapped my arm around his waist.

"She can be, but she's a pit bull when you cross her—just ask my father," he said. "Want some lasagna?"

"What's for dessert?" I asked as he closed the door.

"Anything you want, sugar."

"You know what I want," I said.

"Are you up to it?"

"Question is, big boy, are you up to it?" I wanted him, and I figured that if I challenged his manhood, he'd finally cave. All men are the same in that regard.

He laughed. "Don't ask questions if you can't handle hearing the answer. Eat your food and I'll show you how *up* to it I am, sugar."

He placed a giant piece of lasagna with cheese oozing out in front of me. My stomach growled at the smell, and the feeling of hunger finally registered. I cut into the slice and watched all the insides squish onto my plate. The hot lasagna spread across my tongue, and I wanted to moan from the taste.

"That good, huh?" City asked as he scooped a chunk in his mouth.

"What? Did I?"

"Yep, you moaned, sugar."

My face became heated. "Well, I'm used to Stouffer's lasagna. This is amazing, City. You don't know how lucky you were to grow up on this type of home cooking." I slid the fork across my tongue and slowly chewed, letting all the flavors dance on my tongue.

"I never thought about it." His fork stopped near his mouth as he looked at me with piercing eyes. "Suzy, you keep making noises like that and I won't let you finish the next bite." He set the fork on his plate and leaned back.

"I need my fuel to get better." I placed another sliver in my mouth, closed my eyes, and made a small sound in the back of my throat.

"You have thirty seconds to finish what's in front of you before I take your ass in the bedroom and give you something to really moan about." He crossed his arms over his chest and looked at his watch.

I shoveled the food in my mouth. I felt torn in this moment, but the lasagna could always be reheated.

"Fifteen." He smiled at me, and I felt everything in my body convulse and scream to be touched. I chewed like a maniac.

"Five."

"Wait!" I held up my hand. "I need something to drink," I said as I hopped off the high-top café chair.

"I got something for you to wash that down with, sugar. Time's up."

181

***

"Slower, Suzette," City said in my ear as he rocked in and out of me. "It's not a marathon. I want to savor being inside you."

"I've just missed you. Missed this."

"We have the rest of the weekend. I don't want to hurt you. Slow." He grabbed my hips and held me still as he slowed his pace. I wanted to scream and claw him, but I knew it wouldn't help to fight him.

He rested his forehead against mine as he encased my body and assaulted my senses. This was more than just sex. He expressed his feelings, and I felt them seep into my body. I stared in his eyes as he stared into mine before he kissed my lips. The pain of the kiss didn't stop me from returning it with fervor.

My fingers dug into his shoulders and I felt them flex under my touch. Each thrust brought me closer to the release I craved. His breathing grew harsh as he curled his arms under my body, tilting my hips.

My hands rested on his hips, unable to reach his ass, as I felt them relax and constrict with each thrust. I wished I had a mirror to watch his ass and back as he moved with my body. I squeezed the soft skin and hard muscle as the orgasm tore through my body. It was stronger than anything I had felt before. My toes curled and my muscles clenched around him as his pace quickened, before he slammed into me one last time, reaching his own bliss.

He nuzzled my neck and kissed the soft skin, making a trail to my lips. "I don't know what I would've done if something happened to you, sugar."

I ran my fingers through his hair and pulled his face to mine, forcing his eyes to see me. "I'm fine, Joey. You saved me." I kissed him and didn't give him a chance to respond. He flipped us over, and I straddled his body before breaking the kiss.

"No more fantasies that don't involve me by your side, but I still want to make them come true."

"I'm looking forward to it." I smiled against his chest as I kissed the skin over his heart. I listened to his heart thud in his chest. I had never felt so content with any person, let alone a man.

City spent the rest of the weekend helping me. Even though it started rocky, it ended with me feeling more loved and adored than I ever had. I couldn't deny my feelings for him any longer. My checklist no longer mattered. He showed me that he would take care of me and treat me in the way I'd always wanted. My doubts about if he was the "one" had vanished, and were replaced by a fate that had been sealed.

HOT FOR TEACHER

CITY

"Yes, sir, how can I help you?" the older lady at the reception desk asked. She leaned forward and rested her head on her hands.

I gave her my devilish grin and a wink. "I'm here to see Ms. McCarthy, ma'am."

"Oh, please, call me Kathy." She batted her eyelashes. "You're here to see Suzy?" She looked surprised, and her voice ended on a screechy high note. Her eyes no longer looked at my face, but traveled down my arms.

"Yes, I'm here to see Suzy, *Kathy*." I arched my eyebrow as she soaked me in, undressing me with her eyes. She looked like a nice enough lady, but I didn't like how she said Suzy's name, and I certainly didn't particularly enjoy the fantasy she must be having in her head. I cleared my throat, needing to pull her out of her lust-induced haze.

She blushed as she started fumbling with papers at her desk. She asked me for my identification and to sign the visitor's log. The school day had ended, but a few students milled around the receptionist area. I could feel their eyes on me. I wanted to laugh, but didn't want to be a total asshole.

Kathy gave me directions to Suzy's classroom in the next building. I needed to make sure she was okay on her first day back to work since the attack. I was sure she'd had to explain the injuries to her face over and over again. People could be fucking merciless.

I checked the sign on the door, and it read "101—Ms. McCarthy's Class." The large classroom had tables set up in neat rows, with cabinets lining the opposite wall. There was no chalkboard in the room like there had been when I was a kid, but a dry-erase board hung on the wall. Math problems that made my fucking head spin were written on the shiny white surface.

I didn't see anyone, but could hear voices talking from an attached room.

"I'm fine. Stop it," Suzy said. I picked up my pace to find out what the fuck was going on.

Entering the small office space, I saw Suzy pinned against the wall with Derek cutting off her escape. She looked like she wanted to become one with the wall and couldn't move farther away from his body. Her eyes grew wide as I reached for the prick and grabbed him by the shirt collar.

"What the fu—" he said, his eyes traveling to my face.

"The lady said stop. I think we've already had this conversation once before, dumbfuck." We were nose to nose, and I'd knock the mother-fucker out.

"Suzy didn't mean it," he snarled.

He sure had a pair of brass balls, but my fists were made of platinum. I fisted his pansy-ass dress shirt, pulling his body to mine. "She's mine, you fucker, and when the lady says *stop* it she means stop and back the fuck up."

"I should've had your ass arrested the first time you hit me. Hit me again and I'll call school security."

"Need someone else to fight your battles, sissy boy? You pick on girls, but can't handle a man all on your own?"

Suzy had tears in her eyes as I looked at her over his head.

"Listen here, buddy, I don't know who the fuck you think you are, but Suzy and I have a thing. She's not yours. Right, Suzy?"

She began to shake her head as her eyes grew wide. He turned his head to look at her, and I couldn't hold back my fist any longer. I punched him right in the jaw and watched the spit and blood fly out of his mouth.

Served the bastard right. I held him upright with my grip as he wobbled on shaky knees and his eyes watered.

If we weren't in her office at a school, I'd beat the piss out of the motherfucker. He deserved to be taught a harsher lesson than one simple fist to the face, but I had to tamper down my anger for Suzy's sake.

I let go of him with a shove and watched him stumble before catching himself on her desk. "I'll have you arrested for this." He wiped the blood from his lip with the back of his hand and glared at me.

"I'll share the little tidbit with security. I'll tell them how I walked in on you sexually harassing Ms. McCarthy in her office. I heard her telling you stop. Who do you think she's gonna back, asshole? You've touched her for the last time. Do it again and I'll bury you."

Suzy walked to my side and put her arm around me. "Derek, you mention a word and I'll make sure they fire your ass. I'll have no problem telling them about this and the other times." Smiling at me, she squeezed my waist. "I have Joseph and Sophia to back me up. Sophia knows all about you and your bullshit." Did she use two swear words in that speech? *That's my girl*, I thought as I beamed with pride.

"You wouldn't?" he asked, smoothing out his shirt, wiping the last bit of blood tricking down his chin.

"Try me, Derek," she snarled, showing the slightest hint of teeth.

"I'd put my money on the blonde." I smirked at the jackass as he stormed out of the room. "You okay, Suzy?" I asked, wrapping her in my arms.

She squeezed my waist and buried her face in my shirt. "Mm, you smell good."

"Answer me, sugar. Are you okay?" I kissed the top of her head.

"Yeah, I'm fine. Derek's an asshole. I don't think he'll be bothering me again." She laughed into my chest.

"I don't want you working with that dick anymore."

"I think he almost peed his pants."

"Promise me, Suzette? You need to go to the administration about him. He shouldn't work here or be near you."

She patted my stomach. "I love when you get all tough guy and use my full name." She laughed, and I squeezed her ass hard enough to make her jump. "I promise, Joseph."

"You seem to like it when I'm buried balls deep inside you, sugar, I don't hear you laughing then," I whispered in her ear. She shivered in my arms as the vibrations of my words touched her ears. "Why don't we put your desk to good use?"

She smacked me in the chest, but I could see the twinkle in her eye. She thought about it for a second before she answered. "No way, mister. I'm not getting fired."

"I thought maybe you went all bad girl on me, using all those curse words on Derek." I ran my finger over her bruise, but she didn't flinch.

"Two? I swore twice?" Her mouth hung open.

"You did, sugar. I'm proud of you."

"You must be rubbing off on me." She pulled away from my arms and smiled.

"Speaking of rubbin'." I looked down, wiggled my eyebrows, and moved my hips.

"Absolutely not." She looked away and started to move the papers on her desk.

I wrapped my arms around her and placed my face in her hair. "Whatcha gonna do, baby, give me a detention?" I asked. I couldn't help but laugh. God, if she was my teacher in high school I would've been all over her. My wet dreams would've been filled with visions of Ms. McCarthy leaning over my desk to help me with my math problems. I'd pray that her blouse would just happen to fall open and give me a glimpse of her beautiful tits.

She smacked my hands. "You're a naughty boy."

"You have no idea, Ms. McCarthy." I kissed down her neck, making my way to her shoulder before sinking my teeth into her delicate flesh. "You've smacked me twice, and I think I need to teach you a little lesson tonight." Her breath caught, and I heard a small moan escape as I ground my dick into her ass.

"Whatcha got in mind, Mr. Gallo?"

"I'm going to make sure you know you're mine." I cupped her breasts, squeezing them, and ran my palms across her hard nipples. "I'm going to fuck you so damn hard my cock will be the only one you'll ever think about. I'm leaving no inch untouched, no pore not kissed, and no hole unfilled."

"Um." She swallowed loud enough for me to hear. *Perfect.*

"Lost for words?"

"Not here," she whispered as she closed her eyes.

"My place, sugar. I don't want anyone to hear you scream when you think you can't come again, but I'll make you."

"Your punishment sounds so much better than detention."

"It's more like a retention program for at-risk little girls," I said as she turned around with a smile on her face.

"You know how to win a girl's heart." She stood on her tiptoes and kissed me.

I smacked her ass and she bit down on my lip, but not hard enough to break the skin.

"Oh, sorry, baby," she said.

"I'll get ya back, sugar. Let's get the fuck out of here or I'm tearing your clothes off right here." I pinched her nipple and felt her sharp intake of breath against my lips.

I needed to get the hell out of the school and take her to my bed. I kissed her goodbye after walking her to her car. I walked to my bike on the opposite side of the parking lot after she drove away. It would be hard as fuck to ride with the raging hard-on in my pants—I needed the walk to cool the fuck off.

25

RIDING' DIRTY

SUZY

RUINED. IT WAS THE ONLY WORD THAT CAME TO MIND WHEN I THOUGHT of Joseph Gallo, a.k.a. City McPierced Cock. He'd ruined me for any other man that could've had a place in my future. How could I go back to a boring anybody with a party pickle penis when I had Joey Sex God Gallo?

Joey made me scream in ecstasy; he'd been the first man I didn't have to fake it with. His voice alone made my skin break out in goose bumps, his kiss made the world vanish, and his cock—well, it was just damn unique and felt fucking amazing.

The idea of punishment didn't sound terrible coming out of his mouth. Anyone else and I would've run for the hills, but not City—he made my body feel like it was on fire. I wanted him to claim every inch of my body. What girl wouldn't want all the pleasure that would involve? I'd be an idiot not to want it.

I studied his body as he drove ahead of me on his sexy-ass Harley. I could see him watching me at the stoplights, and I never wanted the man to have eyes for another woman. He was everything I wanted, but never thought to include in my life plan. His muscles moved underneath his shirt as he hugged the road and gripped the bike. My mind kept replacing my body with the bike as we made our way to his house.

He became an addiction. He didn't ruin just my body, but he found a way to make himself a part of my life in a very short time. He invaded my dreams, and every thought I had involved him.

Watching him reminded me of the first time I saw him. I thought he would murder me on that country road. He looked mean and dangerous, but the only casualty would be my heart. Did I love him? It was a strong word to use in such a short amount of time. Could I go without him? Hell. No. Did I want him in my life? Damn straight. Love was a word I reserved for very few people in my life, and I wouldn't mess this up, no matter how fantastic his cock moved and how hard he made me scream. Love would come someday if he didn't fuck me to death first. Death by dick. Didn't sound half bad.

By the time we pulled into his driveway, my body buzzed with anticipation. It had been less than twenty-four hours since City had been inside me, but this felt...different. Turning the car off, I stared at him as he climbed off the bike and removed his helmet. He approached my car—his movement was like a lion stalking its prey—and I felt my cheeks flush with excitement. He looked handsome. Uniquely perfect.

His beauty wasn't only external. He had that nailed at first glance, but internally he was Prince Charming. Nobody had ever treated me like he did. He had just the right amount of caveman and Casanova to be destructive to a girl's mind—particularly mine.

"Come on, sugar. If I have to wait any longer, I'll fuck you right here in the driveway."

Although his words held promise, I'd never had sex outdoors; I wasn't ready to check that off my bucket list. Grabbing his hand, I followed him inside the small white farmhouse. I kicked off my shoes, and he grabbed me and pushed me against the wall.

His soft, wet lips crushed against mine as I gasped, and his tongue took that as an open invitation. "I can't decide which part of your body to assault first." His tongue slowly glided across my bottom lip. My heart pounded in my chest and he had to feel the rapid pace of the thump. "Do I start with this pretty little mouth?" He nipped my lip, causing a small moan to escape with the thought of my tongue wrapped around his cock. "Do I use this in your tight little cunt or your beautiful, tight ass?" He squeezed my ass, and I could feel his hardness against my stomach. I thought about all the ways he could and would take me, and a tingle ran down my spine.

"Perfect choice. Your mouth it is...to start." His eyes crinkled from the smile on his face. Fuck, I didn't make a choice.

"What? Wait."

"Not your decision. Watching you suck that lip in your mouth makes my cock ache to feel your tongue tugging at my piercing. On your knees, sunshine." The use of the nickname from our first meeting, when my world changed forever, made my insides warm.

Placing his hand on my shoulder, he pushed me on my knees, and I came face to face with his giant bulge. This time I knew what I would see, but it didn't dull the excitement I felt. Reaching up to unzip his pants, I peered at his face. The grin playing on his lips and the twinkle in his eye made my core pulse. His shaft bobbed and brought my attention back to the task at hand: sucking his beautiful cock and bringing him to his knees.

I unzipped his pants and began the task of unleashing his hardness. I rarely felt in control when City had me naked, but I felt empowered kneeling before him. Springing free, the tip glistened with a drop of moisture. My mouth watered as I palmed his cock, squeezing it, feeling the heaviness and hardness of his silky-smooth erection in my hands. I licked the tip, capturing the wetness on my tongue before taking him fully in my mouth. I loved the feel of the piercing, and every time I brought the tip back to my lips, I'd run my tongue over the metal, giving it a light tug. His body quaked with each thrust and pull. His fingers tangled in my hair. He gripped it roughly, trying to control my movement and depth.

I ignored his grip, welcoming the pain as I controlled the depth and speed. "Fuck, sugar, your mouth feels amazing." I squeezed his ass and felt a shudder take over his body. Pulsing my grip, I sucked harder and quickened my pace, and I squeezed my legs together, trying to relieve the ache. He moaned and twitched, and I could almost taste how close he was to losing it. I focused my effort on the tip of his cock, running my tongue along the underside, flicking the sensitive flesh and capturing the ring between my lips as I worked his length. "Fuck," he moaned, and he increased the grip on my hair. "Stop, sugar."

Screw that. I wouldn't stop until his body shook, he screamed my name, and I milked him dry. I grazed his shaft with my teeth and he hissed. "Fuck." I didn't stop in my relentless pursuit of his release. I watch his face as I sucked and licked like a starved woman on a mission—his eyes were closed, head tipped back, and mouth open. I gripped his ass with both hands, digging my fingernails in his skin, taking him fully in my mouth, hitting the back of my throat. I swallowed and tried not to gag. I clamped down on his cock as a moan escaped his lips, driving me forward, seeking the moment he'd say my name.

The feel of his rock-hard ass beneath my fingers, flexing and twitching, made me crazy. I wanted him, wanted to feel him inside me, but I wouldn't stop what I started. I felt in charge for once.

"Suzette," he hissed as my mouth filled with his release.

When his body stopped shaking and his cock stopped pulsating, I released him. I grinned at him, with his wide eyes looking at me with adoration. Swallowing, I licked my lips and captured a small drop seeping from the tip. His eyes had a twinkle in them as he watched me.

"You don't fight fair, sugar," he said with a shaky voice as he kicked off his jeans.

"I didn't see you stopping me," I said, pushing off the floor. He reached out, grabbed my neck, and pulled me to him, as he crushed his lips to mine.

He felt soft and warm. I wrapped my arms around his neck and soaked in the feel of his hands gripping my waist. He pulled my legs around his waist and I wrapped my arms around his neck, wanting the connection. We moved as one toward the bedroom where we'd begun weeks ago—my life hadn't been the same since.

He leaned over the bed, but my body stayed attached to him like Velcro. "It's your turn to scream my name, sugar." He unlatched my hands from his neck, placing them at my side. "Don't move." He smirked as he moved down my body, running his finger across the exposed skin of my stomach from the bunching of my shirt.

His touch felt like electricity, a tingling sensation spreading throughout my body as he traced around my belly button. "Elastic?" The word pulled me back into reality after I'd been lost in my dreamlike state.

"What?" I could barely think, let alone form a coherent sentence.

"You're wearing pants with an elastic waistband." He eyed them with curiosity. "Never met a girl that wore dress pants like these." His fingers grabbed the waistband and released it, snapping it against my skin.

Oh, shit. I had my granny panties on too. I didn't think I'd see him today. I just wanted to be comfortable, since I walked into a barrage of questions about the bruises and busted lip. I covered my eyes. "They're comfortable," I said as I swatted his hand.

He raised an eyebrow at me as he looked at the material. "I'm sure. I think that's why my mom wears them too." His chest rumbled with a hearty laugh.

"Fuck off, City." I chuckled, kicking him with my foot.

"Watch the goods, princess." He grabbed my foot as I made another. "I have a fighter on my hands." He gripped the bottom of my pants and gave them a hard yank, exposing my underwear. *Fuck.* "You're full of surprises today, sugar," he said.

"Hello... didn't think I'd be seeing you today."

"Guess not, based on your attire." *Smug bastard.*

"This is who I am, City. I'm not a floozy and I don't like a string up my ass all day while I teach."

"Oh no, it's sexy. The best part about you is that you're not a floozy. Makes me feel special that you break out the sexy shit just for me."

"Well, since it's sexy, then I can stop with all the lingerie when I see you." I giggled. I'd never do it, but if he wanted to pretend it was a turn-on...

"I don't give a fuck what you wear, sugar, as long as you end up naked."

I didn't want to be the granny-panty-wearing girlfriend to the hot biker. I wouldn't change what worked. I'd wear my sexy lacy shit when I saw him, but maybe, just maybe, I'd throw him for a loop with innocent little pink flowers every once in a while. "You going to shut up and fuck me or sit here yapping about clothing all night?" I snapped.

"Oooh, I got a feisty one on my hands tonight." He moved his body as he covered mine before settling between my legs.

"You got a horny one that just sucked you off. She deserves a reward, and I can think of a million other things you can do with your lips than talk," I said, running my tongue across his bottom lip.

Lust filled his eyes as he tugged at my lips with his teeth. He pulled his shirt over his head as he balanced on one arm. I'd never get tired of seeing his body.

His fingers wrapped around the side of my underwear before he ripped them from my body with one quick jerk. "Hey," I yelled.

"I won't be buying you new ones, so don't ask." He laughed before nestling between my legs and licking his lips. The need I felt for him never waned like I'd experienced with other men—it only intensified.

I closed my eyes as his mouth closed around me and his tongue flicked my clit. The heat of his mouth made me melt into the mattress. I gripped the sheets, needing something to hold on to keep my body firmly planted. He didn't rush as he caressed and sucked every fold and inch of my core. I looked down, wanting to catch a glimpse of his beautiful face between my legs, and I was met with his blue eyes staring at me. His eyes didn't leave mine as he brought my body to the point of release. My body glistened as every muscle tensed.

"Please," I moaned. I was wound so tight; I sat at the tipping point and needed just a little bit more to tip me over the edge. I released the sheets and pinched my nipple between my fingers, rolling it back and forth. His eyes grew wide as he watched my fingers move against my skin.

The orgasm ripped through me, stopping my breath; I was paralyzed through the explosion of sensations. He moaned and lapped at my body as I screamed something that wasn't audible to my ears. My heart thundered in my chest as I tried to catch my breath. I opened my eyes to a very happy looking man.

"Sexy as fuck, sugar. Watching you touch yourself, coming on my tongue, and babbling all kinds of incoherent shit—priceless. You made me hard again. I want to feel you come on my cock."

City ripped open the condom wrapper before settling between my legs. The piercing nudged my insides, causing my body to tighten. I felt the pressure building inside my core as he pumped inside of me. He cradled my ass with his hand, and my world exploded around him—and he followed me over the edge.

Multiple orgasms had always been a myth, something I read about in books, but with him they were a reality. What had started as a journey of lust and carnal exploits had now turned into something more. I saw the man behind the muscles, tattoos, and piercings, and I didn't want to let him go. I didn't want to be Suzy Q, the goody two-shoes anymore. I wanted to be a woman that could let her hair down and be who I wanted instead of what everyone expected.

I wanted to do something that I'd enjoy, or at least I hoped I would. City would freak out if I told him what I had planned. I kept it a secret. I contacted Mikey to see if he'd help me pull it off.

2 6

SURPRISES

CITY

THERE WAS A CHILL IN THE AIR AS I WALKED TOWARD THE DOORS OF Inked. Fall rolled into winter in Florida, and that meant cold nights and days that felt like the Chicago of my childhood. It was a nice change, but I craved the warmth of summer on my bike instead of the coolness that stung my skin.

I pushed the door open to see an empty shop desk as the bell above the door chimed. Mikey wasn't at his usual post to greet me, like he had been for more fucking mornings than I could count. I could hear a female voice and Mikey whispering from the piercing room in the back of the shop.

I put my ear to the door to listen to their conversation, but the voices grew quiet. I knocked. "Hey, can I come in?"

"In a minute," Mikey yelled. "Kind of got my hands full." I heard laughing as I walked away.

I checked my schedule for the day and listened to the voicemail messages. My first appointment called to cancel due to the flu, so I had some extra time. I kicked back on the couch and sent Suzy a message. Last night I'd left her exhausted in bed before making my way home. We'd been spending almost every evening together and usually never slept apart. The poor thing, I had been exhausting her with middle-of-the-night sex. She'd asked me if it was okay to sleep apart for a night and I agreed, although not happily. I understood, but I didn't fucking like it. The boner I woke up with this morning could've used some attention, but I did what needed to be done.

Me: Morning, beautiful. Sleep well?

I felt like a pussy-whipped fool, but for once I didn't mind feeling that way.

Suzy: Not really. I missed you in bed.

I smiled, knowing she felt the same. Never in a million fucking years would I have thought that I'd find love again in my life. Joni's sudden death had left me raw and reeling, not wanting to ever experience that hurt again. Suzy had changed that.

Me: Move in with me?

Did I really just type that shit? We'd been together only a couple of months, but I'd been with enough women in my life to know when it was right. I thought I'd get a quick response, but nothing. I was a fucking moron. I'd probably just scared her away.

The hinges on the door creaked as Mikey poked his head out. "Yo, bro. Wanna come see my handiwork?" He looked a little too happy for this time of morning.

"Who you working on off books?" There wasn't a name on his schedule before ten.

"Special request. Get your lazy ass up and come look, you prick." His head disappeared, and I could hear a hushed conversation.

"Mikey, I've seen every piercing out there." I climbed off the couch to make my brother happy, because he'd harp on me like a bitch in heat for the rest of the day. Plus, he could kick my ass if I didn't. "What's so special about this one?" I asked as I walked in the room and stopped dead in my tracks.

What the fuck?

Sitting in the chair was Suzy, *my* Suzy, with her breast exposed and a small metal hoop through her nipple. I couldn't breathe as I stood there staring with my mouth hanging open. Mikey looked excited and proud of himself, but I wanted to rip his fucking throat out—fighter or not.

Suzy had a sly grin on her face. "You like?" she asked.

Should I be happy or pissed? I blinked, but I couldn't fucking

197

respond. My brother had his hands all over my woman, even if it was for my benefit, and I wasn't there to supervise.

"Earth to City," Mikey said, and I swear to fucking Christ I wanted to knock his happy ass out of the chair.

"You don't like it, do you?" She frowned at me, and her eyes began to glisten.

"Oh no, sugar. It's beautiful. Sexy as fuck, actually." I grabbed her chin and kissed her. "I'll have fun tugging on it like you do mine. It feels amazing."

"You scared the crap out of me. Are you mad?" she asked as I rested my forehead against hers and stared in her eyes.

"I'm not mad. A little pissed my brother had his paws on your gorgeous tits and that you didn't let me be here for it." I turned my head and gave my brother a scathing look.

"Hey, seen one breast, you've seen them all. It's work, bro."

Dickhead.

"I wanted to surprise you, Joey."

"Well you fucking did that in spades, sugar." I kissed her forehead and inspected the piercing closely. "Next time you touch my woman, I get to be here, brother. Got me?"

"Got ya. I swear to God it was all for you. Get that stick out of your ass and look how well it turned out. She has the perfect nipples for piercings."

Did he just fucking say that to my face?

"Mikey, watch it."

"I look at it as another body part to be decorated. Chill the fuck out. I know she's yours."

"As long as we're clear on that fact."

"Crystal." He stood to leave.

"Mikey," I said, stopping him in his tracks. "I wouldn't trust her in anyone else's hands. You did well."

"Means a lot coming from you, Joe." He slapped me on the shoulder and gave us a moment alone.

"You're not feeling sick are you?" I asked. She looked flushed.

"Perfect. I thought it would hurt more than it did, though. I want to get the other one done eventually."

"It takes a while to heal. You're still riding the adrenaline high, but you'll be sore for a long time. Thank fuck you still have one nipple I can touch."

"Oh, just touch?" She smirked. I closed the door and locked it. I had time to kill, and Suzy sat before me with her breast exposed and a look of want in her eyes. "What are you doing?" Her eyes twinkled—she knew exactly what I had in mind.

"We're going to have a chat about my text you didn't respond to, and then I'm going to fuck you bent over that chair."

I loved her surprised face. "What text?"

"Look at your phone." I crossed my arms over my chest and waited for her to read it.

"You want to move in together?" Her eyes grew wide and her mouth hung open.

"Yes, sugar. We spend every night together, so why should you have to make a house payment when I have a place of my own?"

"Don't take offense, City, but your place isn't really my taste. The man cave, barren walls, and cottage feel. Can't do it. You can move in with me, though."

"Whatever makes you happy. As long as I have you in my bed and my bike in the garage, I'm a happy man."

"So that's it? We're doing it?"

"Oh, we're doing it. Undress, sugar. You're not leaving here until I've erased any scent my brother left behind and my cock is satisfied." I started to unzip my pants, and watched her carefully as she began to undress. Her nipple was red and slightly swollen from the piercing, and I'd have to remind myself not to touch it.

"Grip the headrest, ass out." I stroked my cock as she kept turning her head to see what I was doing. I liked to make her wait.

When she turned back around, I smacked her ass, causing her to jump and yelp. "What was that for?"

"Next time, ask before you change your body forever. I won't say no, but I'd just like to be clued the fuck in. I would've given that nipple a little extra attention before you took it off the market for a couple of months."

"Yes, sir." She smiled and rested her forehead against the leather.

***

Packing up my house didn't take long. We decided I would move my things during Thanksgiving break. I didn't put my house up for sale. It was paid off and I didn't see the need to get rid of it. I loved the land that the small farmhouse sat on. I bought it for that reason, and thought that someday I'd build my dream house on the property.

I moved my clothes into her spare room. She bought a small drawing table for me to use in the evenings, and I decorated the space with my work and my Harley memorabilia. I didn't want to invade her space. Moving in together was a giant step, more of a leap of faith.

"Are you sure you don't want to put your clothes in my closet?" she asked, leaning against the doorframe in a tiny purple silk nightie.

"No, sugar. My things are just fine in here." I unpacked the last box of clothing, sliding them in the dresser drawer that she'd emptied for me. "You need your space, especially your walk-in closet."

She sighed as she pushed her body away from the door and walked toward me. "Be patient with me."

"Sugar, come here." Holding out my hand to her, I pulled her in my lap. "Don't do anything different because I'm here. I'm easy to live with. I don't require too much. Your body is the only thing I'm impatient about. It's mine."

Her eyes twinkled and her smile widened. "It's yours, City."

"Whenever I want?" I raised my eyebrow, giving her a sly smile.

"Yes." She giggled as I grabbed her by the waist, lifting her ass on the dresser. "What are you doing?"

"Taking what's mine." My hands drifted up her legs, spreading them, and raised the nightie to her abdomen.

The smile fell from her face and all giggles disappeared as I licked her clit. Her body relaxed, resting against the wall, as a small moan escaped her lips. My dick ached to be buried inside her, straining against my track pants. Her breath hitched as I dipped my tongue inside her. The sweetest nectar didn't compare to the taste of Suzy, and I always wanted more.

Her legs tightened around my head, as her breathing grew shallow. Her thighs began to tremble underneath my grip. I sucked harder, flicking her clit with my tongue to drive her over the edge. Her hands fisted my hair as she pushed my face deeper, and I growled, relishing in the prickling sensation of her tugging my scalp.

"Oh, fuck. City," she screamed as I sucked harder, drawing her entirely in my mouth. Her body twitched, and she shook under my tongue as she came on my face. I could never get enough of her. She gasped for air, swallowing with wide eyes as she looked down at me. The grip on my scalp lightened as she grew limp and her back collapsed against the wall. Her nightie had slipped off her shoulder, exposing her breast and the small silver hoop that I'd been dying to touch, but couldn't.

Adjusting my dick as I stood, I kissed her lips, sucking the last bit of air she had into my mouth. "I'll never get enough of you, sugar." Our tongues tangled, her juice mixing with her saliva. She drove me wild. The feel of her small hands on my shoulders, gripping toughly, her nails digging into my flesh, made me rock fucking hard.

"More," she whispered against my lips.

"Insatiable." I pulled her body forward as I opened the top drawer, pulling out a condom.

I fucked her hard and fast. The wooden dresser slammed against the wall, thumping with each thrust. I prayed it didn't collapse from the abuse. Her legs rested on my shoulders as I gripped her ankles, pumping inside her. Each thrust forced a moan from her lips. My balls tightened as her pussy clamped down on my shaft. Her eyes drifted closed as I tipped over the edge, spiraling into an orgasm so intense my legs almost gave out.

My chest heaved as I tried to catch my breath. Her eyes fluttered open, and her cheeks were redder from the second orgasm.

"That's how to start a day."

"Promise." She smiled at me, running her hands down my bare chest.

"I'd fuck you all day, but we wouldn't get much accomplished, sugar. Your pussy is fucking addictive."

"Ha, your cock isn't so bad either."

"You know what your dirty mouth does to me."

"No, we have too much to do, big boy." She pushed against my chest before hopping off the dresser.

I grabbed her around the waist, pulling her back to me. "I'm not done with you yet, sugar. I own your ass," I whispered in her ear.

"I love you," she said, as her eyes grew wide and she covered her mouth.

"What did you say?" I tried not to smile, but the corner of my mouth twitched; I was unable to hold back my happiness. As her hand fell from her lips, I gathered her face in my hands to look her in the eyes.

"I love you, Joey."

"Sugar, I love you more than I thought I could ever love another woman. I've wanted to say those words to you, but I didn't want you to freak the fuck out."

"I do, City. I love you for everything you are. You're everything I wanted and the only one I think about. You've invaded my heart, and I can't go another day without saying the words to you."

"Say it again," I said as I brushed my lips against her mouth.

"I love you." The whisper of her words on my lips warmed my body and sent a shock through my system.

EPILOGUE

SUZY

CHRISTMAS

The transition of having someone live with me again had been easier than I thought. After Sophia and Kayden moved out, I didn't think I would ever allow someone else to live with me. Not because they were such a problem, but because I didn't think I'd find someone I could get along with. I know I'm not the easiest person in the world, and it's a fact that I'd always accepted. We talked about moving into a bigger place, but I didn't think we could afford it. My place was perfectly adequate.

It had only been a couple of weeks, but it had been wonderful. My house was small, but everything seemed to fit okay—with some adjustment on both our parts. I was thankful that it was Christmas break and that I'd get to spend the holidays with City and his family. My parents decided to go on a Caribbean cruise and leave me behind this year, and my sister had her fiancé's family to be with. If it weren't for City and the Gallo family, I'd be the third wheel at Sophia's apartment.

City had spent the morning making a special breakfast for us before heading to his parents' house. He told me that his mother always made panettone French toast every Christmas, and he wanted to treat me to his mother's recipe. It had been the best Christmas morning since my childhood.

I still hadn't mastered cooking, and stuck with the few dishes I could make edible. His mother had shown me some of her techniques and made notecards for me to follow, but it was useless. She would say, "No worries, love, you'll get the hang of it. It just takes practice." It was nice of her, but I knew that either you had it or you didn't—and I clearly didn't.

"Ready to go, sugar?" City asked from the bathroom doorway as I finished applying my lipstick. He looked handsome in a black pair of jeans and tight gray sweater. I wanted to unwrap him like a present.

"Just about, Joey. Do I look all right?" I turned to face him, and watched as his eyes traveled up the length of my body before he stared into my eyes.

"Always beautiful." He grabbed my face and kissed my lips, and the familiar want filled my body. I didn't know if I'd ever lose that feeling with him. I hoped I never did. "No time for what you're thinking, sugar. We can't be late today."

"I can wait. I'm not a total fiend." I laughed. "Did you load all the gifts?"

"Just waiting on you, sugar."

"Okay, I'm ready."

He held my hand and stroked it with his thumb as he drove. He looked happier than he did when we first met. He didn't look sad back then, but the happiness didn't radiate off him. It made me happy to know that I had put it there.

His parents' driveway was packed with cars as we parked on the curb. "Looks like a full house."

"Sugar, Italians do it big. My mom cooks for an army and invites all the neighbors to dinner."

"Oh, that's nice of her. I didn't get presents for everyone, though." A panicky feeling overcame me. I had met his family a couple of times and just started to feel comfortable, and now I'd have to sit in a room full of strangers.

"We do our gift opening later, after everyone leaves. Stop worrying—everyone loves you as much as I do."

City opened the door to a house of people; it looked to be bursting at the seams. His mom came toward the door with a smile on her face. She had on reindeer antlers and a cheery Christmas sweater. She looked like a mom, and one that any child would've been lucky to have.

"Suzy, love, merry Christmas." She enveloped me in a hug. City cleared his throat, and she chuckled in my ear and ignored him. "I'm so glad you came."

"Thanks, Mrs. G. I wouldn't want to be anywhere else. It smells amazing in here."

She held my shoulders and looked at me. "I made all the classic Italian Christmas dishes. Got to fatten you up, my dear." She rubbed my shoulder and stopped on the bone that sat below the skin.

"Not too much, Mrs. G, but I'll have some of everything."

"I knew I loved you, and yes, we do. Someday you'll be carrying my grandbabies." She smiled at me and made a face at Joey.

He choked and wrapped his arm around her to pull her off me. "Ma, let's not get ahead of ourselves."

"Just looking toward the future, Joseph. I want little ones running around. I'm too old not to have at least one. Try and make me happy for next Christmas, will you?"

"In time, Ma. Just give me a hug and we'll talk about it another day." He made eyes at me over her head, and I knew he was embarrassed, but I thought his mom was cute. Her words scared the piss out of me, but it was something nice to think about. I wanted him all to myself as long as possible.

"Come in and grab something to munch on before dinner's ready. Joseph, go introduce her to everyone."

"Yes, Ma." He wasn't always the most patient man, but that changed when he was around his mom. The reverence that was paid to a mom in an Italian family was something to watch. No one fucked with her or went against her word.

We walked around, and Joey introduced me to the family members that flew from Chicago for a warmer holiday, and the friends of the family. In my family, handshakes were the norm, but here hugs were expected. There was a warmth in the house and love could be felt in the chatter of the guests. I felt at home.

"Suzy," Izzy yelled above the crowd, and I could see her hand waving in the air.

"I'm going to go say hi to your sister. I'll be back," I said as I reached up and kissed his cheek.

He smiled at me with loving blue eyes. "I'll join you in a minute," he said before turning his attention back to the neighbor. They were discussing football and the possible Super Bowl teams. Boring didn't even begin to describe how I felt about the topic.

Izzy looked amazing, like always. Her long, flowing black hair framed her face perfectly. She had on a skintight dress that hugged her curves and showed off her beauty.

"Hey, Iz, it's good to see you."

"Merry Christmas, Suzy. I'm so happy you made it. How's my brother doing?"

"They're talking about football. Thank you for rescuing me." We both laughed and looked over at the two men waving their hands as they spoke.

"Boys and their sports. Did you guys exchange your gifts yet?" The look on her face told me that she knew what City had bought me, and she couldn't wait to get my take on the gift.

"Not yet. Do you know what it is?" I squinted at her. I never liked surprises, and maybe I could get it out of her.

"Oh, I know, and my lips are sealed, babe. City would be pissed if I spoiled his surprise."

A surprise. That means it was something big, and not a frilly dress or casual gift like we'd agreed on. I had purchased clothes and a cross pendant for him, along with new leather riding gloves. He was impossible to buy for, but I threw in some ultra-sexy lingerie that would have to wait until tonight.

"I hate surprises," I grumbled.

"This one you won't, trust me." She smiled and giggled, and my heart began to pound in my chest.

We hadn't discussed marriage, and I didn't know what I'd do if he bought me a ring and asked me in front of his family. *Breathe—you can do it.*

"Hey, big brother, merry Christmas." She wrapped her arms around Joey and they whispered in each other's ears.

The clinking of glass caused everyone to turn toward the kitchen. His mother stood, her antlers shaking with each stroke of her hand. A hush descended over the crowd as she began to speak. "I want to thank everyone for coming today. It wouldn't be Christmas without my family and friends. Dinner's served—feel free to help yourself."

"Your mother is really adorable," I said to Joey as he wrapped his arm around my shoulder.

"Yeah, she loves the holidays. Anytime she can get people to eat, she's a happy woman. Hungry?"

"I just ate a ton of appetizers, but I don't want her upset so I'll figure a way to eat more."

"Better get used to it, sugar. Food's the name of the game in this house," he said as we moved toward the kitchen.

A line had already formed, and he stroked my back as we waited to grab a plate. Every granite countertop in the expansive kitchen had a dish of some sort filled with food. The woman should've opened a restaurant with her culinary skills. Every type of pasta dish, braciole, chicken Parmesan, and meatballs were waiting to be consumed.

We found an open space on the lanai and chatted with the table guests until we couldn't eat any more. I kept eyeing the bottles of wine on the table—Gallo Family Vineyard. Gallo was a common Italian name, and I was sure out of pride they chose this label above the rest. I could hardly move. If they celebrated every holiday with this much food, my waistline would be in serious jeopardy.

The ladies cleaned the kitchen, and I was told under no circumstances was I allowed to help. His mom wanted me to enjoy myself, since I was a guest, while she and her sisters did the dirty work. I dozed off on Joey's shoulder during the chitchat and screaming at the football game on the television, but was woken up for the next round of eating—dessert.

The guests left a couple of hours later, after coffee was served and the football game ended. After the last person walked out, his mother yelled from the foyer, "Who's ready for gifts?"

"Anthony, get your ass in here," Izzy yelled from the floor.

His mother sat down next to the tree and waited for everyone to take a seat. "I love you all, but I miss Thomas. I wish he could've been here with us this year." The smile on her face faded as she wiped her eyes with the back of her hand. I knew little of Thomas, and he was the only sibling

I hadn't met. "He called this morning and spoke to your father and I. He promises he'll be here next year." She cleared her throat. "I'm thankful that Suzy could join us."

She pulled a gift from under the tree and held it out to me. "For you," she said.

I placed it on my lap and looked around, noticing that all eyes were on me. "What?"

"We all take turns, sugar." City patted my leg.

"Oh, sorry. My family, it's more like a free-for-all. Not used to this, but I'll learn."

It took hours to open gifts. They ranged in all sizes and shapes. I watched the family in front of me with joy. I'd never experienced something as loving as the Gallo family Christmas.

"I love everything you got me, sugar. I'll use it all." He kissed my cheek.

I smiled at him and whispered in his ear. "Wait until you see your last gift, but it's at home—for your eyes only." I bit his earlobe and was rewarded with a deep kiss.

"Hey, I know I want grandbabies, but not right here on the couch, please. There's one more gift under the tree, and it's for Suzy." His mother beamed as she handed the last present to me.

The box was small, but not a ring box. City leaned back and stared at me to gauge my reaction. I looked around as I undid the ribbon It's a horrible feeling to be the one left out—to be the surprised and not the one doing the surprising.

Tucked inside was a small business card. I read it, but didn't know what it meant. "You gave me a business card?" I asked, confused.

"No, sugar. Read it. Turn it over."

Mrs. Perkins

Florida Real Estate Specialist

I flipped the card over and recognized Joey's handwriting.

Something to call "ours"

Merry Christmas, sugar

"I don't understand," I mumbled as I turned the card over again.

Joey grabbed my hand as he spoke. "I want to buy a house for *us*. I want you to pick out your dream home, or we can build on my land."

"Joey, we can't afford that, but it's a nice thought." I knew his gesture was sincere, even if it were a fairytale.

His mother started to giggle, and the entire family laughed. I didn't get the joke. "Tell her, Joseph," his mother said as she sat down next to his father.

"Suzy, we can afford it. I can afford it."

"How?" I felt like an idiot.

"Jesus Christ, son. Suzy, our family owns a vineyard in Italy. We've owned it for generations. Joseph doesn't flaunt his wealth, but he has the ability to buy five homes."

I looked from his father to Joey, who sat there with a grin. "Is he telling the truth?"

"Yes, sugar. We all own a portion of the vineyard. We run the tattoo shop because we don't want to sit on our ass all day. We wanted something that was entirely ours and separate from what we inherited."

"Why didn't you tell me?" I felt awkward having this discussion in front of his family, but I figured they knew his reasons.

He stroked my face. "I like my little farmhouse. It was enough for me. I also don't like people to know my business. Too many people want things when they know you have money. Sugar, you have to understand. I thought if I ever—and I didn't think I would—found someone that I loved, I had to know they loved me for me and not my money."

"I do love you for you, Joey." The words came out with ease, and even though I knew he'd lied to me for months, I could understand why. "I'm happy in my home, though. No need to buy another."

"Exactly—'your home,' sugar, not ours. I want something that we pick out together with room to grow. We're cramped, but happy. Anything you want is yours. All I ask is for a big garage for my motorcycles and a space for the guys to hang out."

His mom clapped her hands. "Get lots of bedrooms too. I want an army of grandbabies." Even though the idea of a horde of children made my body break out into a blotchy rash, a big house would be wise.

"Not helping, Ma."

Her laughter filled the room. "Sorry, a girl can dream, can't she?"

"So what do you say, sugar? Can we buy a home for us? It can be a fresh start, the beginning of an amazing journey. We'll take our time until we find the perfect place. I love you, Suzy McCarthy, and this is what I want for *us*."

I didn't really have anything to think about. My last wall had crumbled. Everything I had on my impossible checklist had come true, and Joey was the man I'd always wanted. His family waited for my reply, and the air felt heavy. "Yes, Joey. I'd love to find *our* home and look to the future. I love you too."

His kiss stole my breath, as it always did. I thought back to the words Sophia told me not long ago. Butterflies—I still felt butterflies every time I saw him. The nervous energy never left my body, and I felt the electricity when we touched. When it's right, you know it.

He was the one.

Mine.

BONUS
NOVELLA
INCLUDED

HOOK
me

A MEN OF INKED NOVEL

USA TODAY BESTSELLING AUTHOR

CHELLE BLISS

1

MICHAEL

Spring

WIPING THE BLOOD FROM MY BROW, I GLARED AT TITO. THE WOUND stung as sweat trickled into the open cut just above my swollen eye. He moved quickly, but I had more power. It felt like a game of cat and mouse. I let him feel confident in his abilities, before I made my move to take his ass down.

A sharp pain in my ribs stole my breath as I kicked him in the thigh before the bottom of my palm connected with his chin. As his head flew back, I grabbed him around the waist, lifted him off the ground, and threw him on his ass. When my body crashed on top of him, the dull pain in my ribs became excruciating. I couldn't relent, or release him. I fought through the discomfort and held him down as he kicked and flailed like a trapped bitch.

His grunts grew louder and I took the opportunity to hit him in the face as he was locked in my grip, turning red in the crook of my arm. The back of his heel connected with my calf and the muscle instantly tightened. My body may have been screaming for me to stop, but my determination to win the match had me push through the pain and not let go.

Blowing the whistle, the ref called the match to a close. Releasing

Tito, I limped to my feet and held my ribs, trying to catch my breath. I smiled for the cheering crowd as Tito crawled toward his trainer. I wanted to fall down and sprawl out against the cool plastic material, but I couldn't, not yet at least.

"You won," Rob yelled in my ear as he smacked me on the back.

I winced, closing my eyes to block everything out. Through gritted teeth I said, "Fuck, don't do that shit." I exhaled slowly with shaky breath before opening my eyes to look at Rob.

His eyes grew wide as he searched my face, homing in on my hand. "What's wrong?" he asked.

"My fucking ribs. I think they're broken. I can't breathe," I huffed out, struggling to speak.

"Let's get you checked out. Make sure you didn't puncture a lung or some shit," he said as he wrapped his arms around my body and helped me out of the cage.

***

I closed my eyes and listened to the noise outside the room. Voices carried through the hallways—the cries, yelling, beeping, and telephones made it impossible to rest. I concentrated on my breathing, taking small, shallow breaths to stave off the stabbing pain.

"Mr. Gallo," a voice said from the doorway.

I jerked to sit up, but the pain sliced through my chest like a knife stabbing me. I collapsed against the mattress and raised my hand. "Here," I said, before resting my hand on my chest.

Placing her hand on my shoulder, she smiled at me. "I see you're here for your ribs."

"What gave that away?" I said, a little pissed off.

She pulled her lips in, hiding her smile. "On a scale of one to ten, how severe is the pain?"

"Seven when I breathe too deep, and about a two if I don't move and take short, shallow breaths."

"I need to remove your shirt," she said, touching the bottom of my tank top. "This is going to hurt."

"I can handle it, doc. Do your worst."

Her fingertips touched the flesh of my stomach, and I twitched as her nail grazed the spot just above my shorts. "Sorry," she said, blushing. "It

214

may be easier if you sit up. Take my hand," she said, releasing my tank and holding out her hand to me.

Holding my breath, I used my free hand to pull myself up with her help. It wasn't as painful as when I tried it on my own, but it wasn't comfortable either. "Whew," I said as I inhaled and winced.

"Just sit there, sir, and I'll do the rest." Placing her body between my legs, she reached for my shirt again.

When a beautiful woman says she's going to undress me, then have at it—I'll just sit back and watch.

Her facial features were petite—small nose, high cheekbones, and large hazel eyes. She glanced up at me as she pulled the material up, exposing my stomach. The feel of her fingers moving up the side of my body sent a shiver down my spine.

"Can you raise your arms or shall I cut it off?"

"I can do it." I raised my arms, smiling through the pain, holding my breath.

"There," she said, pulling the shirt over my head. Moving to the side of me, she placed one hand on my back and the other on my chest.

Her touch seared my skin.

"Lie back," she said softly.

With a very serious look on her face, she tried to hold up my body weight as I reclined.

"Which rib is giving you the problem?" she asked, looking down at my chest. She tilted her head; her eyes raked across my skin as her tongue darted out, sweeping against her bottom lip.

I needed to think of something else beside her sexy-ass mouth.

Being in this position, a hard-on would be embarrassing.

"Left side." I tried to think of the fight, or my sister sitting in the waiting room, as the doc's fingertips glided across my skin. I felt her touch everywhere, moving down to my toes. I stared at the ceiling and tried to wipe out all thoughts of her, but it's pretty fucking impossible when a gorgeous woman is touching me.

"Right here?" she asked, pressing down.

My entire body jerked. My head flew off the tiny, crappy pillow and my muscles tensed. "Fuck, doc. Warn a person first, will ya?"

She bit her lip, her cheeks turning pink. "I'm sorry. Guess I did my worst." She chuckled. "I think you need an x-ray to be sure you haven't punctured your lung. How did you do this, anyway?"

"I had a fight and the guy kneed me in the ribcage."

She grimaced and sighed. "Men. I'll never understand them."

"Doc." I placed my hand over hers, stilling her movement before I pitched a tent. "It was a pro fight. I don't do street fights and I'm not into barroom brawls."

"Not much difference in my eyes when someone ends up here. Violence is violence."

I said with a grin, "Oh, come on. You've never hit someone?"

"Not unless I was defending myself." She pulled her hands back and picked up the chart from the table next to the gurney.

"Well, I was defending myself from his damn knee." I laughed. "Ouch, fuck."

"Did you win?" Raising her eyebrows and cocking her head, she stared at me with parted lips.

I wanted to grab her and sweep my tongue inside her mouth. Show her how a real man does it. My strength wasn't only good in the ring, but I could hold her against the wall and make her dirty with barely any effort. "I always win." I grinned, winking at her.

"Cocky bastard," she muttered under her breath.

"My ribs hurt, but my hearing is fantastic, doc."

She ran her hands down her face to hide her smile. "I'm sorry, that was rude of me."

"Make it up to me with dinner." I touched her hand and saw her body twitch from the contact.

She felt it too—the connection, the spark between us.

"I don't date men who use their fists, Mr. Gallo."

"My hands have many other uses that you'd quite enjoy."

She swallowed hard enough that I could hear it, before she looked down at the chart and back at me. "I don't date patients or cocky bastards." She chuckled.

"Don't know what you're missing."

"I have to go order your x-ray, Mr. Gallo, and I have other patients to see. I'll be back to see you as soon as I get the results."

"Just think about it, please? You've wounded my pride." Pretending to be hurt, I gripped my chest.

"Your pride is just fine, it's your lung I'm worried about. Stay put," she said as she started to walk away.

"Where would I go? I can't even sit up without your help."

"Good, then I'll know where to find you." She laughed and walked out the door.

Reaching down, I adjusted my dick in my shorts. Fuck, just talking to her made me semi-hard. The half-pitched tent vanished when a burly man walked through the door with an x-ray machine. Never thought I'd be happy to see a man.

His size made it easy for him to move me. After a few shots, he helped me sit up before he left.

I started thinking of all the lines I'd use on her. I wanted that date, but how could I get her to say yes?

My heart sank when I heard, "Well, Mr. Gallo, it looks like a clean fracture." It wasn't the sexy doctor, but a man that spoke.

"Where's the other doctor?" I asked, wanting to see her before I left.

"She's busy and asked me to give you the good news and get you checked out."

"Fuck," I mumbled. She'd foiled my plans. I sighed. "So I'm good to go?"

"It's going to take about four to six weeks to heal. You can tape them to relieve some of the pain if you'd like."

"I know. It's not the first time I've cracked a rib."

"Here's the paperwork with instructions, and make sure to follow up with your family doctor in a week or so."

"Got it," I said as I took the paperwork from his hand.

Grabbing my shirt, I stalked out of the room to find Izzy. The doctor had brushed me off, and I was pissed.

2

MIA

Summer

HUMAN LIFE SEEMED TO BE WORTHLESS TO MOST PEOPLE. THAT WAS WHAT I'd learned during my time as an emergency room physician.

I'd wanted to help people for as long as I could remember. My mom said I raided the medicine cabinet to fix my Cabbage Patch Kids as a little girl.

Each day as I stood over my patients, trying to revive their lifeless bodies, my education and training felt meaningless. Medicine is still referred to as a *practice*. It hasn't been perfected, and even with today's advances in medicine, not everything can be fixed.

It's a hard fact that I don't always want to accept, but have no choice.

The hardest part of my job, the thing I dread most, is informing a family that we were unable to save their loved one, despite our best efforts.

Those words left my mouth twice today, and it had been soul crushing.

"Call it, Dr. Greco," Dr. Patel said as he stood next to the gurney.

I couldn't stop myself from pushing down again. Sweat trickled down my cheeks, as a lump had formed in my throat. Maybe if I pushed one more time, I could get his heart to beat again.

"I can't. Just give me a couple more minutes." I pushed with such force that I knew that a few ribs had cracked under my palm.

His life hadn't even begun and I would be the one that called his time of death.

"Mia." Dr. Patel placed his hands on mine, snapping my mental focus —to save the boy's life. "He's gone. You've been working on him for over thirty minutes. His injuries are too grave. Call it, or I will."

Dr. Patel had been by my side today, and knew the devastation that we were unable to repair—two car accidents, a gunshot victim, and the little blond-haired angel in front of me—a victim of a hit-and-run driver.

How could someone hit a child and leave him in the street to die?

A child…a goddamn innocent little boy.

I looked at Dr. Patel and was struck by the weariness on his face. His eyes were bloodshot; the tiny creases around them looked deeper with big, dark circles. I could see that the day had taken a toll on him too. I wasn't alone in my despair.

I rested my palms against the boy's chest and felt the silence within, there was no life left to save. "Time of death: seven twenty-one p.m." I closed my eyes and took a couple of slow, steady breaths before I removed my hands. I wanted to run to the bathroom and throw up.

A third life I couldn't save.

"I'll go tell his parents, Mia. You've done enough today," Patel said, placing his hand on my shoulder, giving it a tiny squeeze.

"Thank you, Eric."

I usually argued with him. I wanted to be the one to talk with the families and help console them, but today, I had nothing. He patted my shoulder before leaving me with the boy that would never age or have the opportunity to experience all the joys in life.

I collapsed in the chair against the wall; pulling out my ponytail, I let my hair fall free. Placing my head in my hands, I ran my fingers through my hair as I tried to collect my thoughts.

More patients needed me, but I had to take a moment to myself. I couldn't take another loss; I didn't have anything left to give. Each time I lost someone, a small piece of my heart died.

Light footsteps broke my moment of serenity as I questioned my decision to work in an emergency room instead of an office practice, like most of my classmates.

"Sorry to interrupt, Dr. Greco. I need to prep the body for the family to say their goodbyes," the nurse said as she grabbed a damp cloth to wipe down his bloodied face.

"It's okay. I have patients to see. I just needed a moment to myself."

She gave me a weak smile before beginning to clean the body. I couldn't watch. I couldn't take the sounds of the cries and utter grief that would fill this room. It took everything I had to climb to my feet and pull myself together. The ER had an endless stream of people.

I had one hour left until I could go home and crawl in bed.

I had thought about moving back to Minnesota after I finished my internship, but Florida had become a part of me. I wanted to wear sandals year round, feel the sunshine on my face, and watch the sunset over the Gulf of Mexico from my beachfront home. I couldn't go back—snow and I never got along.

My work had become my life, especially in the summer months when my parents went back home. They were snowbirds, and came to Florida to enjoy the sunshine and warm weather when the deep freeze hit up north. They'd been gone a month, as spring had arrived back home. The quietness of my life had become almost deafening when I wasn't at the hospital. Today I was thankful I didn't have to go home and put on a cheery smile for them.

I felt needed here. I had something to contribute, something that many people didn't. The local population was poor and I wanted to help. It had become my calling. I spent my spare time helping at the free clinic in town and helped raise money for the homeless youth that plagued the county.

I stayed for the clinic, where I volunteered, and the chance to make a difference.

3

MICHAEL

MY MUSCLES REVOLTED WITH EACH KICK; EVERY SINGLE ONE SCREAMED for me to stop, but I couldn't. I worked too damn hard to get to this point in my life to give up now. Sometimes I questioned my sanity for waking up at three in the morning to work out for hours at the gym, but my body had to be strong and I had to be ready to win my next fight.

"Pansy ass," Rob yelled. "Harder. Your ribs have been healed for weeks. Show me what you're made of already, Mike."

He egged me on and did everything in the world to piss me off. Rob had been my trainer for two years. Most days, like today, I wanted to knock his fucking lights out, but I knew his methods were right in the end.

"Your sister hits harder than you," he teased, a shit-eating grin on his face.

My sister, Izzy, was where the friend-trainer line crossed with Rob and me. They dated for a short time. When Izzy dumped him, I didn't think we'd continue working together. In typical Rob fashion, he brushed it off and moved on to the next notch in his bedpost.

"Cocksucker," I said, hitting the target in his hand hard enough to cause Rob to stagger backward.

"Better," he said as he regained his stance. "Ten more minutes and then we'll call it a day."

My drive to be the champion was so strong that I could almost taste the next victory. I wanted to show my family that I had talent and the ability, even though at times, at least in the beginning, their support had been questionable.

I won my first two matches, and with each victory, their support grew and my pop finally started to believe. When my ma said he was bragging to his friends, I knew I had him.

I grew up watching the fights with my pop and his buddies. They yelled at the television and made side bets. He liked to call my fighting career a hobby, but I needed to show him that it was more than that. I was meant to be the champion.

Wanting the gym all to myself when I trained, I paid the owner to wait until six in the morning to open the doors. He liked the idea of the publicity my victory and career would bring to his small-town gym in the middle of bum-fuck Florida, and it didn't hurt that he was Rob's brother, either.

"Bodies" by Drowning Pool pumped through the speakers, and it gave me the last push of motivation I needed. Sweat dripped from my brows and stung my eyes. Doing a roundhouse kick, I almost missed the target, nearly hitting Rob in the head.

"Maniac. I'll knock you on your ass if you do that again."

"In your fucking dreams, buddy." I laughed before landing a solid blow.

My forearms burned, my thighs trembled, but I wouldn't quit.

I had this shit.

"Time," Rob said, putting the targets down.

"I could go another hour," I said.

I knew that shit was a lie.

I ran for an hour before I walked in this morning, and my legs were shaking to the point of weakness.

"Sure you could, tiger." He laughed, holding his stomach. "Your muscles need to rest and recoup. We don't want to overdo it with the match coming up."

"Thank Christ," I mumbled under my breath.

"What did you say?" He cocked his eyebrow as he crossed his arms.

"Nothing."

"Why do you seem so fucking pissy today, Mike? Couldn't get it up last night?"

"That would seem like a fuckin' blessing right now." I sat on the bench to give my legs a break as I pulled the tape off my hands. "Tammy. What a fucking pain in my ass."

"I told you she's a crazy bitch. Stop thinking with your dick so much and use what brain is left in that thick head of yours."

I snorted. That had been the funniest damn thing to come out his mouth in a long time—he sure as fuck wasn't Dr. Ruth. "When did you become a relationship expert? Your shit isn't all together in the lady department, Rob."

"Maybe not, but I told you Tammy was a hot mess. She's got the cling thing going on and is crazy to fuckin' boot."

"Crazy is an understatement, man." I shook my head. I had a silent debate with myself on if I wanted to share the details of the entire fucked-up situation. "I went to her place last night to get a piece of ass."

"And?" He leaned against the wall and listened.

"And the crazy bitch had a scrapbook on her coffee table. Do you know what the cover was?"

He started to laugh as he pulled his lips in his mouth to stop from breaking out into hysterics.

"You do, don't you?" I glared at him.

"I've heard stories about her, but I thought they had to be made up."

"She had a picture of a bride and a groom. Somehow, she'd put our faces on their bodies. I opened it when she went to her room, and the book was filled with her version of *our* future. It was beyond fucked up. Gave me the fucking creeps."

Page after page contained images of our children with names and photos. Little hearts in all colors surrounded the pictures. She had our life planned out, and all I wanted was a little pussy.

She didn't have the brains to hold my attention, let alone make me want to spend an eternity listening to her chatter on about the Kardashi-ans. Tammy wanted status and money, and they were two things I wasn't willing to share with a woman like her.

Tammy knew her role in my life—she was my late-night hookup. I never took her out, never led her on, and never promised her happily ever after.

She always replied, "You'll change your mind," but that never happened.

"Wow, I don't know what to say," Rob said as he walked toward the door to unlock it.

"I ended that shit right there. She cried like we'd been dating for years. What a fucking mess. I don't need the bullshit in my life, especially not now."

"Keep your eye on the goal—fighting, not bitches and pussy."

"Didn't you learn not to use that term when talking about women?" I laughed.

His cheeks turned pink as he looked away from me. "She's your sister, and I have nothing more to say about the experience." He drew the last word out. I knew he had a million things he wanted to say about her, but he kept his lips shut because he knew he'd get a beating.

Rob was crass. He referred to women as bitches once in front of Izzy, and she caught him off guard and knocked him on his ass. It was a proud brother moment. She took down a man double her size, and for one hell of a good cause. My baby sister has bigger balls than most men I knew. Growing up with four brothers made her rough around the edges and not willing to take shit from anyone.

"Good choice." I finished drying the sweat from my body. Grabbing my phone, I threw my bag over my shoulder. "Tomorrow, same time?" I asked.

"You got it." Rob reclined in the chair at the front desk, kicking his feet up and putting his arms behind his head. He looked like he was ready for a nap.

That shit wouldn't fly at Inked.

The screen on my phone lit up.

Tammy—there were at least a dozen text messages from her since I'd walked in.

Tammy: We were meant to be together.

Tammy: You'll come back to me.

Tammy: I miss you.

I told her last night we were through, even though we never really began.

I never asked her to be my girlfriend.

Fuck her and her insanity.

I turned the screen off as I reached for the door. The top of my head hit the door before my chest connected with the glass. I saw stars from the impact. I blinked a couple of times before I noticed a woman on the ground. She was picking up the contents of her purse that had spilled.

"Fuck," I muttered, as I opened the door to a very pissed-off female. "I'm sorry; can I help you with that?" I asked, bending down in front of her.

"Why don't you fucking watch where you're walking?" she seethed, as she placed her wallet and other tiny items inside her black handbag.

"I didn't see you." I grabbed her lip-gloss that had rolled away, and held it out to her.

She grabbed the tube from my hand and glared at me with the most mesmerizing hazel eyes. "Obviously." She scanned the ground.

Instead of helping her, I stared at her like an idiot.

Her hair was an amazing shade of brown, with glints of red that sparkled in the light. The straight, smooth locks hung just past her shoulders. She had a small nose, full red lips, high cheekbones, and large hazel eyes with flecks of gold.

"Hey, I said I'm sorry and I am." Standing, I tried to be a gentleman and held my hand out to her.

Her eyes moved up my body, slowly at first, before she stopped on my face with scrunched eyebrows. Her skin felt like silk against my rough palm as she placed her hand in mine. In one quick motion, I pulled her to her feet. Her crinkled forehead and hardened expression disappeared and were replaced with softness. She pulled her hand away from mine with a weak smile and a reddened face.

"How can I make it up to you?" I asked, still staring. It wasn't her beauty that had my attention, but something about her eyes—a familiarity that I couldn't place.

She used the back of her hand to brush the dirt off her yoga pants. "I'm fine. No need to make it up to me. Just maybe watch where you're walking next time. You're kind of like getting hit by a Mack truck." She laughed. "Hey, I'm sorry I was such a bitch. Just a bad night and shitty morning and you're the icing on the cake."

Tilting my head, I gave her a small smile. "I understand. The last twelve hours haven't exactly been stellar for me either."

She fidgeted with her phone but kept her eyes locked on mine.

"Got everything?" I asked. I needed to leave. I didn't need to complicate my shit any further.

"Yeah, I think so. Thanks for stopping to help."

"I'm not a dick. Well, at least not all the time." I grinned. "How could I not stop and help the beautiful lady that I knocked over? I hope your day gets better from here." God, I sounded like a total moron, but I couldn't stop the verbal diarrhea that leaked from my mouth. "Let me get the door for you." I rushed and pushed it open.

"Thank you," she said, brushing against my body as she tried to fit through the doorway, my torso blocking the small entrance.

A hint of lilac or some flowery shit filled the air, disappearing with the distance between us.

"Maybe I'll see you again sometime," I said, not ready to walk away.

She smiled at me before turning around and walking away.

"Yeah, I'm here every day."

When did I turn into Mr. fucking Rogers? I couldn't stop myself.

"Maybe we can work out together or something," I yelled to her.

I'm officially a pussy.

"Sure." She didn't sound too eager, but then again, she didn't say no. She placed her bag next to the desk and signed in.

I watched her as I walked toward my truck.

My cock was hard last night when I went to Tammy's, and that turned in to a clusterfuck of epic proportions without me at least getting off for my troubles.

Seeing the girl that I crashed into wearing a tight, hot pink workout tank top and black yoga pants turned my dick into granite.

Obviously, I needed my fucking head examined.

***

I flipped on the lights at Inked as I walked through the door to peace and quiet. An ice-cold shower didn't do much to take my thoughts off the hot piece of ass I ran into at the gym.

As I sat down at the front desk, my phone danced across the appointment book. It hadn't stopped vibrating from the nonstop messages.

The girl was fucking clueless.

Last night my exact words to her were, "Don't ever call me again, you crazy bitch." I thought it was pretty cut and dry. My words were simple to understand, but apparently she didn't get the fucking message.

When I heard my sister's car beep in the parking lot, I braced myself for her bullshit. Izzy would have a fucking field day when she heard about Tammy. I held my breath, tapped the pencil next to my jiggling phone, and kept my head down as she breezed through the door, chattering on her phone to her asshole flavor of the month.

Izzy isn't an easy girl—she made the guys earn everything she gave.

Growing up with four brothers hadn't been easy for her—we didn't leave her the opportunity to be easy. Most of her boyfriends got chased away when she was younger. It wasn't like she couldn't handle herself, but we made sure to keep her ass out of trouble.

She threw her bag on the floor next to her station before coming to a dead stop in front of me. I snuck a peek at her. She squinted at me, already reading me like an open book, shaking her head.

"I gotta go, John," she said into her phone, popping her gum and looking at the ceiling. Her hands opened and closed, with her fingertips touching, telling me that he was rambling. "Bye, John. I don't have time for this shit. I'll talk to you later." She pressed on the screen before blowing out a puff of air. She leaned over and spat her gum in the trashcan. Classic Izzy.

"Hey, sis."

"What's wrong?" Cocking her head, she waited, rubbing her finger across her lips.

"Nothing." I didn't want to tell her, but I knew it was inevitable.

"You boys are so bad at hiding shit. I've spent a lifetime studying you jackasses. I know you better than you know yourself. I'm guessing woman problems. Just tell me, because I won't stop asking until you do."

"Tammy."

"Ah, the fruitcake," she said as she giggled.

"What do you know about her?" My phone started to dance across the desk again, and I grabbed it to stop the jerky movement.

"I've heard stories. We've all heard *things*." She made air quotes with her fingers.

My sister had been holding out on me. "What didn't you share with me, Isabella?"

"My formal name. Is someone feeling duped?"

"I swear to Christ, Izzy. Why didn't you warn me? I mean, I would've told you if you were going to date some crazy cocksucker."

"I tried to warn you, but you reminded me that you're a big boy."

If she used air quotes one more time during this conversation I was going to put her in a headlock and mess up her hair until she screamed uncle.

"You told me to mind my own business. So...I thought I'd let you learn the hard way, big brother." She couldn't stop laughing.

I sighed. "Next time slap me, will you?"

"Gladly." Her fingers tangled in my hair, ruffling it just the right way to make me cringe. "So tell me what happened, and why is your phone going crazy without you bothering to look?"

"I don't even know where to start. I ended shit with Tammy and she's been blowing it up for twelve hours."

"Why did you end it? Wait, were you guys really a *thing*?" She leaned over the desk and rested her chin in her hand.

"We weren't anything but fuck buddies, or at least that's what I thought. She, on the other hand, had our future planned out. She made a scrapbook, Izzy. A fucking scrapbook." I slammed my fist down on the desk and started to laugh. "Shit would be funny if it happened to someone else, but she's crazy."

"A scrapbook of what?" Her eyebrows drew together.

"The cover was a wedding photo with our faces glued on the bride and groom. I flipped through the book. It was our entire life planned out and in living color. That shit just isn't normal, Izzy."

She doubled over in laughter, smashing her fist against the desk. "No, wait." She couldn't catch her breath as tears began to stream down her cheeks. "Did you at least take the scrapbook with you? I mean, I need to see this shit."

"Fuck. I was so pissed I didn't even think about grabbing it." I rubbed my forehead, annoyed with myself for being such a dumbass. "She hasn't stopped calling and texting me since last night."

Hunched over, gasping for breath, she held her hand out. "Give it to me."

"What?"

"Gimme your phone, stunad."

She tapped a few buttons, the tip of her tongue sticking out.

"What are you doing? Please don't respond to her, Iz."

She gave me a sour look before turning her attention back to her task.

I sighed, leaning back in my chair, and waited.

"Here," she said, placing it in front of me.

"What did you do?"

"You really need to learn more about your phone, Michael. I blocked her." She rolled her eyes.

"You can really do that shit?" I was stunned; I didn't know it could be so easy.

I would've done it hours ago to avoid the barrage of bullshit.

Izzy just shook her head as she walked away.

Joe and Anthony walked in laughing. They said the usual "hey" when walking past me to put their stuff down and prep their areas for customers.

I checked over the schedule while I waited for everyone to finish. Anthony sat first and began to tap out a beat against the plastic chair. Leaning back, he put his head against the wall, and closed his eyes, looking lost in the rhythm.

By the time Izzy and Joe made their way to the front of the shop, I wanted to rip Anthony's fingers off and shove them down his throat.

Izzy sat down next to Anthony, resting her head on his shoulder.

"Anything new since yesterday, Mike?" Joe asked, leaning against the desk. He cracked his neck with a quick push to his chin.

Izzy laughed as she whispered in Anthony's ear. They looked at me and smiled.

"Totally booked. No room for walk-ins unless anyone wants to work extra."

No one met my eyes.

"Didn't think so." I tapped the pen against the schedule and tried to avoid the looks from the two assholes against the wall.

Joe turned toward them. "What are you two giggling about over there?"

I waved my hands in the air and shook my head. I hoped Izzy would take pity on me. I knew the bullshit that was about to take place if she didn't.

"Talking about the nuptials between Tammy and Mike."

Fucking little sisters and their big mouths.

Joe's head turned quickly in my direction. "What the fuck are they talking about?"

"They're being jackasses."

"You didn't elope or anything stupid like that did you?" Joe asked.

"Fuck no! Give me an ounce of credit, will you please?"

We spent the next ten minutes laughing about Tammy and all the problems our dicks had caused through the years. It's strictly a male issue.

I had to own that shit.

When my first customer arrived five minutes early, I wanted to kiss her feet for saving me from my siblings' harassment.

4

MIA

I GROANED, BURYING MY FACE IN THE PILLOW AND WANTING TO AVOID facing the world. My body felt heavy and I didn't want to get out of bed, but the only thing that could help was working out. Even after a full night's sleep, I couldn't shake my sadness from work last night, and I figured, why the hell not? It was worth a shot.

The only thing that usually helped my mood was a good, ass-kicking workout at the gym.

Then I walked in the gym and the man knocked me on my ass. The impact scared the hell out of me as I fell on my ass, dropping my purse and spilling the contents everywhere.

He was the object of my anger. It wasn't from being knocked down; looking back, I was more mortified by it than pissed. I felt helpless over the lost lives that had piled up during my shift. The night before had been one of the lowest in my short career, but when I looked up into his rich caramel eyes, something inside me shifted.

My brain must have been rattled by the force of my fall.

I'd seen him before. I knew it.

I lost my breath as I stared into his eyes. I'd never had a reaction to someone like I had with him. Something unspoken passed between us as we looked into each other's eyes.

It took everything in me to not react when he helped me off the ground. The moment our skin connected, electricity passed between us. There was a snap, crackle, pop.

I couldn't get him out of my damn mind as I started to run on the treadmill. As my thighs burned and sweat trickled down my chest, I thought about only him.

How did I know him?

Tall with broad shoulders, muscular, tattooed-covered arms, and completely not my taste.

The track pants he wore hid his legs, but there was no doubt in my mind that they were as solid and powerful as his upper half.

When our bodies were inches apart in the doorway, my heart pounded in my chest—if he were any closer, he would've heard the frantic rhythm.

"Hey, Mia." A voice pulled me out of my haze.

Blinking, I looked over to see Rob leaning against the treadmill. "Oh. Hey, Rob."

"You're looking beautiful, as always." He stared at my chest as my body bounced.

"If you don't stop staring at my chest, I'll knock you on your ass," I warned.

He snickered, covering his mouth with his hand, but his eyes remained glued to my breasts. "Promises, promises. Why don't you let me take you to dinner?"

"Rob, I'm sure you're a nice guy." I coughed.

He was the farthest thing from nice. He wasn't an asshole, but he sure as hell wasn't boyfriend material.

"We wouldn't work. I'd spend too much time repairing the injuries I'd give you."

A giant smile crept across his face before he finally looked at my eyes. "You say the sexiest shit, Mia."

"Not happening. Who was that guy that left when I walked in?" I grabbed the towel and blotted the sweat from my chest.

Moving his eyes to follow the path of the towel, he asked, "You mean Mike?"

"I don't know his name. Tall, muscular, walked out right after you opened."

Brawn didn't equal brains when it came to Rob.

"Mike, yeah, he's a friend of mine." His eyes flickered between my breasts and eyes.

If they were friends, then in all probability he was an asshole too. I had attracted more of those in my time than I wanted to admit.

"Tell me about him. I think I know him from somewhere." I couldn't help myself; I had to figure out how I knew him.

"He's a fighter. He has a big fight coming up that I'm helping him train for." Rob flexed and punched the air.

"Is that all he does?" Fighter—code word for "unemployed and a workout junkie."

Rob shook his head and laughed. "Nah, he's part owner in a tattoo shop. He's a piercer there."

A busty blonde walked by and started to set up camp at a treadmill nearby. Rob's eyes wandered in her direction as he licked his lips.

"Thanks. You can go now," I said, wanting to be alone with my thoughts.

He put his hands over his heart and staggered backward as though he were in pain. "You just dismissed me like that? I'm wounded, Mia."

"Maybe the girl over there"—I moved my head in her direction—"will have the remedy."

"You may be right, beautiful. I'm off to find out." Winking, he tapped my treadmill with his palm before whistling as he walked away.

CNN played on the tiny screen in front of me, but I couldn't focus as my thoughts drifted back to Mike. The powerhouse that literally rocked my world this morning was a body mutilator. He pierced and punched his way through life while I patched up the damage caused by fists and dirty needles.

I grabbed my phone from the cup holder as it began to chirp.

Lori: Girls night out. Game?

I needed a night with my friends. I needed to laugh and hear the latest gossip. I had two days off, and an evening to let loose sounded like heaven and a great way to get my mind off work.

Me: I'm in. When and where?

I didn't give a shit if I had to drive to Orlando, I'd be there. My restless night would require a nap to keep up with the ladies, or I would do a face plant on the table after the first drink.

Lori: Ybor City. Be ready to party your ass off. I'll pick you up at 9.

Me: I can drive.

Lori: Fuck no, your ass is getting drunk. I got it all worked out.

She knew me so well. Lori and the girls went out all the time. They lived without their work to weigh them down emotionally. Unlike me, they didn't have to hold someone's heart in their hand and try to get it to beat again. Their pressures were different, but I could never stumble into work nursing a hangover.

Lori was a lawyer, Sarah a receptionist at an advertising agency, and Jamie was a bored housewife.

I wanted to buy a new outfit for tonight. I had a closet full of clothes, but screw it, I deserved something special. I worked my ass off and didn't feel ashamed to splurge on myself every once in a while. International Plaza called my name.

***

I straightened my hair—the humidity in Florida wreaked havoc on my long brown locks—before starting my makeup. I didn't wear much to work; the long hours typically had me questioning their claim that makeup was twenty-four-hour wear. It never stayed put, and caused my eyes to look more tired than they did naturally.

I took my time, giving my lids a smoky treatment to bring out their color before applying an obscene amount of Barely There mascara. It made my eyes look bright and my eyelashes long and lush. Lori texted me that she was almost at my house as I spritzed my body with Gucci Guilty and stared in the mirror—giving myself a once-over.

The short, tight black tube top showed off my stomach and hourglass figure perfectly. My tits didn't stick out too much, but would be noticed without flashing a sign that read "looky here." My form-fitting denim capris made my ass look perky. The leopard print stiletto heels caused my calves to tighten and pulled the entire outfit together.

I sat on the front step as I waited for Lori to pick me up. The neighborhood was bustling. People waved as they walked past with their dogs and sat on their front porches enjoying the warmth of the Florida air. Summer would soon be arriving in full force, and people would be scarce at this time of day. The summer sun felt like a flame against my skin, and even the mornings were stifling from the humidity.

I closed my eyes as Lori's headlight blinded me momentarily when she pulled in. The car shook from the loud bass of whatever hip-hop song she had blasting inside.

"Oh my God, I'm so excited. Fuck, you look amazing, girl." She bounced a little in her seat and held the steering wheel, a giant smile on her face, as I climbed in.

I leaned over and planted a giant kiss on her cheek. "I've missed you."

"Me too, Mia. Got everything?" She applied a layer of lip-gloss before smacking her lips together and checking her reflection in the rearview mirror.

I nodded at her with butterflies in my stomach. "Yep, let's hit it."

Lori and I met in college. I was pre-med and she was pre-law. We became thick as thieves sophomore year. Any free moment we had, and there weren't as many as we wished, we spent together at the beach or clubs. We danced our asses off and loved every minute of it.

When college ended and the real world sucked us in, we didn't have the time to hang out together and drink Coronas on the beach. We were lucky to see each other once a month, and to get everyone together had become virtually impossible.

We could go without speaking for weeks and pick up right where we left off. She was *that* kind of friend. I envied her beauty, though. Her blonde hair had a wave that I couldn't achieve, no matter how hard I tried. Her crystal-blue eyes sparkled in the light, and her teeth were so white they almost glowed in the dark.

"Did I tell you I started seeing someone?" she asked, as she turned the radio down when Justin Bieber started to sing. His high-pitched girl voice made me cringe.

"No. You've been holding out on me."

When most people were getting married and starting their families, we were still in school, finishing our degrees before starting our careers. Families and marriage were put on the back burner. Now that we hovered around the big three-zero, we both felt a pang of jealousy and remorse that we may have missed out on so much for our careers.

"His name is Sal and we work together. We'd been eye fucking for months before things got interesting one night when we both worked late."

"Dirty girl, doing it at work." I shook my head and laughed.

"Jesus, I can't even describe what it's like being with him. The first time I could barely think. We were going over a case. We argued about how to win and he went all cavemen and threw me on the table. It was fuckin' hot."

"Mm, that sounds nice. So are you guys casual or are you officially a couple?" I felt a bit jealous. Hospitals weren't sexy.

"We're not officially dating. We are seeing other people, but then again, who the fuck has the time with our schedule?"

"So, you picked a Guido. Hmm."

"What's your issue with Italian men?" She looked at me, wrinkling her nose, before returning her eyes to the road.

"I don't have a problem with them. They're typically bossy and believe a woman's place is in the kitchen."

"He's not like that." Her blonde hair swayed as she shook her head.

"Mm-hmm, not yet, maybe."

"Bitch, don't rain on my parade." She laughed.

I loved Lori. "Never, doll."

"You seeing anyone?" she asked, just like she did every time we spoke.

My answer was the same: "No."

I tried the online dating sites and they ended in disaster. I didn't want to date someone that lived with their parents or enjoyed sitting at home playing video games.

My world consisted of doctors and nurses, and I wanted to escape that at the end of the workday, not date someone that would want to talk medicine.

"Haven't found the right one." I stared out the side window, watching the palm trees sway in the breeze.

"It's not easy for girls like us." She threw the money in the toll box and waited for the green light. We were close to Tampa and Ybor City. Ybor is one of the oldest parts of the city, with a unique history. Cigar factories used to line the streets, but were replaced with nightclubs and bars.

"I don't want to be anyone's sugar mama. I worked hard for everything I have. I will not have someone leech off me. I want a man, not a child. You know what I mean?"

"Agreed." She nodded. "Text Sarah and let her know we're close."

Lori rambled on about Sal and his amazing cock until we pulled into the parking lot. I smiled and nodded, letting her talk. I applied a little more lipstick as she turned off the car.

"I'm so happy you could come tonight, Mia."

"Me too, Lori. I need a night of dancing with my girls."

"Fuck music, let's get inside and find you some dick." She giggled.

"I don't think my Romeo's inside. I just want to dance and get shitfaced."

"I said dick, not your one true love, silly woman. You need a good fuck to remind you what life's all about," she said as we approached the long line filled with beautiful girls in skimpy outfits.

Lori pulled me forward, bypassing all the waiting people, straight to the bouncer. "Hey, Pete. This is my friend Mia." Lori kissed his cheek.

Pete's face softened with her kiss. His t-shirt looked painted on as it strained against his bulging biceps. His hair was cut in military fashion, flattop and perfect. Pete didn't look like someone you wanted to mess with.

He held out his hand to me. "Hi, Mia. It's nice to meet you," he said, bringing my hand to his lips and placing a gentle kiss on it.

There was no sizzle and pop. I wanted the spark, like Michael gave me, and although Pete had that sexy-as-fuck look, his lips did nothing for me.

"You too, Pete." I smiled, pulling my hand back.

"Your friends are inside waiting for you," Pete said, motioning toward the door.

"You're the best," Lori said, wrapping her arms around his waist.

"Only for you," he said, kissing her hair. "When are you going to go out with me, beautiful?"

"Pete," she said flatly.

"I don't give up easily. Can't blame a guy for trying." He shrugged and patted her ass. "Go on in before the line gets restless."

"Thanks again. Maybe we'll see you inside," she said as he opened the door for us.

The thump of the music made my chest rattle as we stood in the entrance, surveying the bar. People were everywhere, and the dance floor moved with the beat and didn't have a free spot on it.

We spotted Sarah and Jamie at the bar nursing their martinis and checking out the men. Jamie's red hair bounced as she shrieked and clapped when she saw us. She was typically overdramatic, but fun to be around, especially when she had a few too many to drink. She had on a kickass black dress and red heels showing off her long legs. Her thin frame swayed as she grabbed the bar top.

Sarah wrapped her arms around me. "Been too long, girl," she said in my ear. Sarah's blue eyes were glassy.

"I know. We have to do this more often." I checked out her outfit. "Damn, you look good, Sarah."

She grinned and twirled. "I've been working my ass off in the gym. I'm wearing a bikini this year if it kills me." She snapped her fingers, catching the attention of the bartender, and signaled for two more drinks. "He's delicious, isn't he?" Sarah asked, watching him move in the tight space. "I'm taking him home as a treat." She laughed, as her eyes remained glued to his body.

"Always on the prowl," Lori said, before becoming enamored by his body too.

He placed our drinks on the bar and leaned over to whisper in Sarah's ear. Her lips turned up in an enormous smile, her eyes growing wide. He was definitely saying something X-rated. He backed away with a grin that could only be described as sinful. "Would you ladies like a shot?" he asked, never taking his eyes off Sarah.

"Hell yes," she said, still wearing the dopey smile he'd given her.

"A toast," Lori said as she raised her glass. "May your love last thousand years but come in six-inch increments."

We clinked our glasses together and laughed before taking a sip.

"Six seems a bit average, don't you think?" Jamie said as she wiped her lips with the back of her hand.

"Hey, when you're getting zero, six seems like fucking king dong."

"True, true." Jamie nodded and giggled.

"Drink those martinis, because the dance floor is calling my name," I said, grabbing the drink in front of me.

"I'd rather stand here and gawk at all the yummy hotness in this room," Lori replied.

"I know you would, Lori, but dance and gawk. Maybe you'll get felt up," I said around the rim of my martini glass.

"If I could be so lucky." She laughed as she finished the last of her drink. The others were ahead of us by a few sips and we had some catching up to do. "I'm usually the one doing the molesting, though." Lori sighed as she placed her glass on the bar.

Lori wasn't bashful, and made her intentions known to any man that caught her attention. We never judged her for going after what she wanted. Nine times out of ten, she hit a homerun, but I'd never been as forward as her.

"Fuck it," she said. "We're taking a taxi tonight, or sleeping at Sarah's place. I'm not going to be the sober one tonight."

When Prince's "Get Off" started to play, we ran screaming to the dance floor.

It reminded us of our college days, bringing us right back to where we all met at a frat party. The song was dirty as hell, and perfect. It wasn't the same song that we heard in the nineties—the DJ had spiced it up, making it techno—but the words were the same.

The mass of bodies moved to the rhythm, bumping and grinding with the music. I swayed, shaking my ass with the girls as we laughed. The colorful lights moved across the floor. I closed my eyes, getting lost in the beat. The alcohol made my legs feel weak as I continued to dance.

Running my fingers through my hair, I bumped into Sarah and leaned against her. We danced back to back, holding each other up. As I opened my eyes, I had the feeling that someone was staring at me.

I looked around and saw *him*. His eyes were focused on me.

My breathing stopped and my heart stuttered, as my body froze and I returned his stare.

I couldn't look away as he held my gaze. Leaning against the bar, he paid no attention to the man at his side. He raked his eyes up and down my body, and I felt flushed as heat crept up my chest to my neck.

"Why'd ya stop?" Sarah yelled from behind me.

All I could do was shake my head. My body felt frozen in place and my eyes were zeroed in on *him*.

Mike, the brick wall from the gym, stood there, watching me.

The dark pants and a crisp white dress shirt with the sleeves rolled up showed off the tattoos on his forearms. He looked calm and collected, but his eyes were fierce and pierced right through me.

The butterflies in my stomach from earlier came back with a vengeance.

What were the odds that I'd run into him again? Did he follow me or was it some cosmic force pushing us together?

"Mia, are you okay?" Sarah asked, as she stepped in front of me, breaking our eye contact.

My cheeks heated as I exhaled. "Yeah, I'm fine. Let's dance." I turned my back to where he stood, and focused on the music, trying to forget he was there.

Watching me.

5

MICHAEL

"Dude, you okay?" Anthony asked, nudging me in the shoulder.

I couldn't take my eyes off her. "Yeah."

"Who you looking at?"

I motioned toward her with my chin before taking a sip of my beer. "Her," I said.

"The blonde?"

"Fuck no, the brunette in the short jeans." She looked fucking edible.

"You gonna go talk to her?"

"Not yet." The connection was there—a strong enough one that she felt me staring and stopped dead in her tracks. I'd never had an issue with pursuing a woman, but based on her reaction to me at the gym, I'd wait before I approached her.

"Never took you for a pussy." Anthony laughed and slapped my shoulder.

She leaned into her blonde friend and turned.

Fucking women, I'd never figure them out.

The blonde looked over her shoulder at me. Her face lit up before she spoke something into her friend's ear. They danced and laughed, and I became transfixed by the scene before me. Their bodies moved together, hips bumping, tits shaking, and I wanted to go on the dance floor and take her right there.

I swear to shit, God wanted to punish me, and used my cock to do it.

Her face shimmered, and her hair flew through the air haphazardly as they danced together. I envisioned her beneath me, on top of me, and against the wall, re-enacting her moves.

I sipped my beer, the bottle gripped tightly in my hand, as I felt the familiar throb in my dick.

When the song ended, they stood in the center of the dance floor and laughed. I didn't move. I called her over with my finger.

She shook her head, and started dancing when the next song started.

Fuck.

I thought I had the market cornered on cockiness, but she could be *stiff* competition.

Facing me, she put her hands above her head and shook her ass.

I caught a glimpse at her stomach muscles, and I wanted to run my tongue over the smooth skin. It met her hips to create a fuckin' knockout figure.

A man placed his hands on her hips, and she froze, holding my gaze. The cocky grin on her face disappeared, replaced with a pissed-off sneer. She slapped his hand away, but he didn't let go.

What the fuck?

I didn't want the sleazy bastard to have his hands all over her. I couldn't blame the guy, but you don't touch a woman unless she wants you to.

Clearly she didn't.

She turned to face him, her arms waving in the air as she laid into the guy.

His eyes grew large but he didn't back away.

I moved closer to them and waited for the moment to step in. I couldn't let her handle this guy alone.

He reached for her waist, but before he gripped her, her knee rose and met his balls in one quick thrust.

Ouch.

I winced, knowing the pain that just shot through his body. I smiled, knowing he deserved it, as he clutched himself, rolling back and forth on the dance floor.

"Fucker, when I say keep your hands to yourself, I fucking mean it!" she roared.

Clearing my throat, I drew her attention away from the asshole at her feet. I wanted to touch her, but thought better after what I just witnessed.

I liked my balls too damn much to let that shit happen.

She turned slowly, her eyes growing wide as they flickered to the floor. "Hey," she said as I caught a glimpse of her small smile.

"That was quite impressive. You took him down pretty hard."

"Thank you. I have bony knees," she said, laughing. She looked too sweet and angelic to have just taken down the overgrown asshole writhing on the tile floor.

"I don't think we were properly introduced earlier. I'm Michael, and you are?" I held my hand out, wanting to touch her skin again.

She placed her tiny fingers in my palm. "I'm Mia."

I closed my fingers around her small hand, lifting it to my mouth. "You smell different than this morning." I kissed the delicate flesh on the top of her hand gently.

Her scent was sweet and reminded me of fresh-baked cookies. I couldn't forget her flowery scent from this morning.

She laughed, and her eyes twinkled. Honest to God, fucking twinkled.

"Not being a creep. Just making an observation." I'd never been such a dumbass with a woman before. She made me nervous and turned me into a horny teenaged boy.

"It's my lotion. Vanilla Bean Noel." Her cheeks turned pink as she looked behind her and waved to her friends.

"You smell like a cupcake." I licked my lips and now felt like the creep. "Can I buy you a drink, Mia?" I needed to do something to break the awkwardness and my inability to stop saying stupid shit in front of her.

Her eyes returned to mine, the corner of her mouth turned up before she answered, "Sure, Michael."

I held my hand out, letting her walk in front of me. Her hips swayed as she sauntered to the bar. I wanted to smack her ass for the wicked shit it did to my cock.

Leaning against the bar, shoulder to shoulder with her, I motioned for the bartender. "What'll it be? Pick your poison."

I expected her to say she wanted a girlie drink, something that required an umbrella, but I would've been dead fucking wrong.

"Dirty martini, please. Straight up, with extra olives."

The bartender approached, giving Mia the once-over.

It took everything in me not to punch his fucking lights out as he lingered a little too long on her chest.

"What can I get you?" he asked her without looking in my direction.

"Another beer, and a dirty martini straight up with extra olives for the lady," I said, without caring who he asked.

I wanted to take the rag he had in his hand and stuff it down his throat. He gave me a sour face before leaving us. I threw a twenty on the bar, trying to avoid as much contact between him and Mia as possible.

Mia began to laugh as he walked away. "Are you two going to have a pissing match next?"

Her laughter was infectious.

"I didn't like the way he looked at you."

"Used to being the center of attention?" she asked, with a cocked eyebrow and a grin.

"No. Are you clueless to the way he just eye raped you, woman?"

Her grin turned into a giant smile. "He's a man. It's what you *all* do."

"Glad you think so highly of us." I leveled my gaze and grabbed the beer that had been left for me.

"How would you describe how you were looking at me on the dance floor?" she challenged.

"I wasn't eye raping you, sweetheart."

"Call it what you want. Your eyes told a different story, Michael."

"What'd they say?"

"Something along the lines of, 'You and me and a *little* tryst in the bathroom stall.'"

She was a feisty little thing.

"You wouldn't go home with me if I asked?"

She coughed, almost spitting out her drink. "No, not even after five of these babies," she said as she held up her glass before taking another sip.

"I like a challenge. I don't like to lose, either."

She smiled over the rim of her glass. "I've never been called a quitter."

I never liked easy.

My life had been filled with hard choices and challenges that kept me moving to bigger and better things.

Everything came easy to my family. We grew up with money, not the kind that Paris Hilton had that caused her to turn into a fucking train wreck, but my parents made sure we never wanted for anything.

"What do you do, Mia? What makes you tick, besides kneeing a man in the balls?"

She placed her glass on the bar and twirled it in her fingers. "I'm in medicine."

I couldn't take my eyes off her mouth. Her lips were full and red from the lip-gloss, or whatever shit she had coating them. I wanted to know if it tasted like strawberry.

"You're a nurse?" I felt like I had to pull information out of her.

She turned toward me with her mouth set in a firm line. "No. I'm a doctor."

I whistled, being thoroughly impressed by the statement.

Dr. Mia was sexy as hell, and had a brain to match. "Impressive. What kind?"

"I work in the emergency room at County."

"Wow, that's some hard shit. Wait, that's where I know you from." Her sassy mouth, beautiful looks, and sparkling hazel eyes made it all click when she said "County Hospital ER."

"You do?" Her brows shot up as her eyes grew wide. "I hope it wasn't for anything too horrible."

"Cracked ribs a couple months back. You called me a cocky bastard, I believe," I said, smiling as I remembered her playfulness.

The corner of her mouth twitched as she tilted her head. "Ah, it's all coming back to me now. I knew I met you before. Sorry I was mean to you." She blushed.

"Nah, I liked it when you called me that. You said you'd go to dinner with me, and I'm holding you to your word."

Her brows knitted together as her eyes moved around my face. "I don't remember it that way. If memory serves me right, I told you no."

245

"You were supposed to come back after the x-ray, but you sent in some schmuck instead. You blew me off."

She snickered as her eyes flickered to her drink. "Michael, I don't remember blowing you off. It gets hectic, and another patient probably needed my attention more than you."

"I don't envy you, doc. You work a stressful job. I couldn't do it."

"Some days are harder than others." A flash of sadness splashed across her face before quickly disappearing. "It has its rewards too."

"I give you a lot of credit. To hold someone's life in your hands is some heavy shit, and a lot of responsibility."

"Some days I question my sanity. I wonder why I didn't settle for a nice family practice with an office, treating the flu, but I'd probably grow bored quickly."

"Ah, you like the rush," I said, rubbing my chin and studying her body language.

"Yeah, I guess I do. What do you do, Michael, besides fighting?"

"Ah, you remember me now. I'm part-owner of a tattoo shop, where I pierce the willing, but my true love is fighting."

"I spend my nights repairing damage that people like you inflict."

I saw the flash of sadness again before it disappeared. That wasn't the reaction I expected. "I never do anything that isn't asked of me, whether it's in the shop or the cage. Which one are we talking about here?"

"The fighting." Her face hadn't changed.

Most women cooed when they found out, but Mia? Nothing.

"I don't street fight—cage matches, MMA style. They're professional. I have a big one coming up." I smiled and felt proud to be able to utter those words, but Mia still didn't seem impressed, with her lips set in a firm line as she brought the martini glass to her lips.

"Still, it's the opposite of my job. I help people and heal them and you injure them. Maybe they spend more time injuring you. I don't know." She cocked her eyebrow at me and took a sip.

"Don't be silly, woman. It's a job. We all go into the cage knowing someone isn't coming out looking as pretty as they did when they went in. All injuries heal. And wait a minute here…you just injured the hell out of that douchebag. He'll probably never be able to have children because of that wicked knee."

"Fighting for money is barbaric." She shook her head, but I didn't buy her distaste for the sport. "What I did was self-preservation. There's a difference." She looked me straight in the eye and didn't blink.

A bullshitter could smell another bullshitter a mile away.

"Liar." I brushed my fingers against her arm, and she shivered with the contact.

Maybe she didn't like what I did, but I could tell it turned her on.

She didn't smile, but there was a twinkle in her eyes. Her body responded to mine...no matter how hard she tried to deny it.

6

MIA

"I DON'T CONDONE VIOLENCE." THE WORDS FELL FROM MY LIPS IN A FLAT tone, even as my body still vibrated from his touch.

Traitor.

My body betrayed me when Michael touched me. I tried to play it cool.

"Not buying it." He lifted the beer to his lips and took a sip.

I stared at them as they hugged the rim of the glass.

I wanted to smack the cocky grin off his face. His rich brown eyes sparkled, and were filled with mischief as he called me a liar. His words were true no matter how hard I wanted to deny them. Michael was pure man—strong, sexy, and self-confident.

"Can we agree to disagree?" I asked, pretending not to look at his mouth.

He licked the beer from his lips. I had the overwhelming urge to use my tongue to capture the few drops of liquid still left behind. "Want a taste?" he asked with a hearty laugh as he tipped the beer in my direction.

I could feel the blush as it crept up my neck. I wanted to avoid his eyes but couldn't give him the satisfaction. I always believed in fighting fire with fire.

"You missed a little," I said before I reached up and used my thumb to wipe the few drops on his lips.

His eyes stayed locked with mine as I touched his soft flesh, slowing dragging my fingers across his skin.

I placed my thumb in my mouth, closing my lips around it.

He leaned in close enough for me to smell the musky cologne on his neck. "You're wicked," he whispered, his lips brushing against my ear.

Pulling my thumb from my lips, I replied, "I'm just getting started, hot stuff."

He backed away and stared at me before giving me a giant smile. "I may have met my match with you, Mia."

"I'll drink to that." I couldn't help but smile. I forgot how much fun it could be to flirt with someone, especially when they were handsome and a smooth talker.

He made it easy and made me feel sexy.

At work, I never felt sexy wearing my drab scrubs and knee-length lab coat, and with my hair up in a ponytail. I looked half dead by the time my shift ended at the hospital.

"Shot?" he asked.

"I've given thousands," I replied, laughing at my hospital humor.

"You're difficult, Mia." He eyed me as he fiddled with the beer.

"You have no idea, Michael." I laughed, wanting to throw myself at him and give in to any wild sexual ideas he currently had, but I wouldn't allow myself to be so reckless. "What do you have in mind?"

He looked me straight in the eye and didn't crack a smile. "Blue balls."

"Seems like a personal problem. I could write you a prescription, if you'd like."

"Um, fuck no to a prescription, but I'm sure it's nothing you couldn't fix." He smirked. "Wanna help me out?"

I leaned forward, my lips almost touching his as I said, "Usually when someone walks in with an erection that won't subside, we drain the fluid with a very large needle. I'm a pro. Interested in seeing my skills firsthand?"

His mouth hung open as he gaped. "That's just inhumane. I mean,

Jesus, Mia, how could you do that to another human being?" He stepped back, shaking his head.

"Better than it having to be amputated from lack of circulation. So, what did you want to drink, again?" I smiled until my cheek muscles ached. I couldn't remember the last time I had smiled or laughed as much as I had with him tonight.

"Lemon drop. Let's skip the blue balls," he said, swallowing hard, probably still reeling from the thought of the long needle in his dick.

"Good choice, and they're my favorite."

"I gotcha." He looked away and motioned to the bartender.

I studied him as he ordered our drinks. Without talking to him, I'd think he was just another meathead muscle guy without the ability to think quickly and hold a witty conversation, but I would've been dead wrong.

Michael was a conundrum to me—brains, brawn, and beauty. His eyes moved in my direction for a moment, but his attention was drawn away from me by the clinking of the glasses on the bar.

Grinning, he slid the clear liquid in front of me. "What shall we drink to?" he asked as he placed the sugar-soaked lemons in between us.

"To blue balls?" I asked, holding up the shot glass.

"Fuck that shit. Don't ever mention that to me again," he said, picking up his glass. "To new beginnings." He raised his glass and tapped it against mine.

Warmth cascaded throughout my body before the liquid ever touched my lips. I didn't want to read into his words and feel like a fool, but the thought of getting to know this sexy-as-hell man made my toes curl. "Cheers."

I watched him over the rim; he stared at me, never wavering, and I winked as the liquid slid down my throat. It burned for a moment, and I winced from the vodka before I slammed the glass down. I reached for the lemon, needing something to cover the taste of the vodka. He was one step ahead of me, and already had the lemon in his hand.

I blinked slowly. The martini and shot coursing through my system was already starting to cloud my vision. Opening my lips, I stuck out my tongue and waited for him to place the lemon on it.

I closed my lips around his fingers as the sugar made my mouth water. Running my tongue across the coarse pads of his fingers, I sucked the juice and swallowed. His eyes narrowed as he watched my mouth with parted lips.

I had him right where I wanted him. Two could play games.

"Fuck me," he muttered, and looked away as I opened my lips, allowing his fingers to slide out.

"You okay? You look a little off." I covered my mouth with my hand, trying to hide my laughter.

He leaned in, brushing the hair away from my shoulder. "If you keep that shit up, I'm going to find another way to occupy your mouth."

I'd like to say it was the alcohol that caused him to have that effect on me, but I'd be lying. "I don't know what you mean."

He wrapped his fingers around the back of my neck, bringing his lips within centimeters of mine. "You know exactly what you're doing to me. Let's not play games here, Mia." He searched my eyes.

I could feel his warm breath against my lips, and my heart pounded in my chest faster than the rhythm of the music. Looking into his eyes without blinking, I melted against him. "Who said I'm playing, Michael."

I wanted him to kiss me.

He inched close, eyes locked with mine, as I placed my hand against his chest. The rapid tattoo of his heart thumped against my palm, matching the beat of mine.

Leaning forward, I closed my eyes and held my breath. Butterflies filled my stomach and my legs trembled. The warmth of his lips sent shivers down my body.

The noise around us disappeared as he kissed me. Nothing else seemed to exist except him and me.

As I tipped my head back, his grip on the back of my neck increased as he pulled me against his rock-hard chest. The feel of him against me was amazing as he kissed me perfectly. Not too much lip, a dash of tongue as he held me against him. I moaned into his mouth as he bit my bottom lip. I sighed against his mouth, melting into his touch—I wanted to be closer to him.

His tongue soothed the spot that he'd just sunk his teeth into, and my sex convulsed from the tenderness.

We became one, lost in each other.

Pulling away, he whispered, "Damn." He rubbed his knuckles against my collarbone, before releasing his grip on my neck.

Instantly I missed the warmth of his palm. My body swayed, as I stood there in a daze, blinking as I tried to regain my ability to think. Dumbfounded and in a fog from his kiss, I stood there like an idiot, with a grin on my face.

7

MICHAEL

"SEE ME AGAIN." I WASN'T ASKING.

It was a simple statement, and I thought I'd use the moment to my advantage.

"I know you're busy, but I'll make time for you," I said as I gripped her hand, squeezing it.

Her eyes closed and opened slowly before she peered into my eyes. "My life is hectic, Michael. I don't have a normal schedule." She frowned and looked at our hands as I stroked her fingers.

"Fuck normal, Mia. Do you want to see me again or not?" I cocked my head and stared into her shimmering hazel eyes.

"I do." Her face was soft as her frown melted away and her eyes flickered back to mine.

"Tomorrow," I said. "I want to take you to dinner."

"I'm off tomorrow; beyond that I can't make any promises, Michael."

"Give me your phone, doc."

She fumbled as she dug inside her purse, pulling out her phone.

I grabbed it, not letting her back out now, and dialed my number. Smiling, I snapped a quick photo and attached it to my number in her contacts. "I have your number and you have mine. What time do you want me to pick you up?"

CHELLE BLISS

She waved her hands in the air and scrunched her lips. "I can drive," she said, narrowing her eyes.

"I'm driving and paying. No arguments." I wanted to surprise her and hopefully make that sassy-ass mouth speechless. "What time, Mia?" I asked.

"Is six okay? I have to work the next—"

I rested my finger against her lips. "Six is perfect. Text me your address and wear something sexy."

"Yes, sir," she said, giggling before saluting me.

I liked her smartass attitude. She'd sure as hell keep me on my toes.

I grabbed her hand and brought the soft skin to my lips. Inhaling the vanilla scent, I peeked up at her face as I kissed it. She watched me with parted lips and wide eyes. "Until tomorrow, Mia. I don't want to keep you from your friends any longer."

"Tomorrow," she whispered.

I waited for her to disappear into the crowd before trying to find Anthony. He sat on a couch against the wall with a group of girls surrounding him. They were enthralled by the topic of conversation…him.

"Where ya playing next?" the blonde sitting to his right asked, as she stroked his leg.

"Yeah, we want to come see you in action." The brunette bounced in her seat.

I rolled my eyes as my brother looked at me and grinned. "Ladies, this is my brother Mike. He's a fighter."

Fucker.

The last thing I needed or fucking wanted was the attention of these "ladies," as Anthony so nicely put it.

"Oooh," cooed the blonde as she slithered away from him and turned toward me.

"Ready to hit it?" I asked, ignoring them. I didn't feel like making small talk.

"Sure, man." He pushed himself up and kissed their hands. "Next Saturday at the Ritz. I'm going to see each and every one of you, right?"

They replied "yes" and nodded with conviction.

I grabbed his shirt, pulling him away from his *fans*. "You're such a whore at times, Anth."

"I know. Whatever fills the seats, Mike. What girl doesn't like a rocker?" He shrugged and waved at them over his shoulder as we walked away. "Hey, can we stop by the Ritz? I want to ask the owner a quick question."

"Not a problem."

"Tell me about the girl you were talking to," he said as he slapped my shoulder.

I looked at him and laughed. "She's not who she seems to be." Sometimes there are things you keep close to the vest—especially in my big-mouth family.

"I saw her knee that guy in the balls. She seems pretty hardcore."

"She's something else. Impressed the hell out of me, really."

"Hmm," he said as we made our way toward the Ritz.

"What the fuck does 'hmm' mean?"

"Nothing. I think you need a ball buster in your life," he said through a laugh.

"Forget about it, brother."

"Did you make a plan to see her again?" He eyed me with one eyebrow cocked and a silly-ass grin on his face.

"Yes," I answered, as I stopped walking and looked at him.

"Maybe she'll break you."

"I don't need that shit in my life," I said, leaving him to catch up.

"You need to let loose a little, but in the right way. Maybe she's just what the doctor ordered."

"You have no idea, Anthony." I laughed as I grabbed the door handle, opening it to the most ear-shattering guitar riff known to man, and followed Anthony inside.

I leaned against the wall, watching the band as they played for their screaming fans. The looks on their faces reminded me of watching Anthony when he was entertaining the crowds.

His adrenaline rush came from the people that watched him like a rock god, and mine came from beating the piss out of someone.

When I fought, the blood pumped through my body so rapidly that I could almost feel it moving. It's hard to describe to another person. Every muscle in my body grows rigid and screams for release. My breathing increases to the point I feel like my lungs will burst if I suck in any more air. When I step into the ring, everything else fades away. I feel like a warrior, fighting for the thrill and challenge. There's so much adrenaline in my system that I barely feel the blows of my opponent as they land against my body, sometimes crushing my bones.

"I'm ready," Anthony said as he tapped me on the shoulder.

I'd been so lost in my thoughts I didn't notice his approach.

"Yeah. This place gives me a headache."

"Wait until we play here. We're going to blow the roof off this motherfucker."

His smile touched his eyes as he pumped his fists in the air. Anthony didn't care about playing music to make a living; he simply did it for the thrill and the pussy.

He loved tattooing too much to ever give it up, but since we owned the shop, we made our own hours. We worked out a schedule so that at least two of us were there in the evenings.

"You're driving," I said as I threw the keys to him.

"Fuck yeah, I love driving this truck. Bitch purrs when I got her in my clutches."

"Just get my ass home in one piece and stop talking nasty."

Sometimes I wanted to punch him, but I loved the big bastard too much to bloody his face.

"Just don't wreck her," I said as he pulled into traffic.

"I should've been an Indy driver. I feel the need, the need for speed," he hollered as he gunned it.

"Shut the fuck up and drive," I mumbled before closing my eyes, not really wanting to watch his idea of NASCAR.

8

MIA

THROWING DOWN MY BAG, I REACHED OVER THE COUNTER AND GRABBED the phone. Cammie was busy helping a patient book their next appointment.

"Hello?" I said as I surveyed the crowded waiting room.

"I need an appointment as soon as possible," the lady yelled in the phone, panic evident in her voice. "There's something wrong with my baby."

"Is the baby able to breath?"

"Yes," she cried. "She has a fever and is coughing, help me."

"How high is the fever?"

"103.1."

"Bring her in right away. I'll see you immediately. Hurry."

"Thank you," she said before the line went dead.

"Girl, you know we're booked. Whatcha doin'?" Cammie, the slightly round and always bubbly receptionist, asked.

"It's a mom, Cam. You know I can never say no when there's a kid involved."

"Oh Lord, child. Are you going to have time to see her with all this?" She waved her hand toward the waiting room and grimaced.

"Yes, Cammie, I'll make the time. Let me know as soon as she gets here. I'm going to put everything away and I'll come grab a chart."

"It's a full house today. I brewed a fresh pot of coffee—from the looks of you, you'll need it." Cammie felt like a fill-in for my mom when she wasn't around.

"Glad to know I look like shit, Cam," I said. "Thanks."

"Not shit, just tired, Mia. I know you don't sleep well; that's why I always have a fresh pot on hand when you're here. Now, get your butt to work, Mia." She swatted my ass. "We have souls to heal."

"Yes, ma'am."

I put away the free medication I was able to score courtesy of the pharmaceutical rep that visited the hospital this week, before grabbing a chart off the counter and diving right in.

"Mr. Needlemyer," I said from the doorway.

He looked up at me and a smile broke out across his face. "Ah, Dr. G," he said as he pushed himself off the chair, struggling with the simple task. "Looking beautiful as always."

"How are you feeling, Mr. N?" I asked, as he approached.

"Like an old fart." He snorted.

"I hope I look half as good as you when I'm your age." I smiled at him, patting him on the shoulder.

"Eh, looks are deceiving. My insides are worn out, but if I were just a few years younger…" He gave me a wink.

I slapped his knee as he sat down on the exam table. "Mr. N., come on now."

Since the first day I met him, he'd flirted with me… relentlessly.

"So tell me, how are you really feeling? Any problems like dizziness, fatigue, or any changes since last time I saw you?" I flipped through his chart, checking his vitals from his last visit.

"I feel about as good as I can for a man my age. Nothing new to report, doc. Right as rain."

I listened to his heart, checked his lungs, and felt his lymph glands before I wrote a refill for his blood pressure and cholesterol pills.

He sat on the exam table and watched me as he fidgeted with his hands.

"Something you want to ask me, Mr. N?"

"Well, um, kind of. I've been seeing this special lady. I wanted to talk to you about that little blue pill. Can I take it?"

"Do you need it? That's the more important question." I inched closer to him so we could talk a bit quieter. "Do you have a problem getting and maintaining an erection?"

His face turned pink as he looked away, momentarily avoiding my gaze. "I don't think so, but it's been so long since I've been with a woman. My wife died over five years ago. I don't know if the ol' pipes still work," he said, giving me a weak smile.

"Ever had any trouble in the past?"

"Never." He shook his head, looking down.

"With your medical history, I wouldn't feel comfortable prescribing it. If you have trouble with your lady, call me and I'll help you out."

"Doc, be still my beating heart."

"You know what I mean, Mr. Needlemyer." I blushed.

Did men ever lose their dirty minds?

"I do. If I have any problems with," he said, coughing, "I'll call you."

"Here are your refills, and I'll see you next month; just make an appointment with Cammie on your way out."

"Wishful thinking at my age."

"You'll be fine," I said as I laid my hand on his. A knock on the door made him jump. "Yes?" I called out.

"The mother is here with her child," Cammie yelled through the door.

"Coming," I said. "Mr. Needlemyer, I need to go, but remember to call me if you have any problems." I closed the chart and stood.

"Go ahead, doc. I'll be fine."

"Thanks, Mr. N." I waved to him as I shut the door and headed to the waiting room.

I knew there was joy in motherhood, but I'd always seen the other side, where children are sick or injured, and the panic in the mothers' eyes. I wasn't ready to become a mother, not yet. I had a career to focus on and a life to live before I invited a bundle of joy into my life.

After examining the baby and determining that she had a lung infection, I gave the mother antibiotics and directions to help her breathe easier. She left the clinic feeling relieved and looking calm.

The rest of the day was a blur—countless patients with various illnesses. At four o'clock the waiting room had finally emptied. I'd been so busy I didn't spend much time thinking about Michael.

I had a couple hours to get ready for him to pick me up. It'd been a long time since I'd been on a real date.

I wondered sometimes why men didn't ask me out, or never called me for a second date. I think I'm a good catch. I have my shit together... maybe a little too together and independent for some guys.

"Where you rushing off to, doc?" Cammie asked as I tried to sneak out the door.

"I just have some things to do," I replied, stopping in the doorway.

I never was a good liar.

I could see the giant smile spread across her face. She slammed her hand on the desk and began to laugh. "You go, girl. I want all the details. Shoo now," she said, waving her hands at me.

I blew her a kiss, stepped out into the warm sunshine, and felt a sense of renewed hope.

The clinic didn't leave me zapped of energy and emotionally drained like the hospital.

***

I twirled the razor in my hand and debated with myself about shaving. If I shaved, I felt like I hoped the night would end with a roll in the hay. If I didn't shave, it guaranteed that I wouldn't commit a carnal sin.

Running my fingers over my shin, I could feel the prickle of hair. I sighed and caved, deciding to forgo the European look.

I carefully shaved, then rinsed out the heavy conditioner in my hair before climbing out of the shower. The mirror had fogged over, and I opened the door to let in some of the cool air. I had one hour to blow dry, do my makeup, and get dressed.

I towel dried my hair a little first before walking into my closet to pick out something sexy, as Michael had requested. I found the perfect little black dress that had a very low-cut back and stopped just below the knee. It showed just the right amount of cleavage, but it wasn't trampy. It made people stop and stare.

I wanted his eyes on me tonight, and no one else.

I did my best to do a smoky eye, as they call it in all the fashion magazines. I dried my hair before finishing the rest of my makeup.

As the minutes ticked away, my heart started to pound. I could feel my blood pressure rising. I felt flushed and clammy.

I blotted the thin layer of dampness from my skin just before six and then pulled the dress over my head carefully before strapping on my favorite black heels with the red bottoms.

The day I was able to afford to buy myself a pair was the day I knew I could take care of myself—I'd arrived and stood on my own two feet.

I looked in the mirror one last time and turned around, making sure my underwear didn't show and that everything was in the right place.

"It's just a date. I got this." My pep talk helped a little, until the door-bell rang. I'd never really felt nervous on a date before, but there was something different about him.

"Coming," I yelled, as I walked through the house, grabbing my purse and keys.

I opened it to the stunning man leaning against the doorframe, with the sexiest grin on his face.

He whistled, his eyes raking over my body before landing on my face. "Fucking beautiful. Turn around," he said, twirling his finger in the air. "Absolutely stunning." He held his hand out.

"Thank you. You're looking pretty damn good yourself."

He did, too. Wearing a sky-blue dress shirt, tucked into his black pants, the sleeves rolled halfway up his forearms. He looked like he just stepped out of *GQ* magazine.

His mouth enveloped mine as soon as I locked the door and faced him. Pulling my body against him, claiming my lips with as much fervor as he had the night before, he stole my breath. His hand on the small of my back felt like a hot iron against my skin, searing into me.

"Ready?" he asked, as he released me.

"Yes," I said, a little too breathily.

He helped me into his pick-up truck before closing the door and jogging around to the driver side. The truck was modern and decked out. It wasn't a redneck truck but a total boy toy, black and trimmed in chrome.

"Where are we headed?" I asked, pulling my dress down to my knees.

"Sunset Beach for dinner." He adjusted and gripped the steering wheel tightly as he glanced at my legs.

"There isn't a restaurant there."

"I know." Resting his arm behind my head, he backed out of the drive.

I uncrossed my legs and shifted in my seat, and he glanced down before looking back toward the road.

"What did you do today?" he asked.

"Worked at the free clinic in town, and you?"

"I worked out and went to the shop for a couple hours. Tell me about the clinic."

I told him about the work we did, and the residents in the county that lacked simple things like medicine and insurance. He listened intently and asked questions throughout our conversation.

"Kids too?" he asked with a furrowed brow.

"They're the saddest to see." I frowned, looking out the window.

He rested his hand on my knee and squeezed, causing a wave of warmth to emanate through my body. "I never knew there was such a problem."

"Homelessness and poverty is pervasive in this area, Michael. Under-employment is almost an epidemic."

"Is there anything I can do to help?" His eyes were soft when he looked at me, waiting for the traffic light.

"Not unless you have a medical degree." I laughed.

"Don't have that, but there has to be another way I can help. My family does a lot of charity work. My parents are huge in helping people in the area."

"Maybe. We do have a small fundraiser coming up. Last year we raised ten thousand dollars, which helped us update some of the equipment in the clinic, but there's so much more that's needed."

I didn't really want to ask for his help, but if his family already helped organizations in the area, I couldn't turn it down.

"I honestly have never heard of it. I'm sure my family would love to help."

"It's very kind of you, Michael." I smiled at him. His kindness made me feel giddy.

"I've always had a soft spot for kids."

"Do you have any of your own?" I didn't want to pry, but I wanted to know his situation.

Did he have a crazy-ass ex or a gaggle of kids running around all over town that I needed to be aware of before we went any further?

"No kids, you?"

"No, I barely have time to date with work, let alone have a child."

"You shouldn't work so much, Mia. Life's too short not to enjoy it."

Staring out the window, I thought about his words. I did enjoy my life, didn't I? "I do enjoy my life," I said without conviction.

"Are you telling me or trying to convince yourself?" he asked, as we pulled into the deserted parking lot.

"Where's everyone? I've never seen the parking lot empty before."

"It's closed for a private event."

Giving him a confused look, I asked, 'Then why are we here?"

He turned off the engine and turned toward me. "I rented the beach for tonight. It's all ours."

"I don't know what to say," I said as he climbed out of the truck. "Does this man know how to do anything small?" I mumbled, as I reached down and removed my heels before he opened the door.

"Great idea," he said as he looked at my feet. He kicked off his dress shoes and threw them on the driver's-side floor before helping me down.

A small white canopy sat in the distance, near the edge of the crashing waves. The sand felt hot on my soles, the sun still beating against the small glass crystals. It was like walking on warm pillows as it squished between my toes.

"Thank you," I said as I stared at the waves crashing against the shore.

"For what?" he asked, sliding his hand into mine.

"The beach at sunset. It's one of my favorite places and I rarely get to come here." I squeezed his hand, feeling completely at peace.

"It's one of my favorites, too. Great for thinking and getting away from it all," he said as we approached the canopy.

A small, round table was in the middle, decorated with a white linen tablecloth, fine white china, wine glasses, and candles. The floor was the warm sand, and a chandelier hung from the beams. Soft music filled the air, along with the warm breeze flowing off the ocean waves.

It may have been the single most romantic date I'd ever had.

"You did all this in a couple hours?" I asked, in shock.

"I have mad skills, and connections don't hurt either." He laughed.

"I may have underestimated you, Michael," I said as I kissed his cheek and inhaled his musky scent, mixed with the salty ocean air.

"Most people do," he said as he pulled out my chair.

Leaning over, I brushed my fingers against his cheek. "You're sweet," I said, wanting to kiss him.

Grabbing my hand, he planted a sensual kiss on the inside of my wrist, making my knees feel weak. If he kept this up, my panties would be wetter than the sand after high tide.

"Thanks," I said, sitting as I brushed the bottom of my dress against my legs.

Michael lifted my chair off the ground, tucking my legs under the table before taking a seat across from me.

A man dressed in a tuxedo poured champagne and smiled at us both.

Michael looked at me, raising his glass. "A toast," he said, tilting his head.

I grabbed my glass, holding it up to his.

"To new beginnings." He clinked his glass against mine.

That was the second time he'd used that phrase. A warm, gooey feeling oozed through my body as I sipped the champagne, letting the tiny bubbles pop on my tongue. We had run into each other less than forty-eight hours ago, but I felt comfortable with him—content.

I placed the glass on the table. "Tell me more about you," I said, rubbing my fingertips across the crystal stem.

"What would you like to know?" he asked, as he motioned to the gentleman.

"Are you a piercer or a fighter?"

Two dishes were placed in front of us. Each contained a mouthwatering steak with asparagus and a baked potato. The man grabbed my napkin off the table and placed it on my lap.

Looking at him, I smiled. "Thank you, sir."

"My pleasure," he said, before walking away and making himself busy.

"I'm part-owner in the tattoo shop. I don't have the artistic ability that the rest of my siblings have, so I learned everything I could about piercing. I've been doing it for years. I couldn't tattoo even if I wanted to. My hands get pretty messed up sometimes after a fight."

"I still can't wrap my head around the fact that you let someone hit you."

"Only if they're fast enough," he said as he laughed.

"Why?" I cut into my steak, avoiding his gaze.

"It's a rush, Mia. I can't explain it, but it's the greatest high ever."

"I still think it's barbaric."

"Street fighting is barbaric, not MMA matches. We both know what's going to happen. It's sport."

"Softball is a sport and much safer," I said, placing the steak on my tongue.

He laughed, and it was so genuine that it warmed my body from the inside out. "It's a sport for girls. No offense to you."

"None taken," I said as I waved my fork in the air. "Sexist, but I wouldn't expect anything less." I laughed, covering my mouth with the back of my hand.

"Hey, now. My sister would kick my ass if she thought I was sexist."

"Oh? Tell me about her. She sounds like my type of girl." I giggled.

"Yeah, you and Izzy would get along very well. She's the baby in the family, but we're all scared of her. She's an *in your face* kind of girl. She takes no shit, but I guess that happens when you grow up with four brothers."

"She's lucky. Sounds like a great way to grow up."

"She'd see it differently."

"Why?" I asked with a frown. "I'm an only child, and I always wanted someone to play with as a kid."

"She didn't get many dates as a teenager." He laughed. "We scared most of them away."

"I could only imagine, but she was lucky to have brothers that cared."

"You'll have to tell her that."

"So, there are three more of you walking around?"

"Yeah. We're all very different. My brother Thomas is an undercover cop, Anthony likes to call himself a musician, and Joseph is just a tattooist."

"Your poor mother." I shook my head and sipped the champagne.

"She kept trying for a girl, which she got after four boys. Now she wants grandchildren." He smirked at me.

"Oh." My stomach flipped from the look on his face.

He was so drop-dead gorgeous, I'd almost be willing to drop my panties and start working on making her dream a reality.

"Enough about kids. Tell me about your family, Mia." He wiped his mouth and set his napkin on the table.

"My parents are snowbirds, and right now they're back in Minnesota. It's just me here, but I would never move back to the freezing cold."

"Cold has some good points." He rested his head on his hands and watched me as I cut the last piece of steak on my plate.

"Like what?"

"Lying by a fire and being snowed in together."

"Those are the only positives. I think more of scraping my car windows, shoveling snow, frostbite, and other crappy things that go with Minnesota life."

We stared at each other as I chewed the last morsel and finished off the champagne in the glass. The sun hovered over the ocean, and the sky blazed with the most beautiful shades of red and orange.

He stood, holding out his hand. "Come on, Mia, let's go watch the sunset."

"I thought we were," I said, placing my hand in his, feeling the electricity that sizzled between us.

"I want to be a little more comfortable for the show. I have a blanket that's calling our name."

Walking hand in hand, we snuck glances at each other as we approached the blanket. Suddenly I felt shy, and my stomach flipped as I sat down and he moved behind me.

"Come here," he said, placing his legs on either side of me and grabbing my hips.

I closed my eyes, inhaling sharply from the feel of his fingers digging into my flesh. I shimmied my body backward until our upper bodies connected. The warmth that permeated off him felt hotter than the setting sun hanging just above the horizon.

"Lean back, Mia," he whispered in my ear, sending a chill across my skin.

Placing my hands against his knees, I rested my head on his shoulder and stared at the sky. Peace overcame me as I sat straddled between his legs; our bodies connected, and we watched the changing colors over the water. His fingers traced a path around my ear to my neck and brushed the hair off my shoulder.

"It's so beautiful," I said as tears formed in my eyes.

"Not as beautiful as you. Are you crying?" he asked with knitted brows.

"I don't know," I said, laughing and wiping at the corners.

"Do you want me to take you home?" His lips brushed against my temple as he watched me.

"No," I said quickly.

"Then what's wrong, doc?" He wrapped his arm around my chest and gripped my shoulder.

"I'm going to sound crazy."

Damn it. How could I explain the peace and happiness I felt without sounding like a total wack job?

"I'd rather know than sit here and wonder why I've made you cry," he said, stroking my collarbone with his thumb.

I shook my head and sighed, relaxing against his body. "I'm stressed out after work, and sometimes it takes me days to shake off what I've seen at the hospital. It's been a long time since I felt truly at peace, but being here, in your arms and watching the sunset with the sound of the waves, I feel it—serenity that I haven't been able to find in so long."

"I can't imagine the things you've seen." He pulled my body closer, wrapping his arms around me, making me feel safe and secure, enveloped by his warmth and muscle.

"You don't want to, Michael. The people I've lost haunt me at night. I can't remember the last time I slept without a nightmare or sleeping pills." I placed my hand on his arm and squeezed. "So to have this brief moment where I'm reminded of the world's beauty and feel like only the two of us exist brings tears to my eyes. You chased away the demons, if only for a little while." I stared across the water, watching the sky turn purple as the sun kissed the edge of the world.

"Stay in the here and now. Nothing else matters but the two of us, on this beach, in each other's arms. I'm not going anywhere, are you?"

"We can't stay like this forever," I said, turning my face toward him.

"I'll stay as long as you need to help chase away your nightmares, Mia." Grabbing my chin, he pulled my mouth to his.

We stared at each other, and I searched his eyes. They were soft and kind and made my heart feel funny. Michael Gallo did not fit the mold of fighter bad boy. He was a romantic, and made me feel like the only person that mattered in the world.

My body ignited as his lips pressed against mine. He glided his hands across my shoulder until they rested against my throat. My heart danced under his fingertips as he kissed me softly.

Our eyes remained open as I turned in his arms and straddled him. Our breathy moans and the lapping of the waves on the shore were the only sounds, as his kiss became more demanding and I opened to him.

I never wanted to kiss someone as much as I wanted Michael to ravage my mouth and put his hands all over my body. The power of his grip on my back as I kissed him had me wanting more. Pushing him back against the blanket, I sat up and stared down at him, as his hands slid up my legs and caressed my hips.

As I leaned forward, my hair sheltered us from the world as it cascaded around his head. "Make me forget, Michael," I whispered.

His hand stilled. Squeezing my thighs, he leaned forward and nipped at my lips. I collapsed against his chest, my nipples hardening with the contact. His cock grew hard and I gasped in his mouth.

"Sorry, doc. Some things I can't control," he mumbled against my lips.

His hands roamed my body as our lips and tongues stayed entwined. Fisting his hair in my hands, I demanded to be kissed harder. My body ached for his touch. I wanted to be filled and feel alive, as I ground myself against him to relieve the throb I hadn't felt in so long.

A small moan escaped his lips, as he grabbed my hips, his fingers digging into my flesh.

"Not here, Michael. Not like this," I whispered, leaning over him.

"I wasn't even thinking about it, Mia." He looked in my eyes as he pulled my face closer to his. "You want to stay or do you want me to take you home?"

I wanted to stay on the beach in his arms all night, but I couldn't. I wasn't ready to give myself to him, and I knew the longer I kissed him the more I'd want to.

"Take me home," I whispered against his lips, still feeling his hardness against me. A lump formed in my throat as I questioned my decision.

Sitting up, he adjusted my body, breaking the contact that had almost driven us over the edge. "Just promise me that you'll see me again."

The lump that had formed in my throat disappeared, and was replaced by warmth that flowed throughout my body. Leaning forward, I rested my forehead against his and listened to his breathing—rapid and jagged. "I'd love to, Michael. Thank you."

"What are you thanking me for?" he asked, backing away.

"For not pressuring me and still wanting to see me after I turned you down."

"Mia," he said as he grabbed my face, "if anything, it made me want to see you more. I didn't think that was even possible. I like you a lot, and we'll do things at your pace and when you feel comfortable. I didn't do all this just to get in your panties."

"But you were hoping to," I said as I smiled, my face growing flushed.

"I won't lie. I can't wait to rip those off of you and feel your body against mine. It's worth the wait. You're worth the wait," he said, holding my cheek in his hand.

I smiled, resting my hand against his chest. "Want me to take care of that with my needle?" I asked with a smirk, and pointed to his crotch.

His grip on my arms grew tight. "Don't ever, and I mean ever, talk about my cock and your needle again, doc. It was funny at the bar, but right now, not as much." He laughed, his body shaking under mine. "Come on, let's go before you get any more crazy ideas."

I kissed him tenderly, still laughing, as he picked me up and carried me from the beach. Michael wasn't the cocky bastard I thought when I first met him—well, not entirely.

I looked at him in a new light after our first date. There was more to the man, and I wanted to know every inch of him.

9

MICHAEL

IT HAD BEEN A WEEK SINCE I'D SEEN MIA, AND I WAS AT MY BREAKING point. I needed to touch her again. We spent the time apart talking on the phone, texting, and learning a lot about each other.

I found out silly things, like her favorite color, which was purple, and that she loved listening to music and dancing around her house.

When she talked about her work, her mood usually changed. "Happiness" wasn't a word I'd use to describe her feelings about her job. The ER seemed to suck the life out of her. When she lost a patient, she'd share her feelings of despair with me.

It was like a punch to my gut, more damaging than any blow I'd ever felt. I couldn't imagine working in a place that was filled with sorrow.

But when she talked about the clinic, the entire conversation oozed happiness. I heard the change in her voice as she told me about the people and how she felt like she made a difference.

Me: Why don't you just work there full-time? It seems to make you happy.

Sitting on my parents' couch, I tried to pay attention to the conversations around me as I texted Mia. Football season had ended, the basketball playoffs were wrapping up, and baseball season became the main after-dinner attraction at the Gallo Sunday dinners.

"Fuckin' Cubs," my pop yelled at the television.

They were his favorite team, and hadn't won a damn thing since before he was born. Think he'd be used to it by now, but not my pop—he was a die-hard believer, and no Gallo would ever be called a quitter.

Mia: It's all donations with little government funding. No money for that.

"Hey, Ma," I said as she sat across from me, rolling her eyes at her still-cursing husband.

"Yeah, baby." She turned to me and smiled.

"Ever hear of the clinic in town that offers free medical care to the poor?"

Her smiled faded as she shook her head. "No, I don't think I have. Why are you asking?"

I shrugged and turned the phone over in my hand. "Just curious. It's all donation based, and I know how the two of you are about helping local charities."

"What do you know about it? If it's worthy, your father and I would be more than happy to help." She leaned back in the chair, picking up her yarn to work on a baby blanket.

"A group of doctors volunteer their time, but I don't know much else. I'll find out about it and let you know." I glanced down at my phone, on silent around my family to avoid the questions.

Mia: Hey, what time are you picking me up?

"Okay, baby." She placed the blanket over her lap before starting to work on it.

Me: At five, and wear a swimsuit under your outfit.

"Who you making that for?" I asked.

"My grandbaby," she said in a flat, even tone.

"Is someone having a baby I don't know about?" I asked as I looked around the room, but everyone ignored us.

"Not yet." She frowned and said, "Soon, though, I hope."

I looked at Suzy, who was staring at the television, a little too engrossed in the game. She hated sports, but at the moment she was totally enthralled. My brother, Joe, and Suzy could never tell Ma no. It had become the giant elephant in the room, as both of them always pretended not to hear her when she talked about babies.

"I'm not ready for a kid," Joe leaned over and whispered in my ear. "I'm too busy enjoying Suzy and I'm way too greedy to share my time with her."

"She's not going to stop," I said softly.

"I may be old, boys, but I'm not deaf," Ma said with a laugh.

"Busted," I said.

"I'm watching your face as you type feverishly on that phone, Mike. I hope it isn't the crazy lady," Joe said as he leaned back and turned his attention toward the game.

"Hell no. I've been knocked in the head a couple times, but I'm not stupid."

He hit me on the knee with a smile. "Stupidity isn't the issue—our dicks are the problem."

"Amen to that, brother." I laughed. "Nah, this one isn't like that."

Raising an eyebrow, he said, "They're all like that."

"I haven't even slept with her, Joe."

He looked at me in horror. "When did you meet her?"

"That's a complicated answer."

"I'll take your complicated over the Cubs any day."

"We met at a bar over a week ago, and I took her on a date last week, but she treated me in the ER when I broke my ribs."

"Wait. You went on a real date?" He eyed me suspiciously.

"I did."

"And you didn't sleep with her after?"

I shook my head and smiled. "Nope."

"Well fuck me, never thought that was possible," Joe said, hitting my leg and laughing loudly.

There was no way in hell would I share that I rented the beach, and all the sappy-ass shit I did for Mia.

No fucking way.

That was for her and I, and Joe sure as shit didn't need to know. He'd laugh at me and probably call me Romeo for weeks, but I knew the truth about my brother. He was just as big of a softy as me. He swept Suzy off her feet, and she described him as a Casanova.

"I'm not a walking hard-on. I can date someone without fucking them." I looked at my ma, surprised she hadn't yelled at us for our language, but she was wrapped up in grandbaby world.

The couch shook with his laughter. "We're all walking hard-ons, but I'm proud of you, brother. When are you seeing her again?"

Before I could answer, Izzy walked in and stretched out on the floor with her head perched in her hands as she stared at the television.

"Today." Looking at my watch, I said, "One hour, in fact."

"What's today?" Izzy asked, turning around.

"Nothing, Iz. Why do you always have to be so damn nosy?" I sounded like a dick, and I might as well have put a billboard above my head with my response.

She giggled like she did when she was a little girl watching her favorite television show, *Fraggle Rock*. "God, you boys are so easy to read. Don't come crying to me when this one wants your name tattooed on her body. You sure know how to pick 'em, Mikey."

I swiped my hands across my face, shaking my head. "Where's your man, Iz? We've been dying to meet him," I said, looking down at her.

"Hell no, I'm not bringing him around you baboons for a long time. When I do, you'll know he's the one—until then, he's only for me. Learned my lesson long ago with you boys."

"We're not the same. We've grown up," Joe said, before grabbing Suzy's hand and kissing it.

"In some ways," she said over her shoulder, turning her attention back to the game.

"Anyway," I murmured, changing the subject and looking at my ma. "Hey, Ma, can we have dessert now? I have an appointment."

"On a Sunday?" she asked, putting down the needles.

"He has a date, Mom. A hot one, I'd say, for him to be rushing out of here on a Sunday." Izzy smiled at my mom before looking at me with a shitty smirk.

I grabbed the pillow from the side of the couch and threw it at her. "I have a date, Ma. I have to leave in thirty minutes. Forgive me?"

One thing you didn't mess with was the Sunday Gallo dinner. Days like today, they seemed like torture.

"Anything for love, Michael." She smiled.

She didn't have to say it, but I knew my mother well enough that she'd do anything for love, even hand out dessert a little early. The visions of babies danced around in her head too much for her to deny any of us a pass on family time, for the chance of love and that elusive grandchild.

10

MIA

MY PALMS WERE SLICK AND MY HEART FELT LIKE IT WOULD BURST AS I put on the harness. "I can't believe you talked me into this shit," I said, my hands shaking so badly I couldn't snap the latch between my legs.

"I thought you liked an adrenaline rush, and I know you love the ocean. Couldn't think of a better thing to do. Two-for-one deal." He smiled at me, fastening his harness without a problem.

"Just my fucking luck. Yay," I said, and clapped. "But you forgot one thing." I held up my finger and waved it in the air.

"What?" he asked as he stepped closer, grabbing my finger.

"I'm afraid of heights."

"Shit, I didn't know. Probably the one thing we didn't talk about this week. It's safe, and I'll be with you. It's the most amazing view from up there. We have to do it. I promise, you'll love it."

"And if I don't?" I asked, as I tilted my head and smirked.

"Then I'll do anything you want, but I know you will. Plus, you can just hold on to me and scream. I won't think any less of you—well, not much, at least."

I couldn't believe I was going to follow through and let myself be pulled over the ocean by a thin rope. "Fine, but I can't get this damn thing on," I said, frustrated and scared as I threw up my hands in defeat.

"Let me. It would be my pleasure." He kneeled before me, brushing his hand against my inner thigh as he grabbed one end of the strap.

I sucked in a breath, shuddering, as I grabbed his shoulder to steady myself. If it wasn't bad enough that I was petrified to the point of almost hyperventilating, the feel of his skin against mine took my breath away.

He looked up at me, smirking as he brought the latch forward, rubbing his hand against my other inner thigh. I closed my eyes and ignored how close he was to me, how near his hands were to the ache between my legs.

No matter what I did all week, I couldn't get the throbbing I felt from being on top of him at the beach to go away.

The latch snapped. I could do this. The nearness of him dulled my fear.

His fingers brushed against my mound, sending an electric current through my body, as he grabbed the latch. "Safe and secure," he said, pulling on the latch with a chuckle.

I opened my eyes and looked down at him. "I wouldn't use either of those words right now," I said as I smacked his shoulder.

I wasn't talking about parasailing, either.

"Come on, beautiful. There's no turning back now. Up ya go," he said, grabbing my legs and throwing me over his shoulder.

I squealed as I flopped against his body, my chest colliding with his shoulder. I smacked his back, bouncing as I kicked trying to break free. "Put me down!" I yelled through a laugh.

"My view is too damn good to do that, doc," he said, and swatted my ass.

"Pig." I reached down and tried to pinch his ass.

Fucker was rock solid, and I could barely get enough between my fingers.

"Nice try," he said, unaffected by my effort and swatting me on the ass again.

I yelped, the sting from his palm making me wish I could reach back and rub the tender spot. "Ugh," I said as I bounced and grew slack in his arms, finally defeated.

The beach disappeared as he stepped on the boat. "Will you put me down now, please?" I asked, trying to sound sweet as sugar.

"If I must," he said, before placing a light kiss against my hip.

I closed my eyes and tried not to think about it, about him. The feel of his mouth against skin that hadn't been touched in so long had me at my breaking point.

He wrapped his arms around my legs, pushing the harness into me, before pulling my body down against him. He controlled the speed, making the journey to my feet as drawn out as possible.

By the time my feet touched the boat, I forgot how scared I had been. The sexual frustration I felt trumped everything. "You're not safe," I whispered as I looked up at him with one eye, the sun behind his head almost blinding me.

He laughed, pulling me against his shaking body. "Doc, I'll make sure you survive the trip up there." He bent down, rubbing his nose against mine.

"It's not the ride I'm talking about, Michael."

"I know." He smiled and kissed me, his lips shaking under mine from the laughter still rumbling through his chest.

"You two ready?" the attendant asked as he approached with the hook, ready to attach us to the boat. My whole life rested in the hands of a guy in flip-flops and a baseball hat with a pair of Tom Cruise Ray-Bans. Fucking marvelous.

I shook my head against Michael's forehead before he pulled away.

"Yeah, we're ready," he said to the man, with a nod. "You'll thank me, Mia. It's spectacular."

I smiled and kept my mouth shut. Right now, being in the air felt a whole lot safer than standing here touching and kissing Michael. My resolve was wearing thin.

The man attached us to the parasail and the boat. There were so many cords and ropes it made my head spin.

Butterflies filled my stomach as the boat started to skip across the water, and I reached for Michael's hand and squeezed. I could already feel the scream inside me building in my belly.

He turned and smiled, returning my squeeze, before leaning over and kissing my temple.

With the whoosh of the air in my ears, the sunshine on my face, and Michael by my side, I felt a combination of excitement and fear. The driver motioned thumbs up to us. Michael nodded before the man released the lever.

We glided backward and anxiety gripped me as the boat disappeared, turning to a sea of blue. "Fuck," I said, clinging to Michael's arm as I stared at the water passing below my feet.

"Nails," he said, as his arm grew tense under my grip.

I looked at him and yelled, "What?"

His eyes shot to my hand currently in a death grip as he yelled, "Your nails, Mia."

"Whoopsie," I said with a smile, and removed my fingernails from his skin. Blood dotted the surface where my fingers had been. "I'm sorry," I mouthed, the wind making it impossible to hear. "Oh shit," I screamed, as my stomach plummeted and the parasail rose in the air. The rope was rigid and we were the highest we could go. I sealed my eyes shut, scared to look. Gripping Michael with one hand and with the other holding the rope next to my head, I concentrated on my breathing and repeated "I will survive" over and over again in my head.

Michael patted my hand, and I peeked at him through one eye. "Look, Mia, there are dolphins," he yelled, pointing to the water.

I tried to swallow, but my mouth felt like sandpaper. I followed his finger with my eyes. Below us were three dolphins jumping in and out of the wake as they kept up with the boat.

Even though I spent a lot of time at the beach in college, I rarely saw much of anything in the water besides the tiny fish near the shore.

I became lost in their play, taking in the moment and forgetting my fear. Michael stroked my fingers as I watched with a giant smile on my face. It was breathtaking, and reminded me that we were just a small part of this planet.

The parasail jolted, and I almost lost the contents in my stomach out of fear as the driver started to reel us in. Michael squeezed my hand and laughed from the obvious look of fright on my face.

A small pang of sadness hit me as we descended toward the water. The dolphins disappeared below the surface as we hovered over the boat.

"It's all over, Mia. You did it," he said as our feet touched the boat deck.

"I did," I muttered as I grabbed his arms and tried to gain my balance. My legs felt shaky as I wobbled from the sway of the waves against the small boat. "I *never* want to do that again."

"Don't you feel alive, though?" He looked pretty damned pleased with himself.

I couldn't be shitty with him. He looked too sexy with his brown hair tousled and windblown, his cheeks sun-kissed, and his body glistening from the heat.

I smiled, but couldn't lie about the sheer panic I had experienced. "I always knew I was alive, Michael. You almost killed me with fear alone."

"Mia, I thought you'd love it. You said you loved the beach and I thought I'd give you a whole new view." His thumbs rubbed my arms, calming me. "I won't make you go again. I'm sorry."

I shook my head and smiled. "I'm just being an asshole. It's okay, really. It's something I would've never done, and I liked it once I saw the dolphins, but I don't think I could do it again."

"It's off limits." He grabbed my face, kissing me passionately, making my tension melt away. "It won't happen again," he murmured against my lips.

"It's okay," I replied, my mind mush and the fear forgotten.

"Want me to carry you?" he asked, as the boat docked. "I liked helping you when we boarded." He smirked.

"I can do it," I said as I pushed him away and stepped on the wooden dock.

"You ruin all the fun."

"My ass in your face is not *fun*, Michael." I fiddled with the latch between my legs and couldn't get the bastard unclipped.

"It's the best kind of fun there is, Mia." He watched me, rubbing his chin. "You want help with that?"

"No, no. I got it." I still felt buzzed from the rush and fear that had coursed through my system during the parasailing ride. I certainly didn't need his fingers brushing between my legs again.

His laughter filled the air as I yanked and pulled to no avail, trying to break free from the harness. Luck wasn't on my side today. I hung my head and whispered, "Can you help me, please?"

Without a word, he bent down and ran his hands up my legs slowly before grabbing the harness and giving it a quick jerk. "I'm more than happy to help you down here."

"Just unhook me, please," I said, closing my eyes, trying to block out the feel of him against my skin. "You're torturing me on purpose."

"It doesn't have to be torture, doc. I don't have a needle, but I can find a way to ease your suffering." He winked as I looked down at him.

"I'm thirsty," I squeaked out, wanting to avoid thinking about the ways he could help me. If I thought about it too long, I'd give in and throw myself at him.

"Avoiding the offer," he said, with a hint of laughter. "Let's grab a drink and watch the sunset again."

Thank God he let me off the hook. Another stroke of his hand would've sent me over the edge and begging for his cock. He stood and grabbed my hand, leading me to a tiny beach bar with colorful umbrellas.

A reggae band played while we sipped on ice-cold beer and waited for the sun to set. His free hand stroked mine, toying with my fingers, never breaking contact.

Just as the sky started to change to a vibrant shade of red, a crack of thunder caused everyone to jump and scream.

"Come on, Mia," Michael said, pushing out his chair as he stood.

Large droplets of water splashed down on the metal table as I reached for his hand. Thunder rumbled as we ran from the patio toward his car.

My swimsuit and cover-up were drenched as we made our way through the parking lot. My hair slapped against my skin, lashing my face with each bounce. The sky lit up, the lightning in the distance causing the ground to shake as we climbed in the cab, slamming the doors to the truck.

We wiped our faces as small drops fell from our hair. I flipped back my hair, pushing it out of my eyes, and ran my hands down my arms, watching the water splash to the floor. "Jesus, that scared the crap out of me," I said, shaking from the excitement.

"Just when you were relaxing, God finds a way to give your ass a jolt." He laughed, grabbing his chest.

"You're a funny man, Michael. I don't think my heart can take much more today."

He leaned over, pulling me into his arms as he grabbed my chin and tipped it back. "I have something that'll take your mind off of it while we wait for the storm to pass."

His brown eyes held my gaze before he crushed his lips against mine. If the interior of the truck hadn't been hot and steamy enough, being close to Michael, wrapped in his arms and smothered by his kiss, made it close to impossible to breathe.

His hand rested against my back, pulling me closer, and I became lost in his kiss. The feel of his rough thumb pad as he stroked my face made my body feel on fire. The sound of the rain beating against the truck, the thunder rumbling outside, and our breath, frantic and quick, filled the cab.

I climbed in his lap as he gripped my ass and pulled my bottom to him. I could feel his hardness against me, and I ached to feel him inside.

I couldn't deny myself any longer.

"Take me home, Michael. Stay with me tonight." I didn't even have to think about it.

I wanted him.

The light touches, commanding kisses, and feel of his hardness had me wanting more, needing it.

"Mia, I don't know if that's a good idea," he whispered against my lips.

"I want to feel your skin against me. Remind me what it feels like to be loved, Michael. Show me the beauty and make me forget." I held myself up and stared in his eyes. "Please."

His fingers swept against my cheek and I leaned into his touch, closing my eyes. "I'll do anything you ask," he said.

I smiled at him before climbing off his lap. "I don't want to be alone tonight," I said as I put on my seatbelt.

He started the truck and grabbed my hand, stroking it, with a smile on his face. We sat in silence as I stared out the window during the drive.

I wasn't alone in life, but I did feel lonely.

Being with Michael reminded me how much I missed that connection to another person. I wanted someone to hold me until I fell asleep and comfort me when the nightmares came.

Our bodies stayed connected as he drove; the energy never waned.

"Mia, are you sure about this?" he asked as he pulled in my driveway.

Turning toward him, I smiled. "Never been more sure about anything in a long time, Michael."

11

MICHAEL

"You want to just go to sleep?" I asked, giving her one final out. "I don't know if I can do gentle, Mia. I'm giving you fair warning." I held her face in my hands as I pushed my hardness against her.

"Don't be gentle with me, Michael. I'm not going to break." She pushed against my chest, breaking the kiss. "Shower first," she said, pushing me toward the shower. "We're covered in sand."

"Only if you're coming in with me." I smirked and reached in the shower to turn on the water before pulling off my rain-soaked shirt.

As she ran her soft fingers across the tattoo on my chest that spelled *Gallo*, my dick ached and strained in my pants. I wanted to be inside her. Her touch felt like torture.

"Verita?" she asked, running her nail down the letters on my ribs.

Goose bumps dotted my flesh. "It means 'truth' in Italian," I said, trying to keep my voice even.

Walking behind me, she kissed my shoulder before sinking her teeth into my flesh.

Inhaling sharply, I tensed. "If you do that again, we won't make it to the shower," I said, on shaky breath. I wanted to feel her nails rake across my balls as she sucked me off. "My turn." I turned around to face her.

I slowly lowered the straps of her swim dress, holding it between my fingers, as the material clung to her skin. As her dress slid from her body, it cascaded to the floor. She stood before me in nothing but her black bikini. Her breasts made my mouth water, as her nipples grew hard with the cool air. She stood stock-still and looked at the floor with her cheeks turning a light shade of pink, as I took in her beauty.

I placed my fingers under her chin, forcing her eyes to mine. "You're breathtaking." A small grin spread across her face, but there was uncertainty in her eyes. "Stunning, actually. You still want this, Mia?" I had to know for certain that she wanted to be with me.

She nodded and palmed my dick through my swim trunks. I shuddered, the ache turning into a throb with the warmth of her hand. Reaching down with a smirk, she pushed from the sides of my trunks, but it caught on my stiffness.

I chuckled when her eyes grew wide, and I heard her swallow.

She yanked harder, before they slid down my hips and fell to the floor with a thump.

As I stepped forward, my cock brushed against her soft, wet skin. Closing my eyes, I inhaled, needing a moment to get my hunger under control.

I wanted to slam her body against the wall and take her, but I wasn't here to hit it and quit it.

Leaning into me, she grabbed my sides and squeezed, her breath catching as my cock bobbed against her stomach.

I ran my mouth along her cheek, relishing the softness of her skin. There was a connection there, something greater than us, and out of our control. We both needed this.

The running water and the sound of our breath filled the room as our lips smacked against each other. I kicked the trunks free from my feet, hissing into her mouth, as her fingers grazed the tender, aching flesh of my dick.

I craved her touch more than I thought possible.

She lightly touched the top of my shaft before running her nails across the head, moving underneath. Her hand stilled as she felt the first piercing and she froze.

I'd failed to mention my hardware.

I grinned, opening my eyes to see her expression.

Her eyes grew wide as she peered down before continuing to feel the underside of my cock.

"Never felt a Jacob's Ladder before?" I asked with a smirk.

"No, I've seen them, but never felt one." She palmed my cock and pulled it up, getting a better view. Biting down on her bottom lip, she gawked at it like it was going to bite her.

"Wait until you feel it inside, sweetheart," I whispered in her ear, as I slid her thong down her legs, waiting for her to step out.

I picked her up and she wrapped her legs around me. It took everything in me not to sink my dick into her as I reached in the shower to check the temperature.

With one foot in the shower, she stopped me, digging her feet in my ass. "Wait."

Fucking hell. My cock was going to explode at any moment. Just carrying her was enough friction to set me off.

"What's wrong?" I asked, resting my forehead against hers.

"We need a condom. Do you have one?" she asked, biting down on her lip.

"Fuck, I don't. Didn't plan on sinking my cock balls deep in ya, doc." I laughed. "Do you?"

"I have one. It's in the top drawer on my nightstand. Put me down and I'll go grab it." She started to pull away.

I shook my head, pulling her tighter against my body. "Hell no, we're not leaving this position. You feel too fucking good to put you down now."

She giggled as I carried her to the bedroom. Leaning over, I held her ass, keeping her in my arms, as she reached into her nightstand.

"Don't look!" She tried to cover my eyes with her hand as she opened the small drawer.

"Whatcha got in there?" I asked, even though I could see through her fingers.

The drawer overflowed with lace panties, and my eyes zeroed in on a sex toy. I liked a girl that didn't have a problem with masturbation. I'd give my left nut to watch her use it on herself.

"Nothing. Stop peeking." She dug her heels in harder, rubbing my cock against the warmth of her pussy.

CHELLE BLISS

I was about to explode if she wiggled any more against me.

Her hand moved through the drawer as she put on an acrobatic act to stop me from seeing the contents. "Got it," she said as her hand emerged with a condom before she pushed the drawer closed.

I captured her fingers in my mouth as they fell from my eyes. Sucking the soft digits, I ran my tongue along her succulent flesh.

She held the condom up to my eyes as her eyes rolled back in her head. "You play dirty," she whispered.

I released her fingers as I squeezed her ass roughly in my palms. "You have no idea, Mia." I kissed her, not wanting a reply.

She fisted my hair, sucking on my bottom lip as I carried her into the shower. As her back collided with the cold tile, she gasped in my mouth.

I rubbed my throbbing cock against her pussy, loving the sounds of her moans. She felt velvety soft, and I didn't know how much longer I could wait to be inside.

I wanted to touch her; holding her body up in my arms just wasn't doing *it* for me. Moving to the small corner bench, I placed her body on it and stood.

"Condom?" I asked, stroking my shaft.

She watched with wide eyes, and placed the condom in my palm softly.

I tore open the wrapper with my teeth, as she stared, mesmerized by my movement. I rolled it down, paying careful attention to each piercing, not wanting to tear the thin latex.

I picked her up and placed her in my lap as I sat down, my ass hanging over the edge slightly. I licked a trail to her collarbone, the saltiness filling my tongue as I continued my descent to her breast. I leaned her body back, holding her in my grip as I tried to get a better angle. I captured her nipple in my mouth, and her head fell back, a moan escaping her lips. I ran my tongue over the hardness and bit down.

"Jesus," she said as she rubbed against my cock, writhing in my arms.

Reaching between us, I ran my fingers through her wetness before I found her clit. As I rubbed, making tiny circles, her movement became more demanding, and she pressed herself against my hand. "Not yet. I want to feel your pussy squeeze the life out of my cock when you come."

286

"I make no promises if you don't do it soon." She took control of the situation as she pushed harder, rocking her hips. Her moans grew louder.

I moved my hand, denying her what she had been so close to accomplishing.

She glared at me, stilling her body against me.

Leaning back, I stroked my cock against her body before I pushed... slowly. I had to go slow; I felt like I'd come at any moment if I didn't move at the torturous pace.

I held her by the hips as I gripped her roughly. I didn't want her to slam down on my shaft and take it deep, at least not yet. I pulled her body down, impaling her with my cock as I sucked her nipple.

When her pussy was an inch from having my entire shaft buried inside her, I thrust my hips upward, burying my dick inside her.

She let out a gasp as the tip hit her cervix. "Oh," she said as her eyes closed partially, and I pulled out just as slowly as I went in, not releasing her hips or giving her the ability to fuck me.

"Feel them?" I asked, studying her face.

"Yes, oh. My. God. I. Do," she said, stumbling on each word as I moved in and out of her.

I couldn't control myself anymore. Fuck this. I never liked slow. I wasn't built for it.

Her feet were barely touching the floor as I pulled her down my length. I controlled her like a rag doll in my arms as I fucked her.

God, she felt fanfuckingtastic.

My thighs burned as I plunged inside of her, pulling her against me with each thrust.

The impact was volcanic.

The sound of our skin slapping and the water sloshing in the shower filled the small space, echoing. Her moans grew louder with each collision until she trembled in my arms.

I couldn't hold out any longer. I picked up the speed, using my dick as a battering ram and her pussy as the object of its blow.

Her body bounced in my arms, her limbs moving on their own as her head fell back, exposing her neck.

"Eyes on me, Mia. I own this orgasm. I earned it."

CHELLE BLISS

Her head snapped forward and she stared at me with glassy eyes. Her
tits bounced with each blow—a spectacular fucking sight.

My brute force drove her over the edge as she screamed, her pussy
milking my cock. I rammed into her as my balls grew tight and my dick
began to jerk. My entire body tingled as all my muscles grew stiff.

I began to shake.

Fuck.

I couldn't remember the last time I came with such intensity. It was
better than any high I ever chased in my life. Mia had become my new
addiction.

12

MIA

WRAPPING A TOWEL AROUND MY BODY, I LOOKED AT HIM WITH A SMALL grin. "Michael, will you stay tonight? I'm not looking for anything more from you, but I'd—"

He put his finger against my lips. "I'll stay, Mia. I want to." He pulled his finger away, smiling.

He looked beautiful with a towel around his waist and tiny droplets of water sliding down his muscular torso.

"I mean, I don't want—"

He shook his head, wrapping me in his arms. "Woman, I said I want to. No one makes me do anything I don't want to. There's nowhere I'd rather be than with you. Can you stop talkin' and get that fine ass in bed?"

Biting my lip, wanting to laugh, I nodded and broke free from his embrace.

"Which side?" I asked, as I walked in the bedroom. "I tend to sleep in the middle."

"The middle it is, then—get in and scoot over and I'll work around you," he said, following me.

I nodded, looking down at my towel. "Let me grab some pajamas first."

I took one step away from the bed before he grabbed the towel and pulled, stripping me bare. "Seen it all, doc. Felt it too. No clothes, just us and the bed."

Shrugging, I said, "Okay," with a soft voice.

In the center of the bed, I watched as he folded my towel and disappeared into the bathroom. A moment later, he emerged stark naked, in all his glory. The phrase fit him perfectly. It was a damn glorious sight.

I stared, licking my lips as he walked toward the bed. It's not often a person can actually see the flex and release of a muscle with such definition.

The man didn't have an ounce of body fat anywhere that I could see. Even his ass had felt rock hard underneath my heels earlier.

His cock twitched, and I quickly looked up at his face. My sex ached from the battering it took earlier. I missed that feeling, the one that reminded me of being pleasured.

"Like what you see?" he asked, winking at me as he lifted the sheet.

"Not bad," I said, trying to seem indifferent.

He slid across the material and pressed his body to mine.

His hard to my soft felt amazing.

Brushing the hair off my forehead, he asked, "You sleep on your back or your side?"

"I toss and turn mostly." I stared into his soft brown eyes.

He smiled as his hand stilled against my hair. "Good, I sleep on my back," he said, rolling over. "Come here."

I scooted across the bed as he lifted his arm. I put my head on his chest, sighing, and smiled against his skin. The hardness under my cheek softened as he wrapped his arm around me and started to stroke my arm.

I moved my legs a couple times, trying to get comfortable.

"Put your leg over me. Make yourself comfortable."

I adjusted my body, placing my hand that had been smashed between us on my leg, and wrapped it around his bottom half.

Placing his arm back on my shoulder, he whispered, "Good now?"

"Perfect," I said as I placed my hand against his hard pec.

I stroked the spot between his two pecs, watching the path of my fingers until my eyes felt heavy. Mindlessly running my finger back and forth, I didn't feel the need to toss and turn like normal.

I felt at peace.

"Just close your eyes, Mia." He stroked my forearm and dug his fingers in my hair, massaging my scalp.

I mumbled against his skin, unable to speak, lost in the feel of him all over me.

***

Stirring my cup of coffee, as I watched the cream swirl in the cup, I felt more rested than I had in years.

Michael did this.

I felt so safe in his arms that I didn't wake up once last night with a nightmare. I didn't think I'd had a dream at all, as a matter of fact.

Michael kissed me goodbye early in the morning after we talked about seeing each other again soon.

The relationship wasn't going to be easy, but he promised he wasn't kissing me goodbye.

"You must have had a real good time this weekend, doctor." The voice pulled me out of my happy thoughts. A nurse leaning against the counter studied me with a shitty-ass grin.

"Yeah, it was decent." I didn't feel like talking to her. It was none of her damn business.

Pointing at my neck, she laughed. "From the love bite on your neck, I'd say it was a little more than decent."

I dropped the spoon and my hand flew to the spot that he'd bitten the night before. "Shit," I muttered, covering the spot.

"Happens to the best of us." She giggled and shrugged.

"I have to go cover this up before I see patients. Nice seeing you."

I didn't know her name and felt kind of shitty about not addressing her properly, but there were too many damn people that worked in the hospital to memorize them all.

I started to walk away, but she called out to me, "You're not even going to give me any details? I did help you out."

I called out over my shoulder to her, "I'm in a rush, but maybe another time."

I heard her mumbling nasty words as I closed the door to the bathroom.

"Fuck," I said as I leaned closer to the mirror, inspecting the red mark on my neck.

We were both too caught up to put much thought into anything, especially a hickey.

I pulled a tube of cover-up from my purse and dabbed the cream over the spot on my neck and sighed. It screamed "love bite." I pulled my ponytail to the side as I tried to hide it.

It shouted "hey, I'm hiding something."

I walked down the hall and nodded at the few people who walked by before making it to the heart of the ER. "Who needs to be seen?" I asked Constance, the station supervisor, as I leaned over the counter, staring at her mountain of paperwork.

"Room seven needs assistance, I think. Check the board." She didn't look up at me as she shuffled the papers.

My eyes looked over each row and stopped dead on one name.

Gallo.

Unable to move, I stared at the board, and heaviness settled over my body. My heart ached as it hammered inside my chest, wanting to burst.

"What's wrong, doc?" Her warm hands touched my fingers, breaking my trance.

"Gallo in room seven," I said, swallowing the lump that had formed in my throat.

"Motorcycle accident, serious injuries. Is there a problem, Dr. Greco? You're white as a ghost."

I shook my head without looking at her. I needed to know if Michael lay in that room. "No, I'm okay. Let me get in there and help."

As I walked down the hallway, I felt like my shoes were filled with cement. I stood outside the room, gathering my thoughts before I walked in.

Even if it were Michael on that table, I had to help save his life.

I needed to separate myself from our…whatever we were.

Holding my breath, I approached the gurney slowly.

A dark-haired man lay motionless on the table covered in blood and dirt. Dr. Patel stood over him, shining a light in his eyes, as nurses hung IVs.

"What do we have, doctor?" My voice cracked.

The heaviness in my chest eased when my eyes flickered on the man's face again.

It wasn't Michael.

"Mr. Gallo, can you hear me?" Patel shouted to him, but he was unconscious. Looking up at me as he placed the light in his pocket, Patel spoke quickly, "Dr. Greco, we have an adult male thrown from a bike but wearing a helmet. His leg is mangled and we've controlled the bleeding. We're still assessing the damage before sending him to surgery. We need to cut his clothing off and check for other injuries."

Grabbing a pair of scissors, I looked at his face before I started to cut the material around his injured leg. "Head trauma?" I asked, looking at the dried blood on his face and neck.

"The helmet took the brunt of it, but he's been in and out of consciousness. We've started him on pain meds for his leg and hand. He came in conscious, but the pain meds knocked him out. We need an x-ray on that leg for the surgeons." His hands never stopped moving as he checked the patient's body for visible damage.

"X-ray, please," I yelled to the nurse near the doorway before she scurried away.

His blood pressure was elevated and needed to be brought under control before surgery.

"Have you started him on anything for his BP?" I asked.

Patel squinted at the monitor and grabbed a small vial from the cart, filling the needle before pushing the liquid into the line.

"Clear the room, please," the technician said, standing in the doorway with the portable x-ray machine.

"After the films are taken, he can be prepped for surgery," Dr. Patel said as we walked into the hall.

I felt useless.

I hated coming into a room late and feeling left out of the diagnosis, which usually happened at the start of the shift.

"He'll need surgery to repair his leg and most likely his hand." Dr. Patel rubbed the back of his neck and sighed.

"I can go talk to the family while you handle the transfer papers if you'd like," I offered.

I needed to see Michael if he was in the waiting room.

Patel nodded, giving me a small smile before going back into the room when the technician called out, "All clear."

My stomach started to cramp as I walked toward the waiting room. I knew the other Gallos would be there.

This wasn't the way I wanted to meet them.

When I pushed opened the door, the first person I saw was Michael. My heart raced and I wanted to jump into his arms. I had the urge to kiss him and tell him how worried I was when I saw his name, but I couldn't.

I needed to remain calm and do my job.

His pained eyes met mine, and the cocky grin he wore so well was missing.

"Gallo family?" I said, staring in his eyes.

"Yes," an older woman said, standing as she wiped her tear-stained face.

I moved toward her, grabbing a chair, and positioned myself close to Michael.

"I wanted to let you know he's being prepped for surgery. Although we don't know the full extent of his injuries yet, we know his leg needs surgery, being badly damaged in the wreck." I looked at Michael, and swallowed as my nose tingled. "His hand is broken and may also need to be repaired. We won't know more until he's in the operating room."

"Was he awake, doctor? Can I see him?" the older woman asked, as she leaned forward, choking on her words.

"He's been in and out of consciousness, ma'am. You can see him when he's in the recovery room."

"Will he live?" the blonde at her side asked, clutching the woman's hand.

"All I can say is that he's currently stable, but his injuries are serious."

I could feel Michael's eyes on me, almost boring a hole in my skin, as I talked with the two women.

Tears began to stream down the younger woman's face as she choked out, "Just make my Joey all right."

I patted her knee, trying to reassure her. "We'll do everything in our power to help him." I stood, looking at the entire family. "You can move to the surgery waiting room when you feel ready. Don't hesitate to ask for updates and watch the monitor on the wall. It'll indicate when the surgery begins and finishes."

Reaching out, the older woman touched my hand. "Thank you, dear."

I nodded before I looked at Michael, giving him a weak smile.

"Come on, Mother, let's go wait where the nice doctor told us for our boy," the older gentleman that sat next to Michael said. Grabbing her by the waist, he helped her walk, allowing her to lean on him for support.

I envied them. They loved each other. I smiled at them until screaming drew my attention toward the hall.

"Outta my fucking way," a woman yelled as she walked into the room.

"Isabella, watch your mouth," the mother said, her voice stern.

Frowning, the woman looked at the floor, not making eye contact. "Sorry, Ma. What happened to Joe? Is he okay?" Her eyes glistened as a tear slid down her cheek.

The mother touched her face, wiping away the tear. "He's going to surgery. We'll know more soon, baby girl. I know you adore your brother. He's strong and a fighter. He'll be okay," she said, wrapping the girl in a loving embrace.

"He has to be, Ma," Isabella said, crying on her mother's shoulder.

"There, there, baby. Come on, let's go." She rubbed her back to soothe Isabella's sobs.

The older man motioned for everyone to follow him as he walked toward the door.

I turned and looked at Michael, pleading for him to stay with my eyes.

"I'll meet you guys in a second. I need to talk to the doctor," Michael said to his father after everyone else cleared the room.

13

MICHAEL

"DON'T BE TOO LONG," POP SAID, WATCHING US WITH HIS HEAD TILTED, rubbing his lip.

Holding up my hand to him, I said, "Five minutes, tops."

Nodding, he walked out, leaving us alone.

Mia threw herself in my arms with such force that she almost knocked the wind out of me.

Wrapping her legs around my waist and her arms around my neck, she said, "Oh my God, Michael. I was so scared it was you in that room." Her voice broke as the words came out quick. "I wasn't happy it was your brother, but I was relieved it wasn't you."

Leaning back, I put my finger against her lips, stopping her from going any further. She blinked, the corners of her mouth turning up.

"I'm fine, doc. How's my brother, really? Not the bullshit stuff you tell all the families. Lay it on me."

"Sorry," she said, wiping her eyes and swallowing. "It's hard to say right now. He's unconscious, so it's hard to determine the extent of his injuries until he's been fully evaluated, Michael. Thank God he wore a helmet." She slid down my body, resting her hands on my chest.

Holding her cheek in my palm, I caressed the soft skin. "Is he going to live?"

She leaned into my touch, closing her eyes. "I can't answer that with certainty." She didn't open them as she spoke. "I know they will do everything they can, Michael."

I inhaled and held my breath, trying to not break down into tears.

Joe and I had a bond. He was my rock and my best friend. We'd busted each other's balls for as long as I could remember. I couldn't even begin to think about a day without him in my life.

I *wouldn't* think about it.

I rested my forehead against hers. "Just keep me posted, Mia. If you hear anything or if you get any information before us, please don't keep it from me. The waiting is driving me fucking crazy."

She cupped my cheeks and whispered against my lips, "I will, Michael. I'm so sorry."

We stood there for a moment, not moving, touching each other before I kissed her and let her go. "I better go before someone comes looking for me. I need to be there with them."

"I wish I had met them under different circumstances." She frowned, wiping the corner of her eye.

Tipping back her chin, I kissed her lips softly and smiled. "They won't remember. It'll be a blur after all is said and done." I rubbed my nose against hers. "Message me when you get any information."

"I will," she said, before we walked in opposite directions.

***

After I'd been pacing for an hour and staring at the monitor that stated *Joseph Gallo—Surgery in Progress*, my phone vibrated in my pocket.

Mia: They're starting now. No internal injuries and he woke up before surgery.

I exhaled the breath I'd held in as I pulled out my phone. The sick feeling in my stomach and the lump in my throat subsided as I read her message.

I hated hospitals and wouldn't feel at ease until he walked out of the front door.

Me: That's good news, no?

I looked around the room at my family—I couldn't keep the news to myself. They looked as shitty as I felt.

"I have news," I said as I stopped in the middle of the room.

Everyone looked in my direction with hope in their eyes.

"How?" Isabella asked, scooting forward in her seat. "Doesn't matter," she said, shaking her head. "What is it?"

"My friend who works here said Joe has no internal injuries and that he woke up before surgery. They're working on his leg and hand now."

"Oh, thank God," my ma said as her body visibly relaxed in my father's arms.

"He's going to be okay?" Suzy asked, as she jumped from her seat and approached me.

"Yes, Suzy, babe. He's going to be okay," I said, wrapping her in my arms. I rubbed her back until my phone started to vibrate. I looked over her shoulder to read the message.

Mia: It's great news. Still going to be a long recovery, but he'll survive.

Suzy clung to me, her silent sobs of joy dampening my shirt. Needing the comfort as much as she did, I rested my head against her hair and held her.

"I was so damn scared, Mike," she said, fisting my shirt in her hands.

"I know, Suzy. We all were. You know Joe. He's not going out that easy. He loves you too much to go out that way."

Instead of that consoling her, she cried harder into my chest, breaking out into a sob.

"He's never going back on that goddamn bike. Over my dead body," she muttered into my shirt.

I bit my lip, trying to hold in my laughter. "Good luck with that, Suz. But if anyone can keep him off that bike, it's you."

She patted my stomach as she backed away.

He was so head over heels in love with her that he'd do just about anything to make her happy, but his bike might be a bone of contention.

I knew why my brother loved her so much. Suzy was a special kind of girl—the needle in the haystack. Why he hadn't married the girl was one thing I didn't understand.

They had recently begun building a home on his property in the middle of nowhere. They called it a "love shack," but it was more like a grand palace. My mother was giddy when she learned they would have five bedrooms. She started planning for her future grandchildren immediately like a woman possessed, hence the baby blankets.

I tossed my phone on the side table as I collapsed in the chair and rested my head against the wall. I couldn't relax, even though my eyes burned and my body felt heavy.

Out of the corner of my eye, I noticed the phone dancing across the *Time* magazine, and I scooped it up. I rubbed my eyes as I looked at the screen.

Mia: *I'm in the hallway, come out.*

Looking around, I saw her standing in the corner as she motioned for me. My heart sank until I noticed the smile on her face, but I couldn't shake my paranoia about the entire situation.

"I'll be right back," I said as I stood and walked out.

"Hey," she said, walking to me.

"Everything all right? Something wrong with Joe?" Reaching out, I grabbed her hand and squeezed.

"Nah, he's doing great and your family will be able to see him soon." Peeking over my shoulder, she looked in the waiting room. "I wanted to make sure you're okay. I needed to check on you."

I smiled, brushing my thumb across the back of her hand. "Aw, you got a soft spot for me, doc?"

She punched me in the shoulder. "You ass. I was being nice and thoughtful, but you're smug as always, I see." She laughed, the joy touching her eyes.

"I'm doing okay. Everyone is relieved and waiting to see him."

"His surgeon will be in soon to talk and give you the details." She smiled and closed her eyes, exhaling. "I'm glad he made it, Michael." She blinked slowly as her face softened, the smile gone.

"Me too, Mia." I slid my hand up and down her arm before grasping her hand again. "When's your shift end?"

"I don't get off work until tomorrow," she said, moving closer.

"I'm sure I'll see you around tonight and in the morning. I'll be in and out, but can I see you after work tomorrow? Away from all this." I waved my hand in the air.

"I'll be exhausted and useless, but if you want to…I'm yours." Her large hazel eyes sparkled as she smiled.

Warmth spread through my body; from my core it radiated outward to my limbs. "Text me when you're done if I don't see you before then." I touched her cheek. I wanted to lean forward and kiss her, but I stopped myself.

It took everything in me not to give in to my craving.

"I have to go," she said, touching my hand.

The electricity between us felt as strong as the first time we touched.

"I'll text you when I'm done," she said, and pecked me on the lips.

"Don't forget me," I whispered, swiping my finger against her soft cheek.

"One thing you aren't is forgettable, Michael."

She smiled before walking away, and glanced back before turning the corner, disappearing.

Looking at the floor with a stupid grin on my face, I walked toward the waiting room and was met with a pair of black leather boots.

"Who's the girl?" Izzy asked, with a shitty grin and her arms across her chest.

My big-mouth sister should be the undercover cop. She never let anything get past her.

Looking at her with my mouth set in a straight line, I responded, "My friend."

Grinning at me, she turned her head to the side, essentially calling bullshit. "Uh huh," she muttered before moving to the side, letting me pass.

Her stiletto boots click-clacked against the floor as she followed me. She stopped in front of our ma as my ass hit the chair.

"Ma, Michael's friend is a female doctor at the hospital. They looked to be a little more than friends, too." Izzy smirked as my mother looked at me and then back to her.

"Isabella, leave your brother alone," my ma said in a stern voice, as Izzy sat next to my father and rested her head on his shoulder, glaring at me.

Patting the chair, my ma called to me, "Come sit with me, Michael."

I moved to the seat next to her and winked at Izzy.

My ma squeezed my leg before turning to me. "Did she say anything about your brother?"

I told her everything Mia had shared with me about Joe.

I could see my ma's entire body relax with each word. "Is she your girl, son?" she asked, with a small smile on her face when I finished.

Laughing, I shook my head. "I don't know what we are, Ma. We just met a bit ago."

"It was nice of her to give you information about Joseph. She a good girl, baby?"

I didn't want to get into a debate on her meaning of good. To me, she was that and more. "Yes, Ma. I think she actually is." I grinned, thinking about her tiny snores as she slept.

"Don't let that one go, you hear me?" She arched her eyebrow as she stared at me.

"We just met, Ma."

"A mother knows, son." She winked.

"You just want grandbabies. Let me get to know her first, but I'll hold on tight if she's the one for me, Ma."

"Good, Michael. Now go grab me a cup of coffee, please?"

"Light and sweet?" I asked as I stood.

I'd do anything she asked me to do. I loved my ma.

She was my first love.

"No other way," she said, laughing.

"Anyone want anything? I'm headed to the cafeteria," I asked, happy to be leaving the room for a bit. I needed to stretch my legs and get some fresh air.

Standing up, Anthony replied, "I'm coming with you. I need to get out of this room for a while."

"We're good," my pop said, placing a hand on Izzy's shoulder as she tried to stand, forcing her back in her seat.

My sister's face turned red and I expected to see fire come out of her nose, but she remained quiet, for once.

***

I stirred the sixth packet of sugar in my ma's coffee as Anthony paid for his drink.

Someone poked me in the shoulder. "Mikey," a female voice purred in my ear.

Fucking shit. I knew that voice.

Tammy.

Psycho Tammy.

Scrapbook Tammy.

Closing my eyes, I felt the need to slap my ear like a gnat buzzed around it, annoying me.

"Where ya been, baby?" she said, grabbing my ass.

I jumped, and the coffee spilled, scalding my hand. "Fuck," I said, gritting my teeth.

I crumpled the packets in my hand and turned around. I didn't really need her fucking bullshit right now.

"Sorry." She smiled as I glared at her. Her smile fell. "I've missed you." She reached out, trying to touch me.

"Tammy." I backed away, my ass bumping into the counter.

"Mikey, I've been thinking about you for days." She wrapped her arms around me. "Why haven't you texted me back?" She stared in my eyes, pouting.

Anthony made faces at me as I looked to him for help. He knew all about her kind of crazy, and loved to see me miserable whenever possible.

Dickhead.

Grabbing her arms, I peeled her off me. "Tammy, we're nothing. You need to get some help."

Her mouth gaped open as she gasped for air.

Holding her firmly, I quietly said, "I don't want to see you or get another text from you. Forget I ever existed." I pushed her body away from mine.

She glared at me. "How could you say that, Michael? We're engaged." Holding her hand in front of my face, she wiggled her finger. A very large diamond ring sparkled on her finger.

She was fucking crazier than I thought.

Shaking my head, I tried to remain calm. "I don't know who gave that to you, but it wasn't me. We. Are. Not. Engaged."

Anthony doubled over in a fit of silent laughter, his body shaking as he grabbed his chest.

Her eyes grew wide, and she covered her mouth with her hand as she shook her head.

302

"Seriously, Tammy, get some fucking help. I didn't give that ring to you. Don't ever say those words to anyone. We. Are. Nothing. You hear me? Nothing." I gritted my teeth; my jaw ached as I tried to keep myself from screaming.

She shook her head vigorously. "Don't say such hurtful, mean things, Michael."

When she reached out to touch me, I grabbed her wrist and stopped her. "I got too much shit going on right now to deal with your crazy bullshit." Releasing her wrist, I stepped back and glared at her. "Stay the hell away from me."

I smacked my brother on the back of the head as I walked by him and away from Tammy. I needed to get the fuck out of here.

"But I'm having your baby!" she yelled, her voice echoing through the cafeteria.

I stopped dead, my body stiffening as my blood turned cold.

What the fuck did she just say?

Bitch just played her last damn hand, and I sure as fuck wasn't going all in.

I turned around, pointing at her. "I have to go, Tammy. I'll deal with your ass later. Don't call me. I'll call you when I'm ready." I dropped my hand to my side. I squeezed my hands into hard fists before leaving her in the dust.

14

MIA

Walking into the bathroom, I saw the nosy nurse who'd pointed out my hickey in tears. It was too late to turn around without looking like a total asshole.

Just my fuckin' luck.

She leaned on her hands, bending over the sink, her tears plopping into the bowl.

I sighed, wanting to walk away.

I really didn't give a shit what made her sad, but my humanity won.

Asshole conscience.

"Are you okay?" I asked as I approached.

"No," she said, sliding the back of her hand across her face, wiping the tears.

"Sorry, I'll leave you be." I stepped back and reached for the door handle.

"No, don't go," she said, turning toward me. "Everyone leaves me," she wailed, her body almost collapsing against the counter.

"Fuck," I muttered under my breath as I rushed to her side.

How in the hell do I get involved in these situations?

"I'm here. What can I do?" I asked, sounding thoughtful, surprising myself.

"There's nothing anyone can do." She hiccupped as she cried.

"Everything is fixable." I patted her back and stared at the ceiling. "I only have another moment between patients. I'm sorry."

"My fiancé left me and I'm pregnant." She choked on her words, starting to fall forward again.

I held her, pulling her upright. "That's terrible," I said, trying to be horrified.

"How could he be so mean? He acted like we never meant anything to each other."

I had the words on the tip of my tongue, but I bit it instead. "Maybe he'll change his mind."

If the man had any sense, he'd run for the hills or go into witness protection.

"I have to win him back." Standing up, she looked into my eyes. "He needs to understand all he's giving up by walking out on *us*."

"Oh, I'm sure he has no idea." I knew I sounded snarky, but whatever.

"I can do it, you're right." She blotted her cheeks with her fingers and smiled. "Thank you so much." Her tears vanished.

Cuckoo.

Wrapping her arms around me, she squeezed so hard I thought my ribs were going to crack.

"I have to go," I said, pulling away.

"Oh, sorry," she said with a half-smile. Mascara had smeared down her cheeks and her eyes were red and swollen. "You helped me more than you'll ever know." Her smile grew wider.

"Don't give up the fight," I said, walking out the door.

"I won't," she yelled, as the door swung shut.

I shook my head and wondered what the hell happened to my *normal* stressful day at the hospital. Today had been one for the record books.

***

The night had been relatively calm compared to the nutty nurse and thinking Michael had been seriously hurt.

His brother was in ICU for the night post-surgery. When I'd looked at his chart earlier, it stated that he would be moved to a regular room tomorrow if he did well through the night.

The ICU was quiet and the lights were dim as the sounds of the ventilators, heart monitors, and other machines filled the hallway. I wanted to check in on him and see if he needed anything.

Michael's brother crouched in the hall outside his room, leaning against the wall, typing on his phone. Looking up at me, he smiled. "Hey," he said, trying to stand, but he fell over, catching himself on the wall. "Fuck," he mumbled.

Rushing to his side, I reached for him. "Hey, are you all right?" I asked.

Waving me off, he said, "Yeah, just exhausted. This has been a day from hell." His shoulders slumped as he sighed.

"Why don't you try and catch a couple hours sleep in the visitor's lounge? He wouldn't want you to make yourself sick."

"I will soon. You looking for Mikey?" He grinned, making the bags under his eyes more pronounced.

Laughing at the nickname, I replied, "Yeah, is he still here?" I looked around.

"He's inside, but he was asleep when I came out here," he said, pointing to the room behind him.

"I'll just text him. Everyone may be sleeping and I don't want to disturb anyone."

He laughed. "My family *is* the disturbance. They're loud and obnoxious in the most loving way, but I don't blame you for not wanting to go into the lion's den." He shook his head. "At least not armed."

I barely knew any of them, but I wanted to. They seemed loving and playful, just my kind of people. The funny smartass personality must be hereditary.

"You make them sound horrible." I said, shaking my head, laughing.

"Nah, just Italian."

"Don't wake him. Just tell him I stopped by and have him text me in the morning. I'm going to try and get some rest while the ER is slow."

"Okay, doc. I hope to see you again soon." The sides of his eyes crinkled as he smiled at me.

I nodded and walked away, leaving Michael to sleep. I wanted to catch a few minutes' rest in the doctor's lounge while I still could. I thought about the Gallo boys as I made my way down the corridors. They were all handsome, but Michael was heart-stopping.

I flipped off the light in the lounge before I collapsed on the couch. My head began to spin from exhaustion when I closed my eyes. Lying on the lumpy couch, I covered my face with my arm and thought about Michael.

"What?" I asked as someone touched my shoulder. "My eyes were closed for only two seconds. Jesus," I mumbled.

"It's been an hour, doctor, and someone is at the desk asking for you."

"I'm coming," I said, rubbing my eyes, waiting for them to adjust to the harsh fluorescent lighting. I grabbed the Visine from my pocket, dropping the liquid in the hope of alleviate the stinging.

I prayed I didn't look like the walking dead. I sure as hell felt like it.

Walking like a zombie, my mind clouded, eyes blurry, I made my way to the reception area. Michael stood there looking exactly how I felt. Fidgeting with his hands, he leaned against the desk and looked around.

I touched his back lightly, trying not to startle him. "Michael, everything all right?"

He rubbed his hands across his face as he turned to me. "Yeah, Anth told me you came by while I was asleep. Thought I'd find you down here."

"I decided to sleep a bit too," I said, a yawn breaking free as I quickly covered it.

"Shit, I'm sorry I woke you." He frowned. The lack of sleep and stress had dulled his eyes' luster.

"I'm fine. I needed to wake up anyway," I said, wiping my eyes. "How's your brother?"

The huge smile on his face said it all. "He woke up for a bit and mumbled some nonsense," he said, laughing.

"Anesthesia can do funny things to a person's brain."

"I thought about messing with his head, but my ma would've beat me. He seems okay, but he's pretty fucked up. The surgeon said it's going to be a long recovery. They had to put a metal rod in his leg and there's pins sticking out and shit. His hand is in a cast and his fingers are swollen. Yeah, he's fucked for now." He shrugged. "At least he's alive."

Touching his hand, I caressed the rough skin on his palm near his fingers. "It's going to be tough on him, but your family will help him through it. How are your parents holding up?" Stepping closer, I leaned against him.

He stared at my fingers as I stroked them. "They're doing okay. Worried, naturally, but better now that he's out of the woods. They need sleep. I keep telling them to go home and rest, but they're hard-headed."

He wrapped his arm around me and feathered a kiss against my forehead.

"Seems to be a family trait," I said, laughing and gripping his shirt. I closed my eyes, inhaling his musky cologne.

"Code blue, room two," a voice blared through the hallway.

Damn. I wanted more than a minute against his warm, hard body.

"I have to go." I frowned, resting my head against his chest. "Go home and rest, Mikey, and I'll see you tomorrow or today…whatever it is," I said, pushing off him and starting to walk away.

Grabbing me around the waist, he brought his lips to my ear and whispered, "It's Michael, doc. I don't remember hearing you moan Mikey as you came on my cock."

The vibration of his voice and his breath in my ear made me shiver.

"I have to go. You're a naughty boy, Mikey," I said as I pushed away from his body, freeing myself from his grip.

I could hear his deep laughter as I ran toward room two and the patient in cardiac arrest.

15

MICHAEL

I KEPT A VIGIL AT MY BROTHER'S BEDSIDE WITH THE REST OF MY FAMILY throughout the night. On the verge of collapse, I found a quiet spot to close my eyes. Pulling up a chair, I stretched my legs out, and rested my head against the wall. I wanted to wait for Mia to finish her shift.

I tried to quiet my mind, but all I could think about was Tammy. I didn't believe for a moment that she was pregnant, let alone with my child.

I knew sure as shit we weren't engaged, so why would I even remotely believe her bullshit? The woman was clearly delusional, and I needed to find a way to set her ass straight, and quick, before it blew up in my face.

Using the front of one shoe, I pried the other one off my foot before repeating the process with my toes. I grabbed my shirt, brought it to my nose, and sniffed. Didn't smell as bad as I thought it would after being at the hospital so long.

Rubbing my face, I yawned and crossed my arms, resting them on my chest.

What the fuck was I going to do about Tammy?

Batshit crazy Tammy.

A pregnancy test would show her for the bullshitter she was and put her lies to rest in a hurry, but how?

We didn't have sex more than a couple times in the last six weeks, and I always wore a condom.

I didn't want a baby—at least not yet, and certainly not with a woman like her.

Could someone even know that they were pregnant in that time? I had a dick, and the female reproductive system mystified me.

I tried to force Tammy out of my mind. Just the thought of her pissed me off, making my blood pressure rise.

I thought of Mia, trying to calm my nerves. There was something different about her, but I couldn't put my finger on it. There was a natural ease I felt when she was at my side.

What if they knew each other? Fuck, I never thought of that.

My heart pounded as my eyes flew open. My palms grew sweaty as I thought about the possibility of my worlds colliding in one giant clusterfuck.

I couldn't make myself crazy.

I pushed the thought of Tammy out of my mind and thought of Mia—the feel of her skin, her brilliant smile, and her infectious laugh.

My head fell to the side, scaring the living shit out of myself. I needed my bed, solid sleep, and a good ass-kicking in the gym to set my body and mind right. I felt stiff after sleeping for three hours in an unnatural position.

I cracked my neck, gaining my bearings as I walked back to Joe's room. I needed to check on him.

My parents, Izzy, and Anthony had disappeared while I was gone. Suzy had crawled in bed and carefully placed her body around him. He watched her as she slept in his arms.

I cleared my throat to get his attention.

Holding his finger to his lips, he motioned for me to sit.

"You scared the shit out of us, Joe." I grabbed the chair, setting it down on the opposite side of the bed that Suzy lay on.

"I wouldn't go out like that, brother. I have too much to live for to leave this world," he whispered, looking down at Suzy. "I feel like shit, though."

"You look like shit too." I smiled.

I would've never been the same without him in my life.

He laughed, wincing as his body shook. "Everything fucking hurts. I'm going to be out of commission for a while—a long while."

"Doesn't matter. Just get better, man."

"At least I didn't fuck up my tattooing hand, but I'm not going to be walking anytime soon." He flexed his good hand, balling it into a fist.

"I'll wheel your ass in every day if I have to. Maybe you can get one of those scooters all the old bastards use." I smirked.

Fucking old people drove him nuts.

"Shut the fuck up, asshole," he whispered, glaring at me.

"Well, at least the accident didn't ruin your ability to use such eloquent language." I laughed. The joy I felt with the simple conversation was unexplainable.

"Since when does your ass say eloquent?"

"You aren't the only one with a college education, Joe. Listen, man, some shit went down in the last twelve hours—more shit than just your accident. I need your advice, but I'll wait until your mind is clear."

"My mind's clear as a whistle."

I shook my head. "Nah, your shit got scrambled, and I need it at its best to help me figure out the shit storm that's about to rain down on me." I rubbed my eyes and raked my hands down my face.

"No, fuck? I gotta know now."

"Why me?" I laid my head on his bed, wishing it all away.

The bed moved slightly as the sound of his laughter rang in my ears.

It was the best damn sound in the world.

"You're going to laugh your ass off when you hear about the cluster-fuck," I said, sitting up to face him.

Suzy stirred as her eyes opened, a small smile on her lips. "Mikey," she said, her voice sounding sleepy.

"Hey, Suz. I didn't mean to wake you. Sorry, sweetheart," I said, watching her body melt against him.

"Don't worry. I want to be up. You need anything, babe?" she asked, staring up at Joe.

She looked relieved. Yesterday I thought she was going to have a meltdown and lose it completely.

They had a love that I hoped to find someday. I wanted someone to be my world.

Fuck, I sounded like a pussy.

I needed to sleep and get my head right.

"Nah, sugar. I'm fine just how we are right now." He pulled her tighter against his body and kissed her head.

I watched them with a dumb, jealous grin on my face. I touched my dick to make sure it was still there.

"Did the doctor come in while I slept?" she asked, nuzzling her face into his chest.

"Not yet. The nurse said he'd be in this morning before they move me to a regular room."

"I can't wait to get you home, baby," she said, closing her eyes.

"You just want me in bed and immobile," he teased as he smelled her hair.

"I'd prefer you unable to talk, but being stuck in bed won't be the worst thing in the world." She giggled softly, trying not to jostle him.

Holding my hands up in mock surrender, I said, "All right, love birds. This is my cue to get out of here. Call me if you need anything." I stood and touched my brother's uninjured arm. "I'm happy you're all right, brother. I love you even though you're an asshole sometimes." I squeezed his forearm, looking at the both of them with their mushy grins.

"Love ya too, man." He smiled.

"Bye, Mikey," Suzy said, without moving.

As I walked out of Joe's room, I sent Mia a text.

Me: You done yet with work?

I'd had as much hospital as I could take. The smell of antiseptic and pine made my stomach turn. I worried it would be permanently part of my sense of smell if I stayed any longer.

Mia: I'll be done in thirty.

Me: I'll be in my car waiting or do you want to meet at my place?

Mia: Meet you at your place.

Me: Hungry?

Mia: Famished.

Me: I'll have food, cock, and a comfy bed waiting for you.

Mia: What if I don't want it in that order?

Me: I offer—you choose.

I laughed, shaking my head. I really liked her.

Mia: I'll be there in one hour.

Me: Don't keep me waiting.

I approached my car with a giant smile on my face, and tucked the phone in my pocket. A white piece of paper flapped under my wiper, catching my eye. I ripped it off the windshield and glanced at it before crumpling it in my fist. Slowly, I peeled the crushed paper apart and stared at it.

Mikey,

You can't just leave us like this. How can you deny your own son? I'll never let you go. You're mine and we're yours.

I'll fight for you until my last breath.

I sighed, wanting to vomit, and crumpled the paper before throwing it on the ground. I'd deal with her shit soon and end her games.

Crazy and me did not fucking mix.

16

MIA

I SNUGGLED AGAINST MICHAEL AND RELISHED THE STARK CONTRAST OF his warm skin and the cool sheets against my body.

The soothing of his hand as he rubbed the back of my arm made me melt into him. I slowly moved my fingers over the scruff lining his jawbone; each hair tickled my fingertips. The coarseness on my skin felt like tiny shock waves moving through my hand. Listening to the beat of his heart, I drifted to sleep.

"Mia," Michael whispered in my ear, waking me.

"Mm." I was too tired to speak.

"I need you." His lips brushed against my ear as his hand caressed the skin just above my underwear.

"Yeah," I whispered, pushing my ass against his hardness, still feeling half asleep.

He wrapped his arm around me and pulled me closer, and his fingers dipped inside my panties. His breath felt hot and sounded heavy against my ear. Raking his fingers through my wetness, he moaned as he found my clit.

His damp fingers moved rhythmically against my tender flesh. I squirmed, a small moan escaping my lips. Arching my back, I pushed my ass against his erection. Moisture pooled between my legs; I needed more than his hand to dull the ache.

Moving away from my body, he placed me on my back without speaking. I didn't have to wait as I heard the crinkle of the wrapping before the bed dipped as he crawled between my legs.

I blinked through blurry eyes and watched his dark figure kneeling before me as he slid on the condom.

Leaning over my body, he whispered against my lips, "You okay, Mia?"

"Yes," I said in a sleepy voice, still not fully awake.

When he stroked the head of his cock against my opening, my eyes flew open. He thrust himself inside, waking me.

Warm hands pressed against my ribs before holding my arms above my head.

I relaxed my arms under his grip, enjoying the small grunts that filled the room and the feel of him inside me.

He pumped into me slowly, caressing my insides. Moaning, I felt the orgasm hovering just out of reach. I need more friction, more power to push me over the edge. I wrapped my ankles around his legs, as the pressure from the piercings hit me deep and in just the right way, sending a shock wave through my system.

The force of his thrust increased as he fucked me relentlessly. My fingers curled around his as he held my arms against the pillow. Wet warmth against my nipple made my body jerk. The sensations were overwhelming in my sleepy state.

As he bit down, I cried out, pleasure radiating throughout my body.

I pushed my head against the pillow; my arms grew rigid under his hold and my breathing halted. In the darkness, my eyes filled with vivid colors as the orgasm tore through me. Feeling like someone had knocked the wind out of me, I grew limp under him as he chased his release. Ramming his cock inside me over and over again, Michael cried out, body shaking until he collapsed on top of me.

Rolling away, he snapped the condom, pulling it off. The bed moved as he rolled over, wrapping his arms around me. Michael Gallo spooned.

"Sleep, Mia," he whispered in my ear, planting a soft kiss against my hair.

I closed my eyes, shuffling my ass back, leaving no space between us.

The peace I knew only when in his arms returned as I drifted back to sleep.

Michael seemed on edge when we woke. We both needed the gym to relax and unwind.

I touched his arm as he drove, seemingly lost in his thoughts. "He's going to be okay, you know that, right?" I asked, hoping to make him feel better.

He nodded his head. "Yeah, I know."

I studied his profile. His forehead was crinkled and his eyes seemed vacant. His sparkle and dirty humor had evaporated somewhere between falling asleep and our drive to the gym.

"What's wrong, then?"

"Just some stuff on my mind. It has nothing to do with us, Mia. Just some bullshit going on."

"I'm a good listener, Michael." I rubbed his arm, wanting him to share his worries with me.

Looking over at me, he exhaled and frowned. "I imagine you are, but some things are for me to deal with."

I pulled my hand back, placing it in my lap. "Okay," I said, looking out the window. I didn't have anything else to say.

We pulled into the gym parking lot after riding in silence. He could say whatever was on his mind had nothing to do with us, but I knew bullshit when I heard it.

He reached for my hand, giving it a small squeeze, as we walked into the gym.

"I'm going to run on the treadmill, want to come?" I asked.

"Nah, I need to lift some weights." Bending down, he kissed my cheek. "I'll catch you in a bit."

It felt platonic and impersonal, unlike the sex we'd had during the night.

"Don't forget me, handsome." I started to walk away and looked back at him with a smile. That just sounded needy and totally not me.

He had scrambled my brains.

He grabbed my arm, drawing me to his body. "I could never forget about you, Mia. You need to stop that thought right there. There's no

316

other woman I think about." He swatted my ass and whispered, "Off you go. No checking out anyone but me. Got it?"

Yes, the playful Michael was back!

As I walked away, I looked over my shoulder. "I can't help if someone is in my line of vision. What are you going to do about it, big boy?" I smirked.

His mouth broke out in a drop-dead sinful grin. "I have my ways of making you pay." He winked, and I wanted to jump in his arms and capture his mouth in a kiss.

Whatever had been on his mind in the truck had vanished.

Butterflies filled my stomach as I walked a little bit faster before he sidetracked us both.

"You know where to find me." Using my thumb, I pointed to the treadmills over my shoulder. I turned around, relieved to have a few minutes to myself.

The man had seemed simple to read until today.

I jogged on the treadmill, catching up with my emails. I'd been trying to finish reading a book for a week with no luck, and I used the time to read while I ran. After each page, I watched Michael for a moment before continuing to read.

He started with free weights for his arms. He looked in a mirror, studying his movement, and our eyes met from time to time.

He was stunningly handsome, with rippling muscles and not a lick of fat on him. I knew he worked out like a beast, but for God's sake, couldn't the man have a pinch of something somewhere? I loved the feel of his rock-hard body against mine.

He put the bar behind his head, squatting slowly before standing with a grunt. His face turned red and a vein protruded from his forehead with each lift.

I licked my lips, my book no longer interesting, as I kept my eyes glued to him. That was how he kept that rock-hard ass and the tree-trunk thighs.

I stared, mesmerized by his ass, watching it move up and down. Every muscle in his body rippled as he removed his shirt before lifting the weight again.

Holy fuck, he was hot.

He grunted with each squat. It was different than the one I heard during sex. This was a grunt of exertion and strain, not of pleasure. The effect it had on me was the same. My face grew flushed, as my core convulsed and my heart pounded against my chest. I grabbed the towel off the bar and blotted the skin around my neck.

Our eyes were glued to each other as we moved around the gym. The air between us was thick, the lust evident to anyone paying attention. He placed the weights on the floor and dried off his damp flesh.

I wanted to lick the sweat off his body, and I wasn't a girl that usually enjoyed a sweaty man.

His smile grew larger the closer he came to me before stopping between my legs.

He stood between my legs, staring down at me as I lifted the weight. "Need some help?"

"Nope, I got this. Twenty-four," I said as I pushed the bar up, trying to ignore his eyes raking over my body. "Twenty-five," I grunted, latching it in place, trying to catch my breath. "You shouldn't gawk, Michael." I smiled up at him, breathing heavily.

"I'm not gawking, Mia. I'm just undressing you in my mind and fantasizing about all the dirty shit I'm going to do to you when I get you back to my place."

My mouth gaped open as I sat up and stared. My attempt to slow my breathing was crushed by his words. The dull ache between my legs turned into a throb.

He touched my sternum, following the path the beads of sweat had traveled into my cleavage. "I want you this sweaty when you're under me, coming on my dick, screaming for me to stop." He kissed me whisper light, before backing away with a grin.

Smug bastard.

17

MICHAEL

POINTING TO THE ERECTION ABOUT TO BURST THROUGH MY SWEATPANTS, I said, "I can't believe you're going to leave me like this, doc."

"Yep." She nodded. "You'll survive; it's not a life-threatening affliction," she said, laughing as she adjusted her shirt. "You have to go see your brother, and I need to go home for a while."

"I can't call my mother or Suzy for help. This can only be fixed by you." I grabbed myself, adjusting my dick.

"Absence makes the heart grow fonder," she said, pulling up her pants.

Standing, I walked toward her, and she backed away. "Fuck my heart. It's my dick that's aching." I smiled and tried to touch her, but she moved out of reach.

"Call me when you're done at the hospital, and I'll see what I can do to help you out with that situation." Grabbing her keys off my kitchen table, she moved quicker than I thought possible.

"Come here, woman." I darted to the left, using the edge of the table for traction.

Squealing, she ran the opposite direction. "You may be big, but I'm quicker, Mikey."

I moved to the left and then quickly to the right, trying to throw her off kilter. "Woman, what did I tell you about callin' me Mikey?"

Stopping on the opposite side, she placed her hands on the table and leaned over with a huge smile. "I must have forgotten, but I remember there was talk of punishment, Mikey."

Moving again, I reached for her arm, but she slipped from my grasp. "Fuck, this goddamn hard-on is slowing me down. Rub it for me, please?"

"You're a pig," she said, laughing before sticking out her tongue and closing her eyes.

I moved as fast as I could to grab her. "Got ya. Come on, Mia. I can be quick." Dragging my tongue across her neck, I nipped her earlobe. Her laughter grew quiet as her breasts pressed against me. "Please?" I whispered, sucking on her ear.

She moaned, squeezing my arm. "No," she said in a breathy tone.

I palmed her breast, stroking her hard nipple with my thumb. "I'll make it worth your while." I pushed her backward toward the table.

"I don't want quick. I want long and hard." She bit my lip. "Call me when you're done seeing Joe, and if you're good, I'll make it worth your while," she said against my lips, causing my dick to twitch.

"Cock block." I released her from my grip and adjusted myself.

"I'd classify myself as more of a pussy hoarder than a cock block," she said before kissing my cheek.

It took everything in me not to slam her to the table and rip her pants off her. "You're maddening."

Her laughter filled the room as she walked to the door. Following close on her heels, I turned her and pushed her back against the door. I placed my hands on either side of her. "Are you sure I can't convince you to stay?"

She grinned before rubbing her nose against mine. "No. Go be a good brother. I'll be home later. Hit me up then." She kissed my lips and as she drew away; I pushed my body into hers and captured her mouth. "Still no," she mumbled against my lips.

"I'll call you. I'm going to need some serious help if I walk around with this hard-on all day."

"Probably won't be the first time in your life or the last." She giggled.

We both jumped as my phone vibrated in my pocket. Sighing, I pulled it out and glanced at the screen.

"It's my ma. I better get this."

Nodding, she opened the door. "Talk to your mom. I'll talk to you later," she said as she waved and closed the door behind her.

"Hey, Ma."

"Where have you been all day, Michael?"

"I'm coming, Ma. I had to work out."

"We have to be here for your brother while he's in the hospital. No one likes to be alone."

That was the problem with an overbearing Italian family. Mine had a tendency to be up each other's ass all day, every day.

Joe probably wanted some time alone with Suzy, but knowing my parents, his room had more people in and out all day than the Bunny Ranch in Vegas.

"Ma, you know my fight is coming up soon. I have to make sure I work out every day. I've slacked a bit and needed to blow off some steam. I'm jumping in the shower and I'll be there. How is he, by the way?"

"He's looking better and they moved him to a regular room. He's out of the woods, thank God."

"I'm glad to hear it. Anyone call Tommy yet?"

"No, I don't think he needs to know about it. Joseph will be fine. No need to worry him, Michael."

"Ma, he deserves to know."

My parents aggravated me with the bullshit. Thomas would want to know if something happened to any of us. He was going to be pissed when he found out he was kept out of the loop.

"We'll see. That's for your father and me to decide. Get your butt up here."

Thomas had been able to use his job to avoid Sunday dinners and family events that would bore any breathing human. My parents never harped on him.

Lucky bastard.

"Let me get off the phone and I can get there quicker, Ma."

Her soft laughter filled my ear. I loved the woman, but at times she drove me berserk. "Very true. See you soon, baby."

She called all of us baby. Guess it was better than "jackass."

My parents smothered us with love at times. Suffocated us, but at least we knew where they stood. We loved them unconditionally and wholeheartedly.

"Bye, Ma," I said as I tapped end before she could get another word out.

I walked in the bathroom, thinking about Tommy as I turned the phone over in my palm. I couldn't keep this from him. It just wasn't right.

I sent him a message before climbing in the shower.

Me: Call when you have time, got news.

I showered quickly, wanting to get to the hospital before my ma called again to chew my ass out.

As I grabbed my keys to walk out the door, my phone began to ring.

"Hey."

"Hi, Mike. What's going on? I don't have much time, but I wanted to check in," Tommy said quietly.

"It's Joe. He's all right now, but he got into a bike accident on Sunday."

He sucked in a breath before replying, "How bad?"

"Fucked-up leg and a broken hand. He was thrown, but he had on a helmet, or else we'd be planning a funeral right now."

"Fuck, I'm going crazy not being able to see everyone and know what the fuck is going on." He sucked in another breath before exhaling.

"You smoking again?" I asked.

"Yeah, when in Rome, brother."

I shook my head. I couldn't imagine the life he led or what he had to do to blend in with MC that he'd been assigned to.

"Should I come home?"

"Nah, I just wanted you to know."

"What the fuck took so long to get me the word?" he bit out.

"Ma and Pop didn't want to bother you and make you worry," I said as I climbed in my truck.

"Mike, text me anytime to tell me when bad shit's going down. I'll always call as soon as I can. Don't let them hide shit from me, ya hear me, brother?"

"Yeah. Are you okay, Tommy?"

I felt relieved talking to him. Every day I wondered if he was okay or even if he was alive. Being cut off from him was scary as fuck.

"I'm okay, just some crazy shit going down. I got it, though. Don't worry about me, Mike. Give my love to everyone. I gotta run."

"Take care of yourself, man. Watch your back."

"Tell everyone I love them, Mike. Please give Ma a kiss for me." His breathing had grown a little more uneven.

"Love ya too, Thomas," I said, tearing up as the line went dead.

I hadn't cried since I was a kid and got hurt on the school playground, but hearing Thomas' voice made it hard to keep my composure. It had been over a year since I'd seen him, and I felt relieved knowing he was okay and ready to fight another day.

Wiping the mist from my eyes, I threw the phone on the passenger seat and headed toward the hospital.

***

Walking down the halls of the hospital, I kept my guard up, expecting psycho Tammy to pop out of nowhere. I was sure she was stalking the halls looking for me.

Walking into Joe's room, I said, "I've arrived."

Izzy looked at me and rolled her eyes. "About time, you ass."

"Love you too, sis." I blew her a kiss and smiled. "Thank God for a private room." I laughed as I looked at them all.

Poor Joe. They were here staring at him all day.

"Joe, how ya feelin,' man?" I approached his bed and kissed him on the cheek.

He puffed out a breath, adjusting his body. "Bored to death and ready to get the hell out of here."

"I can only imagine, but I think you're going to be here a while. Sorry I wasn't here sooner."

"Don't worry about it. You have shit to do. When's the fight?"

Sitting on the edge of his bed, I replied, "Couple weeks."

"I want a front-row seat. I'm so pumped for you. Going to win this one?" He raised an eyebrow.

"Hell yeah. I got this shit in the bag if I stay on track. Have you ever seen me lose a fight?"

He shook his head. "Never, and you never answered about the front row."

"I have tickets for everyone. I grabbed a couple extra too." I bent my knee, putting it on the bed.

The room was filled with chatter. Izzy and Suzy were talking about clothes or some girl shit. My parents talked to Anthony in a whispered tone that I couldn't make out. I never knew my family could talk this quietly.

There was a brief lull in the conversations around us as Joe said, "What did you want to talk to me about?"

I hung my head and rubbed my eyes with my thumb and index finger. Fuck, bring on the Gallo Inquisition.

"What's he talking about?" Izzy asked behind me. Naturally she'd be the one person to pipe up after hearing that statement.

Turning around, I looked her straight in the eye and showed no fear. "Male shit, Iz. Don't concern yourself with it."

Her eyes became slits as she glared at me. Izzy knew me as well as anyone sitting in this room, and I prayed she knew when to drop the subject. "Always playing the penis card. Such bullshit."

"Isabella," my ma chimed in. "Did I raise you to speak that way?"

"I'm a grown woman, Ma, and yes you did. You had four boys and a girl. How else would I talk?"

My ma and Izzy broke into a fit of laughter.

I looked at Joe and I mouthed "later" to him.

He tipped his chin, not making any other movements. He knew as well as I did how nosy this group was, and I needed to deal with Tammy on the down-low.

"Why don't we all go to the cafeteria and let the boys have their talk?" My ma always tried to be diplomatic.

"Great idea, my legs could use a stretch," Pop said. "Come on, baby girl." Standing, my pop held his hand out to Izzy.

She sighed and put her fingers in his palm. "For you, Dad, anything you ask." She had him wrapped around her little finger.

They worked each other well and knew how to get their way. Izzy gave in on the small things because she knew my pop would always have her back; she'd always be his little girl.

"I'm going to stay here," Anthony said as he looked at my parents.

324

"I'm playing my penis card." He smirked at Izzy.

I swear to shit I could see a vein pop out of her forehead.

"We'll be back in ten minutes," Pop said, yanking Izzy out by the arm.

We sat in silence as we waited for them to walk far enough away that we wouldn't be overhead. Anthony poked his head out of the doorway. "All clear," he said.

"What the fuck is up, man?" Joe asked.

"Tammy has gone off the rails." I shook my head, still not believing her bullshit.

His eyebrows scrunched as he looked at me. "Tammy?"

"Scrapbook crazy girl? Did you hit your head harder than we thought?"

He laughed and grabbed his side. "Fuck, I remember her now. I've had other things on my mind than your women."

"She isn't one of my women. She saw me in the cafeteria here and she claimed we were engaged, dude."

"No fucking way." His mouth hung open as he looked at me.

"Yes, I told her to leave me the hell alone and she said how could I just leave her since we were engaged. When I denied her and I went to walk away…" I didn't want to finish the sentence. The mere thought of her words made my stomach churn. "She yelled out that she was pregnant."

His body stilled as his eyebrows drew together. "With whose kid?" Joe asked.

"Mine, dumbass." I shrugged.

"Is that even possible?" Joe asked, trying to sit up.

"Fuck no. I don't think so. I mean, I'm not a doctor, but if I remember my human bio class, there's zero chance."

"Were you careful?" Joe asked, as he rubbed his forehead.

Anthony just sat there, shaking his head as he played on his phone.

"Yes, and we only did it a couple of times. She couldn't possibly know if she was. Could she?"

"Shit, I don't know, but you need to find out, Mike."

I rested my head in my hand, running my finger through my hair. I had to find the craziest bitch in the county and stick my dick in her.

"I got to work this shit out and shut her ass down." God was getting the last laugh.

"I'd say you better do something before that shit blows up in your face." Joe pointed at me and shook his head. "Fight crazy by facing her head-on and putting her down."

"I'll figure it out. You have your own shit to deal with." I motioned to his fucked-up leg.

"Eh, a mere flesh wound," Joe said with a straight face.

We all started to laugh as we got the reference to Monty Python. The best movie scene ever made. When the guy loses limbs but still states it's just a mere flesh wound, until he's jumping on one leg without arms and spewing blood everywhere…epic. I think we drove my mother crazy for months re-enacting it as kids.

"You need my help, Mike?" Anthony asked.

"Nah, it's my mess to deal with, Anth. I just don't want it ruining whatever Mia and I have going on."

"Who's Mia?" Joe asked.

"Girl I met at the gym. She's a doctor here and we've been spending time together." I rubbed my eyes and raked my hands through my hair. "I really like her and don't want Tammy fucking it up."

"A doctor? I'm impressed, Mike. Wait, why was Tammy here?"

"She works here too. I'm so screwed if she runs into Mia."

Anthony looked up from his phone. "Oh, fuck. You better get it handled quickly before the shit hits the fan."

"Just once I'd like my dick not to cause problems," I said, looking up at the ceiling.

"Keep sticking that shit in any pussy around town and your problems will never go away."

"Just because you found Suzy doesn't mean you're the authority on relationships, Joe."

"No, but I knew when I found something so damn good that I'd do anything in the world to make her mine."

"Pussy whipped," Anthony muttered under his breath before laughing.

I had to get control of the situation.

Why did her ass have to go off the hook as Mia came into my life?

18

MIA

Michael hadn't seemed himself all week, distant and preoccupied. I asked him repeatedly to share whatever bothered him, but he said no and I stopped trying to pry. Sometimes, there are things I don't feel like sharing as I deal with the situation. I gave him his space and hoped he'd tell me in his own time.

My week had been busy, almost to the point of hectic. I worked at the hospital and the clinic every day. Michael trained, spent time with his family at the hospital, and kept the tattoo shop running.

His life was just as full as mine. We had to be creative when it came to seeing each other while his brother was at County. I met him early one morning to watch him train with Rob. There was a small ring that had been set up in the gym just for Michael and Rob to practice.

I was tempted to jump in the ring and take out some of my stress on the target or Rob, but I didn't want to make a fool out of myself. I used the time to run on the treadmill as I watched Mike kick Rob's ass. It brought a smile to my face.

Saturday night, Michael brought the DVD of his fight in New York to my house. He fought Victor "The Mauler" Torrez.

Sliding the disc into the DVD player, he explained that the match wouldn't be fought in a boxing ring and that he didn't box. I was clueless to MMA rules. To me it was just a fancy name given to a sport where two men beat the shit out of each other.

As soon as the match started to play, I knew I was right with my first assumption about what he called a sport—it was barbaric.

There was something about watching Michael that had me shifting in my seat and made me feel flushed.

Fuck, he looked sexy and powerful as he jostled from leg to leg on the video.

"Look at this next hit," he said, sitting next to me on the couch, punching the air.

His foot swept the other man's legs out from underneath him. Michael struck him in the face. Sweat and blood flew through the air as he connected with his jaw. High-definition television showed a little too much detail for me.

"That's called a ground-and-pound move." Staring at the television, he was transfixed, with a smile on his face.

"Did you win?" I asked, covering my eyes to avoid seeing the man struggle.

He turned to me with a look of shock on his face. "You'll have to watch to find out, but what do you think?" He said, laughing.

"You won or you wouldn't be showing this to me," I said with a smile before turning back to the television.

Although I knew the outcome, it made my stomach hurt to watch the footage. My heart beat in my throat as I sat on the edge of the couch, watching the recording through my fingers.

Michael squeezed my knee, patting it gently. "I can't wait to get back in the cage."

"How long did you say until the next match?" I looked at his face.

"Just a couple of weeks. I'll be cutting way back on my schedule at the shop for final preparations."

"Where is it?" I asked, praying it was far away.

How would I feel seeing him fighting with another man in the flesh instead of on a recording? The roar of the crowd with each blow was shocking, and in person had to be almost deafening.

"Right here in Tampa. I wanted in because it's close to home. You're gonna come, right?"

"Um, yeah, I guess I'll be there." I turned my attention back to the television as his fist made contact with the opponent's jaw again. His head flew back and I could see the satisfaction on Michael's face. "What made you travel to New York for this fight?"

"I want you there, Mia," he said, ignoring my question. "You have to watch at least one in person. That was a huge fight. It was on pay-per-view and helped get my name out there. I want to make a name for myself in this industry."

"Why would you do this when you're a successful business owner?" I looked at him, totally confused by the man I knew and the one I saw on the screen. The fighter scared the hell out of me, but the man to my side made me feel safe and comfortable. I thought of him as a softy, although I'd never tell him that.

"I do MMA for the thrill and the challenge. I'd give up working in the tattoo shop to fight full-time. Wait, here's the end, you have to watch." Touching my chin, he pushed my eyes back toward the television.

Michael had "The Mauler" on the ground in a chokehold. Their legs were twisted together, their bodies entwined as he squeezed the man's neck, cutting off his airway. I couldn't look away no matter how much I wanted to—I was transfixed—and then they released each other.

"What just happened?" I asked, confused why it ended suddenly.

"I won. The ref ended it because the guy was losing consciousness. Stupid rule, but..." He shrugged with a tiny grin.

"Oh," I said as I turned my attention back to the screen. His chest heaved from exertion; his eyes looked fierce, as tiny droplets of sweat slid down his body. Maybe high-def was a good thing after all.

"I could watch this recording a million times," he said, switching off the television, turning toward me.

"You probably have," I said, smirking.

"Smartass woman." He started to tickle me on my ribs.

I squirmed, trying to break free. "Stop!" I yelped as he pushed me back into the couch.

His fingers moved across my ribs as I tried to find my breath. "I have to teach you a lesson." The weight of his body made it harder to breathe.

I laughed and tried to pry his hands from my side. "Michael, stop. I can't breathe," I huffed out through the laughter, pushing at his fingers.

His hands stilled as he hovered over my body, face to face. "You're so fucking beautiful when you have a smile on your face." His eyes roamed my face as his erection pushed against my leg.

He was hard as a rock.

"Is it me or did the fight turn you on?" I asked.

I would never admit it, but my body ached for him. God, I was such a hypocrite.

"Your laughter did this to me, not the fight."

"I highly—"

He covered my mouth with his hand and placed a kiss on my neck. "No more talking for you."

I giggled behind his hand and my tongue darted out to taste him. "I thought you loved my voice," I mumbled behind his fingers.

"Shh," he whispered, running his nose down my cheek before he licked a path down my neck. The warmth of his tongue sent tiny sparks straight to my core.

My fingers dug into his back as I held him to me, enjoying the feel of his tongue. I wanted more. I craved him.

When his lips met my collarbone, my body flinched as my sex convulsed. I could feel the wetness between my legs. My body was a traitor, but at this point, relieving the throb was all that mattered.

My head fell to the side and I opened my eyes. The clock read six—I would be late to work. I pushed Michael off in a panic.

"What's wrong?" he asked, frowning.

"I'm going to be late to work. You have to go and I have to get ready." I jumped from the couch, pulling down my shirt.

"Your fucking job is getting in the way," he said, sitting up.

I hushed him with my finger. "We both have a lot of shit to do. I'll be off tomorrow if you can find the time to squeeze me into your busy schedule."

He smiled behind my finger. "I'll make the time. I'll do everything early so I can spend time with you."

"Michael, I'd say you're smitten if I didn't know you any better. Are you always this easy?"

"Smitten doesn't even begin to explain what I am at the moment, doc." He grabbed my hand and placed it on his cock. "Rock hard is more like it. You're always leaving me fucking hanging."

I chuckled as I stared into his eyes.

The man probably never had to wait for sex. Woman probably hung on him and begged for it.

"If you can't get it to subside, you know where to find me and my needle, handsome." I kissed his lips before moving out of reach, trying to avoid being pulled down on top of him.

"I've always had a fantasy of doing it in a storage closet where we could get caught." He smiled as he adjusted himself in his pants before standing.

Crossing my arms, I stared at him and shook my head. "I could be fired for that, Michael."

"Not if we're quick and quiet. It's the thrill of getting caught that makes it so fucking great." He winked as he looked down at me.

I swallowed hard, my mouth feeling dry suddenly. "I'll take your word for it."

"You'll see," he said as he brushed his finger across my lip.

I sighed. The man liked to live life on the edge, and so did I. I fully expected a visit to the hospital in the coming days.

"Okay. Now scoot. I have to get ready. People's lives depend on me." I pushed him toward the door.

He pouted and grabbed his chest, pretending to be wounded. "I'll show myself out."

He pulled me into a kiss. I wrapped my arms around his shoulders as he held my head in his hand. The velvety texture of his tongue and the hint of mint left me wanting more.

I moaned, my lips following his mouth as he pulled away.

"A little something to remember me." He released me and made his way to the door.

"Hey, what's your MMA nickname?" I called out to him.

"Why do ya ask?" he asked with one hand on the doorknob.

"Curiosity."

"Michael 'The Iceman' Gallo." He smiled and left.

I stood there and tried to think of him as "The Iceman," but he should be called the "The Raging Inferno."

19

MICHAEL

WALKING THROUGH THE HOSPITAL, I LOOKED OVER MY SHOULDER, paranoid that I'd run into Tammy. I still hadn't done a damn thing to deal with her the last week.

I'd been too fucking busy with the shop, family shit, and Mia.

With a smile, I pushed open the door to Joe's room, and found it empty. The bed was neatly made and everything was back in its rightful place, but no Joe. My smile evaporated.

"Can I help you?" a nurse asked behind me.

Walking out of the room, I approached her. "That's my brother's room. I was coming to visit."

"Ah, they released him a couple hours ago. He went home, darlin'." She smiled.

"Thanks, ma'am," I said before walking away.

Pulling out my phone to text my ma, I headed to the elevators.

Me: Mom, why didn't anyone bother to tell me they released Joe?

I loved that my ma had finally decided to join this century and learn how to text. It was easier to keep the conversations shorter, because she always found something else to say when we actually spoke. If I ignored her texts, she'd call anyway, but for the most part it was the best way to communicate with her—at least for me.

Mom: We weren't there when it happened. We're not going to see him until tomorrow. Let him rest and enjoy your night.

My night would be spent without Mia. I had plenty to do. The shop needed to be organized and cleaned, and I could use an extra workout. The match would be here before I knew it.

The elevator arrived, and I pushed the button for the first floor. I leaned against the wall and thought about what to do first. When the doors opened, I saw a sign for the emergency room and the decision was made for me.

I sweet-talked the receptionist. I explained that I was Mia's boyfriend and I was here to see her, but only if she wasn't busy.

"Let me go see if she is. Take a seat and I'll be right back." She smiled as she stood from her desk, smoothing her skirt with her palms. She swiped her badge and disappeared behind the door.

I cracked my neck, rolling it on my shoulders, as I sat in the chair and stared at the door. The people sitting in the chairs around me looked miserable. They were coughing, moaning and grimacing. I knew the people beyond the doors were worse than those sitting here.

The door opened; the receptionist stuck her head out and motioned for me to come.

"She's in between patients right now. Come on." She opened the door, and I stepped into the noisy corridor. "She's grabbing a cup of coffee down the hall on the right, last door." She pointed, smiled.

I nodded and smiled. "Thanks."

"Mm hmm," she said, eyeing me up and down, before leaving me to find Mia.

I debated if I should walk in and surprise her or wait in the hallway. I didn't want to scare the shit out of her. The hall was empty as I approached the door marked "Staff Only."

I leaned against the wall, crossing my arms as I waited patiently for her.

A few people gave me dirty looks as they walked by at the other end of the hall, and I smiled and waved. Fuck them. I couldn't wait any longer. I knocked on the door to get her attention. "Mia, are you in there?"

The door cracked open and she smiled at me. "Hey, what are you doing here?" she asked, stepping out into the hall.

"I've come to live out my fantasy." I smirked, resting my shoulder against the doorframe.

Her hazel eyes grew wide as a smile spread across her face. "Why are you really here?" She crossed her arms and laughed.

"Came to see my brother, but my family forgot to mention that he was released."

"Good for him."

"Now I'm the only one in need of attention." I stepped closer to her. "Can you spare a moment to take a look?" I looked down and back at her.

"Is stamina your problem?" Her eyes twinkled.

She was a total fucking ball buster.

"Why don't you tell me, doc?" I whispered against her lips. Her hair was perfectly slicked back into a tight bun, with her lab coat over her scrubs. The scrubs I could've done without—not sexy at all.

The corner of her lips twitched as she grabbed me by the shirt, pulling me down the hall. "I don't have long," she said, looking around to see if the coast was clear before pushing me inside the storage closet.

Fuck yes. Finally.

I locked the door and turned my attention on her.

Kneading her ass in my hands, I ravaged her mouth. Hard breaths and small moans fell from our lips. Finding her breast, I squeezed gently, caressing the hard nipple under my fingertips. Her body quaked at the contact. My dick ached to be inside her, not content with rubbing against her leg through my pants.

"Fuck, Mia. I want you," I growled, my erection straining to break free.

We nipped each other's lips.

She smirked, reaching in her pocket. She laughed, pulling a condom out.

"Did you know I was coming?" I unfastened my pants without hesitation. My cock sprang free and bounced off her stomach.

"I knew it was a possibility," she said against my lips.

"Better not be for anyone else, Mia." I grabbed the wrapper from her hand and tore it open with my teeth.

"There's no one else," she said with a straight face.

"Turn around, hands on the wall."

As she placed her hands on the wall, I pulled her scrubs and underwear down to her knees. The lab coat covered her ass, but I'd handle it.

Pushing down on the small of her back, I tapped her feet apart, giving myself a better angle. I placed the condom over my rock-hard dick carefully in the dim light. It glided easily against the silky wetness as I rubbed the tip against her.

She wanted it.

Grabbing her hips, I thrust myself inside in one quick move.

She cried out when I was fully seated, and my piercings stroked her depths.

"Shh. You're going to get us in trouble," I whispered in her ear, placing my hand over her mouth.

I pumped into her, searching for my release as I held up her lab coat. My body slammed against her ass, moving her with each thrust.

There was nothing tender about this type of fucking.

For the first time in a long while, I didn't care about my partner getting off before me. Mia always left me with a hard-on, and for once, I'd leave her wanting more.

Releasing her mouth from my grasp, I used both hands to steady her hips, and pulled her against me. She fucked me back, moving in my hands, as my cock disappeared inside of her.

Watching my dick move in and out was better than any porn movie I'd ever seen.

She whimpered as I pounded into her flesh. God, she felt fucking amazing—tight and wet as her pussy pulsated against my shaft.

She'd be sore and hopefully walking a little differently for the rest of her shift.

Biting down on her neck to stifle my moan, I gripped her tighter and pumped into her one last time.

"Fuck," I said against her neck, my teeth still biting down as my body twitched and shook. Dizziness and exhaustion overcame me as I rested my face in her back, trying to catch my breath.

"Hey, that's not fair," she said, wiggling her ass with my cock still inside her.

"All is fair in love and war. I'll make it worth your while, Mia…
tomorrow." I grinned against her coat before I felt her body stiffen.

I pulled out, grabbing a piece of crappy brown paper from a roll on
the shelf. I folded the condom inside before stuffing it in my pocket. She
bent down to grab her pants, and I could see the redness my body had
caused when it slammed into her.

I smiled, knowing she'd feel me on her for a while.

"You're an asshole," she said, glaring at me as she smoothed out her
scrubs and coat.

"I'll own that." I smirked, stuffing my dick inside my pants and
zipping them.

I kissed her on the lips, rubbing my nose against hers. "You made my
fantasy come true, and we didn't even get caught."

"Yeah, but I would have at least liked to get off too." She glared.

"Tomorrow," I said as I tapped her on the nose. "Lemme make sure
your clothes are right before we walk out." She turned around slowly, and
I checked her out from head to toe. "You look like nothing happened."

"Good." She smiled.

"Shit, I didn't do it right."

Her laughter filled the small space as she opened the door. We walked
into the hallway and she closed the door behind us. "Where are you
headed now?" she asked.

"I'm going to head to the gym. Enjoy your night, doc. Think of me." I
winked at her.

"I'm sure I will. That was so unfair, Michael. It's going to be the
longest shift of my life," she said, frowning.

"Gives you something to look forward to." I reached out to grab her
hand.

"You!" someone yelled from down the hall.

We both turned toward the voice as I pulled my hand back to my side.

At the end of the corridor was my worst nightmare.

Tammy.

Motherfucker.

I closed my eyes and held my breath as I waited for my fucking world
to fall apart.

I went from ecstasy to agony in under one minute.

20

MIA

MICHAEL LOOKED LIKE A TRAPPED ANIMAL AS A NURSE WALKED TOWARD him screaming. Not just any nurse, but the one I had soothed in the bathroom days ago.

Her hands were balled into fists at her sides as she approached with a red face, sneering.

I looked at her and back to him.

Fuck me, it couldn't be possible. Was he?

No, no.

Son of a bitch!

"Where the hell have you been?" She placed her hands on her hips, standing toe to toe with him.

"Do you know her?" I asked, hoping I was wrong.

She turned her glare toward me. "This is the asshole I was telling you about."

"Wait a minute," Michael said. "Let me explain." His face turned white as he reached for my hand.

Suddenly, my mouth felt dry as her words hit me full force. "He's your fiancé?" I asked, still in shock. I stared at them, blinking as my mouth hung open.

"Yes *and* the father of my baby." She smiled as she stood there with her hands on her hips. Her right eye ticked at the corner.

My heart sank as a wave of nausea hit. "Is this true, Michael?" I asked, turning to him, needing to hear his answer.

I looked at him and could see sheer terror.

He shook his head with wide eyes. "No, it's not true at all. Please, let me explain, Mia." He tried to touch me again, but I backed away.

I felt like a fool.

How did I honestly think I was the only woman in his life?

I knew better than to believe the bullshit of a smooth-talking, beautiful man, but I listened to my heart instead of my head.

I looked at the floor, shaking my head as I tried to decide if I should stay or go.

"Tammy, you're a crazy bitch. I'm not your fiancé. For fuck's sake, don't do this to me," he pleaded with her, as the veins on the side of his neck protruded and visibly pulsed.

"What's this, then?" she asked, thrusting her hand in his face.

He gawked, his mouth moving but nothing coming out.

"You asked me weeks ago before I even told you about the baby," she said, pushing her hand closer to his face.

She shoved the large princess-cut diamond ring in my face and wiggled her fingers, with a wide grin. My chest ached as my heart thundered against my insides.

I felt sick. I wanted to curl into a ball and cry.

"You knew about the baby?" I asked in horror.

His nostrils flared as he blinked slowly. "She's not having my baby, Mia," he said through gritted teeth.

Tammy pushed on his chest. "How can you deny your own child?" she screeched.

"Shut the hell up, Tammy," he roared as a crowd began to form in the hall.

I had never been so embarrassed in my life. I hung my head, gathering my thoughts.

I needed to get the fuck out of here.

"Mia, you've got to believe me. She's crazy and making it up," he begged, holding out his hand to me.

Looking at his hand, I took a step back. "She has a ring, Michael. I don't know what to think. I need time." Wiping the tear with the back of my hand as it slid down my cheek, I said, "Don't call me anymore."

"But Mia." His eyes were large and sad.

"No," I replied quickly. "Don't touch or talk to me. You need to work things out with your fiancée and future mother of your child. There's no room for me in your life. I don't date cheaters, and I certainly don't fall in love with men that run out on their responsibilities."

His hand dropped to his side as he stared at me. "Mia, you know she's crazy, right?"

"I'm right here, dickhead," Tammy yelled, punching him in the arm.

His arms flexed and his hand twitched. "Don't fucking touch me, you insane bitch. I know where the fuck you are; you're like a crazy nightmare that won't go the fuck away."

"I don't have time for this bullshit." I shook my head, tears threatening to turn into sobs. "You two deserve each other," I said before turning my back to them.

"Mia," Michael yelled as I walked away.

Hanging my head, I hid my eyes from the onlookers that had gathered in the hallway. I could hear their voices as I disappeared in the bathroom.

Finding an open stall, I closed myself in and shut the outside world out. I sat on the toilet and rocked. Silent tears racked my body. I realized the only person that had made me feel safe had turned into my biggest fear, heartache, and devastation.

Michael Gallo crashed into my world and turned it upside down.

I couldn't sit here and cry over a man that I'd only known a couple of weeks, even though I wanted to. Patients waited for me. I couldn't spend another moment wallowing in what could've been and will never be.

Fuck Michael Gallo and that crazy whore too.

Anger bubbled inside as I stood and walked out of the stall to dry my face.

My phone started beeping, text messages coming in rapidly from Michael. I turned the ringer off and stuffed it in my pocket before reaching for the door.

It was going to be a miserable shift at the ER.

21

MICHAEL

"SIT DOWN, BABY. TELL ME WHAT'S WRONG," MY MA SAID, PULLING OUT a chair for me.

She really was sweet, and I felt shitty to throw this on her, but I needed her.

"I didn't know who else to come to, Ma." Sitting down, I rested my hands in my lap. I stared her straight in the eye as I leaned back and figured out how to break this to her.

"I'm always here for you. You look like shit, Michael." She reached out and caressed my cheek, with a small smile.

I smiled and leaned into her touch as she soothed me. "I don't even know where to begin with this clusterfuck," I said, scrubbing my hands across my face.

"Only because you're so upset will I let that word slide in this house today."

"Sorry, Ma." I shrugged. "All right, here it is." I let out a breath before speaking. "About six weeks ago I started seeing this woman, Tammy."

"Seeing as in dating or..." She looked at me with one eyebrow higher than the other.

340

I sighed, wishing I could avoid the entire conversation. "We weren't dating. We hooked up a couple of times."

"God, I hope you used protection." She shook her head. "All these horrible diseases out there today."

"Ma, can I tell you the story or are you going to interrupt me?"

She laughed, patting my hand. "You go ahead, son. Sorry. I'll sit here and listen." Resting her head in her hand, she stared at me.

Her facial expression changed as I told her the story. Her eyes were as big as saucers and her mouth hung open by the time I finished. "Can I ask some questions now?" she asked.

Nodding, I motioned for her to ask.

"So you didn't ask her to marry you?"

"Nope."

"And she's not pregnant either?"

"Nope."

"Are you sure she's not pregnant?" she asked, tilting her head as she rubbed her chin.

"Fuck if I know, Ma. I wore a condom the couple of times we did it. Not one busted and all came from my pocket."

"You said she's crazy, how crazy we talkin'—Kathy Bates *Misery* crazy or what?"

"She could be Kathy Bates' daughter." I laughed.

"Jesus Christ, son. Didn't we raise you boys right?" She rubbed the back of her neck. She shook her head, leaning back in her chair, and stared at me.

"You did, Ma. Sometimes we just kinda let our other head do the thinking." I looked down at the table, flicking a crumb near my arm.

"We're going to have to talk with your father about this. We may need to call George and get a restraining order against her. Maybe you can get a pregnancy test done, and if necessary, an ultrasound to determine the date of conception." Her cheeks puffed out before letting the air escape slowly.

"I hoped she would just forget about me and move on. She ruined everything with Mia."

I was miserable without Mia. I never felt lonely, ever, but I felt the emptiness when she had walked away from me, from us, in the hospital a couple days ago. The longest two days of my fucking life.

"Is Mia the doctor from the hospital?"

"Yeah, you know about her?"

"Your siblings can't keep a secret worth shit, son, except for Joe. He's like a rock, and it makes me nuts." She laughed, her smile almost kissing her eyes.

"Well, Tammy confronted me when I was with Mia. Mia's confused and doesn't know what to believe. She hasn't returned my phone calls or replied to a text in days, Ma. I have to fix this."

Her smile fell. "Have to be crafty, son. Outthink her. Fight fire with fire." She paused and scrunched her lips. "Maybe you can get Tammy to go see a doctor and let you come." She patted my hand. "You can verify the pregnancy or lack thereof, and we'll proceed from there. It would give you tangible proof sooner than waiting for the court system, but if she's dangerous, then you need to stay the hell away from her."

"I got it, Ma. I can handle her. I'm not worried about her hurting me. She's already done enough damage. I'll do it. I'll call her. I think she'll go for it if she thinks there's any chance of us getting back together."

"It's playing in dangerous territory, but I leave the decision up to you. Just be careful, Michael."

I didn't have a choice.

I had to risk it all to win back Mia.

I needed to show Tammy for who she really was—a liar.

"I don't need this bullshit right now, Ma. My fight is in a week and I have too much going on to deal with this. I need it to end now."

"You'll do it, son. I'll talk to your dad tonight and he can call George. He'll get the paperwork ready to put the restraining order into action. You can call him and find out what to do next."

As I stood from my chair, I bent over and kissed the top of her head. "Thanks, Ma. You always have great advice." I inhaled the strawberry scent of her shampoo and was instantly brought back to my childhood.

Reaching up, she stroked my cheek as she said, "That's what I'm here for."

As I started walking to the door, her voice stopped me.

"Michael," she yelled.

"Yeah, Ma?" I paused, not wanting to miss her parting advice.

"Keep it in your pants, son. Got me?"

"Hear ya loud and clear, Ma." Shaking my head, I opened the door and left to set the plan in motion.

Searching through my phone contacts, I couldn't find her number.

Damn it.

Izzy had blocked her. I headed to the shop to find my sweet little sister and see if she'd be willing to help me smash Tammy once and for all.

Leading up to my match, my schedule at the shop had almost been nonexistent. I tried to work out and practice as much as possible without having to worry about the day-to-day operations.

Piercings were by special appointment. I'd only had to go in twice in the last ten days. Joe wouldn't be back for weeks. That left Anthony and Izzy to deal with running the business and tattooing.

Everything seemed to be in order as I walked through the front door of Inked. The waiting area looked tidy, just as I had left it, and the familiar buzz filled the shop. Soft voices came from the tattooing area. Death metal—Izzy's choice, I'm sure—played quietly so it blended in as background noise.

"Honey, I'm home," I yelled, walking toward the work area.

"Michael?" Izzy's voice echoed. "Get your ass back here, man."

Her face lit up as soon as she saw me. She snapped off her gloves and kissed me on the cheek. "Hasn't been the same without you here, driving us crazy and keeping our asses organized." She squeezed me, smashing her face in my chest.

I loved my little sister. Why? Because of moments like these, but definitely not her mouth.

"Thanks, Izzy. Sometimes you can be sweet...sometimes."

"Don't get too used to it," she said, sitting back down and putting on a new pair of gloves.

"Hey, how are ya?" I said to her client, whom I'd seen before. Couldn't remember his name for shit.

"Trying to survive your sister here. She's not as smooth as Joe with the needle." He winced, closing one eye.

"No one's as smooth as he is. He'll be back soon, though. You should've waited."

"I can hear you both," she said as she rubbed salve into his skin. "I can do this dry if you'd prefer." She snickered.

"No, no," he replied. "Please, you're doing beautiful work."

I laughed and turned my attention toward Anthony. "How you holding up being here with her by yourself, Anth?"

He smiled as he leaned back in his chair and stretched. "She's been pretty good without you and Joe here." His back cracked, and he sighed.

I could never tattoo and sit in the same crippling position for hours. I didn't have the patience to deal with customers for extended periods of time, and I certainly couldn't handle working on the same design for six hours like they sometimes did.

Piercing was quick, with little time for chatting.

"They're the ones that make me the way I am." She shrugged, talking to the man in her chair. "Anthony is my partner in crime. Isn't that right, Anth?" She laughed.

"Oh, how I know that shit. You two give me a headache most days," I said, shaking my head.

"You speak the truth, Izzy." Anthony laughed as he worked on the design. "What brings you by to visit us working people?" Anthony asked as he shaded in a rose.

I cringed because I knew her ass would be so ecstatic to hear the words. "Well, I need Izzy."

Her eyebrows shot up. "What? Are you feeling okay?" she asked as she looked up.

I rolled my eyes, sitting down in Joe's chair. "Yes, I need you to unblock that number you got rid of for me the other day."

"That girl with the damn scrapbook?" Her eyebrows drew together and a small crease formed between them.

"Yes, Tammy. I need you to unblock her number."

She sat back, tilting her head, and leveled me with her stare. "Why in the fuck would I do that?"

"Please, I just need you to. For me, Izzy, please," I said, pulling the phone from my pocket.

"You need to explain it to me first. I'm thinking you're the one that bumped your head, not Joe. I can't believe you're asking me to do this shit."

"Everything has turned into a mess. Mia won't see me or talk to me and it's all Tammy's fault."

"Still not giving me enough detail here, Mikey." She went back to working, not finding my request important enough to stop. "If she fucked everything up, why in the hell do you want to talk to her?"

"She's claiming I asked her to marry me and that she's pregnant with my baby." There it was, out in the open. I might as well have put that shit on a billboard now. Izzy never kept a secret.

"Wait, what?" She stood suddenly. "You drop that shit on me like it's nothing while I have a needle in someone's skin?"

"You asked for details, and those are *the* details."

"Give me fifteen minutes to finish this and we're going to have a talk before I do what you're asking me to. I want to know what the fuck happened with the doctor, too."

"Fine, I'll wait." I sighed and kicked my feet up on the customer chair. "How's Joe?" I asked. "Anyone see him lately?"

"He's well. You should go see him. He's been home for two days," Anthony said.

"Kind of had other things on my mind," I muttered.

"I know, but I'm sure Suzy is smothering him to death at this point," Izzy said, laughing.

"Joe loves that shit. He's probably milking it for all it's worth." Anthony mimicked a blowjob.

I missed being here every day. I missed the four of us as it had been weeks ago.

Everything had changed in my life in the last week—the highest high to the lowest low.

I wanted so badly to talk to Mia. I wondered if she knew how to block someone like Izzy had done on my phone. I hoped she hadn't blocked me. She hadn't read a damn message I sent her. I couldn't help myself. I had to keep trying.

Me: Mia, please talk to me. Tammy's lying and insane. You have to believe me! I miss you, doc.

I stared at the screen, hoping my message would show *read,* but nothing. It just sat there delivered and unread.

I opened Facebook and searched for her page. She'd posted something yesterday. I shouldn't have looked, because it made me feel more rejected than I already did.

She'd posted a quote from Cicero; "Nothing is more noble, nothing more venerable than fidelity. Faithfulness and truth are the most sacred excellences and endowments of the human mind."

I sat there, stunned into silence by her words, as I waited for Izzy to finish.

I still caught myself thinking of Izzy as a little girl. I pictured her with her pigtails flopping, playing hopscotch in the front yard, or begging us to play football. She always felt left out because we worried she'd get hurt. She turned into a tomboy in her teenage years before she realized the power of being a female.

Izzy was a tagalong, and we hated it when she was a little girl, but as she grew older, we'd used it to our advantage. We scared away more men than she'd ever know.

She was ours to protect...no matter the cost.

I had been lost in thought when she walked back into the work area after her client left. "All right, let's go outside and you can tell me what happened."

"Thanks, Izzy," I said, following her out back.

We walked into the Florida evening sun, and my skin felt like it was being burned. There wasn't a cloud in the sky, just a brilliant blue color and the sun shining brightly.

"Why do you want to talk to that psycho?" She crossed her arms over her chest, leaning against the building in the shade.

"I want to catch her in her lies," I said as I ran my fingers through my hair. "It's the only way I can do it quick."

"Why not just go to the police? I'm sure they can speed shit along if you tell them you're Thomas' brother."

"I will if I have to, but I need to prove to Mia that she's full of shit, Izzy. I can't have this hanging over my head with the fight coming up, either." I moved my neck from side to side, trying to crack it. I gave it a push before hearing the bones crack.

"What's your plan?"

"I'm going to pretend I give a flying fuck and ask her to take me to the doctor with her. I want to be the proud daddy. I'm hoping they can confirm that she isn't pregnant, and that it will at least win some favor with Mia. Hopefully it will get Tammy out of my life once and for all." I kicked a stone, watching it skip across the back parking lot.

"Could backfire in your face, brother."

"It's not my kid even if she is pregnant."

"It only takes once." She rolled her eyes like I was a fucking idiot.

"No shit, Sherlock. I used protection every time. She's grasping at straws."

"Fine, but when this shit blows up in your face, just remember I told you so."

"Oh, I'm sure you'll remind me every day, baby sister." I laughed.

"Give it to me," she said, holding out her hand.

Giving her my phone, I watched as she tapped the screen, and within seconds handed it back.

"You really have to show me how to do that," I said, scrolling through my contacts and stopping on Tammy's name.

"Nope. I'd miss out on all the good shit if I taught you boys everything."

"You're right. I'd give my left nut not to have to deal with your ass sometimes. Thanks, though, for this." I wrapped her in my arms, kissing the top of her head.

"Just let me know if you need reinforcements. I know Ma told you you're not allowed to hit girls, but that rule doesn't apply to me." Her smile grew so large it almost touched her eyes. "That's the bonus of not having a dick and being part of the pussy party." She laughed, slapping me on the chest.

"You're my go-to chick for an ass beating, Izzy." I smiled at her. She really could be adorable.

"Go get your shit straightened out. You have a fight to win, and I may or may not have something very important bet on the outcome."

My smiled faded. "You didn't bet on my fight, did you? Please tell me you at least picked me to win."

She nodded. "Fuck yeah. Who else would I pick? You're going to break that dude's neck."

"Only if I can get my mind in the game before that day. My life needs to even out so I can concentrate on one thing at a time."

"Well, what the hell are you still standing here for? Get." She shooed me.

"Yes, ma'am." I saluted her as I walked away.

I reminded myself I had a mission as I sat in the hot car, waiting for the air conditioning to kick in. I had a mission. I gave myself a pep talk, psyching myself up. "You can do this. You have to do this. " I held my breath and hit the call button. My stomach flipped with each ring.

"Michael?" she asked in almost a whisper.

I heard her voice, and I had to choke down the bile rising in my throat. "Hey, Tammy." I almost convinced myself that the hello was sincere.

"Oh my God. I'm so happy to hear your voice, baby. I've been waiting for your call."

I closed my eyes and gripped the steering wheel. "I'm sorry I've been a dick. Think you could forgive me?" I asked through gritted teeth.

"You know I love you, Michael. I could never stay mad at you."

Her voice made my skin crawl. "How's the baby?" I asked, rolling my eyes.

"Safe and sound. Growing bigger every day," she replied in a cheery voice. Clearly she had an entire jar of screws lose in her head.

"I was thinking..." I stopped and gave myself a moment to carefully form my next words. "I was wondering if we could go to the doctor so I can see the baby on the monitor, like an ultrasound. I told my mother and she said it's the most amazing experience to see the baby in the womb."

She gasped. "You told your mother?"

"I did. She's so excited to finally have a grandbaby. I want to show her a picture of *our* baby. What do you think?" I held my breath. *Please be crazy enough not to question my lie.*

She sucked in a breath. "Okay, I know a doctor at the hospital that I can call, I guess. Maybe she can get us in," she said with a shaky voice.

"Tell her it needs to be as soon as possible. I can't wait any longer, and it would make my mom really happy."

"I'll try and track her down at the hospital tonight. She may be there when I go into work."

"Perfect," I said, feeling relieved. "Listen, I gotta run. I'm supposed to be at my brother's. Text me when you have the details."

"I will, Michael. I love you." She drew out the words.

Cue the creepy music from *Psycho*.

"Back at ya." I tapped the end button, unable to spend another second on the phone listening to her and lying through my teeth.

She deserved the deception.

22

MIA

I ignored Michael, his calls, and his text messages. The anger inside me hadn't waned since I found out about Tammy.

He was the first guy in a long time that I'd let into my life. We weren't on the fast track down the aisle, but I had spent more time with him in the last couple of weeks than I had with any other man in the last few years.

I didn't drown my sorrows in ice cream and cry myself to sleep. I may have shed a tear or two after the shock wore off, but that was all Michael Gallo had been worth. I had too much on my plate to walk around all day upset about the shitty end to our relationship.

I did my shifts at the hospital and volunteered more than usual at the clinic. I filled my free time with work and kept my mind off *him*.

I hadn't been to the gym to work out since it all exploded in my face. I couldn't see him. Not yet. I didn't have anything to say to him.

I stood on throbbing feet, filling out my last chart, about a child that had arrived via life-flight, before I could head home. She had drowned in the family pool and was found by her mother. The little girl had been revived to the point that she was breathing upon arriving in the ER. Brain damage was almost a certainty with the lack of oxygen for an extended period. Talking to the parents was bittersweet. They were happy that their baby had survived, but mortified about the possibility of complications and the possibility they'd never have their little girl back.

Every day the hospital chipped out another piece of my heart. Between losing patients, talking with families, and a general feeling of helplessness—I felt broken. I was a shell of the person I used to be before I started med school with big dreams and foolish hopes.

"Guess what?" a woman asked in a giddy tone, distracting me from the chart.

I ignored the voice, signing my name and flipping the chart closed. The outline of a person standing a little too close caught my attention, but I still I ignored her.

"Hey, I'm talking to you," she said again, not moving.

Hell. I sighed before turning. "What?" I took in the sight of her —Tammy.

My blood turned ice cold as I stared at her smile. An overwhelming urge to claw her eyes out hit me, the fantasy in my mind bringing me a moment of joy.

"Michael and I are back together." She smirked.

Well, isn't he quick? She's as big of an asshole as he is. He'd been texting me since the day I left him in the hall with her and they were already back together.

"That's great news. I'm very happy for you." I gave her my best fake smile. "I'm kind of in a rush. My shift ended and I need to go."

The smile on her face faded. "I wanted you to know since you were so supportive, but I know there was something going on between you two. When I found you in the hallway it was obvious." She crossed her arms.

"Nah, we're just friends. You two are back together and you have a bundle of joy on the way. I'm truly happy for you both." My cheeks hurt from the smile; I still needed to make the bullshit happiness I pretended to feel be a little more believable.

She squinted at me, her mouth set in a firm line. "You slept with him, didn't you?"

I looked her in the eyes as I spoke very slowly. I wasn't about to jump on the crazy train. "Michael and I are and *were* nothing. He's yours."

"Oh my God, you did. You're a fucking whore. You're the reason he broke up with me in the first place, aren't you?" She bit her lip, gnawing on it, glaring at me.

I could almost see the wheels in her head spinning. Fucking great.

"I'm out. You can talk to Michael about me, but I don't have time for your bullshit, sweetie." I knew I sounded patronizing, but I couldn't get in a fight with a pregnant woman.

"I'll have a *long* conversation with him when we go to the doctor tomorrow for our first visit. He can't wait to see his baby and show it to his mother." Her phone rang, distracting her before she could continue.

I took the opportunity to get the hell away from her. "Good luck and congrats," I said, walking away before she could catch up to me.

"Wait, wait!" she screamed only a few footsteps behind me, her heels clicking on the tile floor.

I stopped in my tracks, closing my eyes. "What?" I asked in a clipped tone.

"I wanted to show you our engagement photo." She thrust her phone in front of my eyes.

If she had a knife in my chest, she'd turn it, just to make the pain that much worse.

I glanced at the photo and looked away quickly, not wanting it to be thrown in my face more than it already has. Something about the photo was off. "Wait, let me see that again." I grabbed the phone.

"Look all you want, sweetheart. He's mine, and this time, I'm not letting him go." She released the phone with a giant-ass smile on her face.

Touching the screen, I enlarged the picture. The faces weren't right. They didn't match the bodies. I stood there gawking at it until Tammy grabbed it from my fingers.

"He's so romantic. He proposed at the beach," she said, staring at the picture.

It was creepy, and her mind must be totally twisted. I hadn't realized until then how entirely off she was, and the depths of her craziness.

"It's a fairytale," I said. *This bitch lives in La La Land.*

"More than I could've ever dreamed of, really. He's mine, all mine." She hugged the phone, moving her body side to side.

"Yep, all yours." I smiled. "I really have to go." I needed to get away from her. "Good luck with your ultrasound," I called out as I walked away.

I snuck a glance over my shoulder. She stood in the middle of the hall with her hands on her hips, glaring at me. Her very presence put me on edge, but her delusions told me she was far more dangerous than I had imagined. I was the enemy to her.

I wondered if Michael knew about the type of over-the-top nutty that was his fiancée. I asked the security guard to walk me to my car. I didn't explain, but I never needed to. I felt a little more at ease as I drove home, but I looked in my rearview mirror every few seconds to make sure she wasn't following me.

Sitting in my driveway, I opened my text messages, my finger hovered over Michael's name and his last message.

Michael: *Goddamn it, Mia. I need you.*

My resolve wavered until I thought about Tammy. I wanted no part in their crazy bullshit. I would've described him as romantic and an amazing lover, but fuck, there wasn't a cock in the world worth this hassle.

I wasn't going to come between them.

My body felt heavy from a long shift on my feet, my mind was in a fog, and my heart ached. A small part of me wanted to see why he needed me, but I convinced myself it was a ploy.

The day had been emotionally draining already without opening my heart to him again and rubbing salt in the wound.

I pulled down the room-darkening shades and closed the drapes. I tossed my clothes to the floor before I grabbed a glass of water and my sleeping pills. I needed for this day to be over.

I climbed into bed and closed my eyes, wishing the day away. Sleep didn't come easy. Every time I drifted off, a different nightmare would wake me up. Images of patients and their horrific injuries and the screams of the injured, faceless people startled me awake. The last one dealt with Tammy waiting to slice my throat open in my car after work.

The sleeping pills were supposed to help knock my ass out, but tonight, they sure as hell weren't doing the trick.

I turned on the television, giving up on sleep, and looked through the guide. There had to be something happy to watch to help replace my nightmares. *Sleepless in Seattle* had an hour left, and I'd seen it a dozen times. I flipped to the channel and watched with stinging eyes. I needed the happily ever after.

I could recite the lines in the movie verbatim. When they meet on top of the Empire State Building at the end, it always brought me to tears.

I drifted off to thoughts of Sam and Annie.

23

MICHAEL

"I HOPE YOUR ASS HAS BEEN WORKING OUT, MAN. COUNTDOWN IS IN single digits. What the fuck have you been doing?" Rob said as I landed another blow.

"I got this, Rob. Shit's been going on in my personal life that I've had to deal with, and I'm still dealing with it." I stretched my shoulders, cracking my neck, readying myself for the next round. My heart hurt more than my muscles ached, but I couldn't stop.

"You need to get everything worked out before the fight. You need your head in the game. An hour here and there will not make you a champion."

"Oh ye of little faith. I took down 'The Mauler' and I sure as fuck can handle 'The Heat.' One problem will be taken care of today, and then I just have to win Mia back," I said as I grabbed a bottle of water, downing it before crushing the plastic.

Mia walking away and shutting me out hurt more than any injury I'd ever suffered in the cage. She gave me something good and pure to look forward to each day, but it was ripped from me by the devil.

His eyebrows shot up in surprise. "You hooked up with Mia, huh? You're a lucky son of a bitch." He shook his head but smiled. "She did ask me about you."

"When?" I asked, feeling hopeful.

"Weeks ago. Wanted to know who you were." He shrugged.

"Oh. I'd say we more than hooked up. I really like her, man."

"Before you grow a pussy, can you at least train while you pour your heart out?"

"I'm done talking, dick. I'm going to make you pay for the pussy comment."

I spent the next hour doing just that. Cocky bastard talked a good game, but he wasn't as fast as me. Rob knew the moves; his technical skills couldn't be beat. He used to be part of the circuit, but a nasty injury ended his fighting career.

I took my anger out on him. My jabs, kicks, and takedowns were aimed at him, but in my mind, Tammy received each piercing blow. The bitch had crossed the line, making me miserable, and today I would call foul.

"Jesus, that's the hardest you've hit me in a long time, man," Rob huffed, grabbing his shoulder.

"I don't have another outlet for my anger. You're my personal punching bag," I said, wiping the sweat from my eyes.

"Save some of it for the cage. He won't know what hit 'em. Maybe you shouldn't straighten the shit out first." He smirked.

"Fuck you, Rob."

"Kidding, Mike." He laughed. "Let's call it a day. Be here tomorrow morning at five. We don't have a moment to waste."

I collapsed on the bench, every muscle screaming as I rubbed my thighs. "I'll be here. Be ready for another ass kicking." I smirked. I never hit him hard enough to hurt him. I had more power in me than I ever took out on him. "Today I get everything ironed out and I'll be back on track. My mind will be focused."

"I hope so. If you want to get another big match like New York, you can't lose the next one."

"Shut the fuck up. I got this. I'm not losing. He won't be an issue." I pulled the tape off my hands, squeezing them to get the blood to flow to my fingers.

"That's the type of thinking that'll get your ass knocked out."

"Aren't you supposed to be in my corner?" I looked at Rob as he stood in front of me.

He had a cocky grin on his face; the bastard was trying to get me riled up more than I already was with the Tammy bullshit. "I am. Just reminding you to get your shit straight."

"Okay, Mom. I gotta go do just that. Now shut the fuck up and get outta my face."

Putting his hands up, Rob said, "I'm out. I expect a full report tomorrow. Bring some of that piss and vinegar with you for training. We're sparring for real, and I better not be able to take you down or you're in real trouble."

Pointing at him, I smiled. "Keep spouting your shit and I'll make sure you walk into the match with a limp."

He laughed as he walked away and unlocked the doors. I looked through the glass, trying to will Mia to walk through the door.

"She hasn't been here in a week. You can stop looking, pussy."

I didn't reply. She was avoiding me, and it stung more than his words.

***

I stared at Tammy as she looked around the exam room. She had a triumphant smile on her face and excitement oozed off her.

The thought crossed my mind that this could be a huge mistake. What if she really was pregnant? I shook my head, removing the thought, as someone knocked on the door.

"Come in," Tammy said, looking at the door with her hands clasped in her lap and moving her dangling feet.

A heavyset woman with gray hair entered the room. "Good morning, Tammy. How are you feeling today?" she asked as she sat down on the stool next to the exam table.

"I'm doing really great, Dr. Singh."

Kicking back, I put my hands behind my head to watch it unravel. I wanted to speak, but I figured that if the doctor had a brain she'd figure out Tammy's scam quickly.

"That's always nice to hear. How far along do you think you are?" The doctor asked, looking down, flipping through the file.

"I'm not sure. Not too far." Tammy fidgeted with her hands, looking down.

"You said the pregnancy was confirmed, though, right?"

"Yes, my family doctor confirmed it, but Michael"—she looked to me and back to Dr. Singh—"he's the dad and wanted to get an ultrasound picture as soon as possible."

"It's nice to meet you, Michael." Dr. Singh nodded at me and smiled.

"You too, doc. I want to know when the bundle of joy will be entering our lives." I couldn't just come right out and say I didn't believe a word that came out of Tammy's mouth—at least not in front of her, anyway.

"Well, let's see if we can get you a photo and determine a due date for you."

"Is it too early for that?" Tammy looked worried, but I honestly thought she was too nuts to really grasp the enormity of what was about to happen.

"No, I can see the stage of development and can give you an educated guess. Depends how far along you are, sweetie." Dr. Singh patted Tammy's leg.

"I can't thank you enough for doing this so quickly. I know how busy you are," Tammy said with a smile.

"I always try and help out the hospital staff the best I can. You're lucky I had a cancellation."

I was bored with their chitchat to the point where I had started to become annoyed. "Ladies, I don't mean to be a jerk, but I'm on pins and needles here." I rubbed my neck and tried to calm myself down.

"I know you're both excited. Lean back, Tammy, and lift your shirt," Dr. Singh said, pulling over the ultrasound equipment. She grabbed a paper cover-up, tucking it in Tammy's pants, pulling them down to expose her belly. She squirted blue liquid on her stomach as Tammy began to laugh.

"I know it feels funny, but at least it's warm. Now, let's see what we have here."

Swallowing hard, I moved to the edge of the seat. My legs began to shake as my stomach felt like someone was inside beating the fuck out of it.

The wand glided across her stomach as the doctor stared at the screen. She leaned forward and stared before moving the wand a bit.

I had no idea what the hell I was looking for, but it didn't stop me from trying.

"That's strange," Dr. Singh said, her face almost pressed against the black-and-white screen.

"What's wrong?" Tammy looked panicked as she bit her lip, sitting up on her elbows.

"I don't see anything." Dr. Singh moved the wand again and squinted at the monitor.

The angels began to sing in my head, and I felt vindicated as relief flooded my body.

"Wait," Dr. Singh said.

Fuck, no way did something magically appear.

My heart stopped and every ounce of air left my lungs.

"False alarm," she said, frowning.

Jesus fucking Christ, she almost gave me a heart attack. I started to breathe again, almost dizzy, on the verge of a panic attack.

"Tammy, I don't see an embryo, sweetie. Are you sure you were pregnant?"

"What do you mean 'were'?" Tammy's mouth hung open.

"I don't see anything at all." The doctor shook her head and looked at me with sad eyes.

I wanted to fist bump her, not cry.

"I lost the baby?" Tammy's lips began to quiver and her eyes glistened.

The crazy bitch actually was an amazing actress. I'd give her a fucking Oscar.

"I can't say that you were ever pregnant, but if you were, then yes, I'm sorry," Dr. Singh said as she put the wand in the holder.

Every muscle in my body relaxed, and I felt exhausted as I watched the doctor wipe Tammy's abdomen.

"I can't believe it," Tammy whispered as she wiped away tears.

"You can try again. This is common in the first trimester." Dr. Singh was trying to be supportive, but I'd bet money based on her facial expression that she didn't think there ever was a baby. "Sometimes tests can be wrong, sweetie."

"Stop calling me that!" Tammy yelled, covering her ears.

Enter psycho Tammy.

"You're lying about my baby." Her hands fell to her stomach as she cradled herself. "He's in there." She caressed her stomach.

Dr. Singh looked stupefied. I was sure she was used to a bit of crazy dealing with hormonal pregnant women all the time, but Tammy was her own special brand.

"You can always get a second opinion." The doctor rubbed her head before she started to scribble in the file.

I sat there, not wanting to cause a scene in the doctor's office by confronting Tammy with her lie.

"I will. You obviously don't know what you're talking about."

The doctor's eyebrows shot up. She saw the crazy. Recognized Tammy for who she really was—cuckoo.

"It's your right as a patient," the doctor said.

Tammy jumped off the table, adjusting her pants as tears streamed down her cheeks. "Let's get the fuck out of here, Michael. I need to find a real doctor." She glared at Dr. Singh.

The doctor looked at me, dumbfounded. "I'm sorry," she said with a halfhearted smile.

I shrugged and tried to hide my smile. "Don't worry about it, doctor. It's not your fault."

"What the fuck? Yes, it is. She's lying to us, Michael." All the tears on her face had disappeared, replaced by coldblooded hatred.

"Let's go, Tammy. Let's get you out of here." I held my hand out to her as I bit my lip.

No one spoke as we walked out of the room. Tammy walked right by the checkout desk before bursting into the waiting room. "She's a fraud," she yelled at the room full of women with swollen bellies.

"Shh," I said as I clamped my hand around her mouth from behind. "Save it for outside," I whispered in her ear.

I kept my hand on her mouth as we left the doctor's office.

As soon as we made it outside, she yelled, "I can't believe her. There's a baby in my belly." She rubbed her stomach and stared at her hands.

"Let's just get you home." I wanted to drop her off and immediately file for a restraining order. My suspicions were correct, and it was time to put Tammy in the past.

"Will you stay and hold me?" She looked at me with wide eyes, clinging to my shirt.

"I will." I hated lying, but with Tammy it was easy. I didn't flinch with my words. "Come on, get in. I'll stay as long as you need," I said as I held the door open.

She gave me a weak smile as I closed the door and fought every instinct I had to run. After I climbed in, she curled up to me. She held my arm as I drove, and I didn't look at her or return her touch. We drove in silence.

"You're coming in, right?" She looked up from my shoulder with a meek smile on her face as I pulled in her driveway.

"Yes." I wasn't going to fucking cuddle, either. This time I wouldn't leave her house without the scrapbook safely in my possession. "Let's get you into bed so you can rest."

Her smile grew wide as she looked into my eyes. "I can't think of anything that would make me happier, Michael." She climbed out of the car and waited for me.

Holding my arm, she opened the front door.

"Go get ready and I'll be right in. I'm going to make us some tea," I said, wanting her to go away.

"Oh, okay," she said as she stood on her tiptoes, kissing my cheek.

"Take your time, put something comfy on, and I'll meet you in bed."

She walked away with a giant smile on her face, looking back at me before disappearing inside her bedroom.

I turned on the water, to hide any noise, before I looked through the living room.

Where the fuck was the scrapbook? It wasn't on the coffee table, like it had been the last time I was here. I started to panic, my heart pounded, and sweat beaded on my brow. I needed to find it and get the fuck out of here.

As I walked by her television, I spotted it. Victory was mine. I grabbed it and tucked it under my arm.

Turning off the water, I stood in the kitchen, out of her line of sight from the hallway. "You okay in there?" I called out to her.

"Yeah, I'm going to jump in the shower to freshen up. Okay, baby?" she replied from the bedroom.

"Go ahead. I'm just finishing up with the tea. I'll be waiting for you."

"I'm hurrying," she yelled.

As the shower turned on, I waited, listening for her to climb inside. I left the house as quietly as humanly possible before jumping in my truck and breathing a sigh of relief.

I could only imagine the scene when she walked out and didn't see me there. She wasn't my issue to deal with anymore; it was for the law to handle.

First stop would be Izzy to put the block back on my phone, and then to George. I needed to sign the restraining order and have it executed.

Mia was the next thing to resolve.

I had to get her back.

She was the one prize I couldn't lose.

24

MIA

I STARED OUT OF THE SLIDING GLASS DOORS THAT LED OUT TO MY LANAI, sipping a cup of coffee. I inhaled the sweet scent as I watched the palm trees sway in the summer breeze. I needed to blow off some steam. Running was the best option, but out of the question in the blazing sun and humid air. Even early in the morning, the humidity outside was enough to make your hair instantly frizz and your skin damp within seconds.

I tapped my coffee cup with my finger and weighed my options. Pass out from running outside or head to the gym and possibly run into Michael. Why couldn't my life be simple anymore?

A pounding on the door made me jump and spill my coffee.

"Fuck," I muttered, wiping my hands on a napkin. Nothing like a peaceful morning ruined by a Mormon searching for a new convert.

I trudged to the door, annoyed with the interruption. Instead of a gaggle of religious people, Michael stood there with a package tucked under his arm, looking really pissed off.

My heart hammered, wanting to burst through my chest.

"Mia," he said, holding the doorframe.

"What do you want, Michael? Haven't I made it clear that I don't want to see you?"

He closed his eyes, letting go of the doorframe and taking a step forward. "I can't let you shut me out." He shook his head as he opened his eyes.

"It's not your decision to make." Crossing my arms, I didn't let a bit of weakness show through. That's the problem with men—they want control, and I wasn't used to giving it up.

"Fucking hell," he muttered as the hardness in his face melted away. "I *need* to talk to you."

I didn't move. "We're talking. Say what you need to say and go."

I had to stay strong, when all I wanted to do was jump in his arms and make up. I wanted to erase the last week. I needed to be strong. I'd never play second fiddle to anyone.

"Can't I come in?" He straightened, taking another step forward.

I held out my arm, stopping him. "Here will do."

He balled his hands into fists as he stared at his feet. "First, Tammy is *not* pregnant. I had that confirmed yesterday by a doctor." He paused.

I took that opportunity to jump in. "That's lucky for you. I ran into Tammy yesterday and she told me you two were going to get an ultrasound." His eyes widened as I spoke. "I was also told that you're very much back together and happier than ever."

"We are not back together. I spent yesterday afternoon filing a restraining order against her."

My stomach filled with butterflies as he reached to touch my arm, but he pulled away at the last second.

"I needed her to trust me to prove she wasn't carrying my baby. She's nothing to me," he pleaded.

"Are you so careless with women, Michael? We're here to be used?"

He stiffened and glared at me. "Are you fucking kidding me right now? I've never used you. I did nothing to make you feel that way, Mia."

"I felt dirty in the hallway of the hospital when Tammy flashed her ring in my face. I felt used and worthless. No one has ever made me feel that way." I choked back the tears that wanted to escape. "I've never allowed anyone to make me feel that way until you came into my life." I shook my head, and my shoulders fell.

"Mia, sweetheart," he said tenderly. He touched my arm, and the electricity passed between us. The snap, crackle, pop. The spark hadn't died, no matter how hard I tried to smother it.

"Tammy's not in my life. I never promised her a relationship or a forever, and I never asked the crazy woman to marry me. You have to believe me." He rested his hand against my cheek, and I wanted to melt into his touch, but I didn't.

"I want to, Michael. I really do." I looked into his soft caramel eyes and felt his sorrow. It was like a punch to the gut. "How do I know it's really over between the two of you?"

"My lawyer is taking care of it."

"Sometimes the law can't stop someone like her. It's a can of worms I'm not sure I can handle right now. I have enough shit happening in my life without looking over my shoulder all the time."

"I'll protect you." He smiled.

It was megawatt strength, and amazing. It sent a thrill through me that he wanted me so badly, but could I willingly lay myself out for this man?

He grabbed my chin, bringing my eyes to his. "Don't throw what we have away, Mia. There's something that brought us together. I feel like I've known you forever, and I don't want to be without that feeling. I can't lose you."

I felt at home in his arms, and truly at peace when he entered my life. I closed my eyes to break the connection. The enormity of the moment sank in as I opened them. "I don't know," I said, staring at his chest. He'd be able to see my vulnerability if I looked at him.

"How can you deny what's between us, Mia?" His soft lips touched mine, and I couldn't pull away. I leaned into him, inhaling the soft, musky scent that was purely Michael. "We have something here that can't be denied," he said against my lips.

"Michael—" Before I could finish the statement, his mouth enveloped mine, effectively shutting me up.

He wrapped his arms around me. The touch that I had missed for days almost brought me to my knees. Pushing me into the house, he kicked the door closed behind us. I couldn't deny him any longer. I couldn't lie to myself and say what we had wasn't magical in some way.

I pulled away and stared into his eyes. "Only me?" I asked. I needed the affirmation that I was it for him. I wouldn't be in competition with anyone else for his love and affection. I'd never let myself be *that* girl.

"No one else," he said before capturing my mouth.

The sound of his breath as he devoured my lips sent an electric pulse through my body. I loved everything about this man, down to the small noises he made when we kissed.

"I'm scared, Michael," I whispered as he broke the kiss.

"Of what?"

"You." I sucked in a breath.

He held me at arm's length. "Mia," he said, lifting my chin. "I won't break your heart. For the first time in my life, I've found something worth fighting for, someone more important than me." His eyes searched mine. "Give me a chance to prove it. I'll do everything in my power to make you happy."

"How do I know I can trust you? I want to believe you, but what if I was the other woman, Michael? I can't just pretend like nothing happened without knowing for sure." I stared into his eyes.

"I have proof. I brought this to show you." He held out the large brown envelope.

"What is it?" I asked, not sure I wanted to open it.

"Just look. I want you to see Tammy for who she really is. My statement to the police is in there, along with evidence and screen shots of her text messages. She never mentioned a baby, Mia. She lied and tried to trap me." He pushed the envelope forward into my hands.

I walked to the couch and set it on the coffee table. Michael sat next to me, not speaking, as he watched me. I removed the contents one by one. A book and a couple of sheets of paper were inside. Setting the book on the table, I grabbed the papers and flipped through them.

I read the text messages first, paying close attention to the timestamp. Not one said anything about a baby, just Tammy begging him to come back to her. The messages went from pleading to downright mean and threatening. The conversation was entirely one-sided. They were all from before we met. He had ended it with her. I wasn't the other woman.

"What's this?" I asked, holding the black book in my hand.

"Take a look. It's an eye-opener for sure. Tammy made it."

I nodded, opening the cover to reveal the first page. It read "Michael

& Tammy Gallo," with a picture of them on their wedding day. Only it wasn't them. I started laughing.

"I told ya," he said, running his fingers across my hand.

"No, it's just..." I tried to stop laughing. "She showed me a picture like this, but an engagement photo."

"Just great." He reached for the book.

I batted his hand away. "I'm not done," I said as I turned the page.

"Knock yourself out. It gets more bizarre the deeper you go." He leaned back and relaxed.

The engagement photo she had showed me was next, followed by a series of wedding shots. When I came to a page filled with children, I stopped and the laughter I had fought so hard to stop bubbled to the surface.

"Madelyn Gallo," I said, still laughing as tears formed in my eyes.

"Don't forget about Mason," he said, sitting up. "She picked out all the names." He smiled.

"She's seriously a wack job." I shook my head, still stunned by her audacity. "Didn't you know she was this nuts before you slept with her?"

"We were never a couple. I didn't figure it out until I found the book. I walked out of her house that day and never looked back." He rubbed my arm and grabbed my chin. "Mia, I never lied to you. Not about Tammy or anything."

I searched his eyes. With all the information and the sincerity on his face, I knew he spoke the truth. "I believe you, Michael."

"About damn time," he said, moving to kiss me.

"I'm still mad at you," I mumbled against his lips.

Pulling away, he rested his forehead against mine. "Take it out on me in the bed, Mia. I can't wait another minute to feel you under me."

"Wait," I said, pushing him away.

His smile evaporated. "What?"

"I said I believed you, not that I'd have sex with you." I shook my head and tried to make the statement believable. All I wanted to do was make love to the man and fall asleep in his arms. I missed his body against mine as I slept.

He gave me a cocky grin, the one that I loved. "Are you mine, Mia?" he asked, the corner of his mouth twitching.

CHELLE BLISS

"I haven't decided," I lied. There was nothing that I wanted more than to be his.

"Let me help you with that decision," he laughed, as he picked me up and hoisted me over his shoulder.

I laughed, swatting his ass so hard my hand stung.

"That's it baby, I like it rough," he said, chuckling, as he walked toward my bedroom.

I bounced on his back, biting his shoulder blade, smacking him again.

"Damn," he said as he spanked my ass twice, making me yelp. "I'd say we both have some emotions that need to come out. I'm going to fuck every bit of pissed-off out of you and show you who you belong to."

"I wanna see you try," I said, giggling.

He threw me on the bed, and all the air left my lungs as I hit the firm mattress with a bounce. He looked large and imposing standing at the foot of my bed. His shoulders were broad and the muscles in his neck were corded tightly. The t-shirt stretched across his torso looked like it would rip with the slightest movement. His brown hair lay across his forehead in a mess. He looked delicious and more handsome than ever.

"I'm up for a challenge," he said with a smile, as he removed his t-shirt.

Fuck, he really was beautiful. I sat up on my elbows and watched him undress. Every movement made his muscles stretched and contracted. He wasn't wasting a moment or doing a seductive striptease. I needed to feel him.

This wouldn't be lovemaking or rekindling—this was anger banging.

He pushed me back against the bed, opening the tie of my robe. He pushed it open, exposing my nightie. "Still mad?" he asked, his hands gliding across the cool silk on my abdomen.

"Yes." Damn, my voice wasn't strong. I knew he didn't hear the conviction behind my words.

He sat on his knees, grabbing the material with both hands. His palms slid effortlessly against the smooth nightie. His hands stopped just under my breasts before making the journey back down to my bare thighs. He grabbed the bottom of the nightie, pulling it from the middle, and tore it in half.

"Michael," I yelled. The air conditioning caressed my skin and goose bumps covered my flesh.

He laughed. "Quicker this way."

"I could've just taken it off, for fuck's sake."

"That *was* for fuck's sake, Mia. I'm sick of waiting. It's been days since I've been inside you."

I hit him square in the chest as he leaned over my body. Why did men have to destroy shit in the name of passion?

"Oh, yeah. Just like that. I like a little fight in you." His eyes turned dark.

"I hate you." I glared at him.

"No you don't," he said as his mouth clamped down on my nipple.

I arched my back, crying out in ecstasy.

He moaned against my trapped breast, causing a vibration to skate across my skin and my core to pulsate as I pushed him. "Don't fight it; you know you want it, doc."

I sighed, lying back to enjoy the feel of his lips on my skin, because I did want it. I ran my fingers through his hair before gripping it tightly in my fists. I held his mouth in place as tiny shocks shot through my body. The familiar ache between my legs became almost unbearable. I dug my heels into his ass and ground myself against him.

He tried to lift his head, but I pushed it harder against my chest, almost smothering him. I could feel his laughter against my torso as his body shook in my grasp.

"Put your cock in me," I said, releasing my heels, to give him the ability to move his lower half. I felt powerful, even if it was a lie. He could overpower me in a minute, but he let me play the game.

His lips popped off my skin and he looked into my eyes. "Don't you want to kiss a little first?"

"This isn't lovemaking, Michael. You're fucking me. Put it in or get the fuck out." I sounded harsh and strong, and it sent a thrill through me.

His eyebrows shot up, a small smirk on his lips. "That's fuckin' hot, doc."

"Shut the fuck up and do it." I kicked him in the ass.

"I love when you talk dirty to me. It makes me rock fuckin' hard," he said as he reached down and fisted his cock before rubbing it against me.

"Stop!" I yelled, frozen in place. "Get a condom from my nightstand."

"'Put it in. Stop. Any other commands?" he asked, as he reached for the drawer.

"You forgot, 'shut the fuck up.'" I laughed. I didn't know what had gotten into me, but I liked it.

"Kinda rough on me, aren't you?" he asked, as he unrolled the condom, paying careful attention to his piercings.

"I'm just getting started, big boy."

"You just made my balls tingle," he said as he nestled between my legs. Hooking his arms under my thighs, he pulled my body to his. "Let's get one thing straight, doc, I'm in charge here," he said as he stroked the tip of his shaft against me. "This is my pussy." He smacked my clit with the head.

"I don't see your name on it," I said, winded from the sting.

"It will be, but for now, possession is nine-tenths of the law," he said as he rammed his cock into me in one quick thrust.

My back arched as he pulled out and pushed back in with greater force. I wouldn't have described him as gentle the other times we'd been together, but this was rough and raw.

With the next thrust, I smacked him in the face. He flinched, stopping to stare at me through slitted eyes. "What the fuck was that for?"

"What you put me through."

His eyes searched mine for a moment before he pounded into me again.

I smacked him harder, but this time he didn't flinch. "For not being straight with me," I said quickly, before he could ask.

His eyes grew dark as his mouth set in a firm line. He pummeled me and I swung again, but he captured my hand. "You got two free shots, no more." Leaning forward with my wrists in his grasp, he held them above my head.

I fought to free myself, bucking against him. His muscles contracted with each thrust, and the sight of him alone could have me on edge. I bit my lip to quiet the moans that I wasn't ready to give to him.

Beads of sweat formed across his skin as he pounded into me.

He released my hands and I grabbed his biceps, curling my fingers around the thick muscles. Using my grip to push myself against him, I met his thrusts, our bodies slamming against each other. My body bounced off him, and the pressure of his cock hitting my depths drove me closer to the brink.

Our bodies collided, the impact hard enough to cause the headboard to hit the wall with a loud thud. I planted my feet into the mattress, using them to steady myself as I continued to push into him. It only took a few more thrusts before my body tightened and I spiraled into the most glorious orgasm of my life.

It wasn't the body-tingling orgasm that I'd experienced before. This was earth shattering—life changing, no one else would ever compare. Colors burst behind my eyelids as I rode the wave of ecstasy until I gasped for air through blurry eyes.

Michael wrapped his arms around me, cradling me against his chest as he cried out in his own rapture. He twitched, and his body shook in waves.

Releasing my body from his arms, he held himself above me. "Jesus Christ," he huffed out before shaking his head. "That was amazing. Fuck, I've never felt anything like that before."

I didn't reply. My mind was muddled from the bliss it had just experienced. He rested his forehead against mine; his harsh breath skidded across my skin. "Getting you pissed off has its advantages."

Not in a million years did I think we'd be in this situation when I sat there staring out the window sipping my coffee. I figured I was through with Michael Gallo, but after a kiss and mind-blowing sex, the craving was back worse than ever.

My vision blurred as I thought about all we'd been through the last couple of days. I didn't think the Tammy situation was over, but Michael said he'd handle her. I had no doubt in his abilities, but her craziness couldn't be planned for. She was the most dangerous form of opponent.

"What are you thinking?" he asked as he turned over, stretching out across the bed. He slid his hand under my body, pulling me to him.

"I don't know what to think." I snuggled into him and let the tears flow.

"Hey, hey. Don't cry. I know it was good, but I've never brought a girl to tears before."

"You ass," I said, smacking his chest. "I'm scared, Michael."

"Of what?"

"You, Tammy, this," I said, waving my hand over his body.

"Don't worry about Tammy. She's being dealt with. Don't be scared of me or us. We got off track, thrown off by a person nuttier than a Snickers bar."

I bit my lip to stifle a laugh. "You have such a way with words." I couldn't hold it in any longer. I laughed and buried my face in his side.

"Well, how would you describe her?"

I looked up at him, and the tears of worry turned to those of uncontrollable laughter. "You hit the nail right on the head."

"That's enough about her. Let me just enjoy the feel of you in my arms. No more talking, doc."

I snuggled into his side and closed my eyes. I'd never slept so contently as I had when I was in his arms. Closing my eyes, I let his warmth and steady breathing lull me to sleep.

25

MICHAEL

I STROKED HER ARM UNTIL HER BREATHING DEEPENED AND SOFT SNORES fell from her lips. I didn't know if I should be proud or a little disturbed at how easily she slept in my arms. I'd do anything to keep Mia in my life and make her happy. I wasn't anywhere near ready to get down on one knee and propose, or to whisper the words "I love you" in her ear, but I cared for Mia and didn't want to be without her.

I slept for a short time and watched her sleep after I woke. She had small, faint freckles on her sun-kissed cheeks. Her eyebrows were thick and dark, but neatly groomed. Her nose fit her face and had a delicate, narrow shape. Her lips were luscious and thick and were made for kissing. The filthy things she said to me this morning had almost made my heart stop. All blood in my body went to my dick as she smacked me around a little.

"Hey," she said in a drowsy voice.

"Sleep well?"

"Like a rock." She yawned and nuzzled her cheek against my pec.

"What do you want to do today, Mia? I want to spend the day with you." I brushed the hair from her eyes.

"I'm going to the clinic for a couple hours this afternoon."

"Can I come?"

She looked at me and smiled. "Yes, but it won't be a happy day. Have you ever noticed the real poor people in this area?"

"I have seen the homeless people on the corners."

"They're the tip of the iceberg, Michael. It's the ones that you don't see that are the most heartbreaking. The little kids that come in dirty and in need of basic medical care."

"If it's that sad, why do you do it? Why not just stick to the ER?"

"It's rewarding, and I feel I'm making a difference. The ER has its own type of rewards, but mostly it's filled with sadness." She sighed as she rolled out of my arms. She sat up, pulling her knees against her chest.

I sat up, running my fingers across her damp cheeks. "Why don't you find a way to work at the clinic, then?"

"There's no money; it's all volunteers. We get some money from the state and county, but it's minimal, laughable actually."

"Maybe my family could help. What would you guys need to fund the clinic?" I pulled her in my lap and wrapped my arms around her.

"I don't even know. I haven't looked at the books." She sagged against me, resting her head on my shoulder.

I kissed her shoulder. "You give me a figure and I'll see what I can do to make it happen."

"What is it exactly that your family does to have all this money, Michael? I'm all for charity, but if it came by criminal means then I'd have to decline."

"You mean like the mob?" I laughed. Stereotyping at its finest.

She turned her head, looking me in the eyes without smiling. "Ah, yeah. I couldn't take dirty money." She shook her head.

"You just made my day." I laughed, squeezing her tightly. "Totally stereotyping, but funny as hell, Mia." I held her chin in my grasp and kissed her on the lips. "We own a vineyard in Italy. It's been in our family for generations."

"Why do you work at the tattoo shop and fight, then? You could just sit at home all day."

"My parents didn't raise us to be lazy. We were taught to work and be appreciative of what we have. I fight for the fun and challenge. The shop feels more like a hobby than a real job."

"I get it. I couldn't sit on my ass all day either."

She turned in my lap and the friction against my dick made it start to harden. She held my cheeks in her small hands and stared in my eyes. All the craziness of the past week had vanished.

All that mattered in this moment was us.

"You have a big heart under that Superman exterior, Michael. You're a big softy." Her fingertips rubbed against the five o'clock shadow on my face, and I could feel every hair move under her touch.

"Don't tell anyone. You'll ruin my reputation." I laughed. "What's pressing against your ass isn't soft."

She giggled as she rested her forehead against mine. "It'll have to wait until we get done at the clinic. There are needy people waiting for me."

"I'm needy," I said as my dick twitched against her ass. "Real needy."

"You're horny, there's a difference." She smacked my shoulder.

Her smile made my heart ache. I'd do whatever I could to help her make her dream of working at the clinic full-time a reality. She deserved to have that smile every day.

"Tell that to my cock." I took the opportunity to kiss her neck as she tipped it back, laughing. Her heartbeat thundered against my lips as I inhaled the sweet vanilla scent.

God, I wanted to eat her.

"Remember, I have a needle for that problem."

"You and the fuckin' needle, woman." I pushed her off me. "Get up, let's go, or I'm not letting you out of this bed all day."

She snickered as she climbed off the bed and walked into the bathroom.

It felt like we hadn't missed a day together. The air between us had been cleared, and Tammy was an inconsequential part of the past. I climbed off the bed and threw on my t-shirt and shorts, and went into the kitchen to wait for her.

I helped myself to a cup of coffee, since I knew she'd take more than a few minutes to get ready. Her cheeks had been tear-stained and her hair had that "I just got fucked" look. I called the one person I knew who would be interested in helping me make Mia's dream a reality.

"Hey, Ma," I said, and sipped the black, velvety liquid.

"Hey, baby. How are you?"

"I'm great, actually. I'm over at Mia's and I think we patched things up."

"Hmm," she said with a small laugh. "You're a big boy."

"That's what she said, Ma." I chuckled at my wittiness.

Her laughter grew loud until there was silence and static. She must have covered the phone so I wouldn't hear her giggling. "Son, there are things a mother doesn't need to hear, and I changed your diapers so, I know. That poor girl."

"All right, enough about that. I know we're pals, Ma, but I called you for a reason." I sat down, placing my cup on the table, and stared at Mia's neatly manicured yard.

"What is it, baby?"

I explained to my mother the work that Mia did at the clinic. I shared all the information I knew and told her about Mia's dream to work there full-time and help the people in the area.

"What do they need?" she asked without hesitation.

"Money."

"I know that." She laughed. "How much?"

"I don't know. They get some funding from the government, but not enough. The doctors that volunteer help pay the rent, and they get some medicines for free."

"Find out all the details and come see your father and me. I'm sure we can work something out. I'd love to help any way I can."

"Thanks, Ma. I'm going to spend the day there snooping around, and I'll stop over when I get a chance."

"Hey, how's the training coming? Your fight is soon." She sighed into the phone. I knew she hated the violence and could never understand why I chose to enter the cage.

"Really good, and now that Mia and I patched things up, I can finally focus on kicking that guy's ass."

"Make sure you stay focused. I don't want to see my baby hurt."

"I'm like a brick wall, Ma."

"Don't be too cocky, son. Your father is calling me. He wants a cup of coffee. He's lucky I love him."

I wanted a love like theirs—long-lasting and unbreakable.

"You'd go pick the beans if he asked just to make that man happy."

"Let's not give him any ideas, Michael. Call me later, okay?"

"Love ya. I'll talk to you tonight."

"Love you too."

Mia wrapped her arms around my neck, kissing my cheek. "That better have been your mother or I'm getting that needle ready as soon as we get there."

I grabbed her hands and leaned into her kiss. "It was. You're dying to stick a needle in my dick, aren't you?" I laughed.

"Just remember that it's always an option." She laughed against my ear, and I closed my eyes and let the happiness sink in.

I stood, grabbing my keys off the counter. "Let's go, Dr. Jekyll. I'm driving."

"We can take my car." She stayed by the table.

"Nope, I'm the man, so I drive." I opened the door and waited for her.

As she walked by me, she said, "Let's not start the macho bullshit."

"My dad drives my mom around all the time. I just grew up with some beliefs. Let's not kill them yet. You relax and talk and I'll be your chauffeur."

She sighed but nodded. I opened the truck door for her and waited for her to get situated before I closed her in and jogged around to my side. Her eyes were glued to me as I made my way around the truck.

"You really have the chivalry thing down," she said as I sat.

"It's one thing my ma always taught me. How to be a gentleman when necessary."

We held hands and listened to music, stopping on the song "Happy" by Pharrell to sing along. How could I not shout the words at the top of my lungs?

"Is this it?" I asked, as I pulled into the parking lot.

"Yep. I know it's not pretty, but it gets the job done." She shrugged.

"Yeah. This place doesn't look like much, doc."

"I know. The people that come here deserve better."

"I hope you don't pay a lot in rent." I stared at the old brick façade. A tiny sign that read *GS Health Clinic* hung above the door, but the average person driving by would miss it entirely.

"No, we rent the space for pretty cheap. The owner gives us a deal because he likes what we do."

"Does the inside look any better?"

"It's old but clean. We spend the money we have on rent and supplies."

"Let's get inside. I want to check it out." There wasn't an open spot in the parking lot, and that told me that there was a need for this clinic.

"How do you know the people really can't afford medical care?"

"They have to bring in their government assistance paperwork and proof that they've been denied Medicaid."

"Seems fair, and keeps it legit." I followed Mia into the building and a bustling waiting room. People of all ages and races sat patiently in the space.

Mia stopped and smiled at the woman behind the desk. "Cammie, this is Michael. He's going to hang out here today."

Cammie looked at me with the warmest smile on her face as she held out her hand. "It's always nice to have an extra set of hands around. Especially ones as big and strong as yours." She laughed as she stroked my fingers.

"I'm all yours," I said as I looked at Mia.

The stress that was evident on her face at the hospital was gone. Her demeanor at the clinic was different...she was radiant.

"You just offered yourself up to the devil," Mia said, laughing.

"I can handle her," I said, winking at Cammie.

Her face flushed before she cleared her throat. "We have a full house today. Lots to do, Mia. You leave this hunk in my hands, child."

Mia picked up the schedule and studied it before she replied, "He's all yours. I know you'll take good care of him."

"Mm hmm," Cammie said.

Mia kissed my cheek and started to walk away. "You're just going to leave me here?" I asked.

"You'll be just fine. Cammie knows the most about the clinic. Pick her brain if you want to know about the finances."

"Okay, I'll be waiting for you, doc." I patted her ass before she stepped out of reach.

"One second," Cammie said as she held her finger up. "Mr. Johnson," she called into the waiting room.

Leaning against the desk, I watched Cammie interact with the patients. She had a way with people, making them feel important. She was the beating heart of the clinic. She'd be my link to getting this place on track and keeping it running like a well-oiled machine.

"So, what can I help you with, Michael?" Cammie asked as she swiveled her chair in my direction.

"I want to talk about funding, Cammie. I want to help the clinic financially and see about having Mia here full-time. She loves this place."

She clapped her hands. "Wow, I think I just fell in love with you. If Mia wasn't my girl, I'd snatch you from her."

I laughed at the ease with which she spoke to me.

"You know anything about accounting, handsome?" She winked.

"I do. I have a business and I do the books."

"Perfect. I'll let you in the office and you can take a look. It may be easier and quicker than if I told you everything. We're so busy today that I couldn't give you my full attention, no matter how badly I wanted to."

"That would be fine, Cammie. I can see what's going on and how I can help."

She showed me to a tiny office in the back. I could hear Mia speaking with a patient in the next room. The words were muffled, but it was her voice. Cammie had the office organized and the files up to date, which made the task of determining their financial need easier.

They had a couple thousand dollars in the bank, and Cammie said that rent was the biggest expense. The place needed to be rehabbed from the inside out.

I searched the filing cabinet for the rental agreement. They paid a thousand a month, which was cheap for commercial space. I made a list of needs with an estimated cost to keep the place in check, with some extra financial padding. The first step would be purchasing the building and the land it sat on, then giving the place a facelift.

It certainly was doable, and it wouldn't take much financially to make this a stable non-profit that wouldn't have to scrape by to make ends meet.

As I was rubbing my eyes, the door opened and Mia walked in. "How's it going in here?" she asked, wrapping her arms around my neck and settling in my lap.

"Good. I have a plan and just spoke to my ma and the landlord."

"Oh?"

"We're going to make it happen, Mia. I already have the wheels in motion." I leaned back in the chair, lifting her to move with me.

"You don't waste any time, do you?" She rubbed her nose against the tender skin of my neck and inhaled.

I cupped her ass and squeezed. "You're going to owe me something big for all this."

"What do you want?" She smirked.

"I'm going to think *long* and *hard* about that before giving you a definitive answer."

"You do that. I just wanted to say hi. I have to go. There are a bunch of people out there waiting to be seen." She patted my shoulder before trying to climb off my lap.

I pulled her back down, running my lips down her jaw. "I want some sugar first."

She laughed and rolled her eyes. "Only a kiss."

"What else would I mean?"

The kiss was soft and sweet. I smiled as she winked at me before walking out the door.

I spent the afternoon jotting down notes, making lists, and calling everyone I knew to help make this place the best it could be. It would be Mia's dream and her little bit of serenity.

26

MIA

It was finally the night—Michael's MMA match.

I wanted to look stunning.

Picking through my closet, I found my favorite black pencil skirt, a white cami, and my kickass Jessica Simpson peep-toe heels. I spent extra time on my makeup, and straightened my hair.

I felt tense as I drove to the arena to see him before his fight. I sat in the car for a few minutes to calm my nerves before I made my way to the doors. My stomach gurgled as I followed the extra-tall security guard through the backstage area to a door that read "Michael 'The Iceman' Gallo."

After knocking on the door, I smoothed my skirt, wiping my hands against the soft material. My legs were wobbly as I waited for someone to open the door.

Why in the hell was I so nervous? I didn't like the thought of Michael fighting another man, but my stress level was high enough that someone would think that it would be me stepping in the cage.

The door cracked opened and Rob smiled. "Hey, Mia," he said, opening the door.

"Hey, Rob," I said as I entered the dimly lit room.

"Yo, dude, Mia's here," Rob yelled, causing me to jump. "Sorry, didn't mean to yell in your ear."

"Oh, it's okay. I'm just jumpy." I saw Michael sitting in a chair, looking more stiff than normal, and turned to Rob. "Is he okay?"

"Yeah, he's doing great. He gets moody before a fight."

Nodding to Rob, I moved toward Michael, stopping in front of him. I placed my hand on his head, running my fingers through his hair as he kept his eyes pointed at the floor. "Michael," I said as I stroked his hair.

He didn't say a word, but reached out and wrapped his hand around my calf. He slid his fingers up my leg and under my skirt, gripping my thigh roughly.

"No sex before the match," Rob said before walking out.

Michael's eyes slowly moved up my body, stopping at my breasts before settling on my face. His grip tightened as he pulled me closer, resting his head against my abdomen.

"You okay, Michael?" My hand stilled in his hair.

"I can smell you," he said hoarsely.

"Dick," I said as I swatted his back. "You had me freaked out, and you're being a pig."

His body shook as his laughter grew and filled the room. "I'd rather pound your tight, wet pussy than beat this guy's face to a pulp right now." His fingers slid against the edge of my panties and stopped.

"You can have me all night long after you win your match. The quicker you end it, the sooner you'll have me in your bed," I said with a shaky breath.

His finger glided across the satin material of my underwear and rubbed against my clit. My breath caught in my throat as I stood before him, lost in his touch.

"We have a few minutes, and I know just how I want to spend them," he said, wrapping his other arm around my waist.

His fingers dipped inside my panties as I fisted his hair and closed my eyes. My head tipped back as he brought me to the brink of orgasm. My body swayed as his grip increased, steadying me.

My calves stung from the tension and the orgasm that was just out of reach. I opened my legs as far as possible in the restrictive skirt and leaned into his touch.

"You want to come?" he asked roughly.

"Yes," I pleaded.

"After I kick some ass." He smirked, removing his hand from my panties and dragging the wetness down my leg.

"Fuck," I muttered.

"Doesn't feel so good, does it, doc?" He laughed before sticking his fingers in his mouth, licking them clean.

I glared at him. It was funny when I did it to him. To leave me like this now felt downright cruel.

"You're a bastard."

My entire body had been tense, and he had made it so much worse. I was wound so tight at this point I worried walking would cause me to orgasm. I ached that badly.

He patted my ass as he stood and wrapped me in his arms. The warmth of his naked flesh seared through my thin silk camisole. "We'll finish after I win. I want to take my time with you tonight."

I rubbed my cheek against the smooth skin of his pec. "I should hate you right now, but I can't."

"You two done in there?" Rob yelled, knocking on the door.

"He's a pain in the ass," I said, sighing against his chest.

"I know." He kissed the top of my head, burying his nose in my hair. "Yeah, come in."

Rob plopped down on the couch across the room and watched us.

"I better go, Michael. You have to get ready and I need to find my seat." I peered up at him, getting a last look of his beautiful face. I worried it would be bloody and bruised the next time I touched it.

"I'll text Izzy to meet you in the corridor." His kiss burned my lips as he crushed his mouth against mine. "Thanks, Mia, for coming." The smug asshole winked. "I know you hate the very idea, but you being here means a lot to me."

"No other place I'd rather be." I slid my hand down his arm, moving away from him. "Oh, and Michael?"

"Yes."

"Kick his ass, handsome," I said, trying to help him relax.

He winked, and his smile made my heart melt.

Fuck, I hated the thought of that beautiful face being hit. I hated everything about what was about to unfold before my eyes.

I waved to him with a faint smile as I left. I could hear the cheers of the crowd echo through the corridor backstage. I followed the noise, finding Izzy waiting for me near the arena entrance.

Her mouth moved as she waved for me to follow her, but it was so loud I couldn't hear her words. I smiled and nodded before following her to the seating area.

"Down front," Izzy yelled in my ear, as I looked around the arena.

The crowd was larger than I would have expected for a MMA match. Not everyone had such great disdain for the sport as I did. I hated the idea of two men beating the crap out of each other for a title, but I promised Michael I'd be here.

The entire Gallo family, with the exception of Mrs. Gallo, sat in the front row, looking as anxious as I felt.

"I found her," Izzy said as we sat down.

They were a stunning family. The men were all cut from the same cloth. Handsome, rugged, and muscular, and the sister was a spitfire. Even Mr. Gallo was classically handsome and didn't show his age.

"It's nice to see you again, doc," Joe said, a couple of seats away.

"Call me Mia, please. I see you're getting around better these days."

"Physical therapy works wonders. I wouldn't miss this fight for the world. Suzy would have had my balls if I didn't bring her tonight." He turned and kissed her cheek as she kept her eyes glued to the cage.

"Hello, my dear," Mr. Gallo said, taking my hand, planting a soft kiss on it. "You've missed some matches already."

I winced as I watched them clean the floor. There was blood and sweat everywhere. "This isn't my idea of entertainment, Mr. Gallo. I'm only here for Michael," I said, trying to stop my stomach from spilling its contents. "Where's Mrs. Gallo?"

"Oh, she hates the very idea of him fighting. She stayed home tonight to read. So, how's he doing? Is he ready?" he asked.

I shrugged as butterflies filled my stomach. I hoped he was ready, because I really couldn't take watching him being beaten. "He seemed pretty calm when I left him to finish preparing."

Our conversation was interrupted as the announcer spoke: "Ladies and gentleman, the main event you've all been waiting for is about to begin."

The crowd stood, and the screaming made my eardrums throb. Loud music began to play, and I knew it was Michael's song, "Bodies" by Drowning Pool. It had been playing in his dressing room before I left. I covered my ears as I stood, facing the back of the arena.

"Weighing in at 260 pounds, I give you the one, the only, Michael 'The Iceman' Gallo."

The crowd screamed before chanting, "Ice Man, Ice Man."

Michael wore a black silk robe as he entered through the dark curtain and started to walk down the aisle. The crowd went crazy, and people tried to grab him on his way down the ramp into the arena. Bloodcurdling screams from female fans professing their love to him made me laugh. I could see how this could be an adrenaline rush.

I had the perfect vantage point to watch him. I stood with one leg in the aisle and leaned over to watch him. He stared straight ahead, as he walked with his shoulders pushed back, looking bigger than ever. His lips were set in firm line, and there was no happiness in his eyes. The sparkle had been replaced with fierceness. He looked mean as hell, but I knew the real man underneath.

Michael held his fists up to the crowd as he stopped in front of me, turning to face them. He glanced at me from the corner of his eye as a small smirk danced on his lips, but quickly vanished.

The excitement of the moment wasn't lost on me.

He walked into the cage, stopping dead in the center. He shrugged off the robe, exposing his beautiful physique and breathtaking face. The cheers grew louder, mainly from the females, as he stood there bouncing up and down, moving his neck from side to side.

I wanted to run into the cage and jump in his arms and beg him not to fight.

"And now we bring you his opponent. Weighing in at 257 pounds, we give you Tommy 'The Heat' Ramirez."

All eyes in the arena turned as a man in a red robe emerged. He looked almost as big as Michael, but scarier, maybe because I didn't know him like I did Michael.

I swallowed the lump that formed in my throat, and my chest began to ache.

Both of these men would leave bloody and bruised before this was all said and done. I worried about Michael getting hurt, and his male ego if he lost.

"Isn't this exciting?" Izzy said, pulling on my arm.

"Captivating and scary as hell," I responded before turning back to watch "The Heat" enter the cage and mimic Michael's previous movements.

"He's going to kick Tommy's ass," Izzy said as she stared at the fighter.

"I hope so." I gnawed on my lip as I watched Michael size up the competition.

He was ready, and chomping at the bit to get his hands on the guy.

People jumped up and down as the men readied themselves for the fight. I sat there almost breathless and scared for what would unfold before my eyes.

Both men stood in the middle of the cage, staring each other down. It would be comical if I didn't understand the brutality that was about to happen.

I was transfixed as I studied Michael's every movement.

The men touched hands before the referee screamed, "Let's get it on." Before he moved out of the way quickly.

Ramirez lunged at Michael and kicked him in the thigh. I could hear the snap of the skin from the impact. I closed my eyes, cringing, before peeking to see what happened next.

Michael seemed unfazed by the strike, hitting him back with an elbow to the face. Ramirez' face lurched back before he shook it off and steadied himself. The men moved around the cage exchanging kicks and jabs, and I could feel the lump inside my throat growing larger. I touched my throat, resting my hand there as I stared at Michael.

Michael looked magnificent as he moved around the cage and kept pace with Ramirez. He backed Ramirez against the fencing, holding him in place, striking him with the meaty part of his palm square in the chin. I grimaced when I saw blood drip from the corner of his mouth.

Michael wrapped his arms around the man's lower half and picked him up, tossing him to the mat.

I stood, my heart hammering in my chest, praying it would end.

"Hey, lady, you're blocking my view," a man behind me yelled.

I turned around and glared at him before taking my seat. "The Heat" kicked Michael right in the balls. Fuck. Holding himself, Michael backed away, trying to regain his composure.

I had no idea what that felt like, but shit, it had to hurt.

Michael came back at Ramirez a moment later, with more anger than I had seen before. Ducking down, he swept his leg across the mat, knocking Ramirez on his ass.

I gnawed on my lip, but I couldn't look away. Seeing Michael in action, I knew he was made for this. He was a fighter.

Snaking his legs around the man, he held him in place. Ramirez beat on Michael's back, wiggling like a worm, but he couldn't get out of the hold. Michael slammed his fist into the man's face, and I watched in horror as it bounced off the mat.

Blood trickled down his chin as Michael held him in his grip.

"He's winning," Izzy said as she stood, screaming, "Kill 'em Michael!"

I held my breath and prayed it was over.

"Ice Man, Ice Man," the crowd chanted as they rose to their feet.

Ramirez kicked free, both men jumping to their feet.

Fuck, it wasn't over. I exhaled, feeling lightheaded, as Ramirez struck Michael in the ribs. He winced, leaning forward and running his fingers across the spot.

I shook my head, scared that it could be the end for Michael. He had fractured those ribs months ago. They were vulnerable.

Michael straightened and bounced, shaking off the pain before spinning and kicking Ramirez right in the face. His head snapped back as blood flew from his mouth before he fell backward onto the mat.

The crowd stood and began to cheer again as Michael moved around the unconscious Ramirez and yelled something at him.

I stood, gripping my neck, and waited for it to be over.

Grabbing Michael's arm, the referee held it up as Michael pumped his fist in the air with a giant smile on his face.

"It's over?" I asked, as I grabbed Izzy's hand.

"It is. He won! That guy never stood a chance against him." She smiled.

Michael looked like a champion. He was one. I closed my eyes and let out the breath I'd been holding in.

A small cut had formed on the side of his left eyebrow and blood oozed down his face, but he looked relatively unharmed. His body glistened under the bright lights, showing off each ridge and valley.

A giant grin crept across Michael's face as he walked toward us. He looked at his family and then to me as he approached. Wrapping his arm around my waist, he smashed me into his sweaty torso and kissed me.

I collapsed against his body, exhausted from the nervous tension.

Pulling away, he stared into my eyes and said, "That wasn't so bad was it, doc?"

"I fucking hated every minute of it, Michael."

"Liar." He smirked and turned toward his father.

The simple statement and the cocky smirk reminded me of the bar where we had officially met each other. Same statement, same smirk, and totally Michael.

His dad held out his hand and grabbed Michael's shoulder with the other. "Good job, son."

"Thanks, Pop," Michael said as he pulled his dad toward him, kissing his cheek.

The tenderness Michael showed his father was a strange juxtaposition to the cruelty he'd displayed in the ring.

"Couldn't be prouder." His dad slapped him on the back and released him.

Joe and Anthony hugged him as I stayed at his side. Suzy kissed him on the cheek. I watched in awe at the amount of love and support that his family gave him.

After he hugged his family, he turned to me, pulling me tightly against him. The dampness of his skin soaked through my clothes, but I didn't care. He was safe and the fight was over.

"I have to go clean up. You want to come with"—he cocked an eyebrow—"or wait here with my family?"

I touched the open cut near his eye, causing him to jerk away. "You go get patched up and I'll sit with them until you're done."

"I'll be right back, beautiful. You'll come to the next one, right? I know you secretly loved it."

"It's still barbaric," I said against his lips.

"I bet if I touched your panties right now they're as wet as my skin," he whispered in my ear, causing me to squeeze my legs together.

I shook my head and laughed. "You'll have to take me home to find out, won't you?" I smirked.

"You just gave me the perfect reason to make this quick." He kissed me tenderly and walked away. "I'm keeping them as a souvenir too," he yelled over his shoulder.

I collapsed in my seat, exhausted. I couldn't imagine how he felt.

Mr. Gallo took the seat next to me and smiled. "How are you doing, my dear?"

I gave him a small smile. "It's a lot to take in, but I'm doing okay, considering."

"Ah, it's thrilling and scary. I get it. Seems like yesterday Michael was just a little boy. He was always a scrapper." He punched the air. "I always had to pull him off his brothers. He was a rough one, a born fighter."

"I can't imagine him as a little boy, but I'm sure he was handful, Mr. Gallo." I laughed.

He looked so proud as he sat there staring at the cage. "He was never a small boy, but he's grown up into a fine young man. Anyway, Michael told me he's already hired a crew to start the renovations at the clinic. When do you start there full-time?"

"He has, and I'm so excited. I start next week after my time is over at the hospital. I can't thank you and your family enough for everything."

"You need to thank Michael. It was all his doing. My wife and I always like to help out community organizations. What good is having money if you can't help those that need it most?" He smiled, genuine and sweet.

I held his hand. "Thank you, Mr. Gallo. I'll make you proud."

He patted my leg and stood. "I have no doubts, my dear. I'll be right back," he said, smiling, and walked away.

A hand gently touched my shoulder, and I turned expecting to see Michael, but it wasn't him. I swatted the hand away and stood to escape his reach.

"Excuse me," I said, crossing my arms across my chest.

"Sorry, a pretty lady sitting here all by yourself made me curious." His eyes moved over my body.

"Um," I said as I looked around for someone to rescue me, but no one was looking in my direction. "I'm not here alone."

"Oh," he said as he looked around the arena.

"I'm here with Michael."

"Really?" he asked, scratching his goatee.

"Really," I said, tilting my head.

A hand landed on the man's shoulder as he turned quickly to come eye to eye with Michael.

"You bothering my girl, Torrez?" Michael crossed his arms over his chest, giving the man a cold, hard stare.

"Maybe I was—whatcha gonna do about it, Gallo?" Torrez stood, placing his hands on his hips.

"Kick your ass like last time." Michael broke out into laughter.

Torrez punched him in the shoulder. "I let your sorry ass win that match."

"Fucking liar."

"Wanna go for another round?"

"You're more worthy of my time than the pissant I fought today. Mia, this is 'The Mauler,'" Michael said, using air quotes and rolling his eyes.

Now it kind of made sense to me. I had seen him before—he was the guy Michael fought in NYC.

"Don't you two hate each other?" I asked.

"Nah, we went for beers after the match in NYC," Torrez said as he shook Michael's hand. "It's good to see you, man."

"Just remember Mia's mine, Torrez. I'd hate to embarrass you by kicking your ass in public *again*." Michael grinned, holding back a laugh.

"Wait, I don't think I ever said I was yours," I said.

"Possession, remember," he said as he wrapped his arms around me. "You're mine."

I bit my lip. I was proud to be called his...he was a man with the iron fists and a warm heart. Michael Gallo could call me anything he wanted, as long as he spent his nights in my bed.

27

MIA

Liberating. That was how it felt knowing I didn't have to work in the ER anymore. I walked in and quit, not wanting to spend another day working there. Michael's family had found donors and used their own money to have me be the clinic physician on a full-time basis.

I could finally do what I loved. Help people without the nightmares and sleepless nights.

Michael spent his mornings working out and then coming into the clinic before heading to Inked. He gave himself wholeheartedly to making the clinic a success. They were officially starting the remodel next week and, Michael would oversee the project first hand.

Taking a sip of coffee, I looked over the chart for my first patient of the day. Female, unemployed, general check-up—an easy way to start. Grabbing the chart and tucking it under my arm, I walked toward the room. I felt stress free for the first time in a long time.

Closing the door, I set the chart on the counter and turned toward the exam table. My heart stopped and I froze in my tracks.

"Hey, Mia," Tammy sneered.

"How in the hell did you get in here?" I said loud enough that I hoped someone would hear, especially Michael. Fuck, I really didn't need her crazy ass here. "What do you want, Tammy?" I asked, glaring at her.

CHELLE BLISS

"I came to make peace with you. I wanted to apologize for my behavior," she said, hopping off the exam table.

I held my hand up, stopping her. "It's in the past, Tammy. Whatever happened is between you and Michael. Leave me out of it."

"You two aren't together, then?" She cocked her eyebrow and grinned.

"We are together. We're happy. I think you should go before he finds you here and calls the police."

"He's here?" she asked, and looked at the door with excitement in her eyes.

Fuck. That wasn't the response I'd hoped for when I told her that Michael was here. "He's going to be really pissed if he sees you, Tammy. You better go, for all of our sakes."

"Maybe I can apologize to him too." She smiled.

Clearly she was still delusional.

"Tammy, you need to leave," I spoke louder than before, hoping to draw the attention of Michael or Cammie.

I was getting pissed. My hands were balled at my side. I never wanted to hit a person as much as I wanted to smack the shit out of her.

"Not until I can see Michael." Sitting back down, she crossed her legs with that Snickers bar smile she wore so well.

"Fine," I said. Turning my head toward the door and keeping my eyes on her, I yelled, "Michael!" I turned back toward her and we waited, staring at each other.

The door opened and I heard Michael say, "What's up?"

"We have a visitor." I pointed to Tammy without look at him, and held my hands up.

"What the fuck are you doing here?" he said, stepping in front of me, cutting off my view.

"I...I," she stuttered. "I wanted to see you."

"You've seen me and you're violating the restraining order, Tammy. I will have you arrested for coming here." Every muscle in his body tensed as he stood between us.

He trusted her less than I did, but then again, he knew her better.

She slithered off the table and touched his cheek.

He recoiled, taking a step back, almost knocking me over. "Get out," he said, pointing at the door.

"Come on, Michael. We were so good together." She slid her arm around his neck.

She was totally insane. Was I invisible to her?

I bit my lip, trying not to say something to aggravate the situation.

Peeling her off him, he said through gritted teeth, "Are you shitting me right now with this shit?"

"No, I'm just stating the truth." She looked at him with a frown, and hurt in her eyes.

I'm not an angry person, but this bitch needed to be taught a lesson. Tammy wasn't and never would be a threat to our happiness, but to throw shit in my face was too much for me to take.

"You wouldn't know the truth if it slapped you in the face. Go, Tammy. I don't hit women, never have and always said I never would, but you're getting real close to getting knocked on your ass," Michael said calmly.

"You know I like it when you're rough with me, Michael," she said, moving closer to him with a sly smile. "The harder, the better, like old times."

"Okay, I've had enough," I interrupted. I placed myself between her and Michael. He. Was. Mine. If anyone were to knock her on her ass, it would be me.

"I wasn't talking to you, whore. I sucked his cock way before you came along. Sloppy seconds aren't fun, are they?" She smirked.

"Calm down, Mia," Michael whispered in my ear, grabbing my arm.

Motherfucker. My body shook from anger.

"Yeah, Mia. Know your place. I'm sure you don't bring him to his knees like I did. You don't have him smacking your ass as you come on his cock. His body was made for me, and I gave him everything he ever wanted," she said, stepping closer to me.

"You need to shut your damn mouth," I seethed, with clenched hands, wanting to punch her in the face.

"Ladies," Michael said, pushing us apart.

"What's going on in here?" Cammie asked as she looked in the room.

"Call the cops, Cammie. Tammy is violating a court order," Michael replied as he held us apart.

Tammy stood there with her hands on her hips, like she was proving her point. Did she not hear a word he'd spoken?

"I'm fine, Michael. You can let me go," I said.

Michael nodded, releasing his hold on me.

On the inside, my belly was burning and my hands were itching to smack her. I judged Michael and called him a barbarian for fighting, but in this moment, it clicked.

"You listen like a good bitch, don't you?" she asked.

I looked at Michael, and he winced. "He. Is. Mine, Tammy," I said, separating each word to drive the point home.

"He may marry a girl like you, but he'll always come to me for all the dirty things you don't give him. You're plain and boring and probably a rotten lay. He'll always be mine."

I closed my eyes, trying to control my rage. My heart pounded feverishly in my chest, my skin grew hot, and I could hear the blood flowing through my ears.

Michael turned to her, crossing his arms in front of his chest, as he squared his shoulder. "Shut the fuck up, Tammy. Mia's my girl, not you."

"She stole you from me," Tammy said, sounding wounded.

"I did not," I said, stepping around him as he gripped my arm.

"You fucking did," she yelled before smacking me in the face.

Everything else in the room disappeared except her and me. I lunged at her, my palm connecting to her face with a crack. "He's mine," I said as I landed a smack with my other hand. My hands throbbed as we tumbled backward, her body slamming against the tile floor.

"Fuck," Michael yelled as his strong arms gripped my torso, trying to pull me off, but I had my legs wrapped around her body. "Stop, Mia," Michael roared, trying to untangle me.

Blood trickled from her mouth as she lay there crying.

I blinked. I did this to her. I went apeshit and hit her…twice.

I released my legs and leaned over her body, resting my weight on my arms. "I'm sorry," I whispered. "I don't know what happened."

"It's okay, baby girl," he said, lifting me up and cradling me in his arms.

"No, it's not. I just snapped." I didn't know I had that in me. I'd never been pushed to that point in my life.

"She deserved it, Mia," he said, kissing my forehead as he walked out of the room, leaving Tammy on the floor in tears.

"She just wouldn't shut her damn mouth." I looked at her face through the open door; bloodied and tear filled. A wave of guilt rolled over me.

"You hit pretty fucking good for a girl," Michael said, chuckling.

"Shut up, before I pop you one too," I said, reaching for his lips.

I felt the smirk on his face as he laughed. "My, my, how you've changed since that night in the bar. What did you call me? Barbaric?"

"Yeah, well. She clearly didn't understand the English language. I didn't have any other choice, and she hit me first so I'm claiming self-preservation and defense." He was right, but there was no way in hell I'd admit it.

"So, I'm yours, if I heard you right?" he asked.

I sighed and cradled his face in my hands. "Possession, remember?"

"I could never forget. I love you, Mia." His eyes grew wide. He was shocked at his own words.

My heart stopped. I didn't know how badly I wanted to hear that phrase until it slipped from his lips. My insides warmed and felt gooey. I loved Michael, but I would have never been the first to say it. Tears filled my eyes as I looked at him.

"Gonna leave me hanging here, doc?"

I smiled against his mouth. "Just this once...I won't. I love you too, Michael."

He crushed his mouth to mine, and we claimed each other, branding one another with a passionate kiss.

28

MICHAEL

Two months later

MIA WRAPPED HER ARMS AROUND ME AS I LOOKED AROUND THE ROOM, admiring the remodeled clinic. "You did an amazing thing here, Michael," she said, resting her head on my back, smashing her breasts into me. Damn, she felt good.

"*We*, Mia. We did an amazing job." I rubbed her arm and thought about how much life had changed in three months.

I couldn't imagine a day without her. She made me happier than anything else in my life. I quit fighting and trying to climb the ranks. For her, I'd do anything.

My time was spent between the shop, the clinic, and Mia. There wasn't time to fight without sacrificing my time with Mia.

Did I turn into a pussy? Not a bit. I could kick any motherfucker's ass if given the chance.

I had a greater purpose in life—one that mattered and made a difference. I loved seeing the sparkle in Mia's eyes every day. She wasn't stressed and no longer had nightmares as often as she did before quitting her job. She made a difference to the people in the community, and I felt like I played a role in making her dream become a reality.

"Is everyone here?" I asked, turning around.

"If you mean your family, yeah, they're all here. There's a big crowd outside waiting for us to cut the ribbon and open up this bad boy." She laughed. It was infectious.

"I have something for you first," I said, reaching for an envelope I'd left on a waiting room chair.

She grabbed it. Looking up at me she asked, "What is it?" as she tore it open.

"Read it," I said, tapping the folded paper.

She slowly opened the paper; her eyes flickered to me and back to the paper. "Michael," she said, covering her mouth.

"I couldn't think of a better owner than you, Mia." I brushed the small tear that trickled down her cheek.

Tears of joy had never made me feel so kickass. Some of the money came from donations and the rest from my family, and I filled the gap personally. We knew that Mia was the perfect person to be the rightful owner of the building, giving her security that the clinic would always be there.

"I can't believe this, but how?" she said, her eyes moving across the paper as she gripped it with two hands.

"Doesn't matter, Mia. It's yours now." I grabbed her chin and kissed her.

She jumped in my arms, kissing my lips before kissing my face. I laughed, letting her plant soft kisses on my skin.

"I'm speechless. I don't know how to repay you for all this," she said, waving her hands toward the room.

"I can think of a few ways," I said, squeezing her ass as I laughed.

"I'm sure you will." She rubbed her nose against mine, giggling.

"Let's do this, then. No reason to wait any longer." I released her, letting her body slide down mine until her feet hit the floor.

"Ready," she said, wiping her lips and eyes.

We opened the door, stepping outside to a group of about thirty people, including patients, local media, and my family. Mia's smile was radiant as she waved to the patients that she recognized in the crowd.

"This is so exciting," Ma said, grabbing my face and planting a sloppy kiss on my cheek. "And you, my sweet girl," she said, turning to Mia, "thank you for allowing me to be a part of this."

My ma loved Mia as much as I did.

Mia's cheeks flushed. "Thanks, Mrs. G. I couldn't have done it without you." Mia hugged my ma, giving her a kiss on the cheek.

"Come on, ladies. Let's cut this ribbon and get the party started," I said, ready to let everyone in to see the amazing work we'd done in the last two months.

My parents, Mia, and I all stood in front of the red ribbon, with the largest pair of scissors I'd ever seen in my life being held up by Anthony and Izzy. Suzy stood next to Joseph, holding him by the arm as he leaned on his cane. The only person missing was my brother, Thomas.

Flashes from the crowd blinded me as Mia fidgeted at my side. I squeezed her hand, hoping to calm her.

My father held his hands up, motioning for quiet. He turned to Mia and nodded.

"I'd like to thank you all for coming," she said. "The Gallo family has been kind enough to help give the clinic a new life. They helped raise funds to renovate and bring the facility up to date. We're proud to offer the community the best medical care possible." Her voice was strong as she spoke.

She was meant for this, meant to be in the spotlight.

"Without their generosity, none of this would be possible. We will have a full-time on-staff doctor, a nurse, and a receptionist, along with the volunteer physicians that will work in the clinic to meet the needs of all patients. Thank you for coming today and making this moment even more special." With a beaming smile, she looked at me and winked.

Fuck, I loved her.

The crowd clapped and cheered as we held up the scissors before cutting the ribbon. Flashes illuminated around us as I grabbed her, kissing her as the people in the crowd cheered louder.

"Come on, doc. Show the people around," I said.

She smiled at me before turning her attention back to the people. "Come on, everybody, I can't wait to show you all the changes."

The people entered the clinic with the same shocked expression. Their mouths hung open; their eyes looked around as they turned their head, taking in every inch.

Mia showed people round the new exam rooms as I stayed in the waiting room. I watched her walk in and out of the rooms with small groups of people that hung on her every word.

"Is my baby in love?" my mother asked, standing at my side.

I jumped, grabbing my chest. "Ma, you about gave me a heart attack."

She laughed before resting her head on my bicep. "I see the way you look at her, Michael. You wouldn't do all this if you weren't in love with Mia."

Heat crept up my chest to my face. "I do love her, Ma."

"Well then," she said, clearing her throat, "someone better give me a damn grandchild already. I know I taught you boys about birth control, but for the love of God, you or Joseph better make it happen, and I mean quick."

"I've been practicing." I smirked as I looked down at her beautiful smile.

"You've had enough time for that—you're getting older. Don't wait too long, Michael."

"Ma, Joe and Suzy have been together longer, and they live together. Put a little pressure on them first, will ya?" I turned, getting a glimpse of Mia before looking back to my mother.

"Oh, don't worry about that, I am." She laughed. "They're *practicing* too—plenty, from what I hear from your sister. Is Mia coming to the party at the house after this?"

My family was filled with gossips. Nothing stayed a secret for very long.

I swear, sometimes my ma used any excuse to have a party. She loved to cook and have everyone over to talk. She hated how quiet the house had become since we moved out. "Yeah, she's coming. You didn't invite too many people, did you?"

"Baby, do I ever invite too many people?" She smiled at me, but it was a bullshit smile.

Sighing, I said, "Always." I kissed the top of her head.

Her body shook against my arm with her silent laughter. "Never you mind that. I'm going to head home and start getting things ready with your father. Gather the troops when everyone is gone and come over. Don't dilly-dally." She patted my stomach and walked toward my father. He nodded at her and shook the hand of the man he'd been talking with, before they walked to the door hand in hand.

"You did real well, Mikey," Izzy said as she crept up next to me.

"Does everyone feel the need to sneak up on me today?" I crossed my arms over my chest, but didn't turn to face her.

"Cranky ass, aren't ya? I didn't sneak up anywhere. If you weren't so hypnotized by Mia you would've heard me."

I was that obvious. I thought I hung out and blended in with the crowd, but I guess I didn't. "Am I staring at her like a creep?"

Izzy smacked my arm. "Nah, like a love-sick puppy is all."

"Great," I muttered, scrubbing my hands across my face.

"I'm going to go. I have to make a stop before I head to the party," Izzy said, and stood on her tiptoes, grabbed my arm, and kissed my cheek.

"Don't be long, Izzy. Ma will have a cow."

"No worries. I'll be there in plenty of time." She winked and waved as I turned my attention back to Mia.

I shook hands with the people as they left. They thanked me for my family's generous gift to the clinic. I told them that none of it would be possible without Dr. Greco, and they'd nod and smiled.

When the crowd thinned, I sat down, resting my head against the wall. I could hear Mia talking in the back as she continued to walk room to room with the few people left. I closed my eyes and listened to her voice.

Soft, warm lips pressed against mine. As I opened my eyes, I hoped they were Mia's. "Everyone's gone. Are you ready?" she asked as she pulled away.

"Yeah, we better go before Mama Gallo puts out an APB."

She giggled, climbing in my lap. "You make her sound so horrible, but your mom is a sweetheart," she said, resting her forehead against mine.

"You've never seen her other side, Mia. She's Italian and has a temper. No mild-mannered woman can raise four boys."

"I'll remember that," she said, caressing my cheek.

"If we sit here any longer, I'm going to christen the waiting room and maybe one of the exam rooms. How do those stirrup things work again?" I smirked against her lips.

Mia smacked me, shaking her head. "Oh, no you don't. Not today, at least." She jumped off my lap and held her hand out.

"You're lucky my ma is waiting, or else I'd say fuck it, and take you right here, right now." I grabbed her hand.

"Yeah, just my luck." She rolled her eyes and giggled.

To see Mia so happy and full of laughter made everything worth it. The long hours at the clinic and shop, busting my ass to get it done right.

She completed me.

Jesus, now I'm quoting *Jerry Maguire*.

Dick check. Still there. Whew.

I may not be a pussy, but although I'd never admit it, I was pussy whipped.

Mia did that to me, and I couldn't be fucking happier.

***

"All women are crazy," I said as we walked to my parents' front door.

"Let's qualify crazy." Mia coughed.

I called Tammy crazy, but my ma wasn't. Ma was more excessive than crazy. There wasn't an open spot in the driveway, or on their block for that matter.

"What's wrong?" Mia asked, tilting her head.

"I told my ma to have a small get-together. There has to be at least fifty people in that house, based on all these cars."

"Leave her alone. It makes her happy, right?" Mia asked, rubbing my arm.

"Yeah," I said, grabbing her hand and placing a kiss in her palm.

"Everyone is waiting to see you."

"To see us, Mia, not just me." I pushed open the door and shook my head.

"Hey," a few voices sounded as we walked inside.

I couldn't see an open space from the foyer, through the great room, and out to the pool. Wall-to-wall people holding drinks filled my parents' home. I held Mia's hand as we made our way through the house.

"Wait," she said, stopping to grab a photo from a side table near the couch.

"What?"

Holding it close to her face, she asked, "Is this you?" She looked at me and back to the photo.

"Yep, that's me." I forgot my mother had the photo sitting out for the world to see.

"You look so...so..." She swiped her fingers across the glass with a smile.

"Handsome? Buff? Sexy?" I asked with a grin.

"I was going to say young, but we can go with your descriptions if you prefer," she said, and giggled.

"I was a whole lot of trouble back then," I said as I grabbed my freshman year wrestling photo.

Too much of my manhood showed through the tiny maroon singlet, but when I had it on back in the day, I wore it like a proud son of a bitch.

"You haven't changed much since then," she said as I put the photo back exactly where my mother had it.

"Checking out my cock?" I whispered in her ear.

"Shh." She turned, hitting me. "Someone might hear you."

"They're loud and Italian—trust me, they didn't hear a thing."

"I did," Joe said as he smacked my ass with his cane.

"Lucky I don't hit the handicapped, brother." I gave him a giant bear hug. "Where's Suzy?" I asked, looking around.

"Girl talking. It makes me batshit crazy. I love the woman, but being with her twenty-four-seven can be a test to any relationship." He shook his head and laughed. "Thank God I can walk now and go to the shop for a couple hours."

"I haven't talked to the girls lately. Maybe I'll go join them and let you two chat." Mia kissed my cheek.

"Go ahead, love. I'll find Ma and let her know we're here." I patted her ass and watched her walk away.

"You got it bad, bro. It's nice to see I'm not the only one around here being led around by my balls." Joe slapped me on the back.

I sighed. This family—I loved them, but they were all a pain in the ass.

Mia

I felt like I weighed two hundred pounds as I grabbed the open spot next to Suzy on the couch. "My God, do they always eat like this?" I asked.

"Always," Suzy said with a sigh, leaning back as she rubbed her stomach. "I swear I've gained ten pounds since I started hanging out with this family. Everything revolves around food. Doesn't matter the occasion, food is always on hand."

"At least it's good food," I said, happy to be off my feet. The couch felt like lying on a cloud of feathers. The soft cotton material would make it hard to stay awake.

"She's the best cook ever. I look forward to coming here on Sunday. Don't get me wrong, Joey is an amazing cook, but nothing beats his mother's home cooking."

"I wish Michael could cook."

"Whatcha girls talking about?" Izzy said as she plopped her skinny ass between us.

"Talking about your brothers," Suzy said.

"I have all the dirt, ladies. I can tell you some stories that would make you fall off the couch in a fit of giggles," Izzy replied.

"Why isn't Anthony taken?" I asked.

"He likes to play the field. Someday a lady will bring him to his knees and have him begging to be hers. Until then, he prefers the manwhore status. He's gets a little carried away with his *groupies*," Izzy said sarcastically. "Men, total pigs. It's bullshit that he's sowing his wild oats and playing the field, and if a girl did that shit she's easy and a slut."

"Sexism will never die," Suzy replied, patting Izzy on the leg.

"Not in this damn family—too many cocks for it to be equal. Having you ladies around helps, though. My ma and I have always been outnumbered."

She made me feel like I was part of the family. I wanted to fit in and be a member of this tight-knit group. Holidays, including Christmas, had consisted of my parents and me for the last couple of years.

"If you two bitches have kids, they better have vaginas." Izzy laughed. "The world isn't big enough for any more Gallo men."

"I don't think you have to worry about that for a while," I said quickly.

"Yeah, not an issue," Suzy said, sitting up.

"Suzy, come on. Joey has your ass on your back more than a two-bit whore looking for her next fix. Your ass is going to get knocked up sooner or later."

"We're careful, Izzy."

"Whatever. Someone better give my mother a damn grandchild. She's already crocheting blankets, and she's going to get desperate and start bothering me if you ladies don't come through. I'm entirely too young to ruin this body."

"Oh, shut the hell up, Izzy," Suzy said as she slapped Izzy's hand down.

"I'm just saying, Suzy. It's your duty to carry on the Gallo Legacy."

"Fucking great. Don't let Joey hear you say that," Suzy muttered, closing her eyes and pinching her nose between her fingers.

A shadow fell over us, and I peered up to see Joe looking at us with curiosity.

"Let me hear Izzy say what?" Joe asked with a crooked smile.

Suzy looked up, a giant smile painted on her face. "Nothing, sweetie," she said without flinching.

"Babies, Joe. Get on that shit," Izzy said, smacking his good leg.

"I'm on that shit all time, aren't I, sugar?

Suzy's cheeks turned pink as she looked at him "There's always room for improvement," she said with a smirk.

I loved this family as much as I loved Michael. They had become my home away from home, with my parents back in Minnesota. Suzy and Izzy were the sisters I never had and always wanted.

Michael was my savior.

Saving me from my nightmares, from the heart-crushing sadness of the ER, and giving me the greatest gift of all—happiness.

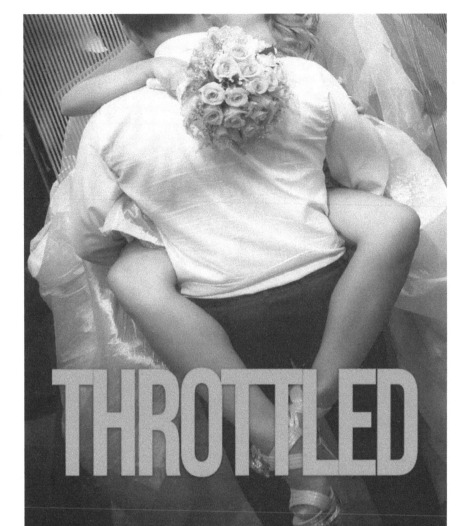

THROTTLED

A MEN OF INKED NOVELLA

USA TODAY BESTSELLING AUTHOR

CHELLE BLISS

1

SUZY

THANKSGIVING

"Push," City barked as his face turned red.

"I am pushing, damn it." I could barely breathe.

"More, just a little bit more," he said through gritted teeth. "One more push, sugar."

I bore down and used my legs as leverage. My face felt prickly and I wanted to give up. It was too much for me to handle. I couldn't do this. Why did I ever think I could? City always made my mind crazy and had me agreeing to do things I didn't want. I knew I didn't have the physical strength to handle this.

I grunted, exhausted. "Fuck, I give up," I said, gasping for air but not letting go.

"You know your filthy mouth does wicked shit to me," he said, winking at me.

"I'm in no mood to talk about your dick right now, Joseph." I glared at him. Sweat broke out near my hairline as my legs began to tremble.

"As soon as we're done, I'm going to show you exactly how hard that mouth makes me."

I glared daggers at him. I didn't want to think about his beautiful cock. "Not happening," I said as I pushed with all my strength. "Are you even helping?" I bit out.

"What the fuck does it look like?"

"Looks like you're standing there getting a kick out of watching me push this damn thing by myself." I grunted, my knuckles turning white.

"If I could push and get this shit done, I sure as fuck would, sugar. You can do this."

I shook my head just as the bed slid into place. "I'm never helping you move furniture again. Shit's for the birds," I said as I collapsed on the bed.

The light streaming through the windows threw a shadow on the bed as City stood between my legs. "You were the one that said I shouldn't do it alone. Who am I to stop you when you put your foot down?"

He looked like an angel with the glowing sunlight behind him. His body was just as divine as it was the night I met him over a year ago. He had a chiseled jaw covered in short, dark hair, his fierce blue eyes shining as bright as the sun, his dark brown hair a mess. I wanted him just as much as I did the first time we touched.

I smiled at him as I admired his ruggedness. "You're still recovering, City. I didn't want you to get hurt. We didn't have to do it right this second, I just made a suggestion."

"Sugar, I know how you are. You don't do suggestions. You wanted it moved and now it is." He leaned forward, hovering over my lips. "I'm not breakable. I'm healed and got the okay to go back to full activity." He wiggled his eyebrows.

I giggled; the man made my heart skip a beat because I loved him so much. "I didn't know you were holding out on me." I wrapped my arms around his neck and kissed him. "You couldn't have moved the bed by yourself anyway. It's too heavy."

"I could've, but it was more fun to watch you struggle." The deep vibrations of his laughter shook the bed.

I smacked his shoulder. "Could not." I grinned.

"Could too. Where was I?" He stared into my eyes. "Ah," he said, grinding his dick into my leg. "That filthy mouth of yours."

"You made me this way. I used to be sweet and pure. Now look at me," I said, digging my fingers into his thick hair.

"I'm looking, Suz, and I'm loving everything about you. I fell in love with the girl I found on the side of the road. You're mine forever now," he said as he pulled my arm down and placed a kiss on the diamond ring he gave me after his accident.

The happiness I felt was mixed with sorrow at the bitter memory of almost losing him. I would've been lost if he died that day. I never realized how full my life was and how much he meant to me until he was almost ripped from my grasp. "Always yours, City. Make love to me," I whispered against his lips.

"There's my cock-loving girl." He crushed his mouth to mine, his hands sliding up the side of my tank top. His touch gave me the shivers; the depth of his voice stole my breath even after a year. I couldn't get enough. I was his cock-loving whore, but only his. He had that effect on me.

Just as the rough tip of his finger touched my nipple, an alarm sounded from downstairs. "Fuck," he muttered, pulling back.

"Ugh, really?" I whined. "Can't we just let it go for a little while longer? Please?" I begged, grinding my panties against him, feeling the hard piercing press against my clit.

He leaned his forehead against mine, drawing in a shaky breath. "We can't. You know how my family is. I can't ruin the turkey. I'll never hear the end of that shit, and neither will you."

I pouted, running my fingernails up and down the back of his neck. "Five more minutes won't matter."

"When have we ever taken five minutes?" he asked, sitting up. "Up ya go. We have cooking to do, woman. Everyone will be here in two hours." He grabbed my arms and pulled me forward.

"I don't know why we couldn't just get everything pre-cooked. I survived Thanksgiving without having made everything from scratch." I collided with his chest, peering into his baby blues with a smile.

"Gallos do not do already prepared. You watch and I'll cook." He kissed the top of my head, reaching under my ass and pulling me into his lap.

"How about," I whispered against his lips, rubbing the rough stubble on his face, "if I help and I get a little City appetizer before they get here."

He smirked, a small laugh escaping his lips. "You want to cook?" He raised an eyebrow.

"I want cock and for that I'll cook." I smiled, nipping his lips.

"You got yourself a deal, sugar," he said as he grabbed my sides and tossed me on the bed and ran. I giggled and kicked, hopping off to run after him.

2

CITY

"You look flushed, dear," Ma said to Suzy as she hugged her. "Are you feeling well?"

I covered my mouth, hiding the smile while Suzy blushed an even deeper shade of red.

"I'm just fine, Mrs. G." Suzy glared at me as she patted my ma's back.

"Are you sure?" Ma rested her hand on Suzy's stomach. "No bun in the oven yet?"

Oh, fuck. Suzy was about to pop her lid. I looked down, holding my face in my hand, unable to look Suzy in the eyes.

"Sorry to disappoint you, but no. No bun, Mrs. G."

"It's okay, love, and stop with the Mrs. G. Call me Ma. Soon it will be official."

"Yes, Ma."

I couldn't look up. Pissed-off Suzy was too damn cute and I knew I wouldn't be able to stop my laughter.

"Son." My ma rested her hand on my shoulder.

"Hey, Mama." I wrapped my arms around her and snuck a glance at my bride-to-be. She had my pop's full attention.

"Happy Thanksgiving, baby." She kissed my cheek, standing on her tiptoes.

"You too, Ma. Thanks for pissing Suzy off for me." I laughed.

"Just don't want anyone to forget about a grandbaby." She smiled innocently.

"We wouldn't forget, Ma. We watch you knit every Sunday."

"Crochet," she corrected me. "Is she really okay? I haven't seen her so red in a while."

I couldn't stop the laughter bubbling out. "She's just fine, Ma. She had her hands full before you got here." I looked over my ma's shoulder, winking at Suzy.

Her mouth dropped open as she realized what I said. Before my parents walked in the door, she was on her knees sucking me off. Her hand cupped my balls while the other stroked my shaft. Pure mother-fucking heaven.

"I know Thanksgiving is a lot of work, Joseph. We appreciate all your hard efforts." She wrapped her hands around my back and turned toward Suzy. "It means a lot to us."

"It was *hard*"—I coughed—"work, Ma, but Suzy took it like a champion." My body shook against my mother as I placed a kiss on her hair.

Suzy's eyes almost bugged out of her head. "Just a little thing, Ma," Suzy said, and then laughed.

I nodded to Suzy, impressed with her quickness. I'd get her later for that comment. "Hey, Pops." I couldn't take the double meaning anymore. I needed to change the direction of this conversation.

"The house looks amazing, son." He wrapped his arms around me, giving me a giant bear hug. I loved that my father wasn't afraid to show us how much he cared.

"We just finished everything last week. I don't ever want to build another house again. What a pain in the ass!" I said as I smacked him on the back.

"The fireplace framed by the ceiling-to-floor windows is breathtaking," Ma said, as she walked to look out at the windows. There was a large pool with a waterfall on the lanai.

"I always thought you'd go with more of a classic Florida style of architecture, but I must say, I love the log cabin look. Reminds me of when your ma and I would take trips to the mountains before we had you kids." He walked next to Ma and placed his arm around her. He rubbed her shoulder, slowly stroking her skin while they rested their heads together.

Ma patted his hands and then turned. "Where's the nursery?" she asked with a large smile on her face.

"It's a spare bedroom, Ma," I said, trying not to laugh. The woman was relentless.

"Someday there will be a baby in there," she said, pointing at Suzy.

A change of subject was needed quickly. "Want a drink, Pop?" I asked, wrapping my arm around him, leading him into the kitchen.

"I'd love a stiff one," he replied, looking around the finished living room.

"Yeah, Suzy had one before you got here." I smiled, looking back at her over my shoulder.

"I'll get it for you, Mr. G," Suzy said as she walked by and elbowed me in the ribs. "Why don't you show your parents all the hard work we've done?"

I hunched over, feeling the sting of her bony elbow as I pretended to catch my breath. "Sure." I smiled at her.

Suzy was a vision. Skin slightly pink and pale, blonde hair flowing down her back with her knee-length white sundress. She looked like an angel, but I knew the truth. The girl came off as sweet and innocent, but she was a tiger and had developed quite a liking for curse words. I rubbed off on her. To say I was proud to call her mine was a complete understatement.

"The house is beautiful," Ma said as she grabbed my arm. "You trying to kill her?" she whispered as we walked into the great room.

"Ma, she gives as good as she gets."

"I'm sure, baby," she said as she patted my stomach. "Wow, the fireplace really turned out better than I thought."

I looked at it with pride. It took me days to get it just right, laying each stone one at a time. "Thanks, it was worth all the hours." The rounded river rock made it a challenge, but I sure as fuck wasn't going to let it beat me.

Ma touched the stones and ran her hand across the large wooden mantel. "I'm speechless. The entire place is…" She smiled, looking around.

"I know, Ma. It's perfect. Turned out better than I could've dreamed."

"Here's your drink Mr. G," Suzy said as she handed him a glass of whiskey on the rocks.

A loud pounding on the door made my mother jump. "I'll get it," I said.

Suzy nodded. "I'll show them around."

The banging continued. "Jesus," I yelled as I opened the door.

Mike's fist stopped in midair, as he was about to land another blow. "Sorry, didn't think you heard me."

"I think the dead heard you, brother." I opened the door, letting him inside. His large body hid Mia. "Hey, Doc. How the hell are ya?" I asked Mia as Michael walked inside.

She smiled, holding out her hand to me. I shook my head, grabbing her, and pulled her to my chest. "I want a hug. We're beyond handshakes, Doc. You've seen me naked, for shit's sake." I laughed, feeling her tense in my arms.

She blushed, her cheeks turning red as she pulled away. "Well, um…"

"It's okay, Mia. I was dying and you saved me. I'm just harassing you."

She swallowed, looking at Mike before turning back to me. "You know how your brother gets." She chewed her lip as she looked around my body to Mike.

"Don't worry. He doesn't give a shit about me. He knows I have my girl. Come on in." I stepped aside, letting her pass. "How's the clinic?" I asked as I followed her toward the sound of Mike's voice.

"I promise I didn't look, by the way." She winked, with a small smile on her face. "It's so great, Joe. Your family has done so much." She smiled, stopping at the counter to watch everyone else in the great room.

"Mia," Ma said, holding out her arms.

I smiled as Suzy wrapped her arms around me, placing her head on my chest. Life couldn't get much better than this. Mike and Pop sat on the couch talking, Ma and Mia greeted each other, and Suzy was at my side.

The front door opened and I turned to see who it was. We were only missing Izzy and Anthony. "Smells damn good in here," Izzy said as she walked into the kitchen.

"Hey, sis," I said, walking over to hug her.

"I brought someone, I hope you don't mind." She smiled, looking up into my eyes. Izzy was never this sweet.

"Who?" I asked, looking up.

Anthony waved and stepped aside. Fuck. "Really?" I whispered in her ear, grabbing her by the shoulder.

"Come on, Joey. He didn't have anywhere else to be. He was in town and I told him he could spend the day with us. I know you made enough food for an entire army." She batted her eyelashes at me.

"He's here now." I shook my head, looking down at her. "Next time ask, Izzy."

"Okay," she whispered in my chest, squeezing me before ducking under my arms.

I held out my hand to Sam as Anthony walked by and grimaced. He felt the same way I did about this fucker. "Nice to see you again, Sam."

He placed his hand in mine, gripping it roughly. "I go by Flash now."

"Whatever," I said, rolling my eyes. "Welcome to my home," I said, pulling him close as I crushed his fingers in my grip. "If you hurt my sister, I'll fucking bury you. Got me?"

"Easy now, City. I wouldn't dream of it. We're just friends." He stood toe to toe with me, gripping my shoulder.

"I don't care who the fuck you think you are or what MC you're in. You're still Sam to me and I can still whip your ass. Just so we're clear." I glared at him. Who the fuck did this punk think he was?

Suzy's arms slid around me as her tits crushed against my back. "Everything okay, baby?" she asked.

"Just perfect, sugar. This is Sam, Izzy's friend."

She released me and held out her hand to him. "Hi, Sam, I'm Suzy. Nice to meet you," she said, smiling, unaffected by his inability to dress up. He had on his MC cut and jeans—classy for the holidays.

"It's my pleasure, Suzy." He pulled her hand to his lips and kissed it gently. "You have a beautiful home."

"Thank you, Sam."

I growled, wanting to punch him in the face. His eyes flickered to me, his lips turning up in a half-smirk before he looked back to Suzy.

"Joe's a very lucky man. I hope you don't mind me crashing the party." Sam's eyes flickered to me with a shitty grin before looking at Suzy. I wanted to rip his head off, the fucking weasel.

"Not at all. Come on in and make yourself at home," Suzy said with a smile.

As Sam walked past me, I glared at him but I knew I should be nice. Suzy stood on her tiptoes, rubbing my cheek and staring at me with her head tilted. "What's wrong, City?"

I looked down at her, giving her a half-smile. Her kind eyes and big heart always did a number on me. "Nothing, sugar. I just don't like him."

"I'm sure he's harmless. Let's enjoy our first Thanksgiving in our new home."

I kissed her hair, taking in the coconut sweetness on the silk strands. "Harmless isn't a word I'd use to describe Sam, but you're right, let's enjoy it."

"No more sex references either," she said as she pinched my ass.

"Sugar, I make no promises when it comes to you and that sweet pussy," I said as I crushed my lips to hers, stealing her breath.

3

SUZY

"WHAT STILL NEEDS TO BE DONE, DEAR?" MRS. G ASKED AS I SIPPED MY white wine. "We're just over a week away." She smiled, her eyes soft. I knew she was happy and excited. The wedding was all we talked about anymore.

"I think everything is ready. I have a couple to-do lists, but it's last-minute stuff." I set my fork down, unable to take another bite. "Maybe you can look over the seating chart with me one more time while the boys watch football after dinner."

Her teeth sparkled as her smile grew wide. "I'd love to help."

"Me too," Izzy said from across the table. "Maybe we can have the boys do the dishes for once." She grinned, looking around the table.

"Oh, hell no," Anthony said. "That's women's work." He shook his head, shoveling another forkful of stuffing in his mouth.

Clinking from all the ladies dropping their forks on the table made me laugh. That wasn't the thing to say at this table.

"No shock why your ass is still single," Michael said, slapping Anthony on the back of the head.

"When have we ever done dishes on Thanksgiving? I'm just saying. It's our job to eat and watch football, and the ladies cook and clean. It's the Italian way." He smirked and his body jerked. "What the hell was that for?" He looked at Izzy.

"Being a dumbass," Izzy said as she rolled her eyes.

"Anthony, you boys can handle it this year. The ladies have wedding plans to finalize," Mrs. G said.

"But Ma," Anthony replied with wide eyes.

"No buts, mister. There are enough of you that you'll get it done quickly. Joseph and Suzy's wedding is more important than football this week." Her mouth was set in a firm line. Mrs. G was sweet as apple pie, but no one, and I mean no one, challenged her.

"Fine, Ma." He covered his mouth with his napkin and mumbled.

I bit my lips, stifling my giggle. "We never went around the room sharing what we're most thankful for."

"You're right, Suzy. The boys were so hungry, I didn't even think about it. Forks down," Mrs. G said, placing her fork and knife next to her plate.

A collective groan filled the room. The boys didn't like anyone getting between them and their food, or their women, for that matter. The two things were non-negotiable.

"I'll start," she said. "I'm thankful for my children and loving husband. I'm thankful for the new additions to the table and new members of the family, Suzy and Mia. I'm thankful that Thomas is safe even though he's missed another holiday. I've been blessed with each and every one of you being a part of my life." She smiled, wiping her eyes.

Mr. Gallo stood and cleared his throat. "I'm thankful to live another year to hopefully see the Cubs win the World Series." He laughed. "I'm thankful that I can be proud of each of my children, Mia and Suzy included. When I met and married your mother, I never dreamed that she would give me such wonderful children and a life filled with such joy. I can honestly say I have no regrets, and for that I thank my lucky stars each day." He tipped his head and winked at Mrs. G before sitting.

She blushed and blew him a kiss. I wanted that life. I wanted that love. The lifetime-enduring happiness that seemed out of reach for most.

"I'm thankful for my uncomplicated single life. No offense." Anthony looked at his mother. "I'm thankful for this meal and having you all part of my life. That's enough sappy shit for me to say in one day." He blew out a breath and smiled.

"Aw, you're so sweet, Anthony, you almost made my teeth hurt," Izzy said. "I'm thankful for having two wonderful parents. I'm thankful for having more women around the table. Being outnumbered sucks." She looked at Flash, and he shook his head before he turned to Michael.

Michael glared at him. "Fine, I'll go, you pansy ass." He cracked his knuckles and put his arm around Mia. "I'm thankful for all of you, but most of all for the woman at my side. I haven't been the same since the day I knocked her on her ass. I love ya, Mia, baby." He leaned forward, holding her chin, and kissed her gently.

All the love around the table made my eyes water. This family had become everything to me. City was the icing on the cake, but they were the silky-smooth filling.

"Pussy whipped," Anthony choked out.

"Shut the fuck up." Michael slapped Anthony on the head without looking, as his lips lingered over Mia's mouth.

City stood, looking down at me with a smile that made my stomach flutter. "On that note, I'll get the mushy shit out of the way. I'm thankful that Suzy has agreed to be my wife. I couldn't ask for a better person to share the rest of my life with. We had a rough beginning, but I knew I had her the moment I kissed her. I'm thankful to Mia for helping save my life after the accident." He smiled at Mia, and she blushed. "I'm thankful for my family…well, maybe not Anthony, but everyone else."

He wrapped his arm around my shoulder, pulling me forward before he kissed me. His lips were warm and sweet from the wine. My nose tickled from the facial hair he'd become so fond of. As he pulled away, I moved with him, wanting more of his mouth. He winked, giving me the cocky grin that always set my body on fire.

I swallowed, trying to regain my composure. "I'm thankful that City is still with me after all we've been through. I'm thankful that he survived and is healthier than ever. I'm thankful for each and every one of you for being around this table, even Anthony." I laughed as Anthony smiled, winking.

All the Gallo men were to die for—they were the panty-dropping variety. Women couldn't say no to them; that was how City stole my heart.

Everyone dug back into their meal, scooping up the stuffing and dreaded green bean casserole, and chatter filled the large dining room. I set my napkin down, sat back in my chair, and let the joy I felt seep inside me.

There was something about a man that could cook. I hadn't gone hungry or worried about which brand of Ragu jarred sauce to use since I met City. He had so many skills, and every first impression I had about him was wrong. He was cocky, I hadn't been wrong about that, but City wasn't the overbearing brute I thought he was when we first met.

City was an artist, a romantic, a loving partner, a cook, and an amazing person. The most diverse and well-rounded person I knew. His artistry when it came to tattooing was beyond amazing, colorful and intricate; he spent hours in his studio upstairs creating designs for clients.

He wasn't easy or simple, but he was mine.

"Sugar, you okay?" City brushed the back of his knuckles against my cheek.

I turned to him, smiling, tears welling in my eyes. "Yeah, babe. I'm great." I wiped the corner of my eye, turning to him and taking in his rugged beauty.

"Why the tears?" he whispered in my ear, rubbing my cheek with the rough pad of his thumb.

"I'm just happy." I touched his hand, moving into his touch, and leaned to the side to kiss him.

He smiled, moving toward me and enveloping my lips in a loving kiss. "I can't wait to call you my wife." He searched my eyes, a small smile on his face. "You'll be mine legally."

"I've always been yours, City." I smiled, warmth flowing through my body. He'd never let me think otherwise. He'd laid claim to me early in the relationship and never let me too far out of reach. No matter how scared I was or how hard I tried to fight him, the pull he had over me was too great.

The cocky grin I could no longer live without spread across his face as he grunted. "There's no going back now, sugar." He crushed his lips to mine, stealing my breath, the familiar dull ache returning between my legs.

"You two are kinda nauseating," Anthony said, pretending to gag.

We both turned to glare at Anthony. City cleared his throat. "Someday you'll understand, brother."

"Not going to happen," Anthony said, grimacing before stuffing a piece of bread in his mouth. "I have too much to offer to be tied to just one woman," he said with a muffled voice and small pieces of bread falling from his mouth.

"Yeah, I can see that. Who couldn't resist such a specimen of a man?" I said, breaking out into laughter.

Mrs. G pushed back her chair to stand; the sound of the wooden chair scraping against the slate flooring sent a chill through my body, reminding me of fingernails on a chalkboard. "All right, boys, the ladies are done and we're going to work on the wedding plans. Get this place cleaned up." She raised an eyebrow and looked around the table. The boys, including Mr. G, nodded at her but grumbled under their breath. "Come on, ladies, we have work to do. We have eight days to make it perfect."

Mia, Izzy, and I rose from our chairs and followed Mrs. G out of the dining room. "I can't believe I'm going to have a sister," Izzy said, throwing her arms around me. "Finally, the tables are turning. We're so close to equalizing the cock in this family," she whispered in my ear, a small giggle escaping her lips.

"That's not possible," Mia said as she walked behind us. "All the vaginas in the world couldn't outnumber those boys. They're too…"

"Full of themselves," Mrs. G chimed in, turning to face us. All of us laughed as we walked up the stairs. Gallo men were unique, and we knew it. "It's my fault. I made them who they are, but never fear, ladies—we control everything, even though they think otherwise."

We sobered, hanging on her every word. "You control them, Ma. We sure as hell don't." Izzy rested her body against the wall outside the wedding war room I'd created.

"I'll share my secrets when we're inside and out of the boys' earshot. They don't need to know who really holds the power. It may bruise their male egos," Mrs. G said, her body shaking with laughter.

"Come on, ladies. Be prepared, it's organized chaos inside." I smiled as I opened the door, standing back to let them walk in first.

"Wow," Mia said as she stepped inside and looked around with her mouth agape.

"Holy shit," Izzy said, stepping into the room with wide eyes as she spun around.

"I wouldn't expect anything less from you, dear," Mrs. G said as she put her arm around me and gave me a tight squeeze as we entered the bedroom.

I smiled at her, blushing. "We haven't made it into a bedroom yet. We're using it for the wedding only right now. It is pretty damn cool, isn't it?"

"Will it be a nursery?" Mrs. G looked at me with hopeful eyes.

"Maybe someday." I smiled, my stomach in knots.

We weren't ready for a baby, not just yet. I had too much City left to enjoy.

"No worries. I have all the faith in you, my sweet Suzy." She released me and walked toward the gown.

My body warmed from her sincerity and love as I took in the most important women in my life, all in one spot and without our testosterone-laden other halves.

"This is stunning," Mrs. G said, running her fingers across the lace skirt of my wedding gown.

"Joey is not allowed in this room anymore. I can't risk him seeing my dress." I shook my head. He begged me to wear it for him, he wanted to dirty it—his words, not mine—before I walked down the aisle. That wasn't going to happen.

"Good idea," Mrs. G said, smiling at me.

I watched them as they looked at every detail I'd laid out across the expansive space. I had a seating chart that looked more like an invasion plan for a war, tables and sticky notes everywhere in different colors to represent our two sides. Izzy eyed the party favors while Mia grabbed my wedding shoes and studied them.

"These shoes are amazing. Everything is going to be beautiful, almost magical." Mia placed the shoe back in the box. "You're so organized. I thought I was anal, but babe, you have me beat by a mile," she said with a small laugh.

"What needs to be done?" Mrs. G asked, staring at the seating chart.

I stood next to her, looking over my work. "I just need to make sure I have everyone seated correctly. I don't know most of the people on here. Joey said this person couldn't sit near that person. I'm so confused and don't want to mess it up."

She touched my hand, looking at me with a smile. "I'll inspect it, but from what I see so far, it's perfect."

"Thanks, Mrs. G."

She looked at me, her mouth set in a firm line.

I gulped, realizing my mistake. "*Mom.* Thanks, Mom," I quickly corrected.

She smiled, her face growing soft as she turned back to the poster board.

"Let's talk about the bachelorette party while Ma is busy." Izzy grabbed my arm, pulling me toward the small table on the other side of the room.

"Maybe she wants to come," I said, looking at Mrs. G.

"Nope, she's staying home with Daddy. I have everything planned out."

"Izzy," I warned, my eyes snapping to her face.

She smiled, looking overly pleased with herself. "Don't worry. I have it all under control," she said, winking at me.

"That's what I'm worried about." I said, leveling her with my stare.

"As a bridesmaid it's my duty to give you a kickass bachelorette party. Whatever happens, just blame it on me. I can take care of those boys."

"Give us the rundown," Mia said, not letting me respond to Izzy.

"Okay, well, we have a party bus picking up all the girls here on Friday night and the boys will have their own," Izzy said. "We'll be spending the evening at Shepard's Beach Resort. I reserved the top floor, where the suites are located, and we'll party our asses off. They have a dance club set up at night and we can drink till we puke and crawl to our rooms." She bounced up and down in her chair. "This shit is going to be so kickass."

I looked down, twisting my fingers in my hands. "No stripper, Izzy." I wasn't asking. I wanted to make it clear that I didn't want any half-naked men touching me.

423

"Don't worry," she said, her smile growing wider as my stomach turned over.

"Izzy, I'm serious." I stared at her, holding her with my gaze.

"Relax, Suz."

"I'm looking forward to a girls' night out," Mia said, squeezing my arm. "Michael doesn't let me out of his sight much. Well, really he doesn't let me out of his bed." She laughed, her face turning red.

Izzy winced. "My ears are going to bleed or my brain will explode with that image. Do not mention my brothers and sex. Ever. Ick," she said, sticking out her tongue like she was going to throw up.

"What about Flash?" Mia asked, smirking.

"He's just a friend." Izzy frowned, looking to her mother.

"He looks like he wants to be more than friends," I added. "You've never brought anyone around for family dinners, let alone a holiday, Izzy."

"Eh, he was in town and he doesn't have any family in the area. We hang out sometimes but it's nothing more than that." She drew in a breath. "He's not right for me, and the guys, well, they'd never allow him to be part of this family."

"What are you girls talking about?" Mrs. G asked as she sat down with us.

"The monsters that you've created," Izzy said quickly, changing the subject.

"Ah," Mrs. G said, turning to me. "Suzy, everything looks perfect. I wouldn't change a thing on that seating chart."

I smiled, happy that I hadn't messed it up. "So Ma," I said, the words still foreign on my tongue. "You were going to share your pearls of wisdom with us about how to handle our boys."

She laughed, her eyes twinkling. "Well, it's taken me many years to hone my skills and learn how to get what I want. It's a fine line, though, ladies. You can't let them know you're the one silently controlling the strings from the background. They like to think they're the puppet master, when in reality we hold all the strings."

"Still not giving me details," Mia said, shaking her head.

"Michael and Joseph are tough boys, and Izzy, any man that steals your heart will be just as tough as your brothers, if not more. This information will be for all of you to file away and use when necessary."

We leaned forward, waiting to hear her next words.

"Always remember to make them think they're in charge." She smiled and laughed. "That's the key. Don't ever make them think otherwise. Love them hard, ladies. Smother them with your love. Be fierce when necessary and never back down. Once you give in, they'll expect it always. When they won't give you what you want, well, that's when you deny them the thing they want most." She paused, wiggling her eyebrows.

"Oh my God, Ma. I don't even want to think about you and Pop having sex." Izzy stuck her finger in her mouth, pretending to gag.

Mia and I broke into a fit of laughter.

Mrs. G shook her head. "Deny them food, Izzy." She laughed. "Your mind is always in the gutter, child."

I couldn't control myself. I sagged into the chair, hysterical, with tears streaming down my face. Izzy glared at her mother, unconvinced by her pearls of wisdom. Mia put her head down on the table, her body shaking from the giggles we'd all developed.

I sobered, sitting up in my chair and leaning my elbows on the table. "That won't work for me, Ma. I don't do the cooking. It's hard to deny a man food when he does all the cooking."

"Well then, you only have one other weapon." She smiled, patting Izzy on the leg.

"For the love of God, Ma. Really. My ears are going to explode and I'll never be able to have sex again if you keep talking." Izzy closed her eyes, rubbing her fingers roughly against her skin. "No more. I can't listen."

"Izzy, dear. I was going to say that Suzy shouldn't snuggle with Joey. Snuggle, Izzy."

"Snuggle?" Izzy looked at her ma with wide eyes. "Really? Who the hell snuggles?"

My laughter returned, worse than before. Izzy and Mrs. G were the cutest two people I knew. I could listen to them talk all day.

"All Gallo men snuggle, Izzy," Mrs. G stated calmly and matter-of-factly.

CHELLE BLISS

"Bullshit," Izzy coughed. "Suzy?" She looked at me for confirmation.

"I'm sorry to blow the image you have of your brother, but he loves to snuggle. He'll never use those words, but there's not a night that goes by that I'm not required to fall asleep in his arms."

"You've ruined the image I have of my brother being the big bad wolf." She shook her head, turning her attention to Mia. "Michael too?"

Mia nodded. "Yep, but there's no place I'd rather be. I feel so safe in his arms. He's like an overgrown security blanket. I don't think we've ever fallen asleep without our bodies being entangled."

Izzy rubbed her forehead, looking to the floor. "My mind is blown. Jesus. I know there's no way in hell Anthony is a snuggler. No goddamn way." She shook her head and looked at her ma. "You did this to these men, Ma."

"I snuggled them since the moment they were born, just like I did you. Even as little babies, their fingers would tangle in my hair, playing with the strands."

"I'm not a snuggler," Izzy interrupted, holding up her hand. "Never have been and never will be."

"You will, my dear. When you find the right man." Mrs. G swept her fingers across Izzy's cheek, tilting her head and smiling. There was so much love between the two women, it radiated off of them.

"Nope. I like my space. I'll never give in. Who knew I was really the one with the penis after all these years?" Izzy laughed, hitting the table.

"Don't let the boys hear you say that," I said, grinning at her.

"What are they going to do? Cuddle me to death?" she asked through her laughter, her body slipping from the chair in hysterics.

426

4

CITY

"Get your ass up and help, Sam. We aren't done. You may think you're a guest, but you help like the rest of us. Earn your meal, *friend*," I bit out, trying to hide my obvious dislike of the man.

He sat at the table like a king, watching us as we cleared the table and started to clean up dinner. "Really? Izzy said I was a guest."

I walked over and leaned over the table so only he could hear. "I don't give a fuck what Izzy said. This is my house and you ate my food. Get your fuckin' ass up and help."

"I knew you were a prick," Sam said as he stood, grinning. "I don't remember your mother treating a guest like this in her home."

"I'm not my mother and I don't like you. Never have and sure as fuck never will." I leaned farther across the table, coming eye to eye with him.

"What the fuck did I ever do to you?" Sam glared, not breaking eye contact.

"I don't like you being with my sister. It's that simple."

"Izzy and I aren't together." He crossed his arms.

"I don't give a shit what you say. I don't like her even being near you. You're trouble, Sam."

"I'm not trouble, Joe. You know me. I've never done shit wrong." He walked around the table, coming to face me without a barrier.

427

"I know you're prospecting with the Sun Devils. They don't play games, Sam. They're the real deal. I don't want my sister involved in their bullshit." I snarled, fisting my hands at my side.

"They're good guys, Joe. I never take your sister around them. She and I spend time together when I come to town to see my parents or go on a run. Nothing more than that." His eyes softened as he stared at me; the glare had vanished. "I'd never hurt your sister. We've been friends since we were little kids. She'd kick my ass anyway. I mean, seriously, Joe, your sister doesn't take anyone's shit."

I shook my head as I laughed. "Good, Sam. Remember that. If she doesn't get ya, I sure as fuck will." I placed my hand on his shoulder, giving it a firm squeeze. "There's a whole line of Gallo men that have my back. Don't get her involved in that MC, you hear me?" I raised an eyebrow as my laughter vanished.

"I got ya, man. Your sister is the only girl that has ever earned my respect. I would never do anything to endanger her," he said as he held out his hand to me.

I stared at him, trying to judge his sincerity. "I'm going to hold you to your word, Sam." I gripped his hand, squeezing it between my fingers, letting him know that I could easily overpower him.

A hand landed on my shoulder as Michael said, "What's going on over here? While you two ladies chitchat, the real men are doing all the work." He looked at Sam before turning to me.

I smiled, increasing my grip on Sam's hand. "We're done, Mike. Just having a little heart-to-heart about Izzy."

Sam gritted his teeth and tried to pull his hand away. "I got it, guys. I'll treat your sister right."

"Damn right you will," Michael said, taking a step forward.

"What the fuck? I've never done anything to her."

"Keep it that way, Sam, and we won't have an issue," Michael said.

"Boys, get your asses over here and clean some shit. Football's on and I'm not going to miss the game. Move it," Pop yelled, causing us all to turn.

"Coming, Pop," Michael said over his shoulder. "Let's go. I think Sam has a clear enough picture of what's at stake."

"I do." He nodded, shaking out his hand after I released it.

I grabbed the remote, turning up the volume on the football game that was just about to kick off. We finished clearing the table, loaded the dishwasher, and polished off the pots and pans while we listened to the game.

Just as I put the last pot away, the girls walked back down the stairs. Their laughter filled the space, overpowering the sports announcer on the television. The guys had piled into the living room, making themselves at home on the couch.

I captured Suzy's wrist, pulling her against my chest. "What's so funny, sugar?" I asked, rubbing my nose against her temple.

"Just girl stuff. Did you boys have fun?" she asked, staring up at me, tears hanging in her eyes.

"You okay? You look like you've been crying." I swept my fingers underneath her eyes, catching a single tear.

"We were laughing so hard, City. I love them so much." She beamed.

"I don't think I want to know what you girls were talking about. They love you just as much, Suzy. You're family now." I pulled her chin up, brushing my lips against her tender skin.

She closed her eyes, parting her mouth for me. My dick twitched, wanting to be inside of that pretty little mouth again. Grabbing the nape of her neck, I held her in place, claiming her mouth. The feel of her soft lips on mine drove me closer to the edge. I wanted to throw her over my shoulder and run upstairs for a quickie. She acquiesced, giving herself to me with her mouth as she snaked her arms around my body. My dick throbbed in my pants; the blowjob earlier wasn't enough to dull the constant ache I felt when near her.

Placing her hand on my chest, she pushed gently. "City," she said breathily against my lips. Her eyes opened slowly, blinking back the haze. "Later. Your family is here."

"I don't give a fuck. They won't notice if we disappear for a few minutes. I need to taste you, sugar. I need to sink my cock in you so deep that my balls slap against your clit until you scream." I held her in place, staring in her eyes, watching them dilate.

"Okay," she whispered, scrubbing her hands across my chest.

I looked over her head at my family sitting in front of the television. "Come on, let's sneak upstairs." I released her neck, putting her hand in mine, and pulled her toward the stairs.

"Shouldn't we say something?" she asked, looking back at them.

"No, they won't notice, I'll be fast." I winked at her as we walked up the stairs.

"We've gone over this. You're never fast."

I reached down, picking her up from under her arms and tossing her over my shoulder. She squealed and giggled.

"Everything okay in there?" Ma yelled.

"Perfect, Ma. Be right back," I yelled down the stairs.

"You've given us away."

I swatted Suzy's ass. "Now I *have* to be quick. Fuck."

She wiggled and laughed, grabbing my ass as I rounded the corner to our bedroom. Kicking the door closed, I released my grip, letting her body slide down mine. Her soft to my hard. I wasn't in the mood to take her gently. She wasn't my bride-to-be in this moment. She was mine, and mine to use.

"I don't think—" she started to say as I placed my finger against her lips.

"No talking." I shook my head, claiming her lips as I unzipped my jeans. As she walked backward, her hands found the top of my jeans. She pulled them down at the sides; my dick sprang free, slapping against her arm.

She moaned in my mouth. "Jesus, babe. You're so hard."

"You did this to me walking around in that hot-ass sundress shaking your ass." I reached under her dress, my eyes growing wide when I didn't feel any panties. "What the fuck, sugar? No panties? You never go without," I murmured against her lips, running my fingers through her wetness.

The silky smoothness of her cunt made my cock grow harder. The familiar ache that I'd been perpetually blessed with since meeting Suzy was almost too much to bear at times.

She rubbed her pussy against my palm. "Please, City. I need to feel you." Her eyes fluttered, her breathing turning harsh.

Grabbing her by the waist, I spun her around to face the bed. "On your stomach, hands on the bed, sugar."

She smiled over her shoulder, her cheeks turning pink. "City, everyone's downstairs. They may hear or come looking for us." She placed her palms against the crisp white down comforter.

"Then you better bend over so we can be quick." I smacked her ass and watched her jump.

She bent over as she rubbed her ass, bringing her sundress up her legs, showing me a hint of thigh. She planted her elbows flat against the mattress and stilled as my hand caressed her ass.

My dick twitched, screaming to sink into her. I grabbed it, stroking the length as I hiked up her dress. Running my cock through her wetness, I sighed, knowing I wouldn't be walking around with a hard-on for the rest of the night.

I pulled her hips up, lifting her slightly off the bed, my dick touching her opening.

"Wait." Her body stiffened as she planted her face in the mattress.

"What?" I asked, with my cock in my hand, ready to push inside.

"Condom?" Her voice muffled by the blankets.

"Sugar, you're on the pill. We're about to be man and wife. We've done it without before. Right now, I want to feel you with nothing between us. I want to feel your silky wetness as I fuck the shit out of you."

She sighed, relaxing her body. "Okay, but—"

"Enough talking. The only words I wanna hear out of you are 'yes' and 'give me more.'" I leaned over her, kissing her shoulder as I jammed my cock into her.

Her body jerked, accepting all I had to give as she melted into the mattress. The blankets were bunched in her hands as I stood, looking down at her.

I slid my hand up her back, tangling my fingers in her hair. Wrapping it around my palm, I grabbed it and pulled. She gasped, her eyes sealing shut as I thrust myself inside her. The flesh of her hip felt cool underneath my forceful grip.

Every time my dick slammed into her, my balls slapped her clit, causing her body to twitch and moans to escape her lips. I thrust harder, needing the release as I watched her body bounce off my shaft.

"You want me to stop?" I bit out, swiveling my hips to touch every inch of the inside of her pussy.

"No," she moaned.

"You love my cock?"

"Yes," she said as she bucked.

I pulled her down forcefully against my body. "This is my pussy." Pulling her hair harder, I wrapped it around my fist, holding it more securely. "I take it when I want, not when you want to give it."

"Yes, yes. Oh God, yes!" she yelled, her pussy convulsing against my dick. She drew her legs in closer together, almost crossing them, making her hold on my cock viselike.

I slid my finger from her hip to her abdomen and down to her clit. It was swollen, and she shuddered as I pinched it, rolling it between my fingertips.

Her face fell forward and she bore down, pulling the blanket between her teeth. She grunted, pounding herself against me as I worked her clit, bringing her to the brink of release.

"Say what I wanna hear." I stilled my hands as I pummeled her.

"It's your pussy," she moaned without hesitation.

I chuckled, biting my lip. Suzy went from saying "heck" to using the word "pussy" without hesitation since she met me. Hearing her say such dirty shit made my spine tingle. "Always, sugar. Come on my cock. Shows me who owns you."

Using two fingers, I covered her clit entirely, making small circles with the soft pads of my tips. Her grunts grew louder, her pussy milking me, as she tensed and stilled. My touch became more demanding, my thrusts rougher as I used my cock as my own personal battering ram. I wanted her to walk funny when she went back downstairs.

"Give it to me, sugar." I tweaked her clit, needing her to come before I did.

She sucked in a breath, not moving, as she came on my cock. As her body relaxed and she grew limp, I used it as an invitation to fuck her senseless. Her body bounced like a bowl of Jell-O underneath me.

The orgasm ripped through me, sending me collapsing on top of her, gasping for air. "Fuck," I moaned as I caught my breath, my knees feeling weak.

"Mm," she hummed as she lay underneath me, smiling.

Planting my palms on the bed, I trailed kisses across her exposed skin as I pushed myself up. Her ass was a light shade of pink from the relentless pounding I gave her. She lay there with her dress hiked up around her waist, her ass still in the air and her body bent over the bed. She looked how I felt: sated and happy.

I tucked my dick back in my pants, leaving the remnants of our mingled orgasm on my flesh. "Come on, let's get back downstairs before people come looking." I ran my fingers down her arm, stopping in her palm to make tiny circles.

"I don't want to," she whispered, her skin breaking out in goose bumps.

"No choice now, princess. Let's go." I grabbed her by the hips and pulled her upright.

She gasped as her eyes widened into saucers.

"What's wrong?" I searched her eyes, watching her face flush an even darker shade of pink.

"Everything just gushed out of me. Oh my God, it's running down my leg." She looked down. "I can't go down there like this." She glared at me.

My body shook from the laugh I couldn't hold in. "Sugar, go get cleaned up. I'll wait for you and we can go down together." I smiled, watching her move from one foot to the other.

"Ugh, this is so not sexy," she whispered, turning toward the bathroom. Her walk reminded me of the marshmallow man from Ghostbusters—her arms far from her side as she took large steps on spread legs. She stalked to the bathroom in the most ungraceful way, but that was my girl. I wouldn't change a thing about her.

As the bathroom door closed, I collapsed on the bed, placing my hands behind my head. She'd be feeling me in more ways than one for the rest of the night. She'd be my wife soon. *My wife.* It still felt foreign to think, let alone say, but there had been no other person in the world that had me the way Suzy did. I was hers completely, maybe more than she was mine.

I closed my eyes. I never knew life could be this fucking fantastic.

5

SUZY

"IZZY, WHAT DID I TELL YOU ABOUT TONIGHT?" I LOOKED AT HER AS WE entered the hotel suite. I couldn't pin it on her alone. She had help planning my bachelorette party. The girls in the wedding party plotted together to send me out of singledom in style. I knew that Izzy and Sophia would be a wicked combination.

The hotel suite was stunning. I'd never seen anything like it. It was larger than my first home and overlooked the ocean. The exterior walls were glass from floor to ceiling. The sunset made it look like an ever-changing picture hanging in a gallery. The red, purple, and orange shades reflected off the water as the sun kissed the horizon.

Izzy stepped in front of me, breaking me from my sunset trance. "I heard you, Suzy. We were good. Sophia helped me and you know that she always has your best interests at heart," Izzy said with a laugh.

Sophia was my best friend. She was my opposite, though, living life a little more carefree, taking chances, and was a little too much like Izzy for my liking. She may be a librarian, but the girl partied like a rock star. Fuck.

"What's wrong, Suzy?" Sophia asked, touching my arm.

"You two," I said, shaking my head.

Sophia's lips parted as she laid her hand against her chest. "What did

434

we do?" Her innocent act wasn't convincing. Motherhood had softened her a little. She had more weight on her body and looked healthy. The happiness that had now filled her life was clearly evident when looking at her.

"I don't trust you and Izzy individually, and I sure as hell don't trust you together." I glared at her, watching a small smile creep across her face. My stomach filled with knots. The two of them didn't follow any of the normal rules, let alone mine.

"Suzy, would I do anything to upset you?" Her brown eyes twinkled as a large smile spread across her face. Crossing her arms, she tilted her head and waited.

I studied the look on her face. "Yes, yes you would. Just the girls tonight, right?" I asked, watching her reaction very closely.

She nodded, her brown hair bobbing against her breasts that peeked out from her V-neck dress. "I only invited the girls. I swear."

The knot in my stomach loosened a bit with her statement. "I just don't want there to be any trouble tonight."

"Oh, there won't be." She shook her head and wrapped her arms around me, drawing me against her body. "I'm so happy for you, Suzy. Do you think I would do anything bad and have to deal with Kayden's bullshit?"

"No," I whispered as I hugged her.

Kayden was her man and the father of her son, Jett. Their love was complicated. The road they traveled to happiness had been filled with bumps, but they made it through and never looked back. Kayden was a man I could rely on, a friend that would lay down his life for me. Sophia had told me that he could be "wicked jealous." Her words for him, not mine.

"Okay then, let's grab a drink. The girls are all about to arrive." She held me at arm's length, smiling and squeezing my hands. "We're here to celebrate before you become Mrs. Joseph Gallo."

"I don't want to drink too much, Sophia," I mumbled as we walked toward the already prepped bar area.

Izzy was pouring herself a hefty glass of Jack Daniel's as we approached. "What'll it be, ladies?" she asked as she set the bottle on the counter.

"Just a glass of wine," I said, looking at the dozens of bottles on display.

"No wine tonight, Suzy. Pick your poison." Izzy smiled, waving her hands over the liquor.

"Bahama Mama." I winced, my stomach rolling at the thought of getting drunk. "Light on the liquor, though."

"Honey, it's your bachelorette party and if you don't get shit-faced drunk and party your ass off then I haven't done my job as a bridesmaid." She smiled as she started pouring the rum in the glass.

I watched, my eyes growing wide as she poured and poured. "That's enough, Izzy," I said, placing my hand on her arm. "I want to make it until at least ten."

She burst into laughter as she set the rum down. "We'll get ya there. We have the whole night planned out. It's going to be one for the record books. When we're old and pissing our pants with dentures in our mouths, we'll be telling stories about tonight." She smiled, pouring the juices and rum in the cup before handing it to me.

I shook my head and grabbed the Bahama Mama from her hand. "That's what I'm afraid of," I muttered as I brought the glass to my lips. The rum didn't smell overpowering; maybe I'd misjudged the amount of alcohol she poured.

The fruity concoction of pineapple and orange danced across my tongue as the liquid slid down my throat, causing a slow burn. I closed my eyes, enjoying the taste, although it was a bit stronger than I wanted.

Izzy tipped my cup. "Drink up, girl. We have a big night ahead of us."

I batted her hand away, pulling the cup from my lips. "Last time I drank too much I ended up in your brother's bed." I smiled, my body warming at the memory.

If I hadn't been tipsy that night, I would've been a total mess the first time I saw him naked. The man had a kickass body, and don't even get me started on his piercing. If I had been stone-cold sober, I probably would've run out of the room screaming once that caught my eye. Even to this day, I get a thrill looking at him naked.

"You're a dirty whore and we all know it." Sophia nudged me, cackling like a loon.

"Am not," I said, my cheeks heating as I glared at her.

"Suzy," Izzy interrupted, "you're with us, your girls. You can drop the good-girl bullshit. We know you're a closet freak. If you weren't, you wouldn't be with my brother." She laughed.

A knock on the door saved me from the conversation. One by one, Izzy and Sophia's friends and mine from work poured into the door. My sister wouldn't be here tonight. She said that she couldn't get off work to be here in time for the bachelorette party. She'd make it for the rehearsal dinner. The girls in this room were more like family to me than my own flesh and blood anyway.

I stood at the window, watching the sun kiss the horizon as I sipped my drink. I felt blessed, surrounded by loving women, marrying the man of my dreams, and officially becoming a member of the Gallo family. The ladies chatted and drank, their laughter filling the room.

"Hey, you okay?" Sophia asked, standing at my side.

"I'm just so happy, Soph. I never thought I could be this happy." I turned to her, a sad smile on my face.

"What's the sad face for?" Her eyebrows drew together as she looked at me.

"I'm not sad. I'm just thinking about what City and I have been through. I almost shut him out of my life by judging him. I would've never known the love I do now. Then the accident happened and he was almost ripped from my life forever." I shook my head, trying to force the sad memories from my mind. "I'm so happy right now...happier than I've ever been before. Is this as good as it gets?" I asked, grabbing her hand and squeezing.

"Nah, there's more good things to come." She smiled, squeezing my hand. "Wait until you hold your firstborn in your arms. There's nothing like it." She smiled, releasing my hand. "I'm proud of you."

My eyebrows shot up at her words. "For what?"

She giggled, covering her mouth. "For staying with City. I know he scared the hell out of you. I know how OCD you are with your lists—even that fucking list of your husband requirements. You threw them out the window and took a chance for once. You listened to your heart and not your head. When I met him, I knew he was right for you." She wrapped her arms around me. "Now, let's stop talking sad shit and party our asses off. I have a night without Jett and Kayden. I want to get drunk and enjoy a night without baby food on my clothes."

I chuckled and squeezed her. "I love you, Sophia. For you, I'll party like it's 1999."

"God, you're such a dork," she said as she laughed, holding me by the arms, shaking her head. "But I love you. I don't know why, but I do."

"Bitches, I better see you two drinking a little quicker," Izzy said as she grabbed my glass and looked inside. "Let me refill this. Sophia, want more?"

Sophia held her cup out, shaking it. "Feels a bit light to me. Another Jack and Coke, please." She handed the cup to Izzy.

"And I'll—" I started to say as Izzy started to walk away.

"Got it, light on the alcohol," Izzy yelled over her shoulder.

"Gifts! Let's do gifts," Sophia said, pulling on my arm.

I loved presents. It's not that I was materialistic; I just never had the type of family where the gifts were piled higher than me. I always received a couple of small gifts for my birthday or Christmas. My family decided to draw names for Christmas that year. Just when I thought it couldn't be more depressing, bam, wrong again.

"Okay," I said, nodding, trying to hide my excitement.

Sophia clapped, drawing everyone's attention. "It's time for presents!" she yelled, pulling me toward the couch.

I sat down on the large U-shaped sectional in the middle of the living room that faced the windows. Everyone fit snugly on the couch as I opened each gift. I felt slightly uncomfortable being the center of attention. I liked to blend in to the background, but I knew the entire weekend would be filled with uncomfortable moments. I was the bride, and as such, I'd definitely be the center of attention.

"Open mine next," Sophia said, holding out a pretty pink box with a giant white bow. I'd opened six presents so far and they'd all been lingerie and nighties to wear for City. He'd love them, but I knew most likely one or two would get ripped. The man was a brute.

Pulling it from her grasp, I smiled nervously, unsure of what was inside. With Sophia, it could be romantic or downright dirty. "I don't trust you," I said, placing the box on my lap and pulling on the ribbon.

She chuckled, covering her mouth. "I wouldn't either."

I stilled my hand, looking up at her with a glare. "Do I want to open this in public?"

She nodded, her smile growing larger. "You do. Don't be a baby and open it already," she said, putting her hands on her hips.

I pulled the ribbon, letting the white material fall away from the present before tearing into the shiny pink paper. When I opened the box, I gasped and put the lid back on. "Sophia," I said, trying not to laugh.

"You have to show us," Izzy said as she stood. She grabbed her phone from her pocket and held it up to take a picture. "Come on, Suzy. We're all girls here. Don't be a pussy."

I sighed, realizing I wouldn't win the battle. "Fine," I said, opening the lid and grabbing the first object. Fuckin' Sophia. I held it up and listened to the whistles and giggles.

"What the fuck is that?" Mia asked.

"That, my dear," Izzy said, snapping a photo, "when assembled, is a spreader bar." Izzy giggled and snapped another picture.

My face grew flushed, but I couldn't help but laugh. "I've never had a problem keeping them open for City." I winked at Sophia. She and I always swapped stories about sex. Before City came into my life, sex had always been bland and boring. I'd lived vicariously through her and always went to her for advice.

"Oh, I know. You've turned into quite the little sex kitten since meeting City. This gift may seem like it's for you, but it's really for him." Sophia smiled and looked very pleased with herself. "Next."

"Whore," I mumbled as I pulled out a pair of nipple clamps.

"I don't want to think of you using any of this shit with my brother. I can never look at you two in the eye again. I know too much. Too much, I tell you." Izzy snapped another photo before taking a seat at the end of the couch.

I quickly pulled out the other objects, crotchless panties and a crop, and held them up before dropping them back in the box. The crop was the one I'd always wanted and admired. It had a heart made of leather on the end. I just loved the look of it, but it had to sting like a mother when hit with it.

Knock. Knock.

"Oh," Izzy said, jumping from the couch. "There's my gift. I had to have it delivered."

I looked at Sophia and she shrugged. Motherfuckers. I knew they wouldn't listen when I said no strippers. I hung my head, rubbing my face, as I heard the door open.

"Why, hello there, officer," Izzy said. She giggled and backed away from the door.

For the love of God—I wanted to kill her right then.

"I heard there's a disturbance up here. I'm here to investigate," the man, who obviously wasn't a cop, said as he looked around the room.

I thought for a moment that I was in a movie. Cop stripper comes to the door and then the real party starts. The last thing I wanted in the world was someone other than my fiancé touching me.

"She's right over there—the blonde in the middle. She's a real handful." Izzy looked at me with a smile, and winked.

I blushed, all eyes turning on me as he started the little CD player he had in his hand. The girls started to scream, scrambling from the couch.

I sat alone, leaning back, and crossed my arms over my chest. He handed the CD player to Sophia as he approached me. He stalked toward me, untucking his shirt and shaking his hips. Izzy held her phone in our direction.

"Don't you fucking dare take a photo of this," I warned. The last thing I needed was this getting into City's hands. He wasn't a jealous man, he knew I was his, but still, there would be a sting.

"You're such a killjoy," Izzy said as she shoved the phone in her pocket.

"Bad Ass" by Kid Ink played as the stripper tried his best to seduce me. He wasn't bad looking—blond hair, thin but muscular, and beautiful brown eyes. He ripped his shirt open, exposing a hairless chest. He turned, shaking his ass in my face as he ripped off his pants. Was he twerking?

I wanted to laugh, but I didn't want to be rude. He was trying hard to impress me, but he wasn't my City. I uncrossed my arms, letting them fall into my lap, as I watched him shake his ass. He turned and I came face to face with his cock, thankful it was tucked neatly in a G-string. Wouldn't work for City and his well-endowed package.

"Smile, for shit's sake. At least pretend to have a good time," Sophia whispered in my ear. "As soon as he's done with you, the rest of the girls will get their shot at him."

I turned to her and glared, but did as she said. I smiled and pretended to enjoy myself. My stomach flipped when he sat on my lap and started rubbing against my chest. He nuzzled his face in my hair as he scooted forward, and all I could think about was City, and how he loved being wrapped in my gold locks.

His small, semi-erect dick touched my stomach, and I cringed. I closed my eyes, thinking about something other than what was happening.

"Hey," he whispered in my ear. "Don't worry, the song is almost over."

I opened my eyes and blew out a breath. I couldn't be the only ambushed bride in this uncomfortable situation.

"Thanks," I whispered, and smiled. His words put me at ease and helped settle my nerves, knowing the torture was almost done.

When the song ended, he grabbed my chin, kissing me on the cheek. My eyes grew wide as I pulled my head back, letting his fingers fall from my chin. He smiled sweetly and turned his attention to Mia sitting next to me. I sighed, happy that it was over and I could relax.

I stood on wobbly legs and approached Izzy. She couldn't stop laughing. "Happy with yourself?" I asked, my hands on my hips.

"Very." She laughed louder. "You're done now, Suzy Q. Drink up. Let the other girls enjoy him for a while. We'll head down to the party around the pool in a bit."

"I need the entire bottle of rum to forget the feel of him against my body." My body shook as I remembered foreign skin against mine.

"Well, good thing for you I brought extra. Help yourself," she said with a grin, motioning toward the temporary bar with her head and wiggling her eyebrows.

"I'm still pissed at you," I said as I pointed at her and glared.

"You love me, don't bullshit yourself." She kissed my cheek and walked toward the gaggle of girls stuffing ones in the strippers G-string.

Grabbing my phone off the table, I checked my messages. Nothing. City and I hadn't spent much time apart since the motorcycle accident, and I missed him. I didn't want to be the clingy, annoying fiancée, but I couldn't help myself, I sent him a text.

Me: Having fun?

I set my phone down and grabbed the bottle of rum and poured half a glass. I didn't know how much to put in a Bahama Mama, but it looked like the same amount Izzy poured earlier. I added the juices and watched the color change to a salmon pink after the grenadine splash. It was as pretty as it was tasty. I sipped it, sat down at the dining room table, and waited for his reply.

City: Miss you, sugar.

That was a vague and cagey reply. He didn't say if he was or was not having fun. I didn't want to know what the boys had planned for him tonight. No one would tell me anyway, or any of the girls, for that matter. I sent him a quick message as I watched the bump-and-grind show taking place on the sectional.

Me: Miss you too.

Sophia sat down next to me and frowned. "Why are you over here and not over there with the rest of the party?" She tilted her head and chewed on her bottom lip.

"Just rather watch that hot mess than participate. I could ask you the same thing. Why aren't you copping a feel?" I raised my eyebrow and challenged her. I didn't need an answer. She felt the same way I did.

"Hell no. I don't need someone pawing at me. I'm here to have a girls' night, not stare at his tiny junk."

I choked on my drink, and wiped the liquid off my chin. "You noticed that too, huh?" I asked.

She laughed, throwing her head back and relaxing in the chair. "Gotta be blind not to. You ready to be Mrs. Joseph Gallo?"

"Yeah, I'm excited, but you know I don't like too much attention."

"Well, you're going to be the center of attention here and there this weekend. Might as well get used to it." She grabbed her Solo cup, downing the last remnants of her drink.

"At least City will be by my side." I checked my phone, but there wasn't a new message.

Izzy ripped the phone from my hand. "Oh, no. This is a man-free night. This is all about us celebrating and partying our asses off. No phones, no Joe. Got it?"

"You're a bitch," I said as she shoved my phone in her back pocket. "If this is your idea of celebration then you're not who I thought you were, Izzy." I stuck my tongue out.

"This is the pre-party. The real fun starts downstairs. The nightclub opened an hour ago. No good club starts until eleven. Keep your granny panties on. We'll be going shortly. Keep drinking." She gave me a cocky grin and walked away.

"I love her," Sophia said, getting up to refill her cup.

"You would," I mumbled before downing the last of my Bahama Mama, a slow burn sliding down my throat and spreading throughout my body.

Mia sat in the chair Sophia had been in. "It's nice to finally get a night away from the guys, isn't it?" she asked, smiling before she took a sip of her drink.

"I guess so. I love City, but I love my girls too."

"There's nothing wrong with that, Suzy. It's good to have some time apart. I've spent as much time with anyone as I do with Michael. I mean, I love him—fuck, most days I can't get enough of him—but I needed tonight," Mia said as she leaned back in the chair, resting her head against the high chair back.

"Are things okay with you two?" I asked, concerned about them. I loved Mike and adored Mia. I wanted them around and loved any time we were all able to hang out. With all of our work schedules, it wasn't easy.

"Yeah, things are great. Sometimes we get in arguments, but that's when he wants to pull his man bullshit, and I eventually put him in his place." She laughed, bringing the cup to her lips. "Gallo men are a breed of their own."

"Yeah, no truer words have ever been spoken."

"Are you ready for the wedding?" she asked me, tilting her head and twirling the cup in her hand.

"Ready as I'll ever be."

"You have that need for control, like Mike. It'll go off without a hitch,

Suzy. Every Gallo will make sure it does. I'll help too. I'll do anything you need that day."

"Thanks so much, Mia. I just want it to be perfect."

"Perfection is overrated," she said, smiling at me.

"On my wedding day, I don't think it is," I said, my stomach turning at the thought of anything going wrong.

"Suzy, it's life's imperfections that stand out and make memories. They're what great stories are made of, and we'll tell them over and over again. Imperfections make the world more interesting. Think about your relationship with City, how you began. Was it perfect?"

I shook my head, the power of her words calming my rumbling stomach. "Hardly. We hit some bumps along the road."

"Does it make your love story less worthy or the journey less sweet?" Mia asked.

"No, it makes me hold on tighter, thinking of what I could've lost."

"Perfection isn't all it's cracked up to be. Just enjoy the day. All that matters is that you're husband and wife at the end of it all. Not if the cake was perfect or if the seating chart was right. Just Joe and you becoming one."

I leaned forward, wrapping my arms around her. "You're right, Mia. Everything else is trivial. Thank you for your kind words. I couldn't have picked a more perfect person for Mike."

"There's that 'perfect' word again. I'm far from it, but we're a good fit," she said, hugging me back. "Now, I'm ready to party my ass off with the girls and worry about the men and wedding later. You in?" she asked, releasing me.

"All in. Let's do it," I said, standing to find Izzy and Sophia. I was ready to dance. Clearly, I'd had too much to drink.

6

CITY

"I can't believe that shit can even be done," Anthony said, holding his stomach as he laughed.

"She has mad skills." Mike shook his head, all of us still stunned.

"When she shot that thing out of her pussy, I almost shit a brick." Anthony scrubbed his hand across his face, shaking his head.

"A ping-pong ball. Jesus Christ, I'll never be able to see anyone play that fucking game again." Mike grabbed the beer from the cup holder and downed it.

We were safely on the limo bus after a rather interesting trip to some shit-ass dive strip club in Tampa. It wasn't my idea of a good time, but since Mike and Anthony planned the entire night, I sat back and tried to enjoy the ride. I felt guilty watching strippers, knowing that Suzy was off enjoying a peaceful night with the girls. Izzy promised me that they were just going for drinks and maybe dancing and that they'd be staying in a hotel room so they wouldn't drink and drive.

"Why the fuck aren't you talking?" Bear said as he nudged Tank.

I shook my head, laughing at the mix of guys on this bus. For some unknown reason, Mike and Anthony decided to invite Bear, Tank, and a few other guys from the Neon Cowboy. They knew each other from Inked since they were not only friends but also clients.

"I'm talking. Just listening about the pussy show." I glared at Bear and then looked at Tank, tilting my head while I studied his face. "What the fuck is that smirk for?"

"You're so pussy whipped." Tank tipped his glass, his smirk turning into a smile. The corners of his eyes wrinkled as he chuckled and took a swig of beer.

"Fuck off," I growled. "I'm not pussy whipped. Why look at ground meat when I have grade-A platinum pussy at home? I know you boys don't know the difference." I smirked, looking to Mike. "Not you, brother, you get the good shit too. You know what I mean."

He smiled, nodding. "I do, but I am still in disbelief. Mia better never shoot anything out of that pussy. Shit's too good to ruin with a ping-pong ball or anything other than my dick, fingers, and tongue," Michael said, making a V with his fingers and tonguing the void.

"Clearly you've had too much to drink," I said, looking at him, unable to contain my laughter.

"Two fuckin' pussy-whipped bastards. You sure you two still have your balls attached?" Bear slapped his knee.

"Why don't you suck my dick and find out, motherfucker?" I smirked as Bear stilled and gagged. "You're just jealous, plain and simple."

He mumbled, bringing the bottle to his lips. "You know I've always been fond of Sunshine. Couldn't be pussy whipped over a better girl."

"We're here," the driver called out as the limo-bus stopped in front of a beachside hotel.

"What the fuck are we doing here?" I looked out the tinted windows, confused by the destination. I didn't think we'd end the evening at a hotel. We'd already seen the strippers, so I didn't think that awaited us inside.

"Shepard's has the best fuckin' nightclub in the St. Pete. Get your old grumpy ass up and let's dance." Anthony stood, taking the glass from my hand.

"One, I don't fuckin' dance without my woman. Two, don't ever touch my beer. Three, this wasn't supposed to be a night for you to find a piece of ass," I said as I climbed off the limo bus.

"Fine, you drink and stew in your moodiness while the rest of us enjoy the ladies, right, men?" Anthony pumped his fist, his body shaking with excitement. "Right?"

Michael cleared his throat, looking away from Anthony. "I'm with Joe. I'd rather drink and bullshit than look at any other women. Mia would have my balls in a sling if I even thought about looking at another woman. I'll hang with my brother while you bastards find your next victims." He laughed as he walked by, and slapped me on the shoulder. "I got your back," he said softly so only I could hear.

"More for us," Tank said, heading toward the door.

"Yeah, this looks like your type of place, Tank." I shook my head. "The girls are going to run away screaming from your ass." The warm air of the Florida night felt good against my skin. The salty smell of the air and the gentle breeze of the ocean were soothing.

"I'll show them what a real man looks like," Tank said. "They're too used to these pansy-ass boys that pluck their eyebrows and wax their body hair. They need a little Tank in their life. What the fuck are those douchebags called again?"

I rolled my eyes. The man was clearly full of himself. "Yeah, I'm sure they do. How the fuck am I supposed to know what they're called?"

"Metrosexuals," Bear said, giving a weak smile.

"What the fuck?" I said, totally in shock. I never ever in a million years thought Bear would know that fucking term. A big, burly biker like him should not know that term. "You reading *Vogue* magazine or some shit?" I raised an eyebrow, studying his face.

His cheeks turned pink as he looked at the ground. "I have sisters, asshole. Their boyfriends are metrosexuals. Beats the fuck outta me. They throw the term around like it's the most glorious thing. Someday they'll figure out what they're missing being with such a pussy."

I laughed along with the rest of the guys. "Had us worried there for a second," Tank said, smacking Bear in the back of the head. "I was about to do a dick check."

"I know you've always wanted to get your hands on my cock, Tank. I don't swing that way. Sorry, buddy."

I smiled as we walked through the lobby. I had the best friends and brothers in the whole fucking world. Before Anthony pushed open the doors to the pool, the glass panes started to shake from the bass of the music on the other side.

"Ready, boys?" Anthony asked, looking like he was about to enter a little piece of heaven.

"Just open the fuckin' doors already," I growled.

He nodded, pushing open both doors at once. We took two steps and stopped dead to take in the sight before us. Girls in bikinis, skimpy dresses, and various other kinds of tiny, barely there clothing writhed and danced to the beat of the techno music.

"Wow, I've been missing out at that hick bar," Tank said, his voice filled with disbelief.

"Neon Cowboy women do not look like that." Bear held his hand out, moving it up and down, motioning toward the crowd, and licked his lips.

"There is sure as fuck is something to be said for city girls." Tank headed toward the crowd, winding his way through the ladies.

At least Tank and Bear didn't come in their camo or some other redneck attire. They wore clean denim jeans, black t-shirts, and boots. We looked like the redneck biker version of the Rat Pack. Our tats were clearly visible on our arms—metrosexuals we most definitely were not.

"Bar," I growled, pulling Tank off the back of some chick. He had her by the hips and she was pushing back against him with a big smile on her face.

"What the fuck, man? I was enjoying myself."

"She had a ring on her finger, dumbass," I yelled over the loud music.

"Who cares? I was looking to hit it and quit it." He laughed, making a smacking motion while thrusting his hips.

"Shots. We need them in mass quantities." Bear threw a fifty on the bar.

"That won't get you far here, Bear." Michael threw an extra fifty on top. "This isn't the Podunk bar you're used to. This is the city, and every-thing is three times as much."

We leaned against the bar, studying the dance floor like a scene from *Saturday Night Fever* as we waited for our tequila shots and beers. I reached in my pocket for my phone as panic started to set in. Fuck.

"What's wrong, Joe?" Michael asked, resting his hand on my shoulder.

"I don't have my phone. Suzy's going to be pissed if I don't text her back."

"I got it in my pocket. You'll get it back tomorrow. Tonight it's all about us and not our ladies. She'll be fine. It's her party night too. Trust me, those girls have her too busy to even bother looking at their phones. So chill the fuck out and drink." Mike shoved the tequila shot under my nose as a smile crept across his face.

"You're right." I grabbed the drink from his hand and turned toward the guys. "What are we drinking to?" I asked, raising the glass.

"Platinum pussy and unlimited blowjobs." Anthony clinked his glass to mine as all the guys joined in with a laugh.

I grimaced as I downed the liquid. Tequila and I were never friends. We slammed the shot glasses on the bar, grabbing our beers to wash it down.

"Another," Tank said, motioning to the bartender. "Same," he yelled as the man approached.

"Gonna be one of those nights, huh?" I said, sipping my beer as I looked around.

The setting was amazing. Suzy would love it here. She didn't like to dance when I met her, but when we were on the dance floor together, our bodies moved as if they'd known each other a lifetime. She knew how to move, but being with me gave her the confidence to feel uninhibited in the sack and in a club.

"Earth to Joe." Bear tapped me in the head, annoying the shit out of me.

I swatted his hand, ready to tear his finger off, and turned toward him. "You wanna lose that finger?" I smirked, moving into his personal space.

"Shut the fuck up and drink, shithead." Bear pushed my chest, knocking me back a step.

Grabbing the drink off the bar, I slammed it back, enjoying the warmth. "Ahh, another," I said as I put the glass down, turning to see everyone's mouths agape. "What?"

"Jesus, you're going to be shitfaced. Pace yourself, brother." Michael threw back his drink, calling the bartender over.

We spent the next hour laughing and drinking. We talked about women. Michael and I spoke of our girls while Tank, Bear, and Anthony talked about their plethora of pussy. The stark contrast of the caliber of pussy the three of them enjoyed was astounding. I knew the club bitches Tank and Bear spent their nights with, and I wasn't too impressed. They could do better, and hell, they deserved more. They may be rough around the edges, but they were good, honest men.

Anthony was just Anthony. He was a manwhore to the nth degree, enjoying life a little too loosely. I couldn't blame the guy, but at some point, you have to give up the chase and enter the adult world.

"Here," Anthony said, nudging me. "You look a little lost in thought, or you're already shitfaced." He laughed, pushing the glass of amber liquid in front of me.

"I'm not even close to being shitfaced."

"I want to do a special toast," Michael said, holding up his glass, waiting for us to follow suit. As we raised our glasses, holding them together, he spoke. "To Thomas. He couldn't be here again, but this one's for him." He frowned, his eyes glistening a little in the club light. "To the best goddamn brother out there. May he stay safe and come back to us in one piece." A weak smile formed on his face as he brought the glass to his lips.

My chest felt tight as I thought about Thomas. I wanted him to be here to celebrate this weekend with us, but he had gone too far under at this point. We were on a no-contact basis the last few months. We could check in with his superior, but beyond that, we hadn't heard from him. "Way to bring a party down," I said, shaking my head. "To Thomas." I downed the tequila before wiping my mouth with the back of my hand.

I looked at Anthony, and his eyes were the size of saucers. He wasn't moving, the shot in front of his lips, frozen in place. "What the fuck, man?" I asked, turning to see what caught his attention.

What the fuck? My heart started to hammer, my mind racing as I fisted my hands at my side. *There's no fucking way.* I shook my head, trying to get rid of the image, hoping it was an optical illusion. Fuck, it wasn't.

Across the pool danced *my* bride-to-be with some motherfucker doing the bump-n-grind. I moved forward, but a hand stopped me, clamping down on my arm.

"Don't cause a scene, City," Bear said, gripping me tightly.

I looked down at his hand, a growl starting deep in my throat. "That's my woman. No one, and I mean no one, puts their hands on her." Pulling my arm from his grip, I stalked across the pool, cracking my neck and preparing for the shitstorm that was about to happen.

Sophia stopped dancing, her mouth hanging open as she nudged Izzy, motioning to me with her head.

"Fuck," Izzy mouthed, shaking her head, her eyes growing wide.

With Suzy's back to me, I grabbed the asshole groping Suzy's collar, removing him from my fiancée. Suzy turned slowly, all the color draining from her face as her eyes found mine.

"Fuck off," I growled, pushing him away as I tried to restrain myself.

"You fuck off, asshole. I'm dancing with the beautiful blonde. She ain't yours." He moved forward, standing toe to toe with me.

I snarled, moving closer to his face. "She's my motherfucking fiancée. You had your shitty-ass hands all over her."

"City," Suzy said, grabbing my arm. "Baby."

I pushed her away, not looking in her direction. "You need to back the fuck off and go find some other pussy. This one is *mine*," I roared, grabbing his shirt and pulling him closer to my face.

"I didn't hear her say no when I started dancing with her, motherfucker." His words were slightly slurred as tiny droplets of his spit hit my face when he spoke. "Her ass felt so good in my hands."

"City," Bear said, touching my shoulder. "Not here, man."

"What did you just say?" I asked, tightening my grip.

"Her ass...you can bounce a quarter off that shit." His mouth slowly turned up into a cocky-ass grin.

As I released him, I pushed him back and swung. I connected with his jaw, the bones crunching under my knuckles. His arms flailed as he fell to the ground and I grasped his face.

"Keep your fucking hands to yourself, dickhead." I spat on the ground next to him. "Worthless piece of shit."

He dragged his hand across his lips, wiping the blood that had trickled out of his mouth. I fisted my hands at my side, waiting to see if he'd retaliate, but he stood slowly and walked away. Pussy.

Bear patted me on the back. "Can't say the asshole didn't deserve it."

"He deserved more. If we were at the Neon Cowboy I would have beat him unconscious, but here it's like a damn show."

I looked around the crowd that had gathered. People were smiling and laughing and looked impressed. Such is city life at a club. They just wanted to see someone get their ass kicked. I closed my eyes, trying to calm my breath before turning to see Suzy.

Her arms were crossed and her head cocked as she glared at me. "You're such a caveman. Does everything require violence?" She snarled.

I'd never seen Suzy so pissed off. She had no fucking right to be pissed. I was defending her honor, *my* soon-to-be bride. "You're pissed at me?" I asked. "Why the fuck are you pissed off at me? You're the one letting him manhandle you."

Her glare turned ice cold as she walked toward me. Her hands dropped to her side as she stopped in front of me. "You knock a guy on his ass and you want to know why I'm pissed off?" She poked me in the chest, her nail digging into my skin. "It's my bachelorette party and I was having some harmless fun. What the fuck is wrong with you?" She smacked me in the chest, trying to push me backward.

I grabbed her wrist, pulling her closer. "Some asswad has his hands on my woman and I'm just supposed to, what? Tap him on the fucking shoulder and say may I cut in? No, I'm going to confront that shithead and do what I have to do. I'm the one that's pissed, and rightfully so. You *let* him touch you. What the fuck happened to faithfulness?" I released her arm as her eyes flickered to the ground.

Her eyes returned to mine filled with anger and hurt. "I was being faithful, you big, dumb oaf. It's a bachelorette party and I'm here with your sister. I wasn't doing anything wrong. You're just being your diffi-cult, overprotective self." She shook her head. "You always want to solve things with your fists. We're not twelve anymore, City."

"Sugar, I'll protect you until my last breath. I don't share, not now and not ever. You're mine and only mine. No one is allowed to put their hands on you, no matter the situation." I grabbed her by the waist, drawing her to my body. "Maybe I'm being harsh, but the thought of someone else touching you just pisses me off. I tried to control myself, but the prick had to keep running his mouth." I touched her cheek, holding her face in my hand.

Her face softened as she leaned into my touch. "He did. I'm sorry. I'm drunk and we're just having some harmless fun."

I leaned in, hovering just above her lips. Her eyes fluttered closed as I inhaled the smell of Suzy. The scent wasn't right. "What the fuck?" I sniffed her cheek and neck. She had a sweaty, musky scent on her skin. "Why do you smell like a man?"

Her eyes flew open and grew wide. "What are you talking about?" she whispered.

"You smell like another man's been pawing you. That jagoff didn't touch your face. Why the hell does your face and neck smell like someone else?" My heart started to pound sporadically; my chest felt hollow except for the flutter of my heart.

"I don't know what you're talking about. I haven't touched anyone." She grabbed my shirt, holding me to her.

"Like fuck you haven't. I can smell him." Nausea overcame me as the realization that Suzy had been that close to another man. Maybe she wasn't the woman I always thought she was.

"City, I haven't touched anyone. You're making shit up."

I backed away, dropping my hand from her cheek. "I find you with some guy with his hands all over you and now I can smell someone all over your skin. Don't you have anything to say for yourself, or are you just going to deny it?"

She looked to the sky and back to me, her eyes glistening in the light. "I didn't do anything wrong," she yelled, her hands fisted at her side.

I shook my head, feeling my heart shattering into a million tiny pieces. The thought of her cheating on me made me feel like death would be preferable. I didn't want to look at her anymore. I couldn't take the lies or the dull ache in my chest. "I don't believe you," I whispered, looking over her. I couldn't stomach looking in her eyes anymore.

"City," she pleaded, reaching for my arm.

I recoiled, moving my body out of reach. "No, not this time, sugar. I need some time to myself," I said as I turned my back to her.

I didn't want to see the hurt on her face. I didn't have to look at her to know it was there, but I was too pissed off to stick around and talk about it. I needed to get away and cool off.

"Bro, where ya going?" Michael said, stepping in front of me.

"I need to be alone, brother. I'm taking a cab home," I said, trying to control my breathing. I closed my eyes and breathed out through my mouth before looking him in the eyes.

"Come on. We have the party bus. We can go somewhere else." Michael gave me a fake smile.

"Fuck that. I'm going home. Take the party bus and enjoy the night. Tell Suzy to stay here with the girls. I need to be alone tonight."

I walked around him, leaving them behind. I found a cab and headed home. I tried to process how the night went so terribly wrong. Did I over-react? Probably. Did someone touch my fiancée? Most definitely. Could we be fixed? Only time would tell.

I closed my eyes; the blur of palm trees made my head hurt more than it already did. I thought about everything we'd been through in the last year. Suzy lost her good-girl image and stole my heart. I wrecked on my bike and almost died. The woman nursed me back to health and waited on me hand and foot.

It may have been a bachelorette party, but the shit still stung. My overactive imagination and the words the cocksucker spoke were like a punch to the gut. I knew my Suzy. She wouldn't cheat, but the thought of someone else touching her made my stomach hurt and my heart ache. I literally pushed Suzy away and turned my back on her. I let my anger rule instead of using my head. I reacted without thinking and would have to deal with it tomorrow.

I rubbed my face, wishing I could wash it all away and go back in time. I'd been a total dumb fuck, and there would be a heavy price to pay and most likely groveling. I wasn't one to grovel and beg, but this was my sugar. I'd do anything for her, to keep her, and make her mine. The closer I got to the house, our house, the more I knew I fucked up.

After paying the cab driver and walking up the driveway, I pulled out my phone and checked my messages. Not a message since I'd left her.

Me: *I'm sorry. I love you.*

The house was eerily quiet. It had been quiet before, but tonight it was deafening. Suzy was missing. Her joy and laughter usually filled the space. The girl was a damn chatterbox at times, and as I walked to the bedroom I realized how much I missed it—how much I missed her. The stillness of our house made me feel uneasy. I wanted my woman in our bed with me. I wanted to hear her giggle as I whispered in her ear before she fell asleep. She was the sunshine in my day; she softened me and filled my life with happiness.

I emptied my pockets, placing my wallet and keys on my nightstand. I removed my clothes, the stench of the clubs clinging to the fabric as I tossed them to the floor. No reply from Suzy as I crawled in bed, laying the cell phone next to me. I didn't want to miss her message. I stared at the ceiling, watching the fan create moving shadows in the darkness. For the first time in months, I felt completely alone.

Fuck, maybe I *was* pussy whipped.

7

SUZY

FUMING. IT'S THE ONLY WORD I COULD USE TO DESCRIBE WHAT I FELT. City had always been a little on the impulsive side, but tonight put the fucking icing on the cake. How could he think I had been unfaithful? I told Izzy no strippers, but did she listen? Of course not, when does she ever listen to anyone?

I'd had too much to drink, but I was still in control. I wasn't sloppy drunk, just at that point where everything was wonderful and nothing got me down. Well, nothing until Mr. "She's Mine" Caveman killed the party. When the guy that City laid out tried to dance with me, I said no and pushed him away. Izzy intervened. Fucking Izzy, said it was my last night and every girl had the right to dance with whomever they wanted before they're officially off the market.

I didn't see any harm in it. It was just a dance and nothing more. My girls surrounded me and they would never let anything happen to me. Furthermore, I don't cheat. It's not in my nature. I'm madly in love with City. I don't mean just that type of comfortable love. I'm talking that "take my breath away, make my stomach flip" type of love that I couldn't imagine being without. But, and this is a huge but, could I deal with his testosterone-laced, fist-throwing macho bullshit for the rest of my life?

If I answered the questions based solely on the amount and way I

456

loved him, the answer would be yes. If I used my brain and really thought about City and his quickness to stake his claim and scare anyone with a cock away from me, the answer would be, "I honestly don't know." He said that's his way of protecting me, and it's how he's built.

The night I was attacked at the Neon Cowboy, his level of protection increased and became almost stifling at times. Somehow I managed to survive the first twenty-something years of my life without his watchful eye and brute fists. The trauma we endured during our relationship didn't help matters. My assault and then almost losing him in the motorcycle accident—they were events that put a strain on our emotions but brought us closer together.

The night we sat in the hospital waiting to hear if he would survive was the longest night of my life. I couldn't form a coherent thought until Mia told us that he'd survive. I felt like my world was ending. I didn't have control and I hated it. Control was something I strived to maintain. I made my lists and planned everything out. Having City's life hanging in the balance and relying on someone else to make him better was maddening.

I didn't think I could ever get mad at him again, but here we were. City walked off and left without talking to me. He didn't want to believe anything I had to say. He jumped to his crazy-ass conclusions and stalked off.

My mind was hazy as I sat on the barstool and watched the club moving to music that was muffled in my ears. I couldn't process anything but my thoughts of City and what the fuck just happened.

"Suzy, let's go upstairs, babe." Sophia grabbed my elbow, trying to get me to stand.

"No," I whispered, not ready to move.

"Come on, I'll go with you. Let's get out of here so we can talk," she said as she brushed my hair off my shoulder.

I looked at her with blurred vision; a line of tears sitting in my eyes hadn't yet fallen. "What's there to talk about? He walked out on me."

"Now listen to me, woman. He loves you and you love him. You both have been drinking and the scene went south quick. You know that isn't how City is, babe."

I blinked, letting the tears cascade down my cheeks. "That's exactly how he is, Sophia. I don't know if I can deal with that forever." My voice cracked as I wiped my cheeks.

"Up ya go, sugarplum, upstairs for you. You've obviously had more to drink than I thought if you're questioning your future with this man." She grabbed me around the waist, helping me stand on steady feet.

"Fine, Soph, but only because I could use a little peace and quiet. There's no one else I can talk to about him and get an honest opinion but you. They're all related or partial to the Gallo family." My legs felt rubbery as we walked past the dance floor and made our way to the outside elevators. "Thanks, Sophia." I smiled at her. She was my best friend, the only person in the world that knew everything about me. We'd been through too much together to not be able to read each other like an open book.

She smiled back at me but didn't say a word as we entered the elevator. I sagged against the wall, trying to keep my balance as it was ascending to the top floor. As soon as we walked into the suite, I kicked off my shoes and threw myself on the couch. Wrapping paper, boxes, sex toys, and lingerie were strewn around the room. Partially empty glasses, bottles of liquor, and champagne sat on the coffee table. The night had started with so much promise.

"All right, beautiful. Spill your guts," Sophia said as she sat down next to me and put my feet in her lap. God, I missed times like these. Sophia and I used to stay up late at night having talks about men and our problems. Life had changed so dramatically for both of us over the last two years. Being here with her, like this, made my broken heart long for the olden days.

"Did you hear what he said to me?" I asked, nestling my head into the soft throw pillow.

"I did. He was drunker than I've ever seen him."

"So what, are you saying I should give him a pass?"

Shaking her head, she rested her hand on my chin. "Never. Fuck that. I've learned you can never give someone a free pass, but don't throw it all away. Look, I fell in love with Kayden, and Lord help me, that man has been a whole heap of trouble. I should've been tougher on him and called him on his bullshit more. I paid the price, but I've learned and now we're in a better place. You need to talk to City and tell him how you feel."

"He hurt me tonight, Sophia." I closed my eyes, remembering how my stomach fell when he pushed me away.

"Physically?" Her eyebrows turned downward as her eyes snapped to my face.

"No, he hurt my feelings. He basically said I cheated on him. The accusations stung." The tears started to flow easier. His words finally sank in, and I processed the entire scene as if watching a bad movie. "He's never been mean to me. Tonight he was just a plain asshole."

Sophia chuckled, covering her mouth with her hand.

"What's so funny?" I squinted at her, not understanding the humor of the situation. "I'm sitting here pouring out my soul and crying, and you're laughing. What the hell, Sophia?"

"You said asshole like it was a word you used every day. Not so long ago you were using terms like 'get the heck out of here' and 'you big b.' The shit just rolls off your lips like it's been part of your vernacular for years." She rubbed my leg, running her nails over my skin. "He's a man, Suzy. They do not like to see their woman near other men. That guy said some nasty shit too. I'm surprised City didn't beat the fuck out of him until he was unconscious."

I sighed, putting my arm over my eyes. "City changed me. I can't deny it. He made it sound like I was a piece of property. I mean, why doesn't he just piss on me like a dog marking his territory?" My eyes were heavy and burning. The tears and alcohol made it hard to keep them open.

"Now you're just being overdramatic. Let's get you tucked into bed and see how you feel in the morning." Sophia moved my legs to the couch and pulled me up by my arms. "A little help would be nice," she said, as she tried to hold me in a sitting position.

"I'm just so tired. Just leave me here." I opened my eyes to look at her, and quickly closed them after seeing she wasn't amused.

"Get your ass in that bed. All the drunk bitches will be back and they'll wake you up."

I stood, using Sophia for leverage, and wobbled. "Yes, Mom. You're so damn bossy." I smiled, leaning forward to kiss her on the cheek. "I've missed you, Soph. I don't know what I'd do without you."

She wrapped her arms around me, embracing me in a tender hug. "You'd be at home making lists about lists." She chuckled, releasing me and helping me toward the main bedroom.

"You're probably right. I was such a boring human being." My voice had become quiet, almost mouse-like as sleep started to overcome me.

"In you go, princess," Sophia said as she pulled back the covers.

I didn't bother to get undressed. I just wanted to sleep. I wanted tonight to be over and to deal with everything tomorrow. Grabbing an extra pillow, I turned on my side, tucking it into my body. I'd grown used to snuggling against City. I needed something to fill the void, and the pillow was my only option.

The lights turned off before I heard the click of the door as I drifted off into a restful sleep. All thoughts and worries disappeared as I dreamed about my City. His deep voice, ice-blue eyes, and the feel of his arms wrapped around me. I could feel the love he had for me even in my dreams. He invaded every part of my life, became ingrained in my entire being.

I loved him even subconsciously.

8

CITY

I ROLLED OVER, FEELING FOR MY PHONE, BUT DIDN'T FIND IT WHERE I left it. Somehow, during the night, I had pushed it under Suzy's pillow. I tossed and turned, waking up feeling like I hadn't slept a fucking wink. There were no new messages or calls on my phone, and no word from Suzy or any of the girls.

Bits and pieces started coming back to me as I lay in bed staring at the ceiling. I'd fucked up, and managed to do it royally. I left Suzy behind without so much as an "I love you," just an accusation and shitty words. I had to fix it. I fucked up and I had to man up and say I was sorry.

I grabbed my head, the throbbing almost blinding as I climbed out of bed. The quiet from the night before that felt deafening now became overwhelming. I couldn't sit around the house today and idly wait for Suzy to come home so that I could ask for her forgiveness. I had to go to her, find her, and mend the shattered pieces of our relationship.

Leaning over the sink, I stared at myself in the mirror, and was disgusted by the person looking back. I was better than this. The man that acted out last night wasn't me. He was a jealous asshole and I'm a lovesick fool. I quickly showered and brushed my teeth before throwing on my jeans and t-shirt. I didn't give a fuck what I looked like; I just had to get to Suzy.

I barreled down the highway, making my way to the hotel. Izzy hadn't replied to a text I sent her before I left. I kept the phone in my pocket on vibrate, but it remained still. I weaved in and out of traffic, needing to not waste another minute away from Suzy.

The closer I came to the hotel, the more butterflies filled my stomach. What if she didn't forgive me? I knew I'd hurt her, and I prayed that our love for each other could overcome the words of the previous night. As I shut off the bike, sitting in the parking lot of the Shepard's Hotel, I texted the only person that may be awake at this hour — Sophia. It was only eight a.m., but I was banking on her above anyone else.

Me: Sophia, it's City. I'm at the hotel and need to see Suzy.

I walked toward the door, waiting for a reply, with the phone gripped tightly in my hand. A lump formed in my throat, worry hanging in the air so thick I could almost taste it.

Sophia: Room 1215. She's still passed out but I'll let you in. You have a lot of sucking up to do.

Sophia wasn't a bullshitter, and she was Suzy's best friend. I knew no truer words were ever spoken.

Me: I plan to do a lot of sucking up. I'll do anything.

Sophia: Anything?

Me: Just open the damn door, woman.

Sophia: You better make it good. I'm waiting.

The elevator ride seemed to take forever, stopping on every other floor to let off guests. Everyone had been downstairs enjoying the complimentary breakfast. When the bell chimed and the twelfth floor was illuminated, I thought my heart literally stopped in my chest.

Fisting my hands at my sides, I squeezed them, trying to release some tension. I lightly knocked, waiting for Sophia to answer, and swallowed hard. My mouth felt dry, my stomach ready to expel the last ounce of alcohol, and my heart was ready to burst from the rapid pounding in my chest.

"Quiet," Sophia said after she opened the door. "Follow me." She motioned and led me through the suite.

Izzy lay on the couch, passed out and oblivious to my presence. Someone else I didn't recognize, mostly because they were facedown, lay on the floor next to her. The hotel suite was a mess. Wrapping paper, boxes, clothes, and glasses were everywhere. The girls had partied harder than I would've thought, but then again, this was Izzy's doing, and she didn't do anything half-assed.

Sophia stopped in front of the door to a bedroom and crossed her arms over her chest. "Now listen here, mister," she said, poking me in the chest.

I looked down at her bony finger digging into my flesh, and smiled. The girl had balls, and big ones at that. I loved Sophia for the simple fact that she was Suzy's friend, but she and I could've been friends if we had met first. She had the piss and vinegar that reminded me of my sister. She was fierce, loyal, and cared deeply.

"She's crushed, and I haven't seen her since I put her to bed last night. She loves you, City, and you better get down on your knees and beg for her forgiveness. Do whatever it takes."

"Yes, ma'am." I nodded. She hadn't told me anything I didn't already know.

"Don't be a smartass," she said, slapping me on the shoulder. "You made her feel trashy and like shit. You need to make her feel like the princess she deserves to be treated as. You've always done that for her. Made her feel good about herself. I was always your cheerleader, even when she wasn't sure about you. So don't fuck this shit up."

"I got this." Fuck, I really hoped I did.

"You better, but I want to tell you a few things first. The guy she was dancing with, she didn't want to dance with him. Not at all, but your sister told her it would be her last dance as a single girl and she couldn't turn him down. She said some bullshit about bachelorette etiquette. Your sister can be very persuasive." She paused, tapping her lip with her finger.

"Fuck, she's a pain in the ass." I sighed, looking toward my sister passed out and dead to the world.

"Second, the smell on her last night was the weirdo stripper your sister hired. Suzy told her more than once that she did not want a stripper under any circumstances. The guy came in and did a quick dance, but Suzy was totally uncomfortable. As soon as he realized that, he broke contact and gave her a sweet kiss on the cheek when he was finished. She didn't touch him at all and he didn't do anything inappropriate." She straightened her back, looking me straight in the eyes. "City, if you would've seen him you would've laughed. You're like an Adonis compared to this man. You're the only thing that has Suzy's eyes and heart. Grovel, my friend, grovel." She leaned over, kissing my cheek before she left me to enter the room.

I stood there staring at the door, and closed my eyes. I'd been a complete tool. How in the fuck did I even think Suzy would allow someone to touch her or that she'd been unfaithful? I knew Suzy inside and out, but I let my territorial bullshit get in the way. My heart ached at the thought that maybe I made our relationship fubar. Was it fucked up beyond repair? Had I crossed the line that she wouldn't forgive? I'd listen to Sophia's advice and beg for her forgiveness. Not as a sign of weakness, but because of the love I had for her. It was the only way I could fight for what I wanted most—Suzy.

I opened the door slowly, trying not to startle Suzy. Sunlight streamed through the sheer drapes along the wall behind her bed. The rays cascaded across the floor, framing the bed and my bride-to-be. I stood at the foot of the bed, staring at her. Her long blonde hair was fanned out across the pillow, making a halo and giving her an angelic look. My heart ached at the thought that I could possibly lose her. Maybe I fucked up so badly that she wouldn't forgive me. Sometimes words are more painful than any physical harm inflicted by another person. Pain evaporates, but words last a lifetime, replaying in our memories and feeding on our insecurities.

Her soft snores and heavy breathing mingled with the sound of the waves crashing on the shore below. She clung to a pillow, holding it against her chest, her arms tightly wound around it.

Sitting on the bed, I tried to keep my movement to a minimum, not wanting to wake her just yet. She was mine, and had been the only person I'd ever used that term with. No one else had a chance to capture my heart, but Suzy and all her sweetness bored into my heart like a cavity from too much sugar.

I kicked off my shoes, needing to touch her, to hold her in my arms. My body ached for her. I didn't feel comfortable in my skin without contact from her. I couldn't explain it, and I'd never voice it in front of the guys. They already thought I was a pussy-whipped asshole.

Grabbing the pillow, I pulled it from her arms, making sure she remained asleep. She didn't move or twitch as her arms fell against her body. I threw the pillow on the floor, crawling under the covers next to her, and pulled her against my chest. Her breathing changed as she snuggled against me, burying her face against my shirt. I closed my eyes, enjoying the quiet moment and the feel of her in my arms. As soon as she realized I was here, there'd be hell to pay.

I peppered kisses against her temple, brushing back the hair on her forehead as I inhaled the smell of the woman that had stolen my heart over a year ago. It wasn't a pure scent; the alcohol she'd consumed the night before permeated her skin. If we had both been sober, last night wouldn't have happened. Really, if I hadn't consumed a few too many shots and seen someone touching what was mine, then it wouldn't have happened.

Her body stiffened in my arms, and I closed my eyes, knowing the moment had been broken. "Suzy," I whispered, trying to hide the fear in my voice.

"What are you doing?" she asked, her voice laced with anger as she pushed against my chest.

"Sugar, don't push me away. I'm sorry." I tightened my grip, holding her head against my chest.

"I don't want to talk to you." She didn't touch me or return my embrace.

"Don't talk, then. Just let me talk while I hold you." I held her tighter, resting my chin on top of her head as I wrapped my legs around hers. I caged her in; there was no escape and I had a captive audience. "I'm sorry I was an asshole last night." I sighed, knowing my words weren't enough to make up for my behavior.

"More like a giant dickhead," she interrupted, not sagging into my embrace like she normally did.

"Call me what you want. All the terms fit. I'm sorry I didn't listen to you last night. I had too much to drink, but I'm in no way blaming the alcohol. I'm solely responsible for my actions. I fucked up, sugar. I didn't mean to imply that you had been unfaithful to me. Seeing you with that guy and then smelling someone on you pushed me over the edge." I

465

inhaled, winded from the words that I had said without stopping. I was too worried to break in the middle of my speech.

"I would never do anything to risk our relationship, City," she said, digging her fingernails into my bicep.

"I know, sugar, I know." I kissed the top of her head and rested my cheek against her silky, golden hair. "Please forgive me. I have no other excuse except for the love I have for you. You've scrambled my brains. I've never felt as territorial or protective over someone like I do with you. When I see someone touching you, I want to rip their hands off and shove them down their throat. I control it most times."

"No you don't." Her laughter broke the tension, making *me* laugh.

"Trust me, sugar, I do. I wasn't going to hit the guy last night but he wouldn't shut his fucking mouth. He kept talking shit and I couldn't hold back anymore. I couldn't stop myself from knocking him on his ass."

"City," she said as she adjusted her body, looking into my eyes. Her lip trembled as she spoke. "I'm not upset about you hitting him. He deserved it. You hurt me by questioning my faithfulness. You made me feel dirty." A single tear formed in the corner of her eye and slid along the bridge of her nose.

I wiped the tear with the pad of my thumb, cradling her face in my palm. "I never want to make you feel that way. You're the most pure and honest person I know, Suzette. I know you're faithful and I never meant for it to sound otherwise. I'm sorry. You consume me and became a part of me. Your love is as vital to me as the air I breathe. The thought of losing you terrifies me." To admit the last sentence scared the shit out of me. I'd never felt so vulnerable in my life. My heart and happiness lay in her hands.

"Promise me you'll never make me feel that way again, City." She blinked, causing more tears to trickle down her cheek. The redness in her eyes made the blue even more breathtaking. "You're the one person in the world that I thought would always have my back. I never expected you to treat me that way, and I won't stand for it. I refuse to be married to a man that treats me like that. If you do it again, I may not be so easy to find."

"I promise, Suzy. I will never act like that again. I love you more than anything in the world. I'd kill for you and give my life to save yours." I enveloped her in my arms, squeezing her tightly against my body.

"You're everything to me and I will do everything in my power to show you how much you mean to me. I will spend every day showing you all the love I have for you and profess my love to you on my deathbed."

"Jesus, you're so morbid. 'I promise' and 'I'm sorry' would've been enough." She laughed, wrapping her arms around my body.

"It takes more than two words to explain the amount of love I have for you, but right now, I'd rather show you." I smirked, grabbing her chin and bringing her lips to mine.

"Oh, how are you going to do that?" she asked with garbled words as she spoke against my lips.

Breaking the kiss, I looked in her eyes. "I'm going to make love to my fiancée the day before our wedding." Her breath hitched as her eyes searched mine. "Tomorrow you officially become Mrs. Joseph Gallo."

"Why can't you become Mr. Suzy McCarthy?" She giggled, rubbing her nose against my cheek.

"Not how it works, sugar. I'm the man and you're the woman, but you can call me whatever the hell you want when we're in private." I smirked, nipping her nose with my teeth.

"Mmm, I like the sound of that." A warm smile spread across her lips as her body melted into mine.

I kissed her lips, gently prodding, trying to find her tongue. I wanted to taste her. "Suzy, why won't you kiss me back?" Maybe her heart hadn't caught up to her words. I prayed to fuck that was the case. When someone won't kiss you and show you the love you want to convey, it's like a stake to the heart.

She covered her mouth with her hand. "I didn't brush my teeth yet. I think a small furry animal died inside my mouth last night." The corners of her mouth peeked out the sides of her hand, the smile touching her eyes.

Laughter bubbled out of me, slow at first, until my entire body was shaking as her words hit me. "Baby, I don't care if you have bad breath. I won't breathe through my nose." I leaned my forehead against hers.

She shook her head, moving her face farther away from mine with her hand still covering her mouth. "Not happening. Either I get up and brush my teeth or you don't get a kiss until after."

"You feel this?" I asked, pushing my erection into her stomach. "I'm not waiting until you find your toothbrush and get lost in the bathroom. I need to feel you from the inside. I don't give a fuck about your breath."

"I'm not going to kiss you," she said firmly, her mouth set in a firm line.

"Didn't say anything about kissing you, sugar. I want to fuck you, and I only care about your pussy right now." I was done discussing the topic. I needed to be inside her and I needed it now. My body craved her and my heart needed her; I wasn't in the mood to be patient.

SUZY

"I LOVE WHEN YOU TALK DIRTY TO ME. YOU JUST WANT TO MARK YOUR territory." I smirked, watching him hop off the bed and unbutton his jeans.

"You bet that sweet ass I'm marking it. I'm going to crawl so far up that pretty little pussy that I'll ruin you for life." He shucked his pants, kicking them to the side as he pulled his t-shirt over his head.

What the man didn't understand is that he had already ruined me. I was destroyed, damaged goods, and no one would ever compare to him. As hard and sexy as he was, the soft and loving side of City was what ultimately stole my heart. The man loved me so fiercely that no one could ever come close. The small looks he stole when he thought I wasn't looking, the loving touches as I fell asleep, and the sweet nothings he whispered in my ear when he thought I was dreaming—those were the things I loved most about him.

I yawned, pretending to be unimpressed by his words and sexy-as-hell naked body. "Well, you can try anyway. I'll let you know if your words ring true."

He grabbed the comforter, yanking it off my body before pulling me down the bed by my feet. I squealed; the quickness of his movements caught me off guard. Pulling me off the bed in a standing position, he quickly stripped me of my clothes.

"So far, a C for effort. You can do better." I smiled, watching the corner of his lip twitch.

He placed his hands under my arms, firmly gripping my waist before throwing me on the bed. He pounced on me, not giving me a moment to catch my breath before smothering me with a perfect closed-mouth kiss. My stomach fluttered like it did the first time he kissed me. The nerves and emotion of the last twelve hours poured out through our lips.

I dug my fingers into his dark locks, fisting the hair in between my fingers as I held his mouth to mine. I wished I had brushed my damn teeth. I wanted to taste him. He pulled away, breaking the connection we had, and looked down at me. The heat of his chest seared my skin and the thump of his heart matched mine. He was just as nervous as me, both of us on edge from last night.

"This will be the last time I'll make love to you before you become my wife." He smiled; his teeth sparkled in the sunlight.

"What about tonight?" I asked, totally confused.

"Sugar, I can't see the bride the night before the wedding. We've talked about this before. I'm going to stay at my parents'."

"I don't like that idea. That's two nights not sleeping in your arms." I sighed, rubbing my thumb across his unshaven cheek. The roughness matched the man more perfectly than the silky skin I felt some days.

"Me either, but it's only for one night. We can't break tradition."

"Make it good, then, handsome. Make me still feel you when I walk down the aisle tomorrow." I always felt him for hours afterward. The days when he was insatiable, I could feel him for days, often sore the next time he wanted to fool around. Knowing that this was the last time before we were married warmed me and turned me into a puddle of goo.

Growling, he brought his mouth down on mine. I moaned, the regret about brushing my teeth growing. His tongue darted out, sliding across my lips before traveling down my jaw to the sweet spot on my neck. Goose bumps and shivers racked my body as the warmth of his mouth and coolness from his breath skidded across my skin.

When he captured my nipple in his mouth, nibbling on it with his teeth, my entire body convulsed. The rough stubble of his face, the sharp pinch from his hold, and the silky smoothness of his tongue flicking the hardened tip had me seeing stars and moaning his name. I held him to me, fingers wound in his hair as he sucked and flicked until I begged.

"Please, City. I want to feel you," I said.

Grunting as he held my nipple between his lips, he lifted his hips and fisted his cock. The cool metal rubbing against my clit made me twitch before he rubbed the tip through my wetness. As I thrust my hips forward, trying to force him to put his dick inside me, I could feel the deep, low laugh in his chest.

"So ready, sugar. You're always ready for my cock," he whispered against my breast.

"Yes! Yes," I chanted, growing impatient with his lack of thrust.

Swiping it through my wetness again, he placed the piercing against my clit and made tiny circles, capturing my clit with the motion. The combination of the hard metal and smooth tip drove me closer to the edge, but I didn't want to come like this. I closed my eyes, sealing them tightly, trying to stave off the orgasm that was about to rip through me.

"No," I whispered, "not like this."

"You want to come on my cock? You want to feel me thrusting in and out of you as your pussy squeezes me like a vise?" he asked, his voice low and husky.

"Don't make me beg," I said, keeping my eyes closed, moving my hips, trying to escape his cock circling my clit.

Without warning, he rammed his cock inside me in one quick thrust. My eyes sprang open; I felt completely filled as a tiny spark of pain shot throughout my body. He pulled out slightly and stilled, staring down at me with a cocky grin on his face.

"Is that how you want it, sugar?"

"Don't stop. I'm so close." I pulled back and pushed myself forward, fucking him. I couldn't take the lack of motion.

Slipping his arms under my back, he held my shoulders, as he began to rock into me. Each lash of his cock against my G-spot sent tiny shock waves through my system, making my toes curl. I grabbed his hips, relishing the feel of his muscles constricting as he moved inside of me. Our bodies worked in unison, driving me toward an orgasm I knew would leave me breathless and with blurred vision.

His hips started to rotate as he pulled out and rammed back into me straight. The movement intensified the pressure building inside of me. His breathing became ragged as he maintained the momentum, driving into me without mercy.

Colors dotted my vision, the light almost blinding, as everything in my body coiled and released at once. I felt like a slingshot pulled to the max and then let go, flying forward with no escape or ability to control the outcome.

I screamed, "City," as my body became rigid and my breathing halted. My head flew off the pillow, my body grounded by his hold on my shoulders as my curled toes started to cramp.

My core convulsed around him, the hardness of his cock giving nothing as he continued in the pursuit of his orgasm. His moans turned to growls as he stiffened above me, emptying himself inside me. Gulping for air, he collapsed on top of me, his body twitching with aftershocks.

I closed my eyes, listening to our mingled breaths as I enjoyed the afterglow. The feel of his weight crushing me made me feel encapsulated, as my body grew limp underneath him.

His breathing slowed as his breath skidded across my ear; the low growls of pleasure bringing a smile to my face. As he pulled out, everything he'd just worked to achieve slid down my body, forming a pool on the bed. I still hadn't gotten used to the feel of a man coming inside of me. I felt like I wet myself and couldn't stop it.

"Let me grab a washcloth," he said as he pushed off the bed.

I grabbed his arm, stopping him. "Let me. I'm dying to brush my teeth. I want a proper kiss." I smiled at him, trying not to run my tongue across my dirty teeth.

He collapsed against the mattress, staring up at the ceiling as he rested his hand on his chest. "I'll be waiting." He grabbed my arm with his free hand, sliding his palm down my arm. "Make it quick," he said with a crooked, happy smile.

I groaned as my feet touched the floor. The aftereffects of an evening of overindulgence and wicked high heels hit me. I swayed, grabbing the mattress to steady myself.

"You okay, sugar?" City asked as he sat up and touched my hand.

472

"Fine, baby. Just not as young as I used to be. Can't party all night and bounce right back."

"I doubt you partied all night too much even in your college years." He laughed, covering his mouth with his hand.

"I didn't sit in my dorm room and study all the time," I said sarcastically. It was all bullshit. I rarely partied. The number of times I had been drunk in college I could count on one hand, but sometimes I didn't like to be reminded of just how much of a good girl I had been.

"Uh, huh," he said, resting his head on his hand as he watched me walk away.

I flipped him off, a small chuckle escaping my lips. He knew me too well. Knew I could never escape my good-girl qualities even though I liked to pretend I had a badass side. I knew I was a cream puff, and I accepted it, though I did so begrudgingly.

My mascara was smeared down my cheeks, the result of my crying last night over City. I looked as bad as I felt. My hair was a tangled mess, makeup half on but not in the right places, and my eyes were swollen. Thank God the wedding wasn't today. I'd have to live with horrible wedding pictures for the rest of my life.

Grabbing the tube of toothpaste out of my toiletry bag, I stood on my tiptoes and leaned into the mirror. Shit, I looked horrible. I quickly backed up, not needing the up-close reminder of last night. After washing him from my body, I covered my toothbrush with paste. I needed to clear the funk out of my mouth. My mouth felt drier than the Mojave Desert on a blistering summer day. Just as I stuck the toothbrush in my mouth and started scrubbing, I heard my phone chirp.

"Suzy, your mother sent you a text," City yelled from the bedroom.

Fucking great. I loved my mom, but she added an extra bit of pressure and stress to an already nerve-racking situation. Weddings are supposed to be blissful, but no one seems to tell you about all the turmoil and decisions that need to be made. My mother could be judgmental at times, and I often felt like my decisions weren't good enough.

I pulled the toothbrush out of my mouth, balancing the paste remnants on my tongue as I yelled, "What's it say?"

I scrubbed my teeth, my motions more feverish at the thought of my parents being in town. She always watched City with a suspicious eye when she didn't know I was looking. She was happy that he had money, although it wasn't the reason I fell in love with the man. I would've been with him even if he were only a tattoo artist. It's a good job, and he's talented. She couldn't get beyond his looks. He had a roughness about him, and the tattoos didn't exactly win him any points in her mind. She'd bust a cork if she knew about the piercing that decorated his lower extremity, or if she ever found out that I had my nipple pierced.

"She just wants to know if she should be at the rehearsal dinner early to help."

I spat the toothpaste into the sink, cupping water in my hand and swishing. The last thing I wanted was my mother there for her type of help. Everything was ready and all we needed to do was show up, including her and my father.

I washed my face quickly, erasing the nightmarish mess from the smudged makeup before returning to the bedroom.

"She's become such a pain the last few months," I said as I crawled in bed.

"She's still your mom and she loves you," he said, grabbing my hand and planting soft kisses across the top.

"You grew up with a different type of mother, City. Your mom has made me feel more like a daughter than my mother ever did. Don't get me wrong, I love her, but she doesn't know how to make me feel loved." I closed my eyes when they watered as I thought about what it would've been like to grow up calling Mrs. Gallo Mom. I always felt like my parents had to fit me into their schedule, and often there wasn't a slot for me unless I had called in advance.

"Let's just get through the next thirty-six hours and everything will go back to normal. You have the Gallo family now, and they're not letting you go."

I'd felt like a member of the family since that first Sunday dinner so long ago. They made me feel like I belonged and had always been there. My sister and I had never even really been close. I didn't ask her to be a part of my wedding party. Izzy had become more of a sister to me than she ever had. We don't get to choose our family, but we do choose those people we let into our life, and with whom we spend time with going forward. For me, the people I wanted nearest were the Gallos. They were a loving and diehard-loyal group. Above all else, they had each other's backs and no one could tear them apart. They accepted each other for their flaws, embraced the bad with the good, and loved unconditionally.

"We should go soon. I have a ton to do before the rehearsal dinner tonight." I snuggled into his side, enjoying the last moment of peace.

He pulled me tighter against his chest, rubbing the tender skin on my upper arm as he kissed my hair. "It'll all work out. Somehow it will all fall into place."

"I'm sure you're right." That statement was a total lie. I couldn't give up my incessant need to be in control and plan every last detail.

"You can't control everything in life, but I know you try like hell. It's one of the things I love about you."

"Tell me five other things you love, City." I swiped my fingers across his chest, stopping on his nipple to tug on his piercing.

"Where do I start?" he said before rattling off a list that left me feeling more loved than I had ever felt before. The list wasn't filled with vain things like my beauty, which would fade over time, but the things that made me as a person. My success, education, kind heart, and silliness were just a few things he listed without much thought.

"I love you, City," I said, moving my body to plant a wet, sloppy kiss on his lips.

Breaking our connection slightly, he whispered, "I love you too, sugar." He kissed me with as much fervor and passion as he did the first night we met.

We made love one more time before dragging ourselves from the hotel room and heading home to prep for the chaos that awaited us. Wedding weekend was in full swing and there was no turning back.

10

CITY

NEVER IN A MILLION FUCKING YEARS DID I THINK I'D BE STANDING IN A church dressed in a tuxedo—not as a groom, at least. I wasn't a cynic. I'd just never found anyone worthy of my time or commitment until Suzy walked into my life. Sometimes when we least expect it and stop looking, fate has a way of playing its hand. Mine came in the form of a drop-dead gorgeous girl broken down on a deserted street. I thanked my lucky stars each goddamn day that her car was a piece of shit.

"You look a little nervous, son," Pop said, slapping me on the back, pulling me from my thoughts.

I rubbed my hands together; they slid easy from the sheen of sweat that had formed over my entire body. I wiped my brow, feeling more nervous than I had ever felt in my life. "I am, Pop. Just never thought I'd be standing here."

"Amazing the place hasn't burst into flames," Anthony said, and laughed. "We surely aren't the churchgoing crowd, and Lord knows we've broken more than one commandment." He fidgeted with his bowtie, pulling it away from his neck.

I laughed. His words were true, but that wasn't why I was nervous. I turned to my Pop, who had a smile on his face. "Did you feel this way when you married Ma?"

476

He nodded, his smile growing larger. "I was scared as hell, son. It's a big step to take in one's life. It's a serious commitment, but times are different now. I didn't live with your mother before we got married like you've lived with Suzy. It was a leap of faith." He grabbed my shoulder, squeezing it gently. "Do you love her, son? The type of love you can't be without for even a day?"

"I do, Pop. I know she's the one. She makes me a better person, and I want to be surrounded by her and make a family. I want to be in your shoes one day. Suzy is more than I deserve."

"She isn't more than you deserve. You two were made for each other. Just like your mother and me. She brings peace and tranquility to my life, and gave me an amazing family. My life would've been meaningless without her."

I didn't doubt that marrying Suzy was the right decision. The events of Friday night scared the shit out of me. The thought of losing her drove me half insane. I'd never wanted to need someone in that way, but I did with her. I needed her in my life, needed her to be mine, and wanted to spend the rest of my days on Earth with her.

The door creaked open as Ma poked her head inside. "Where's my baby boy?" she asked, opening the door with tears in her eyes.

"Why ya crying, Ma?" I asked, as she wiped the tears.

"Damn, I'm going to mess up my makeup." She pulled a tissue from her bra and blotted the skin under her eyes. "I just saw Suzy and she looks stunning. I'm the happiest woman in the world today. They're tears of joy."

"How is she, Ma? Is she okay?" My heart pounded, my throat feeling constricted by the button-up shirt.

"She's better than okay; she's glowing and ready for the ceremony to start." Ma wrapped her arms around me, holding me against her as she spoke. "You've made me a happy woman, Joseph. I couldn't love Suzy any more than I do if I had given birth to her myself." She rubbed my back as she kissed my cheek.

"You just have baby Gallos in your mind, Ma," Michael said as he kicked back in a chair against the wall. He looked so put together and calm.

"So what?" she asked as she placed her hands on her hips and turned toward Michael. "I'm old, boy and all I want is a baby...just one damn baby. Is that too much to ask?"

"Not really, Ma, but it'll happen when it happens. We're still young and enjoying our life," Michael said, leaning forward, resting his elbows on his knees.

"By the time I was your age, I had four children. I enjoyed every bit of my life, and maybe more so since it was filled with such love. Children don't end your life, Michael, they add to it."

"Bullshit," Anthony muttered, covering his mouth and coughing.

Ma narrowed her eyes at him. "Anthony, you better stop acting like a playboy and living your hollow existence. You have to settle down some-time, and when you do, you'll regret all the years you spent alone."

"I'm rarely alone, Ma." He smiled, his hair flopping over his forehead.

"I mean emotionally alone." She stared at him, waiting for him to respond, but he didn't. "Okay, I want a picture with my son on his wedding day. Where's that damn photographer?"

Pop walked toward the door, pausing as he opened it. "I'll go get him."

As the door clicked shut, my ma turned to me. "Nerves are normal, son. Once you see how breathtaking Suzy is in her dress, everything else will fade away." She rested her head on my chest as she held my hand.

"I know, Ma. I'm just ready to get this started. I hate waiting; I've never been a patient man." I kissed the top of her head, getting lost in the strawberry scent from my childhood.

"You don't say." She laughed, squeezing my hand. "Just like your father." She sighed, drawing her body closer to mine. "I wish Thomas could've been here. I'm more worried about him than I've ever been, Joseph."

"I know, Ma. I haven't spoken to him in a while. He's too deep under-cover now. I don't like it, not one fucking bit."

"Y'all are going to burst into flames with the language in this room. We are in a church," Izzy said as she entered the room with Pop and the photographer.

"If you haven't, then no one will, Izzy," Anthony said with a laugh.

"Enough. Let's take some photos. We have five minutes until you boys need to be at the altar."

Five minutes felt like an eternity as we took more pictures than I wanted to count. My line of sight would have a perpetual dot from the camera flash. By the end of the night, I'd have dozens of tiny blobs in my eyes and possibly be partially blind. We took photos as a group, the Gallo family minus Thomas. We took turns taking pictures with our parents; it wasn't often that we were all dressed up and in one place together.

I was thankful when there was a knock on the door and a voice said, "It's time."

Cracking my neck, I straightened my back and headed for the door. Ma grabbed my arm, stopping me. "I'm proud of you, baby." She smiled and released me.

I nodded, leaving the tiny room and heading toward the church. Anthony and Michael filed in behind me as we stood in our designated spot at the top of the altar in front of the crowd. The church was packed with people, many faces I didn't know. Ma and Suzy went overboard on the invites, but my mother insisted that her friends be invited, besides our gigantic family that had flown in from all parts of the world. The Gallos didn't know how to do anything small.

As the music started, the doors in the back of the church swung open and the entire church stood and turned. The attention no longer on me, I squinted down the aisle, catching a glimpse of Suzy. She looked like an angel dressed in off white.

The tulle straps created a V, encasing her breasts. The fact that I knew the word tulle disturbed me slightly, but Suzy had educated me about bridal fashion...whether I wanted to know it or not. The bodice was form fitting; a wide ribbon around her waist held a large fabric flower just below her left breast. The bottom of the dress was loose with layers of tulle that flowed and shifted as she walked. It wasn't over the top of puffy shit, it was perfect and totally Suzy—classy and sweet. I couldn't wait to rip the fucking thing off her. A veil covered her face, more traditional than I thought she'd be. I desperately wanted to see her.

She walked arm in arm with her father, slowly moving down the aisle, facing forward. I rubbed my hands together, the last bit of nerves leaving my body, replaced by excitement and a calm that I hadn't expected. When she stopped in front of the first step, our eyes connected. Through the thin veil, I could see the smile on her face as the priest approached her and her father.

The priest stepped down and said, "Who gives this bride away today?"

"I do," her father said, releasing her hand and lifting her veil. He placed a chaste kiss on her cheek before stepping back.

Suzy ascended the stairs, stopping in front of me with teary eyes.

"I love you," I whispered, trying not to become misty-eyed myself.

With a smile on her face, she tilted her head and said, "I love you too."

Sophia reached around and grabbed the flowers from her. Suzy held her hands out to me, and I grasped them with both of mine and squeezed. With one last smile, we turned toward the priest and waited.

We stole glances at each other as he spoke; his words were lost on us. With our hands in each other's, we faced forward and tried to pay attention, but it was impossible. I leaned over, close enough for only her to hear. "You look beautiful, sugar."

She blushed, squeezing my hand. The priest cleared his throat; clearly, we had missed something, as we were so lost in each other.

"The rings," the priest repeated.

I turned to Michael, my best man and brother, and held out my hand. He placed the two platinum bands in my palm and I closed my fingers around them. I had hers engraved with *You're mine, sugar.* A simple statement, and she was from the moment she walked into my life. I handed him the rings and we watched him bless the metal, saying a prayer over them before returning his attention to us.

"Suzette, repeat after me," he stated, turning toward her.

"I, Suzette McCarthy, take you, Joseph Gallo…" She repeated his words, never breaking eye contact with me. She slid the ring on my finger, a smile on her face, as we both felt the power in the moment. Her voice never wavered as she finished with "Until death do us part." She wiped a tear from her eye as she finished. I had to fight every urge I had to wrap my arms around her and kiss her.

"Joseph, repeat after me," the priest said, holding her ring in his hand.

I repeated the words, without missing a single one, letting the power behind the statement seep into my veins. We were connected, a single soul in front of the eyes of God, joined in holy matrimony. We never broke eye contact, keeping each other grounded in the moment.

As I slipped the ring on her finger, I held her hand in mine, running my fingertips against her dampened flesh. We stood there for a few more minutes after I finished my part of the vows and stared at each other. He could've said the church was on fire and we wouldn't have known. I always looked at Suzy, usually watched her sleep, but to stand here and just look into each other's eyes was some heady shit. I loved this woman, more than I loved anyone or anything in my life, including myself.

"I give you Mr. and Mrs. Joseph Gallo," the priest said as we both turned to him. "You may now kiss the bride."

Without needing another word, I grabbed her by the waist and pulled her to my body. Stopping briefly above her lips, I searched her eyes and could see only joy. I crushed my lips to hers as the crowd began to whistle and holler in the background. Their voices faded away as I kissed her, my wife and bride.

When we backed away from each other, we both had watery eyes. As we turned toward the people, now on their feet, I grabbed her around the waist and held her to my side. Our friends and family clapped and cheered as we made our way down the aisle and out of the church doors to the small bridal suite.

As soon as I closed the door, I pulled her into a kiss. Not the small kiss I gave her in front of the family, but one that left us both breathless and needing more.

"We did it, sugar. You're mine forever," I said, as I swiped my fingers against her cheek.

"No, baby, you're mine." She smirked, a devilish expression on her face as she leaned in and captured my lips.

11

SUZY

AFTER WE GREETED THE GUESTS AT THE DOOR, MY FEET WERE ON FIRE. The shoes I had picked were beautiful and made me feel almost the same height as City, but the damn things were like torture devices. I loved how the satin ribbon of the high heels intertwined and laced up my feet, stopping around my ankle with a bow. It was too bad the dress was so long that no one could see them. I grabbed City's arm, leaning over to rub my ankles.

"You want to go change your shoes?" City asked, watching me with a concerned look.

"You think we can sneak away for a minute upstairs? I'll never be able to dance in these."

"It's our wedding, sugar. We can do anything we want." He smiled and winked at me. He turned toward his mother and said, "Hey, Ma, we're going to run upstairs and get different shoes for Suzy."

She smirked, not believing the reason for our hasty exit. "Sure, just don't be too long, son. We have a wedding to celebrate."

City nodded, holding my hand and pulling me from the line. As we walked out into the hotel hallway, he grabbed me by the waist and scooped me up into his muscular arms. I squealed from the sudden movement and sighed as I rested my head on his chest. The intense pain in my feet turned into a dull throb as he carried me to the elevator.

"It's great that we had the reception in a hotel. Makes life so much easier," he said.

Reaching up, I touched his cheek, still not believing we were married. "We really did it, huh?" I asked.

"We did, sugar. Now comes the fun part," he said as the doors to the elevator opened.

"Dancing?"

"Fucking my wife," he said, a deep growl low in his chest.

He quickly adjusted me as the doors to the elevator closed. Pushing my back against the wall, he pressed the STOP button on the elevator as soon as it moved. Holding me against the wall, with one arm supporting my weight, he quickly undid his zipper and reached under my dress.

His eyes twinkled as a naughty grin decorated his face. "No panties again. It must be my lucky day."

"I wanted to give you a surprise when you put your head under my gown for the garter."

"Don't give a shit about that right now. I want to fuck my wife, right here, right now."

I didn't speak, just threw my head back as he thrust inside of me. I wrapped my legs around his waist, holding him to me as he moved. He nibbled on my neck and kissed my lips as he pulled out and slammed back into me. The building tension from the day quickly drove me to the edge as his body slammed into my clit.

I panted, so close to the edge as he rocked his cock into my core. Within minutes, our bodies shook and we both came on bated breath. Our bodies were dotted with perspiration, and our breathing was ragged as he rested his forehead against mine. He must have pressed the STOP button, because the elevator began to move again as he pulled out and zipped back up.

As he cradled me in his arms, I felt utterly loved, completely content, and totally sated. He carried me to our suite, placing me on the couch as we entered. He knelt down and undid the cloth straps on my heels. Grasping my feet in his large hands, he massaged the ache out of them.

I moaned, throwing my head back against the couch cushions. "That feels so gooood."

"I should feel insulted that you're moaning more now than when you were in the elevator." He laughed, pushing harder on the tender flesh.

I giggled, kicking my feet out of his hands. "I'm okay now. Let me grab my shoes before they send out the search party." He backed away, grabbing my hand and helping me stand. "Fuck," I said as his come dripped down my leg.

"What?"

"I feel like I just peed myself, damn it." I sighed. "I can't go down there like this." I lifted up my dress, touching the wetness with my fingers.

"You grab your shoes," he said as he stood, "and I'll grab a washcloth."

"Okay, but you get to do the honors," I said as I walked to the bedroom with my legs as bowed out as possible. I didn't want it to get on my dress any more than it already had.

City entered the bedroom behind me, disappearing into the bathroom for a moment. I grabbed the pair of white tennis shoes I had brought just in case I needed some relief, and waited for him.

"Just stand there and let me do it all, sugar," he said as he knelt down and disappeared under my dress. He wiped my legs gently before taking great care, and probably joy, in wiping his come from between my legs.

"Don't get any ideas," I said, feeling a tingling from the warm washcloth.

"I can control myself only for so long." He laughed as his head popped out from under the layers of lace. "Give me your shoes."

I handed him my shoes and stood still looking down at the man I loved. I held his shoulder, trying to maintain my balance as he placed each shoe carefully on my feet and laced them up tight. They felt like tiny pillows, relieving the pressure in the muscles of my feet.

"Better?" he asked, running his hands up my legs.

"So much better. Thank you, City."

"It's my job to take care of you," he said as he stood and grabbed my chin. "I plan to spend my lifetime doing just that, sugar."

"Mmm," I mumbled as he leaned forward and kissed me.

I could've collapsed in his arms and fallen into a peaceful slumber, but there was a party going on downstairs and we were the main event. We couldn't miss it even if we were exhausted. As we entered the ballroom, the party was in full swing. The DJ was playing instrumental music before dinner, and many of the party guests surrounded the bar in conversation.

"Hey, sister," Izzy said as she walked toward me. "I'm so excited to be able to say that and it be true. I've always wanted a sister." She wrapped her arms around me, squeezing me a little too tight.

"Can't breathe," I whispered.

"Man up," she said as she released me.

"I'll be back, ladies; I'm going to grab a drink at the bar with my boys," City said as he kissed my cheek and left us alone.

"Where's your sister?" Izzy asked, looking around the crowd.

"Don't know, and don't give a shit either."

"You know you've turned into a badass with a potty mouth, Suz." She smiled, shaking her head.

"City. It's all his fault."

"I'd like to think I played a part in it too." She laughed.

"You're always getting me in trouble, Izzy."

"Me?" she asked, holding her hand to her chest.

"Always."

A man cleared his throat next to us and we both turned in his direction. "Excuse me, ladies, I don't mean to interrupt."

"Well then don't," Izzy said, looking the stranger up and down.

He was big and handsome as hell. He reminded me of an Italian version of the Rock. Muscles bulged from his suit, and he had close-shaven black hair, shimmering green eyes, and knockout lips. They were the puffy kind that fit his strong jaw line perfectly and called the name of countless women.

"Don't be rude, Izzy," I said, turning to face him. "How can I help you?"

"I'm a friend of Thomas' and he asked me to drop off a gift on his behalf." The man held out an envelope and waited for me to take it.

"Is he okay?" Izzy asked before I could thank the gentleman.

"He is, and he's very sorry he couldn't make it," he said, looking down at Izzy as if he was not sure of how to take her change in attitude.

"Don't mind her," I said to him, my eyes flickering between the two. "Thomas is her brother."

"Ah, you're *that* Izzy," he said, his lips turning up into a smile. "I've heard a lot about you."

She snarled, not entirely liking the shitty grin on his face. "And you are?" she said, holding out her hand for him to take.

"James." He grabbed her hand and stilled. "James Caldo."

"Never heard of you, Jimmy," she said with a twinkle in her eye.

"Perfect," he said as he brought her hand to his lips and placed a kiss just below her knuckles.

I could feel the electricity between the two of them. Izzy basically eye-fucked him as he kissed her hand. As soon as he looked up, her face went back to a pissed-off sneer. The girl could play a good game, but as an observer, I could see the lust.

I coughed, breaking the moment of awkwardness for myself. "Thanks, James. I'll give this to Joseph for you. Why don't you stay and enjoy the wedding?" I said, smiling at the man. He'd taken the time to get dressed up and I wanted to see Izzy squirm, in all honesty.

"What?" Izzy asked, turning toward me.

"We have plenty of food and I'm sure the Gallos would love to talk with you about their Thomas." Izzy gave me the death glare. "You can keep James company tonight, Izzy. You didn't bring a date." I smiled, and I could almost see the venom dripping from her fangs.

"I'd love to stay. Thank you. Izzy, would you like a drink?" he asked, still holding her hand in his.

"Only because Suzy would want me to be a gracious host," she said, looking at me out of the corner of her eye.

"I don't want to put you out or anything. I'm a *big* boy and can handle myself. I just thought you could use a drink to unwind a bit. You feel a little tense, and that mouth of yours could get you into trouble."

"I don't need a babysitter, Jimmy, but I'll take the drink."

"It's James," he said, squeezing her hand.

I'd been around Izzy enough to see when she was attracted to someone, and she was to James. She may not want to admit it—Izzy often picked guys that she could push around—but I had a feeling James could give her a run for her money.

486

"You two kids play nice," I said as I waved and walked toward my husband. I curled my arms around his waist, leaning my head on his back as he stood talking to Michael. "Hey, baby. Someone dropped this off for us."

"What is it?" he asked as he grabbed the envelope from my fingers.

"A card from Thomas."

I could feel his chest tighten before he tore the envelope open. His eyes scanned the card, his eyebrows drawing together as he read the message from Thomas.

"What does it say?" I asked, dying to know what Thomas wrote.

City sighed, pinching the bridge of his nose before handing the card to me. "Read it for yourself, sugar."

"Are you sure?" I asked as I opened the card. He nodded and closed his eyes. Inside was a brief message from Thomas.

JOE,

SORRY I COULDN'T BE THERE for your wedding. I'm in deep...too deep to get away, even for your wedding.

I'm safe, my cover still intact. Shit's worse than we thought and I'm trying to bring them down as soon as possible. I couldn't take the chance of blowing my cover and risking the lives of our family. This is the path I've chosen, and I refuse to risk anyone's life but my own.

Please know I love you and can't wait to meet Suzy. Give my love to everyone.

LOVE ALWAYS,
Thomas

I CLOSED the card and handed it back to City.

He shoved it in the inside pocket of his suit. "Who gave it to you?"

"The man over there." I pointed down the bar where James and Izzy stood with shots in their hands. "The one with your sister."

"Who is he and why is he having a drink with my sister?"

"He's Thomas' friend and I invited him to stay and enjoy himself. Izzy will take care of him."

He rubbed his face. "That's what I'm afraid of," he said, his chest expanding before he exhaled.

"Don't worry, City. They're like oil and water," I lied. "You don't have to worry about him. He knows all about your sister from Thomas."

"That may not be a good thing either. I'm going to go introduce myself," he said, trying to break free of my grip.

"Oh no you don't. Give them some time to talk."

"I want to talk to him about Thomas," he said, turning to face me with no smile on his face.

"Come on, kids," Mrs. Gallo interrupted. "It's time to be seated for dinner."

I smiled at him, happy that he couldn't barge into the conversation his sister was having with James. It looked heated and made me giddy inside.

"I would say you're both in cahoots if I didn't know any better," he said before kissing my lips.

"You're going to need some fuel for our wedding night." I laughed, burying my face in his chest.

"Sugar, I could live off you alone."

"Pfft," I said, pulling him toward the table at the front of the dance floor. "I wasn't born yesterday, City. You do need to eat."

He leaned down, his hot breath against my ear. "The only thing I need to eat is your pussy."

My core convulsed; the sated feeling I felt before evaporated and was replaced with lust and an ache between my legs. "Don't you start," I said as I took my seat.

"I've only just begun," he whispered in my ear as he pushed in my chair.

I smiled, looking at the crowd, wishing I could run out of here and back to the suite with him. It would be hours before we could escape this place. I figured I'd use the time to torture him as much as he tortured me.

Our guests started clinking their glasses as the rest of the wedding party was seated. I leaned over, placing my lips on his and inhaling the scent that was distinctly him—musky and male and pure sex. I ran my hand up his leg, resting it against his cock and squeezing. His body twitched as he sucked in a breath. He broke the kiss, looking at me with a mischievous grin.

"Do it again and I'll take you in the bathroom and fuck you. I don't care who's in there."

I bit my lip, trying to hide my laughter. He wouldn't dare. I loved this man, caveman attitude and all.

I played nicely as we tried to eat our food, constantly interrupted by the clinking of the wine glasses. It was cute at first, but then it just became annoying. I was starving, and eating had become impossible. After ten minutes of trying to choke down the steak, we both gave up and headed into the crowd to greet the guests we missed earlier.

The rest of the evening was fantastic. It was amazing being surrounded by so much love. Everyone I cared for was there. Sophia and Kayden, minus the little bundle of boy. My friends from work, the boys from the Neon Cowboy, and everyone else that played a role in our life. My parents and sister were there too, but they mainly stayed with my side of the family and stuck to themselves. Pity, really. The two sides would probably never mingle, but then again, I could choose whom I spent my time with.

The most memorable part of the evening was our first dance as husband and wife. We picked "All of Me" by John Legend as our song. It was City's choice; I loved it and couldn't deny him his request. It was perfect. It was our story tied up in one song. It was written for us, or at least it felt like it had been.

City sang it in my ear as he held me against his body and we danced. Tears formed in my eyes. The man could be romantic, and I believed every word of the song. Hearing his deep voice in my ear professing his love through lyrics made me melt. I buried my face in his chest, wiping my tears against his jacket as the song came to a close.

He grabbed my face, looking into my eyes before he kissed me. The love I felt in this moment was almost overwhelming. Sometimes his touch made me feel weak in the knees, like a teenage girl that was lovesick.

I was blessed to spend an eternity with this man.

12

CITY

W E SPENT TWO WEEKS IN I TALY, TOURING MY HOMELAND, AND I SHOWED her the vineyard my family owned. It had been her first time outside of the US and I wanted her to experience the beauty that Italy had to offer. Suzy fell in love with the people of Italy. The culture is so different than in America. Life was slower; people enjoyed the simple things and didn't move through their day at breakneck speed.

Although neither of us wanted to say goodbye to Italy and head back to reality, the moment we walked into our home, everything felt right. I carried her over the threshold, not wanting to break tradition and also being told by Suzy that it was a requirement. I laughed when she refused to walk into the house until I picked her up and carried her inside.

Waking up in our bed made me feel more rested than I had in over a month. Suzy slept peacefully at my side with the sheet covering half her body. Her breasts were exposed, her hair flowing around her head, as she softly snored.

I kissed her neck, feeling her pulse under my lips. She stirred, a small moan coming from her lips.

"Morning, sugar," I said against her skin.

"Morning, husband." She stretched, the sheet cascading down, exposing her entire body.

"I love the sound of that," I said as I partially covered her body with mine.

I slid my hand up her side, stopping on her breast, feeling the fullness in my hand. I rubbed my palm against her nipple, feeling her twitch. I grabbed it with my fingers, giving it a slight tug.

"Ouch," she said, her face contorting.

"Sensitive today. Is it time for your period?" Typically that was the only time she complained that my touch was too tough or abrasive.

"I haven't been keeping track. It must be," she said with a yawn as I cupped her tit in my palm.

"They feel fuller than usual," I said, squeezing them lightly.

"I probably gained ten pounds in Italy. The food was so amazing."

I looked down at her. I knew her body like I knew my own. I'd spent hours worshiping it. "Suzy, are you...?" I sucked in a breath. Suzy's body hadn't changed in the year since we met. No amount of pasta or Gallo family meals had added a curve to her hourglass perfection. Missing her period and her overly sensitive nipples had my mind spinning.

"Oh no," she said, sitting up quickly, grabbing her breasts. "I can't be."

"I'm greedy and want you all to myself, but when it happens I'll be the happiest man alive, sugar." I touched her stomach, resting my hand against her skin and smiling.

"I'm on the pill, but I missed a couple days with traveling. I can't be," she said, blowing out a puff of air, resting her hand against mine. "I'm sorry I forgot my pill, baby."

"I fucked you so much there should be quadruplets in there." I laughed, moving to rest my head against her abdomen. She snaked her fingers in my hair, massaging my scalp. "There's no greater honor than for a woman to carry a man's child. Don't ever say you're sorry. When it happens it happens, but let's try to not have it happen so soon." I kissed her stomach, making a ring around her belly button.

"Your mom would be so damn excited," she said, pulling my face up.

"You'll make her the happiest woman in the world someday, Suzy." I kissed her lips, enjoying the feel of her against me. "But would you be happy, sugar?" I asked, looking into her eyes.

"I'm not ready to give *us* up yet," she whispered. Suzy swallowed hard and rubbed her forehead. "City, what if I am?"

"If you are," I said, rubbing her cheek with my thumb, "I won't be pissed off. You'll be carrying a part of us and we'd still have nine months to ourselves before our world would be rocked."

"I'm not ready," she whispered, her eyes closing as she frowned.

"Sugar," I said, touching her chin and forced her to look into my eyes. "You can handle anything. You're stronger than you think, and I'll be here with you when it happens. Let's not worry about something that we can't control. We'll find out soon enough if you are or aren't. You worry too much. I'm sure it's just the stress of the travel. Let me help you forget." I smiled as I watched her gnaw on her lip.

"You're right. I'm sure it's from the stress of the wedding and travel. How are you going to make me forget?" she asked, and wiggled her eyebrows.

I crushed my lips to her mouth, devouring her lips. She melted into my touch, her mind occupied by the feel of my rough hands gliding across her soft skin. I made love to Suzy in our bed for the first time as husband and wife. Life couldn't get any better.

CHRISTMAS

Suzy and I decided that we'd wait until Christmas day to share the news with the Gallo family. My parents had everything they could ever want, and buying a gift for them was a bitch. The one thing we could give them that they couldn't get anywhere else was the news of their first grandchild.

"You ready for this?" I whispered to Suzy as we sat down on the couch.

"Who's going first this year?" Anthony asked, sitting next to Izzy on the floor.

"I'll go last," Izzy said, leaning back, looking uninterested.

"That's total bullshit, Izzy. You always want to be first," Michael said, sitting down next to Mia on the love seat.

She placed her hands on her chest as she spoke. "Being the baby earns me the right to always go first. I was left out of everything growing up. Christmas day was mine, all mine."

"Please, you were so far up our asses, you were never left out of anything," Michael said, laughing and wrapping his arm around Mia.

Suzy leaned over, whispering in my ear. "I'm kind of nervous. Everything is about to change." Suzy turned her attention back toward the family.

I nodded, leaning over so only she could hear. The shit was about to hit the fan, but for once, it would be a great thing. "Just be ready to have your eardrums shattered." I laughed. God, the Gallos could be loud, but I imagined my mother's happy screams would be near window-cracking volume.

"Why don't we start oldest to youngest," Anthony said.

"That's not necessary; your father and I don't need presents," Ma said, sitting in her chair next to the Christmas tree.

My parents had outdone themselves this year. The Christmas tree almost touched the ceiling. They never went with an artificial tree. My pop had to cut down a tree each year. My parents spent days finding just the right one on their property before cutting and hauling it inside. Thank God they had boys, because it took all of us to help him carry it inside and set it up. Ma spent days decorating it, adding ornaments that dated back to our childhood. The woman kept every decoration we ever made, and they lined the tree.

"Ma, stop. You and Pop deserve presents. You've always spoiled us and now it's our turn to give back," Izzy said, turning toward Ma. "Not really happy about the oldest-to-youngest thing, but I can wait."

"You're a sweet dear," Ma said, leaning forward, stroking Izzy's cheek.

I rolled my eyes. The sugarplum fairy must've invaded my sister's body.

"Open my present first, Ma," Izzy said, reaching under the tree and pulling out a small box wrapped in red glitter paper and a silver bow, which she handed to Ma.

Ma shook it, putting it next to her ear. "Hmm, I wonder what it is."

"Just open it," Izzy said, bouncing on her knees.

"Patience, Isabella. It's a virtue," Ma said, pulling the ribbon and removing the bow.

"Virtues and me don't get along," Izzy said, her laughter growing loud.

"You're a Gallo, none of us do," Pop said as he smiled at Izzy and chuckled.

Ma opened the box, a giant smile spreading across her face. "Oh, Isabella, it's beautiful." She pulled a bracelet lined with rubies and diamonds from the box.

"It's our birthstones together, Ma," Izzy said, crawling closer to her. "Can I put it on you?"

"Yes, I'd love that." Ma handed the bracelet to Izzy. "It's beautiful. I love you, baby girl." Ma leaned forward, kissing Izzy on the head as she snapped the bracelet around Ma's wrist.

"Love you too, Mama." Izzy moved the bracelet so the stones sat on top and were visible, before crawling back to her spot next to Anthony.

"City, why don't you go next," Michael said, winking at me.

"Did you tell him?" Suzy mouthed at me with wide eyes.

I shook my head, because I hadn't said a word to anyone. "No, brother, you go ahead," I said, trying not to spoil their gifts by going before them.

"I can't follow up Izzy's gift. You always give strange things to Ma, so I'd rather go after you," Michael said as he slapped his knee.

Everyone laughed, and Mia elbowed him. I always bought Ma something special and meaningful. The woman didn't care about price; she only wanted something that was heartfelt and meaningful.

"I hadn't planned on giving Ma our gift so soon, but we'll go now just to make you happy," I said with a smirk. He'd shit a brick in a moment... it served his ass right for his shitty comment.

"I want to give it to her," Suzy said, placing her hand on mine before pushing off the couch.

We'd spent hours talking about the best way to break the news. Suzy decided to have a shirt made that said "World's Greatest Nana," along with the first ultrasound photo tucked underneath. Damn kid looked like a jellybean, but I knew it was enough to make my ma squeal.

"Izzy, can you give me the big box with the snowman paper, please," Suzy said as she approached the tree.

Izzy grabbed the box, shaking it as she handed it to Suzy. "Is it an ugly Christmas sweater? You know a girl can never have too many of those." Izzy smiled as Suzy ripped it from her hands.

"Shush it, you. I'm still mad at you," Suzy said, sticking out her tongue at Izzy. She turned toward my parents, sitting in their favorite chairs next to the tree, side by side. "We had something made for you this year, Mom." Suzy handed her the box and came back to sit at my side.

"That's so sweet of you, dear," Ma said, tearing the paper slowly.

"It's for both of you," I said, grabbing Suzy's hand, giving it a squeeze.

"Thanks, son," Pop said, watching Ma open the box.

As she pulled the shirt from the box, Izzy said, "I knew it. Ugly Christmas clothes. Nice, brother."

"Izzy," I warned.

My ma's eyes grew wide, her lip trembling as my pop grabbed her arm. Her mouth dropped open as she read the shirt. "Really?" she whispered.

Pop reached in the box, pulling out the ultrasound photo and bringing it close to his eyes.

"What the hell is it?" Michael asked.

Ma turned the shirt around, a giant smile on her face. "Promise me you two aren't joking?" she asked, holding the shirt in the air.

"We would never joke about that, Ma," Suzy said, squeezing my hand and leaning into my side.

The shrill scream from my ma had me covering my ears. She hopped from her seat, coming at us quickly.

"Fuck," Michael said, clearly understanding the error of his previous statement.

My ma was so lost in her baby haze that she didn't even flinch at his statement. She stopped in front of us, tears just starting to stream down her cheeks. "When?" she asked, clutching the shirt in her hand.

Suzy laughed, hopping to her feet. "August," she said, wrapping her arms around my ma.

"Oh my God, August is so far away, but there's so much to do," Ma said, grabbing Suzy and squeezing her tightly.

I stood, walking toward my pop, holding out my hand. "Congrats, Grandpa," I said, waiting for his response.

He placed his hand in mine, pulling me toward him, embracing me. "I'm proud of you, son. Damn proud. There will finally be someone to carry on the family name…about damn time." He laughed, patting me on the back.

"Only if it's a boy, Pop," I said, sighing and feeling completely content.

"Look around; boys are genetic. Girls are an anomaly in this family."

Ma grabbed me, pulling me from his arms. "And you, how could you keep this from me?"

"We wanted to be sure, Ma. Don't be mad," I said, kissing her cheek.

"I'm not mad. I don't know if I've ever been as happy as I am right now," she said, resting her head on my chest. "A baby, finally a baby," she whispered, her tears soaking through my shirt.

Over my shoulder, I could see everyone surrounding Suzy. She beamed, a giant smile on her face and her cheeks slightly pink. She didn't like attention, but she'd better get used to it. She'd be the center of attention until the baby arrived.

Anthony touched her stomach. "Wow, it's going to be like the movie *Alien*. That's some scary shit, Suzy." He smiled, patting it before moving like the creature that busted out of John Hurt.

Mike batted his hands away from Suzy. "Stop it, you dumbass. You're scaring her. Congrats, doll. I'm so excited to finally be an uncle." He smiled at her, wrapping her into his arms, but holding her like she was breakable.

"Maybe someday Mia can be an aunt?" she asked as she pulled away to see his face.

Mike laughed, nervously looking at Mia. "We'll see. I'm still trying to figure out if she's 'the one,'" he said, and laughed.

Mia smacked his ass, causing a loud crack to fill the air. "You could only be so lucky," Mia said. "Come here, Suzy, give me a hug, Mama. Are you ready for this?"

I watched my family as they showered her with love. We weren't the main attraction anymore; the world would now revolve around the baby.

Suzy huffed out a breath. "Ready as I'll ever be." She shrugged before hugging Mia.

"Congrats, Suzy," Izzy said, pulling Mia off Suzy. "Remember, that baby better have a vagina." Izzy poked her in the stomach and bent down next to her belly. "Hey, little girl, Auntie Izzy will teach you everything you need to know about life," Izzy said, rubbing her hand over Suzy's stomach.

The color drained from Suzy's face, as her eyes grew wide. "Izzy, we don't know the sex yet, but boy or girl, they'll be lucky to have you as an aunt." Suzy looked at me with her eyes bulging like she was scared to death of Izzy getting her hands on our baby. There were worse things than having Izzy teaching a girl how to be strong. Izzy could be a pain in the ass, but she was a tough cookie. The man that could tame her would have to be a beast, if it was possible at all.

RESIST
me

A MEN OF INKED NOVEL

USA TODAY BESTSELLING AUTHOR
CHELLE BLISS

1

FLASH

IZZY

"I DON'T LIKE THE IDEA OF YOU GOING TO BIKE WEEK, IZZY," JOE fumed, slamming his beer on the worktable and glaring at me.

"I'm not a fucking child anymore, Joe. You can't tell me what to do." I stared at him, holding his gaze. I'd always been the little sister, the one everyone wanted to protect. When I was a child, I'd found it flattering, but now? Now it was just a fucking pain in my ass.

"We're not saying you're a kid, babe. Too much bad shit happens during Bike Week. It's not safe for you there. We're just looking out for ya." Michael leaned forward, running his fingers across the back of my hand.

"I can take care of myself. It's just for the weekend. Flash will be with me. I'm not going alone." I sat back, tilting my head to watch their reaction. I knew it wasn't going to be pretty.

"Flash?" Joe asked with wide eyes. "I thought I told you to stay away from that dumbass prick." He ran his hand down his face before squeezing the bridge of his nose. "It was bad enough you brought him to Thanksgiving dinner. I hate that asshole more than I ever did."

"Fucking unbelievable, Izzy." Michael shook his head.

"There's nothing wrong with Flash. He's harmless, but he'll look out for me."

Flash wasn't a pussy, but he wasn't a Gallo man either. I didn't give a shit. He was a friend and we hung out when he came through town. We had never been a couple, but he knew how to please me in bed. I liked being with him. He was uncomplicated and not looking for a relationship. He breezed into my life from time to time and exited just as quickly.

"Izzy," Joe warned. "He was a good kid, but now he's prospecting to get into the Sun Devils MC. I know what shit goes down in a club. I've spent enough time at the Neon Cowboy to know what the life is all about. What the fuck do you think Tommy would say if he knew you were going there with Flash?"

I loved my brothers. I truly did. But for shit's sake, they could be overbearing.

"I don't know what he'd say because I haven't seen him in over a year. I'm not Flash's old lady or his whore. We're going as friends. I'm going and you two can't stop me. He'll protect me." I smiled, crossing my arms.

"Flash is a fucking pussy." Michael hit the table with his fists. "Mia could protect you better than him. Jesus Christ, Izzy, why are you so damn hardheaded?"

"Didn't you two teach me how to protect myself?" I glared at them.

"Yes," they answered in unison.

"I can handle myself. I know how to kick ass and bring a man to his knees." I tried to hide my smile. I knew the double meaning wouldn't be lost on them. "I'll be good."

"It's not your behavior we're worried about, baby girl," Joe growled, cracking his knuckles. "Michael and I can't risk jail because we have to kick some fucker's ass for touching you."

"Speak for yourself, old man. You're still pretty fucked up from the accident, but I'm always down to kick ass, brother." Michael laughed. "Anthony is going to be fucking livid when he hears this shit."

I smiled at them. "He already knows, so shut it. I love you both and appreciate everything you've done for me, but I'm an adult. Have a little faith in me for once. Who's the first person you two run to when shit goes bad?" I arched my eyebrow and laughed. "Me. You're always coming to me for help. I'll be fine." I waved my hands. "Don't try and stop me. I promise to be safe and not go anywhere alone while I'm in Daytona. I'll stay with Flash and won't do anything stupid." I stood, completely done with the conversation.

"You'll call us every day," Michael insisted, giving in. He knew he wasn't going to win this battle.

"Text," I replied. "I'll text you every day while I'm gone, but that's all you're getting." I headed toward the front desk to cash out my tips.

"Fine." Michael sighed, shaking his head. "Don't like this shit one bit."

"Not my problem," I called out from the front of the shop.

"Women are a fucking pain in the ass," Joe said to Michael, and they both laughed. "And shut your fucking mouth. I'm healed from the bike accident, dumbass. I can kick your ass right now to prove it too."

"I don't hit the disabled." Michael laughed.

My boys. Their banter and laughter made me smile as I grabbed my money and slammed the drawer closed. I had everything I wanted in the world: four fantastic brothers, one that was MIA—Tommy—a flourishing business, a growing clientele. And I was totally unattached.

What more could a girl ask for?

2

FLASH IS A DUMBFUCK

IZZY

ROLLING INTO DAYTONA WAS AN UNFORGETTABLE EXPERIENCE. THE entire beachfront was lined with row after row of bikes, babes, and badass boys. Flash and I checked into the shitty, seedy-ass hotel, but at least it seemed clean and had a bed. I chuckled when I caught a glimpse of the old coin-operated machine that caused the bed to vibrate. We'd find a way to make that useful.

After throwing my bag down on the floor, I collapsed on the lumpy mattress. The vibration of the three-hour bike ride still hadn't left my system as I stared at the brown spot on the ceiling.

"Hey, baby." Flash crawled on top of me, crushing me with his weight. "I want to taste you before we head out." He planted soft kisses on my neck before biting down on the tender flesh of my ear.

I moaned, tangling my fingers in his hair. "You know how I like it," I whispered, pulling on his scalp. "Do me good." I pushed his head down my body, not wanting to waste any time.

"Don't I always?" He licked his lips as he unbuttoned my jeans.

"Mm-hmm. Usually." I smirked as I lifted my ass, allowing him to slide the denim down my legs.

Flash was a beautiful man. He didn't resemble the scrawny kid I used to play kickball with at recess. His blue eyes, killer smile, and chiseled body made my mouth water. I was sure I wasn't the only girl out there who enjoyed his beautifully bent cock—not broken, just curved. It wasn't too wide or thick, just total perfection. Each stroke hit just the right spot, and I'd never found another one since. It was the reason I always welcomed him in my bed.

He threw my jeans across the room before he nestled between my legs. "No panties," he mumbled as he kissed the skin on my lower abdomen. "Landing strip too. You know how I like it."

"Just for you," I lied.

It was the start of bikini season in Florida. I wouldn't be caught dead with stubble or razor burn. I pulled my knees up, planting my feet flush with the comforter, to give him better access.

He inhaled, a gleam in his eye. "You smell better than I fucking remember. You have the sweetest pussy, Iz. Fucking fantastic." Sticking his tongue out, he flicked my clit as he gripped my hips, holding me in place.

A jolt of pleasure shot through my body as I arched my back, pushing my head into the mattress. Warmth cascaded across my body as he latched on to me, sucking my flesh. Letting my knees fall toward the bed, I lay before him, spread eagle and wanting more than his mouth.

His hands slid under my ass as he squeezed it roughly, kneading it with his fingers. He sucked and licked my core while he stared in my eyes. Our gazes were locked as he rubbed his fingers against my opening.

"You're so wet, baby. I can feel how much you've missed me."

"Stop talking, Flash." My body was overly sensitive from the long bike ride. The slightest touch of his lips sent tiny shockwaves down my legs, causing my toes to curl. "Make me come and maybe I'll let you stick your cock in me."

"I'm taking that shit," he muttered against my flesh as he thrust two fingers inside me.

I cried out, the pleasure too intense as he latched on to me. He rhythmically sucked and finger-fucked me until I screamed through the breath-stealing orgasm.

"It's my turn now, Izzy." Flash patted my thigh as he sat up.

"I said maybe." I closed my eyes, lost in a post-orgasm haze.

"I'm taking it. No maybe about that shit. I earned it," he murmured as he nudged my legs farther apart.

I smirked, closing my legs. "You didn't earn shit. Eating my pussy *was* your reward."

"I'll stick it in your ass, then, but I'm taking something," he said as he flipped me onto my stomach.

I reached back, covering my ass with my hands. "Oh, no you don't!" I yelled. Then I felt a sharp sting on my ass as the sound of the smack he'd just landed filled the air.

"You know you want my sweet cock, Izzy. Don't play hard to get. It's not a good look on you."

I laughed into the blanket as the bed sprang back from the loss of his weight. He opened his bag on the old wooden desk next to the television. The man could wear a pair of blue jeans. He looked in the mirror and caught my eye before turning with a condom in his hand.

"Liking what you see, baby?"

"Eh, it's all right," I mumbled putting an unimpressed look on my face. I did, but no fucking way would I ever tell him and let my foot off his throat.

With a smile, he unbuttoned his jeans and pulled them down before kicking them off. His cock bobbed as he straightened, waving at me in all its hard glory. He tore the wrapper open with his teeth, sheathing his stiff, curved member before walking toward the bed.

"Not even going to take your shirt off?" I asked, staring at his cock. Then I forced myself to look at his face.

"You didn't." He pointed to me with a shitty smirk.

I didn't even care. All I'd wanted was his mouth on my pussy and the orgasm that had been just out of reach during the trip to Daytona. "I'll fix that. You, off the bed and totally naked," I commanded, pulling my tank top over my head.

After grabbing the back of his collar, he pulled it over his head, exposing his washboard abs. Fuck. He was a sight. Then he crawled up the bed, his cock swaying and a shitty-ass grin on his face.

"I know you want it. You need my dick more than you'll ever admit, Izzy. No one makes you come like I do," he whispered in my ear as he rubbed his hard length against me. "You want it?"

"If you think you're man enough to give it," I challenged. I loved when Flash felt like he needed to prove himself. He worked harder at it, fucked me better, and outdid himself each time.

"I'm busting that shit, Izzy. I'll show you how a real man fucks." He stood on top of the bed, pulling me up by the hips. "Ass up, princess," he said as he smacked my other cheek.

I giggled into the comforter. Dipping my stomach toward the bed, I pushed my ass in the air, wiggling it.

"Don't move," he said as he landed another blow to my already stinging flesh.

My laughter became uncontrollable as I buried my face deeper into the blankets, trying not to hurt his pride. Flash was hot. But controlling? Not one bit. I'd let him play the part for the pleasure of feeling his cock in me.

He pushed into me in one quick thrust. His fingers dug into my hips as he pounded me. I moaned each time the head of his cock stroked my G-spot. I fisted the sheets, closing my eyes, and tried to remember to breathe. His body bounced off mine, slamming into me to the hilt before he withdrew. As our bodies collided, my ability to keep my upper body in place began to slip. I reached back, wrapping my hands around his ankles, holding our bodies together.

He rested his palm against my lower back and placed his finger against the one hole I'd never given him. I opened my eyes, looking behind me. He towered over me with a hand on my hip, his abs clenching and relaxing, and a trail of spit falling from his lips. I squeezed my eyes shut, trying to get my body to relax as he rubbed the saliva against my flesh.

"Fuck," he muttered as he pulled out his cock and pushed his thumb inside my ass.

I whimpered, wanting the feel of his cock as I dug my fingernails into his ankles. He rammed his cock into me, filling me in both holes. Pleasure shot through my body as he worked one in and the other out. Moving out of sync and in absolute fucking perfection.

"Who's fucking you, Izzy? I want to hear you scream my name." He stilled.

I mumbled, not able to form words.

His thumb dug deeper, pulling upward, hooking me. "What's my name?" he growled, taking out his cock.

"Flash. Fucking Flash," I answered in one quick breath, burying my face in the comforter.

He pummeled me, his balls slapping against my clit, the curved shaft stroking my G-spot, his thumb caressing my ass. The second orgasm tore through me without warning as I chanted his name.

I lay there panting as the world came back into focus. My grip slipped from his ankles as I became putty in his hands. Flash picked up the pace, slamming into me a couple of times before resting his chest against my back and twitching. He gasped behind me, trying to catch his breath. Our bodies were stuck together by sweat-soaked flesh.

"Fuck, darlin'. I've missed ya," he panted in my ear as his cock slipped out.

"I missed your cock, Flash." I chuckled, earning me a swift smack on the ass. I started to crawl off the bed, ready to hit the town and get out of this shithole of a room.

Flash grabbed my foot. "Where are you slithering off to?" he asked as he pulled me against his body.

"I wanna shower and go out. I'm ready for a little fun." I sighed.

"Just lie here for a minute. I'm tired and I want to hold you." He jerked me back, holding me tighter to his chest, and nuzzled his face in my neck.

I relaxed against him. He did feel really good, but I wasn't here to snuggle. Flash and I had never had that type of relationship.

"You want more pussy this weekend? If you do, you'll rest while I shower and take my ass out. Understand what I'm saying?" I looked at him, seeing only his eyes as he bit down on my shoulder.

He released me, pushing me off the bed. "What the fuck ya waiting for? Go shower, wench."

I laughed as I grabbed my bag and flipped him off. Pussy was the great equalizer and always won when you needed to get one over on a guy who thought he was "the man."

***

When he'd said that he'd take me out and show me the town, I hadn't thought that included the shittiest biker bar in all of Daytona Beach. The place reeked of cigarettes; the air was hazy from the smoke. A band was playing behind a cage like in that movie 'Roadhouse'. I walked through the door with Flash at my side. The floors were filthy and the men inside didn't look much better.

"None of your mouthy bullshit that I love so much when we talk to these guys, got it?" Flash cocked an eyebrow at me, standing like a statue as he waited for my answer.

"I'm not mouthy," I insisted, crossing my arms over my chest.

"Darlin', ya are, and I fuckin' love it." His smile grew wider, giving me a glimpse of why they called him Flash. He had a perfect smile filled with shiny, pearly-white teeth, one that could charm the pants off any girl. It did funny things to my brain, and I couldn't say no to him. "In this bar, with these guys, it's not the place. Understand? I'm a prospect, and that shit won't fly here."

I slid my arm around his waist, looking up into his baby blues. "I got it. I'm to be seen and not heard?"

He grabbed my shoulders and stared back at me. "That's how these guys are. You don't like something they say, just keep quiet."

The last thing I wanted to be was a piece of arm candy that faded away in the background. It was not how I'd been raised. "Let's get one thing straight, Flash. I know you're badass and all, but I don't stand in the shadows for anyone. *Understand?*"

"Fucking hell," he muttered, rubbing his face.

"I'll play the part this once, for you, but hear me now, mister. I'm not a club whore and I sure as hell ain't your old lady. I don't know what in the hell we are exactly, but if you want to be more than whatever the fuck this is"—I waved my hand in the air between us—"I will not stay quiet and be a mindless twat."

"Calm the fuck down, woman," he croaked as he wrapped his fingers around my wrist. "I don't think of you that way. This is for them." He turned his attention to the table full of rough-looking men about twenty feet away. I could handle big and burly. I hadn't grown up a pussy. "Just please do this for me and I'll make sure to make it worth your while," he said, wiggling his eyebrows and giving me a cocky-ass grin.

"I won't make a scene and walk out, but you owe me big time." I tore my wrist from his grip.

"Whatever you want, Izzy. You know that." His eyes softened as he looked down at me.

"I'm going to use my *silent* time to come up with something really *big*." I swiped my fingers across the small hint of chest hair just below his throat.

"I can do big." He laughed and grabbed my hand to pull me toward the table.

"Fucker," I muttered to myself as I followed behind.

He looked over his shoulder and said, "I heard that."

When he stopped suddenly, I ran into his back, and it felt like hitting a brick wall. I used his body as a shield from the men at the table. I didn't know if I had an off switch, but this wasn't really the place for me to test it. I just needed to keep my eyes down and pray their little hello didn't last long.

Flash leaned over the table, shaking their hands as I stood behind him pretending to be invisible—something I'd never done for anyone. Ever.

When he'd said that he wanted to take me to Bike Week in Daytona Beach for the weekend, I hadn't been able to imagine anything better than the feel of the wind in my hair, the sand between my toes, and a shitload of hot bikers. What could be bad about that?

I hadn't expected this, and I didn't like it one bit. Flash would have to pay and pay dearly to make up for this "be seen and not heard" bullshit.

"And who do we have here?" a rough voice asked, pulling me out of my thoughts on how to torture Flash.

Flash shifted and reached around to grab my hand, tugging me to his side. "This is Izzy, my woman." He tightened his grip on my waist.

I glared at him.

What the fuck? I wasn't his woman. We had an agreement, but to call the naughty shit we did a relationship was overstating it just a tad. I gave him the stink eye and saw the corner of his mouth twitch.

"Well aren't you stunning, Izzy. Is that short for Isabella?"

I turned my attention to the genius and smiled the biggest bullshit smile I could muster. "Yes, it is." I swallowed the other words I wanted to say, still smiling like an idiot.

He wasn't a bad-looking man for someone his age. His long, gray hair was pulled back in a low-slung ponytail, making his emerald-green eyes stand out. A small patch of salt-and-pepper facial hair framed his thin lips. He looked a little like Santa Claus on crack. The vest covering his black t-shirt was the same cut as the one Flash was wearing, but it had more patches—including one that stated he was the VP.

"Why don't you sit down with us and have a drink?" He lightly patted the empty chair next to him, never taking his eyes off me.

Flash moved in front of me and started to sit, but the VP grabbed his arm.

"I meant her, you idiot. Not you."

Flash stopped dead, with his ass hovering just above the seat. "Oh, sorry, man."

What type of man would let another one talk to him that way? The way he'd said "idiot" hadn't been the same as when my brothers called each other "jackass" or "dumbfuck." His dislike for Flash was clearly evident in his tone, but Flash did as he was told, like a good soldier.

I slid into the wooden chair as Flash gripped my shoulder. "Thanks," I whispered, folding my hands in my lap.

"My name's Rebel," he said as he brought my hand to his mouth, running his prickly lips across my skin. "These are the guys." He placed my hand on his leg, patting it, and then grabbed his beer.

Flash's grasp on my shoulder hardened, but I didn't dare look up at him.

Fuck. How had my dumb ass gotten into this situation? Flash was a stupid bastard. I should've listened to Joe and Mike, but then again, I never did.

"Hey," I said, slowly looking around the table. I tried not to linger on any one man too long.

They all said, "Hey," and smiled—except for one man. The long hair hid his face as he picked at the label on the bottle. His reaction to me wasn't friendly or welcoming like the others'. Nope, he was avoiding me.

"So, Isabella," Rebel said, pulling my attention back to him. "Can I call you that? You don't mind, do you?" He leaned into my personal space and squeezed my thigh. The stench of cigarettes and stale beer invaded my nostrils.

Flash gripped my shoulder and Rebel held my thigh. I knew Flash wouldn't do shit. He was the prospect, the one trying to get in the club, and Rebel knew it. I just needed to be agreeable and get the hell out of here for my sake and for Flash's pussy ass.

I bit the corner of my lip before responding. "Sure." The only people in my life who called me Isabella—who I allowed to call me by my full name—were my parents. I didn't think telling Rebel to go fuck himself would be good for anyone.

The tiny hairs on the back of my neck rose, and I felt like someone was watching me. Without looking, I noticed him staring at me out of the corner of my eye as I kept my attention on Rebel. It bugged the fuck out of me. I wanted to get a glimpse of him, just for a second, but Rebel wanted my total attention.

"Flash, go fetch me a beer and get something for the beautiful girl too," Rebel demanded, staring at me, paying no attention to Flash or anyone else.

My eyes flickered to his face as he barked orders to Flash. "I'm fine. I don't need anything to drink." The last thing I wanted was to drink anything that wouldn't allow me to be in control. Being around Flash was one thing, but I didn't trust the men sitting at the table.

Flash didn't move. He kept his hand on my shoulder, squeezing it lightly, and I could almost feel the tension radiating from his body.

"What the fuck are you waiting for? Get the fucking drinks, boy!" Rebel roared, slamming his fist on the table.

I jumped. The anger that oozed out of him put me on edge. My heart stuttered in my chest and I wanted to get out of here. Flash released my shoulder, leaving me alone with Rebel.

Rebel leaned over, twirling my hair with his fingers. "So, darlin' Isabella, tell me about yourself."

I looked down at my hands, trying to stop the urge to bat him away. "Not much to tell," I whispered.

He pushed the hair over my shoulder, running his fingertips down my skin, lingering on my collarbone. "I doubt that, Isabella." As he drew out my name, rolling the last bit off his tongue, his breath tickled my nose.

Small prickles slid down my neck, the hair still standing at attention. I leaned back in my chair, trying to escape his invasion of my personal space, pissed off that Flash had brought me here and then left me like a pansy ass.

"Tell me about you, Rebel." I was deflecting. A man like him had to be full of himself, drunk off power, and I prayed it would take the focus off me.

"Tsk, tsk," he said, shaking his head. "I know all about me. I want to know about you." His eyes bored into me as he started to slide his hand up my leg before settling on my thigh.

I swear to shit I wanted to rip Flash's dick off and shove it down his throat. I didn't care if I ever fucked him again. His cock was not worth this bullshit.

"I'm a tattoo artist," I said with a sigh while looking into his eyes, knowing that I wasn't going to get out of the situation without being cordial. It wasn't one of my better traits, but I knew how to play the game. "It's my life." I plastered a fake smile on my face, trying to maintain eye contact with him. I wouldn't show weakness. I was a Gallo girl, not a shrinking violet.

"I love a girl who does ink. Maybe I should come to you next time I need some work done. I wouldn't mind dropping my drawers for you, beautiful."

I wanted to heave. The mere thought of seeing any of this man's junk or ass made me gag. "I'm between gigs right now," I lied, biting the inside of my cheek.

"The MC has a shop. Job's yours if you want it." Rebel squeezed my thigh, running his hand farther up my legs, stopping mere centimeters from my pussy.

"Just like that, huh?" I couldn't keep my mouth shut. I didn't want to seem too eager to please, or too easy. "Maybe my skills are shitty. Then what?"

He inched his chair closer, squeezing my thigh again. "If your ink skills are shitty, I'm sure we can find *other* ways for you to earn."

"Listen," I said, about to lay into him and give him the nicest "fuck off" he'd ever had, but the sound of Flash slamming the drinks on the table stopped me from finishing the statement.

"Flash, you fucker," Rebel said, releasing my leg and leaning back in his chair. "You spilled my beer," he growled, wiping the glass with his finger. He turned to me, drawing his fingers into his mouth and sucking them as he stared.

Sam, a.k.a. Flash, didn't speak. Cool biker nicknames were reserved for badasses, and Sam had lost that right when he'd pussied out on me. He hadn't stood up for me, and left me high and dry in the hands of Rebel.

As Rebel grabbed the bottle to bring it to his lips, I turned and gave my "I hate you" scowl to Sam. He shrugged, grimacing before giving me a halfhearted smile. I closed my eyes, trying to calm the fuck down, because at this point, I wanted to tell Sam exactly how I felt and get the fuck out of the shitty-ass bar. I counted to five like they'd taught in a college psychology course I'd taken on a whim. I slowly opened my eyes to find Rebel staring at me *again*.

Sam leaned down, resting his hand on my shoulder, and whispered in my ear, "Want to get out of here?"

What a clusterfuck. Would he have balls big enough?

"I'm getting tired," I complained, standing to say goodbye. Before my ass was five inches off the chair, Rebel had his hand on my wrist, pulling me back down.

"I wasn't done talking to you." He smiled, licking his lips.

My eyes flickered to Sam, who now had wide eyes and an "oh fuck" face. I narrowed my eyes at him, wishing he'd man the fuck up, but nope. He must've checked his cock at the door. I turned back to Rebel, looking down at his hand, which was still wrapped around my wrist. *Be diplomatic, Izzy. Do not piss off the MC vice president.*

I turned my wrist, breaking the hold he had on me. "I-I," I stuttered, trying to figure out something other than, "Keep your fucking hands off me."

Just as I opened my mouth, a voice called out to Rebel. "Leave the fucking girl alone, you horny ol' bastard."

I turned to look in the direction of the gravelly voice, where Rebel's attention was now focused. My breath vanished and a dull ache settled in my chest as I sat there wide-eyed and in shock. The blue eyes shooting daggers across the table at me I'd seen before—I knew them. They were mine looking back at me.

The smile I loved so much and the handsome, boyish looks were gone. His features were hard. Small lines had formed around his eyes since the last time I'd seen him. He didn't look like the man who had pushed me on my swing set and taught me how to throw a punch to defend myself. The man's lips were set in a firm line as his glare focused entirely on me. He didn't look anything like the brother I remembered, like the Tommy I loved.

"You want a piece of this ass?" Rebel asked, looking from me to Thomas. "I wouldn't blame you, Blue. It's mighty fine," he said as he turned back toward me, running his finger down my jaw.

I snarled, moving my face away from his fingers. Rebel gripped my hair, yanking my head back and holding me in place.

"Where do you think you're going, Isabella?" He stared into my eyes, a smirk on his face.

My heart started pounding, growing louder by the second as it beat out of control. This was bad, a real fucking nightmare.

"I want her," Tommy said, slamming his hand down on the table. "You got the last piece of ass and this one's mine."

Rebel laughed, releasing my hair. "Want me to get her warmed up for you, brother?"

"I don't want your filthy hands on her. She looks too innocent and pure. I want to take that from her," Tommy replied, laughing with the rest of the guys, his eyes only on me.

"If you don't do it, Blue, I will," Rebel promised.

"Oh, I plan to do all of her, and she's going to like it."

Thank God the words were coming out of Tommy's mouth, because I'd be totally fucked otherwise. Sam released my shoulder. The fucker still hadn't said a word. He'd stood there like a fucking idiot and stayed silent.

"Don't I get a say?" I whispered, grinding my teeth. "I'm not a piece of property."

"Flash brought you here, darlin', and you came out of your own free will. If Blue wants you, he gets you," Rebel said, laughing like a hyena. "You can thank Flash later."

I turned to Sam as his eyes dropped to the floor. "Don't you have anything to say?" I hissed, the venom dripping from my voice.

He shook his head as he kicked an imaginary piece of dirt on the floor.

"Fucking pussy," I muttered before turning back to look at Thomas.

A small smirk played on his lips; he knew I could never hold my tongue.

Rebel slapped Sam, his laughter filling the air and mingling with the other guys'. "Even the girl can see you're a pussy, Flash," he teased, wiping his mouth with the back of his hand.

I would've pissed myself by now if it hadn't been my brother claiming me for the night. I had fucked up, and although Tommy might have smirked, I knew I was in big fucking trouble.

3

CLUELESS

IZZY

"WHAT IN THE FUCK WERE YOU THINKING?" TOMMY SCREECHED AS HE slammed the hotel room door and locked it.

"Clearly, I wasn't," I quipped as I sat on the bed, avoiding his eyes. Fuck. I looked at the ceiling, my stomach flopping around like I was about to be chastised by my dad.

"I know you do some dumb shit, Izzy, but this takes the mother-fucking cake." He paced near the door, checking the peephole, as he ran his finger through his hair. "How in the hell do you get mixed up with an MC guy?" He stopped pacing, turned toward me, and tapped his foot.

I shrugged, not really having a good answer for him.

"A shrug. I get a goddamn shrug?" he groaned as he walked toward me. "Izzy, look at me," he barked.

I looked up into his piercing blue eyes and could see a storm behind them. My mouth suddenly felt dry and I was at a loss for words—something totally out of my realm of comfort.

"Thomas," I whined, trying to find the right thing to say.

"You are in over your head, Iz. This is some serious shit. If I hadn't been there tonight or if Rebel had decided that he wanted you for himself, you'd be fucked, and so would I." He rested his hands on either side of me and leaned into my space. "I mean that literally. This is a fucking nightmare."

I blinked slowly, taking in the sight of my very pissed-off brother, and sighed. "I just wanted to have fun, Thomas. I wasn't expecting all this bullshit." I swallowed and concentrated on breathing through my nose. Pissed-off Thomas was a scary fucking dude.

"All this bullshit?" he whispered. "All this bullshit is what comes with an MC. They make their own goddamn rules." He backed away, grabbing my hand as he sat next to me. "I have to keep you safe and get you the hell away from these guys." He pinched the bridge of his nose and exhaled loudly.

"I'm sorry," I choked out, tears forming in my eyes. "I thought Flash would protect me. He promised a weekend getaway." God, I sounded like a fucking idiot. Mike and Joe had warned me. They'd pleaded with me not to go, but as always, I did whatever the fuck I wanted to.

"Flash is a fucking pussy and a complete moron. I worried he'd recognize me, but he was too young to remember me. Plus, he's an idiot. Nice kid, but dumb as a box of rocks."

"Why are you still here, Tommy?" I inquired. He'd always be Tommy to me—my big brother who had been missing from my life for more years than I'd like to admit. "Why haven't you come home?"

He looked up at me; his shoulders slumped before he spoke. "I'm in deep, sis. I've moved up the ranks. I'm sergeant-at-arms now. I'm in the inner sanctum and doing everything I can to bring this club down. I don't want the shit to be half-assed, either. I need to bring it to its knees. Cut off the head and burn the body. Leave nothing behind."

"It's so dangerous." I knew my statement was obvious, but I didn't have anything else to say. The thought of something happening to him made my heart feel like someone was squeezing it in their fist, and I didn't want to feel it pop.

"It's my job, Izzy. I have to see it through. I promise I'll come home to everyone, and I'll do it soon."

"You better. Ma is beside herself with worry. Joey is going to have a baby. The family is changing and you're not there to see," I grumbled. I wanted to run out the door with Tommy in tow and head home.

"Joey's going to be a dad?" he whispered, his eyes growing wide.

"Yes. You're going to be an uncle soon. You need to come home."

"I will, love. I will." He wrapped his arms around my shoulders, bringing my face against his chest.

I rested my hands on his shoulder blades, gripping them for dear life. I didn't want to let him go. I couldn't remember the last time I'd seen my brother, let alone been able to touch him. How was I going to be able to walk out the door and leave him behind?

"Now what?" I asked, my voice muffled by his t-shirt.

"Well, everyone thinks I'm banging your brains out." He blanched and gagged. "After, I have to bring you back." He sighed, pulling away from me as my hands slipped from his back. "Let me make a call. Do you have your phone? Mine isn't safe."

I grabbed my purse, which I'd dropped on the floor when I'd sat down. I rummaged through the contents, pulled out my phone, and handed it to him.

"Who are ya going to call?" I asked. I did not want any of my other brothers in harm's way. It was bad enough that I'd put Tommy in this fucked-up predicament, let alone the others.

"I only have one person near by I can trust to get you out of this clusterfuck." He tapped the buttons on my phone but didn't look up at me.

"Who?" I asked. "Don't call Mike or Joe either," I pleaded, lying back on the bed.

"Fuck no, woman. I'm calling a law enforcement buddy. Only he can pull this off without it looking like I had anything to do with it." He stood, bringing the phone to his ear.

Well okay, then. He still hadn't answered my question. I looked around the hotel room as he walked away from the bed. This place was an even bigger shithole than the place Sam and I had booked for the weekend. The room hadn't been updated since it had been built in the '70s. The color scheme was straight out of *The Brady Bunch* on meth. Mustard yellow, burnt orange, and avocado green decorated the flowery wallpaper and the bedspread. I didn't want to even think about all the things that had been done on this bed. It had to be crawling with germs.

I stood, walking toward my brother, stopping to look out the peephole. The green shag carpeting did not make me want to kick off my shoes and feel the lushness. It was matted and trashed.

"Hey," Tommy said into the phone. "I need your help."

I turned, studying him as he moved around the room. He would've worn a path in the carpeting if the shag had still been good. I grabbed my purse and sat down on the bed, pulling my lip-gloss from my purse as I listened.

"My sister's here. I need you to help me get her the fuck out," Tommy said, running his fingers through his hair. "I know. She showed up with one of the prospects and Rebel almost claimed her for the night, but he offered her to me—thank fucking God." Tommy stopped and listened before moving again. "Yeah, Izzy," he said, his eyes darting to me.

My eyes grew wide. The person on the other end knew who I was, but I didn't know them.

"She's the only fucking sister I have, James. What the hell kind of question is that?" Tommy glared at me as James spoke on the other end of the phone.

I looked up at him, my mouth dropping open when I heard his name. James Caldo. He was the smug bastard who'd come to the wedding uninvited to drop off a card for Tommy. We'd shared drinks—way too many drinks. I'd woken up the next morning slinking out of his hotel room without saying goodbye. I'd gotten what I'd wanted, gotten the hell out, and never looked back.

James was…how do I say it? Hot as fuck, but a little too bossy for my liking. He reminded me of my brothers, but times ten on the macho bullshit. I'd waited for him to grunt, "Me caveman. You're mine," after he'd fucked me into a coma after the reception.

If I hadn't been plastered by an abundance of Jack and Coke, I wouldn't have been seduced by him and ended up in his bed…against the wall…on the floor.

Fuck. Why did he have to call James? My stomach started to flutter, a wave of nervousness filling my body. My leg began to shake, a nervous habit I had when I couldn't control a situation, as I sat there and listened.

Maybe I wouldn't have to see him. *Oh God, please don't let me have to see him.* Maybe they'd devise a plan to get me out and that would be that. I closed my eyes, fell back on to the bed, and stared at the ceiling. I listened while crazy scenarios played in my mind.

Maybe James wouldn't help because I'd hit it and quit it. Would he be that cruel?

Maybe he'd want payback with me on my hands and knees as a thank-you for my rescue. The sound of that wasn't bad, but I would be subservient to no one, and certainly not James.

"Yeah. I can find a way to get her on my bike after we leave here," Tommy said, sitting down next to me. He scowled at me, maybe having heard something from James about what had happened that night. "Okay. I'll have her text you when we're leaving the bar, and you handle it from there. I trust you, James. Only you. She needs to be safe and brought home. She shouldn't be here. Can you do that for me, brother?" He stood again and walked into the bathroom, closing the door.

I exhaled, letting go of the breath I had been holding while thinking about James. I didn't like the sound of this one bit. I closed my eyes and tried to block out the sound of the outside world and focus on Tommy's voice, but it was no use. I couldn't hear a fucking thing over my heart beating like the drummer in Anthony's band. I wanted to run in the bathroom and throw up, but I stayed glued to the bed, waited for my brother, and closed my eyes.

The sound of the bathroom door smacking against the wall made me jump. I sat up quickly, looking toward the noise to see Tommy staring at me.

I gave him a fake smile and tilted my head. "Everything worked out?" I asked, my voice hoarse as I tried to hide my curiosity.

"Fucking perfect," he grumbled as he moved toward the window, peeking through the now yellowed, sheer drapes. "How well do you know James?" he asked, turning to me.

"Um," I said. Fuck. *Lie—do not tell him the truth.* "I met him at Joey's wedding. He brought your card and we had a drink together." I kept the fake smile plastered on my face, speaking quickly so as not to trip over my words.

"Just a drink?"

"Maybe two," I replied, still smiling as my eyebrows shot up. God, I was horrible at the angel act.

"James seemed to be very interested in helping get you out of here.

Maybe a little too eager," he complained as he moved to stand in front of me.

I looked up at him. He could be intimidating, but he'd always be just my brother. I didn't have anything to fear from him, but I wouldn't tell him about my night with James. No fucking way.

"He's your friend, Tommy. Naturally, he wants to help out. You called him for a favor, and as any good friend would do, he agreed to help."

Tommy shook his head, a grin slowly spreading across his face. "You've never been a good liar, Izzy. I'll kick his fucking ass if he tries anything with you." One of his eyebrows rose and the muscles in his jaw ticked. "No one touches my sister," he warned, the tiny grin disappearing.

"Thomas, I'm not a child. We had a couple of drinks, and even if I wanted more—which I don't," I insisted as I stood. "But if I did…it wouldn't be any of your business." I poked him in the chest, driving the point home.

His head dropped, his eyes staring at my finger as I held it against his chest. A rumble started underneath my finger and bubbled out through his mouth. He threw his head back, his laughter filling the room before he looked back at me.

"Izzy, love," he said, grabbing my face, his blue eyes shining with tears. "That has to be one of the funniest damn things you've ever said."

"What the fuck? It wasn't funny." I poked him harder and with my nail. "I'm a woman now, if you haven't noticed. I make my own decisions." I tilted my head and glowered at him.

He was still laughing as he wiped his eyes. He shook his head as he spoke. "You'll always be my little sister. Flash is going to get his ass kicked." His laughter died. "He won't know why, but I will. He'll be hurting because I know he dirtied you. He's not worthy of you."

"Flash is just a friend," I said, because it was the truth.

"He's been in your pants, sister. Don't try and bullshit me." He glared at me, studying my every twitch. "He'll pay."

I sighed, blowing out the air I'd stored in my cheeks. "Whatever," I blurted.

"James better not touch you either."

"I don't like James like that. I thought you boys were bad growing up, but he makes you guys look like pussycats."

Tommy's eyebrows drew together. "You got all this over a couple of drinks?" His jaw worked back and forth as he ground his teeth together. The sound sent shivers through my body.

"Yeah." I kept it simple. No need to throw up a flag that alerted his big brother Spidey sense that James had fucked me senseless.

"Swear?"

"Yep."

He sighed and wrapped his arms around me. Then he kissed my temple, and the warmth of his body felt great against me. He was my brother, and I had proof that he was safe and alive.

"We'll leave here in ten minutes. We have to make it believable, Izzy."

I looked up at him. "What do you mean make it believable?" I questioned, scrunching my nose as I thought about what that could mean.

"They have to believe that I had sex with you," he said.

"Fuck," I muttered, gnawing on my thumbnail.

We smudged my lipstick, tore my shirt at the bottom, and messed up my hair. The bar was dark enough that hopefully it would pass. The most important part would be my attitude.

"Don't pretend to like me, but don't hate me either. You aren't attached to Flash, but you didn't have a choice in coming with me, either."

"I love you, brother. You're cute, so it's not like I would've had to bang Rebel."

"Do not say the words *bang* and *Rebel* in the same sentence." He cringed, opening the door for us to head back to the bar. "When we get there, just stay quiet and let me talk. I want to get us the fuck out of there as soon as possible so James can grab you."

I sighed, wishing the fucking night were over and that I were in my bed...at home and on the other coast. "You know how quiet and I work out, Tommy."

He stopped dead in his tracks and turned. "From here on out, I am not Tommy. Blue is my name. For fuck's sake, Izzy, do quiet for me just this one time," he pleaded before walking away.

"Men suck," I mumbled.

As I approached his bike, Tommy turned and faced me. "I won't see you again for a while, Iz. Although I'm pissed about you being here, I'm happy at the same time. I've missed you, baby girl." His face softened as he held his arms out to me.

I looked around, wondering if someone was lurking in the shadows, unsure if I should hug him.

"It's okay. Come here." He motioned with his finger, beckoning me into his arms.

I wrapped my arms around his waist, holding on to him for dear life. What if I never saw him again? I couldn't think that way. Thomas was the toughest man I knew. If anyone could live through all this bullshit and come out on the other side unscathed, it would be him.

"I'll miss you," I said, choking back the tears. I squeezed him tighter, rubbing my face against his t-shirt. "Come home soon."

He released me, wiping the tear off my cheek with the pad of his thumb. "Don't cry. I got this." He grinned, his beautiful blue eyes twinkling from the streetlight. "Let's get this shit over with so I can know you're safe. You listen to James and do whatever he says, Izzy. He'll keep you safe."

I rolled my eyes, unable to hide my annoyance. My shoulders slumped as I thought about being trapped with James for any amount of time. It would be a total clusterfuck.

"Fine," I sang, grabbing the helmet and putting it on my head. "I don't like it, but I'll try to be good."

"He'll keep you alive. Remember that." He climbed on his Harley and turned the key.

"Got it," I said as I nestled behind him and encased him in my arms.

I rested my cheek against his back as we took off, headed back to the guys. I use that term loosely; they were more like animals that could talk.

If my brother had known the sordid details of my night with James, he wouldn't have asked me to obey his every command. James hadn't contacted me after the wedding, and for that, I was thankful. I hadn't had to avoid his calls or block him from my phone. The man knew how to take a hint, but thrusting the two of us back together without being able to be in control freaked me the fuck out.

Why did I care so much about seeing him again? I closed my eyes, getting lost in the memory of the night that happened four months ago.

James had been more of a man than I'd ever been with. He was a true alpha and didn't take bullshit. Bullshit and me were the best of friends. He'd called me on everything, and I'd felt like he could read my thoughts. I didn't want to be the type of woman that people could figure out. He knew when I was full of shit, and I didn't like when anyone could figure me out so easily. I wasn't a girl. I was fierce and no one's pushover. Isabella Gallo was not subservient.

4

THE GREAT ESCAPE

IZZY

WHEN WE WALKED BACK INTO THE BAR, NO ONE REALLY SEEMED TO CARE. Rebel gave me a once-over and quickly patted "Blue" on the back. They exchanged words as I sat down, my unhappiness evident from my tear-stained cheeks. They thought it had been caused by the sex I hadn't wanted, but really, it had been at the thought of saying goodbye to my brother.

After a round of drinks with Thomas's arm draped around my shoulder, protecting and claiming me all at once, the group decided to head out for the night. Parties were happening all over Daytona, and they had club business to attend to before they hit the sack.

"She's riding with me," Tommy declared as we walked outside and were greeted by the thick, humid Florida air that smelled like the ocean.

"Whatever you say, brother," Rebel conceded as he threw a leg over his bike.

"Where's Flash?" I asked, looking around one last time for him.

"Fuck Flash, darlin'," Tommy snarled, holding out the helmet to me.

"But—" I started to speak but saw his lips set in a firm line as he glared at me.

"He's been sent off to do club business with some other members." He shoved the helmet in my hands. "Get the fuck on. We don't have time for your bullshit girl stuff," he barked, turning around and starting the bike.

The roar of the engine made me jump, and I quickly put on the helmet and pulled the straps tight. Climbing on the bike, I realized that this would be the last time I'd touch my brother for months. The guys took off just as I nestled myself behind him.

When the roar of the bikes and the distance between them and us was sufficient, Thomas turned to me and smiled. "Make the call, Izzy. Love ya, kid," he said before turning around and quickly taking off, hot on the tail of the other guys.

I hit dial, ringing James's phone to alert him that we'd left the bar. Thomas had said that James would stop us shortly after leaving the bar, and he'd had me put a baggie of cocaine in my pocket. James would do a search for some bullshit reason and place me under arrest.

Daytona was crawling with cops and DEA during Bike Week. Undercover, I presumed, since I didn't see a crazy amount of police presence, especially not with the amount of bikers that flooded the city during the event.

Rebel led the pack and we pulled up the rear. Tommy had wanted it that way, figuring it would be easier to be pulled over by James. I tried not to think about what was about to happen as I held on to him, taking in all that was my big brother—strong, kind, caring, and protective.

He'd made me laugh as a little girl, holding on to my hands and twirling me in the air like I was a blade of a fan. My mother would scream, but Tommy and I would just laugh and collapse in a heap of giggles. His face had been softer then; the years of undercover work and biker-life wear and tear hadn't yet entered his life. I wondered if he could ever go back to that fun-loving, carefree guy again. I hoped he would, but living this life had to alter you in some form and stick with you for the rest of your days.

My heart stammered in my chest as the sound of police sirens filled the air. I opened my eyes, the red and blue lighting bouncing off of Tommy's jacket. I gave him a squeeze as he slowed the bike and waved off the rest of the guys.

We pulled off to the side of the road as the police cruiser stopped behind us. The lights continued to flash, but the screeching siren noise turned off before I heard a car door slam.

"Sir," the familiar voice said as he approached us.

The sound of his voice alone had my pussy clenching. Fucking cunt had always been a problem. I didn't like James. It needed to cool its fucking jets and not think about his cock. James wasn't the man I wanted...I couldn't top him.

Thomas sat still, peering in his side mirror until James came to a stop at our side. The others were far enough away, leaving us behind to deal with the cop issue.

"Get her the fuck out of here. Blow is in her left jacket pocket."

"Hey, Iz," James slithered out as he slowly looked me up and down.

I lifted my chin, staring him in the eye without a smile. "Jimmy," I replied, the corner of my lip twitching.

God, he looked fucking good. No, good wasn't the right word. He looked fucking amazing dressed in the law enforcement uniform. The brown dress shirt hugged his muscles, looking like a second skin against his tan flesh. The shitty polyester pants the force handed out clung to his muscular thighs, showing off every dip and crevice in his body. The gun sitting around his waist reminded me that he wasn't a man to be crossed, though I liked to push his buttons. He could easily overpower me, and for some reason, the thought turned me on.

His jaw ticked as I spoke his name. He hated when I called him Jimmy, said it reminded him of a child. I'd used it to only piss him off, crawl under his skin like he had mine.

Tommy handed over his license and registration, shoving it in James's hand as he openly gawked at me.

James turned his attention to Thomas and cleared his throat. "What the hell are you going to tell them?" he asked, motioning toward the red taillights off in the distance.

"I'll figure some shit out. She's just another pussy to them. She's not a club whore or an old lady. She's inconsequential."

"Men are such fucking pigs," I bit out. "How can you even be around those douchebags? You don't think that way, do you?" I asked, looking at Tommy.

"Fuck no. I'm just playing the part. Ma did not raise me to think that way."

James laughed, drawing my attention in his direction. Why did he have to be so damn handsome? I mean, Jesus. Why couldn't he be plain and not fantasy inspiring?

"And you?" I asked him, wishing I could wipe that shitty smile off his face.

"Oh no, doll. I love women. Not all of them are just a piece of ass. Not even the ones who slink out of my hotel room before the sun rises." He grinned.

My eyes grew wide as a lump formed in my throat. He wouldn't dare tell my brother. Would he? I mean, the man had cockiness down pat, but he wouldn't be dumb enough to clue my brother the fuck in on our sex Olympics.

Tommy shook his head and turned to look at me. "Can I trust you to listen to him?" he asked, squinting as he peered at me.

"I'll listen," I said, as James began to chuckle. I moved my eyes from Thomas to glare at James. "I can't promise I'll do as he asks, but I'll listen and do what I feel is right."

"Izzy, for fuck's sake. Just fucking listen for once in your life. I know you bow down to no man, but this is your life we're talking about. I have enough shit to worry about and don't need to worry about you getting home safely," Tommy snarled, keeping his eyes focused on me.

"I'll be good to her," James promised as he stopped laughing and cleared his throat. "I won't let her out of my sight and I'll keep her safe. You couldn't put her into more capable hands." James smiled, giving me a quick wink.

I turned to Tommy, unable to take the smug smile on James's face any longer, and spoke the words he wanted to hear: "Yes, I promise to do whatever is necessary to get home safely."

"Off the bike, ma'am. I need to search you. You too, Blue," James barked out, stepping away from the bike.

We climbed off, me with the assistance of my brother, and turned our backs to James. He frisked Tommy first. I straightened my back and watched him as he touched my brother, moving quickly and thoroughly

CHELLE BLISS

and finding nothing. It was all for show. I knew I wouldn't be so lucky. As he turned his attention to me, I closed my eyes and waited.

I knew he wouldn't be so quick when touching my body. He wouldn't make it obvious to my brother or the eye of an outsider, but I remembered what his hands had felt like on my body. The amount of pleasure the strong hands had given me. The feel of them on me and in me was like nothing else I had ever experienced.

"Back on the bike, sir," he ordered. "Ma'am, hands behind your head and do it now!" he roared, as I was lost in my memories.

As Tommy took his place on the bike, keeping a lookout for any stragglers from the club, I sighed and tangled my fingers together behind my head. Thankfully my back was to him. In this position, my breasts were pushed out farther, leaving myself exposed. He started at my wrists, brushing against my skin with the tip of his rough fingers. Tiny sparks shot down my arms, a direct line to my nipples. I opened my eyes, sucking in a breath before closing them again.

I didn't have to see his face to know that he had a grin dancing across his lips. His giant hands swept down my arms and stopped just above my ribcage. The tips of his fingers grazed my breasts as his hands slipped down the front of my torso before he searched my waistband.

No matter how hard I tried to control a reaction or think of anything other than his hands on me, my body responded. I twitched and silently swore. I rolled my eyes at the feeling of being defeated. He knew in that moment that he had an effect on me. I was fucking doomed.

I could feel his breath against my ear. My body shuddered as my heart skipped a beat, before it was gone and his hands slid down my legs.

Please don't...

Fucker.

His thumbs touched the holy land as his hands glided up my legs. As he reached the V of my legs, I swear to shit my heart stopped dead in my chest. I sucked in a breath, trying to calm my insides as my head dropped.

I was happy when his hands left my legs until he caressed my ass, all in the name of a search, but I knew he was enjoying it too much when he gave it a quick, hard squeeze.

"Must you?" I whispered as he moved closer, reaching into my pockets.

"Yes," he whispered back, his mouth coming close to my ear. "Think of all the *fun* we're going to have as I give you a *ride.*"

"You're an asshole," I hissed, turning my face to look at his profile.

"That's one part of you I haven't *yet* explored," he whispered in my ear, low and close enough that Tommy couldn't hear.

I gulped, closing my eyes and using all of my self-control not to turn around and give him a piece of my mind. I couldn't react in front of my brother or the other eyes that could possibly be on us.

"What do we have here, ma'am?" James asked, pulling his hand from my pocket and dangling the small bag in front of my face.

"It's not mine, officer," I pleaded, shaking my head and playing the part.

"Place your hands behind your back. I'm placing you under arrest," he said, grabbing my arm, gingerly moving it away from my head and down to the small of my back.

"Must we do this?" I asked, looking toward Tommy.

Tommy winked, not giving any other physical indication that everything was okay.

"We must, doll. Give me your other hand."

I wrinkled my nose and ground my teeth as I felt the cold steel of the handcuffs slap against my wrist. Great. Not only was I being placed in his custody, I was starting off bound and in his possession without a means of escape. Being with the men of the MC had felt less scary than what I felt about being a captive for James.

"I'll leave them loose so they won't pinch, but you can't get out. Not yet at least," he said as a low, slow laugh tickled my ear.

I glared at Tommy, not looking at James as he marched me toward the back of the police cruiser. He placed his hand on my head as he helped me into the back seat.

"Stay put," he ordered as I moved my legs inside.

"Where the fuck am I going, genius?" I blurted out, the anger dripping from my voice. My hands were restrained behind my back and I was about to be locked in the police car.

"You better watch that smart mouth of yours, doll." He grinned, leaning against the frame of the car.

"Or what? Are you going to rough me up, Jimmy?" I snuggled back into the seat, adjusting my body and trying to find a comfortable position.

"I'd hate to add resisting arrest to your charges." His grin turned into a smirk as he wiggled his eyebrows and licked his lips.

"Just get this shit over with so we can get the fuck out of here," I hissed, not finding him charming at all.

"As you wish." He slammed the car door, leaving me with my thoughts as he approached Tommy and spoke with him.

I watched through the windshield as they exchanged some heated words—or at least they made it seem like they were. A dull ache settled in my chest as I watched them speak. This would be the last time I'd see my brother for some time. The not knowing was the worst part. Tommy looked over at me a couple of times as they finished their conversation. My nose began to tickle as tears threatened to fall.

When James slid into the front seat, he didn't speak. He turned on the car and started to pull away after Thomas had sped down the road.

"When are you going to let me out of these fucking cuffs?" I asked. My wrists already felt the bite from the metal digging into my skin.

"Tomorrow," he answered calmly, looking at me in the rearview mirror. His eyes changed from the smile I couldn't see but knew was there.

"You can't keep me like this until tomorrow." Anger built inside me. My body was almost vibrating as I stared at him in the mirror.

I knew I was now a pawn in his game. I'd have to play by his rules. I was pissed at Thomas for leaving me with James, and at asshole Flash for being an idiot and not realizing the amount of shit he was bringing me around this weekend.

James looked at the road, the corner of his eye crinkling as he spoke. "Harder for you to run away like that. Plus, you look fucking sexy when you're pissed off, Izzy."

"Jimmy, look, I didn't mean—"

"James." His eyes momentarily flashed in the rearview mirror before leaving me again.

"James," I hissed, holding the end, letting the letter stick between my teeth. "I'm sorry about what happened." I looked down at my knees, chewing the inside of my lip.

"I'm not," he said flatly.

"It wasn't nice of me to leave without saying goodbye. I was a jerk. Can you forgive me?" I wasn't really sorry for anything, but I wanted the damn cuffs off my wrists.

"It won't work, Izzy."

"What?"

"Your fake apology," he said as he pulled up to the red light and his eyes returned to mine. His face had a red sheen from the traffic light. He looked like the devil I figured he really was. He'd torture me as long as I was in his custody.

My mouth dropped open and a scream was crawling up my throat. "It wasn't—"

"Yes, it was."

I closed my mouth, grinding my teeth as the car started to pull away, and his face changed color. "I had fun with you and we both got what we wanted out of that night." I swallowed, remembering the feel of him against my skin. Those sweet-ass lips that were pissing me off right now had brought me so many orgasms that I'd lost count, the amount of alcohol I'd consumed not helping my memory.

"Maybe I'm sensitive and wanted a kiss goodbye?" he said, tilting his head up to look at me. I could see the corner of his mouth as it almost kissed his eyes. He was enjoying himself.

I sighed and pushed my shoulders back. Glaring at him, I said, "That's total bullshit."

"Maybe so," he said, looking away, "but I did want that kiss."

Fuck, his voice was sexy. It matched him entirely...big in all ways. "You're not going to play fair, are you?" I whispered, but I already knew the answer.

"Did you?" he retorted with a clipped tone.

"I'm sure you did the walk of shame many mornings, James."

"Doll, I've never been ashamed of spending the night in the company of a beautiful woman—especially you."

A knot formed in my stomach, and it felt like James had reached inside and was using his giant hands to untie it. He made my belly feel funny, and I didn't like it. I pursed my lips, not taking my eyes off the back of his head.

"It was easier for both of us," I whispered, trying not to give anything away in my voice.

He shook his head. "Can't stop the bullshit from rolling off your tongue, huh?"

"Are we there yet?" I was annoyed and pissed off. James did not get to question me on my truthfulness.

"To the police station, yes, but not the entire trip."

"I can find my way home. I'm an adult woman."

"Why don't you start acting like one, then?" he asked sarcastically.

I felt like he'd punched me in the chest. No one talked to me the way he did—no one with a dick, at least. The only people who could get away with calling me on my shit were my girls, but not a man. Not even my brothers or father.

"I am acting like an adult. I can rent a car and get myself back to Tampa. It's only a couple of hours away."

"Izzy, listen up, because this is how it's going to go." He pulled the cruiser over on the side of the road, rolling to a stop. He turned around, resting his arm on the back of the passenger's seat. "I promised your brother *I* would take you home. I promised him *I* would keep you safe. I will not just release you to fend for yourself." He licked his lips, and my eyes moved to his mouth as he continued speaking. "It's late, after two a.m., and I'm tired. We're going to return the car and then find a hotel for the night and drive back in the morning. That's the plan, and I don't want your brother to worry that I'm not following the plan. He has enough shit on his plate right now. Understand?" He glared at me, waiting for my response.

"Wow. Didn't know you knew so many words." I smirked, watching his jaw as he tried to stop a smile. "Fine, but I want my own room," I requested, knowing that I didn't have a choice in the whole "how to get Izzy home" plan, but I sure as hell wasn't going to share a room with him.

"One room, double beds," he growled, turning around and pulling back on to the road.

"No fucking way. I will not share a room with you."

"It's for your own protection."

"Not happening," I declared, looking out the tinted window, seeing the police station sign in the distance.

"Yes, it is. Don't fight me on this, woman."

"I don't want to spend the night in your room."

"Our room, and you do."

"Jesus, you're infuriating."

"Touché."

"Ooh, he knows French too. Didn't know cavemen were bilingual."

"Must you always be a smartass?" he asked, parking the car in the "reserved" space.

"Nothing good can come out of sharing a room," I said as I sat up, unable to stop the anxious feeling. I had to get the hell out of this car.

"I remember a lot of ear-shattering moans the last time we shared a room. I'd say only good can come from it," he murmured, a low, smooth chuckle escaping his lips before he climbed out of the car.

"Fucker," I muttered as his door slammed.

"Out you go, doll," he said when he opened my door, the hot, humid air hitting my skin. He reached in and grabbed my arm, trying to help me up, and I fought the urge to pull away.

"I hate that term," I said, climbing out with his hands still on me.

"Doll?" He smirked, giving my arm a light squeeze.

"Yes. It's patronizing," I hissed as I turned my back to him.

"As long as you call me Jimmy, I'll call you doll. And what the fuck are you doing?" he asked, grabbing my shoulder.

"The cuffs. I want them off." I glared at him. Why did he have to make everything so fucking difficult?

"I can't take them off yet. You never know who has eyes on the station," he said, and laughed.

"You're a prick."

"You're hitting every word I like to hear—come, prick, fuck. What else do you have to say?" He smiled as he grabbed my upper arm and pulled me toward the station doors.

"Let's just get this over with." I sneered at him as I tried to keep up with his large steps.

"I'm going to enjoy this," he whispered in my ear as he opened the door and waited for me to pass by. "So fucking much."

My body shuddered. This gravelly tone of his voice shorted the wiring in my brain. I'd spent too many years trying to block guys like him out, and I'd been successful. James was an entirely different beast. I didn't know how to deal with him. He always had a reply. It was fucking infuriating.

I closed my eyes, taking the final step into the station and hopefully to freedom—or at least an escape from him.

5

ISABELLA

JAMES

WE ONLY SPENT A FEW MINUTES AT THE POLICE STATION RETURNING THE uniform and equipment they let me borrow to rescue Izzy from the clutches of the MC. She sat on the chair, her eyes never leaving me as I talked with a few of the officers. If looks could kill, I'd be dead and buried.

After we finished at the police station, Izzy and I headed to find a low-key hotel just outside of the county. I wanted to be far enough away that no one would find us, but close enough that, if shit went down, I could get backup. She climbed on the back of my bike after protesting and arguing for a few minutes. She knew it was futile. I wasn't letting her out of my sight.

Feeling her body wrapped around mine—her thighs squeezing me tight, her arms holding on, and her tits against my back—was fucking perfection.

When Thomas had called and asked if I'd help rescue his sister, I'd jumped at the chance to see her again. It wasn't that I loved her—fuck no. I'd only spent a night with her, but there was something about her.

No one had ever sneaked out of my bed the next morning without saying a word. Izzy was the exception to that rule, and for that, I gave her props. She was her own person. I knew she didn't play by anyone's rules but her own. Thomas spoke of her often, and I could feel the love he felt for her with his words.

Thomas and I had met back during training. We'd both joined the DEA right after college. I knew it was where I wanted to be, and had dedicated my life to ridding the world of drugs. I knew it wasn't possible, but I'd do my best to not make it easy for the sleazeball criminals who preyed on the innocent.

I'd joined because I'd lost my little sister to an overdose. She was only seventeen and I was in my sophomore year at Florida State. Getting the news that your one and only sibling has died is indescribable. It crushes your soul and had made me question everything in my life. I'd felt like I'd lost direction in my life, and the only thing I'd wanted was retribution. The only way I knew how to do it legally was to join the one group that had the ability to stop the flow of illicit drugs. The DEA became my home and my new family.

Yes, I still had my parents, but they'd fallen apart after the death of my sister. They weren't the same people anymore. They walked through life as shells of their former selves, the sorrow too much for them to bear.

When we met, we were excited and looking to kick some major ass in the drug world. We spent a lot of time talking about our families—his happy and mine not so much.

We each had sisters, his alive and mine dead. Even though I could never touch my sister again and I couldn't protect her, I still loved her more than anyone else on Earth. We spent our nights drinking too much beer and talking about life. Our conversations always veered off course and would turn to our sisters as the main reasons for us being there.

Thomas said that Izzy wasn't into drugs but he always felt a need to protect her, and others like her who didn't come from such a loving family. I'd wanted to join because the same drugs had reached in and plucked my sister from my life.

I was out for payback. After we graduated training, Thomas and I were partnered with veterans and taught the ropes. Years later, we were paired up, and it felt like coming home. He was the brother I'd never had. I was his go-to person when he was placed undercover. I was his link to the DEA and his call of last resort. I kept tabs on him and picked up information when he found a way to get it out.

His case was solid, but at times, I worried about Thomas. I'd never admit it to him—he'd call me a pansy—but he was in deep. Deeper than I'd ever thought possible. He'd been able to move up the ranks and solidified his position with the club. I made sure to do my best to keep his cover intact and my ears to the ground in case shit went down.

Leaving him for the weekend to drive his sister home was a sacrifice I wasn't sure I could make, but how could I say no to him? I didn't want him to go through the same loss that still squeezed my heart and hung heavy on my soul even after ten years. Loss is loss and it never goes away. We learn to deal with it, but the desperation and longing never fade. I didn't want Thomas to experience what I had.

I found a replacement in the agency, someone I trusted to cover for the weekend while I made the round trip with Izzy. I felt at ease knowing that he was protected and I could do the one favor—the only one, in fact —that Thomas had ever asked of me. His family was his number-one priority.

I'd felt shitty after fucking Izzy when I brought the card on his behalf to his brother's wedding. I felt like I knew Izzy after having heard stories about her ball busting for years. I'd seen pictures of her, but her beauty in person couldn't be conveyed in a photograph.

Her smart mouth, killer body, and bombshell looks had my cock throbbing and my mind reeling as I had a drink with her at the bar. A back-and-forth conversation over Jack Daniel's left me hard as a rock, and I needed to crawl inside that sweet cunt of hers. After too many drinks to make a proper decision, I sure as fuck wasn't thinking of her brother, and invited her to my room.

I wasn't surprised when she accepted, following me to the elevator as the party raged on. As soon as the elevator doors closed, I had her against the wall. I claimed her mouth, her tongue sweet from the Jack and Coke lingering on the surface as I devoured her. Caging her face in my hands, I stole her breath and replaced it with my own.

When we reached my floor, I broke the kiss. She didn't move as her eyes fluttered open, and her breathing was ragged. I grabbed her hand, pulling her toward my room, a little too eager to feel her skin.

The chemistry was off the charts. We tore at each other's clothes as soon as the door shut while our lips stayed locked. The need I felt to be inside her bordered on animalistic as our heavy breathing and pants filled the room.

I dropped to my knees, looking up at her, and said, "I need to taste you." She was a vision. She had on thigh-highs that connected to a garter belt and cock-hardening stilettos.

She didn't reply, but spread her legs. I cupped her ass, bringing her body forward as I swept my tongue through her hair. I could smell her arousal as I flicked her skin with my tongue. I wanted to worship at her altar.

I lifted her with my hands, placing her legs over my shoulder as I feasted on her. I sucked like a starved man, licking every ridge and bump as she chanted, "Fuck yeah," and "Oh my God." I didn't relent when she came on my face, her legs almost a vise around my head. I dug in deeper, sucking harder as I brushed her asshole with my fingertip. Her body shuddered, the light touch against the sensitive spot sending her quickly over the edge.

It's not that I didn't want to take her in every way, putting my cock in every hole and making her dirty, but I wasn't ready to go there—not yet, at least. I wanted to feel her pussy squeeze my cock and milk me. I needed it.

I don't know what time we both passed out. I'd never had sex so much in one night, but even after it all, I wanted more. She was the one person I couldn't get enough of, and it didn't sit well with me. When I woke up and found her gone, I won't lie, that shit stung. In the end, I knew it was for the best. I didn't need the headache in my life.

I couldn't tell Thomas what had happened—no way in fucking hell. He'd murder me and hide my body. That shit I knew. I hadn't chased her or tried to contact her. Let that shit stay buried in the past.

"Turn around or close your eyes," she said.

Lost in the memory of our first night together, I blinked. "What?" I asked, shaking my head, trying to clear my mind. I took in the surroundings of a very different room. It wasn't the lush accommodations from the night of the wedding, but a crappy, run-down motel.

"I need to undress," she said, tapping her foot as she stared at me. "I don't have my bag of clothes and I can't wear this shit to bed."

"I've seen it all."

Her clothing didn't do much to hide what I already knew lay underneath. The skintight jeans that narrowed around her ankle just above the black high heels had my dick aching. I wanted to feel the bite of them against my skin as I pounded into her.

"I was drunk," she groaned, her eyes growing into little slits.

"Are you saying I took advantage of you?" She couldn't be fucking serious. I didn't do that shit. She'd wanted it as much as I had. I'd known from the moment she'd called me Jimmy that she'd wanted me. I'd known enough about her from Thomas that I'd had her MO down pat.

"I wasn't thinking clearly. You aren't my type." She wrinkled her nose, twirling her finger like I was going to roll over like a dog and face the other way.

"Doll," I teased.

"Fuck you and that 'doll' bullshit. Turn. The. Fuck. Around," she hissed.

Laughing, I kicked back on the bed and covered my eyes with my hand. "Happy now?" I asked, leaving space between two of my fingers to get a clear view of her undressing.

"Very." She turned around, facing the opposite direction as she removed her Harley tank top that framed her breasts but left little to the imagination.

Underneath, she was wearing a black bra that lay just below her shoulder blades. She reached back, unhooking the straps with her fingers. Black nail polish decorated the tips, and I wanted to see them wrapped around my cock and her eyes watering from choking on taking me to the back of her throat.

She bent down, pulling off her jeans, and her breasts fell to the side, giving me a marvelous view. They were full, round, and natural. I licked my lips as my mouth watered, while watching her tits sway as she stepped out of her jeans.

She climbed in the bed opposite mine, lying back, her tits on full display and her tiny black G-string the only thing she'd left on. Yeah, like that would protect her and keep her pussy safe from me.

She pulled the covers up to her chin, closing her eyes for a moment, and then said, "All done. You can look now."

I turned to my side, resting my head on my hand, and smiled at her. "Now close your eyes," I commanded, watching her face contort.

"For what?" she asked, staring at the ceiling, avoiding eye contact.

"I need to get undressed too, and I don't want you to catch a glimpse."

"Please, Jimmy." She laughed. "I've seen it all." She rolled over and smirked.

"Felt it too, but I still want you to turn around or close your eyes."

She rolled her eyes, throwing her hands down and slapping the mattress at her sides. "Really? You worried that I'll jump on you and beg for your dick?" She made a *pfft* noise with her lips, blowing out a quick breath of air, causing her hair to blow away from her face.

"Just do it, doll. I know if you see it you'll be begging for me to crawl in that sweet cunt of yours and fuck you like no man has done before or since me." I twirled my fingers, giving her the same patronizing gesture she did me.

She stuck her tongue out and covered her eyes with her hand. "Just get fucking undressed so I can go to sleep already. I'm exhausted," she said, resting her other hand against her breast.

I could see that she was doing the same as I had—left a space between her fingers so she could peek. I knew she wanted me.

"I bet I could find a way to wake you up," I taunted as I sat up, pulled my shirt off, and threw it across the room, just catching the back of the chair.

I pushed my shoulders into the mattress, lifted my ass, and contracted my abs, knowing that she was watching and taking in the view. I unbuttoned my jeans and pushed them down at a painfully slow pace just to prolong her show. I wasn't the type of man who wore underwear, either.

As soon as I lowered my jeans below my thighs, my dick sprang free, bobbing as if waving hello and calling her over. I knew it remembered Izzy as much as I did.

Izzy sucked in a breath as soon as my cock entered the room devoid of covering, the piercing shimmering in the light.

"You okay over there?" I asked, smirking because I had further evidence that she wanted me. She wanted me badly.

"Yeah. Just a piece of dirt in my mouth." She swallowed and

coughed, playing the lie to the fullest.

I wrapped my hand around my shaft, stroking my length as I spoke. "Want something to wash it down?" I had to bite my cheek to stifle the laughter I felt coming to the surface. The only thing better than fucking her was fucking with her mind.

"No," she breathed.

"You sure? I can find something to help that tickle in your throat. I have something close at hand." Fuck, I felt like a creeper. Only to her would I say such fucked-up, bigheaded shit to, because she was Izzy—ball-buster champion of the world.

"I'm fine. I don't need anything you have." The corner of her mouth twitched.

Damn, her cockiness was such a fucking turn-on. No one had ever made my dick as hard as she did. The torture, too much for even me to bear anymore, made me kick my jeans off the rest of the way and toss them to the floor.

"Shit," I mumbled, remembering that I'd left my gun on the stand next to the television. I never slept without it next to me in bed or on my nightstand.

"What?" she asked in an annoyed tone.

"My gun is by the TV. I need to get it. Keep your eyes closed," I demanded as I placed my feet on the floor and faced her bed. I'd called dibs on the bed closest to the door in case anything happened. I'd be the one to protect her. I'd step in front of a bullet before I'd let anyone hurt her.

"They're still covered, Jimmy." She smiled, thinking she was slick.

"Uh huh," I said as I climbed to my feet and stretched, my front on full display for her peep show.

Her mouth parted and her tongue darted out, sweeping across her bottom lip. I wouldn't call her out on peeking because, fuck, it was just too much fun to watch her suffer in secret.

I stalked toward the television, taking small steps until I stopped and grabbed my gun. I lifted my head, catching a glimpse of her in the mirror that hung on the wall. Her fingers were spread apart for a moment, a smile playing across her lips before she closed the gap. Maybe she knew I'd caught her, but if she did, she didn't confess.

CHELLE BLISS

I walked back, my dick swaying and bobbing as it passed close enough to reach out to touch her as I gave her a full show. I wanted her to remember what I had to offer physically. She couldn't fight it forever.

After I pulled the covers just above my waist, I said, "You can look now." I turned off the light and flipped on the television, needing some lighting in the room. I had to keep an eye on Izzy and be able to see if anything were to happen.

She nestled in her pillow, placing her hands above her head, the sheet slipping just enough that I could almost see the pink skin that lay underneath. I silently prayed the sheet would slide an inch lower, exposing her piercings and the hard nipples that were outlined by the thin material.

"Good night," I yawned, trying to be a gentleman. "Sweet dreams."

"Yeah," she whispered as she closed her eyes.

I rolled toward her, resting my hand under my pillow as I watched her. Her face illuminated by the television, shadows playing across her features, she was even more stunning at peace. She looked like a different person as she slept. Her face was softer, but I knew the bite those sexy, full lips held when she was awake.

I didn't feel guilty for staring at her, watching her chest move up and down as her breathing slowed and grew shallow.

Would she sneak out again? The woman was more pigheaded than any other person I'd ever met. She wouldn't risk her life…would she?

I couldn't take the chance. I had to find a way to keep her in the room, and I knew just how I'd do it.

I waited, watching the clock and her body as she slept. I needed her to be in a deep enough sleep that small noises wouldn't wake her. When I felt she was ready, with small snores falling from her lips, I gingerly climbed out of bed, trying to avoid the box spring creaking with my weight.

I walked quietly to the bag I had set near the end of the bed and unzipped it, listening to it snag on each tooth as I pulled it open. I grabbed my cuffs, holding them together in my palm. I stood and approached her bed, trying not to wake her.

I'd never been so thankful for a shitty, old, '70s-style bed frame. It was perfect to attach the handcuffs to in order to keep her exactly where I wanted her. I opened the cuffs, connecting them to the bed, wincing as I closed it around the wood slat.

Her hand rested just below and in the perfect spot to quickly put them on before she'd have a chance to react. As I reached out to grab her hand, she moved and her face turned away from me. I held my breath and prayed she didn't wake up as I stood next to her. My balls and dick were too close and at eye level. I wanted to keep them and have them intact and functioning. I didn't need her attacking me.

I pushed down on the pillow with the metal as I slid it under her wrist. As soon as they were closed, her eyes flew open and she yanked her arm, but it stopped, held by the handcuff.

"What the fuck?" she screamed, pulling against the cuff that trapped her. "Get this shit off of me, James."

I laughed, moving out of the way of her kicking feet. "Calm down, Izzy."

"How the fuck can I be calm when you did this shit?" she fumed, holding up her arm and shaking her wrist.

"I wanted to make sure you didn't sneak out again." I shrugged and smirked. "I used the only way I knew. Thomas said to 'use any means necessary,'" I said, making air quotes.

"I don't think he meant naked and handcuffed."

"Details," I muttered.

She grabbed the wooden slat with her free hand and began jostling it back and forth, trying to break it free from the frame.

"Stop," I warned. "You're going to hurt yourself."

"Is this really necessary?" she complained, lying still and glaring at me.

"Yep," I crooned as I crawled back in bed.

Minutes passed as I heard her moving in bed, tossing and turning the best she could with one arm suspended above her head.

Finally, she stopped moving, the sheets crinkling as she turned to me. "James," she whispered.

"Yes?" I answered, closing my eyes. Hearing her whisper my name with that sugary-sweet tone had made the bottom of my stomach drop like I was on a rollercoaster ride and had just plummeted from the first hill.

"I'm scared."

Now that I *knew* was a load of shit. From what I knew of and had experienced with Izzy, she was never scared—or at least she wouldn't admit to it. She was hatching a plan, but I'd play along.

I glanced over at her, taking in her beauty and feeling slightly guilty, but not enough to make me undo her cuffs. Izzy restrained was priceless. She was like MasterCard—everywhere I wanted to be.

"I got ya. I won't let anything happen to you."

She had let the sheet drop down a bit when she'd turned. Her nipple was almost showing, and my hands and mouth itched to feel her.

"Will you lie with me?" She pouted with sad eyes, trying to pull me in and break me down.

Obviously she didn't give me much credit in the intelligence department. Did men always fall for her bullshit? I imagined that, with having four brothers, she was well practiced in getting her way and using her femininity to her advantage.

"That I can do, Izzy." I didn't bother to tell her to cover her eyes. I threw back the blanket and climbed to my feet. Fuck it. I could play too.

Her eyes grew wide as they traveled up my thighs and became fixated on my cock. "You could've warned a girl."

"I don't see a girl here, and you're well acquainted with what I have." I smirked, rounding the bed, not looking over my shoulder. I didn't have to see her to know that she was staring at my ass, taking in my bare skin. "Like what you see?" I teased.

"Yes," she whispered.

There were two things I knew with her words. The first thing I knew was that her answer wasn't a lie. She was affected no matter how much she wanted to deny it. The second was that the niceness that had oozed out of her mouth was bullshit. There were no weapons near her, and I assumed she hoped to charm me with her nakedness to gain her freedom.

"You sure about this?" I asked as I stood on the opposite side of her bed, stark naked and unashamed.

She nodded and pulled back the blankets for me to climb in next to her.

I slid across the stiff sheets that sounded more like paper than cotton as my body moved closer to her. I punched the pillow a couple of times, trying to find comfort in my limited amount of space, but it was useless with Izzy this close to me. My semi-hard dick had grown rock solid with her proximity.

"James, will you hold me?" she asked, turning to me with those same doe eyes.

"Always," I said as I faced her, placing my front to her side. I rested my hard length against her thigh and saw her eyes grow wide before a small smile played on her lips.

I couldn't hide how attracted I was to her. I'd never had the capacity to turn off a hard-on. There was only one way to tame the beast, and she was currently at my mercy.

Turning her face toward me, she stared in my eyes, and I could see emotion behind her wild sapphire eyes. As part of the agency, I'd been trained in reading emotion and knowing when someone lied during an interrogation. Izzy wasn't hard to read, since I knew her personality from firsthand experience and Thomas's stories.

"Kiss me," she blurted out, and bit her lip.

"I thought you'd never ask."

There was nothing more I wanted in this world than to taste her again, but I wouldn't get to taste all of her like I wanted. It would be an appetizer. Just enough to drive me mad and remind her of our night together.

I leaned over, hovering just above her lips as I looked into her eyes. "Last chance," I warned, waiting for her to respond.

"I want you, James," she whispered against my lips before moving her mouth to meet mine.

Her mouth felt soft, and I craved to feel her lips wrapped around my dick, sucking me off and choking on my hardness. What started as a gentle kiss turned hot and heavy as my need for her intensified. Leaning over, I held her face in my hand, resting my thumb against our mouths.

She didn't smell the same. The stench from the biker bar had almost washed out her perfume. I hadn't been able to be near a woman who wore the same scent without growing hard.

Her mouth was unforgettable. The way it moved across my skin, devouring my lips, and took all of me was something I could never wipe from my mind.

She moaned as I swept my tongue against hers. I nipped her lips,

CHELLE BLISS

drawing them into my mouth and sucking with enough pressure to cause them to be swollen tomorrow. I wanted her to remember where I'd been.

Moving my hand away from her face, I let it fall to her neck, feeling her pulse race under my palm. What started as a plan had turned into something more, something that could swallow us whole and suck us in so deep we wouldn't be able to turn back. She dug her nails into my back, scraping down, and rested her hand just above my ass.

As she whimpered in my mouth, pushing her leg against my dick, I pulled back and looked at her. "You want me? " I asked, resting my forehead against hers.

Breathing raggedly, she swallowed and answered, "Yes," as she slid her hand down to my ass and squeezed.

I smirked, moving myself on top of her before taking her lips again. I captured her moans and tiny whimpers in my mouth as I pushed my cock against her G-string, driving her closer to the edge.

"James, my hand," she whispered, grinding her pussy against me. "Please. I want to touch you."

I was tempted to free her hand. I wanted to feel her fingers roam my skin and her fingernails scratch down my back, but I hadn't been born yesterday.

Sliding my tongue down her neck, I latched on to the sensitive spot near her collarbone. She cried out, flinching from the pressure of the bite. I fisted the thin scrap of lace she thought was underwear, ripped it from her skin, and tossed it on my floor.

She sucked in a quick breath, pushing her hips into me. "Hand," she whimpered.

Hearing her beg made my dick harder than it had been before. I could feel her wetness against my length as I feasted on her skin. She was right where I wanted her—horny and ready to take all of me.

Placing my hands on either side of her, I captured her lips, moving my hips to glide against her heat. I backed away, stared in her eyes, and pushed myself off her.

As I stood, her eyes grew wide and she pulled at the restraints. "What the fuck?" she thundered.

"I know your game, Izzy," I replied as I walked toward my bed.

She kicked the mattress and grunted. "I don't know what the hell you're talking about. Get your ass over here and finish what you started."

I smiled, sitting on the edge of the bed, my cock standing at attention, and looked at her. "You started it. You only want me to take off the handcuffs, and that shit ain't happening."

"I wanted you, James." She stilled in the bed and stared at the ceiling.

"You'll get me when you're not trying to play me for a fool."

"I wasn't," she pleaded, closing her eyes and exhaling.

"The next time you have me, you'll be begging for it, and maybe, just maybe, I'll give it to you."

"I won't beg."

I smiled, fisting my shaft as I stroked the length. "I won't fuck you again until you're begging for me to fuck you. Fuck you like I did months ago."

She turned toward me, her eyes staring at my dick. "I won't beg."

I continued to move my hands up and down, teasing myself just as much. "You. Will. Beg."

"You're an asshole. I've never begged a man for cock," she said through gritted teeth with her body uncovered and on full display.

"Those were boys, Izzy. I'm a man. I remember how hard you came with me, how many times you came on my cock and in my mouth. You fuckin' loved it."

"I was drunk," she protested, stroking the space between her breasts with her fingertips as she moved them up to her neck and traced the same path down toward her belly button.

Sweet fucking Jesus, watching her touch herself made me want to throw my brilliant plan out the window and fuck her senseless.

Her olive skin was highlighted with tattoos. Most of her tattoos were hidden from public view. They were for her personal enjoyment. She had a dragon down her left ribcage with the word "Gallo" underneath. Near her left breast, she had an intricate hibiscus flower in vibrant reds and oranges. The leaves and vines wrapped around her breast, almost cradling it. For a tattoo artist, she hadn't overdone the artwork yet.

Her piercings captured my attention the most. Her nipples and the hood just above her clit were pierced. I wanted to yank on it with my teeth and scrape against her clit, causing her to chant my name. The small piercings hanging from her nipples had me fantasizing about the ways I could put them to use. I imagined restraining her using those alone. Fuck, I needed to stop thinking about fucking her.

"Not an excuse. I didn't take advantage of you," I said, pulling on the tip, running my fingers over the apadravya. "And I know you loved feeling this," I declared as I gave the piercing a tug, "stroking you from the inside."

"I'll admit, the happydravya is a nice touch," she conceded, pursing her lips.

"Happydravya?" I asked, tightening my grip around the shaft.

"It's a nickname for that type of piercing."

I released my cock, too close to coming, and placed my legs in the bed as I swiveled around. "Go to bed."

"That's it?"

"Yep. That's it, doll. You won't get my cock until you're on your hands and knees, begging for me to fuck you. It won't be as a ploy to untie your hands."

"Asshole."

"I'll fuck you there too. I'm taking all of you the next time I sink my dick in you balls deep." I punched the pillow, resting my head against the lumpy mess.

"You're so full of yourself," she whispered as she lay on her back and pulled the covers over her breasts.

I smiled, knowing that she was right. I was an asshole and full of myself, but she was right there with me. The girl had confidence and bullshit down pat. She was a master and could get her way with any man—anyone but me. I was impervious to her charms.

"You'll be full of me again someday soon."

"Fuck off," she hissed.

"Good night, Isabella," I crooned as I switched off the lamp and closed my eyes.

She didn't reply. I could hear her breathing, jagged at first, begin to slow. Once she was asleep, I allowed myself to think of making her mine as I drifted off.

Isabella Gallo wasn't an easy target, but nothing worth having ever is.

She didn't know it yet, but I had my sights set on her, and I always got what I wanted.

6

LYING TO MYSELF

IZZY

My body was covered with sweat as I kicked off the sheets. James had invaded my goddamn dreams. Motherfucker had gotten into my head last night with his smug bullshit.

The brown '70s alarm clock on the nightstand read eight. The drapes were closed and blocking out the sunlight, but the illumination of the television made James glow like an angel. Not an angel sent by God, but a fallen one put on Earth to torture me. The numbness in my arm had woken me from the wet dream I'd been having. Once again, I'd been denied the orgasm I needed and wanted.

The blankets had shifted as he slept. One leg rested on top, the other still underneath and hiding. I sat up, placing my back against the headboard, and took in his wicked beauty.

He was exactly how I liked him best—silent.

I'd never had the chance to really look at him. I couldn't bring myself to give him the satisfaction of drinking him in. He towered over me. He was wide too, more than twice my width, and he easily overshadowed me. Not only was he bigger than I was, he was cockier too.

He looked like a giant in the tiny-ass bed. The man needed a California king to look like a normal-sized person. His feet touched the end and almost hung off as his head rested just below the headboard. Even when he was sleeping, when his muscles should be the most relaxed, everything was taut and hard.

His washboard abs looked like a product of Photoshop, and flexed with his breathing. His black hair was longer than the last time I'd seen him. It lay across his forehead in a wild mess, touching his eyebrows. His lips twitched slightly, and I ached to touch them. They were full and made to be kissed. It was a shame they usually spouted such smug shit.

I admired his tattoos, which flowed down his shoulder and ran up his ribcage. He must've spent hours in the chair. It wasn't colorful artwork— all of it was black with gray shading. Waves stretched across his side, reaching from his hip to just under his armpits. Riding the waves were koi fish and Japanese-inspired flowers. His shoulder piece was as unique as the other. The claws of the dragon touched his pec, ran down his shoulder, and ended a couple of inches above his elbow.

Each one of my brothers had a dragon tattoo, and even I had one on my ribcage. It was a family thing—a symbol of our togetherness and all that bullshit. I'd just thought it was a kick-ass tattoo.

The fact that James had a dragon tattoo could enter him into the Gallo brotherhood without needing extra ink. I hoped he never discovered that simple fact. He'd probably go off about how we had been made for each other. Yada, yada. The man probably thought he was God's gift to women.

"Like what you see?" his deep-sleep voice asked.

I closed my eyes, knowing that I'd been caught, and sighed. "Just looking at your ink and nothing more."

"Sleep well?" He rubbed his eyes and yawned.

I jiggled the cuffs in the air. "How do you think I slept?" I growled.

"Stiff?" he asked, a playful smile spreading across his lips.

"Sounds like your problem, not mine." I laughed, but inside, I was secretly dying.

We had been so close to having sex last night. What had started out as a plan to get him to let me go had turned into something more. The memories from Joey's wedding night came flooding back, and I wanted more. I'd rather him think it had all been just an act. That was preferable to admitting that I wanted him.

"Can you take these off now? I have to pee."

James stood, stretching his muscles and showing off his body. The man had no shame. I didn't either. He grabbed the key off the desk near the door and sat on the bed, staring at me.

"What?" I snapped, annoyed and over the entire situation.

"I like you like this." He smiled, rubbing his chin as he ran his finger across his lips.

"Well, you better memorize it, because you'll never see me like this again," I muttered, chewing the inside of my cheek.

"I bet I will, Izzy. You can't resist me forever."

"I didn't know you were trying, Jimmy."

Starting at my wrist, he lightly ran his fingers down my arm and traced a path to my chin. He stroked my cheek and stared into my eyes. "I'm telling you now. I love a good chase and a worthy adversary. You. Will. Be. Mine," he said calmly, swiping his thumb across my bottom lip.

I swallowed hard, trying to get the lump that had formed in my throat to disappear. "I don't go for the caveman shit," I insisted, trying not to let him hear the delight his words had caused me.

"You do. You just won't admit it." He leaned forward, kissing the corner of my mouth.

I closed my eyes, savoring the scent of him. He smelled amazing. The light hint of musk and leftover cologne invaded my senses.

I turned my face and said, "I have to pee or I'll do it right here."

"You always have an excuse. Keep running, but I'll get you in the end."

What a cocky-ass motherfucker. I'd grown up with cocky. I knew it well. My ability to sniff it out had been honed since I was a child. I'd spent years trying to avoid it. It wasn't that I wanted a pussy; I just didn't want someone who felt like they owned me. No one told me what to do. I was Izzy Gallo. Slave to no one and master of my destiny.

I glared at him, about ready to start shifting in the bed from having to go and the effect James was having on me. "Please let me up," I said, playing the sweet card.

"Do your business and then let's hit it. I want to get you home as soon as possible so I can get back to Thomas," he replied as he reached for the cuff. Holding my wrist, he worked the key in the lock, freeing me.

After pulling my wrist down, I rubbed it, soothing the spot the metal had rubbed against all night. "Thomas should be your priority right now," I said as I rolled off the other side of the bed and away from him. "Not me."

"I'm a multi-tasker." He laughed. "Plus, your sweet ass is the one in front of me, so you take the top spot."

As I walked by the bed, he reached out quickly and swatted my ass. I jumped, turning to face him, and glared. "What the fuck was that for?"

"I couldn't help smacking that beautiful ass. Next time I do it, I'm going to be buried inside you and you'll be begging me for more."

I grabbed my clothes off the floor near his feet and stood, leaning into his space. "You'll be the one begging, Jimmy. You bet your tight, hard ass on that one."

The corner of his mouth turned up and his emerald-green eyes sparkled. They were an amazing shade of green. A picture would never capture their beauty and the depth of color. I needed to stop thinking of how beautiful he was and stick to my guns. James would not get what he wanted from this girl.

"Doll, I'm flattered you noticed my tight, hard ass." He laughed, grabbing my face quickly and planting a kiss on my lips.

I felt the spark, just like the one I'd felt the first night he kissed me in the elevator. We had electricity—enough that we could probably light up a small town for a year—but no spark was worth dealing with his smug ass every day.

Pushing him away, I smacked him. "Don't ever do that unless I want it."

"Oh, you did," he said, shaking his head and breaking out into laughter.

I placed my open palm against his head, pushing him backward. "Clearly we need to go over when no means no."

I could hear his laughter as I walked toward the tiny bathroom. After closing the door, I tossed my clothes to the floor and leaned against the cool wooden surface. Sealing my eyes shut, I rested my hands on the door, and breathed.

James had my number. I was so totally fucked. I didn't know if I should be happy or totally pissed off. I liked the idea of the chase. Fuck, it could be fun as hell, but knowing what it meant if I were to be captured did not make me overly excited. I loved a good sparring partner as much as the next person, but James was an entirely different animal. He wasn't a pushover, an easy victim. No, he was the worst kind of all—a clear-cut victor and an opponent I couldn't beat.

I had to channel my inner Tyson. The man had known that Holyfield would kick his ass and he wouldn't win with his fists alone. He'd resorted to biting the dude's ear off to not show his weakness. I'd be like Mike. Play dirty or lose it all.

A small knock made me jump. "What?" I yelled as I slowly peeled myself off the door.

"Just wanted to make sure you didn't slip out on me. I didn't hear any activity."

Where the hell would I have gone? There wasn't even a window in this craptastic bathroom. "I'm almost done," I sang, hovering over the toilet.

I heard his footsteps as he walked away, giving me privacy. It had never felt so good to go to the bathroom. Shivers racked my body from having held it so long. Afterward, I threw on my clothes and washed my face. What I wouldn't have done for some makeup and a toothbrush. The motel had been kind enough to supply not only soap, but also a small bottle of mouthwash. I cracked open the top, taking a mouthful and swishing it around. Using my finger, I scrubbed my gums and teeth before spitting it out. I wasn't high maintenance, but this was a little beyond my comfort zone.

As I opened the door, my eyes took in James—fully naked and leaning against the wall.

"Have you no shame, man?" I asked as my eyes traveled up his body and stopped on his face.

My face felt flushed and my belly dropped. I wanted to jump on him, wrap my legs around his hard body, and rub my pussy against him. I hated him. His devilish grin, his sparkling eyes, and his beautiful face pissed me off. The man played games and played them well.

"What's to be ashamed of? I saw you staring last night. I thought I'd give you one last look before I got dressed."

"You're obviously delusional." I glared at him and started to walk past him.

He grabbed my wrist, pulling me back. "Stay right here."

"Why?" I asked, looking down at his grip on me.

"I don't trust you not to bolt. You stay right outside this door or I can handcuff you again. I prefer the second option, but I leave it entirely in your hands."

"I'm not going anywhere. Just do what you need to do so I can get the hell away from you." I tore my wrist from his hand and sneered.

"You're never getting away from me, Izzy. Right here." He pointed to the spot outside the bathroom, close enough that he could keep his eye on me while he was inside.

I saluted him, feeling the need to be a smartass, as he stalked into the bathroom and left the door ajar. "Where's my phone?" I asked. It wasn't in my pants pocket where I'd left it.

"Nightstand."

"Can I grab it, master?" I asked.

I heard him suck in a breath, pausing a moment before answering. "You don't know what those words do to me, and yes, you may."

I rolled my eyes just for the sheer satisfaction, because there was no one else to see me do it, and walked toward the nightstand. As I grabbed my phone, something on the floor caught my eye. Sticking out from under the bed skirt was my black lace G-string. Unable to help myself, I picked it up and stuffed it in his bag next to the door.

"Where are you?" he yelled from the bathroom.

"I'm coming!" I yelled back as I headed toward my assigned spot.

Jesus, the man was a control freak.

"Mmm, I like the sound of that," he said as he walked out with a smile.

"Get dressed already." I sat on the bed, crossing my legs, and enjoyed the increased pressure on my core. Why couldn't he have dressed while I'd been in the bathroom? "Or I'll leave without you." I wouldn't, but he didn't need to know. I didn't even know where the fuck we were to have someone to pick me up.

"Keep your panties on. I'll be ready in two seconds." He grabbed his clothes, pulling on his jeans first, tucking his dick inside, and then zipping them. His t-shirt he slowly pulled over his head, thinking he was torturing me.

I didn't stare at him, but I watched him out of the corner of my eye as I pretended to check my phone. The only messages I'd received overnight were from Flash. He seemed to be in a panic.

"Who ya texting?" James asked as he looked over my shoulder, catching me off guard.

"Flash is worried."

"Fuck Flash. Put that phone down." He grabbed my hand, plucking the phone from my grip.

"He's my friend," I said, glaring at him.

"He sold you out and left you at the hands of the MC. That's no friend I ever want."

"You don't know him."

"I know enough about him. Do not respond to him. If you never listen to me again, Izzy, please do on this one thing." He ran his fingers through his hair, taming the strands that had wandered when he had put on his shirt.

"I know he's a pussy. Trust me. I'm pissed the fuck off at him, but I want to tell him that I'm fine."

"You wait to do that shit when I have you on the other coast and in the protection of your family."

"You worry too much," I argued, grabbing the phone and pushing it in my back pocket.

"You don't worry enough." He lifted his bag, touching the small of my back as he opened the door. "Let's go."

I squinted when the bright Florida sun hit my face as we walked out of the dark motel room. I hooded my eyes and looked around. We were in the middle of nowhere and far from home.

"This is going to be a long-ass ride."

"You make it sound like a bad thing," he said as he walked to his bike, grabbed the helmet, and held it out to me.

I approached, ripping it from his grasp. "Three hours on the back of your bike doesn't sound like a joyride."

"You say the word and I'll pull over and give you something to smile about," he murmured as he touched my cheek.

With my free hand, I batted his hand away from my face and put the helmet on, cinching the straps tight. "In your dreams," I huffed out, standing next to the sleek Harley V-Rod Muscle bike. I'd spent enough time around boys with their toys to know my Harleys. It wasn't traditional, but it matched his personality perfectly—strong, sexy, and loud.

"It'll be my reality. Just you wait, beautiful." He climbed on, twisting his body before patting the back seat.

I stared at the sky, closing my eyes and making a silent plea to put distance between us. Why had I fucked his brains out the night we met?

Holding his shoulder, I adjusted myself. Wrapping my arms around his torso, I smashed my tits against his back and smiled. I'd make the ride just as uncomfortable for him as he always made me. I'd invented games.

7

UNFORGETTABLE

JAMES

THE GIRL HAD GAME AND MAD FUCKING SKILLS. I'D NEVER MET A FEMALE who was as full of shit as I was. Izzy was everything I'd ever wanted in a woman—fierce, strong, driven, and full of attitude.

Riding with her on the back of my bike for over three hours should've been boring and tedious. I was finding out that nothing we did together could be described with those words.

She'd taken every chance to brush against my dick when we were stopped at a light. Running her hand down my thigh, all in the name of stretching her back. She hadn't just held me to stay on the bike. She'd felt me up and I fucking knew it.

As I pulled into her drive, I could feel my semi-hard dick I'd been sporting for the last twenty miles start to stiffen. It wouldn't happen today. I had shit to do, including a long ride back to Daytona.

I parked the bike, securing it in place before turning off the engine. Izzy pushed off using my shoulder and plucked the helmet from her head. Leaning over, she shook out her hair, flipping it like a wet dream. She was a fucking tease.

"Thanks for the ride." She smirked, holding out the helmet.

"Can I use the bathroom before I head back?" I asked. I figured I could have a little more fun with her before I walked out of her life for a short time. I knew I'd be back. No one could keep me away from Izzy Gallo.

She rubbed her face and stared at the ground. "If you must," she mumbled, bringing her eyes to meet mine.

In the sunlight, her eyes matched the color of the Gulf on a sunny day. Turquoise with hints of sky blue. They were lush and big for her face. I didn't speak as I hopped off the bike and stretched.

She walked away, heading for the door, and I followed behind, admiring her ass. Looking over her shoulder, she glared at me before stopping in front of her door and unlocking it.

The house sat on a canal, the Gulf of Mexico not far away from the multistory dwelling. The façade was white with muted orange trim, and it stood three stories tall. Following her inside, I took in the beauty of the living room. It was like Izzy—loud and unforgiving and alive with vibrant color. Large windows lined the back of the house as the sun cascaded through the room and shone on the dark wooden floors.

"Restroom?" I asked, looking around, taking in the layout of her home.

"Over there," she replied, motioning to the left with her head.

I walked away, finding a hallway where she had pointed. I stopped when I passed an open door that held a bedroom. I didn't think it was hers. It was all white and too plain for her tastes. I continued to the next room and found the Holy Grail.

This was Izzy's bedroom. The walls were painted a deep red with black trim. Black curtains hung from the floor-to-ceiling windows. Along the opposite wall was a king-sized bed with black satin bedding. It wasn't feminine, but totally her.

"Find it?" Her voice carried down the hallway, forcing me back into the hall.

"Yeah!" I yelled, and moved toward the last door on the right.

After I was done, I didn't bother looking around before I headed back to find Izzy. She was standing in the kitchen, moving with ease, a coffee pot in hand.

"Want a cup before you head out?"

Look at Betty fuckin' Crocker. "Sure," I said, my voice uncertain.

"It's the least I can do. I need you to make it back to my brother safely."

"Well, I'm kind of hungry too." I smiled, taking a seat at her breakfast bar.

"I don't cook, and you're pushing it."

"I'll grab something at the gas station down the street," I responded, propping my chin on my hand and staring at her.

She blanched. "I have some leftovers from my mom's place." She opened the fridge and bent over to look through the contents.

It was a perfect ass shot. I grinned, watching her move.

"How about some pasta?" she asked with her head still stuck inside.

"Perfect." I leaned back, looking away before she turned around. I wouldn't fuck with pasta from Mrs. Gallo. Thomas always raved about it.

She pulled off the plastic wrap and splashed a bit of water on the plate before sticking it in the microwave. "Is my brother really okay, James?" she asked with her back to me.

I sighed, wishing I could fuck with her mind, but I wanted to put her at ease. "He's doing okay, Izzy. He's smart and tough. He's made it deeper than any other agent." I tapped my foot on the floor, feeling uncomfortable while trying to shovel a load of bullshit at her.

No one in the life was safe. It could all end without notice, in the blink of an eye.

"That doesn't sound so promising." The microwave beeped, and she grabbed the plate from inside. "Will he be done soon?" she asked as she placed the pasta in front of me.

"Hopefully. We're trying to get him out ASAP, but you know your brother. He wants more. He's never content."

She grabbed a fork from the dish strainer and held it out to me. "That's how all the Gallos are. We always want more." She smiled.

"I'm counting on it, doll." I snatched the fork from her hands before she could throw it at me. I knew she hated it, but I wanted to change the subject from Thomas to something that made me happy.

"Just eat and shut up." She took the dishrag from the sink and wiped down the counters.

Shoving the first forkful in my mouth was sheer happiness. Even a couple of days old and dry, the taste exploded in my mouth. I hadn't had homemade sauce this damn good since my grandmother passed years ago.

"Mmm," I mumbled, taking another forkful. "I never pictured the domestic side of you." I laughed, placing the noodles on my tongue.

"Someone has to clean. I do it all myself, except cook. That is my weakness. Never had the patience for that shit."

Swallowing my food, I offered, "I could teach you."

Her hand stilled as she looked at me with big eyes. "You cook?"

"I've been known to, yes. I'd love to get your mom's recipe for this sauce."

She shook her head and stared. "That is for Gallo family members only. It's a closely guarded secret. So, what do you cook?" She leaned over the counter and gawked at me as I attacked the pasta.

"Anything you want. I had to learn to cook, being single. I couldn't maintain this body and eat shit food all the time."

"Interesting," she mumbled, watching me shove the fork in my mouth. "Never took you as a Paula Deen."

I laughed, almost choking on my food. "I think of myself as a better-looking version of Emeril."

"His food is so damn good. I'll never believe you can cook like that."

"Someday you'll find out." I wiped my face after I inhaled the pasta.

She pulled my plate from the counter, setting it in the sink. "I won't, but I'll take you at your word."

I smiled but didn't respond to her remark. She turned me down at every opportunity, but I was fine with the chase. Fuck, I loved a good game of cat and mouse. It was one of the reasons I'd joined law enforcement.

"It's quite a place you have here," I said, swiveling around on my stool.

"Want to see the upstairs? It's my favorite part of the house."

"Sure. And I'd love that cup of coffee."

"You can bring it up with you," she said as she grabbed two cups. "Black?"

"Yes, please."

She filled the cup, adding sugar to hers before turning around with her hands full. "Here," she said, placing it in front of me. "Let's go."

Once I took my cup, I followed her closely up the stairs I hadn't noticed before. I had been lost in my thoughts of her and all the dirty things I wanted to do to her.

"This is why I bought the place," she said when we reached the top.

As I made my way behind her, the stunning landscape came into view. She had a view of the Gulf of Mexico in the distance. The sun shimmering across the water made it look like a sheet of glass covered in glitter.

"Stunning," I muttered, sipping the coffee.

"Come outside on the deck and have your coffee before you go." She pulled open the sliding glass doors.

"I'm not used to the nice-girl act," I said as I followed her.

"I'm not always a twat." She laughed, sitting down on the swing, facing away from me. "Close the door, please."

"I'd never call you a twat, Izzy. You have such a mouth."

"You love my mouth, from what I remember, James."

"I so fucking do." I sighed as I closed the door and made my way toward her. As I sat, I said, "This is a little slice of heaven."

"It's my serenity. When shit gets bad or my life feels overwhelming, this is where I come to center myself."

Listening to her talk while we sat together, I felt like I was seeing the real Izzy for the first time. She had her guard down and was speaking to me differently. There was no sarcasm in her voice, no smartass comment —just Izzy. I liked this side of her, but the other one made me wild and drove me crazy.

A comfortable silence settled between us as we sipped our coffee and gently rocked back and forth. The last thing I wanted to do was get back on my bike and leave her, but I had to. Duty called. If I didn't go back and something happened to her brother, I'd never be able to make her mine. All hope for the future would be killed.

"I better go," I said. "Thank you for the perfect ending to the last twenty-four hours." I didn't look at her as I spoke. I stared off into the distance, taking in the beauty of the Gulf and longing for this life.

I loved my job, but some nights, I wished for someone to be mine, someone to spend my life with. I didn't want to lead a senior-citizen life-style. I wanted a partner, someone I could spar with and make love to at the drop of a dime. Izzy was what I wanted; she just hadn't accepted her fate. She couldn't resist me for long.

"This has been nice. The rest, not so much. I could've done without the cuffs, James." She turned to me and smiled.

I laughed. "You'll learn to love them." I winked at her, and her cheeks grew flushed.

"In your fucking dreams," she shot back, rolling her eyes.

I reached up, stroking her cheeks, and leaned into her space. "I know many uses for handcuffs besides arrest. Imagine your body at my mercy. I could feast on your flesh for hours, Isabella," I murmured against her lips.

She blinked slowly and stared into my eyes. "You say such pretty shit, but I'll pass on the offer."

Running my hand to the back of her neck, I gripped her roughly, holding her in place. "I could have you right now if I wanted. Don't kid yourself. I don't buy your bullshit. You want me as much as I want you. You haven't forgotten how good my cock feels inside you."

Her eyes flashed and her tongue darted out, swiping against my top lip. "You'll never—"

I captured her words in my mouth, crushing my lips to hers to quiet her. The smart-mouthed woman I fucking craved was back, and I couldn't control myself. I didn't want to listen to her lies. I knew I'd have her again.

As my tongue slid across hers, mingling her taste with mine, the sweetness of the sugar from her coffee made my mouth water. She tasted so fucking good. I'd leave her with a reminder of what I felt like and how I tasted.

The tiny hairs on the back of her neck rose, brushing against my fingers as we kissed. She panted into my mouth, kissing me back with her hand resting on my forearm. Her body spoke the words she was too afraid to say.

I backed away, breaking the kiss, and stared at her face. We were both breathless and didn't release our grip on each other.

"What were you going to say?" I asked, trying to calm my breathing.

"I don't know," she said, her voice breathy and her face flushed.

"I can show myself out." I stood and grabbed my coffee cup off the small table next to the swing.

Izzy sat there looking like a deer in headlights as I reached to open the door to the house. "Wait!" she yelled, standing on shaky legs.

"Yes?" I asked, turning to her.

"I can at least show you out," she said.

I smiled and released the door handle.

"It's more for self-preservation, really." She opened the door, trotting down the steps in front of me. "I want to make sure you don't leave a reason to come back."

"I don't need to leave something behind," I said as I reached the last step, following her into the kitchen and toward the front door. "I'm all the reason you need." I walked up to her as she stopped by the door and pressed her against the flat surface, brushing my lips against hers. "My cock is a good reason. I remember you mumbling something about God when I was finger-fucking you. And then…then there's my mouth; you almost suffocated me to death. Do I need more reasons?"

She glared at me and exhaled loudly, her breath hitting me in the face. "James, I think it's you who can't forget my pussy. It was so damn good you keep coming back for more. We'll see who's begging." She ducked, weaving out of my grasp, and laughed as she stood behind me.

I hung my head and smiled. The girl had smartass perfected. "Maybe we both have a problem." I straightened my back and turned toward her. "We'll find out soon enough. Thanks for the meal and coffee, doll."

A flash of anger clouded her eyes before a small smile spread across her lips. "You're welcome. Keep my brother safe, ya hear me?"

I opened the door and waved, leaving her behind. "I will. That I promise you, Isabella."

I climbed on my bike, smiling as I pulled away, and caught a glimpse of her standing in the door watching me head away from her home. No one did that if they hated the person. The girl had it just as bad as I did. Now I had to figure out how to get her to admit it.

8

GALLO FAMILY CLUSTERFUCK

IZZY

I SPENT THE REST OF SATURDAY AT HOME RELAXING. NO ONE EXPECTED me at work, so I didn't bother. I answered a few text messages and lay around. Even Flash got a short response. I told him that I was fine but too pissed to talk to his sorry ass. He took the hint and left me alone. I mean, what the fuck could he say anyway? "Sorry I left you at the mercy of an MC guy so he could rape you"? He was a total dumbass.

I didn't feel like hearing bullshit from my brothers if I went into the shop. I'd have enough explaining to do showing up at Sunday dinner, but I had to go. I needed to tell everyone that I had seen Tommy. They'd be relieved that he was well, but totally pissed off at me.

I rubbed my face as I stood outside my parents' front door. I could hear everyone inside laughing and carrying on. We were never a quiet bunch.

"Here goes nothing," I whispered to myself, trying to put on a happy face and come up with a bullshit excuse.

I opened the door, walked into the foyer, and dropped my purse next to the stairs. "I'm here!" I yelled, heading toward the great room.

The smell of pasta sauce filled the home and made me think of James. He'd looked so damn hot sitting in my kitchen, scarfing down pasta like it was the best fucking thing he'd ever eaten. I wanted to plop my pussy on the plate and let him attack it like it was his last fucking meal.

I shook my head, clearing James from my mind. The man had me all crazy and losing focus.

"What the fuck are you doing here?" Anthony hollered, standing from the couch and stalking toward me.

"Nice to see you too, brother." I smiled, wrapping him in my arms and patting him on the back.

"You weren't supposed to be back until tonight. What happened?" he asked, backing away and looking me up and down. "Are you okay?"

"I'm fine, Anth. Really. Bike Week just wasn't for me."

Out of the corner of my eye, I saw Joey and Mike striding toward us. *Here we go. Let the inquisition begin.*

"Hey, guys," I said, turning toward them and holding out my arms.

"Don't give us that bullshit, Izzy. What happened?" Mike growled, coming to halt and glaring at me.

"I just wanted to come home. I'm not built for that life." I looked at Joey, trying to wrap him in a hug.

"I call bullshit, little sister. You better spill and spill quick before I track Flash's ass down and beat him to a bloody pulp," Joey snarled.

I pinched my nose between my fingers, trying to massage away the stress. "Honestly, I'm fine, guys. I made it home in one piece. I just missed you, is all."

"Bullshit," Anthony coughed, and looked at the floor.

Glaring at him, I sighed. "Listen, I'll tell you all about it, but I want to say hi to Ma and Pop first."

"You will spill, Izzy." Joey crossed his arms over his chest and did his best to look intimidating. He wasn't to me; I'd known him my entire life. I knew the man underneath the big, hard exterior.

"I know, I know." I threw my hands up, walking away to find Ma, who was in the kitchen, pouring the sauce over the angel hair pasta.

"Hey, Ma," I said as I wrapped my arms around her from behind. I loved her more than life itself. She was everything to me, even though she thought I favored my pop over her. I did at times, only because he was a pushover and I loved him for it.

"I'm so happy you're here, baby girl. I thought I heard you walk in."

"Probably heard the three stooges out there."

She laughed, her body shaking in my grip. "They can be a pain in the ass, can't they?" She giggled, turning in my arms.

"Ma, I haven't heard you use that language in a long time." I kissed her cheek, a small laugh escaping.

"Sorry. I'm just stressed. Dinner!" she yelled over my head and toward the four men, who were now sitting in the living room along with the other two females in my life, ones I adored like they were my sisters.

I flinched, covering my ears as she yelled. Years of raising five children had given her the lung capacity to not need a megaphone to be heard over the loud, obnoxious cackles of their voices.

"Jesus, Ma. Warn a girl before you yell in her ear. Will ya?"

She chuckled and grabbed the giant bowl of pasta from the counter. "I want to hear all about your weekend. Was it exciting?" she asked as I followed her to the dining room.

Everyone was already seated. They must've run when they'd heard her voice. No one kept her waiting—at least not if they liked their life too much. She wasn't to be fucked with.

"It wasn't what I'd expected." I sighed.

I sat down in my usual chair next to Joey, who sat at the head opposite my father. My mother always took the seat to his right; often, I'd catch them holding hands while they ate. Suzy sat next to Joey in the same manner my parents sat. Mia and Michael were across the table next to my mother, and Anthony sat on the other side of me. We all had our places, but there was always a void at the table—Thomas's spot.

All eyes were on me. I felt them. They were waiting to hear why I'd returned early. The only ones not paying attention were my parents. My ma was speaking with my father and dishing him out a heaping helping of pasta.

"So, dear, tell us about your trip," Pop said after Ma filled his plate.

Smiling, I began to speak. "Well, it was a train wreck of sorts." I looked down at the table, grabbing my napkin and placing it across my lap. I rested my elbows on the table and caught Joey's watchful eye. "Don't say it," I warned him, holding up my hand.

"Are you okay?" Ma asked, continuing to work her way around the table.

"I'm fine, Ma. I wasn't hurt."

"What the hell did Flash do?" Michael asked, cracking his knuckles as he glared at me. I knew that suspicious look; he'd used it on me many times as a child when pulling information out of me.

"He didn't do a thing. That's the problem." I laughed, preferring to freak everyone out for a moment.

"Izzy," Pop warned.

"Not like that, Pop. I saw James," I croaked out for some unknown reason, hoping to take the heat off Flash.

"Oh my God," Suzy screeched, with a giant smile.

"Who the hell is James?" Anthony asked, looking at me with knitted brows.

I opened my mouth to speak, but Suzy, in her excitement, answered for me. "He's Thomas's friend. He brought the card from Thomas to the wedding. Izzy met him there."

I nodded to Suzy, not worried about anything else she'd say about James. No one, not even Suzy, knew that I'd slept with James the night of the wedding. That information I hadn't shared with a soul. I knew when to keep a secret, and that was one I'd hold close to the vest.

"Isabella, did he have anything to say about your brother?" Ma asked, and I couldn't hold out any longer.

"Well, that's the thing." I swallowed, readying myself for the barrage of questions and some pissed-off brothers. "Flash took me to a biker bar and we ran into his club."

"I told you to stay the fuck away from that MC," Joey interrupted.

"Language, son," Pop said, and then returned his eyes to me. "Go on."

I shifted in my seat, worried that the dinner would turn into a free-for-all, but I knew the information about James would both be a relief and a worry. "When I got there, one of the men at the table wouldn't look at me. He was acting funny." No one was eating, and everyone was staring at me. "When he finally made eye contact with me, I knew it was Tommy," I said, leaning back in my chair.

A collective gasp sounded around the table as my words seeped in.

"Is he okay?" Ma asked, dabbing at her eyes.

"Yeah, he's good, Ma." It wasn't an outright lie. He was okay, relatively speaking.

"Did you get to talk to him?" Pop asked, resting his fork next to his dinner plate.

"I did. We spent an hour alone together." I nodded and smiled. The last thing I wanted to do was add more worry to their lives. "He promised me he'd be home soon and he asked me to send his love. He misses us all."

"How did he look?" Joey inquired, leaning forward with his hands clasped over his plate.

"He looked tired, but otherwise good," I answered.

"How *exactly* did you get time alone with him?" Anthony asked, the perpetual scowl on his face intensified.

"That's not important," I snapped, glaring back at him and biting my lip.

"Like hell it isn't. Spill it, sister," Joey growled with snarled lips.

"Jesus," I muttered. "He kinda called dibs on me for the night." I smiled, pretending like it was no big deal.

"I'll kill Flash!" Joey yelled, slamming the bottom of his fist on the table.

"Fuck," Anthony groaned.

"Dead man walking," Mike growled.

"Calm the shit down!" I yelled over their ramblings.

"What's that mean?" Ma asked, confusion written all over her face.

Pop shook his head, patting my mother's hand. "I'll explain it later, love," he said to her.

"No matter how it happened, I was able to spend time with Tommy," I said, looking around the table. "I wouldn't trade my time with him for anything—not even the nonsense I had to go through to be with him."

"Tell me more about what he said," Ma said, ignoring the others at the table.

I spent the entire dinner talking about Tommy and answering questions. Knowing that he was alive and breathing was something we didn't know on a day-to-day basis. Not being able to hear his voice over the phone or get a text message were the hardest parts to deal with.

He'd been missing from Sunday dinner for so long that it had become the norm. His seat was never filled; it sat open, waiting for his return.

I ate my last forkful of pasta, placing my napkin on my plate, and sighed. I felt relieved to get the information off my chest and be done with the questioning by my family.

"Thanks for the great dinner, Ma."

She patted my shoulder as she walked by me on the way to the kitchen. "Thank you, Isabella."

I smiled at her, nodding. As she left the room I looked over at my brothers, who were still wearing scowls. They were like little girls who couldn't let shit go easily.

"We're not done here," Joey barked, standing from his seat and carrying his plate in the kitchen.

"Oh boy," I whispered, breaking out into a fit of giggles.

Pop winked at me. He always knew when shit was going down. He had my back. That I knew. He'd make sure the boys didn't get too crazy.

As I stood, plate in hand, Suzy stood too, following behind me.

"James, huh?" she teased, elbowing me as we entered the kitchen.

"Yeah." I rolled my eyes, placing my plate on the counter next to Ma. "Want help?" I asked her as she rinsed the pans.

"Nah, baby. Go sit with everyone. You've had a long weekend. I'll be fine."

I sighed, turning and running into Suzy. She smiled and winked at me. She wanted to know only about James, and it made me uncomfortable. I walked by her and made my way toward the family room and my usual spot on the floor.

"Did you talk to him?" she asked before my ass hit the carpet. She settled down next to me instead of next to Joey.

"Who?" I asked, playing stupid.

"James," she groaned. "Come on. I know there's more there than you're saying." She grinned, tilting her head and studying me.

"We spent some time together."

"Ooooh," she whispered, positioning herself next to me as she sat Indian style.

Suzy was now five months pregnant, and showing. I couldn't imagine having a lump sticking out of the front of me. I always lay on my stomach and would be uncomfortable during the entire pregnancy. I winced thinking about childbirth and babies. I loved them, but fuck. I was nowhere near ready to become a mom.

"Don't you have a man to sit next to?" I hinted, motioning toward Joey.

"Nah. He's okay for now. They're talking sports." She rolled her eyes and put her finger in her open mouth and stuck out her tongue, making a gagging sound.

"What else is new?" I turned toward the television, hoping she'd drop the topic.

"I know there's more to you and James than you're saying, Izzy." She nudged me with her side, almost knocking me over.

"What are you talking about?" I asked, shaking my head and looking into her eyes. "There's nothing between us."

She giggled, covering her mouth with her hand. "I saw you two sneak out of the wedding reception."

I looked at her, my mouth gaping open, shocked by her words. "You never said anything to me before."

"I forgot with the honeymoon and then the baby." She rubbed her belly in a circular motion as she spoke. "You mentioned his name and it all came back to me."

"Lucky me," I whispered, resting my head in my hands.

"Did you sleep with him?" she asked, wiggling her eyebrows.

"No. Wait. When?"

"I knew it!" she roared, breaking into a fit of laughter. "Tell me all about it." She fluttered her eyelashes, moving closer to my face. "I won't tell a soul." She crossed her fingers.

"He got me out of Daytona, but no, I didn't sleep with him this weekend."

"Tell me you did on my wedding night. I want all the juicy details."

"It was such a huge mistake," I whispered.

"Why?" she asked, her eyebrows shooting up and her smile vanishing.

"I knew it the moment I woke up in his hotel room. I got my shit and got the hell out of there."

"Oh, no. You hit it and quit it?"

"Where in the hell did you hear that phrase?" I asked as I started to laugh.

"I've been hanging around you for too long." She laughed, biting her lip.

Talking to Suzy always made me feel better. I knew what I told her never made its way to Joey. He never questioned me on anything I confided in her, and I knew without a doubt he'd ask if it had. My brother couldn't keep a secret. No one in my damn family could, except my girls.

"What are you two talking about?" Mia asked as she stretched out on the other side of me.

I was now in the middle of a Mia and Suzy sandwich, and I couldn't be happier. These were my girls. The sisters I hadn't had growing up, but I was thankful for them now.

"James," Suzy blurted, drawing her lips into her mouth.

"Me likey," Mia said, and laughed.

"How do you know him?" I asked, turning to her, confused.

"Suzy told me about him at the reception. We watched you slink out with him and not return." She cocked her eyebrow and stared at me.

"Fuck," I muttered. "Did anyone else see?"

Mia shook her head, pursing her lips. "I don't think so, and if they did, no one has said anything."

I looked toward the ceiling and sighed. "Thank Christ for small miracles."

"Is he the one?" Mia asked, a giant smile on her face.

"What? I've seen him twice in my entire life. That's quite a leap, Mia."

"I knew about Michael after only a couple of dates."

"When the hell are you two going to get married, then?" I asked. "If you're so sure, why wait?"

She shrugged and picked at her nail. "I'm waiting for him to pop the question."

"Fuck that old-school thinking. Ask him to marry you," I insisted, shaking my head.

"No way in hell would I do that. Michael's too old school and he'd have a coronary."

"Have you two talked about marriage?" Suzy asked.

573

"Yeah. Neither of us is ready to take that plunge."

"He'll ask when the time is right. It took Joey's accident before he popped the question," Suzy said.

"I'm not worried, ladies. I love Michael and we're in a really good place. The clinic is doing so well right now, and living together is enough for me."

"Makes shit less complicated," I said, cracking my knuckles.

"When you're in love, everything is complicated," Suzy said, smiling and rubbing her belly. "Joey has made my life complicated since the moment I met him."

"You didn't fall in love with him right away." I remembered how he'd had to chase Suzy and make her admit her feelings.

"I don't remember not loving him. Sometimes you can only lie to yourself for so long."

"I don't believe in love at first sight," I lied, but didn't even convince myself with that statement.

"Girl, sometimes there's a spark you can't ignore." Suzy rubbed my shoulder. She was always so touchy-feely.

I hung my head, as the girls seemed too ecstatic about my time with James. "Ladies"—I cleared my throat—"I don't do relationships, and certainly not with a man like James. I fucked him once and that's it."

"What do you mean a man like James?" Mia asked with raised eyebrows.

"Mia, you keep wiggling those things up and down and you're going to get a cramp." I laughed, slapping the floor.

She scowled. "Shut the fuck up and spill it, woman. Your deflection doesn't work on me."

"Fine. You two are nosy bitches."

"That's the pot calling the kettle black." Suzy giggled.

"You both know how Mike and Joey are, right?" I whispered.

They looked at each other with dopy smiles, and nodded.

"I don't *like* how they are, and James makes them seem like kittens compared to him."

Mia's mouth opened into an O shape, and Suzy's smiled grew wider. Half of my sisterhood understood my dilemma.

"What's wrong with how your brothers are?" Suzy asked, looking over her shoulder at Joey.

"Um, hello. Bachelorette party ring a bell?" I asked, shaking my head. "They're bossy, demanding, and cocky as hell."

"Yeah," Suzy whispered, turning back to me with that lovesick-puppy look. "I've grown to love it."

"I can't believe I'm going to say this, Suzy, but that man has seriously scrambled your brains." I rested my face in my hands, hiding my eyes and wondering what happened to my girls.

"I get it," Mia said, touching my shoulder. "I get it more than anyone here. Mike made me crazy at first. I had been on my own too long to put up with his bossy bullshit, Izzy."

"Add Joey and Mike together and they don't equal James."

"Fuck me," Mia whispered.

"Exactly." I sighed. "He's too much for me, ladies."

"I felt the sizzle and pop between you two, Izzy," Suzy said.

"Suzy, it was electric, but that doesn't mean I want the man as a part of my life."

"You're scared 'cause he has you nailed," Suzy replied.

"He nailed me all right," I said, trying to hold back a laugh. "And it was fucking amazing."

"I don't see you with someone like Flash. You need someone who won't put up with your brother's bullshit. James is that man. Don't you think so, Mia?" Suzy asked, looking toward Mia.

"That's hard to say, but she definitely needs someone who will tell these boys to go to hell. No wimpy guy will survive in this family. No way in hell."

"He drove me home Saturday." I don't know why I felt the need to share that fact with them, but maybe they needed to understand the caliber of man I was dealing with here.

"And?" Suzy asked, moving closer to me.

"Let's go outside or for a walk. I can't tell you where the others will hear." I sat up, quickly moving to my feet. I held out my arms, helping Suzy and her growing belly off the floor. "We're going to sit outside and enjoy the fresh air," I told the guys, not caring if they were okay with it or not.

They grunted and waved goodbye as the three of us wandered onto the lanai and sat around the table. I faced the living room so I could keep an eye out for anyone heading our way.

"Mia, reach back and close the door all the way," I said, motioning toward the glass siding door with my chin.

"This must be juicy," Suzy shrieked, rubbing her hands together.

I loved her. She was sweet and pure, and she always wanted to think the best of everybody. Usually, she was misguided, but thankfully, she was my biggest cheerleader. Someone like her needed a man like Joey to protect her. It wasn't that she was weak; Suzy was just naïve and way too kind for her own good.

"First off, I did *not* have sex with James this weekend."

"Darn it," Suzy whispered, snapping her fingers as Mia laughed.

"Tommy called James and had him bring me home."

"Sounds like no big deal to me," Mia said, leaning back in the chair, twirling a piece of her long brown hair in her fingers.

"It is a big deal. When I slept with him on your wedding night"—I looked at Suzy before I continued—"I didn't stick around for a goodbye. I grabbed my things and left before he woke up."

"Oh, you're a bad girl," Mia crowed, laughing. "That takes balls."

"Hey, I am who I am. Well, Friday night he didn't want me to 'run away' again."

"Oh boy," Suzy said.

"Anyway"—I turned back to Mia—"he waited for me to fall asleep and he handcuffed me to the bed." I put my head on the table, banging it lightly against the glass surface.

"I like him already," Mia whooped.

"He didn't?" Suzy asked with her mouth hanging open and her eyes as large as saucers.

Lifting my head, I answered her: "He did." I nodded, a small smile playing on my lips. "I tried to convince him to free me, but my charms didn't work."

"Did you try to seduce him?" Mia asked, covering her mouth and laughing.

"Fuck yeah, I did, but he didn't fall for it."

"He left you like that?" Suzy asked. "All night?"

"All night."

"Hold up. How did you try and seduce him?" Mia inquired, leaning forward, clasping her hands together in front of her.

"Well…" I sighed. "I told him I was afraid. He crawled in bed with me and we started to make out."

"Ooooh," Suzy cooed, resting her hands on top of her blossoming belly.

I laughed at her response. It was sexy looking back at it, but when it had happened…well, fuck, it had been sexy then too.

"I asked him to free my hands because I wanted to touch him."

"What did he do?" Mia asked, her right eyebrow shooting up toward her hairline.

"He ripped my panties off and left me in the dust and handcuffed to the bed."

"He plays dirty." Mia laughed. "Yep, I like this James guy."

"Oh fuck off, Mia," I hissed, but couldn't hold on to the fake anger. "He's so fucking bossy."

"He knows your game, sister, and that's why you're scared." Mia smiled, her eyes teary from her laughter.

I blew out a breath through puffy cheeks. I knew she was right. My schemes didn't work and he seemed to know my next move.

"I don't like him," I whined, crossing my arms over my chest.

"Yes, you do," Suzy argued, nodding as she smiled.

"No, I don't."

"You so do. You're fucked." Mia cackled, leaning in her chair and throwing her head back.

"I'm totally fucked," I whispered, closing my eyes as I tried to come to terms with this knowledge.

I didn't want to like James. Men like that always rubbed me the wrong way, but when James did it…well, it sent sparks through my body.

It was a traitor.

9

THE CHASE

JAMES

BIKE WEEK ENDED, AND THIS YEAR HAD BEEN RELATIVELY QUIET compared to previous ones. The Sun Devils MC, along with Thomas, headed back to Leesburg—a town north of Tampa, and their home base.

It had almost been a week since I'd walked out of Izzy's house and headed back to Daytona. I couldn't get her out of my mind. She was like a wet dream I couldn't shake. Her smile, her taste, her smell—everything about her had stayed with me, and I wanted more.

It didn't help when I found her G-string shoved in with my shit. I'd walked out of her house with a hard-on, wanting to slam her against the door and take her. The throbbing in my dick and aching in my balls needed some attention, and I'd do what I needed to do to make it happen.

I twirled my phone in my hand, wondering if I should pull the trigger. Send her a text and find my way in. I couldn't wait any longer. It was fucking killing me. Either I'd die of blue balls or boredom. Izzy Gallo was the only thing that held my attention. It was ten p.m., but I figured she had to be awake. She didn't strike me as the type of girl who turned in early. Plus, she might still be at work.

Me: Hey, beautiful. Thinking of me?

Within seconds, my phone beeped with a reply.

Sexy Fugitive: Who the fuck is this?

I smiled as I thought about how I'd added my number to her phone while she'd slept. I woke up in the middle of the night to check on her and saw the screen light up. It captured my attention, and I couldn't stop myself from sending a message to steal her number. I saved it and added mine to her contact list. I didn't use my name. No, that would have been too boring. I put myself in as…Man of My Dreams.

I laughed, picturing her pissed-off sneer as she looked at her phone and read my message.

Me: I can't stop thinking about you.

Sexy Fugitive: Creep.

I typed with a dopy-ass grin on my face.

Me: Only for you, doll.

I didn't have to add in the nickname she claimed to hate, but I thought I'd clue her the fuck in if she didn't already know it was me.

Sexy Fugitive: What do you want, James?

Me: You.

What more could I say?

Sexy Fugitive: Well…you know where to find me.

I stared at the screen with my eyebrows knitted together, rubbing my chin. Was this an open invitation or was she busting my balls?

Me: You can't resist me forever.

Sexy Fugitive: Catch me if you can.

Me: Catching isn't the hard part… It's keeping you that's the challenge.

Sexy Fugitive: You seem to be the type of man who doesn't take no for an answer.

Me: I always get what I want, Izzy…always.

Sexy Fugitive: Smug bastard.

I laughed. No matter what she called me, I knew she liked me. Even when her words were venomous, I still knew. She tried like fuck to deny the connection we had, the electricity that flowed through our bodies when we touched, but I felt it.

Me: You know you want me…

No quick response came from Izzy. With an aching dick so hard it was ready to break off my body, I crawled out of bed. I put on some clothes and set my sights on her. I had the weekend off, and the last thing

CHELLE BLISS

I wanted to do was spend it in this sleepy Florida town. I wanted her and I couldn't stay away any longer.

Izzy Gallo would be mine tonight.

As I locked my front door and headed for my bike, my phone beeped in my pocket.

Sexy Fugitive: *I can't talk now. I'm working.*

I wasn't surprised by her text. She never wanted to admit her attraction to me. The entire time I spent with her last weekend had been a barrage of bullshit denying what her body betrayed.

Me: *When do you get off?*

Sexy Fugitive: *As often as I want.*

Fuck. My dick hardened, straining against the denim, as I thought about the sounds she made as she came.

Me: *On my way...*

Just as I was about to shove my phone in my pocket and climb on the bike, she replied.

Sexy Fugitive: *Now?!?!*

Me: *On my way, and I won't take no for an answer this time. I'm bringing my handcuffs too.*

Sexy Fugitive: *Fuck.*

Me: *Two hours, Izzy, and you're mine.*

I didn't wait for her reply. I put the phone on vibrate, placing it in my back pocket. Throttling the engine, I thought about her screaming my name, and took off toward the only woman who felt right in my arms.

She'd be mine tonight.

Her days of running were over.

***

I pulled into Izzy's drive just after midnight. Her sleek black Infiniti sat in the driveway, and the front porch light illuminated my pathway to her pussy.

I almost expected her not to be home. That would be something she'd do. She'd avoid me and play hard to get, denying herself the one thing she was too stubborn to admit.

I turned off my bike, stretching as I climbed off, and then secured it

580

for the night. I didn't plan on leaving until the next morning at the earliest, but I hoped to stay the whole weekend.

It was rare for me to have this kind of time off in my line of work, but since returning from Bike Week, the club had been lying low and things had been calm. I'd been told by my supervisor to take some R&R for the weekend and be ready to hit it hard when I returned on Monday. His ideas of R&R were different than mine—mine did include hitting it hard. I planned to fuck Izzy until she couldn't even remember her name, let alone her smartass attitude.

I knocked gently, trying not to startle her even though she knew I was on my way. I heard voices and rustling inside, and I leaned in, trying to hear their words.

"You better get the hell out of here," Izzy said, her voice muffled by the thick wooden door, but I could still make them out.

My heart started to pound so hard I felt like I'd just run a forty. My mind started to race with thoughts that someone was inside and it wasn't me.

"Izzy!" I yelled as I banged on the door. "Open up!"

"Go, Flash. I won't ask again!" Izzy yelled, quieter this time, but loud enough that I heard with my ear pressed up against the door.

Hearing his name made my blood run cold. I knew exactly who the little prick was. Flash was a prospect in the MC Thomas had been working undercover in for over two years. Flash was also the cocksucker who'd brought Izzy to Daytona and thrown her to the wolves.

"Fuck no," he replied. "I'm staying right here. We're going to have a little chat."

I'd had enough. I was getting in the house if I had to bust down the motherfucking door. Leaning back, I shouted, "Izzy, I'm going to bust this door down if you don't open the fuck up!" I pounded on the wood, the door jumping under my fist.

"Coming!" Izzy sang, her shoes clicking against the wood floors as she moved closer.

I needed to calm myself. Murder wouldn't be the best way to start the weekend.

As soon as she opened the door, I took quick stock of her appearance. She looked unharmed and calm, but maybe a little frustrated.

"Izzy, what the fuck is going on?" I barked, looking over her head to see a pair of boots resting on her coffee table. "What the hell is he doing here?" I touched her cheek, caressing her skin with the pad of my thumb.

"He's harmless, James." She looked at my face but didn't make eye contact.

"Izzy." I gripped the back of her neck, forcing her eyes to mine. "He's not harmless. I know exactly who he is, and he's leaving your house with or without my help."

"No," she pleaded, placing her hand on my chest.

"Yes, doll, he is." I released her, grabbing her shoulders and picking her up as I moved her out of the way.

The door closed behind me, her heels clattering as she followed me. I rounded the corner, getting a full view of Flash leaning back on the couch, his arms outstretched and his feet up. "I think the lady asked you to leave," I growled as I fisted my hands at my sides.

I didn't want to spill blood and break shit in Izzy's home. Breaking shit from hot fucking, I enjoyed. Doing it to beat some punk's ass? Not so much.

"I came here to speak to you," he answered as he rose to his feet and looked at Izzy before turning to me with a smile. "Man to man."

I stepped closer to him, breaking his line of sight with Izzy. "I have nothing to say to a piece of shit like you." My voice echoed in the house, the wood floors carrying it throughout the open space.

"There are things I need to explain," he said.

"James," Izzy begged, grabbing my arm from behind. "Just talk to him." Her face was soft, all smartass gone. This was Izzy asking me to do something I didn't want to do. Not one fucking bit.

I looked over my shoulder, staring in her eyes, and nodded. I turned back toward Flash. "You got five minutes and then I'm showing you the fucking door."

"Outside." He started to walk toward the French doors that led to a staircase to the backyard.

"Wait for me in your room," I ordered, holding her by the arms. "If shit gets bad, I don't want to worry about where you are."

"James, really. I'm a big girl." She smiled, crossing her arms over her chest.

"I never said you weren't. This is for my sanity. I'll let him speak his piece and I'll fill you in when I come up."

"I don't like being told what to do," she hissed, pulling away from my grip.

I rubbed my face. The woman could be trying at times. "I'm asking you to please do this for me."

She nodded, glaring at me as she walked down the hallway, and disappeared in her bedroom. I made a beeline to the backyard, ready to get Flash the fuck gone.

"Make it quick and get the hell out," I grunted as I descended the stairs and stopped in front of Flash. "You have two minutes to convince me why I shouldn't beat the fuck out of you."

"You don't know who I am," he growled, moving a step closer to me.

"I know exactly who you are."

He shook his head and reached into his back pocket. "You don't."

"I know all I need to." I kept my eyes trained on his hand, ready to fight back if he pulled a weapon.

"I know you're law enforcement, James. DEA to be exact," he replied as he pulled a black wallet from his pocket.

My stomach sank as he spoke. That information was a closely guarded secret. I wondered if he knew about Thomas.

"How do you know that?" I asked, stepping closer to him.

He flipped open the wallet, flashing an ID and badge at me. "I'm FBI," he whispered. "Not many people know that about me. Not even Izzy. I live the life and I'm totally immersed."

"Fuck," I grumbled, raking my hands through my hair.

"I'm prospecting, trying to make a name for myself within the club. I'm not supposed to take a dominant position inside. I'm their ears and eyes on the inside."

"How the fuck didn't I know this?" I asked as my nostrils flared and my anger turned toward the law enforcement branch of the US government.

"My boss thought it would be better if I was treated like everyone else." He swallowed, turning his back to me. "I only found out about you and Thomas"—he paused—"when Blue took Izzy out of the bar."

"How could you be so reckless?"

"I know, I know. I didn't think shit would go down like that." He shook his head as his shoulders rose and fell.

"Reckless as hell, Flash."

"Sheer stupidity. I have no other excuse." He sighed.

"How did you find out about us?" I didn't understand how he knew about us but we had no fucking clue about him.

"When she left with him, I freaked the fuck out and went to my contact. Immediately, my supervisor was informed and they called me in. I was told about the two of you and reassured that Izzy was safe."

"That's all it took, huh?"

"Listen," he said, turning back to face me. "That girl in there?" He pointed toward the house and continued. "I love her. There's no one like her. I know she'll never be mine, but fuck, I'd kill for her." He closed his eyes, regaining his composure. "They were worried I'd blow my cover and start ripping shit up to find her."

"You love her?" I repeated, glaring at him as my heart started to pick up speed, the sound of blood gushing through my ears.

"I do," Flash responded, rubbing the bridge of his nose.

"Fuck me," I muttered.

"James, she doesn't want me. She never has. We've been friends since we were kids. We'll never be anything more."

I felt bad for Flash. To love a woman and not have the feeling returned had to be fucking gut wrenching, but there was something he wasn't saying.

"You've fucked her?" I inquired, trying to contain my rage.

"That's not important. We're only friends," he answered quickly, holding his hands up. "I'm not a threat, James."

"All men are threats," I growled.

"Not me. I'm too busy building my career and focusing on my work right now. Plus, I know when I'm not wanted. She's all yours."

"All mine?" I laughed. "You must not know her as well as you think you do, bud."

He shook his head, kicking at the dirt. "She told me tonight when I came by that she wouldn't see me anymore. She dropped your name and I tuned out. Izzy has never spoken of another man. Don't listen to her bullshit. She acts tough as nails, but she's a powder puff."

His words shocked me. Izzy had talked about me...mentioned me when breaking off contact with Flash. One of us was being bullshitted, and I hoped it was me. I knew she wanted me physically, but maybe, just maybe, there was more to us. Either way, I'd do whatever I could to convince her to give us a shot.

What could go wrong?

The connection we had, the lust I felt, and the current that surged between us couldn't be ignored any longer. I'd make sure of it.

1 0

HARD TO SWALLOW

IZZY

As I watched from the window, Flash and James talked, and it didn't seem to be a pissing match. My heart raced as they'd stood toe to toe in my backyard. I'd expected it to go down very differently. I had figured one of them would end up bloodied before it was said and done. Who the fuck was I kidding? Flash would've been the one a heaping pile of broken bones after James had beaten him. Instead, they'd acted like grown men. They'd spoken low enough that I hadn't been able to make out the words, even after cracking my window to be able to hear better, and the handshake at the end had sure as fuck thrown me for a loop.

No fists were thrown, Flash disappeared between the houses, and James made his way up the stairs and back into the house. I walked down the hallway toward the kitchen as I heard the back door close. "Everything okay?" I asked as I turned the corner and almost ran right into James.

He was grinning with his head tilted and the corner of his mouth curved. He looked proud with his chest puffed out. Any moment, he might have broken out with "Me Tarzan" by the way he carried himself. His eyes were fiery yet playful.

"Perfect," he whispered, grabbing my chin.

My belly sank—but in the most wonderful way—as he held my face

586

in his hands. I felt his hot, sweet breath against my skin, and the small hairs on the back of my neck stood up. Just like when you're waiting for something that you know will scare the holy fuck out of you to happen— James was my holy fuck. He scared the piss out of me.

"Izzy," he growled.

"Yes?" I responded, my voice weak.

"You want me?" His eyes pierced me, held me in place even though my mind was screaming for me to run.

I looked down, unable to maintain eye contact, or maybe I just didn't want to look into the eyes of the boogeyman. "Yes," I whispered, placing my hand on his muscular forearm. I needed the extra support when saying those words. Letting James in was the biggest leap of faith I'd ever taken in my life. I just hoped there wasn't a rocky bottom I'd dive into headfirst.

"Just give me tonight," he breathed, moving his lips closer as he kept his eyes locked on mine.

"One night," I said with wide eyes as I swallowed hard. I felt like my airway was closing and I couldn't breathe.

"Just feel me, Izzy. Feel us and how our bodies respond to each other."

He didn't wait for me to respond as he crushed his lips to mine. He gave me the air I hadn't been able to find moments before. Wrapping his arms around me, he pulled me close and held the back of my head.

"James," I moaned into his mouth as his hand grabbed my ass, squeezing it roughly.

He pulled away, grinding his rock-hard dick into me. "I'm not taking no for an answer tonight. I barely survived last weekend, having you so close and not sinking my dick into you. It's heaven, and I won't let you deny me again."

Well fuck. How could I say no to that? Shit, I didn't want to say no. The man did me better than anyone ever had. The entire week, all I'd thought about was him. The asshole had even invaded my dreams. I tried to put him out of my mind when I was awake, but once I closed my eyes, my subconscious took over, and it, along with my extremely wet pussy, both wanted James.

Pushing me against the wall, he placed his lips against my neck and nibbled just below my ear. Goose bumps broke out across my flesh as tingles cascaded across my skin like water drops finding their path to my feet and rooting me in place. I clawed at his t-shirt, wanting to feel his skin. When I pulled it up, my knuckles skimmed his ribs.

As he sucked in a breath, he stole the air in my lungs. Releasing me, he pulled the shirt off his body, revealing his mouth-watering chest. I placed my palms against his hard pecs, kneading the muscles with my fingers as he kissed a path down the opening of my tank top. His hands found my thighs, looping underneath. As my feet left the floor, I wrapped my legs around his torso, grinding my pussy against him. He carried me down the hall, his lips back on mine, as he held me tight against his body.

His grip lessened just over the threshold of my bedroom doorway, causing me to slide down him. I grinned, looking into his eyes and seeing the desire on his face.

He took a step back, crossing his arms and cocking his head. "Strip," he commanded.

My body swayed as his words hit me like a ton of bricks. "What?" I blurted, shocked by the forcefulness in his voice.

"Strip, and make it good." He didn't move or change expression.

"Excuse me? Is that any way to talk to a lady?" I barked, kind of turned on but not willing to share that little nugget of information.

I glared at him, my eyes raking over his body and stopping dead on his crotch. I could clearly see the outline of his long, thick cock straining against the material. I knew how it felt to have that monster inside me, and it made my mind mush. I started to slowly take down the straps of my tank top without waiting for his response.

"Don't I get music or something?" I quipped, cockiness in my voice as I removed the material from my arms. I turned as I gathered the tank in my hands. Bending at the waist, I stuck my ass in the air as I shimmed out of my shirt and then tossed it across the room. Shaking my hips, I started to hum as my ass bounced, and I peeked at him between the gap in my legs.

He leaned against the wall with his arms crossed, and studied me. He seemed pleased with what I was doing. Turning around, I held my hands over my breasts, covering my hard nipples as I shook them in my hands.

Bouncing them in my hands, I licked the top of my breast. The skin feeling like velvet against my tongue.

"Fuck," he hissed, his lips turning up into a snarl as his nostrils flared.

My body warmed from his reaction, and I felt a sense of confidence in my movements. Stripping for someone when it's your idea is entirely different than doing it when being told to. James's reaction made it fun, and I figured why the fuck not tease him in the process?

"You like when I cocktease you?" I asked, opening my fingers, letting my nipples show. A black lace bra covered my breasts, leaving little to the imagination. I rolled my nipples in between my fingers as I licked a path to my other breast, peeking up at him through hooded lashes.

"Lose the clothes, Isabella."

He dropped my formal name, once again causing the bottom of my stomach to flutter.

"Yes, master," I responded, curtseying to him and unable to hold my smartass comments.

His face changed as he squinted at me. "Those words make me so fucking hard," he whispered.

Was James one of *those* men? Was he the type of guy who got off on being in total control and wanting a sex slave in the bedroom?

After I peeled off my pants, leaving nothing between him and me except my lace black panties and bra, I stood still, my tongue sticking out as it hovered just above my breast. I wanted to be touched, and if he wouldn't do it, then I sure as fuck would be the one to take up the task.

"Crawl to me," he demanded.

I shrugged, thinking, *What the hell? Why not?* and dropped to my knees. Moving slowly across the wooden floor, I crawled to him like a cat stalking its prey. Sticking my ass up in the air, I raised my shoulders as I approached him.

Funny that I didn't feel weird or humiliated crawling to him as he'd asked. It turned me on, and from what I could see from being eye to eye with his dick, he was hard as a rock.

"Unzip me," he said, his voice softer.

I looked up at him, taking a moment to drink him in. Yeah, I was totally fucked. Perching up on my knees, I pulled his zipper down, releasing his cock.

It was bigger than I remembered, especially up close. Then again, I might have had half a bottle of Jack by the time we'd ripped each other's clothes off in the hotel room.

Palming his thickness, I stuck my tongue out, capturing the small drop of liquid off the tip. Divine saltiness spread across my tongue as I leaned in to take him in my mouth.

"Wait," he said, grabbing my face with his hands.

"James," I groaned, leaning back on my heels to look up at him. "Make up your mind."

"No hands. I want only your mouth on me," he growled. This was a side of James I hadn't expected, but I liked it.

I nodded, gripping his thighs with my hands before I slid his jeans down his legs to give me better access to his hardness. The hair lying across my back moved as he wrapped his hand around it, fisting it tightly. Small tingles started at my neck before shooting down my spine and straight to my core. I ached to be filled by him, and would do whatever it took to have him thrust me over a cliff of ecstasy.

I gripped his firm, muscular thighs, placing my fingers just below his ass. I dug my nails into his flesh. He hissed, sucking in air as I swirled my tongue around his piercing. The metal felt soft compared to his throbbing cock as I slid the length of him across my tongue until it touched the back of my throat. I gagged slightly, pulling him out to relieve my body's reflex to repel the contents.

"Take all of me. You can do it." He thrust his hips forward, jamming his cock to the back of my throat.

My eyes watered as my ability to breathe was cut off from the foreign object filling my mouth. He gripped my hair roughly, pulling his cock from my lips before sliding it in over and over again. His grunts and moans spurred me on and kept me focused.

Drool pooled at the corners of my mouth, slowly oozing from the sides as he pummeled my throat with his rock-hard dick. Tears streamed down my cheeks, my fingers digging into my skin as I took the torture, wishing it were my pussy on the receiving end of the blunt force trauma.

Just as I felt his cock grow bigger, filling my mouth further, he moaned, "Fuck." Then he pulled my hair back, releasing his dick from my mouth. "Not yet. Not like this," he moaned on a shaky breath. His fingers slipped from my hair and slid across my face, capturing the moisture from my chin. "You're so fucking sexy right now."

I blinked, wondered how I possibly looked sexy. I had drool on my face, blurry eyes, and tear-stained cheeks. That didn't fit my idea of fuckable, but then again, I didn't have a cock.

A thought occurred to me as I kneeled before James. I thought women who acted like I just had—following sexual commands without question —were weak, but that's not what I'd felt. I'd felt empowered and in control. Even though James barked out the orders, I was the one to carry them out, and I held his world in my hands—or in this case, my mouth.

A small smile spread across my face as I used my tongue to grab the moisture from the corners of my mouth. His eyes zoned in on my tongue as his cock bobbed. "Fuck, Izzy," he hissed, holding his hand out to me. "Off your knees before I lose control staring at that fuckable mouth."

I grabbed his hand, letting him pull me from the floor, and slid up his body. My tits rubbed against his skin. Feeling the hardness against my throbbing nipples sent a shiver through my body. Having him in my mouth and remembering our first night together had driven my body so close to the edge that I knew it wouldn't take much for me to come.

I stared in his eyes as he held my face in his palm and my neck in his grip. Just as I was about to start rubbing my pussy against his leg, unable to bear waiting any longer, his free hand glided down my body toward the promised land. I silently thanked the gods for taking pity on me. As his fingers slid through my wetness and his palm massaged my clit, my head fell back and my body moved forward on its own.

"James," I moaned as I slid my hands up his arms and dug my nails into his shoulders.

"You're so fucking wet," he murmured.

His finger rubbed my G-spot, driving me closer to the thing I wanted most—an orgasm. A second finger joined the first, stretching me and making me feel full as the others stroked my outer parts. Shivers racked my body as he worked my pussy to the point where, at times, he stole my breath. The pressure was so intense that I could barely form a thought. Wetness and warmth filled my senses as he licked a path up my neck, stopping at the spot where I could feel my pulse beating rapidly under his tongue.

"James." It was the only thing I could say. My mind had become muddled. Everything in my body was tight and ready. I pushed up on my tiptoes, trying to get more leverage and work his fingers deeper inside me.

His hand stilled. "You want my cock?" he whispered against my neck.

I nodded my response. I wanted to come, but I wouldn't mince words with him putting me so close to an orgasm that I felt like I would explode.

"You just want to come," he grunted, pushing my neck forward and forcing my eyes to his.

Heat crept across my face as I looked into his eyes. It pissed me off that he could read me so well. I'd prided myself on being unreadable my entire life, but James had an ability that unnerved me.

"I want you," I pleaded, nipping at his lips.

His fingers began to move at a torturous pace. Slowly, he rubbed my insides as he pulled out and pushed back in with force, but kept his palm clear of my clit.

"Tell me what you want," he insisted, digging his fingers in my neck.

"I want you to fuck me." I could feel the buildup again as my pussy clenched down on his fingers, trying to keep him inside.

"Ask me nicely." He smirked against my lips as his cheeks rose, almost touching his eyes as his hand stilled again.

I sighed, knowing that there was only one way to get what I wanted. I could fuck around and play a game with his mind. I knew he wanted me as much as I wanted him. The proof of that was pressed against my hip.

"James, will you fuck me?" I asked, not breaking eye contact.

"Please," he said before nipping at my jaw and massaging my insides without the in-and-out motion I fucking craved.

He wanted me to beg—something I'd never done for anyone in my life. People begged me. I'd never wanted anything enough to beg. If I couldn't get it for myself, then it wasn't worth having or lusting after.

James was different. He was something I couldn't get without groveling and giving more of myself than I wanted to. I was too close to coming to turn back now and tell him to get the fuck out of my house. A small part of me wanted to tell him to take his junk and leave, but the part I wanted to punch in the face later said, "Please fuck me, James. I want you." Fucking traitorous words. Later, I'd kick my own ass.

His smirk turned into a smile as his fingers slipped out of me. He placed the fingers that had just been inside me into his mouth, and swirled his tongue around them. "Mmm," he murmured as he licked my juices off. "You taste fucking fantastic. Just how I remember."

"You're an asshole. If you're getting your rocks off by making me beg and then you're just going to—" I didn't get to finish the sentence, as he moved my face to his and swallowed my words with his lips.

When he backed away, I was breathless and wanton. I would've professed my love and a horde of children to this man for a single orgasm. He'd driven me so close and then pulled away so many times that I no longer was Izzy Gallo, kick-ass chick—I was Izzy Gallo, cock slave to James. I only mildly hated myself for it.

I swayed as he removed his pants, dug in his pocket, and then discarded his jeans to the side. James stood before me, naked and magnificent, with a giant, cocky-ass smile on his face. As he slipped on the condom, I took in his hotness. He had the entire goddamn package—piercings, tattoos, rock-hard muscles, and a beautiful fucking cock. The only downside to James that I could think of was his mouth, but even though I wanted to smack it sometimes, it did crazy fucking things to me. Things I didn't like to admit.

Before I could move, he lifted me with one arm under my ass and impaled me on his cock with a grunt.

"Fuckin' heaven," he moaned, pushing farther inside.

All negative thoughts about the smug bastard standing gloriously naked in front of me vanished as his piercing stroked me from the inside. Turning us, he pounded into me as he pushed my back against the wall.

Using his arm and the solid surface behind me, he battered my body. Drawing my nipple into his mouth, he drove my body higher, granting him deeper access to my pussy and bringing my tits closer to his face.

As he bit down, I hissed, "Fuck." The pain was soon forgotten as his strokes increased and the mounting pressure returned, more intense than before.

I clawed at his flesh, scraping his skin, as he pounded me into the wall with each blow. He grunted, moaning against my nipples as he sucked and bit on the tender skin.

My eyes found the mirror across the room. There was just enough light for me to clearly see his body as he thrust inside me. His ass cheeks clenched and released as he pushed himself deep, driving me closer to the edge. My arms were wrapped around his torso as I stared at our reflection. The pink streaks caused by my fingernails were visible clear across the room.

Watching him fuck me, and the feeling of his dick slamming into me, made it impossible to stave off the impending orgasm.

"Fuck yes!" I screamed, hitting my head against the wall. "Harder!" I demanded.

My toes curled as his fingers gripped my ass and his cock pulverized my pussy in long, thick strokes.

He released my nipples, pulling my body down harder on his cock. He moved his mouth next to my ear and said, "Come for me, Izzy. I want to feel you squeeze the life out of my dick."

All the muscles in my body grew rigid as he moved his hands to my waist, forcefully pulling me down against his cock. I bounced off his body like a rag doll. Everything around me ceased to exist except James and his dick.

My nails slid against his skin, tearing the flesh as I screamed through the best fucking orgasm of my life. I mumbled and chanted like a person in a trance as one orgasm passed and another started to build.

"Don't you dare come again," he growled, pulling me from the wall and walking toward the bed.

My eyes flew open as I stared at him. "What?" I asked, swallowing hard and trying to catch my breath.

"Not yet, doll. Not like this," he groaned as he stilled inside me.

As we approached the bed and he started to lay me back, I wrapped my legs tighter around him. My pussy ached from the devastation he'd just inflicted upon it, but I wanted more.

"Let go," he ordered as he released me and pulled at my legs.

"No," I cried, pulling him in deeper and increasing my viselike grip.

He looked down at me and smiled. "Such a selfish girl," he whispered as he ran his fingers over my lips, tracing a path down my body.

His fingers stopped at my breasts, circling around each one, as his fingernail scraped against my nipple.

"I'm not selfish, James, I'm horny." The first orgasm, even in its intensity, hadn't done enough to quell the ache and throb I felt when I was around him. His fingers, mouth, and dick made me want more. That was exactly why I'd done the walk of shame out of his hotel room months ago. He scared me.

"Izzy," he barked, bringing my attention back to him as he pried my legs apart. "Flip over, beautiful. I'm not done with you yet."

My pussy convulsed with his words. That divine clenching of both happiness and anticipation. I shifted, and he slipped from my body. A dull ache was left by the emptiness inside me as he walked away.

"How do you want me?" Why I asked this question, I had no fucking clue. Did it matter?

He bent down next to his pants, and the sound of metal clinking filled the room. My heart stopped in my chest as I closed my eyes and knew what he grabbed. I looked over my shoulder, finding him approaching the bed as he twirled them around his finger.

"I brought these just for you." He leaned over, touching my skin with the cold metal, and dragged it down my spine.

I sucked in a breath, the sensation intense against my hot damn skin. I closed my eyes, enjoying the feel of the icy hardware, and when I opened them, James had a very smug grin on his face.

"Hands behind your back, Isabella." He smirked—as he probably assumed I'd do just about anything right now.

"What are you going to do?" I asked, more concerned with him leaving than anything he'd do to me physically.

"I'm going to get mine now," he said, holding the handcuffs in the air with one hand as he stroked his condom-covered cock in the other. "You want this?" he asked, fisting it rapidly and looking down at his dick. "Then you'll get these." He shook the cuffs, causing them to make a loud clatter.

"Promise you won't leave?" I pleaded, needing to be sure before I handed over total control. Before, when I'd crawled to him and let him fuck my face, that hadn't been giving him free rein, but being restrained and naked left me vulnerable and at his mercy.

CHELLE BLISS

"I'd never do that. I want to bury myself inside you until I can't fuck you anymore. Hands," he commanded.

I swallowed, placing my hands behind my back and burying my face in the comforter. He moved quickly, grabbing my body and pushing me up the bed. Before I could respond, a cuff was around my left wrist and attached to the headboard. The bed dipped and rose as he climbed off and back to his feet.

My stomach sank. The nasty feeling of being duped entered my bones. "Where the fuck are you going?" I snarled, panicking as a lump formed in my throat as he bent down.

As he stood, he said, "To get these," and jiggled another set of hand-cuffs in his hand.

"Thank shit for small miracles," I whispered low enough so he wouldn't hear. I turned forward, feeling the bed dip as he returned and hovered over my body.

"Give me your hand," he said, holding out his with the handcuff in his grip.

I sighed, reaching out and willingly giving my hand to him. Butter-flies filled my stomach as he restrained my right arm to the headboard. I lay there splayed out before him, for his enjoyment and use.

He pushed my hair to the side, biting down on my neck as he slid down my body. His hard shaft left a trail of tingles as he glided across my skin. I looked over my shoulder to see him kneeling between my legs.

"Mmm, so fucking beautiful," he groaned as he squeezed my ass roughly, kneading it in his grip. "I want this."

Closing my eyes tight, I said, "James."

There was no fucking way his dick would go in my ass. No goddamn way. He was too fucking big for that to happen. I started to thrash as he spread apart my ass cheeks, rubbing his thumb over my opening. My body locked up, my ass clenching to stop the assault. I'd let him restrain me. I'd given up complete control.

"You'll love it," he replied as wetness filled my crack.

"Where did you—" I started to ask, but as his fingertip pushed inside, my mouth quickly shut.

Pain sliced through me for a moment and was replaced by a fullness I hadn't anticipated. James had huge hands and, in turn, thick, long fingers.

"I'll make it feel good," he whispered, working his finger inside me as he began to stroke my pussy opening with his other hand.

I'd had anal sex before. I even enjoyed it, but something about James and his size scared the shit out of me. My palms began to sweat; the thought of the pain as he filled me made me nervous.

My eyes rolled back in my head, the pleasure making it impossible to keep a watchful eye on him. I pushed against his hand, needing the pleasure of his fingers pounding into my pussy to forget the burn in my ass. More wetness fell against me before he added a second finger in my ass, driving me over the pain-pleasure threshold. Too many feelings were mixed in my body as my mind turned off from all thought or ability to yell stop.

They worked out of unison from each other. As he moved one hand in my pussy and the other out of my ass, I found myself spiraling dangerously close to an orgasm I thought would stop my heart. The pleasure building up from deep inside had my heart pounding uncontrollably. This could be the destroyer of all men who might grace my future. James was wrecking me and doing it on fucking purpose.

My hands moved, trying to grip on to something to ground myself, but it was futile. I couldn't reach a fucking thing, and I didn't have the strength to shimmy up the bed as he worked my body perfectly.

A moan fell from my lips even as I tried to bite back the words. "Oh, yes. Fuck me, James."

Just then, his fingers left my ass. I buried my face into the bed, both happy and relieved at the loss of fullness. I mumbled something incoherent even to myself as he still thrust his fingers inside my cunt.

Scooping more wetness from my pussy, he rubbed my juices against my ass before jamming his cock into my pussy.

"Still so fucking wet," he said, moving his face close to my ear. "I want your ass, Izzy."

I sucked in a breath, fear gripping me because of his size. "James," I moaned. I wanted to say no, but everything the man did to me felt fanfuckingtastic.

A few thrusts later, he removed himself from my core and rubbed against my asshole. As he pushed the tip inside, I whispered, "You're too big," and bit down on the comforter.

"It'll fit. You're so fucking ready for me."

Problem was, he was fucking right. I didn't like when James was always right.

"Push out. It'll make it slide in easier," he grunted, placing his hand underneath me and stroking my clit.

"Fuck," I moaned, pushing down with all my strength as he circled my clit with his fingertips. "Yes," I wailed.

I pulled at the handcuffs, wrapping my fingers around the cold metal chain connecting the two parts, and took what he gave me.

"Fuck," he moaned, seating himself fully inside of me.

I moved, grinding my pussy against his hand and hoping it would urge him to move. The only thing worse than being fucked in the ass was someone stopping with their dick inside you. I needed the movement and the friction against my pussy. I needed to come. My body was wound so fucking tight I thought my heart would burst.

"Selfish," he whispered, his hot breath licking my ear as he began to rock in and out of me.

"Just fuck me and shut the fuck up," I hissed, pushing back against him.

His palm came down fast on my hip as he slapped it hard enough to cause me to focus on another point of pain. "You're not the boss anymore, Izzy. I am." His words surprised me more than his palm, and the funny thing was...I liked it.

"Yes, sir," I spouted back, feeling the need to be a smartass.

"Always have to be such a tough-ass," he grunted, gripping my hip and thrusting inside me. He pinched my clit and rolled it between his fingers.

I cried out. The orgasm that had built broke loose. I screamed until my throat was sore and my voice hoarse. I grew limp, my body and mind both sated and in post-orgasmic bliss, as his thrusts grew more punishing.

I squeezed my eyes shut, praying for his release and my freedom. My body couldn't take much more of James and come back unscathed. His movements became sporadic as he hissed, "Fuck," and collapsed against my back.

Our bodies were slick with sweat as he lay on top of me, crushing me against the mattress.

"Jesus," he murmured between labored breaths.

I moved, his dick feeling like an unwelcome guest.

He shifted, pulling his cock from my body as he rolled off me. "Sorry," he said as he stroked my ass with his fingertips.

"James, let me go," I whispered, and yanked at the handcuffs.

"I may keep you like this all night." He traced a path up my ass cheeks to my spine. "I like you so willing and ready."

I glared at him, turning my head in his direction. "My arms are getting numb," I bit out, trying to not yell.

"I'll never believe your bullshit." He laughed, climbing off the bed.

"Where the fuck are you going?" I roared, worried he'd leave me like this all night.

"Getting the fucking key," he responded, bending down and retrieving it from his jeans pocket.

"Oh," I mumbled, feeling like a fool.

As he climbed on the bed, the mattress dipped, much like my stomach from his nearness. As he released my arms, he rubbed my muscles and eased the tension inside. The feeling of his strong hands massaging my limbs felt amazing.

"Mmm, so fucking good," I muttered as he continued the same treatment on my other arm.

"Stay here. I'll be right back."

I watched as his beautiful, tight ass walked to the bathroom until he closed the door. Hearing water running, I closed my eyes and thought about James. I was currently in the love phase of the love-hate relationship I had with him, but I was certain that, soon enough, the orgasmic haze I was in would wear off and I'd slide on the other side of that thin line.

I cracked open an eye as the door opened. He was approaching the bed with a washcloth. "Let me clean you," he whispered, crawling next to me in bed.

Without speaking, I opened my legs and relaxed. The warmth of the towel against my pussy and ass relieved the throbbing I'd felt a moment ago. His cock had been brutal, but his kindness and the fucking orgasm made it all worth the abuse.

"Ouch," I hissed as he pressed it against my asshole.

"It'll help. Just lie still," he whispered, working the soft cloth against my skin.

I did as he'd said without a fight. I didn't have the energy to argue with James tonight.

Leaving the washcloth against me, he stood and pulled back a corner of the sheets. "Up you go," he said, cradling me.

I wrapped my arms around him, rubbing my nose against his neck, and inhaled. He smelled like musk, sweat, and sex.

He placed my head on the pillow, climbed over top of me, and settled in the bed. After covering us, he cocooned me in his arms.

With my back to his torso, I closed my eyes and exhaled. My eyes were heavy as I blinked, straining to keep them open.

"Sleep, sweet Izzy," he whispered, increasing his grip around my body.

I drifted off, listening to his breathing in my ear, blissfully sated and exhausted.

James would be the death of me.

11

FINDING AN INROAD

JAMES

I WOKE THE NEXT MORNING TO IZZY'S LIGHT SNORES IN MY EAR. DURING the night, she'd shifted, turning her face toward me and wrapping her body around mine. Now, we were in the same position with her face buried in my chest.

I didn't want to move. Izzy looked sweet and almost angelic lying in my arms, curled around me. I knew that, the moment her eyes opened, her wicked tongue and smartass words would be nonstop. The girl needed to stop running—or at least pretending to.

I never believed in love at first sight. Lust, yes, but not love. The problem was that I did love Izzy Gallo. She wasn't like other women who'd spent time in my bed; she was in a class all her own.

I didn't have to peel back the layers to find out who the real Izzy was. Her brother had already told me almost everything I needed to know about her. He had shared pictures with me, told me stories about his wild sister, and sung her praises for years. I had seen the fire in her eyes when I stared at her picture and listened to him talk about her. Meeting her in person had brought it all to life.

I loved her spirit. She grabbed life by the balls and played by no one's rules but her own. I wanted a woman who would challenge me. Ladies caved too easily and gave no chase, but not Isabella. She was my prime target.

I eased her body away from mine, sliding out of bed to make a pot of coffee and some breakfast. I wanted to start the morning off on the right foot. If she hadn't been so exhausted last night, I was sure she would've had a few choice words to hurl in my direction.

Sliding on my jeans, I looked at the bed and Izzy sprawled out amongst the dark sheets. The material hung just below her belly button and her breasts were uncovered, a tangle of brown locks framing her body. I wanted to crawl back in bed and wake her with my dick, but I knew she had to be sore from the pummeling I'd given her last night. I wanted her to remember where I'd been and how I felt filling her from the inside. Izzy Gallo wouldn't be forgetting my territory for days.

I checked the coffee maker, the grounds and water already inside, and pushed the "on" button before heading outside to my bike. I grabbed the bag I'd packed, hoping I'd be spending a couple of days here, and stopped to look around the neighborhood.

A light fog covered the houses in the distance and hadn't broken up yet from the sun. The birds chirped as a few people milled around the neighborhood walking their dogs and hurrying off to God knows where at this time of day.

The aroma of freshly brewed coffee hit me as soon as I walked back into the house. I needed to clean up before the princess woke from her slumber.

After washing my face and brushing my teeth, I grabbed two cups of coffee and headed to the bedroom. Izzy hadn't moved while I was gone. I set the cups on the nightstand and kicked off my jeans, setting my phone on the nightstand. Once I'd crawled back in bed, I stretched out next to her and stared for a few minutes before I stroked her skin.

It was as smooth as silk and free from imperfections. Her long, dark lashes rested against her cheeks while she slept. I traced her lips with my fingers, restraining myself from devouring her whole. I kissed her softly, enjoying the velvety feel of them against mine until she began to stir. Her eyes fluttered open as her lips turned up into a small smile.

"Good morning," I whispered against her lips.

"Good morning," she said after turning her face away from mine and yawning.

"Sleep well?" I moved the hair away from her neck and planted a light kiss against her pulse.

"I'm so tired," she mumbled, curling against my body and drifting back to sleep.

"Izzy," I whispered, kissing her cheek.

"No," she moaned without opening her eyes.

"I brought you coffee." I ran my fingertips over her skin, tracing tiny circles and watching a line of goose bumps break out across her skin.

"What time is it?" she groaned, rubbing her eyes.

"A little after eight."

"Why are you up so early?"

"I don't need much sleep."

Her blinks were slow as she stared up at me. "Did I hear you say coffee?" she asked with a groggy voice.

"I brought you a cup just how you like it."

"I don't want to move," she said, closing her eyes.

I pulled her body against me and stroked her hair. "Just sleep. We have all day," I whispered.

"Wait. What?" she asked as her body stiffened in my arms.

"I have all weekend off. I'm all yours for forty-eight blissful hours." I smiled, biting my lip as I waited for her to freak out.

To my shock, her body relaxed and melted into mine. "Good. I can go back to sleep," she said, closing her eyes and making noises of pleasure as I caressed her back.

Her breathing slowed as she drifted back to sleep. I held her, stroking her body as she snored softly. I'd expected her to throw me out or have a fit when I said that I'd be here for the entire weekend, but to my surprise, she'd fallen back to sleep.

That was the thing about Izzy. She was a woman full of surprises. I couldn't nail down what her reaction to anything would be. She kept me on my toes, and for that, I'd be more than happy to keep her on the edge of her seat.

Just as I was about to drift off to sleep myself, my phone beeped and startled me. Izzy didn't move when I jumped or when I rolled backward to grab my phone.

Tapping the screen, I saw a message in my inbox.

Thomas: Checking in. Quiet week. Hope you're doing something more fun than I am.

Fuck. A wave of guilt rolled over me, settling deep in my stomach. Thomas was risking his life while I was busy fucking his sister. I couldn't admit it to him, at least not yet.

Me: Good. Took the weekend off.

No reply came, as was usually the case. One message a week was what we were allowed before he'd wipe his phone clean of any remnants of our communication.

Izzy stirred in my arms, touching my face. "Everything okay?" she asked.

"Never better." I turned off the screen and tossed the phone toward the end of the bed.

"Did you say something before about the entire weekend?" she yawned.

"Yep. I'm all yours," I replied, kissing her forehead.

"Um, I have to work today." Her body shook in my arms as she stretched.

"I'd love to see the shop."

"Wouldn't you rather do something else?" She pulled from my grip.

"I'll find something to do today after I drop you off. We can go out later when you're done."

"I work late, though."

"Don't you own the joint?"

"Well, yeah."

"Maybe you can get off early."

"I was hoping to get off now," she said, and laughed, covering her mouth with her hand.

I inched closer, bringing my body to hers. "That I can do," I growled in her ear.

"James," she said, pushing against my chest.

"Hmm mmm." I nibbled on her ear before nipping a path down her neck.

She moaned as I bit down on the tender flesh above her collarbone. Using my tongue, I tasted her skin as I captured her nipple in my mouth and sucked hard, flicking it.

"Keep going." She laughed and dug her fingers in my hair.

Izzy and I stayed in bed for a couple of hours, feasting on each other and drifting back to sleep. Finally, after showering, we were ready to head to the tattoo parlor a little after noon.

As she locked the door, she turned to me and said, "James, I've never brought anyone to the shop." She kicked at the ground with her right foot and looked down.

"Izzy, I met everyone at the wedding. I'll tell them I was in the area and you let me crash on your couch."

Looking up, she rolled her eyes at me. "Yeah, 'cause that's believable."

"Listen, little mama. We can play it however you want to. I can say I fucked you mindless last night or that I just crashed at your place. I'll let you explain it. I thought it would be nice to see the shop Thomas has told me so much about." I climbed on my bike, lifting the stand as I straddled the machine.

"Skip the mindless fucking part," she said, walking toward my bike.

"I'll be your secret." I winked at her, patting the back seat of my bike, and hoped she'd let me give her a lift.

"It's not that I want you a secret. I just haven't figured *us* out yet. I don't know what I want." She squeezed in behind me, gripping me with her thighs. She felt so fucking good wrapped around my body.

"You want me," I replied, laughing as I turned on the engine and revved it. I took off before she could respond, and headed toward her business.

She yelled in my ear when I needed to turn. I didn't tell her that I already knew where it was because of Thomas. Our jobs were dangerous and we had to share everything in our lives with our supervisors. Our families were monitored for their safety, and files were built about them. Thomas knew my life just like I did his. There were no secrets—until now, at least.

She climbed down, shaking out her hair as I turned off the bike. "I can't believe I agreed to this shit," she said loud enough for me to hear.

As I got off the bike and stretched, I said, "They'll be more concerned about Thomas than what I'm doing here with you." I twirled my keys in my hand as I followed her toward the front door.

"Let's hope. This shit could blow up in my face."

"What could go wrong?" I grabbed the door, opening it for her.

"Hey!" she yelled as she walked inside.

The reception area was empty, but there were voices and movement coming from the back.

"Yo! Back here," a male voice called out from the tattoo area.

"Come on," she whispered to me, motioning for me to follow.

I took a moment to look around the shop. It was stunning. Totally unlike some of the seedy shithole tattoo parlors I'd been in. This joint was classy, with colorful walls and beautiful decoration. It had Izzy written all over it.

"Hey, I brought someone," she said as we walked into the back.

Mike, Joe, and Anthony stopped, looking up in unison. One by one, smiles crept across their faces as they recognized me.

"James," Mike said, standing to shake my hand.

"Hey, Mike. Good to see you again." I shook his hand, squeezing it firmly.

I didn't feel out of place seeing the Gallo guys again. I'd met them all at the wedding. I'd spoken with each one of them, sharing the information about Thomas that I was able to without putting him at risk.

"Yo, James," Anthony said, nodding to me without standing up.

I smiled, giving him a nod back.

"James, I'm surprised to see you here," Joe said as he stood and held out his hand to me.

I smiled, taking his hand in mine and shaking it roughly. "I just wanted to see how Izzy was doing."

"Ah." He looked at me with squinted eyes and the corner of his mouth twitching. "I heard all about last weekend." He released my hand, a dull throb in my joints where Joe had squeezed back as I hard as I had him. We were that type of man. We never showed weakness.

"Oh, did you?" I asked, a giant smile playing across my lips.

"Izzy never listens to us. We told her to stay the hell out of Daytona and stay the fuck away from Flash." He sat back in his chair, looking at his sister. "She has to learn everything the hard way. Thank Christ she had four brothers to watch over her."

I laughed as I looked at Izzy and practically saw steam coming out of her ears. No woman liked being talked about in this way, especially Izzy. She wasn't weak and didn't always need to be under the watchful eye of her brothers.

"Yeah, Daytona was rough. She's home safe now and Flash is of no worry. I took care of him."

"Good man," Joe said, opening the drawers to his station and placing tiny cups for the ink on the perfectly laid-out paper sheet to keep the area clean.

"How's Thomas?" Mike asked, leaning back in his chair.

"He's well. It's pretty quiet in the MC right now, but he's kicking ass."

"When the fuck will he be home, man?" Anthony asked.

I felt every eye in the place on me, waiting for the answer to a question I couldn't give a simple answer to. "Soon. He's so close he can taste it. You know Thomas. He won't stop until he gets the job done."

"Izzy said she saw him last weekend," Joe said.

"Yeah. We both did." I didn't feel the need to expand upon the information. The details of which I was sure Izzy hadn't given to them fully.

"She said he looked okay but a bit worn," Joe prompted.

"The life he's leading wears on a person, especially someone like Thomas."

"I just want him home and safe," Izzy commented as she walked up beside me and stopped.

I reached out, wrapping my arm around her, and drew her close. "He'll be home soon, doll," I promised, kissing her temple.

She stiffened in my arm. I looked down at her and followed her eyes to see three very curious faces.

"Want to share something?" Anthony inquired with one eyebrow reaching for the sky.

"Nope," Izzy responded, quickly moving out of my grasp.

I grinned, happy with what had been done but knowing I'd probably catch shit for it.

"I'll let you guys get to work. I'm going to head out for the day." I nodded at them and turned to Izzy. "What time should I pick you up?"

"We don't close until late," she responded, looking up at me.

"Iz, you don't have any appointments after six. You can take off after that," Mike chimed in.

"Perfect," I said, turning to him and winking.

She glared at him. "Thanks," she hissed.

"I'll be back at seven. Walk me out?" I asked, pulling her against my body.

"Fine," she bit out.

"Oh hey, James," Joe called out as we started to walk away.

"Yeah?" I asked, turning around to face him.

"My parents would love to talk with you. Mind going over there tomorrow for Sunday dinner?"

I smiled. The entire weekend was turning out perfect. I couldn't have planned it any better if I'd tried. "I'd be more than happy to see them. I've heard amazing things about your ma's cooking."

"For the love of all that is holy," Izzy muttered, rolling her eyes as she fisted her hands at her sides.

I laughed when her glare was now trained on me. "You okay with this?" I asked her, putting her on the spot with her brothers there for the show.

"Yep," she barked. "Peachy."

She was pissed off, and I loved it. When Izzy was angry, she looked even more beautiful.

"Good," I said to her, and turned toward Joe. "I'll be there."

I grabbed her by the shoulders and ushered her toward the front of the shop and away from the watchful eyes of her brothers.

"Pissed off?" I asked as I stopped near the door.

"Not with you. Not entirely, at least." She looked down and bounced on her heels.

"With them?" I motioned with my thumb over my shoulder.

"Yes." She sighed. "They're nosy bastards. And you." She poked me in the chest. "What the fuck are you doing being all touchy-feely with me in front of them?"

"Just letting them know how it is," I growled, drawing her against me.

She didn't relax or melt into me like she had done when we were alone. "Only I let them know how it is."

Moving my head back, I looked down at her and grinned. She was a pussycat. "I'll behave from here on out."

She rolled her eyes and pursed her lips. "I don't believe a word that comes out of that sexy-ass mouth."

"Probably smart." I laughed, squeezing her tighter as I kissed her lips. Backing away, I stared at her. Her lips were parted and her breathing a bit uneven. She fucking wanted me and she couldn't hide it any longer. "I'll be back at seven."

"Okay," she whispered as I released her.

As she walked away, I reached out and smacked her ass. "Be ready, doll. There's no rest for the wicked."

"Jesus," she whined. "Will you ever get enough? I ache all over."

"When it comes to you, the answer is no. I want that body destroyed by the time I head home. I want you to remember who owns that pussy."

"Caveman asshole."

"Speaking of which, I want more of that too."

"Get the fuck out of here," she demanded, shoving me toward the door.

"Until later, doll," I grunted as I touched her face, letting my fingers slide from her cheek.

I climbed on my bike, heading out to chill on the beach for the day and catch some rays. I'd be back for Izzy well rested and ready to ravage her body all night long. I didn't want to miss a moment together. I'd have her ass loving me and wanting no one else but me before I walked out the door tomorrow.

12

SUNDAY FUCKIN' FUNDAY

IZZY

AFTER TWO NIGHTS WITH JAMES, MY BODY ACHED LIKE I'D DONE THE Tough Mudder obstacle course. Just peeing was a major issue. Everything hurt—even my face from smiling too much. James had entered my life like a hurricane, slowly building over time and then creating total and utter devastation in his path.

I'd always lived my life like a free spirit. I never gave a fuck what anyone thought of me and I was never apologetic for my actions. The words "slut" and "whore" left a bad taste in my mouth and made me want to rip the nuts off any man who'd muttered them. I acted like many men did; I used people for the physical aspect but never promised them anything more. I wasn't into relationships or being tied down. Having a man tell me what to do and how to act was my biggest fear, and something I'd run from at every opportunity.

Men seemed okay with how I behaved for the most part. Only a few had hurled insults because they'd wanted more. Those boys had ended up on the floor, gripping their balls and crying like babies. Each one of them had thought they could get me, capture my attention long enough for me to fall in love, and be the one. They hadn't been man enough to be worthy of my time, let alone a lifetime of sacrifice.

After having spent thirty-six hours with James, I knew I needed to end it. Not because he wasn't worthy of my time, but because he was too much of what I wanted. There was a problem. I wasn't ready for someone like James to come crashing into my life and turn shit upside down.

When I opened my eyes this morning and watched him sleep, I knew what I had to do. I needed to gracefully bow out of whatever the fuck this was. James was a big boy and I was sure he'd understand. Maybe I could be his hookup when we both had an itch that needed to be scratched.

I knew I was scared, but fear was enough to make me lash out and run away. James had a way about him that altered the axis on which I teetered. I knew how I liked my life—uncomplicated and simple. He was a complication of epic proportions.

No one bossed me around—not even my four very demanding brothers. When James bossed me around, I bowed and said, "Yes, master," giving more of myself than I ever had with anyone.

"You ready, Izzy?" James asked, walking out of the bathroom as I sipped my coffee.

Setting it down on the counter, I turned to face him. God, he looked amazing. He wore a plain black t-shirt that clung to every inch of his torso and arms, and dark blue jeans that hugged his thighs. His feet were bare. The fucked-up part of it all was that I even loved his motherfucking feet.

"Yeah," I said, watching him approach.

"You look beautiful." He kissed my temple, wrapping me in his arms.

I closed my eyes, letting myself enjoy the feel of him against me. "James, we can't do this at my parents'," I whispered against his chest.

"Do what?" he asked, rubbing my back with his palm.

"Touch like this," I responded, pushing him away. The feel of him had become too much with what I knew I had to do.

"I'm not fucking you, Izzy. It's only a goddamn hug." He crossed his arms, looking down at me.

"My parents are old-fashioned," I lied. My parents were used to my touchy-feely brothers and their girls. Hell, even my parents were prone to public displays of affection. It was one loving and nauseating family.

"Okay, Izzy. I'll keep my hands to myself if it makes you happy." He smiled weakly, his shoulders falling as he exhaled.

"Good. That makes me happy."

"That's all I want. Your happiness is my highest priority."

Fucker. Why did he have to be nice? I'd rather him be an asshole and tell me to get down on my knees and suck his dick. That would make tonight so much easier.

"Ready to go?" I asked as I grabbed my coffee cup and set it in the sink.

"Yep. I'm starving."

I smiled, knowing that he'd enjoy the food my mother had prepared. I was sure word had spread like wildfire about his appearance at Sunday dinner. She'd probably spent all night preparing a feast for the guest of honor. I prayed my brothers hadn't spilled their guts about what they'd seen in the shop yesterday, but they all had loose lips.

"We're taking my car," I told him as I locked my front door.

"Whatever you want, Izzy." James headed toward the passenger's side door of my Infiniti as I unlocked the doors.

We didn't speak on the trip, as I turned the radio volume up high enough to make it impossible. James toyed with my fingers and stroked my arms as I drove. I fought everything in me to not close my eyes and get lost in the feel of him against me. His simple, loving touches were almost enough to push me over the edge and pull the fucking car over and beg for his cock.

I dragged my hand away from his as I parked the car on the street in front of my parents' home. Turning the radio down, I said. "We're here."

"Finally," he replied as I shut off the car. We climbed out at the same time, making our way to the front door. "Wait," he growled, grabbing me around the waist. "I want to kiss you before we go inside. It's a long time not to be able to touch you."

I nodded, biting my lip as I stared up at him. His eyes matched the color of the leaves that had just bloomed on the tree behind his face. His dark olive complexion made his eyes seem brighter than they were. Before I could reply, he kissed me, wrapping his arms around my back as he drew me in.

I melted into him, moaning slightly at his taste. James's kiss was like a hit of a crack pipe for an addict. "Stop," I mumbled against his lips. "Someone will catch us."

"Shh," he whispered before delving deeper inside my mouth.

Just then, the door popped open and I heard, "Oh heavens."

Fuck.

My mother had caught us red-handed. I pulled back, heat creeping across my face as I looked at my ma.

"Sorry, Ma."

"Oh no, child. Nothing to be sorry about." She laughed, looking between James and me. "James," she crooned, smiling at him and holding out her arms.

"Mrs. Gallo. It's nice to see you again," he replied, hugging her.

"It's very *nice* to see you again, and with my Izzy too." She winked at me over his shoulder, still tightly holding on to him.

"Ma, we're not together."

"Looks like it to me, dear." Her smile grew wider as she watched me and released him. "Let me get a good look at you, James." She snickered as she held his arms and drank him in.

"Ma, you're embarrassing him." I crossed my arms over my chest, watching my mother rape him with her eyes.

James laughed, leaning forward and kissing her on the cheek. "It's always a pleasure, Mrs. Gallo."

"Oh, sweetie. The pleasure is all mine," she whispered, looking over her shoulder at me. She linked her arms with his and ushered him into the house. "James is here!" she yelled as I closed the door.

I'd already known this was going to be a long-ass day, but having my mother catching us in a lip lock made it that much worse.

"Me too!" I screeched, feeling a little left out.

Suzy and Mia both rounded the corner from the family room with giant smiles on their faces as they looked at James.

"James," Suzy cooed, holding out her arms to him. "I'm so happy you're with Izzy."

"We're not together," I said.

"Uh huh. Sure, hon." Mia laughed, drinking in James at such a close proximity. "I've heard a lot about you, James."

He turned to me, winking with a grin on his face. "You have? That's interesting," he replied, looking back to Mia. "I hope they've all been nice things."

She nodded as her smile widened. "Yep. Izzy's told us all about you," she said as she looked down at his crotch and wiggled her eyebrows.

"Oh," James said, and laughed.

"For the love of all that is holy, shut the hell up, Mia." I pinched the bridge of my nose. A sense of doom seeped into my body.

My ma leaned over and whispered not so quietly to Mia, "They were kissing outside."

"You were not," Suzy said, smacking me on the shoulder. "I knew you liked him," she whispered—also not so quietly.

"Would everyone just shut it, please?" I begged, ready to run out of the house like a little girl throwing a temper tantrum.

"What's all the commotion in here?" Pop asked as he entered the foyer with his eyebrows knitted together. As soon as he saw James, his face lit up like a fucking Christmas tree. "James, my boy," he said, holding out his hand to him before pulling him close. "How the hell are ya, and my boy Tommy?"

"Fine, Mr. Gallo. I'm just fine, and so is your son." James shook his hand, gripping his forearm.

I glared at my girls as they stood there with dopey-ass grins on their faces, staring at James. "Traitors," I mouthed, snarling my lips.

Suzy stuck out her tongue while Mia shrugged and laughed. My ma, on the other hand, was watching James and my pop very closely.

"Come on and sit with the men. Dinner will be ready soon," Pop offered, motioning toward the family room with his head.

"Hello?" I whined, wondering where my greeting was.

"Sorry, baby girl," he said, stopping and walking in my direction. "I got caught up in the moment." He wrapped his arms around me and kissed my cheek.

"Seems to be a problem in this house," I groaned.

"Let's go, son. They'll call us when it's time to eat," Pop said to James.

Son? Really? What the fuck just happened?

James gave me a wink before he disappeared with my pop to lounge in front of the television and bullshit. Ma smiled at me and quickly excused herself to check on dinner.

I turned my attention to Mia and Suzy. "What the fuck just happened?" I asked.

They laughed and shrugged. They were no fucking help.

"Just nice to have someone new here for a change," Suzy responded.

"A fucking homeless guy wouldn't get that kind of reception," I bit out.

"Maybe if he was as sexy and locking lips with you he would." Mia laughed.

"Fucking lying bitches," I muttered, walking away from them.

I did love those girls. They were lying through their teeth, but they knew what had gone down between James and me. They were looking for some juicy gossip and they'd get it, but not today.

"Need help, Ma?" I asked as I walked in the kitchen to find my mother straining the pasta.

"You talk and I'll cook," she replied, keeping her back to me.

"I'd rather cook." I leaned against the counter and watched her.

She looked at me with a smile on her face as she tossed the pasta, washing away the last bits of water. "I'm sure you would, but I want to know how James just showed up this weekend."

"The boys invited him to dinner, Ma. I didn't have anything to do with it. I'm sorry." I crossed my arms, watching her.

"Baby girl, I know that. I mean how did he end up locking lips with you at my front door?" She laughed, knowing that I hated talking about this shit.

"I saw him last weekend and he dropped in to check on me."

"Isabella, I wasn't born yesterday." She snickered as she poured the pounds of perfectly cooked pasta in the serving bowl.

She always had her ears to the ground. She knew everything that went on in this family.

"It's a long story, Ma."

"Do you like him?" She stopped, turning to face me with a grin.

"He's okay," I lied, feeling my cheeks warm.

"Just okay? Looks like he's more than okay, dear." She scooped sauce over the pasta, tossing it to keep it moist.

"Eh. He's not my type." I shrugged, hoping she'd drop it.

But in true Mama Gallo style, she replied, "You doth protest too much."

"Ma, he's bossy," I whined, grabbing the bowl of pasta off the counter.

"Bossy or doesn't put up with your bullshit?" she asked, following me into the dining room.

"We'll talk about it later." I sighed as I placed the pasta in the middle of the table.

"Fine, but I won't forget." She turned on her heels and walked back into the kitchen.

"Dinner!" I yelled toward the family room, and joined my mother in the kitchen.

We filled our arms with her chicken parmigiana, an enormous salad, homemade garlic bread, and a dish piled high with meatballs and sausage.

"You cooked for an army," I said, trying to balance the dishes in my arms.

"I wanted to make sure no one left here hungry." Her feet clattered behind me into the dining room.

Everyone had found their seat around the table, James sitting in the chair next to mine. He rose to his feet, moving toward me quickly, and grabbed two dishes from my arms.

"Thanks," I whispered, placing the other bowl on the table.

"Everyone have everything before I sit down?" Ma asked, standing near her chair.

"We're good, darling," Pop said as he patted her hand.

"Guests first," she said, passing the bowl of pasta to James.

A collective groan filled the room as James had first dibs on each dish. My father went next before the rest of us were able to fill our plates.

"James here said Thomas is doing great and hopes to be home soon," Pop said as he filled half of his plate with pasta.

James nodded, grabbing my leg under the table as he waited for the next dish to be passed his way. "He's an amazing agent."

"How about our Izzy? She's pretty special, isn't she?" Ma remarked as I tried to swallow a sip of water but ended up choking on it.

James patted me on the back as I tried to catch my breath while coughing up the water that had gone down wrong. "There's no one like her," he replied, smiling at me.

I held up my hand, trying to set shit straight, but I couldn't stop choking. God was playing a wicked trick on me. Everyone was in James's corner and no one had my back. *What the fuck?*

"You okay?" Mike asked with a grin on his face.

I glared at him as I tried to clear my throat and rid it of the invasion. "I'm ooo—" I croaked out before choking again.

"So are you two seeing each other?" Suzy asked, biting her lip as she stared at James and tried to ignore me.

"I guess you could say that," he replied, squeezing my knee.

"Wait," I whispered, my throat finally clear enough to speak. "We are not."

"You have a habit of kissing just anyone, baby girl?" Pop asked with his fork in midair.

Goddamn it. I closed my eyes, wiping away a tear that had formed while I'd been choking. "No, Daddy. I just don't want anyone to get the wrong idea, is all." I smiled halfheartedly, hoping that it was enough to stop his line of questioning.

"No one is thinking anything. That's why Suzy asked. We're curious. You've never brought anyone to Sunday dinner before." He stuffed the pasta in his mouth and began to chew.

I shook my head and sighed. "I didn't invite James. The guys did." I motioned toward my three jerkoff brothers around the table.

James leaned in to my ear and whispered, "Way to make me feel welcome, doll."

I glared at him before turning my venom toward my brothers. "You know I feel this is family time."

"James is the closest thing we have to Thomas right now, and for that, I'm grateful that he's here. He's welcome any Sunday he'd like to join us for a nice home-cooked meal," Ma insisted.

"Thank you, Mrs. Gallo. Your cooking is superb. Better than any Italian restaurant I've ever been to, and the closest to my grandmother's cooking I've ever found." He smiled, turning toward me and winking.

I was in a losing battle. I was sinking fast, making a total asshole out of myself, and no one would throw me a fucking life vest. James had turned into the golden boy, and I felt like a major cunt for saying that I hadn't invited him, because in all honesty, I liked having him around and I knew my family did too.

"We mean it, son. You're welcome here any time," Pop reiterated between forkfuls of pasta.

I hung my head, playing with the food on my plate as I wallowed in my asshole behavior. James pushed the hair away from my face and moved into my personal space.

"You and I will work this out later. Eat," he whispered, reaching down and stroking my leg. "You're going to need your energy."

The man was sex crazed. Every part of my body hurt, and there was no way in hell I could have sex with him again. I wouldn't be able to walk right if we did it one more time. He couldn't honestly be serious…could he?

I turned, looking into his emerald eyes, and saw the seriousness behind his words. I ate the rest of my dinner in silence, letting the family talk to James and monopolize the conversation. I'd never sat silent for so long at the dinner table before today. I'd let them ask their questions and hear about Thomas's work within the MC. I knew it was helping dampen the fears each one of them had about his work.

After dinner, we all fell into our usual spots—me on the floor with Anthony and the others on the couches and chairs around the room. James stretched out next to me, facing the television as he twirled a piece of my hair out of view of my parents. They wouldn't have cared, in all honesty. I knew that about my parents, but I worried they'd see how I responded to him. They already didn't believe that he meant nothing to me. I'd have a lot of explaining to do the next time the girls cornered me alone.

James Caldo was like a parasite, although a fucking sexy one.

13

THROWN FOR LOOP

JAMES

I COLLAPSED NEXT TO HER, COMPLETELY WINDED FROM AN ORGASM TO end all fucking orgasms. Izzy Gallo was a beast in the sack. She fucked like a porn star and took everything I had to give. Every moment I spent with her and her family, I fell a little bit farther into the rabbit hole, and I knew I'd never be the same after this fucking weekend.

"Jesus," I murmured through labored breaths.

"I don't know if I can even walk," she whispered, rolling over and resting on her back.

"I can't remember a better weekend in forever, Izzy." My words were true. It had been the most relaxing forty-eight hours I'd had in years.

It wasn't just that it had been relaxing—that I could do with a cold beer and a weekend of football. This was different. She made every minute enjoyable. Just watching her squirm at her parents' had been enjoyment enough.

"I don't think we should see each other again," she said, putting her back to me.

What the fuck? "Excuse me?" I asked, turning toward her. "You can't be fucking serious."

"Dead fuckin' serious, James."

"Izzy," I whispered, grabbing at her shoulder as I tried to roll her back toward me. "Look at me."

"No," she barked, pulling her body from my grip. "I don't want to see you again."

"Not this shit again," I muttered as I ran my hands through my hair. "Can't even let me enjoy the goddamn afterglow before you start spouting your bullshit. I don't believe a word of it."

"Believe what you want, James. This isn't working out for me."

"Seemed to be working out just fine when you were grinding your pussy on my face and chanting my name." I stared at the ceiling, thinking about what my next play should be to stop the train of destruction that was heading straight toward me.

"That was fucking, nothing more."

"It was more than that and you know it." I curled toward her, trying to hold her body against me.

She went rigid in my arms. "You should go before it gets dark," she whispered.

"That's it, huh? Fuck my brains out and toss me out like a piece of trash?" I asked, mystified at her thought process.

"Yeah," she replied, her body flattening against the mattress.

I knew she was scared, but I was too pissed off to try and calm her fears. I bit back like a wounded animal.

I climbed off the bed, grabbing my jeans off the floor and sliding them on. "We're not done, Izzy. I won't stick around for us to say things we'll regret. Shit we can't take back."

"The only thing I regret is spending the weekend with you."

"You're a fucking liar!" I roared, so pissed off I could barely see straight.

"Think what you want, but you're not my type."

"You just want a pussy you can boss around. I have a dick, babe. One you seemed to love this weekend. You get your head on fucking straight and give me a call when you're ready."

"Not happening, James," she replied as she turned to face me.

I'd already raised my voice, but I couldn't fucking help it. The woman was maddening. "I'm exactly what you need and want. You're too fucking scared to admit it."

She shook her head as she crawled out of bed and started to dress. "You're not all that."

"When you grow the fuck up, call me," I said as I stalked toward her.

"You're a total dick," she hissed, moving to slap me.

I grabbed her wrist, pulling her to my body. Gripping her hair in my fist, I gave it a slight tug as I hovered over her lips. She gasped, holding my shoulders.

"You know you want me," I growled, my lips a breath away from hers. "I wrecked you for any other man. I own your ass, Izzy. I'll let you run, but you can't resist me forever."

I crushed my lips against her, holding her by the hair. She moaned into my mouth as her body betrayed her every word. Backing away, I released her and left her standing in her room half naked and speechless.

The ride back to Leesburg gave me plenty of time to think of my next move. I'd give her space—for a little while—before I came crashing back into her life. We had that spark, that something special that couldn't be denied. Come hell or high water, Izzy Gallo would admit that she wanted to be with me.

***

"Who pissed in your damn Cheerios?" Bobby teased as I walked in the office on Wednesday morning.

Bobby was my regional supervisor, but I often told him to go fuck himself. We had one of those relationships. He didn't hold back when pointing out the obvious.

"No one. Just a shitty-ass week," I snapped, throwing my bag on the floor and collapsing in my chair.

"Ah. Pussy problems." He laughed, kicking his feet up on the desk.

"Shut the fuck up," I snarled through gritted teeth.

"You better sort that shit out and get your head in the game," he said, riffling through a file. "There's movement on the coast within a rival MC. We need to keep an eye on Thomas and make sure he's safe."

"I got his back," I grunted, pulling myself toward the desk.

"Not when you have pussy on your mind."

"I got this shit, Bobby."

He stood and walked toward my desk. Leaning over, he placed his fists against the surface. "Sort your shit out. Got me?"

"Yes, sir." I knew he was fucking right.

One thing I'd gathered about Izzy through conversations with Thomas was that she was the most stubborn person he'd ever known. Izzy wouldn't be the one to make the first step or reach out to me. I knew I had to be the bigger person in this nonexistent relationship.

I needed to at least contact her and hope she had changed her mind. If she hadn't, I needed to find a way to help her do that. I needed to break down her walls. Finding the crack was the problem. Once I did, victory would be mine.

Me: Thinking of me?

Hopefully she hadn't blocked my number. The girl was feisty enough that she'd do something like that. Try and remove all temptation from her life. I knew that if she responded, I had her.

I threw the phone down on my desk, grabbing a cup of coffee before going through some surveillance footage that had been gathered the night before. When I returned to my desk, I had a message waiting. I smiled to myself as I read her words, feeling victorious.

Sexy Fugitive: Hey.

It wasn't much, but it was a reply. The name I'd put in my phone when saving her number fit our situation perfectly. I tapped my pencil against the desk, debating on how to respond.

Sexy Fugitive: I'm sorry.

I almost fell off my chair as I read her message. Izzy didn't seem like the type of girl who used those words often. Her stubbornness did not allow her to admit when she was wrong or regretted something. My heart started to pound as I saw a glimmer of hope for us.

Rubbing my chin, I wondered if I should ask about which part. It could be about a myriad of things, including fucking me or kicking me out of bed afterward.

Me: For?

I'd let her be the one to explain her need to apologize. No way was I going to fuck up the one inroad I had. No fucking way in hell. Once that shit vanished, it would be gone for good.

I set my phone down, starting the video on my laptop of the MC in action last night. We had surveillance cameras everywhere outside their compound, and in areas Thomas had told us were usual spots where club business took place. When we were finally able to bring them down, we'd have video proof to back up the allegations.

Letting it continue to play, I picked up my phone to read her reply.

Sexy Fugitive: For being a bitch.

Her message was still vague and cagey, but perfectly Izzy. She wasn't a fucking fool. No one likes to admit they were wrong, especially not someone as stubborn as she is.

Me: I wouldn't use that term.

Sexy Fugitive: I didn't mean to be a cunt.

I cringed at her colorful wording. *Cunt* wasn't a word I threw around when describing a woman. That shit would be immediately met with a punch to the face or a kick to the balls.

Me: I hate that word, especially when thinking about you, unless…

Sexy Fugitive: Unless what?

Me: Unless we're talking about your beautiful, selfish pussy and how it milks my cock.

I waited a moment, but there was no quick response. I turned my attention back toward the screen, watching as the prospects, including Flash, exchanged a duffel bag with an unknown man for a package. I didn't know what was inside, but the group was heavy in the drug trade in the central Florida region. Most likely it was heroin or meth.

Sexy Fugitive: You scare me, James.

I knew I'd come on strong, but fuck. I didn't want to waste time playing a bullshit game. I'd laid my feelings out for her, made my intentions known. Izzy wasn't just another easy fuck to me.

Me: Nothing to be scared of, doll. I'm not the boogeyman.

Sexy Fugitive: You're scarier.

I paused the video, Izzy taking precedence over the grainy images on my laptop.

Me: Why?

Sexy Fugitive: I don't want to like you.

I deconstructed her words. She didn't want to, but she did. I smiled, rubbing my lips as I chose my next words carefully.

Me: What scares you most?

I needed to cut off the head of the beast. Face her fear head on and alter her perception. The last thing in the world I wanted was a scared Izzy Gallo. She needed to know that I wasn't the enemy.

Sexy Fugitive: I swore off men like you.

Men like me? What the fuck did that mean? I knew I could be demanding in the bedroom, but besides that, I was like every other red-blooded American man. She wanted easy, someone she could control. That shit I was not down for. Just like her, no one told me what to do.

Me: Men like me?

I wanted her thoughts. She needed to voice her fears to me. Maybe it wasn't my demanding ways in the bedroom. I didn't want to expand until I knew her reasoning. I always believed in not giving too much information without knowing the enemy you faced. My enemy in this battle was Izzy's fear.

Sexy Fugitive: You're demanding and bossy.

I laughed when I read her message. Izzy wasn't a fucking cream puff. Those exact words could be used to describe her.

Me: The only time I'm bossy and demanding is when we're fucking, doll. I like things done my way in the bedroom.

I had particular tastes. Most people do. I didn't do missionary style with rose petals spread across the bed. I liked shit raw and rough, and I wanted to be in total control. That's not to say I wouldn't hand over the reins from time to time, but I was a man, after all, and the bedroom was my domain.

Sexy Fugitive: You want shit done your way all the time.

Me: That's bullshit. I like you because you're the most aggressive and strongest woman I've ever met. I don't want a pushover who's going to do everything I ask.

Sexy Fugitive: You want me to fight back?

Me: Outside of the bedroom, yes. I love that fucking smartass mouth of yours. When you get mouthy, it makes me rock fucking hard.

Sexy Fugitive: And inside the bedroom?

Would Izzy understand the difference? Would she be able to give herself willingly during sex? She'd seemed to enjoy herself this weekend when I'd told her to strip. She'd had me by the balls during her striptease.

Me: I'm the boss in the bedroom.

Sexy Fugitive: I don't know if I can deal with that.
Me: Did you like when I told you to strip?
Sexy Fugitive: Not at first.
Me: And then?
Sexy Fugitive: I liked teasing you as I danced.

Sitting there, I thought of her naked, shaking her ass and hips as she took off her clothes. Her dark olive skin and brown hair had made me hard in the dim lighting of the room. It had taken everything in me not to throw her to the ground immediately and fuck her brains out.

Me: Did you like when I fucked you?
Sexy Fugitive: Yes…

The *dot dot dot* told me that she wasn't happy with admitting it, but she had nonetheless.

Me: Was there anything I did that you didn't like?

I wanted to know where her head was with what I did to her. Maybe I moved too fast, but I wouldn't apologize for who or what I was.

I started the video again, needing to get my head in the game. I wanted to nail these motherfuckers as soon as possible so I could get the fuck out of this town. Five minutes later, there still wasn't a reply from Izzy, but I knew we weren't over.

14

OPINIONS ARE LIKE ASSHOLES

IZZY

"HEY, TERRI," I SAID AS HE WALKED THROUGH THE DOOR, INTERRUPTING my conversation with James. I knew it was shitty spot to leave him hanging, but I didn't have a choice. It would be hours until I could answer the question.

"Hey, babe. I'm ready," he said, cracking his neck.

I winced and patted the chair in front of me. The piece was a monster —an entire back design. I had done the outline previously, and today, we'd finish it. The dude, although not a pussy, didn't like to talk while he got inked. He put on his headphones and blocked out the world while I worked.

My workstation was set with everything I needed, so I was ready to go when he arrived. After a few kind words, I got down to business. I shaded the massive design while he faced the opposite direction.

Since I'd kicked James out on Sunday, I hadn't given myself much time to reflect on what had happened. I'd kept myself busy with work, friends, and family. The last thing I'd wanted to do was linger on my epic fuck-up. I hadn't meant to be such a bitch to him, but I hadn't known how else to handle the situation.

I hadn't been able to even face him when I told him to leave. I hadn't wanted to see his face—I couldn't see it. I would've taken the words back if I'd seen the hurt I'd inflicted. The rub of the entire situation was that I did like James—maybe more than I was willing to admit.

Even when he was a bossy asshole, I liked having him around. The banter between us was wicked fast, and his ability to call me on bullshit was matched by no one outside my own family. Maybe it was his ability to read me that unnerved me the most.

No one in my family, especially my brothers, had ever liked any man I spent time with. James was the exception. He had been welcomed with open arms, treated as family, and invited back.

Would I be willing to let him in my life? Would I still be me after he invaded my world?

I didn't like weak women. They drove me fucking insane. The girls who changed and made themselves the perfect woman for their man. I wanted to be me, and would do everything in my power not to lose myself. I saw it happen all the time with my friends as they settled down, and although I loved them dearly, it pissed me the fuck off.

Would James try and change me? Did he want a meek woman who would agree to everything he wanted? He said that he loved my smartass mouth, but would he feel that way later? Was he just saying the words I wanted to hear to get back into my bed?

I took a page out of Suzy's playbook as I worked on Terri's back. I needed to figure shit out about James. I needed to go through the pros and cons and see which side won. I mean, that's a rational way to make a decision, right?

James had a lot of pros. He was funny, smart, kind, and respectful to my family. He loved my brother, and he was handsome and sexy as hell. He had a dirty-ass mouth, and he was an amazing lover, Plus he made me feel good about myself.

His cons were a mixed bag. He pissed me off…a lot. He was bossy (although that could be a pro in the bedroom—fuck, I did like it). He was too smart for his own good, knew my game before I could play my hand, and didn't put up with my bullshit. He was a arrogant prick, he knew how sexy he was, and I liked him too much.

The list of reasons not to be with James was longer than why I should give him another shot. In all fairness, the list of bad qualities weren't truly bad. I remembered him saying that I wanted a man I could control, and based off the cons, I'd say his words were true.

Flash was an example of a man who didn't know how to handle me, and for that, I let him hang around and come back for seconds. I didn't have to worry about him overtaking my life and losing myself. Flash didn't ask for much, just a fuck every once in a while and nothing more. He'd tried once and I'd shut that shit down quick. He'd accepted it and we'd continued as friends with benefits.

I'd tried to steer clear of men like my brothers my entire life. Suzy had changed since she'd met Joe, but she hadn't lost herself. It was the opposite, actually. She was stronger than she had been the first time I met her. She spoke her mind, slung profanity like a true Gallo, and seemed more confident. A strong man like Joe helped the real Suzy shine.

Mia was just Mia. Mike hadn't changed her at all. She had still been the same sassy, no-nonsense chick since the day I met her. She didn't put up with his bullshit. She called his ass on the carpet and met him head on in every situation.

Mike and Joe had enough testosterone and bossiness in them that they could rule the fucking world if they put their minds together. The fact that I'd never thought about their inability to change the women in their lives was surprising. I'd thought it happened in every relationship, but maybe I'd just focused on the people I knew who had lost themselves instead of those who had become stronger with the love of a good man by their side.

"I need a piss break," Terri uttered, pulling off his headphones.

I almost didn't hear him, lost so deep in my thoughts as I dissected everything I knew about love and all of my fucked-up theories.

Moving my hand away, I set down the ink gun. "Sure, Ter. Take as long as you need." I leaned back, stretching my muscles. I felt stiff after sitting for a couple of hours hunched over his back.

I felt like a doormat—totally used and exhausted after not having slept well for three nights. I hadn't felt like I'd slept when I woke in the morning. It was like I had lain there in a trance as the night had passed, haunted by the words that had been thrown around before James left. I felt guilty, and it wasn't an emotion I knew how to deal with.

"What's wrong, Iz?" Joe asked as I stood to stretch.

"I just haven't been sleeping well." I rolled my neck on my shoulders, trying to relieve a headache I felt building.

"Is this about James?" Mike piped in, leaning back in his chair and watching me.

"I don't know. I'm just a fucking mess."

"Izzy, you know I hate any man who is with you or wants to be with you. Yes?" Joe asked, placing dollops of Vaseline on the plastic wrap laid out on his station. "I mean every fucking one of them." He set the small, round inkwells on top, prepping his workstation for his next client.

"I know, Joe. I remember you threatening the lives of more than a few." I laughed, bending over to stretch my lower back.

"I like James," he said, causing me to stand up and look at him.

"You've got to be shitting me," I said, completely in shock.

"He's not a shithead. He's a solid guy. Works hard, likes your brothers, and seems to adore you. Fuck, he fit right in with the family too."

"He adores me?" I shook my head. "Clearly you saw something else than I did."

"I saw the way he looks at you, Iz," Mike agreed, getting up from his chair and coming over to my workstation.

"Like a piece of meat he can control." I knew my brothers didn't want to hear about my sex life, and I sure as fuck didn't want to tell them, but I thought my words could be taken many ways.

"I'm going to talk to you as a friend and not my sister," Mike said, looking down at me with a smile. "Shit's going to be hard to swallow, but I'm going to say my piece."

"Here we go," I whispered, sitting back down and waiting to hear his pearls of wisdom.

"He looks at you like I look at Mia and Joe looks at Suzy. He looks at you like he worships the very ground you walk on, Iz. Men are bossy creatures—it's in our nature. If you find one who isn't, then they don't have a set of balls," Mike explained, shaking his head. "Every boy you liked was a total pussy and not worthy of your time. They wanted in your pants and that's why we ran them off. James is an entirely different animal."

I sighed, knowing that my brother was right. I knew the look on his face when he stared at me. I was sure it was a reflection of how I looked at him, but it didn't mean I liked it.

"He's bossy, Mike. I don't think I can deal with that caveman bullshit."

"You deal with ours just fine." Anthony laughed across the room as he walked toward his seat.

"You guys are different. You're my brothers and you do things to protect me and make me happy."

"Who's to say James isn't the same?" Joe asked, swiveling his chair around to face me.

"I have to love you because we're blood," I said, avoiding his question.

"I try to stay the fuck out of your business, sister, but for once, you're wrong," Anthony interrupted.

"When you guys need help, I'm the first person you run to, and now you think you know what's best for me?"

"We come to you for help because you're the toughest chick we know. You're always one step ahead of everyone and everything. You're a force to be reckoned with, Isabella," Joe said.

I hated when they dropped my full name. It showed that they were serious. Where the fuck was Terri? I wanted him to get the fuck back in here so this conversation would be put on the back burner.

"Listen, boys, I don't need a man in my life to complete me. I'm not weak." Fuck it. I was the fiercest bitch I knew. People didn't fuck with me unless I let them. Many men had been brought to their knees by a swift kick to the balls by me. The only people in the world I let talk to me this way were in this room.

"Weakness is walking away," Mike muttered, grabbing his chair and pushing it close to my station. "It takes strength to face the unknown and do it in the name of love."

"You've been listening to too much Barry Manilow or Lionel Richie or some bullshit. Who's filling your head with this nonsense?" Where had my tough-ass brother gone? I mean, a year ago he wouldn't have been telling me that it took strength to take a chance on love.

"Listen here, smartass. Love doesn't make you weak. You're stronger as a couple than you are apart. If he's the right man, he'll know how to bring out your strengths. He'll make you a better person. If you lose your-self, then you weren't strong to begin with. Man the fuck up and take a chance for once. Prove you got a set of balls on you like you always claim."

Mike was challenging me and being all philosophical and shit. I turned toward Joe, hoping he'd have something better to say. "And you?" I challenged.

"What he said," Joe replied with a smile and a wink.

I looked over at Anthony, who was staring at the ceiling, avoiding eye contact with me. "Anth, I know you have something to say. Tell them they're wrong."

Slowly, he brought his eyes to mine and shrugged. "You know I think relationships are bullshit, Iz, but I think James is a great guy."

"When did everyone jump off team Izzy and hop on the James train?" I asked, ready to pull my hair out.

Before anyone could answer, Terri walked back into the work area. "Sorry," he coughed, plopping his ass back in the chair.

"No worries, Ter. You rescued me," I said as I picked up the gun and got back to work.

Terri was a big-ass biker around fifty, and he had an old lady at home. He'd been coming to the shop for a couple of years and I knew some things about him, but we didn't spend much time chatting like two old friends.

"Ter, let me ask you something before you disappear into your Led Zeppelin haze."

He placed the headphones around his neck and leaned forward, displaying his back. "Sure thing, kid. Shoot."

"You're married, right?"

"Twenty years."

"You happy?"

"Well, yeah, or I wouldn't be married anymore."

"She a pushover?"

"What?"

"You like your woman weak?"

He shook his head, turning slightly to look over his shoulder at me with his unibrow arched inward. "Babe, I don't do weak."

"Is your wife a 'yes, sir' kind of woman?"

"She's the toughest woman I know."

"You seem like a badass dude, yet you're with a tough chick. Why?"

"I said that I don't do weak. I wanted a partner. If I just wanted someone who would fill my bed, I would've stuck with club whores, kid."

"I thought tough guys liked weak," I said, placing the needle against his skin and starting on the heart I'd woven with the skull.

"Weak pricks like weak chicks. I want someone to keep me on my toes. You have some fucked-up thoughts on men, babe."

I thought about his words, letting them sink in before I spoke. "I have four brothers who act like the missing link between modern-day man and cavemen," I said, laughing to myself as I pictured them beating on their chests.

"They're men and not pussies like boys are today. Video games, manscaping, and metrosexuals have fucked up society. We're raising a generation of pansy-ass motherfuckers. Your brothers are solid dudes. I'd want them at my back when shit went down."

"Huh," I said, knowing that his words were true. My brothers always had my back and were there when I needed them. I'd never feared shit because of them.

"We done?" he asked, holding his headphones in his hand.

"Yep," I answered, not looking at my brothers as I continued to work. I knew they were all smiles with shitty "I told you so" looks on their faces.

Opinions were like assholes—everybody had one.

15

PLAYING DIRTY

JAMES

Four hours had passed since I'd sent Izzy the message asking her what she didn't like. She could've been writing a goddamn novel to describe everything that drove her ass crazy. Just when I was about to lose my shit, my phone beeped.

Sexy Fugitive: Sorry. I had an early client and it took for fucking ever... HUGE piece of work covering his entire back.

At least I knew her quietness hadn't been intentional.

Me: I thought you were giving me the brush-off... again.

Sexy Fugitive: I don't even know where to start, James.

Me: Anywhere you want, beautiful. Tell me one thing you didn't like.

I was possibly inviting disaster.

Sexy Fugitive: You're bossy.

I laughed as I read her words. Izzy was a bossy little thing too. She wasn't a patsy for anyone, especially someone with a dick between their legs.

Me: Only when I need to be.

Sexy Fugitive: So all the time basically you feel the need.

She was a ball buster. Her brothers had raised her right and hadn't sheltered her.

Me: When I feel the need to protect something important, then yes.

Sexy Fugitive: I'm capable of protecting myself, James.

Me: Never said you couldn't, but I'd rather be your shield and take the brunt of anything thrown your way.

A few minutes passed and I waited, sipping on a beer as I let ESPN play in the background. Seventy-two hours ago, I'd walked out of her house and waited for her to make the first move. It hadn't come, but I'd been man enough to suck it up and take the first step.

Sexy Fugitive: You're cocky.

Me: Wait a second here. Are we listing your traits or mine?

She had cocky down pat. The girl had the shit in spades.

Sexy Fugitive: Don't be an ass. We're talking about you.

Me: Confused me there for a second. I am who I am just like you are who you are… Smug, bossy, and beautiful.

Sexy Fugitive: Flattery will get you nowhere.

Me: I know. You like the challenge as much as I do.

Sexy Fugitive: Bullshit. You're infuriating.

Me: And it makes you wet.

Sexy Fugitive: You can't be serious.

Me: I'd never joke when talking about that sweet-ass pussy of yours, Izzy.

I had a hard-on just thinking about her. It took everything in me not to hop on my bike and have this conversation face to face.

Me: Touch yourself. I'm sure you're wet right now.

Her reply was swift and made me laugh. She didn't like the thought of me being right.

Sexy Fugitive: Fuck off, James.

Me: If you were here, I'd have you on all fours, begging for more.

Sexy Fugitive: Maybe I'd want to be on my back and looking in your eyes.

Me: Lying through your teeth, doll. You'd be slamming yourself against my cock, taking all I had to give.

Sexy Fugitive: STOP.

My dick throbbed, aching for release. My balls had to be blue with the way they felt. Bastards may burst at any moment. I needed inside Izzy and I didn't want to wait. I knew that if I jerked off, it wouldn't fucking help. My hand didn't compare to her milking the life out of my dick.

Me: Panties soaked?

Sexy Fugitive: I didn't wear any today.

She didn't understand how her trying to shut me the hell up was a total cocktease. I loved it. I could go out and find some nameless woman who would lay herself out and offer her pussy to me to relieve the ache deep in my balls. I didn't want that. I only wanted her. After having a few tastes, I was hooked. No one else would ever compare.

Me: STOP.

Sexy Fugitive: I'm almost dripping thinking of you jamming your hard, long cock inside me.

She was the devil.

Me: STOP.

Sexy Fugitive: My fingers don't feel as good as your dick driving into me.

I closed my eyes, rubbing my hard-on through my jeans as I thought about her fingering herself. I refused to let myself come until I was buried deep inside her.

Me: You're wicked.

Sexy Fugitive: Spank me.

I thought that she needed a visual. I unzipped my jeans and pulled out my cock. Gripping it from the base in one hand, I snapped a picture and sent it to her. *Let her choke on that.*

I gave my cock a quick squeeze, trying to stop the ache before I shoved it back in my jeans. Tonight, I'd need an ice bath to quell my hard-on.

Sexy Fugitive: You don't play fair.

Me: When it comes to you...no fuckin' way.

Sexy Fugitive: I have a client. Gotta go.

Me: Think of me when you touch yourself tonight.

Sexy Fugitive: Arrogant asshole.

I left it at that. I had her.

16

MOTHER KNOWS BEST

IZZY

"WHAT'S TROUBLING YOU, ISABELLA?" MA ASKED AS SHE SAT DOWN next to me at her kitchen table.

James and I had been texting for the last twenty-four hours—a constant volley of messages to drive each other insane. I didn't know what I wanted anymore. The world seemed to be conspiring against me when it came to James. Was I the only one who thought we were a terrible idea?

"James," I whispered without looking at her as I rubbed the smooth wooden table with my fingertips.

Placing her hand over mine, she stopped my nervous motion. "Izzy, look at me."

I met her soft, kind eyes. My mother was and would always be my best friend. I looked up to her and how she lived her life. From the outside, people would assume that she didn't run the show, but make no bones about it—she was the boss of this family.

"What are you so scared of?" she asked, stroking the back of my hand with her thumb.

"He's just so…"

"Perfect for you?" she asked, smiling wide.

"Ma, are you crazy?" I asked, flabbergasted by her question.

"I know when a man is smitten. I've seen you with other men, Izzy. No one got the reaction out of you that James did."

"Isn't that a bad thing, Ma?"

"Oh, honey, no. Your father still gets a rise out of me. It's what keeps us going after all these years of marriage. Without the fire between us, we would've ended long ago."

"But you and Pop love each other."

"Fiercely," she said, staring out the window as she watched my dad tend the garden. "Even after all these years, he makes me batshit crazy."

"Pop isn't bossy like James."

"Isabella, you look at your father through rose-colored glasses. Salvatore was the bossiest man I've ever met."

"Not Daddy," I said, following her eyes to watch him as he hand-picked some tomatoes.

She laughed, patting my hand. "Child, that man made your brothers look soft. I've worn him down throughout the years. Don't tell him that, though."

I giggled, thinking of my mother laying into my dad. "I remember what you told us before Suzy and Joe were married."

"Men like to think they have all the power, but we really know who rules the roost."

"Ma, if you start talking about sex, I'll puke right here."

"James will make you happy."

"He makes me miserable. What if I become one of those women who changes for her man?"

She shook her head, turning her attention back to me. "Izzy, baby. I raised you to be strong and independent. That'll never happen. A man like James needs someone who is his equal. I can see it in his eyes when he looks at you."

"What do you see?" I asked, wondering how I missed all the signs.

"He looks at you like your father looked at me when we dated. Hell, he still looks at me that way now."

"Like a piece of meat?"

"Like a challenge worth the fight, baby girl."

"I don't know, Ma."

"Have I ever given you bad advice?"

I thought about it for a moment before I answered her. Shaking my head, I said, "No."

The door opened as Dad walked in. "Baby girl, what are you doing here?"

"That happy to see me, Daddy?" I asked, jumping to my feet to kiss him.

"I'm always happy to see my favorite child."

I slapped him on the shoulder and smiled. "You say that to all of us."

"You're my favorite daughter," he said, setting the tomatoes on the counter.

"Your only daughter."

"You mince words. Give me a hug," he demanded, holding out his arms.

I buried my face in his chest, wrapping my arms around my dad. Even at his age, he was still toned and muscular. It was in the male genes in the Gallo family. They didn't breed them small.

He stroked my hair and spoke softly. "What's troubling you, Isabella?"

"You and Ma are scary," I said, moving from his arms to look up at his face.

"Why?" he asked with knitted brows, lines creasing his forehead.

"She asked the same exact question."

"What was your answer?"

"James."

"Ah. I like that man."

I rolled my eyes, releasing my grip from my dad's shirt. "Who doesn't?"

"I know you're sweet on him too, baby girl."

"Dad—"

He put his finger against my lips. "I always have your best interests at heart. No one will ever be good enough for my baby girl, but James is a man's man. I know he'll protect you when shit gets bad. I won't ever have to worry about your safety."

"I'm kind of old for you to worry, Daddy," I grumbled, smiling and rubbing his face.

"You'll always be a little girl in pigtails to me, Isabella. The little tiny thing playing with her Barbies in her room or trying to tackle her brothers in the backyard when they played football. You may be a woman, but I don't see you that way. I just can't." He sighed, brushing a hair away from my face.

"I love you, Daddy."

"Love you too, baby girl." He leaned forward, kissing me on the cheek. "What did you say, my love?"

My mother sniffled, rubbing her eyes as I turned to look at her. "I said the same, sweetheart."

"There is just too much loving going on in this room. I need to go."

"Where are you headed off to today?" my pop asked as I grabbed my keys.

"I have to work and then I'm headed out with the girls tonight."

"Mia and Suzy?" Ma asked.

"Yep. It's a girls' night out. The boys are all going to play poker at Joe's place while we have drinks."

"Just be careful," he said as I kissed him quickly.

"I will, Daddy."

"Call me tomorrow, dear," my ma said as she walked me to the door.

"I will, Ma. Love ya."

"Love you too, my sweet child."

After we kissed goodbye, I headed to my car feeling entirely different than what I'd felt when I'd arrived.

Maybe I needed to give James another chance. Either that or I needed my head to be examined. I'd think about it over drinks.

***

I downed another shot of Patron, sucking on a lemon before I wiped my lips. My legs felt numb from the three shots I'd already ingested.

"Izzy, you may want to slow down," Suzy suggested, sipping her virgin something or other.

"I got this shit," I said, slurring my words as I threw the lemon on the napkin in front of me. Picking up my phone, I typed out a little message to James.

Me: What are you wearing?

I giggled, figuring I'd turn the tables on him. He wasn't the only one who could send nudies.

"Okey-dokey," she whispered, rubbing her belly and frowning. "I can't carry you out of here tonight."

Cocky Bastard: *How much have you had to drink?*
Me: *Enough.*
Cocky Bastard: *Clearly you've reached your limit.*

"What?" I asked, missing what Suzy had just said.

"I can't carry your drunk ass out of here," she repeated.

I blinked, my vision partially clouded and my mind a little muddled. "Mia can do it," I slurred, laughing before I typed another message.

Me: *You're always so serious. Do you even know how to have fun?*

I set my phone down on the table, resting my head in my hand.

"Bitch, I'll roll ya out, but I sure as fuck am not carrying you anywhere."

"Whore." I laughed, moving my head to rest on the table.

"I think we should get the check," Suzy said, touching my chair.

I lifted my head, squinting toward her to bring her face into focus. "Don't you dare! We're not done here."

"What's crawled in your snatch and died tonight?" Mia asked, polishing off her martini.

"James." I smiled, the dopey grin spreading across my face. I felt heat creep up my neck and settle in my cheeks. My entire body overheated. I pulled at the scoop neck on my shirt, trying to cool off.

Cocky Bastard: *I think I showed you a good time not so long ago. Let me remind you.*

Suddenly a picture of his cock, piercing and all, popped up on my screen. I blushed as I stared at it, almost in a trance.

"He has your panties in a wad," Mia teased, raising her hand to get the attention of the waitress.

"He hasn't been in my panties since last weekend," I croaked with a frown as I scrubbed my hands across my face.

"Missing him?" Suzy asked with a cocked eyebrow.

"I kicked him out of bed." I set my phone down on the table and looked at my girls with a giant-ass smile. I was proud that I'd kicked his ass out of bed.

"You did what?" they asked in unison, moving backward as if I'd slapped them.

Mia leaned forward, confusion all over her face. "Back the fuck up. You kicked him out of bed?"

"Shameful," Suzy muttered, shaking her head and staring with her beady blue eyes.

"I did," I yelped, slamming my hand down on the table. I tossed my head back and giggled, thinking that the entire situation was funny. I stopped when I realized that I was the only one laughing. "What?" I asked, calling over the waitress.

"Why the fuck would you do that?" Mia asked.

"Hello? James is a bossy fuck."

"He's sexy too."

I smirked and looked at Suzy. "I know."

"Are you going to be a hardass your entire life?" Mia asked, handing over cash to the waitress and shooing her away.

"I wasn't being a hardass."

"No, you're being a pussy," Mia spat.

"Am not." I stuck out my tongue at her and snarled.

"And a child."

"I'm drunk," I blurted, burping and covering my mouth.

"Have you at least talked with him?" Suzy asked, taking another sip of her drink.

"When is that baby going to pop out so you can drink with us again?" I asked, leaning over the table and poking her belly.

"More months than I wish to count."

"It better have a pussy, dear Suzy. No more cocks in this family." I sat back down just as the waitress approached. "Ahh, perfect timing," I howled as I grabbed the drink off her tray and set it in front of me without spilling a drop.

"We want it to be a surprise," Suzy said, smiling.

"Surprises suck," I shot back. "To pussy!" I yelled, holding my glass high before taking a sip. To my shock, it wasn't what I'd ordered. "What the fuck is this?" I asked, looking at the drink.

"I cut your ass off," Mia replied.

"You're such a party pooper."

"You'll thank me tomorrow."

"Are you going to see him again?"

I turned my head to look at Suzy as her words registered with me. My brain had to work overtime to process each phrase. Clearly Mia had been right in cutting off my drinks.

"Who?" I asked, swaying in my chair.

"For the love of God," Suzy whined, looking toward the ceiling.

"Is he there?"

"Who?" she asked.

"I dunno…God?"

"Jesus, girl. Get your shit together," Suzy scolded me, biting her lip to stifle a laugh.

"Why? We leaving?"

"Are you going to see James again?" Suzy said, leaning forward, almost resting her belly on the table.

"You don't have to be so serious," I said, blinking slowly and opening my eyes wide. I felt like I was sitting there with my eyes closed, looking through slits.

"Mia, I'm gonna choke her ass out. You talk to her." Suzy leaned back in her chair as she glared at me.

"James, Izzy. Are you going to see him again?"

"Fuck," I muttered, trying to look at my phone, but my eyes were almost crossed. "We were texting and he said I'm to call him as soon as I get inside tonight and he'll be over after work tomorrow or at least that's what he said."

"I like him," Suzy said, a sappy grin on her face.

"You would," I said, resting my head in my hand. I felt like I had a bowling ball rolling around in my head. I just wanted to lie down for a bit.

"Come on, princess. It's time to get you home. You're going to need your beauty sleep if James is coming over tomorrow," Mia said, grabbing me under the arms from behind.

I slapped her hands away. "I can walk."

"Fine, tough ass. I want to see this shit on those heels."

"I'm a pro," I bragged, trying to climb off the high-top chair.

"I'm filming this shit to blackmail you later," Mia said, pulling the phone from her purse.

"I'll kill ya," I said as I slipped, grabbing the table for support. I steadied myself and turned to her. "Mia, put that shit away and help me."

"You're one crazy bitch."

"You girls love me anyway." I smiled, wrapping my arm around Mia as she helped me to the door.

I must've passed out in the car, because before I knew it, I was sitting on the couch in my living room with Mia and Suzy.

"Gimme your foot," Suzy demanded, bending down in front of me and touching my leg.

"What are you doing?" I asked, giving her my leg without hesitation.

"Helping your hot-mess self get undressed," she crowed, unstrapping my shoe.

"I can do it," I argued, falling back into the comfy cushions. "Just leave me here."

"Don't you want to go to your bed?" Mia asked, standing behind Suzy.

Mia looked like a giant Greek goddess from where I sat. Her long hair moved as if a soft breeze were circulating in the room. Clearly, I was three sheets to the wind and way beyond my limit.

"No, don't move me," I begged. "Everything just stopped spinning."

"Fine." Suzy stood and smoothed her pretty pink maternity dress.

"Are you sure, love?" Mia asked, tilting her head and staring at me.

"Please just leave me here. Go home to your bossy-ass men and leave mc in peace."

"Love ya, Iz," Suzy said, patting my leg.

"You're a crazy whore," Mia said with a small laugh as she bent down to kiss my cheek. "I love ya too."

"I love you bitches, but if you don't get the fuck out, I'm gonna scream."

They threw their hands up as Mia said, "We're going. I left aspirin and water next to you. You're going to need them."

"Fuck off, bitches."

The sound of their heels grew softer as they walked toward the front door before I heard the lock engage.

I sighed, happy to be alone in peace as I let my heavy eyelids close and drifted off to sleep.

***

"Wake up, beautiful," I heard a man say in my dream. "Isabella." The deep voice rang in my ear.

As I felt something touch my lips, my eyes flew open to see a pair of green eyes staring back at me.

I blinked, clearing my vision. The alcohol must have clouded more than just my eyes, because he looked like... Fuck. For the life of me, I couldn't remember his name.

"Am I dreaming?" I asked, reaching up and grabbing his cheek.

"You have to come with me," he demanded, letting me clumsily paw at his face.

"No," I said. My head fell back. I was too tired and drunk to deal with this fucked-up dream. "Lemme sleep."

"Thomas needs you," the man said, waking me from my dream.

"What?" I asked, sitting straight up and blinking rapidly.

"Come on, girl. He's hurt and asking for you," the thick, gravelly voice whispered in my ear.

"Oh my God," I cried, pushing myself off the couch only to fall back down against the cushions.

Thomas needed me. He was hurt. Thomas needed me. He was hurt. His words kept ringing in my ears as I tried to stagger to my feet.

"Let me help you up," Green Eyes said, wrapping his arms around me as he lifted me from the couch. "Hurry, Isabella. We don't have much time."

"What the fuck are you waiting for?" I asked, laying my head on his chest as he carried me from the house. "I need to get to my brother."

Those were the last words I spoke before passing out in Green Eyes's arms.

644

17

NAGGING FEELING...

JAMES

I COULDN'T SLEEP. IT WAS TWO A.M. AND IZZY STILL HADN'T CALLED. I didn't know if she was just being difficult or if I should listen to the nagging feeling in the pit of my stomach.

Everything had been going smoothly since we'd started texting each other on Wednesday. We had worked out some issues and come to a general understanding. I knew shit would be rough, but this was fucking ridiculous. She couldn't possibly be so cruel to not call. She had to know I'd be out of my fucking mind.

I dialed her number, letting it ring until her voicemail picked up. I tapped end and redialed, but still nothing. Tomorrow, I planned to drive up to her place in the late afternoon and whisk her off to dinner, but I couldn't wait. I had to know where the fuck she was. I'd probably get kicked in the fucking balls, but I'd go out of my mind if I didn't know she was at home, safely sleeping in her bed.

I grabbed the keys to my bike and started toward the door, but stopped. I tossed the bike keys on the table near the door and picked up the keys to my 1969 GTO. She had power and speed and I needed both right now.

I sped down I-75 headed toward her house. I gripped the steering wheel, my fingers damp with sweat. I tried to control my breathing and nerves as I drove. Working myself up wouldn't help get me there any quicker.

What if something was wrong? My stomach turned as I thought about the possibilities. My mind, maybe, was a little too imaginative. If something bad had happened, I would've heard by now. Being in law enforcement and seeing all the bad shit in the world doesn't help keep one's imagination at bay. Every sick crime scene flashed through my mind, replacing the victim with Izzy.

My blood turned cold the closer I got to her house. I hit redial over and over again until it went right to voicemail. I knew what that fucking meant. Either she had turned off her phone, it had died, or someone else had turned it off for her. There weren't any other options.

I slammed my fist down on the steering wheel, pressing my foot down against the pedal to pick up speed. I didn't have time to waste with worrying about the cops pulling me over. They'd have to chase my ass down and follow me to her house if they wanted to catch me.

My heart jumped out of my chest as my phone rang. When I looked down at my phone, I expected to see Izzy's number flash across my screen, but it wasn't her. I pressed speaker, placing the phone on my dash.

"What the fuck?" I barked as the call connected.

"Where the fuck is Izzy?" Thomas asked, breathing heavily.

"I'm on my way to her now. What the fuck is going on, Thomas?" I gripped the steering wheel so hard I could have snapped it from the dashboard.

"Flash just called me. He said Izzy was in danger. Somehow Rebel found out who she was. He knows who I am too. Find her, James, and do it now!" he roared, a loud slamming noise filling the air.

"I'm pulling on her street now," I growled, looking around the neighborhood as I sped down the road.

"I don't know who knows what at this point, brother. Find my goddamn sister."

"On it," I barked, fear gripping my insides.

"Call me back. I'm headed that way with Flash in tow."

"Give me five," I replied, stopping the car in her driveway. I tapped end, jumped from the car, and ran up her front steps.

Turning the doorknob, I realized that it was locked. I reared back and kicked in the door.

"Izzy?" I thundered, flipping on the light in the entry.

With no sign of her, I walked down the hallway to her bedroom, but it was empty. Her bed hadn't been touched.

"Izzy?" I continued yelling, running from room to room, but she wasn't there.

A lump formed in my stomach and I felt like throwing up. Izzy was gone and Rebel fucking knew about her and Thomas.

I walked toward the front door and something on the floor caught my eye. Turning, I saw a single shoe lying on the floor and her phone on the coffee table.

I ran from the house, dialing Thomas as I jumped back in the car. "She's gone," I bit out, slightly winded and in a total panic as I started the car.

"Gone or missing?" he asked, anger oozing in his voice.

"One shoe on the floor and her phone on the coffee table. She's missing."

"Fucking Rebel," Thomas muttered, his breathing growing harsh and loud. "Flash and I are an hour out. We need to figure this shit out and what our next move is."

"Fuck," I hissed, trying to think of where they would've gone.

"Stay the fuck there and make calls. Do not leave in case she shows up. We'll be there in sixty."

"Hurry the fuck up!" I snarled, and hung up as I climbed out of the car.

Once back inside, I dialed Bobby and began to pace. *Ring. Ring.* Where the fuck was he? *Ring.* I didn't have time to wait for his lazy ass to pick up the phone. *Ring.*

"Hello," a groggy voice said.

"Bobby, wake the fuck up. Izzy's been taken and Thomas's cover may have been blown."

"Wait, what?" he asked through a yawn.

"Jesus, fuck. Thomas called me tonight. Said Izzy was in danger and that Rebel found out who he is."

"Fuck," he spat, a loud thump sounding on the other end of the phone.

"Get your ass out of bed," I growled, ready to jump through the phone and choke his ass.

If my life—or Izzy's, for that matter—depended on this asshole, we were in fucking trouble.

"I'm up. Let me make some calls and get back to you," he said, disconnecting the call.

"What the fuck?" I yelled, my voice echoing through the house.

I called everyone I knew—local law enforcement in Leesburg, DEA, and FBI. All were working to bring down the MC, but the problem was that no one communicated with each other.

No one had seen Rebel. They'd lost track of him when he left the compound hours ago and he hadn't been spotted since.

Just when I was about to start climbing the fucking walls, I heard a car outside followed by two sets of footsteps up the stairs. Reaching for my gun, I drew as Thomas and Flash burst through the door.

"What the fuck did you find out?" Thomas asked, looking around the room.

"Nothing. No one knows shit," I ranted, running my fingers through my hair.

"Flash made some calls on the way here. Everyone is searching for them. They can't get far without us hearing about it."

I glared at Flash. "Did you open your fucking mouth?" I asked, charging toward him.

His mouth dropped open and his eyes grew wide as he stepped backward to avoid my grasp. A set of arms grabbed me from behind, pulling me away.

"Calm your shit down," Thomas ordered.

"Thomas, he's the only douche who knew who you were!" I roared, prying his hands from my body.

"Listen, fucker," Flash snarled, moving toward me. "I went into Rebel's room to leave a package on his bed and I found a file sitting in plain sight."

"What a fucking clusterfuck," I hissed, scrubbing my face in my hands. "What was inside?"

"A picture of Izzy with her full name and address and a complete file about Thomas."

648

"Think he told others?" I asked, looking at Thomas.

He shook his head and winced. "I don't think so. No one seemed to act any differently. Rebel was the only one missing at the compound when Flash called me."

"Did you at least grab the fucking file?" I asked Flash.

"I'm not a fucking moron."

"When did you know about this?" Thomas asked, stepping in between Flash and me.

"When you called." As soon as the words left my mouth, I knew my mistake.

"What the fuck do you mean when I called you?" He glared at me, invading my space. "How the fuck did you beat us here?"

"Well, I—"

"You didn't give that file to Rebel, did you?" Thomas asked, standing nose to nose with me.

"Fuck, man. No fucking way!"

"James, I'll fucking kill you if I find out you sold me out, and if Izzy's hurt, I'll bring your ass back from the dead and kill you again."

"You don't even know how your words slice right through me."

"Who else could have given him that information?"

"It wasn't me," I insisted, turning toward Flash.

"Fuck, dude. You know I love Izzy. I wouldn't risk her life. I told you that man to man, James."

"What the fuck am I missing here?" Thomas asked, looking between us.

"James has a thing for your sister," Flash told Thomas.

There went any hope of explaining it when the time was right. *Let's add more gasoline to the flames.*

"What?" Thomas screeched, turning toward me, red-faced, with the veins of his neck popping out.

"*Thing* isn't really the right word," I said, looking him straight in the eyes.

"You're going to start talking as soon as we get her back safe."

I nodded, knowing that I should've already been straight with him about my feelings for Izzy. Thomas deserved to know how I felt about her and that I wasn't using her for sex. Flash had made it seem tawdry and sordid, but it was nothing like that.

My phone rang, breaking the uncomfortable silence as Thomas and I stared at each other. I lifted the phone to my ear without losing eye contact.

"Yo," I barked, chewing the inside of my lip.

"I got some news," Bobby said, the sound of papers moving in the background.

"Hit me."

"Rebel was spotted with a female at a motel in Bushnell. I just got the tip," he said, then he covered the phone and spoke to someone. "Sorry. The wife."

"Text me the information. We're heading that way," I said before disconnecting the call. "Motel in Bushnell," I said, grabbing my keys from the table and running toward the door. "Move your shit, Flash. We're taking my car."

As we climbed in the car, Thomas shotgun and Flash in the back, I threw my phone to Thomas. "Handle it," I said, starting the GTO and taking off toward Izzy. Thomas rattled off the address to the motel while tapping the screen on my phone.

"Should we call backup?" Flash asked, leaning forward and sticking his head between us.

"No," I snapped, gripping the steering wheel tighter. "Sit the fuck back. I don't need your face all up in my shit."

"Asshole," Flash mumbled. "How do you want to handle this, Blue?"

"We're going to find out who else knows and then we're going to kill the motherfucker," Thomas said, not looking up from the phone screen.

"Shouldn't we arrest him?" Flash asked, his eyes wide as I watched him in the rearview mirror.

"Fuck him. He deserves to die after taking Izzy," I said.

"What the fuck is this shit on your phone?" Thomas asked, holding out my phone and staring at me.

"What the hell are you talking about?" I asked, glancing at him out of the corner of my eyes but not daring to take my focus off the road.

"This shit with my sister, motherfucker."

"We're friends," I said calmly, wishing we weren't having this conversation.

"There's some shit in here that can't be unseen," Thomas bit out, growling as he continued to scroll.

"Stop fucking reading it, then."

"A fucking cock shot? Really? What the fuck? That's my little sister and you're sending her pictures of your junk?"

"Give me my goddamn phone," I growled, reaching over as I tried to rip it from his grasp.

"After we kill Rebel, I'm kicking your ass."

I nodded. "I deserve it."

If she were my sister, I'd do the same. I'd want to beat the living fuck out of anyone who touched her or harmed her virtue. This was Izzy, and I wasn't her first, but I planned to be the last damn man she ever bedded.

"Shut the fuck up and drive!" he shouted, tossing the phone back into my lap.

We drove in silence as we made our way to Bushnell. The highway was empty during the dead of night, a streetlight near an exit the only change in scenery.

As we pulled off the highway, Thomas spoke first. "This is how this shit is going to happen. I'll get the information from the desk clerk while you and Flash make sure no one leaves the motel."

The closer we got, the faster my heartbeat pounded in my chest. All the horrible things I'd imagined when I thought she hadn't made it home safe amplified. Knowing that she was in the hands of Rebel, an MC vice president, made my fucking stomach churn.

"Okay," Flash said, pulling himself forward.

"Then when I get the room number, you'll wait outside"—he turned to face Flash—"and James and I will go inside and deal with whatever clusterfuck we find."

"But I want to go inside too," Flash whined.

"Man the fuck up. We need someone to keep an eye out in case others show up."

"Fine," he snapped, slapping the front seat before he slumped in the back seat.

"Fucking pussy," I mumbled, trying to stop myself from turning around and punching him in the face. "Who's getting Rebel?"

"Let me deal with Rebel. You get Izzy out of there," Thomas said, turning to look out the window.

I flipped off the headlights as we approached the motel. The contents of my stomach began to churn inside me. Sweat dotted my brow as nerves racked my body. Jesus, I was so scared of what we might find inside. I'd kill the motherfucker with my own bare hands if he'd hurt her.

Thomas went inside as Flash and I watched the motel, making sure no one left.

"You got a problem with me?" Flash asked, my eyes flickering to him in the rearview mirror.

If looks could kill, he'd be a dead man. "This shit is all your fault," I said, my voice laced with anger.

"How the hell is this my fault?" he asked, glaring at me.

"You thought it was a great idea to bring her to Bike Week," I spat out, wishing I could wrap my hands around his pencil neck.

"I thought we could have some fun. How did I know all this shit would happen?" he asked, running his fingers through his hair.

"Don't they teach you anything at the mighty FBI? You don't fucking mix personal and business. Ever."

"James, wouldn't you call sleeping with Izzy a conflict of interest there, buddy?" A smug grin spread across his face.

"Fucker, I didn't bring her into my world. I went to her, never the other way around."

Thomas walked out of the office, motioning to us to follow. I grabbed my gun as I climbed out, and we both ran toward him on quiet feet.

"Room 103. Guy inside said he only saw Rebel and no one else," Thomas informed us, pulling the magazine from his gun and looking at it. "Ready?" he whispered, stopping before the room and jamming the magazine back in place.

We nodded, removing the safeties from our guns as we approached the room that hopefully held Izzy.

Thomas motioned to Flash to stand in the parking lot, pointing to his eyes and then around the exterior of the building. Flash was to be our lookout. Thomas lifted his chin, standing off to the side as I used my leg and reared up, kicking in the door.

Charging into the room, I looked around and saw Izzy lying on the bed, unconscious. My heart sank as I ran to her. A heat and searing pain sliced through my arm as a loud bang filled the room. My body jerked sideways as I reached for her.

I didn't look or stop to help Thomas; he could handle Rebel without a doubt. He'd given me a task and I'd follow it—save Izzy and get her the fuck out.

I carried her outside as another gunshot went off. She looked like an angel, resting and blissfully unaware of the shit going down. As I laid her on the hood of my car, I grabbed her face and placed my ear near her nose. She was breathing and reeked of liquor. I lifted her arms, studying every surface of her body. She was unharmed and had simply passed the fuck out.

"Watch her!" I yelled at Flash before running back into the room.

Kicking the door closed, I took in the scene before me. Thomas had Rebel on his knees with the gun to his head. Rebel was bleeding from his leg, his hands behind his head and his chin up in defiance.

"I want to know how you found out about me," Thomas roared, his hand almost shaking as he held it to the top of Rebel's head.

"Go fuck yourself," Rebel sneered, spit flying from his mouth as he spoke.

I stepped forward, wondering what I should do next. I was torn between my duty to the DEA and my feelings for Izzy. Rebel knew information that could end her life and Thomas's.

Thomas raised his hand, smacking Rebel with the butt of his gun. "You want to get out of this room alive? You better start fucking talking."

"You're a traitor and a fucking rat. You might as well kill me, because I'll put your ass in the ground otherwise. I'm dead either way," Rebel bit out, wincing from the pain. "I brought you in and helped you move up the ranks. Fucking shoot me, you pussy."

"Who. The. Fuck. Knows?" Thomas said, moving to stand in front of Rebel with the gun still trained on his head.

"Fucking sucks not knowing something, doesn't it, *Blue*?" Rebel growled, kneeling and bleeding all over the floor.

Thomas moved quickly, pointing the gun at Rebel's shoulder and pulling the trigger. Rebel's body swayed backward before he righted himself.

"First chance I get, I'm going to taste the pussy on your beautiful sister." Rebel laughed.

I closed my eyes, seeing red as my stomach turned at the thought of Izzy being in danger. Fisting one hand at my side with my gun still in the other, I fought the urge to push Thomas out of the way and shoot the motherfucker in the head myself.

"I bet she tastes as fucking sweet as she looks." Rebel smiled, bringing his hand to his face and licking his fingers.

I couldn't stand the shitty look on his face. I didn't want to listen to him talk about Izzy anymore. Lunging forward, I pushed Thomas out of the way, and Rebel's eyes grew wide.

I pulled the trigger, watching Rebel's body fall back in a heap on the shaggy green carpet. Leaning over his bloodied body, I spat in his face. "Rot in hell, motherfucker!" I shouted, a growl rising in my throat.

"What the fuck?" Thomas asked, hitting my arm.

I looked at him and shook my head. "You two would never be safe with that motherfucker around. He deserved to die."

"I didn't get the information out of him," Thomas groaned as he sat on the bed.

"No one knew. If they did, he would've had backup here with him. He had to know we were going to come after him."

He sighed, setting his gun next to him on the bed. "You're right. Fuck, this complicates shit with the club."

"Only thing it does is move you up higher in the ranks, brother," I said, sitting next to him and staring at Rebel's body as the blood almost reached my boots. "What do you want to do with the body?" I asked, debating if we should bury him somewhere along the highway or make it look like a setup.

"You take Izzy home and Flash and I will handle it," Thomas said, standing from the bed as he stuck his gun in his waistband. "Is she okay, James?"

"Izzy?" I asked, nodding. "Yeah, she's just passed out. Hopefully she won't remember a damn thing."

"Fuck. No one can know about Rebel's death. Got me? No one besides the few people we called. Especially Izzy. Do not tell her." Thomas moved toward the door and walked out.

I stood and rubbed my face with my hands. When had my life gotten so fucking difficult? Everything used to be so damn simple.

Thomas was hovering over her, checking her for injuries when I stepped outside.

"I checked her. She's fine," I said, pushing him away and scooping her into my arms. "I'll get her home."

He nodded, glaring at me as I held his sister in my arms. She nuzzled my neck as tiny whimpers fell from her lips.

"Shh, doll. Sleep," I whispered in her ear as I held her body tightly.

"Flash!" Thomas yelled, causing Flash to jump.

"What?"

"Get your ass in the room. Let's get Rebel and get the fuck out of here. James is taking Izzy home," Thomas said, motioning toward the motel room.

Flash looked at Izzy and me, then nodded at Thomas before disappearing into the room.

I laid Izzy in the front seat. "You be careful, brother," I said as I gently closed the car door, trying not to wake her.

Thomas stepped closer, standing toe to toe with me. "I'll text you when it's done. Keep her safe," he said, holding out his hand to me.

"You're okay with this?" I asked, taking his hand in mine.

"Fuck no. I'm still going to kick your ass when everything is said and done, but for now, you make sure she's okay."

"I'll wait until she wakes up and then I'll head back up to make sure shit doesn't go down in the MC."

"No, you stay clear until you get the all-clear from me. Do not come back. Stay with her and don't leave her side. Do you understand me?"

"I can't leave you without backup," I said, shaking my head. I didn't like it one bit.

"I'll be fine, James."

"I can't bear the thought of losing you, Thomas. You're like a brother to me, man."

"I don't have time to stand here and argue with your stubborn ass. Let me ask you this: Do you love her?" he asked, lifting his chin and motioning toward his sister with his head.

My feelings for Izzy ran deep—deeper than they had for anyone ever before. Was it love? To be truthful with myself and him, I replied, "Yes."

"Then keep her safe, James. I can handle the club, and Bobby will be around for help. Flash too. Now get the fuck out of here and take her home. Make sure she's sleeping."

"Not a problem," I said, smiling and turning my back to get in the car.

My head jerked to the side, pain shooting across my jaw as his fist connected with my face. I turned quickly, gaping at him.

"What the fuck was that for?" I asked, rubbing my jaw.

"Keep your dick in your pants," he said before leaving me standing outside with a stupid-ass grin on my face. "Get your fucking arm looked at too."

"I'll patch up my arm when I get her home," I said, touching the wound on my arm. It wasn't anything I hadn't dealt with before. I could patch it up with a first aid kit and a knife.

I pulled away as he closed the door, leaving them behind and speeding toward Izzy's before she woke.

18

DREAMS

IZZY

I SQUINTED, COVERING MY EYES AS I CRACKED OPEN AN EYE. EVERYTHING in my body ached. My head throbbed and my stomach churned—both casualties of having overindulged the night before. Reaching out, I grabbed a spare pillow and yanked, trying to cover my face. The pillow didn't move, stopped by something heavy. Turning, I saw him. I had to still be fucking drunk.

Rubbing my eyes, I looked to my side again and saw James sprawled out and naked at my side. The sheet had slipped below his waist, showing off a very erect and hungry-looking cock.

I turned away, staring at the ceiling and wondering exactly how fucked up I had been. I didn't remember him coming over—or even inviting him, for that matter. I bit my lip while trying to remember the events of the previous night.

I remembered leaving the club with help from Mia, and the girls bringing me inside. I didn't remember the car ride at all. Although hazy, I remembered them leaving me dressed on the couch before I heard the door close.

How the fuck had James gotten here? Did I have sex with him again and this time didn't actually remember it?

Covering my face with both hands, I played the night before back like a movie. Drinks, home, sleep…and then Green Eyes. I'd thought I'd dreamt him showing up in my house and scooping me off the couch, but I hadn't.

The churning in my stomach increased as liquid climbed my throat. After rolling out of bed, I ran to the bathroom and slammed the door. I grabbed the toilet, not bothering to lift the lid before I emptied the contents that were coming out one way or another.

Heaving over and over again, I prayed for something cool and comforting. As the urge to throw up passed, I rested my head against the cool plastic toilet seat. "I'll never drink like that again," I whispered. "Just make me feel better and I'll swear off alcohol forever," I promised God, even though I knew it was a vow I wouldn't be able to keep.

Moaning, I sprawled out on the tile floor, resting my cheek against the cold surface. I hated being cold, but right now, it was the only thing I craved. My body was covered in sweat and I felt like I was on fire. When I closed my eyes, the only sound I heard was my breathing as I wished for death or sleep. Anything was better than how awful I felt.

"Up you go, beautiful," James said as he scooped me into his arms.

"Leave me here," I whispered, wishing for the cold tile instead of the heat from his body. "I wanna die."

"Shh. I'll make you feel better," he whispered, feathering kisses against my forehead.

"Don't even think about sex," I groaned, lifting my head to look at him.

He wrinkled his brows and smirked. "I'm not an asshole, doll. It wasn't even a thought in my mind."

"What's that poking me in the ass?" I said, laying my head against his chest.

"My dick has a mind of its own." He laughed, gently placing me in my bed and pulling up the blankets.

I touched his arm, running my fingers along the bandage. "What happened?" I asked, looking up at him.

"Nothing for you to worry about, Izzy. Just a small wound," he said, cupping his bicep in his hand.

I kicked at the sheets, using all my energy to keep the heat at bay.

"I'm so fucking hot. I don't want blankets," I whined, moving the sheets off my body and sprawled out stark naked.

"Kinda hard not to think about fucking you when you're lying like that, Izzy," James groaned, pinching the bridge of his nose and shaking his head.

"Stop looking and make yourself useful." I closed my eyes and motioned for him to go away.

"What would you like, mistress?" he asked, a lightness in his voice.

"Fetch me something cold, and medicine for my head." I dismissed him with my hand as the corners of my lips twitched. I wanted to laugh but stayed in character. The playful side of James was something I hadn't really experienced before, but I sure as fuck liked it.

"How about I grab a giant fan and keep a cool breeze flowing across your skin?"

I opened my eyes, taking in the sight of James standing at the end of my bed, naked as the day he was born, with a smile on his face.

"Leave me in peace. Go fetch my things," I demanded, throwing my arm across my face to block out the light.

"Right away."

I moved my arm, making space enough for me to watch him walk away. I giggled softly as his beautifully naked ass strutted toward the door. He looked over his shoulder and winked, catching me peeking at him. I didn't have the energy, or else I would've thrown a pillow at him before he walked out.

I rubbed my face, trying to calm the throbbing in my head. It felt like the drummer from Anthony's band was inside, banging away on the cymbals.

The bed dipped, and I opened my eyes to see a smiling James staring at my flesh like a rabid dog. "Down, boy," I teased, pushing myself up on my elbows. "The last thing I'm thinking about is sex."

"Fuck," he muttered, handing me the aspirin and water. "It's all I can think about when I'm around you."

"Do men ever grow up?" I asked before placing the pills in my mouth and taking a gulp of water.

"I sure as hell fucking hope not." He took the water from my hand and set it on the nightstand.

Lying back down, I sighed and closed my eyes. His fingertips began to trail a path up my arms, moving gently across my skin. The light touches made goose bumps break out across my body. Shivering, I sucked in a breath as he drew a tiny circle on the space between my breasts.

"James," I whispered, my breathing altered by his movements. "Why are you here?" I opened my eyes to look at him.

He smiled as he guided the hair away from my face. "You didn't call me like I'd asked. I was worried, so I jumped in my car and headed over."

"What if I were with someone?" I asked, biting my lip.

"Wouldn't have happened," he said, lying down next to me, resting his head in his hand.

"How do you know?"

He cupped my pussy, gripping it in his hand. "This right here is mine."

"Actually, it's attached to me," I said, smirking at him.

"I thought we'd cleared this shit up already."

"That you're a caveman pig? Yes, that we've agreed upon." I laughed, grabbing my head as the pounding made me wince.

"God's paying you back for those nasty words." He snorted, increasing his hold on my core. "You agreed to let me back in, and 'in' means the entire package. No one else touches what's mine, especially when it's attached to your body. It's the only thing I care about."

"James, you're getting all mushy. I don't do mushy."

"I know, doll. You like it rough." He laughed, dragging his hands from between my legs to my thighs. He began to trace small circles down my legs before starting the same path upward.

"Shut the fuck up," I whispered. "Hey, how did you get in?"

"Broke the door down," he said matter-of-factly.

"What the fuck? Jesus, you could've knocked."

"Iz, you didn't hear me bust open the door, so you sure as fuck weren't going to hear me knock."

"I'll get you a key so you don't have to break any more of my shit."

He grabbed me by the waist, pulling me against him.

"You're so fucking hot," I shrieked, trying to inch away.

He nuzzled my neck as his hand mindlessly stroked my ribs. "Tell me how you really feel."

Using the last bit of strength I had, I slapped him on the shoulder. "You're still a cocky bastard."

His face grew serious as he looked down at me. "Izzy, I want to tell you that I—"

I covered his lips and shook my head. "Don't," I said, swallowing hard, afraid of what he was going to say.

He smirked and spoke against my finger. "I think you should brush your teeth." He broke into laughter, the entire bed moving under his weight.

I closed my eyes, thankful and a little bit hurt that I'd jumped to the conclusion that he had been about to profess his undying love to me. We weren't ready, and I sure as fuck could barely think the words, let alone say them. I cared for James. No one fucked me like him. He had the mix of animalistic sexuality that I hadn't known I'd wanted.

"Fuck off," I snapped, lashing out at him as I rolled from the bed. "You're not smelling as fresh as a daisy either."

"Better than vodka vomit," he replied, covering his mouth as he laughed.

"Patron," I said, hanging my head and vowing to never drink tequila again. "He and I go way back."

"Tortured love affair?" he asked as his eyes followed me in the mirror next to the bathroom door.

"Story of my fucking life," I said, smiling at him.

He stretched out across the mattress, looking at home in my room. Closing the door, I turned and looked at myself in the mirror. "Fuck," I muttered, moving my face closer to get a better look at my reflection. Smashing my cheeks, I blinked twice, hoping it was just the alcohol affecting my vision. No such luck. I looked like death. Heavy black bags had formed under my eyes with my mascara smeared all around them, framing them and drawing attention to the nightmare.

I grabbed a washcloth and a bar of soap and washed all evidence of the night before away. Brushing my teeth, I tried not to gag. Toothpaste and vomit didn't make the task easy. I cupped my hands together to pool water in my palms before bringing it to my mouth and swishing it around.

When I went back into the bedroom, I still felt like shit, but at least I thought I looked better.

"Let's talk, Izzy." He patted the mattress next to him and motioned to me with his hand.

I rolled my eyes, pain shooting through my head by the simple movement I'd done a million times. "Now? I'm too sick to talk."

"It's the perfect time to talk."

"Ugh," I whined, sliding in next to him. "Why?"

"'Cause you aren't as big of a smartass when you're like this, and I need you to be serious for a few minutes."

"Oh boy," I whispered.

"Just shut it, woman." He placed his finger over my mouth. "I'll talk, and you pipe in when you don't agree."

"So no talking?" I asked, knowing that wasn't going to fucking happen.

"If that's possible," he said, and laughed.

"Not a fucking chance."

He rubbed his eyes, trying to hide the smile on his face. "Izzy, I want to give this a shot between you and me." He paused.

I stared up at him and blinked.

"I know I can be demanding—"

I giggled, covering my mouth and quickly turning my face back to stone.

He sighed and continued. "I *am* demanding. I need control in the bedroom. It's hard to explain it."

"Are you a swinger?" I blurted.

"Fuck no. What kinda shit do you have in that head?"

I shrugged and waited for him to go on.

"I don't want to control your life. I want a partner, but inside the bedroom or anywhere I'm taking you...I'm the boss."

"Okay. I don't have any complaints when it comes to you and sex."

"Good," he said, and smiled, lightly touching my cheek. "Are you into kink?"

I smiled. Kink should be my middle name, but I'd play dumb for his sake. "Like what?"

"Why did you call me master when we had sex?" he asked with one eyebrow cocked.

"Felt right, and I was being a total smartass. I've been to a kink club in Tampa with my girlfriends once or twice to check shit out."

"What?" he asked, his eyes growing wide.

"You know. We were curious. There was so much talk on the news about submission. We wanted to see what all the fuss was about." I shrugged, feeling my cheeks turning pink as heat crept up my neck.

"Did you do anything when you were there?"

"James, I may have been easy for you, but I don't just fuck around with every cock that comes my way."

He sucked in a breath. I thought I'd given him a little too much information.

"Let's just say it was eye opening."

"Did you like what you saw?"

"Let's say it piqued my interest."

"Did it make you wet?" he asked, running his knuckles down my cheek before resting his hand on my neck.

"Some things." I smiled, heat spreading throughout my body.

"Which things?"

"Have you been to one of those clubs?" I asked, throwing the question in his court.

"I have."

"Really?" I whispered as images of James dominating women flooded my mind. "Tell me more. Do you like to hit women?"

"Fuck, I'm not a sadist, but I like to dominate women sexually."

"Women or me? I don't think I could handle you doing shit to other women."

He laughed, rubbing his nose against my cheek. "I want to dominate you, Izzy." He nipped my ear. "No one else."

"Not in a club either," I said, turning to face him.

"Never. I don't want anyone seeing what's mine."

"I'm willing to try everything once."

"You're a natural submissive, Izzy," he said, smiling at me.

I reached up, laying my hand against his forehead, and laughed. "Are you feeling okay? One thing I'm *not* is a submissive, James."

"You didn't say no when I told you to strip and handcuffed you to the bed."

"I liked stripping for you. It was sexy."

"And the handcuffs?" he asked, touching my wrists where the cuffs had been.

I closed my eyes, remembering the feel of him overpowering me and being unable to stop him. It sent a tingle through my body and made my pussy convulse. I opened my eyes and shrugged.

"It was all right," I said, pursing my lips.

"Sweetheart, I remember how hard you came when I tied you up. Don't lie to me," he said, running his finger across my bottom lip.

"Arrogant," I whispered, licking his finger with the tip of my tongue.

"I'm right. There's a difference."

"I can already see how it's going to be," I said, pouting, crossing my arms over my chest.

"I ask only three things, Izzy."

"What?" I asked, removing the fake pout from my lips and replacing it with a smile.

"You're only mine, no other men. Secondly, don't run away. The last thing I ask is that we get tested, you get on the pill, and no more barriers between us. I need to feel all of you."

"Sounds like a hell of a lot more than three," I teased. I gnawed on my lips, looking around the room as if I were debating the three things he'd asked. I sighed before I replied, "I can do that."

"Try not to bust my balls too much, 'kay?"

"Only when you're being a total asshole. I'll save it for those special occasions." I smiled, a giggle escaping my lips. "So when people ask me who I am—and they will, trust me—do I say I'm your submissive?" I asked, and pulled at my lip, waiting for him to answer.

"You're my girlfriend, Isabella."

"So I'm not your submissive?" I asked, still fidgeting.

He lay back, covering his face with his hands. "You're so difficult."

"You have no idea. I'm just getting started, Jimmy."

He jumped up, jostling the bed, and started to tickle me. I laughed uncontrollably with tears streaming down my face. Grabbing for his hands, I yelled, "I can't breathe!" as he pawed at my ribs.

He stopped, his face quickly sobering. "Are you okay?

"Psych!" I screeched, jumping on top of him and straddling him.

"I can see this shit won't be easy," he mumbled, pushing his hardness against me and laughing.

"Nothing in life that's worth having ever is," I whispered, leaning over and kissing him.

19

WILD WILD LOVE

JAMES

"I'M ON MY WAY, DOLL. YOU READY FOR ME?" I ASKED, CLIMBING ON MY bike and placing the key in the ignition.

"I'm already naked," she said, her laughter tickling my ear.

"Fuck," I muttered, scrubbing my face with my hand. "I already have blue balls."

"Hurry or I'll start without you." She laughed and hung up.

I stared at the screen, shaking my head. She was the biggest prick-tease I'd ever met. I shoved the phone in my pocket, started the bike, and took off.

I spent every possible moment I had free with Izzy. Working with Thomas to take down the Sun Devils and living an hour away didn't leave us much time together. I knew things would change eventually, but for now the distance worked. With her phobia of relationships and my overly bossy attitude—her words, not mine—the time we spent apart helped calm her fears. It had been a month since Izzy finally agreed to be mine.

We talked on the phone, texted nonstop, and Facetimed. I was able to convince her to masturbate while I watched, and it was the sexiest damn thing I'd ever seen. By the time I was able to see her, my cock ached, my balls were blue, and I couldn't control myself. We didn't spend too much time with clothes on when I visited.

I thought about how she tasted, the smell of her skin, the feel of her hands as I drove to her house. By the time I parked my bike, my hard-on had become as hard as granite.

"Shit," I mumbled, climbing off my bike and adjusting myself. I grabbed my stuff and headed for the promised land.

I didn't bother knocking. She may be a tease, but I knew her ass was naked and waiting, just like she said before she hung up on my sorry ass.

"Izzy," I shouted, throwing my bag down next to the couch.

"Back here," she yelled.

I headed toward her bedroom, unzipping my pants as I walked. As I turned the corner, entering her room, I stopped dead.

"What the fuck?" I said, my eyes growing wide. I blinked and shook my head, wondering if I was seeing things.

"Ya like?" she asked, smiling as she twirled.

"What—" I was stunned. She had on a corset that hugged her every curve as her breasts spilled out the top. Black thigh-highs, a matching garter belt, and a G-string, with black stilettos.

"I wanted to do something different." She giggled, walking toward me.

"I can't—" I said, feeling my cock about to break off in my pants.

"You don't like it?" she whispered against my lips, palming my dick through my pants.

"Jesus," I hissed. "I fuckin' love it."

She pushed against my chest. "Wait, I got something else." She walked next to the bed, opening her nightstand and pulling something from inside.

"What?" I asked, a little worried about what she was adding to the outfit. Anything more and I'd explode in my pants.

"These," she whispered, holding up two sets of handcuffs and a crop. Her smile was wide, almost touching her eyes. "I thought we could get a little adventurous."

"Doll, I'm going to show you adventurous." I beckoned her with my finger.

"No way, James Caldo. This is my show."

"I'm not following," I said, wondering when she thought she had the reins.

"You want my sweet pussy?" she asked, sliding the crop up her legs and stopping at her G-string.

"More than I want air," I replied, pushing my pants down. "Get your ass over here."

"I'm in charge tonight, Jimmy," she drawled, hitting her leg with the crop.

"What?" I asked, shaking my head.

"I get to boss your sexy ass around. That's the deal. I get to play too."

"Fuck," I said, my balls aching for release. "Whatever you want, doll. I just need to be inside you." I walked toward her, kicking off my pants.

"Not so fast, mister," she growled, holding the crop out and hitting me in the chest. "I didn't tell you to strip yet."

I bit my lip, keeping the laugh I felt coming from escaping. "Izzy," I said.

"Strip, and make it good or I'll have to give you ten lashes." She grinned, sitting on the bed and leaning back.

I couldn't bring myself to correct her on the type of impact a crop inflicted. "Yes, Izzy," I growled, slowly lowering my pants to my ankles.

"Mistress," she croaked, the corner of her mouth turning up.

"Mistress?" I asked, stopping my movement and staring at her.

"I like the sound of it." She shrugged, causing her tits to pop out of the corset a little more.

I continued with my striptease, dancing around the room and teasing her the best I could. It didn't take long for me to undress, since I only had on jeans and a t-shirt.

"Such a letdown," she whispered, shaking her head and pursing her lips.

"Hey," I said.

A loud slap echoed in the room as I felt a pinch on my hip. Looking down, I saw the crop retreating from my body. "You did it too quick." She laughed.

"I did not," I said.

She swatted me again and giggled.

"You hit me one more time for no reason and I'm going to take you over my knee and spank your ass," I growled, stalking toward her.

"James," she murmured. "I didn't say you could touch me."

"Izzy, I'm about two seconds from coming just looking at you. Get your ass naked and suck my dick."

"Tsk, tsk," she said, placing the heel of her shoe against my abdomen. "Get on your knees and eat my pussy," she commanded, pointing to the floor between her legs with the crop.

That was an order I'd gladly follow. I dropped to my knees, pulling her body forward, and ripped the G-string from her body. Placing her legs over my shoulder, I leaned in and licked her. She flinched and whimpered, "James."

I held her waist, keeping her in place as I latched on to her wetness. Groaning, I devoured her as she writhed under my hands.

"Harder," she chanted, pushing her pussy against my face.

I obeyed, driving her closer to the edge. I listened to her breathing, waiting until the right moment to pull away.

"Don't stop," she demanded, looking at me with an evil glare.

I smirked, going back to feasting on her as I inserted two fingers into her depths. Curling my fingers, I stroked her from the inside and licked at her clit like a man possessed. All I wanted to do was jam my dick inside her. I'd give her this moment to feel in control before I took over.

"Yes, yes!" she shouted, her entire body growing rigid. "Fuck," she hissed, trying to pull away.

I didn't relent, sucking harder while flicking her with my tongue. "Another," I murmured against her pussy, sending her spiraling into a second orgasm.

I backed away, wiping her juices from my face. "Your playtime is over, doll," I growled, pulling her off the bed like a rag doll and impaling her with my dick.

"James," she screeched as I filled her, throwing her head back and gasping.

"So fuckin' good," I groaned, pausing to gain my bearings. "Don't move," I said, holding her back in my hands.

"You don't have a condom on," she whispered, looking at me with large doe eyes.

"We're clean, babe. I needed to feel all of you. It's been too damn long since I've been inside you," I said, grabbing her by the waist and easing her off my shaft.

She blinked, a small smile spreading across her face. "Okay," she whispered.

Still kneeling, I slammed her back down on top of me, repeating the motion until I felt my balls about to explode. I stilled, not ready to come, and grabbed her face.

"I've missed you," I murmured, bringing my lips to hers.

"I missed you too," she whispered, staring in my eyes.

I kissed her, holding her body tight, still planted deep inside. Breaking the kiss, I licked a trail down her neck to her breasts, still spilling over in her corset. Looping my tongue inside, I pulled her nipple from its restraint and sucked. Her pussy convulsed, milking me and matching the rhythm of my mouth.

Unable to restrain myself any longer, I pulled her off me, letting my cock free from her vise. I thrust my hips as I yanked her body down, slamming into her.

"Fuck," I hissed, my body on the verge of orgasm. I kept battering her pussy, driving myself toward the release my body needed. Finally feeling her core gripping my cock, I hammered into her at a quicker pace. Sweat trickled down my back, and my body and balls overheated as she clawed at my skin.

My vision blurred and shivers raked my body as I came. "Izzy," I gasped, unable to catch my breath.

As my world came back into focus, I saw Izzy pouting. "What's wrong, doll?" I asked, nuzzling her neck.

"I wanted to be the boss," she whined, crossing her arms in front of her chest as her bottom lip trembled.

"Jesus," I mumbled, rubbing my nose against her soft skin. "We have all weekend," I said, moving back to look at her.

"Promise?" she asked. "I really want to beat your ass with this thing." She snickered, smacking the floor with the crop.

I shook my head, laughing as she smiled innocently. "You're too much."

She bounced, stroking my semi-erect dick with her inside. "Yes," she shouted, slamming down on top of me.

"Keep doing that shit and I'll show you how to really use that."

"Oh?" she asked, her eyebrows moving toward her hairlines.

"I have so much to teach you."

"I can be a really good student," she said, batting her eyelashes at me.

"I'm sure you were anything but, Izzy." I laughed, holding her under the ass and climbing to my feet with her legs wrapped around me.

"James," she whispered.

"Yeah?" I asked, setting her on the bed and collapsing next to her.

"I really did miss you." She buried her face in my side, hiding her eyes.

I grunted, unsticking her from my body. "When this shit with your brother is all over, I want you to live with me," I said, staring down at her.

"With you?" she asked, pursing her lips.

"Ah, yeah. You didn't hear me wrong, doll."

"Babe," she said, reaching up and touching my cheek, "I'm not leaving this house."

"Fine, I'll move in here," I said.

"Don't you think it's too soon?"

"You want someone else?" I asked.

"No."

"Miss me when we're apart?"

"Yes."

"Love how I fuck you?"

"Uh, yeah. Dumb question."

"Lo—"

She placed her hand over my mouth. "You can move in here."

I laughed, falling on to my back. She was easy. Say any word that started with "lo" and she freaked the fuck out. I knew it was the best way to get her to agree.

"Wise girl," I mumbled, feeling her pulse under my lips as I kissed her neck.

"Just remember I'm the boss," she moaned as I bit down.

"You're the queen of the castle, but I'm master of the bedroom."

"Okay," she whispered.

"Or any other room I want to fuck you in."

"Okay."

"Why are you so agreeable tonight?" I asked.

"I think you literally fucked me stupid." She giggled.

"I'm leaving my shit here this weekend."

"Okay."

"Izzy, you're fucking killin' me here. You never just say okay to everything." I brushed a few stray hairs that had fallen across her face. "What gives?"

"I'm scared," she confessed, covering her eyes.

"Of me?" I asked as I peeled her hands away from her face.

She nodded, biting on her bottom lip. "Yes," she whispered.

"Isabella, don't ever be afraid of me."

"What if I lose myself?" she asked, opening her eyes and stared at me.

"You're too strong for that to happen. I'd never let that shit happen either. I love you for the fireball you are. Your sassy mouth and sharp tongue make my dick hard."

She laughed, "Your dick is always hard."

"Only because of you."

"What if we fight?"

"Makeup sex, doll. It's fucking fantastic," I whispered in her ear.

She turned to face me. "James, what if something happens to you?"

"I'm not going anywhere."

"You don't know the future," she said, closing her eyes and breathing deeply.

"I waited all my life to find someone that lights my fire like you do, Izzy. Nothing can put out that flame. Come hell or high water, I'll spend eternity lo—" Her hand flew to my mouth. "Stop doing that," I hissed, pulling her hand from my face.

"Don't say it."

"As I was saying," I said, holding her hands above her head, "I'll spend eternity by your side and worshipping you."

"Why me, James?"

I looked at her, taking a deep breath before speaking. "Your brother talked about you all the time. I felt like I knew you before we met. That night at the reception when I saw you and you threw your attitude at me…I can't explain it. In that moment I knew I wanted no one else but you."

She smiled, blinking slowly. "But I ditched you." She grimaced.

I laughed, running my hand down her arm. "I wouldn't have expected anything less."

"Really?" she asked, her eyebrows knitting together.

"Really. I figured you'd run away. When I touched you for the first time, it was like fireworks exploding under my skin. I never felt that with anyone before, Izzy. Never in my entire life," I said, grabbing her hand and linking our fingers. "I knew I'd have you again and that someday I'd get you."

"Liar."

"You didn't feel it?"

"Fuck," she mumbled, looking down before bringing her eyes to mine. "Yes. Why the hell do you think I ran out of there?"

I chuckled, pulling her against me. "I told you I love a good chase. I knew you couldn't resist me."

"It's kinda hard when you keep finding ways to pop into my life."

"Divine intervention," I whispered, crushing my lips to hers.

"Bullshit," she muttered into my mouth.

"Izzy," I said, pulling her lip between my teeth.

"Yeah?"

"Shut the fuck up and suck my cock," I growled, pushing her head down toward my dick.

Her eyes flickered as a grin spread across her face. "Yes, master," she teased, climbing down my body.

2 0

TIME KEEPS ON TICKIN'

JAMES

Two Months Later

"JAMES," MRS. GALLO CROONED, HOLDING OUT HER ARMS TO ME. "IT'S been far too long since we've seen you."

Izzy cleared her throat as her mother nuzzled against me, rubbing her hands down my back. "Ma, really? Must you paw him?"

Mrs. Gallo pulled back, sticking her tongue out at Izzy. "I'm just giving him a hug, dear."

"Looked like more than a hug."

"She's always been so sensitive," she said to me, ignoring Izzy.

"For fuck's sake," Izzy said behind me.

"Watch your language, Isabella."

"Oh, she notices me all of a sudden." Izzy's voice was laced with sarcasm.

"You should hear her, Mrs. Gallo. She has the dirtiest mouth I've heard on a woman." I looked over my shoulder and winked.

"It's her brothers' fault. Her father and I didn't teach her to speak like that." Mrs. Gallo shook her head, peeking over my shoulder at Izzy.

"Oh please, Ma. I've heard you drop more F-bombs than anyone I know. Give up your Mother Teresa act."

"She's a mouthy one, isn't she? How do you deal with her?"

"I'll whip her into shape, Mrs. Gallo." I turned to Izzy with a smile so large my cheeks hurt.

"You do that, dear. Lord knows her father and I didn't do a good enough job."

"What the hell?" Izzy muttered, pushing past us to get into the house.

"Thanks, Mrs. Gallo."

"For what, James?"

"Busting her balls for once." I laughed.

"Oh," she said. "I've been doing it for years." She smiled, laughing and looping her arms with mine. "Any news on Thomas?" she asked as we entered the foyer.

"He's well, but I can't say much else. I'm sorry."

She nodded, her face beaming from the smile on her face. "No worries. Any news is better than no news. It's been a tough couple of years."

"It shouldn't be much longer." I couldn't give her a timeframe, but after Rebel's death, things had been kicked into overdrive. The MC was heading for a cliff, they just didn't know it yet.

"James, how the hell have you been, son?" Mr. Gallo asked, holding out his hand as he approached when Mrs. Gallo headed toward the kitchen.

"Couldn't be better, Mr. Gallo." I shook his hand, watching as Izzy followed her mother while giving me the evil eye.

"Don't mind her. All the ladies are touchy in this house lately."

"Must be the heat," I said. Wondering where to take that topic of conversation, I decided to switch course. "How are your Cubbies doing?"

"There's always next year." He shook his head and sighed. "Someday before I die, I'd like to see a championship. The rest of the men are watching the game. Join us?" he asked, tilting his head and smiling.

I liked Mr. Gallo. He was my kind of man. Strong and protective, but he knew how to laugh. He loved his wife. That was evident the last time I was here. He cherished her, and I wanted their kind of relationship with Izzy. I hoped maybe someday we'd get there.

"Sure." I peeked into the kitchen on the way, seeing Mrs. Gallo and

Izzy talking at the kitchen table. "Hey," I said as I walked around the couch to find an open spot.

They all waved, keeping their eyes glued to the television. Suzy was the only one to look at me and smile before she patted the seat next to her.

Joe turned toward her, making a face. "Here," he said as he stood and lifted Suzy, depositing her in his spot.

I sat, feeling slightly uncomfortable, and looked around the room without moving my head. The couch dipped as Joe sat between Suzy and me.

I gaped at him. My eyebrows drew together as a confusion spread across my face.

"Just lookin' out for what's mine. You got me?" he asked, raising his eyebrow at me.

"I do."

I could see why Izzy wanted to run away from me. All the men in this family were cavemen. We were cut from the same cloth.

Joey's head jerked forward, and I turned to see Izzy standing behind him.

"What the fuck was that for?" he asked, turning to glare at her.

"Being a jerk." She snickered, crossing her arms over her chest.

"Jesus. You're lucky you're my sister."

"Izzy, doll, I've never seen your room," I said, changing the subject.

"What?" she asked as she turned toward me.

"I want to see your room. Did your parents change it?"

"Nope. Looks exactly like it did the day I moved out."

"Show me," I blurted, getting up from the couch.

"Ma!" Izzy shouted. "How much longer for dinner?"

"Thirty minutes!" Mrs. Gallo yelled from the kitchen.

"Is it okay, Daddy?" Izzy asked, looking at her dad.

"You're a grown woman."

She laughed, drawing her lips into her mouth. "They like you," she said, pulling me by the arm up the stairs.

"Ya think?"

"I've never been allowed to bring a boy up to my room," she mumbled as we hit the top step.

"I like the sound of that."

"That doesn't mean I haven't had a boy in there, though, James. Don't get too excited."

I stopped, pulling her into me as she grabbed for the door handle to what I assumed was her bedroom. "Have you ever fucked a *man* in your childhood bedroom?" I murmured against her lips.

She sucked in a breath, blinking slowly. "No," she whispered.

I covered her hand in mine and turned the doorknob, opening the door. "You're not scared?" I asked as I closed the door, locking it.

"Of what?"

"Getting caught," I said, starting to undo my zipper.

She shook her head. "Nope. They won't look for us. They think you walk on water." She laughed.

Picking her up, I walked toward the bed, placing her on her back. My hand glided up her leg, taking the bottom of her dress with it. I smiled as I realized that she'd listened this morning and hadn't worn panties.

"I didn't want them ruined," she said, wrapping her arms around my neck.

"Smart girl." I rubbed my nose against hers as I cupped her mound. "You're already wet." I dipped a finger inside, watching her eyes close.

She moaned softly, pushing her head back into the blankets.

Covering her mouth with my free hand, I hissed, "Shh. Quiet."

Moving my hips, I placed my dick close enough to grasp it with my hand and slam it into her body. She gasped, biting down on my fingers.

"Fuck," I muttered.

"Not so easy to stay quiet, is it?" she said, smiling underneath my palm.

"Quiet, girl," I commanded, slapping her hip before I slid my hand underneath her ass.

She opened her mouth, pulling my fingers inside with her tongue. I pounded into her as she sucked my fingers. The extra sensation made my vision blurry, and I picked up the pace.

She moaned, sending vibrations through my fingers straight to my balls. Staring down at her, I watched her tits bounce out of the top of her dress. She looked so fucking beautiful underneath me as I possessed her.

Moments later, my world exploded as I pushed inside her one last time before collapsing.

"Damn it," I growled, swallowing as I tried to catch my breath.

She wrapped her legs around me, holding my body in place. "I didn't get to come," Izzy whined, kicking me in the ass.

"You'll get yours." I smiled, pushing myself up.

"Who's the selfish one now?" she teased, unwrapping her legs from my body.

I stuffed my dick back in my pants and zipped it up, returning my outfit to its original state. I held out my hand, helping Izzy off the bed.

"If you're a good girl, I'll let you play mistress again tonight," I whispered, brushing my lips against her mouth.

A smile spread across her face as her blue eyes blazed. "Only if I can use the whip again," she said, clapping her hands as she bounced.

"I've created a monster." I laughed, picking her up and tossing her over my shoulder before I swatted her ass.

"Mmm, I liked that." She giggled before biting the sensitive spot just below my shoulder blades.

"Fuck, Izzy," I growled, slapping her ass a little harder.

"You better watch yourself, Jimmy. I'm gonna get you later," she said through her laughter as we descended the stairs.

I pulled her body down, letting it slide against mine until we were eye to eye. "You already got me, Izzy Gallo. Bring it." I cradled her face in my hands and kissed her hard, demanding entrance into her sweet mouth.

I finally felt at peace and secure with Izzy. Although we hadn't professed our undying love to each other, I could see the sadness in her eyes every time I had to say goodbye and head back to Leesburg to work. We spent a couple of days every week together, but it was becoming harder to stay apart.

My phone rang in my pocket, echoing throughout the hallways. I sighed, pulling it from my pocket. "I gotta take this. It's work."

She nodded and walked away as I hit answer.

"Yeah?"

"Get your ass back here now," Bobby barked, his breathing fast and hard.

"What the fuck, Bobby? It's my day off, man," I whispered, trying to not draw the attention of the family.

"The bust. Thomas called. It needs to happen tonight. It's all hands on deck, James. Wipe the pussy off your face and stick your dick back in your pants. You have two hours to get the fuck back here and be ready."

"Are you sure?" I asked, pinching the bridge of my nose as panic started to grip me.

These were the final hours of the thing Thomas and I had been working years to accomplish. This was our chance to bring the MC to its knees and bite off the head of the snake. One fuck-up and everything could go wrong.

"You got a dick?"

"Yeah. Dumbass question."

"Well, so is questioning my orders. Get the fuck off the phone, kiss your lady goodbye, and get the hell back here ASAP." A loud bang in my ear caused me to pull the phone away from my head before the line went dead.

"Izzy!" I called, waiting for her to come back so I could spill the news.

"Yes, Jimmy," she answered as she walked in with a confused look on her face.

"I gotta run, doll." I kissed her on the forehead.

She gripped my arms, staring into my eyes. "Everything okay?"

"Yeah. I got called into work. Tell your folks I had to run and that I'm sorry."

"I wanted to play mistress tonight." She stuck out her lip, pouting at me.

"I'll be back in a couple of days and we can play mistress all you want."

"Jimmy." She pulled me closer, her grip tightening around my biceps.

"What, Izzy?" I leaned forward, resting my forehead against her.

My heart ached from having to say goodbye. I'd told her I'd be back in a couple of days, but I didn't know when I'd see her again. With the case wrapping up, I could be buried under a sea of paperwork and court dates.

"Promise me everything will be okay?" she whispered with sad eyes.

"I promise," I lied. I couldn't promise a goddamn thing except that I would do everything in my power to be back in her arms as quickly as possible.

"Bring him home to my parents and yourself back to me." She leaned forward, tenderly kissing my lips.

"I will. We'll be here together before you know it," I said, kissing her one last time, inhaling and memorizing her scent and taste. "Izzy, I lo—" She placed her finger against my lips.

"Don't," she whispered. "Tell me when you come back to me."

I nodded and released her, touching her hand until my fingers slipped from hers as I walked out the door. She waved from the doorway as I jumped in my car and sped off to the one thing that could bring me back to her forever.

We needed to put an end to the Sun Devils MC and I needed to bring Thomas home safe.

***

Ready for Thomas Gallo? He's deep undercover, but when the woman he loves is in danger, he'll do anything to save her life. *Tap here to read Uncover Me now*

TWO TORTURED SOULS. ONE GREAT LOVE.

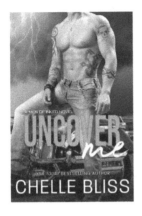

I lost track of my life. Spiraling down the rabbit hole, I lost myself and became one of them. Becoming consumed was easy.

Was I Thomas Gallo, good guy and respected cop or Blue, Sergeant-at-Arms of the Sun Devils MC? Before, I could answer with certainty, but now, there's a darkness that has settled deep in my soul.

Roxanne grew up as part of the MC, a victim of her birth. Her life has been treacherous, setting her on a course of torment and destruction.

When our worlds collide, secrets are revealed. Trying to save us from damnation, I fight for redemption and the woman I love.

Tap here to read Uncover Me Now
or visit *chellebliss.com/books/uncover-me*

FREE BONUS READ!

Want to know what happened the night Izzy and James met? ***Tap here to download Resisting for FREE.***

BE A GALLO GIRL...

Want to be the first to hear about the next Men of Inked book or everything Chelle Bliss? Join my newsletter by <u>tapping here to sign up</u> or visit *menofinked.com/inked-news*

Want a place to talk romance books, meet other bookworms, and all things Men of Inked? Join Chelle Bliss Books on Facebook to get sneak peeks, exclusive news, and special giveaways.

LOVE SIGNED PAPERBACKS?

Visit *chelleblissromance.com* for signed paperbacks and book merchandise.

Men of Inked
MYSTERY BOX
DELIVERED EVERY 4 MONTHS

SPECIAL EDITION PAPERBACKS & EXCLUSIVE MERCHANDISE!

CHELLEBLISSROMANCE.COM

Visit chelleblissromance.com to learn more!

ABOUT THE AUTHOR

I'm a full-time writer, time-waster extraordinaire, social media addict, coffee fiend, and ex-history teacher. *To learn more about my books, please visit menofinked.com.*

Want to stay up-to-date on the newest Men of Inked release and more? Tap here to join my newsletter or visit *menofinked.com/inked-news*

Join over 10,000 readers on Facebook in Chelle Bliss Books private reader group and talk books and all things reading. Tap here to become part of the family or visit at *facebook.com/groups/blisshangout*

Tap here to see the Gallo Family Tree or visit *menofinked.com/books*

Where to Follow Me:

facebook.com/authorchellebliss1

instagram.com/authorchellebliss

bookbub.com/authors/chelle-bliss

goodreads.com/chellebliss

amazon.com/author/chellebliss

tiktok.com/@chelleblissauthor

x.com/ChelleBliss1

pinterest.com/chellebliss10

Printed in the USA
CPSIA information can be obtained
at www.ICGtesting.com
CBHW010922180524
8520CB00011B/163